Barbara Taylor Bradford was born in Leeds, and by the age of twenty was an editor and columnist on Fleet Street. Her first novel, *A Woman of Substance*, became an enduring bestseller and was followed by twenty others, most recently *Just Rewards*. Her books have sold more than seventy-five million copies worldwide in more than ninety countries and forty languages, and ten mini-series and television movies have been made of her books. She lives in New York City with her husband, television producer Robert Bradford. Visit www.barbarataylorbradford.com for more information on the inspiration behind the Ravenscar series.

Visit www.AuthorTracker.co.uk for exclusive updates on Barbara Taylor Bradford.

Also by Barbara Taylor Bradford

Series
THE EMMA HARTE SAGA
A Woman of Substance
Hold the Dream
To Be the Best
Emma's Secret
Unexpected Blessings
Just Rewards

Others
Voice of the Heart
Act of Will
The Women in His Life
Remember
Angel
Everything to Gain
Dangerous to Know
Love in Another Town
Her Own Rules
A Secret Affair
Power of a Woman
A Sudden Change of Heart
Where You Belong
The Triumph of Katie Byrne
Three Weeks in Paris

BARBARA TAYLOR BRADFORD

The Ravenscar Dynasty

HARPER

This novel is entirely a work of fiction.
The names, characters and incidents portrayed in it are
the work of the author's imagination. Any resemblance to
actual persons, living or dead, events or localities is
entirely coincidental.

Harper
An imprint of HarperCollins*Publishers*
77–85 Fulham Palace Road,
Hammersmith, London W6 8JB

www.harpercollins.co.uk

This paperback edition 2007

First published in Great Britain by
HarperCollins*Publishers* 2006
1

Copyright © Barbara Taylor Bradford 2006

Barbara Taylor Bradford asserts the moral right to
be identified as the author of this work

ISBN 978–0–00–786623–6

A catalogue record for this book is
available from the British Library

Set in Sabon by Palimpsest Book Production Limited,
Grangemouth, Stirlingshire

Printed and bound in Great Britain by
Clays Ltd, St Ives plc

For my husband Robert Bradford, who has lived with these characters for over twenty-six years, and has never lost patience with them or with me. With my love.

Contents

PART ONE

Powerful Allies

Edward & Neville

'Princely to behold, of body mighty, strong and clean made.' *Sir Thomas More*

'Yet there was magnanimity in him, and if he is not quite a tragic protagonist, he is a memorable human being. He refused to admit that there were disadvantages he could not overcome and defeats from which he could not recover, and he had the courage, and vanity, to press his game to the end.'

Paul Murray Kendall

'Their relationship, like their division of authority, was amiable and undefined.'

Paul Murray Kendall

ONE

Yorkshire – 1904

Edward Deravenel galloped ahead at great speed, leaving his brothers behind, rapidly gaining the advantage. He urged his white stallion forward, oblivious to the icy weather, the lash of the wind on his face.

At one moment, half turning in the saddle, glancing behind him, Edward laughed out loud, his hilarity filling the air as he waved to his brothers: George, trying to catch up, his face grim in its determination . . . Richard, struggling even farther behind, yet laughing and waving back. But then he was the youngest, and much less competitive, the baby of the family and Edward's particular favourite.

For a split second Edward considered slowing down and allowing Richard to win this race, which had come about so spontaneously a short while before, then instantly changed his mind.

George would inevitably contrive to finish first, by pushing Richard out of the way in his overriding desire to be the winner. Somehow he always managed to do this, whenever he had the opportunity, no matter what the circumstances. And this Edward could not permit. Not ever. He strived to make certain Richard was never

3

humiliated, never diminished by George, who was older than Richard by three years.

Edward continued at a gentler pace along the narrow path, glancing down to his left as he did. The plunging cliffs fell steeply to the rocks and the beach; six hundred feet below him the North Sea roared under the gusting wind, like polished steel in the winter sunlight.

The surging waves frothed and churned against the jagged rock formations, while above him kittiwakes, graceful and buoyant in flight, squawked stridently as they wheeled and turned against the pale sky. Hundreds of these beautiful white gulls with black-tipped wings made their homes on projecting ledges of rock on the cliff faces; as a child he had watched them nesting through his binoculars.

He shivered involuntarily as the sudden remembrance of a tragedy of long ago hit him. A man in his father's employment, who had been bird-watching, had plunged to his death from this very spot. Now, instinctively, Edward veered away from the precarious cliffs, headed in the direction of the dirt road which led across the moors and was much safer terrain.

This morning the moorland was dun-coloured and patched with slabs of frozen snow, and there was no question in Edward's mind that he much preferred riding up here in the warmer months.

He mentally chastised himself for taking his brothers out on this January day. He had realized, rather late, that it was far too bitter, especially for Richard, who tended to catch cold so easily. He dare not contemplate his mother's ire if the boy fell sick because of this ill-conceived outing on the cliffs.

Swinging his head, he saw that the boys had again slowed and were lagging behind, were obviously even more fatigued by the long ride. He must spur them on, encourage them to move forward, get them home without delay and into the warmth of the house.

Beckoning to them, he shouted, 'Come on, chaps! Let's get a move on!' And he set off at a brisk canter, hoping they would follow suit.

Once or twice he glanced behind him, pleased that they had heeded his words and were hard on his heels. Within minutes, much to his profound relief, their ancestral home was in his direct line of vision and he couldn't wait to arrive there.

Ravenscar, the beautiful old manor house where the Deravenels had lived for centuries, stood on high ground, was set back from the sea, and dominated the surrounding landscape. Dark-green trees, ancient, tall and stately, formed a semicircle around it on three sides, and these in turn were backed by high stone walls; the fourth wall was a natural one – the North Sea. This stretched into infinity below the tiered gardens and sloping lawns that ended at the edge of the precipitous cliffs.

As Edward drew closer he could easily make out the crenellation along the line of the roof, smoke curling up from the chimneys, and the many mullioned windows glittering in the sunlight. Within seconds he was bringing his horse to a slow trot, riding through the black iron gates and up the long, tree-lined drive. This ended with some abruptness in a small, circular courtyard covered with gravel and with a sundial in its centre.

The house was built of local, pale-coloured stone

that had mellowed to a soft-golden beige with the passing of the centuries. An Elizabethan house, it typified Tudor architecture with its recesses and bays, gables and battlements and many windows of differing sizes. Ravenscar was one of those grand houses from the past, utterly unique, with a lovely symmetry and a charm all of its own. To Edward there was a sense of timelessness about it, a quality of serenity and peace dwelling in its gently flowing façade, and he understood why his forebears had always cherished and cared for this treasure.

The Deravenels had lived in their house by the sea since 1578, the year it was finished. Before then, for many centuries, the family had occupied the fortified castle that had stood at the bottom of the gardens on the edge of the cliffs; a ruin now, it was nonetheless a well-maintained ruin. This stronghold had been built in 1070 by the founding father of the dynasty, one Guy de Ravenel, a young knight from Falaise, liegeman of William, Duke of Normandy.

Duke William had invaded England in 1066, claiming his right to the English throne through his cousin, the deceased monarch Edward the Confessor, who had promised him that the throne would be his one day. But for political convenience, Edward the Confessor had reneged on that promise and passed over William in favour of his wife's brother, Harold, bequeathing the throne to the man who became, briefly, Harold III.

Believing his claim to be absolutely legitimate, William had crossed the English Channel with the six knights who were his trusted childhood friends, and a large army. He defeated Harold III at the Battle of Hastings, was proclaimed William the Conqueror and crowned on Christmas Day of 1066.

Some time later, William had despatched Guy de Ravenel to the north to act as his marshal. Based in Yorkshire, Guy had followed William's orders, had kept the peace, by force when necessary, built defences and forts, and ensured the north's loyalty to his friend the Norman king. And Guy had been enriched by William because of his staunch loyalty and unparalleled success.

Ever since that time, some eight hundred and thirty-five years ago, descendants of Guy de Ravenel had lived on this long stretch of coastline high above the North Sea. Nearby was the ancient seaport and spa of Scarborough; a little farther along the expansive stretch of coast was a picturesque fishing village with the quaint name of Robin Hood's Bay. Both dated back to Roman times.

Moving forward, Edward rode out of the courtyard and around to the back of the house, heading for the stable block. He clattered into the cobbled stable yard, his brothers following behind him, and jumped off his horse with his usual vitality and energy. As he hurried over to his youngest brother, he greeted the stable lads cheerfully; a moment later he was reaching up for the eight-year-old Richard, exclaiming, 'Let me help you down, Dick!'

Richard shook his head vehemently. 'I can manage, Ned. I truly can,' the boy protested, stealing a surreptitious look at George through the corner of his eye. He knew only too well that George would tease him unmercifully if Ned helped him to dismount.

But Ned paid not the slightest attention to Richard;

he put his strong arms around him, obviously determined to lift him out of the saddle. Richard sighed, swallowing another protest that had sprung to his lips. Accepting that he now had no other choice, he slipped his riding boots out of the stirrups and reluctantly slid into his brother's enfolding arms.

For a split second, Edward held Richard close to his chest, hugging him tightly, and then he put him down on the cobblestones, noting, as he did, that the youngster's narrow face was pinched with cold and drained of all colour. My fault, he chided himself, regretting even more than ever his thoughtlessness of earlier that morning.

'Thank you, Ned,' Richard murmured, staring up into Edward's face through his steady, slate-grey eyes. His eldest brother was six feet four, broad of chest, very strong and athletic. His brilliant eyes were as blue as the speedwells that grew in the summer meadows, and his thick hair was a stunning burnished red-gold. To Richard, and every woman who met him, Edward Deravenel was the handsomest man alive, with a warm, outgoing and endearing personality. He was affable, inordinately friendly, and blessed with a beguiling natural charm that captivated everyone. Richard loved him more than anyone else in the family, was completely devoted to him, and he would be all of Edward's life.

'Inside the house as fast as you can,' Edward cried, giving Richard an affectionate push towards the side door, which led to the mud room. 'And you, too, George, my lad. No dawdling around this morning.'

The two boys did his bidding, and as Edward followed them at a quick pace he called out to one of the stable lads, 'The horses have been ridden hard this morning, Ernie. They need your very best rub-down, and put the heavy wool blankets on them before you give them water and feed.'

'Aye, Master Edward,' Ernie shouted back, glancing at him. He and the other stable lad took the reins of the three horses and led them across the yard in the direction of the stables and the sheltered stalls where the tack room was also located.

Once Edward and his brothers entered the mud room they felt the warmth of the house surrounding them. Shedding their black-and-white checked caps and thick woollen Inverness capes and hanging them up, they scraped their riding boots free of dirt. A moment later they all went down the corridor at the back of the house, heading toward the Long Hall at its centre.

'I shall ask Cook to make us a small snack and hot tea,' Edward informed them, an arm on each of their shoulders. 'Perhaps she'll be able to rustle up some of those delicious Cornish pasties of hers.'

'Oooh, I hope so,' George exclaimed, and added, 'And sausage rolls as well. I'm very hungry.'

'And what about you?' Edward asked, glancing down at Richard. 'Aren't *you* ravenous?'

'I will enjoy the hot tea,' Richard answered, smiling up at his brother. 'But I'm not really very hungry, Ned.'

'We'll see about that when you smell some of Cook's tidbits. You know how they make your mouth water,' Edward said and shepherded his brothers into the Morning Room.

The boys raced over to the huge fire roaring in the grate, stood warming their hands, glad at last to be thawing out.

After doing exactly the same thing, Edward swung around and went back to the door. 'I'm going to have a word with Cook. I'll be back in a few minutes.' Closing the door behind him, he left them to their own devices.

Mrs Latham, the cook at Ravenscar, glanced up expectantly when the door to her kitchen opened. Instantly her mouth broke into smiles. 'Why, good mornin', Master Edward!' Her surprise and pleasure were evident.

'Hello, Mrs Latham,' he responded in his usual polite manner, giving her one of his most beguiling smiles. 'I've come to beg a small favour. I know how busy you are on Tuesdays, but would it be possible for you to make a large pot of tea and something to eat for us? The boys are famished after their ride on the cliffs.'

'By gum, I bet they are!' She wiped her big, capable hands on a tea towel and strode across to the long oak table standing in the middle of the huge kitchen. 'I've just been baking a few things –' She broke off, waved a hand in front of her morning's work and added, 'Pork pies, fishcakes, Cornish pasties, sausage rolls and savoury tarts. Take a look, and take your pick, Master Edward.'

'How splendid,' he said, grinning at her. 'A veritable feast, Cook. But then you're the best in the world. No one has your remarkable skill in the kitchen, no one.'

'Oh, get along with yer, sir. It's a real flatterer yer are.' This was said with a hint of pride at his compliment. Straightening her back, she added, 'I knows yer all like the Cornish pasties, and Master George is ever so fond of my sausage rolls. I'll get a tray ready for yer, sir, and send young Polly with it in a tick, once I've made the pot of tea. Does that suit, Master Edward?'

'It does indeed, Cook. I can't wait to sample some of this fare, it smells delicious. Thank you so much, I do appreciate it.'

'My pleasure,' she called after him, watching him walk over to the door.

Swinging his head, he grinned at her, waved and was gone.

Mrs Latham stared at the door for a moment, her eyes filled with admiration for him. Edward Deravenel was blessed with the most pleasant nature as well as those staggering good looks. She couldn't help wondering how many hearts he would break in his lifetime. Scores, no doubt. At eighteen he already had women falling at his feet. Spoil him, that they will, she thought, clucking to herself, turning to the ovens. Aye, they'll all spoil him rotten, give him whatever he wants, and that's not always a good thing for a man. No, it's not. I've seen many a toff like him ruined by women, more's the pity.

She swung around as the door opened again and muttered, 'There yer are, young Polly. I was just wondering where yer'd got to –' Cook broke off and clucked again. 'Bump in ter Master Edward, did yer, lass?'

The parlour maid nodded and blushed. 'He's ever so nice ter me, Cook.'

Mrs Latham shook her head and sighed, but made no further reference to Edward. Instead she continued, 'Set a large tray, please Polly. I'm preparing a mornin' snack for Master Edward and his brothers. When it's ready yer can take it ter the Morning Room.'

'Yes, Cook.'

After crossing the Long Hall, Edward made his way back to the Morning Room where he had left his brothers. He was lost in thought, contemplating his return to university. Today was Tuesday, January the fifth; in two days he would travel to London and go up to Oxford that weekend. He was looking forward to returning and especially pleased that he would be reunited with his best friend and boon companion of many years, Will Hasling, who was also an undergraduate.

His attention suddenly became focused on the end of the corridor. He had just caught a fleeting glimpse of a dark skirt and jacket, a froth of white at the neck, a well-coiffed blonde head. And then there had been the click of a door closing.

He hurried forward, passing the Morning Room, not stopping until he reached the last room at the end of the corridor. Pausing at the door which had just closed, he listened intently. There were no voices, only the sound of someone moving around, the rustle of papers. Tapping lightly on the door, he did not wait to be summoned inside. He simply walked in.

The woman in the room stared at him, obviously startled.

Edward closed the door, leaned against it. 'Hello, Alice.'

The woman took a deep breath, then exhaled. After a moment she inclined her head, stared at him, but said not one word.

Stepping forward he took hold of her arm just as she started to move around the desk, wanting to put it between them.

Holding her arm, pulling her closer, he leaned forward and murmured, 'Alice, my dear, you didn't come to see me last night. I was devastated . . .'

'Please,' she whispered, 'let go of me. Your mother might walk in at any moment. Please, Master Edward.'

'Not *Master Edward*. Surely you mean Ned . . . that's what you whispered to me in the dark last week.'

She looked up into the handsome face, was momentarily blinded by the vivid blue eyes, and closed her own.

Edward was instantly alarmed. 'What is it, Alice?' he asked in concern. 'Are you ill?'

She opened her eyes, shook her head. 'No, no, I am not ill. But I can't see you anymore. I'm afraid of . . . what might happen to me if we were to continue our . . . intimacy.'

'Oh, Alice, darling, don't be frightened –'

'And then there's your mother to consider,' she cut in peremptorily, her eyes darting to the door. 'She would be furious if she found out about our liaison. You know she would dismiss me at once. And I do need this position . . .' Her voice trailed off and she swallowed hard.

Looking down into her pretty face, Edward saw the tears glistening in her hazel eyes, and he noticed the fear and anxiety gripping her. He nodded. 'Yes, I'm afraid you're correct, Alice.' He studied her for a moment. If

13

she had been from the working class, or even a woman of his own class, he would have pressed his suit, certain that there would be no serious repercussions. But Alice Morgan was from the middle class, and also very vulnerable, and because of that he knew he must show consideration to her. She was the widow of a local doctor with a small child to support, and she did indeed need this position as his mother's secretary. And so because he was a compassionate young man and had a kind heart, he let go of her arm and stepped back.

A rueful smile touched his lips and he let out a small sigh. 'I won't trouble you any further, Alice,' he said in a very low voice. 'You are perfectly right, everything you have said is true. And I don't wish to be a nuisance to you or cause you any difficulties.'

Leaning forward, she touched his cheek with one finger, and then she swiftly edged around the end of the desk, where she stood looking at him.

'Thank you,' she said in a voice as low as his had been. 'Thank you for being such a gentleman.'

He left without glancing at her again, and as he closed the door behind him he did not hear her say, 'It's not because I don't want you . . . I do. But I know you're the kind of man who can't help but break a woman's heart.'

TWO

Cecily Deravenel, matriarch of the family, was aware that Edward had followed Alice into the office. She had been walking along the minstrel's gallery above the Long Hall when she had seen first one and then the other enter the room.

Neither Alice nor Edward had noticed her, and she had continued on her way, heading for the wide, curving staircase which led to the ground floor. As she was descending Edward had suddenly come out into the corridor in a great hurry and rushed into the Morning Room, closing the door sharply behind him.

Once again, Cecily's presence had gone unnoticed, and this pleased her. She had no wish to confront her eldest son about his interest in the young widow whom she employed.

Cecily Deravenel had always been a good judge of character and she knew Alice Morgan very well. She trusted her to handle the situation with practicality, decorum and the utmost discretion, since she was well brought up, a proper young woman. Fully understanding that it was a passing fancy on Edward's part, if it *was*

15

anything at all, Cecily was nonetheless relieved that he would be going to London on Thursday, and then back to Oxford at the weekend. She knew how much Edward loved university life, and his studies would absorb him completely, as they always had. Also, his absence would bring the matter of Alice to a close, if it had not already died a natural death, or been terminated by one of them a few minutes before. Even if it had been non-existent, she was glad he was going. At Oxford he was safe.

She sighed under her breath. He could be wild, even reckless at times, acting impulsively, without considered thought. And, women of all ages found him utterly irresistible.

It had long ago occurred to Cecily that temptation was always under his feet and in his way; in fact, poor Edward was forever stumbling over temptation, more so than the average man.

It would take a saint to resist everything thrown in *his* face, she muttered to herself, as she stepped into the Long Hall, still thinking about her son.

Cecily was a tall and regal woman in her mid-forties, handsome, graceful and elegant. She was usually dressed in fashionable clothes even when she was here at Ravenscar, the family's country seat.

This morning she was wearing a navy-blue wool day suit with a long skirt slightly flared from the calf, and a matching tailored jacket over a white cambric blouse with a high neck and frilled jabot. The jacket was short, ended at her narrow waist; it was cut in the style of the moment, with puffed sleeves which became narrow and tight from elbow to wrist.

Cecily's hair was one of her loveliest features, a glossy

chestnut which she wore upswept on top of her head; arranged in a mass of curls, these moved forward to the front, just above her smooth, wide brow. This was the latest and most fashionable style, as every woman in England, from every station in life, was copying Queen Alexandra. Ever since Queen Victoria's son, Albert Edward, had ascended to the throne as Edward VII, his queen had become the arbiter of fashion, style and taste. Edward's wife, a Danish princess by birth, was much admired by the public as well as those in the top echelons of society.

When Cecily was living at Ravenscar she wore little or no jewellery, unless there were house guests in residence or she and her husband were entertaining members of the local gentry. Today was no exception. Her choices were simple: small pearl earrings, her gold wedding ring and a fob watch on the lapel of her jacket.

Now Cecily looked at the watch and smiled. The small hand was just moving onto eleven. Her husband forever teased her, insisted that he could set his pocket watch by her, and in this assertion he was absolutely correct. She was the most punctual of women, and every morning at precisely this hour she set out on her tour of the downstairs rooms at Ravenscar.

What had begun when she was a young bride had, over the years, turned into a daily ritual when she was in residence here. She needed to be certain that all the rooms in this grand old house were warm and comfortable, that everything was in order with not one thing out of place. She was fastidious about this, as in most things.

Over twenty-six years ago, when she had come to

Ravenscar as Richard Deravenel's wife and the new mistress of the manor, she had at first been startled, then terribly saddened to find this Tudor jewel, glorious in its overall architecture and design, to be so utterly unwelcoming, so uninviting. The sight of it had filled her with dismay and she had baulked, momentarily.

The rooms themselves were of fine proportions, with many windows that flooded the interiors with that lovely crystalline Northern light. But unfortunately these rooms were icy cold and impossible to occupy for long without freezing to death. Even in summer the cold penetrated the thick stone walls, and because of the nearness of the North Sea there was a feeling of dampness, especially in the wet weather.

Richard had explained to her that the house was basically only suffering from neglect, that its bones were good, as was its structure. In effect, his widowed mother had grown parsimonious in her old age. She had closed off most of the house, since her children lived in London, and had occupied a suite of rooms which were easy and cheap to keep heated. The remainder of the house had been ignored, and for some years.

When walking through it, that day long ago, Cecily had quickly discovered that the warmest place to be was the huge kitchen, along with the small rooms which adjoined. It was in these rooms that the cook and staff lived, because of the warmth that emanated from the kitchen fire and ovens. All the other rooms were covered in dustsheets, closed off to the world.

Richard, trusting Cecily's judgement, had told his young wife to do what she wanted. Within a week of her arrival she made sweeping changes. Every room was thoroughly cleaned as was every window; the walls were repainted, the wood floors polished. Fires were soon blazing in every hearth, and great quantities of wood were chopped, the logs stored in the cellars, so that fires could burn throughout the year if necessary.

In London, Cecily purchased beautiful Turkey carpets and the finest Persian and Oriental rugs from the most reputable importers, as well as beautiful velvets, brocades and other luxuriant fabrics in rich jewel colours. The rugs went down on the hardwood floors, the fabrics were cut and sewn into handsome draperies for the many windows, furniture was polished and reupholstered if necessary. Because she had fine taste, a sense of style and a good eye, within a few months Ravenscar had been transformed, brought back to vibrant life through Cecily's tireless and loving ministrations.

In a certain sense, none of this happened by accident. Cecily Watkins Deravenel was accustomed to homes of great splendour, as the daughter of a titan of industry who had made an immense fortune in the industrial revolution of the Victorian age. She had grown up in a world of stunning beauty, amidst priceless objects of art, sculpture, great paintings, and fine furniture, as well as tremendous, almost overwhelming, luxury. And so it was these particular elements which Cecily sought to introduce at Ravenscar, because she herself loved them and was comfortable with them. She succeeded, although only in part in the beginning, because it took a great deal of effort and time to collect unique and beautiful artifacts. Only now, after twenty-five years of painstaking work, had she finally accomplished what she had set out to do so long ago.

One of Cecily's latest innovations had been the introduction of electric light throughout Ravenscar, which she had installed several years earlier. Gone were the gas lamps at long last, finally abandoned and replaced with shimmering crystal chandeliers and bronze wall sconces which bathed the rooms in a refulgent glow during the day as well as at night.

Today, as she walked down the Long Hall, glancing around as she did, Cecily noticed damp patches near a line of windows facing the sea. She made a mental note to point them out to the handyman, so that they could be dealt with promptly.

Entering the corridor off the hall she opened doors to different rooms, looking inside, checking the fires, the state of the furniture, and the general appearance of everything. Sometimes she went inside, straightened a floor-length cloth, or corrected the way a curtain fell. And her eye, always keen, sought the slightest imperfections.

Half an hour later Cecily found herself standing outside the Morning Room, hesitating, debating whether to go in or not. Finally making up her mind, she turned the knob.

Three heads swung to face the door as she stepped inside . . . three of her four sons . . . three of her seven children. She had borne twelve babies but only seven had lived and grown up.

George, at eleven, was more irrepressible than ever, and failed to hide his feelings. He was grinning at her now, his face open and revealing. He came to see her constantly . . . to confide, even to admit his misdeeds and mistakes, but also to carry tales, and frequently she had thought he had a touch of envy in his nature, and perhaps even treachery as well. But this morning he looked positively angelic; with hair the colour of wheat, he was the blondest of all her children.

There was such a contrast between him and his brother Richard it was quite startling. There *he* was, sitting next to his adored Ned, his face so very grave, and now he offered her a solemn sort of smile, a sad smile for a little boy of eight. How steady his slate-grey eyes were; such a serious child, so dedicated in everything he did, her Richard. For a split second she wanted to ruffle his black hair, but she knew he would not appreciate that, because he would think she was babying him. He was the darkest in colouring of all her children, dark like her, and he had inherited some of her traits, her stoicism, her stubbornness particularly.

Finally, Cecily's eyes came to rest on her eldest son. Edward, too, was smiling at her, a loving smile. His eyes were so vividly blue they startled her, but then they had since his childhood. His red-gold hair, inherited from his Normandy forebears, resembled a polished helmet above his face, and as his smile grew wider and his white teeth flashed she thought of those women who fell all over him – yet he was so young, still only a boy . . . not even nineteen . . .

For a long time she had believed that his inherent wildness did not negate his other qualities, especially his natural ability in so many areas. And he *was* very able. She never underestimated him, although his father occasionally did. Even so, her husband was fully aware, just as she was, that with Ned family loyalty was deeply ingrained in him, bred in the bone. Family came first; she knew it always would. She relied on it.

As Cecily stood there for a moment longer, she stopped ruminating about the three boys present, thought for a moment of her second son, Edmund, gone to Italy with his father several days ago. Edmund, who was seventeen, seemed the most responsible of her sons, and he had begged to accompany his father on this business trip. He was practical, had his feet firmly planted on the ground, and was very much his own man. It was his two elder sisters whom Edmund most resembled, at least in his colouring . . . They had light brown hair, hair which her fourteen-year-old daughter Meg characterized disparagingly as *mousey*. Meg was blonde, but not quite as blond as George.

Edward said, 'Please come and join us, Mother, won't you? We've been having a snack. Would you like to partake of something . . . a cup of tea perhaps? Should I ring for Polly?'

'No, no, but thank you, Ned,' she replied, walking across the floor to the sofa. As she seated herself on it, George jumped up and rushed across the room, fell onto the sofa next to her, leaned against his mother possessively. Automatically, she put her arm around him protectively. Years later she would remember this gesture from his childhood, and wonder why she had done this so often then. Had she somehow had a premonition that he would one day need protecting?

Ned ventured, 'I wonder, Mother, if you know when you plan to return to town?'

'In a week. I told your father we would all be waiting

at the Mayfair house when he returned from Italy. Of course, you yourself will be at Oxford by then.' She glanced down at George, lolling against her, and then across at Richard, before adding to Edward, 'Mr Pennington will be joining us at the end of the month. He will tutor the boys as he did last year when we were in London. And Perdita Willis has been engaged as governess to tutor Meg. Where is she by the way? Have any of you seen your sister since breakfast?'

Ned and Richard shook their heads, but George spoke up, murmured, 'I saw her going up to the attics.'

'When was that?' Cecily asked swiftly.

'I can't really remember the exact time, Mother.'

'Force yourself,' she said a little sharply for her.

'Oh, about an hour ago,' he muttered.

'I wonder why she was going up there?' Cecily frowned, looked puzzled.

'Oh, heavens, Mother! I think *I* know why,' Edward announced. 'I've suddenly remembered. She told me her friend Lillian Jameson is being given a spring ball for her sixteenth birthday. Meg said she was going to look in those trunks up there –' Edward broke off, glanced at the door which had opened to admit his sister.

'There you are, darling!' Cecily exclaimed, rising, moving towards her daughter Margaret. 'I was just wondering where you were and Ned said you'd probably gone to look in those old trunks.'

'Yes, I did, Mama,' Meg answered, gliding into the room; she was as graceful as her mother, and she looked pretty this morning in a red wool dress, black stockings and black shoes.

23

Cecily knew Meg was blossoming into a very pretty girl indeed, and smiling at her youngest daughter, she murmured, 'You didn't mention that Lady Jameson is giving a spring ball for Lillian's birthday.'

'It's not actually definite yet, Mother. The invitations haven't gone out. And they won't for weeks and weeks. If it happens at all. Well, you see . . . Lillian is *hoping*, and so am I. It might be rather fun, don't you think? However, her mother hasn't actually said yes.'

'Are boys going to be invited?' George asked, sitting up straighter, staring at her intently.

Meg laughed. 'You're incorrigible, George, truly incorrigible. Imagine *you* thinking *you* could be invited.'

'Why not? I'm a Deravenel. We're invited everywhere.'

'The likes of Papa, not you,' Meg said with cool authority. 'You're too young to go to cotillions, dances, that sort of thing.'

'No, I'm not, am I, Mother?' He gave her an appealing look.

'Well, George, perhaps . . . at this moment, let's say. By the spring you'll certainly be a little older,' Cecily replied quietly, wanting to mollify him.

'There, you see, Margaret! Our mother says because I'll be older by spring I could go. I'll think about it, and maybe I will come after all . . . I shall give it considered thought, as Papa always says.'

Edward chuckled. 'I hope you'll ensure I get an invitation, Meg,' he teased, winking at his sister, wanting to make light of all this, since George looked sulky.

She laughed and nodded. 'Of course I will. And if you come you'll be the envy of every other man there.'

He looked surprised. 'Why?'

'Because all the young women will be falling at your feet,' George announced. 'Everybody says you're a ladykiller.'

'That's enough, George,' Cecily cut in, although she spoke mildly. 'None of that type of vulgarity here, if you please.' Turning to Meg, she asked, 'Well, did you find anything interesting in the trunks?'

'Oh, yes, Mama, I *did*: some wonderful frocks, all beautifully packed away in cotton bags. They're like new. Will you come and look?'

'I'll be happy to,' Cecily answered, taking her daughter's arm. Laughing, the two of them went out together.

The attics at Ravenscar were large, and ran the entire length of the house, under the eaves. Since she was such a stickler for cleanliness and perfect order, Cecily had them cleaned and dusted once a month. Because of this, it was easy to find everything, and her neatness and talent for organization meant easy access to the chests, boxes and trunks which were stacked there.

Earlier, Meg had taken out several gowns, and laid them across a sofa which had been covered in a dustcloth. The gowns were made of silk, a light featherweight silk, since they had been designed to wear over bouffant underskirts, or hoop skirts, which had been so prevalent in the middle of the Victorian era.

Meg ran over to the sofa and picked up one made

of pale green silk and held it against her. 'I thought this colour would suit me. What do you think, Mama?'

Cecily stood facing her daughter, studying her for a moment. Then she nodded her head. 'I must agree with you, it's a pretty colour and perfect for you. I am sure we can have several of them remodelled to fit you. Madame Henrietta is such a good dressmaker, and innovative, she'll create more up-to-date designs.' Reaching for another gown, Cecily handed it to Margaret. 'Let me see how this shade looks: it's such a lovely blue, it reminds me of cornflowers.'

'And Ned's eyes,' Meg murmured as she took the dress, held it in front of her.

'Ah, yes, that is true,' Cecily acknowledged, Ned's eyes indeed. They were close, Edward and Margaret, with only a few years difference in their ages. Meg, like Richard, adored her eldest brother. He could do no wrong as far as she was concerned, and for his part Ned was protective of her, had kept a watchful eye on her since childhood. In turn, it was Meg who took charge of her younger brothers when necessary, mothering them when Cecily was away, guiding them in so many different things.

'The blue is enchanting,' Cecily now exclaimed, liking the way the colour enhanced Meg's grey eyes. 'We shall take the green and blue to London with us next week, and before we leave do go through the other trunks. Perhaps you'll find several more which can be remade.'

'Oh, how kind, Mama, thank you so much.' Margaret stepped closer to her mother and hugged her in a sudden show of affection, the silk frock crushed between them.

Cecily, who was not a particularly demonstrative

person, began to laugh. 'It's my pleasure, but Margaret, my dear, you're ruining the dress.'

Meg let go of her mother at once, and shook the frock out. 'I don't think any real harm has been done,' she murmured, scrutinizing it with some intensity.

With her head slightly tilted to one side, Cecily studied Margaret for a split second, realizing once again how pretty she had become, with her flowing fair hair and those large grey eyes, which were so beguiling. Instantly Cecily's thoughts turned to the girl's future, her marriage prospects. Meg would grow into a lovely young woman, that was clear. And she would definitely make just as good a marriage as Cecily's two eldest daughters Anne and Eliza had done.

'I shall speak to Lady Jameson next week when we return to town, Meg, in an effort to ascertain what her plans actually are. It has suddenly occurred to me that perhaps your father and I should consider giving you a small afternoon tea dance later this year, to celebrate your fifteenth birthday.'

'Oh, Mama, that would be wonderful!' Meg was startled by this suggestion, which was so unexpected, but the happy smile on her face revealed her genuine pleasure at the idea.

Cecily had also startled herself. She was not usually so spontaneous or impulsive, and normally spent days in deliberation about important things such as this. She wondered if she had made an error in bringing up the idea of a party for Meg, but immediately decided she could not backtrack now without upsetting her daughter. She would talk to Richard next week, but she was perfectly certain he would make no objection. He had always been quite content to leave such matters to her . . . the raising of their children . . . the running of their homes.

Richard. Such a good man. So devoted to his family, a wonderful father. The best husband any woman could ever have. She could not wait for him to come home. Her life was empty without him by her side, and lonely.

She hadn't really wanted him to go to Italy but he had felt obliged to do so. There was some sort of problem at the marble quarries they owned in Carrara, and as the assistant managing director of Deravenel and Company, he agreed with Henry Deravenel Grant, the chairman, that he was the best person to investigate the situation. And so off he had gone with Edmund, who had never been to Italy before and was genuinely excited about making the trip.

Her brother Rick and her nephew Thomas went along to keep her husband and son company; Richard and Rick had been extremely close friends for many years, enjoyed each other's company and travelling together. Also, Rick hoped to buy some paintings and sculpture in Florence; he was in the process of remodelling his town house in London and only the very best in art and artifacts would do. He was something of a connoisseur and had a great eye, and he had said to her only two weeks ago that the thought of Florence made his mouth water.

Rick and she had been close since childhood, and after their father's death it was Rick who had taken over the family business. If her father had been one of the greatest magnates in industry, then Rick had surpassed him a thousandfold; today he was one of the richest men in the country, and because of his flair and genius in business her own inheritance had increased. This was a great relief to Cecily. Her husband was always at odds with Deravenels when it came to money, and it was a company that really belonged to him at that. At least he should have been running it, not Harry Grant. Like all the Lancashire Deravenel Grants, he was incompetent when it came to finance. As for Harry's French wife, Margot, she was a woman who was riddled with overriding ambition and greed who managed Harry like a puppet master and sought to run the company herself. She probably *is* running Deravenels, Cecily now thought, and more's the pity.

'Shall we take the frocks downstairs, Mama?' Meg asked, interrupting her thoughts.

'Oh, yes, of course, let us do that, my dear.' Cecily looked at her fob watch and exclaimed, 'Good heavens, it's almost time for lunch.' But as they went downstairs her mind went back to the Grants; they were never far from her thoughts. Henry Grant's father had always cut her husband out, cheated him, and the hatred had escalated over the years. Now, Margot Grant was making things even more intolerable. There was going to be another battle between Richard and Henry, of that she was convinced.

THREE

'There's a sea fret coming up,' Richard said, swivelling around on the window seat in Edward's bedroom, and looking across at his brother. 'I can't see any of the fishing cobles out there, Ned, it's thick like a fog.'

'Well, it really is a fog in a sense,' Edward responded. 'A fret usually comes up when cold winds blow in from the sea over the warmer land, in summer too, sometimes, as well as winter,' Edward explained, glancing up from the box of books he was packing. 'And there wouldn't be any fishermen out this afternoon, you know. Tonight perhaps, if the fog lifts, Little Fish.'

Richard grinned. He loved this name Edward had given him years ago; sometimes Ned called him Tiddler, which also meant little fish, and this pleased him. Having nicknames bestowed by Edward made him feel very special indeed. 'I'll be glad to go to London next week,' Richard said, introducing another subject. 'Even though I have to work hard because Mr Pennington is coming back to be our tutor.'

Edward caught something odd in his voice, and

asked, 'Don't you like it here at Ravenscar?' As he spoke he frowned and then gave Richard a piercing look. 'Perhaps it's too cold for you here in winter, I realize that. On the other hand, I enjoyed winters at Ravenscar, when I was young. There's always so much to do.'

'Yes. I love it here, Ned, but I like London because *you're* not so far away . . . I mean you're at Oxford and I get to see you more when I'm in London.'

Touched by his brother's expression of his love and his need, and pleased that he could articulate it so well, Edward put down the leather-bound book he was holding and walked across the bedroom, sat on the window seat next to the younger boy. Placing an arm around his narrow shoulders, giving him a quick hug, he said softly, 'I'll miss you, too, old chap, very much. And you're quite correct, Oxford *is* much closer to London than it is to Yorkshire. And listen, I'll come to town often, so that we can spend some time together. Would you like that?'

Richard's young face filled with pleasure and his slate-grey eyes shone. 'Do you promise me, Ned?'

'I do, Dick, I do promise you.'

The eight-year-old visibly relaxed, his tense body growing slack as he leaned against Edward in a companionable way, fully at ease with him, as he had been since his toddler days. 'Things are not the same when you're not at home . . . I do miss you so.'

'I know how you feel, I miss you too, Tiddler, but I'm not all that far away. Perhaps I could write to you occasionally.'

'Oh, Ned, would you? How wonderful to have a real letter from you every week.'

Edward began to chuckle. 'I didn't say *every week*. But look here, Dick, it's not as if you're a boy alone when I'm at university. Meg is around, and you have George. Also, Edmund will be at home with you.'

'Yes, I know,' Richard answered in an uncertain voice. 'I love Edmund, but he's so busy, and sometimes he seems a bit . . . impatient.'

'I know he's a very busy fellow indeed.' Edward laughed, added, 'Doing what I don't know. But George is all right with you, isn't he?'

'Oh, yes.'

Glancing at him swiftly, Edward asked, 'Does George bully you too much? Tell me the truth, I don't want you to lie to me.'

Richard stared at his brother askance, and exclaimed, 'I never lie, and I wouldn't fib to *you*. George *doesn't* bully me.'

'I'm glad to hear it, but I do recognize that at times he can become over-zealous, shall we say, about certain things.'

'I can defend myself.' There was a sudden flash of pride, a defiant tilt to Richard's dark head.

'I know you can. After all, I taught you.' Edward gave him a light punch on the arm and stood up. He glanced out of the window, noticed how the sea mist was now obscuring everything; even the battlements at the bottom of the garden far below had been obliterated this afternoon.

Turning, Ned strode across the floor, went back to

the table where the large box stood. He put in another volume and then checked it off on his list.

Richard, watching him from the distance of the window seat, asked, 'Will Edmund go to Oxford one day?'

'I expect so, and George, too, and you yourself, Dickie boy. When you're old enough. That's what Papa wants, that we all should be Oxford-educated. Does that suit? Would you like to go? To be an undergraduate?'

'Oh, yes, I really would. Why does everyone call it the city of dreaming spires?'

'Because there are so many churches and buildings with spires and they look beautiful in the light.'

'It's very old, isn't it? Meg told me it was.'

'It is indeed. Twelfth century.'

'Can I come and visit you one day, Ned? *Please*. I would like to see everything at Oxford. Will you take me to see everything?'

'Of course, old chap, and especially the Bodleian, that's *my* favourite.'

'What is it, Ned, the Bodleian?'

'A library, a very lovely and very ancient library.'

'Oh, I'd love to see it! Meg told me that in the Civil War Oxford was the Royalist capital, and that it was *besieged* by Cromwell's parliamentarians, but it wasn't hurt by them.'

'That's correct.' There was a knock on the door and Edward called, 'Come in.'

The door opened and Jessup, the butler, entered, inclining his head. 'Master Edward, please excuse me.'

'Yes, Jessup?'

'Your mother wishes to speak with you. She's awaiting you in the library.'

'Thank you, Jessup. You may tell her I shall be down in a few minutes.'

'Mrs Deravenel did ask me to say that it was a matter of some urgency, Master Edward.'

'Very well. Then I shall come right away.'

The room wasn't quite right. There was something curiously *wrong* about it.

Edward stood in the doorway of the library, hesitating, not wishing to enter.

It was far too dark, darker than usual, and this was not normal. It wasn't like his mother not to have the electric lights blazing; she loved sunshine and brightness, which was why she had had the electricity installed in the first place.

Only two small lamps were turned on in the vast room, even though it was late afternoon and gloomy as dusk descended outside. The shadow-filled room seemed decidedly odd to him, off-kilter. Unexpectedly, he was filled with sudden unease, felt a sense of desolation, and even of foreboding enveloping him.

Opening the door wider, he finally went inside, peering ahead in the dim light. He could make out his mother standing next to a high-backed wingchair at the far end; behind her, wrapped in shadow, a figure lurked, stood staring out of the window, his back to the room. Edward couldn't discern who it was.

Slowly he approached his mother, his mind racing, every one of his senses alerted to trouble. Fear, he decided, fear is present here, and the hackles rose on the back of his neck at this unexpected and irrational thought.

Taking a deep breath, he murmured, 'You wanted to see me, Mother.'

She said nothing.

Stepping over to the fireplace, Edward switched on a lamp standing on a small occasional table, turned to his mother. He noticed how dark her eyes were and huge in her face, and how they were filled with apprehension.

Alarmed, he stared at her more intently, waiting. Now he realized her face was without expression, wiped blank, or so it seemed to him, and it looked as if it had been carved from stone. She was very pale, all the colour had drained away.

'What has happened? What is it?' he pressed, his voice sharp, rising and filling with urgency.

A shudder rippled through her and Cecily reached out, gripped the back of the chair as if to steady herself, her knuckles gleaming whitely in the faint glow from the lamp.

Edward felt that fear spreading out from her, touching him, and he asked again, '*What's wrong?*'

In a rush of words she said in a low, tense voice, 'It's your father ... there's been an accident. A fire. Your father ... and Edmund.' She stopped, choked up, finished bleakly, 'They're both dead, Edward.' Her voice broke, but she somehow managed to keep a strong hold on her emotions. In a wavering voice, she managed to say, 'My brother and your cousin Thomas ... they, too, were killed in the fire.'

Stupefied, disbelieving, Edward gaped at her. He found it hard to take it in, couldn't quite comprehend what she was saying. He was frozen to the spot where he stood, unable to move or speak.

The figure near the window turned around and walked forward. Immediately Edward realized it was his cousin Neville Watkins, eldest son of Rick and brother of young Thomas.

'*I* brought the bad news, Ned,' Neville announced, his voice thick with emotion. The cousins clasped hands for a moment, and Neville exclaimed, 'It was I who brought death and sorrow here!'

Edward shook his head vehemently. 'No! It's just not possible,' he cried. 'Not my father. Not Edmund. Not Uncle Rick and Tom. It simply can't be, not our family gone like that in the blink of an eye.'

Cecily's heart clenched at the sight of Edward's pale and stricken face, the tears welling in his eyes; his devastation was palpable to her. Although she shared his overwhelming pain and sorrow, his utter disbelief that this tragedy had occurred, at this moment she thought only of her son. 'How can I comfort you?' she asked, shaking her head helplessly. Tears began to seep out of her eyes, slid down her cheeks unchecked.

Edward did not respond. He was rendered speechless by the news. She knew he was in shock just as she was herself.

It was then that Cecily Deravenel uttered the words Edward would never forget for the rest of his life. 'Oh, Ned, Ned, has no one ever told you that life is catastrophic?'

For a long moment he was transfixed, staring at her, and then he swung around and rushed out of the library without saying a word. All he knew was that he had to get away, escape this death-laden room. He had the desperate need to be alone in his terrible grief.

Edward half stumbled across the Long Hall, making for the double doors that led to the garden. Once he was outside he fled down the paved path, through the tiered gardens, past the lawns until he at last arrived at the ruined battlements of the old stronghold on the promontory at the edge of the cliffs.

The sea fret had lifted. It had begun to snow and the tiny crystalline flakes stuck to his face, his burnished hair. He barely noticed. He was oblivious to the weather in his anguish.

Ned stood in the small, round enclosure which had once been a watchtower looking out over the North Sea. He pressed his face against the cold stones, his mind in a turmoil. How could they be dead? His father, his brother, his uncle and his cousin. It didn't seem possible. And it certainly didn't make sense . . . how had they all died together? Where had they been? When had it happened? Tragedy had struck not once but four times.

Papa is dead. And Edmund. Only seventeen . . . my lovely brother, so special, so full of promise for the future. And Tom, cousin Tom, with whom he had grown up. And Uncle Rick, the only other senior member of their closely-knit families, whom everyone depended on. They had all been constant, loyal to each other.

Papa and Edmund. Oh, God, no. His throat closed and tears flooded his eyes as grief finally engulfed him.

A bit later he heard a step on the cold stones, felt a warm cloak go over him, a comforting arm slip around his shoulders.

'Weep, grieve, let it come out, Ned,' Neville Watkins murmured against his ear. 'As I did last night.'

Within moments the two cousins went inside and stood conferring in the Long Hall. 'When did you receive the news?' Edward asked. 'And who was it that contacted you?'

'Aubrey Masters from Deravenels,' Neville answered. 'He telephoned me last night as soon as he heard what happened in Carrara. He thought it better that Aunt Cecily and you and the children were told in person by me, rather than receiving a telephone call from him or a telegram. Much too impersonal, he said. I told him he had done the right thing.' Neville's face was deathly white and taut as he continued, 'However, I had to come to grips with my own grief and my mother's distress before coming over to Ravenscar. I left Ripon as soon as I was up to it today, and came by carriage this afternoon. I hope you don't think I delayed too long.'

'Neville, of course I don't! You're as grief-stricken about your father and brother as I am about mine.'

'We must go to Florence,' Neville now said. 'And then to Carrara, Ned. We have to arrange for their bodies to be brought home for proper burial here in Yorkshire. And we must do some detective work whilst we are there.'

Edward did not respond for a split second and then he murmured quietly, 'You obviously don't think it was an accident, do you?' His voice trailed off, and his eyes locked with Neville's.

'No, I don't think it was an accident. I am relatively certain it was somehow planned, not sure how.'

'You're suggesting foul play, perhaps?'

'I am, Cousin.'

'My father was a target, is that what you are intimating?'

'Yes, I am, Ned.'

For a moment or two Edward did not speak, as he sifted this information. Finally he asked, 'Where was the fire?'

'At a hotel our fathers and brothers were lodging in. Other people were killed, too, by the way.'

'Oh, my God, how terrible. Do you believe Henry Grant is behind it?'

'Not Grant personally,' Neville answered, looking reflective. 'In my opinion he's a doddering fool. However, I consider that French wife of his to be a clever woman in certain ways, and capable of double dealing. And so are his subordinates. They're a dangerous lot, capable of anything.'

'What did you mean by foul play, Neville?'

'Just that. If so, we must avenge the deaths of your father and mine and our brothers. I think your father may have been silenced because he has been making too much of a fuss lately about his role at Deravenels. He's been persistently reminding the current management that he is the one who really should be chairman, and that the Lancashire Deravenel Grants stole the company, grabbed the top jobs and took control of the overall management. It happens to be the truth but none of them like to hear it. And so they targeted your father to shut him up and retain control. That's the long and short of it, in my opinion. I think you must do something about this, Ned, and I am here to help you. I shall back you all the way, and I shall protect your back at all times.'

Edward nodded. 'Thank you, Neville, thank you. We shall make our plans later, but now I feel I have to go to my mother, to comfort her, and then we must give the other children this tragic news.'

FOUR

Cecily Deravenel was known for her stoicism and iron-willed self-control, but both had vanished. Edward became acutely aware of this when he found his mother in her private suite of rooms upstairs.

After knocking on the door, he had walked straight in without waiting for her assent, knowing instinctively that she needed him, needed his comforting presence.

His mother was seated on a love seat close to the fire, in the small parlour which adjoined her bedroom, staring into the flames. When she turned her head, gave him a direct look, he saw at once her ravaged face, the bloodshot eyes, the despair surrounding her, totally enveloping her like a caul. Her grief was so apparent, so acute, he forgot his own for a moment, and hurried to her, alarm touching his face.

Sitting down next to her on the love seat he put his arms around her and drew her close to him.

Cecily resisted, out of habit really, but only for a split second, and then she collapsed against him, holding onto him, weeping as if her heart was breaking. And it was, he was certain of that.

41

Edward had never had trouble understanding this elegant and regal woman who appeared so aloof and oddly remote to many people. He had been privy to her true self since his childhood, and he knew how gentle and loving her heart was, how deeply she loved his father, and he himself and her other children. She had never been anything but an understanding wife and mother and was sympathetic, sensitive to everyone's needs, a constant and loyal ally to her family. And she was a compassionate woman, ready to help anyone in need, and especially those who worked on the estate who adored her, called her an angel.

His mother cherished her relationship with her brother, and depended on him. Aside from their strong filial relationship as siblings, Rick handled her financial affairs and managed the fortune which had been left to her by their father, Philip Watkins, the late industrialist.

Now the two most important mature men in her life – her husband and her brother – had been ripped away from her in an instant, and with a terrible and frightening suddenness. Her life had changed so abruptly, so unexpectedly it took one's breath away; all of their lives had changed, in fact, and nothing would ever be the same again. Not for his mother, not for him and his siblings.

Neville Watkins had become head of the Watkins family; and he himself was suddenly head of the Deravenel clan, the Yorkshire branch. What this actually meant troubled him enormously . . . Total responsibility for the family, for everything their father had taken care of all his life, plus their stake in the Deravenel Company.

Ned was not quite sure how he would manage to juggle all of this, being at university, and also unfamiliar with the workings of the company.

On the other hand, Neville was thirty-two, married, with two small daughters, a seasoned man-of-the-world, a brilliant businessman held in very high regard by his peers, whilst he himself was not yet nineteen, considered a boy by most. Nor was he as experienced as his cousin and certainly he did not have his wisdom. At least not yet.

Nonetheless, he and Neville Watkins would have to pick up the pieces carefully and take charge of their families, endeavour to bring all of their lives back to normal as soon as possible. Ned was fully aware that this would take a certain amount of time. There was a mourning period to get through, and many adjustments to be made. He also accepted that he had a lot to learn, and very rapidly, if he was to handle things properly and for the good of everyone. A balancing act, he thought. It will be a balancing act on a tightrope.

And he must keep a cool head at all times. That was implicit. He was aware that there was now only one person he could trust, apart from his mother, and that was Neville Watkins. His cousin and he were bound together as never before, and Ned knew he needed him, needed his guidance and support if he was going to succeed . . .

His mother's voice broke into his thoughts when she said, 'I'm so sorry, Ned, for giving into my grief. However, I'm afraid I really can't help it. Do forgive me.'

'Mother, there's nothing at all to forgive!' he exclaimed swiftly, looking into her tear-stained face, taking out a handkerchief and gently dabbing her wet cheeks. 'It's vital to let your grief come out. Bottling it up doesn't help. It's a natural thing to grieve, you know. And it's very *necessary* if one is to come to terms with it. People who push grief inside become ill.'

'Yes, you're correct,' she responded. 'We have difficult times ahead, but we must find a way to keep going, lead normal lives if we can. I have the children to think about, their welfare to consider. They are going to need me, Ned, and they will certainly need you, too, although I think *you* are truly going to have your hands full with other things.'

Nodding, Edward stood up. 'We ought to go and speak to them, if you're feeling a little better. We don't want one of the servants to accidentally blurt out the news –'

'They know, Ned. I've already spoken to them,' Cecily cut in, looking up into his blue eyes. 'Naturally they have taken it extremely badly. As I knew they would. I came in here a few moments ago in an effort to pull myself together. I was trying to calm myself when you walked in. And yes, we had better go and comfort them, reassure them that everything will be all right.'

'Are you sure you're up to it now?' he asked, eyeing her.

Cecily's voice quavered slightly as she answered, 'I believe so, yes, Ned. I *must* come with you, it is vitally important for their wellbeing.'

He gave her his hand; she took it and rose. Together

they left the room. Slowly they climbed the stairs leading up to the nursery floor which the younger children still used.

The moment he saw his mother George leapt up from the chair where he was seated and rushed to her, flinging himself against her body so hard she staggered slightly. He wrapped his arms around her, needing her protection, approbation and love. 'Oh, Mama, why did it happen? Why? Why?' he wailed, tears filling his smokey-green eyes. 'WHY?' he demanded in a louder voice, his young face full of grief and anger intermingled. 'I want to know why Papa and Edmund are not coming back. *Please tell me, Mama.*'

'If I knew I would of course tell you, George,' Cecily softly responded, holding the boy closer, glancing down at him, her heart full. She smoothed her hand over his blond hair and went on, 'None of us quite understand yet what happened, George. Ned is going to find out if he can, and then he will tell us.'

Turning to face his brother, George asked a little plaintively, 'You will, won't you, Ned?'

'I will indeed . . . As soon as I know, you'll be the next.' Edward drew closer to his mother and brother and put his arms around them both protectively, holding them close to him for a few moments. Suddenly he became aware of Meg standing near the window sobbing; George's volubility and Meg's weeping only served to make him conscious of Richard's absolute quietness, the pool of stillness surrounding him. The

45

youngest of his siblings was huddled in a chair at the far end of the room, his face the colour of bleached bone, the light grey eyes almost black in the dimming light of late afternoon. The boy looked so sorrowing Edward felt heartsick.

Moving away from his mother, who was still holding George, Edward hurried across to Richard. He stared down at the youngest member of the family, and noticed at once that the pinched, drained look of earlier had settled on the child's face yet again.

'Don't be afraid, Dick,' Edward murmured softly, leaning down to the boy. 'I'll look after you.'

Richard nodded and struggled to his feet. Gazing up at his adored Ned, he whispered, 'I want to know everything, like George. I want to know about Papa and Edmund.' Tears came into his eyes and he said in a trembling voice that was almost inaudible, 'I said Edmund could be impatient . . . I wish I hadn't said *that*.'

'I understand, but it's all right, Dick, really it is.' Reaching out, he pulled the youngster into his arms and held him tightly, stroking his dark head. 'I will keep you safe. Always.'

'You do promise?' the boy whispered.

'I do promise. And you must try to be brave and help Mama.'

'I will, Ned. I promise, too.' He hesitated and then asked, 'Are you going to Italy?'

'Yes, I have to, and Cousin Neville is coming with me. We'll find out everything, and then I'll tell you.'

'You will come back, won't you, Ned?' Richard asked, his voice tremulous, his eyes suddenly awash with tears.

'Of course I'll come back . . . Ravenscar is my home,

and you're here, aren't you? I shall always come back to you, Little Fish.'

Richard nodded, and glanced at Meg. 'She's been crying a long time.'

'I shall go to her at once, perhaps I can console her.'

A moment later Edward was holding his sister in his arms, trying to calm her, soothe her, give her comfort.

Meg wept against his shoulder for a while, and then finally, taking deep breaths, she managed to gain control of herself. Slowly her shoulders stopped heaving and the sobs lessened. When she lifted her hands to her face and wiped away the tears with her fingertips, Edward saw at once the anguish in her eyes. The whole family had been totally bludgeoned by the tragic news Neville had brought earlier in the afternoon. They would be a long time recovering, if they ever did.

Edward said quietly to Meg, tilting her face to his, 'Our Mother needs you at this terrible time, Meggie darling. You must endeavour to be strong for her, help her with George, and especially with Richard, who suffers in silence, as you well know.'

Meg could only nod, not trusting herself to say a word. She had been extremely close to her father and Edmund, and the pain she had suffered since hearing of their deaths had seared through her like a hot iron. She was well aware that she would never be that carefree young girl again and would mourn them for the rest of her life. She felt she had grown old in a few minutes.

After a while, taking more deep breaths she said, 'How long will you be gone?'

Edward shook his head, his eyes suddenly bleak. 'I don't honestly know. A week, perhaps two, I just don't know how long it will take to –' He broke off abruptly. He had been about to wonder aloud how long it would take to bring the bodies back to Ravenscar. And then he had realized he simply could not mouth those words.

Edward could not sleep. All manner of troubling thoughts jostled for prominence in his mind, each one of them more dire than the other, and yet he did not seem able to focus on any problem in particular.

When he had come up to bed, an hour or two ago, he had believed that in the quiet and peacefulness of his bedroom he would be able to quickly sort everything out in his head, but this had not happened. And sleep had remained elusive as his busy mind had raced and raced.

Sighing, he tossed back the bedclothes in exasperation and got up. After putting on his thick woollen dressing gown, he padded over to the fireplace and threw two more logs into the grate. Instantly, sparks flew up the chimney, the fresh logs began to crackle, and in the sudden burst of bright firelight he saw that the carriage clock on the mantel read one-thirty. He was surprised how late it was.

After stepping into his slippers, Edward pulled a wing chair closer to the fire and sat down, his mind still churning. This day had been the worst of his life, one he would never forget. Sorrowful and grieving, his mother and the other children had sat at the dining table with him and Neville, not touching their food.

None of them had eaten, and not much conversation had taken place either. Each and every one of them was too stunned and shattered by the news of the tragedy that had so diminished their family, and Neville's as well.

Eventually his mother had shepherded the children up to their rooms; she had returned a short while later, had invited Neville and himself to join her in her sitting room just off the Long Hall. They had dutifully followed her, glancing at each other questioningly as they hurried behind her.

Within minutes, Jessup, the butler, had brought them a tray of brandy balloons and a decanter of cognac, placed it on a side table and departed. Ned and Neville had been the only ones to pour a drink for themselves; his mother had declined as she usually did.

Once the three of them were settled in front of the fire, Cecily had seemed reflective for a short while, and then she had looked at Ned intently. 'I know you and Neville must go to Italy,' she had begun, and then hesitated before continuing. 'I just want to caution you to be scrupulously careful. And you also, Neville. Pay attention, and don't leave anything to chance.'

They had both immediately promised her they would be on their guard at all times, and would look after each other.

Nodding her understanding, Cecily had then told them in a low, subdued voice, 'There are powers at work here we know nothing about. We must all be alert and very, very cautious.'

'What do you mean, Mother?' Edward had swiftly asked, frowning.

'I can't give you a proper explanation, I simply know that I have this instinctive feeling of . . . *danger*.'

'I never ignore a woman's intuition,' Neville had murmured. 'It is usually infallible.'

Cecily had gone on: 'And you, Ned, will have to go to work at Deravenels, and as soon as possible when you return.'

Startled, he had literally gaped at her for a split second. 'Am I not to return to Oxford then?' he had asked.

'No, you cannot. Your father is dead. You are, by the rules of primogeniture, his heir. So you must now go to work at Deravenels. *That* is the *family* rule . . . when the heir of a Deravenel is over sixteen or reaches sixteen, he must take his deceased father's place. Obviously, not in the same capacity, in this instance as the assistant managing director, but somewhere a little way down the ladder. But the heir must go into the company, he has no choice. It has always been that way.'

'I understand. Now that you've mentioned it, I do recall Father explaining about this old family rule several years ago.'

Neville had then volunteered, 'And remember what I said earlier, Ned, I will help you any way I can.'

All he could do was nod. His mother had turned to face Neville. 'When do you plan to leave Ravenscar?' she had asked somewhat abruptly.

'Tomorrow morning. My carriage will take us to York, and we will then proceed to London on the afternoon train.' His cousin had paused for a moment, taken a swallow of the brandy, and finished, 'Once in London

I shall make plans for us to leave for the Continent on Friday or Saturday.'

'I would appreciate it, Neville, if you would kindly stay in touch with me, and you, too, Edward.'

They had both promised they would.

At this juncture his mother had pushed herself to her feet, and they had also jumped up. At the doorway she had swung her hand and said, very quietly, 'This has been the most horrendous day for everyone, and I must go and make certain that the children are resting quietly . . . there have been far too many tears today, and so much heartbreak.'

Left alone he and his cousin had talked for a while longer, mostly about their imminent travel plans, and then they had gone upstairs to retire for the night. Now Edward stared into the flames, thinking about his father's death.

Revenge. Edward turned the word over and over in his mind. Neville truly believed that deadly factions within the Deravenel Company had hired someone to get rid of his father. However, Edward knew that Neville had nothing concrete to go on, no hard evidence; it was pure supposition on his part, a supposition tied to what Neville called his gut instinct.

Edward was well aware that his father had been complaining and grumbling about the way the company was run for a number of years, and of late his voice had become louder, more strident and insistent. His father's chief target was Henry Deravenel Grant, who had descended down the Lancashire line of the House of Deravenel. Henry was chairman of the board, and his father's cousin. 'An absentee landlord,' his father had called him disparagingly, along with a number of other choice names.

But would Henry's colleagues resort to foul play? Edward wondered. They could have quite easily rendered Richard Deravenel useless by restricting his power in the company. Or they could have forced him into retirement.

Sitting back in the chair, closing his eyes, Edward pondered on these matters for a long time, but he did not have any answers for himself. None at all. What's more, additional questions flew into his head, and again all of them were unanswerable. One question, in particular, stood out . . . *why* had his father gone to Italy to look into problems at the marble quarries in Carrara? Surely that was a job for Aubrey Masters, head of the Mining Division. And why had Edmund, Uncle Rick and Thomas been killed if his father was the target? He was truly baffled, and it suddenly struck him that he would remain in a state of bafflement until he arrived at Carrara and started asking pertinent questions of the local authorities, as well as the manager of their quarries. Only then perhaps would he have a better understanding of the fire, the cause of it, and the manner in which his family had died.

As he continued to gaze into the roaring flames, Edward remembered that he had not looked in his father's desk. He had meant to do so earlier, but he had become so distracted by the children's plight, their sorrow and their need for him, it had slipped his mind. Rising, he hurried out of his bedroom and along the corridor, quickly went down the wide staircase into the Long Hall.

Within seconds he was turning on the lights in his

father's spacious study and striding over to the desk positioned near the window. He knew exactly where the key was hidden; some time ago his father had shown him the hiding place. 'Just in case you ever need to get into my desk when I'm not here,' his father had explained.

Kneeling down in front of the mahogany Georgian partner's desk, Edward pushed his head and shoulders into the space between the sets of drawers and reached his hand towards the back for the key. It hung on a hook on the section of the desk just beyond the knee space.

Slowly, carefully, Edward searched each drawer. His father had been meticulous, and everything was neatly placed. But he came up with nothing of any importance. There were no notes, no records, no diaries, and no files on anything to do with his father's work or the Deravenel Company. Everything in the desk was innocuous, personal, and of very little consequence.

Sitting back in the chair, feeling frustrated, Edward let his eyes roam around the study, thinking of his father, and how much he had loved this particular room at Ravenscar. Every piece of furniture in it he had chosen himself and placed; he noted his father's collection of ancient coins, the many photographs of the family in silver frames, and his treasured books. The Moroccan-bound volumes were carefully arranged in low shelves placed against one of the long walls.

And then there were the portraits . . . the paintings of so many Deravenels, from long ago to the present. Guy de Ravenel, the founder of their dynasty, his likeness somewhat faded now in the extremely old painting.

And, on the other wall, there was the recently-completed portrait of his father, commissioned by his mother and hung there by her only a few weeks ago. As he stared at his father's image a lump came into Edward's throat. He swallowed hard, pushing back the incipient tears. How he would miss him.

His eyes continued to another wall, and he spotted a couple of Deravenel Turners from Wales, along with portraits of the Deravenel Grants from Lancashire. The Grants might spell trouble, but certainly the Turners were relatively docile, and there were not many of them left, only two or so he believed. That line had dribbled down to nothing. Well, that was how his father had put it . . .

A rustling sound, followed by a faint cough, brought Edward's eyes to the door. He was startled to see his brother Richard standing there, bundled up in his woollen dressing gown, staring at him.

'What on earth are you doing up at this hour, Little Fish? It's the middle of the night!' In a flash Edward was on his feet, hurrying across the room to his small brother, concerned for him. Leading him over to the fireplace, Edward went on, 'It's very late for you to be up, old chap.' He sat down, brought Richard close to him.

'I couldn't sleep. I went to your bedroom, Ned, but you weren't there.' Looking into his face intently, Richard frowned, and asked, 'You *will* come back, won't you?'

'I certainly will, I promised, didn't I?'

'Yes. But you see, well, Ned, I don't think George and I are old enough to look after Mama and Meg . . . but you are. So you *have* to come home.'

'I understand what you're saying, and I'll be home in a flash, don't you worry. Once I've done my business in Italy I'll be back. But you know, Dick, I have a feeling that the two of you *could* keep an eye on things for me, couldn't you? Or should I say four eyes?'

Richard forced a smile, but his slate-grey eyes were sad. 'I suppose so.'

Funny how his eyes look more blue at times, Edward thought. Then they become the colour of wet slate, and sometimes they even turn black. They reflect his moods, I suppose. 'Come along, old chap, let's go upstairs,' he suggested. 'It's time we both went to sleep, don't you think?'

Richard simply nodded. Taking hold of Ned's hand, he allowed himself to be led out of the study, across the Long Hall and up the wide staircase. It was only when they came to the first-floor landing that Richard tugged on Edward's hand. 'Could I sleep with you tonight, Ned? Like I did when I was really, really little and afraid of the dark?'

'It will be my very great pleasure to share my bed with you,' Ned exclaimed, smiling down at the eight-year-old boy, understanding that Richard needed to feel protected, safe and secure tonight. There had been so much pain and hurt and sorrow today.

Edward found himself the recipient of a wide and happy smile from his youngest brother, a smile that touched his heart profoundly.

FIVE

London

Will Hasling stood waiting at the barrier at King's Cross Station, stamping his feet to keep warm, and huddling himself deeper into his long winter overcoat. This was made of grey merino wool and had a raccoon fur collar; the coat was slender and elegant, made him look taller than his five feet nine, and added to the twenty-two year-old's air of prosperity.

A pleasant looking young man, with a warm, expansive smile and light-brown hair, Will hailed from a prominent family of landed gentry in Leicestershire. His father was a landowner of considerable importance, with a stately home on hundreds of acres; the local squire and justice of the peace as well, he was something of a bon vivant. His son took after him in that he, too, enjoyed good food and drink but, unlike his father, rural life did not appeal to Will. Hunting, shooting and fishing held no interest for him.

After graduating from Oxford, he fully intended to live in London where he hoped to work in the City, possibly as a broker with a firm on the London Stock Exchange. He loved London, and especially the way it was these days. He found it glittering, glamorous and exciting, *the* place to be.

In the three years that he had been king, Edward VII had become even more popular than he was as Prince of Wales; everyone in the country adored him, from the aristocracy to the working classes and those in between.

Will, like the entire nation, mourned Queen Victoria's passing, but he also felt that same sense of relief, and expectation, now that Edward was on the throne.

People were happy that the king had moved the monarchy back to London. He had lit the lights, thrown open the doors of Buckingham Palace, welcomed his friends inside, and the dancing had begun. It seemed to Will and his friends that after the constraints and repression of Victorian England a new era had begun – a time of jollity, gaiety, freedom and expressiveness. And he for one couldn't wait to sample all of these excitements and pleasures when he left university.

Stamping his feet again, he moved around trying to combat the icy weather. There was a fog on this Wednesday evening, a fog Will hoped would not turn into one of those dreadful pea-soupers. There had been quite a few of those of late, and they blighted London, made the streets difficult to manoeuvre, whether on foot or in a hansom cab.

Will glanced around as he waited, amazed to see the railway station so busy; but then the majority of L.N.E.R. trains from the north and the northeast came into this particular station, most of them arriving during the early evening. So it was understandable that the place was teeming with folk meeting trains at this hour.

It was a normal mix of people waiting here tonight.

There were a number of women, either accompanied by a woman friend or a man, hovering close to him at the barrier. Plain-looking women in long dark coats and cloche hats, obviously from the middle class. As his eyes roamed he spotted a lot of bowlers and a few Homburg hats, but no flat caps ... funny how one could distinguish a class by its headgear. Not many toffs or working class men amongst the bustle, he realized, mostly chaps from the middle class, just like the women.

Adjusting the silk scarf wrapped around his neck, Will began to walk up and down, his thoughts turning to Edward Deravenel. His closest friend, indeed the man he considered to be his very best friend. He was deeply concerned about him, and had been since he had visited the Deravenel town house in Charles Street in Mayfair earlier that day.

His intention had been to ascertain when exactly Edward was arriving from Yorkshire, wishing to plan their journey to Oxford together, already set for the end of the week.

Mr Swinton, the butler, had answered the door, and he had known at once, as Swinton had invited him to come inside, that there was something horribly wrong. A dour expression had ringed the butler's face and a mournful feeling permeated the house. After greeting him, Swinton had confided the terrible and tragic news.

Will had been shocked and stunned, so much so that Swinton had asked him if he would care to partake of a glass of brandy. He had declined, and had then asked for a few more details. Unfortunately, Swinton had not known very much, and had merely added that Mr Edward had telephoned that morning to announce his arrival at the Mayfair house in the early evening. He was travelling up to town with his cousin, and they would be on the afternoon train from York. And then Mr Edward had broken the sorrowful news.

When Will had inquired how Mr Deravenel senior and Mr Edmund had died, the butler had explained, 'It was in a fire in Italy. Mr Watkins senior and his son Thomas were travelling with them, and they were also killed. A great tragedy for the two families, sir,' the butler had finished in a shaken voice, looking on the verge of tears.

Further shocked and appalled, Will had offered his condolences to the butler, who had been in the family's employ since boyhood, he being the son of an old family retainer. Swinton had thanked him, and the two had talked for a short while longer.

Will had eventually taken his leave, and had placed his calling card on the silver salver on the hall table as he went out. Feeling upset and worried, he had walked back to his rooms at the Albany, his senses positively reeling as he had strode down past Shepherd's Market, through Berkeley Square and into Piccadilly where the Albany was located.

During his walk he had made up his mind to go to King's Cross to meet the York train, to be there in case Edward needed him. And of course he would. To lose a father, brother, uncle and cousin in one fell swoop was something incomprehensible, and certainly Will knew that if such a catastrophe had happened to him he would need his best friend, and all the help he could get.

For Will the rest of the day had been miserable. He had paced his rooms, left his food untouched, and discovered that his concentration had totally fled. He had sat staring into the fire for hours, filled with sadness

for his friend, and wondering how to console him in
his loss.

Now, in the distance, Will heard a train hooting
and he wondered if it was the one he was waiting for.
He hoped so. Moving closer to the barrier, he peered
ahead and was somewhat relieved when he overheard
a man standing nearby tell his companion, 'That's the
York train pulling in now.'

Train whistles blowing. Smoke, steam, fog mingling. Doors
slamming. Hustle and bustle. Busy porters pushing luggage
carts. Crowds hurrying along the platform.

So much activity, so many people, Will thought,
moving his head, craning his neck, scanning the crowd,
seeking Edward Deravenel and Neville Watkins. Within
a few minutes the crowds were dissipating, thinning out,
and suddenly he spotted them walking together along
the platform, followed by a porter with their luggage.
He made the decision to stay put. He was standing just
behind the barrier, the best place of all, he knew that,
and certainly Edward would spot him immediately.

Naturally, it was hard to miss Edward Deravenel. He
was so handsome, so tall he towered over everyone and
stood out most markedly in any crowd. And there was
no mistaking Edward's cousin.

Neville had always had a taste for fine clothes and was
beautifully attired in the latest and most stylish fashions
on all occasions. His reputation for being a bit of a dandy
had preceded him for years; there were even those who
referred to him as the Edwardian Beau Brummell.

Tonight Neville wore a black Homburg hat, in the jaunty style favoured by King Edward, and a black overcoat with an astrakhan collar. It was stylish, elegant and obviously it had been impeccably tailored in one of Savile Row's best establishments.

Although he was not as tall as his cousin, Neville was, nonetheless, a striking, good-looking man, and he held himself regally, walked as if he owned the world.

In a sense, he probably did, now that his father was dead. He would inherit the many companies which his grandfather had left to Rick Watkins, and which Rick had run most successfully for some years. But this aside, Neville was a prosperous man in his own right; his vast fortune came from his own efforts, and there was too the fortune his heiress wife Anne had brought to the marriage as her dowry. Will knew that he was considered to be one of the most important magnates in England.

People standing in front of Will hurried off to greet those travellers they were meeting, and he found himself looking straight down the emptying platform. Edward caught sight of him, and a quick flash of a smile glanced across his handsome face.

Will waved, and went to the gate, clasped Edward's hand as he came through.

Neville nodded, thrust out his own hand, and then when the greetings were over the three men moved towards the entrance to the railway station which also led out to the street.

'Good of you to come, Will. I suppose you've spoken to Swinton?' Edward spoke quickly, raised an eyebrow.

Will nodded. 'I went to the Mayfair house today, to

find out when you were returning from Yorkshire. Swinton told me the horrendous news. Ned, I'm so very, very sorry. This is such a terrible tragedy . . .'

'Yes,' Ned said laconically.

Turning to Neville, Will went on, 'Please accept my condolences, Neville. I know you're as heartsick as Ned.'

'Thank you, Will,' Neville responded a little brusquely, and cleared his throat. 'Did you come in a hansom?'

'Yes, I did. The driver's waiting for me.'

'My carriage will be outside. Would you care to ride with us, or do you prefer to make use of the cab which brought you?'

'I'd like to come with you and Ned, naturally,' Will answered. 'I'll pay the driver off, he'll be happy to pick up another fare here at the station.'

By this time they had reached the exit where several private carriages were waiting, along with a number of hansom cabs. Will glanced around until he found the one he had come in; he hurried over to pay the driver while Neville and Edward showed the porter where to put the luggage.

Within a very short while the three men were seated comfortably in Neville's elegant carriage, being driven across London, heading for Mayfair and the town house in Charles Street where the Deravenels lived.

After making desultory conversation for a few minutes, all three men fell silent, and Will, who was sitting opposite Edward and Neville in the carriage, soon began to realize that both had drifted into their own thoughts.

And with good reason, Will decided: they both have a great deal to think about and to deal with. Several times he was on the verge of saying something and then instantly bit back the words. He was reluctant to intrude on the privacy they appeared to need, and on their grief. Their expressions were sorrowful, and Edward, who was usually filled with vivacity, was positively sombre; Neville's face was closed, bore no expression at all, except for his eyes. And they were cold, pale blue ice.

Will leaned back against the padded seat of the carriage, lost in his own mental meanderings for a short while. He noticed through the window that the light fog had deepened but was not yet so thick that the driver couldn't make his way. He closed his eyes, drifting, the only sound the clatter of the horses' hooves on the road.

A little later Will opened his eyes and saw at once that Edward was studying him intently. Edward said, 'I hope, Will, that you will join me for a light supper, and you, too, Neville?'

Before Will could say a word, Neville shook his head. 'I do believe I should get back to Chelsea. I must attend to our travel plans, but thank you, Edward.'

Edward glanced at Will. 'And what about you, my friend?'

'Of course I'll dine with you, Ned, and I'll help you in any way I can.'

SIX

Edward and Will sat in front of the fire in the small parlour of the Mayfair townhouse, each of them nursing a cognac. Edward was recounting everything he knew about the fire, and the tragic deaths of his family, and when he finally finished, he added, 'However, Neville believes they were deliberately removed. He's suggesting foul play.'

Will, who had been listening attentively to everything Edward had to say, sat bolt upright in the chair. Momentarily stunned, he gaped at Edward, and then exclaimed, 'Ned, that's preposterous –' Will cut himself off abruptly. Leaning forward, he fixed his eyes on Edward intently, and in a quieter voice, added, 'Perhaps it's not so preposterous, after all. There has been bad blood between your father and his cousin Henry Grant for years. Is that what Neville is suggesting? That Henry Grant got rid of your father because he feared him, feared that he would endeavour to take over Deravenels?'

Edward nodded. 'That's the gist of it. But of course Neville doesn't mean Henry, but his subordinates, and he doesn't have anything pertinent or concrete to go on, as of this moment. It's what he calls a gut feeling, an instinct. And you know very well that Neville is a masterful businessman of no mean talent, and he has great psychological insight into people.' Edward sighed. 'He's convinced he is right in this assumption, and I can't argue with him. It seems to me he's correct. And so we are going to Italy to investigate what actually happened. *Really happened.* Maybe we will find something, maybe we won't. And once we've finished checking the facts, we will bring the bodies back for burial. We plan to leave for Florence on Friday, actually, by way of Paris.'

'Where *was* the fire in Florence?' Will asked, wondering why he had not read about it in *The Times*. After all, Florence was the greatest Renaissance city in the world, and a fire anywhere there would be bound to make news.

'It wasn't in Florence, Will. The fire was in Carrara, in the hotel where they were staying. My father had gone to Carrara to look into a problem with our marble quarries. Edmund had begged to go with Father, because he'd never been to Italy, and Uncle Rick and Thomas asked if they might accompany them, because my uncle was eager to buy sculpture and art for his house. Naturally Florence was a very tempting place to visit.'

'I understand,' Will answered, and then hesitated for a moment, looking down into the amber liquid in his glass, his expression thoughtful. After a second, he asked, 'Could I come with you and Neville, Ned? I think I might be of some help, useful to you, and if you don't think I can do anything special for you, do remember I can give you moral support. I'm very good at that, don't you know.'

A smile flitted briefly across Edward's mouth, and

was instantly gone. He glanced across at Will, his expression suddenly quizzical. 'What about Oxford? Your studies? We were supposed to go back there this coming weekend, you and I.'

'That's absolutely true. But isn't this an emergency?' Not waiting for an answer, Will continued, 'We could return together in a few weeks, when this problem has been resolved.'

'I won't be going back to university, Will. This is it for me, I'm afraid. My mother informed me yesterday that I must take my father's place at Deravenels. That's the family rule.'

Will looked crestfallen. 'So you won't be coming back? Not ever? Is that what you mean, Ned?'

'I do. And of course I do regret that. On the other hand, there is nothing *I* can do about it, since that rule has been in existence for several hundred years. Don't forget, the Deravenel Company was originally founded by my ancestor, Guy de Ravenel, once he'd settled in Yorkshire after the Norman Conquest. At that time, he started importing wines, and exporting raw wool, spun wool and woollen goods.'

'It's amazing, when you think about it, Ned. Eight hundred years of trading.' Will shook his head. 'Few companies are that old.'

'Yes, you're right. But it didn't really come into its own as a proper company until the fifteenth century, when Deravenels began trading all over the world, importing and exporting goods . . . everything under the sun, in fact. And we still do. I suppose we are the largest trading company in existence today, and I know my father felt he had entitlement to it.'

'I've never really understood the bad blood between members of your family. What is it all about?'

'It's actually fairly simple, Will. Sixty years ago, Henry Grant's grandfather deposed one of our cousins, who was running Deravenels. He did this by slurring the man's reputation, putting out bad stories about his private life, along with harmful allegations about his abilities. In fact, he made our cousin look incompetent and reckless. Because our cousin had no children, his direct heir was a second cousin, Roger Morton Deravenel. However, this man died, and so it was Roger's son Edmund who was next in line. But he was a child, only seven and obviously he couldn't run the company.'

'Henry Grant's grandfather just grabbed the top position because one man was weak, another had just died and the next in line was too young to run Deravenels,' Will interjected. 'What an opportunity that was. *Irresistible.*'

'That's true, and very suddenly the Lancashire Deravenel Grants were in control, having pushed the Yorkshire Deravenels out. In other words, *us.* Not long after this, our cousin, who had been shoved out, died in mysterious circumstances, and so there was no opposition left. Henry Grant's grandfather was tough, strong, and ruthless, and that's the reason our side of the family has been in second position at Deravenels all these years. But it truly should be ours.'

'Cousins fighting cousins,' Will muttered.

'A family feud of long standing. But we do try to be civil with each other . . . at least my father did. I don't know that I can be.'

Will half smiled, then asked, 'Well, what do you say, old chap? May I join you on this trip to Florence?'

'If you are inclined to do so, then why not? I am quite certain that Neville will appreciate your presence, as indeed I will.'

After Will Hasling had gone home, Edward hurried up to his father's study on the next floor. He went in, snapped on the electric light, and recoiled slightly. The room had a faint lingering odour of the cigars his father had enjoyed, mingled with the scent of the bay rum aftershave lotion he had always favoured.

In his mind's eye, Edward saw his father sitting behind the large Georgian desk at the far end of the room, smiling across at him, and a lump came into his throat as a sudden rush of intense emotion swamped him. He had loved his father, admired him, and he would miss him inordinately, as would his brothers and sisters.

For a moment he thought of walking out, going up to his bedroom, and then changed his mind. He would have to become accustomed to these flashes of over-whelming feeling, the vivid memories, and face them squarely, not run from them. His father was dead, just as Edmund was, and nothing would bring them back. However, the remembered past and their lives existed inside him, were deep in his heart, and so there was really no death in his lexicon. These two men lived on in his heart, and for as long as he was alive then they would be alive, too, and part of *him* forever.

He walked over to the desk, went around its bulk

and sat down in the comfortable black leather chair. He knew at once that he would find nothing of any importance here because all of the drawers had keys in the locks.

Nothing to hide, nothing to find, Edward thought, as he opened the top middle drawer. It contained only a few items, none of any importance, and as he went through each drawer, he discovered the same thing. Basically there was nothing of interest to him, and certainly nothing alluding to the Grants.

Closing the last drawer, Edward sat back in the chair, sighing to himself. He wondered what he had been looking for . . . he had no idea really, but he had thought that perhaps somewhere there might be a piece of damning or revealing evidence about Henry Grant and his cohorts, the men who surrounded him, or his French wife.

Glancing around the room, Ned suddenly saw it more objectively than ever before. He had always liked its warmth and handsome overtones; the deep red-flocked wallpaper, the large, comfortable sofa covered in a matching red velvet fabric, the worn black leather armchairs near the fireplace, the wall of leather-bound books. Despite the general prevalence in most homes of that tabletop clutter of the recent Victorian era, there was a paucity of it here. His father had never cared for lots of bric-a-brac, but then neither had his mother. As in his father's private abode at Ravenscar, there were numerous silver-framed photographs of himself, his siblings, plus several of his mother. And that was the extent of it, except for a silver cigarette box and, over on the long side table, a humidor for his father's favourite Cuban cigars.

It was *his* room now. At least it was his if he wished to make use of it, courtesy of his mother. The town-house belonged to her; it had never been his father's property, but had come to his mother from her father, Philip Watkins, the industrialist. Until his grandfather's death they had lived in a much, much smaller house in Chelsea, one which had been passed down from his other grandfather, Charles Deravenel, to his father. It was a nice house, and relatively comfortable, but extremely modest in comparison to this one. And, of course, it was his mother's inheritance that paid for its upkeep and for the maintenance of Ravenscar as well. He wasn't sure why his father had always been short of money, always endeavouring to make ends meet, and obviously embarrassed by the impecunious situation he found himself in. But no doubt *he* would find out soon enough, now that he was going to be working at the Deravenel Company.

On the train to London, Neville had suggested they both go there tomorrow to question Aubrey Masters, and to have a look around in general. 'It won't do any harm,' Neville had said to him. 'And it's only natural that we would want to go over there together, since our fathers and brothers died together.'

Ned had immediately seen the sense in this, and Neville had offered to pick him up at ten o'clock the next day. The Deravenel Company had large offices in the Strand, 'Which,' Neville had pointed out, 'is the place you'll have to occupy for the rest of your life. But at the top of the heap, if I have anything to do with it.'

Edward knew that Neville was a brilliant strategist,

an incomparable businessman, one with money to burn, if needs be. Whatever else happened, he was secure in the knowledge that Neville Watkins, cousin, friend and mentor, would get to the bottom of the tragedy which had taken place in Italy. But he had no idea how Neville proposed to put him at the top of the heap in the Deravenel Company. That would take a miracle, wouldn't it?

Once again, sleep eluded Edward. At eleven o'clock he got out of bed, went into the adjoining bathroom and splashed cold water on his face. He stood for a moment, staring at himself in the looking glass. He appeared tired, with faint dark shadows under his eyes, but other than that there were no real signs of the pain and grief he had suffered since learning of the family tragedy. In fact, he looked like himself . . . a strapping young man in the bloom of youth, broad-chested with wide shoulders, a slender waist and narrow hips. And he was tall, taller than most men he knew. Moving away from the looking glass, he returned to his bedroom, dressed in fresh linen, took a dark suit from his wardrobe, put it on, then filled his pockets with small change, keys, his money wallet, and the gold watch his grandfather Watkins had left him in his will.

Ten minutes later, bundled up in a dark overcoat and scarf, he went to the butler's pantry, where he found Swinton. 'I'm afraid I must go out on an errand,' Edward said to the butler, adding, 'And please don't wait up for me, Swinton, there is no need for that.'

'Whatever you wish, sir,' Swinton replied, his face unreadable.

Edward inclined his head politely and returned to the front hall. Within seconds he was outside on the pavement hailing a hansom cab that was rumbling down Charles Street. He climbed in as the driver was saying, 'Evenin', Guv, where can I be taking you?'

Edward gave an address in Belsize Park, told the driver he was required to wait, then sat back against the carriage seat. The cab began to move forward and Edward asked himself why he was going to see Lily Overton, tonight of all nights? He had only just learned of his father's death, his brother's death, and that of close relatives. Four of the family gone, and here he was going to see a woman, a woman he knew would give him a certain kind of solace. But it was not her sexual solace he sought or required tonight. It was solace of another kind he craved. He needed to be comforted and soothed; hopefully she would be able to help him out, ease his heartache. One thing he knew for certain was that she would be alone; Lily was not a prostitute. She was yet another widow he knew, older than Alice at Ravenscar, and also well provided for, having been married to a solicitor who had been successful.

He had acquired a liking for older women ever since he had been seduced at the age of thirteen by the wife of the choirmaster at a Scarborough church: a woman who had instructed him in the pleasurable art of sex in a cave on the beach at Ravenscar, just below the ruined stronghold built by his ancestor, Guy de Ravenel. She had been twenty-five and a beautiful blonde with silver-grey eyes. Lily Overton was thirty-two and just as beautiful as Tabitha had been, another blonde-haired temptress who had truly captivated him and held him in her sexual thrall. He closed his eyes and thought of both women; they intermingled in his mind and he suddenly felt the thrill of unexpected sexual arousal.

A short time later, the hansom cab jolting to a sudden stop made Edward sit up with a start; glancing out of the window he saw that they had arrived at the small house where Lily Overton lived.

Opening the door, he jumped out, and looking up at the driver, he said, 'Wait a moment, please.'

'I understands, Guv,' the cabbie said.

The house was in darkness, but Edward noticed the glimmer of a candle flame in an upstairs window. Lifting the brass knocker, he banged hard on the door.

Lily did not appear. Once more he lifted the knocker, but before he used it again her voice said, from behind the door, 'Who's there?' She sounded alarmed and he knew he must reassure her at once, using a code they had devised together.

'Lily? It's me, Ned. Your brother-in-law. I've come to see my brother. Is he at home?'

'Come to the window,' she replied in a low voice, 'so that I can see you, be certain it *is* my brother-in-law outside at this hour.'

Stepping over to the window, Edward waited for her to peep through the lace curtains. Once she had done so, he moved back to the front door and waited; within a second Lily was unlocking it. Before he stepped into the house, he called over his shoulder to the driver of the hansom cab, 'Please wait for me. I won't be too long.'

'Righto, Guv'nor,' came the reply, followed by a quiet chuckle.

Once he was inside the house, Lily locked the front door and then turned to Edward, looking up at him, her light green eyes questioning, her expression puzzled.

In the past he had always sent notes to her by messenger, asking if he could visit her, and she had responded by return using the same messenger, either declining or acquiescing to his request to see her. It was usually the latter. His arrival tonight was unannounced, and unexpected, and she was quite obviously surprised, he realized that. He said quickly, 'Excuse me, Lily, for coming to see you without prior warning, and at this very late hour. I hope I have not inconvenienced you.'

'No, not at all. Perhaps I misunderstood the letter you posted from Yorkshire . . . I was expecting you on Friday . . . before you went back to Oxford the next day.'

'I did plan that. But I returned to London earlier than I expected – this evening, in fact, and I had such a need to see you, to be in your company, if only for a short while, I just had to come here.'

He had spoken softly, in a low tone, and there was a seriousness about him tonight which was unusual. She suddenly wondered what was wrong, for surely something was amiss. Lily Overton was not a stupid woman by anybody's standards, and she detected a strange and unfamiliar sadness in Edward; it seemed to her that sorrow shadowed his brilliant blue eyes, dulling them, and his demeanour was quiet, reflective almost, which was unlike him.

Since their first meeting last year she had found him irresistible, and readily succumbed to his charms whenever he wanted to be with her, whatever the circumstances. Even though he was so young, far too young for her, she cared about him deeply and he was the only man who had ever satisfied her sexually.

Reaching out, instinctively understanding he needed comforting for some reason, she put a hand on his arm and said gently, 'Hang up your coat and scarf and let us go to the sitting room upstairs where we can talk for a while. I was reading there when you arrived on my doorstep, and there's a lovely fire. It's cosy.'

Edward nodded, put his coat in the closet and followed her up the staircase into her private haven. He liked this small but charming room with its dark-rose coloured walls, rose-damask covered sofa and chairs and moss-green carpet. Rose-coloured velvet draperies covered the window, banished the foggy winter's night from sight, and the room was warm and inviting as he remembered.

'May I turn down the gas lights?' Edward asked. 'It's rather bright in here.'

'Of course,' Lily answered, added, 'And could you please throw another log on the fire while I pour you a glass of brandy.'

He smiled at her, added logs to the grate and, reaching up, he lowered the gas lights on either side of the mirror above the mantelpiece; instantly the sitting room was shadowy and more restful, intimate.

Walking over to the sofa Edward sat down. He leaned

back against the needlepoint pillows hoping he could relax here with Lily; his nerves were taut and he had developed a raging headache. But she was always calm, warm and affectionate with him, and she had never failed to have a soothing effect on him.

Within the space of a few minutes she was handing him the balloon of brandy, and seating herself next to him on the sofa.

Looking at him intently, studying him through narrowed green eyes, Lily said finally, 'I *know* there's something wrong. You are troubled, I can tell that.' When he was silent, she asked, 'Would you care to talk to me about it, Edward?'

For a moment he did not answer, and then he said in a subdued voice, 'There has been a terrible tragedy in my family. We are all devastated, Lily, grief stricken –' He broke off, shook his head, as if he still disbelieved the veracity of what he was about to say. And then slowly, still speaking in that same low monotone, he told her about his father and brother, uncle and cousin, and their sudden and unexpected deaths in the fire at Carrara.

Lily was so aghast she was stunned into total silence. She found it hard to take it in, to comprehend what he was telling her . . . to lose four close family members in one stroke was something quite unimaginable. She sat staring at him through tearful eyes, and it took her a moment or two to recover her composure, to find the right words. But at last she said, 'Oh, Ned, Ned darling, I'm so very sorry. It is heartbreaking for you and your family, I understand that . . . a great tragedy, catastrophic. Words are such cold comfort at a time like this, words are just . . . *hopeless*.' She blinked back her tears, and went on in a quavering voice, 'What can I do? How can I help you? Is there anything I can do to comfort you?'

Ned sighed, shook his head. 'Not really . . . just being here with you is enough. You have always been so kind and loving –' His voice trailed off, and he took a swallow of the brandy, put the glass back on the side table. When he turned his face to hers, he looked at her carefully. 'Thank you for being . . . well, for being here. So understanding, so compassionate.'

Lily took his hand in hers, brought it to her lips and pressed it against her mouth, moved closer to him. Placing his hand in her lap, she stroked it. After a few minutes of mutual silence, she murmured, 'Do you want to be with me? To stay here tonight?'

'I really can't,' he answered swiftly, frowning. 'I am meeting my cousin very early tomorrow morning, so I must leave here soon. I haven't slept at all since we received the news.'

'I understand . . .' She paused, hesitated, then remarked quietly, leaning into him, 'You are so *tense*, overwrought really, Ned. At least let me give you a massage before you go, you know how much my massages help you to relax, to feel better.'

Now it was his turn to hesitate before speaking. After a moment of thought, he said, 'I'll stay for an hour, Lily, if that's all right with you.'

'Whatever you want, my darling.'

SEVEN

At thirty-two Lily Overton was a wise woman, and over the years she had acquired a degree of sophistication and worldliness. She had been married and widowed twice. Her first husband had been a surgeon and her second a solicitor who was head of his own law firm, and both men had left her their considerable wealth. She was a widow well placed.

During her marriage to Oscar Overton, the solicitor, she had met all manner of people from all walks of life, and she had benefitted enormously from this. It was because of her wisdom, insight and bright intelligence that she had rapidly come to understand Edward Deravenel, from the first moment they had met.

Their initial encounter had been a year ago, and she found herself thinking about that evening now, reliving it, as she waited for him to return to the upstairs sitting room after going down to talk to the hansom cab driver.

Last January she had been invited to a small dinner party at the Kensington home of her dear friend Vicky Forth, the newly-married sister of Will Hasling. Will had arrived with his best friend Edward Deravenel, and it had been patently obvious to Lily that Edward was instantly drawn to her the moment he set eyes on her. He had gravitated to her at once, making a beeline across the long stretch of drawing room, and had remained glued to her side until they had gone in for dinner, not saying much but focused on her to the exclusion of all else.

Much to her surprise, she had been filled with genuine disappointment when she had found herself seated between Will and a middle-aged banker with a walrus moustache and a slight lisp in his speech; a moment later, she had smiled with delight as Edward was shown to the chair opposite her.

His brilliant blue eyes had barely left her face throughout dinner; they had greedily devoured her as he had left his food untouched. His interest in his female dinner partners on either side had been vague, brief, only just meeting the usual standards of courtesy. His concentration had again been focused entirely on her, and she had understood *exactly* what he wanted from her. It was reflected in the expression in those mesmerizing eyes which left little to the imagination.

After dinner the women had retired to the drawing room whilst the men had remained alone to enjoy their port and cigars. She had been restless, impatient, and on a knife's edge until *he* had appeared in the doorway of the drawing room half an hour later. Relief had flooded through her as he walked towards her, holding her with his eyes, not caring what anyone thought. Neither had she, much to her amazement. Lily had been somewhat surprised that she had remained taut inside, excited and anxious to have him closer to her.

Once he had come to a stop, he had said, 'I need to speak to you alone, Mrs Overton.'

She had simply nodded and he had put his hand under her arm and carefully ushered her to a distant corner near a potted palm.

'I must see you again, and as soon as possible,' he had muttered in a low voice once they were by themselves, his eyes on hers. 'And I do believe *you* would like that, too.' As he had spoken he had inched closer and increased the pressure of his hand on her arm, and there was such naked desire written across his face she had found her mouth suddenly turning dry.

For a moment she had not been able to speak, had simply gazed up at him, totally entranced, under his spell.

'*Please*,' he begged.

Bright colour had flooded her face and she had felt extremely hot, flushed.

'Tomorrow,' he murmured hoarsely. 'Better still, tonight. *Later tonight.* Oh, please say yes.'

Finally finding her voice, she had whispered, 'Tomorrow. In the afternoon. At four.'

'Shall I come to your home? Or do you want to –'

'My home,' she had cut in, dreading the thought of a meeting at a hotel. A public rendezvous would be improper, disastrous, and she had quickly told him where she lived.

The following day, Lily had wondered about herself and her behaviour, asking herself why she had become so quickly entranced by this young man, one who was obviously so much younger than she. And she had known the answer immediately. *Instant attraction.*

Overwhelming sexual desire. On both their parts. And so she had told her housekeeper to leave early that day, had seen her off at two o'clock; fifteen minutes later she had sent the maid home as well.

Alone, she had bathed and perfumed herself, brushed and dressed her golden hair in a loose, girlish style, put on pretty white undergarments and selected a pale-green chiffon-and-lace afternoon tea gown. The style was simple, loose and floating, tied around the waist with a broad, pale-green ribbon belt. Even though it was a cold day she had wanted something young and pretty to wear which also gave him easy access to her. She had already known instinctively what to expect when he arrived; she knew he would make a move on her very swiftly, attempt to seduce within the first half hour. His lust for her had been only too obvious and too urgent the night before.

She had been ready for an hour before he was due, and had paced the floor, prowled around the house, checking on everything, and as she did this she discovered she was hardly able to contain herself. She was trembling, excited inside, acting like a young girl without experience. These feelings had truly taken her by surprise, since she *was* experienced.

Edward had arrived at five minutes to four, for afternoon tea. She had served him herself, and his gaze had never left her. Lily had been fully aware that the absence of staff and her flushed face signalled to him that her aim and intentions were indeed the same as his. But then he had already known that before he had come here today.

He had taken a sip of tea, and so had she; he had talked to her for a short while about Oxford, his close friendship with Will, and how much he liked Vicky Forth, *her* friend.

Lily had listened attentively, loving the timbre of his voice, as she had the night before, a voice which was deeply masculine, mellifluous and cultivated.

And then, unexpectedly, Edward had stopped abruptly, risen and walked over to her chair. Bending over her, he had said in the softest of voices, 'Won't you come and sit with me on the sofa? You seem so far away.'

Before she could even answer he had taken her hand, brought her to her feet and led her to the sofa positioned near the fireplace.

'You're trembling, Mrs Overton,' he had said, sounding surprised, as he had pressed her down onto the sofa, seated himself next to her. 'Are you all right?'

'Perfectly,' had been all she could manage to say.

'I'm afraid I'm not,' he had murmured and immediately drew closer. 'I've been extremely agitated since last night. You see, I haven't been able to stop thinking about you.' When she did not respond he asked, 'Dare I hope that you've given a little thought to me?'

She nodded.

He leaned into her then, put his arm around her shoulders and brought his mouth to her cheek. She had not flinched, had remained quite still as he had kissed her cheek again and found her mouth with his. She had kissed him back. Why pretend, she had thought, why pretend to be overly virtuous when he knows how much I want him. Within the space of a few seconds his hand had been on her breast; he had pulled her closer to him, holding her tightly in his arms and with one dexterous hand he had unbuttoned the front of the gown and slipped his hand inside, lightly touching her nipple. When she had not shown any resistance to these advances, he had grown infinitely bolder, had slid his hand down her leg, lifted the loose flowing skirt of her dress, slipping his fingers along her inner thigh and between her legs. It was at this moment that she had stopped him, exclaiming softly, 'Please, we must stop. This is most unseemly.'

He had pulled away from her gently, staring into her face, an amused look on his, and he had laughed. 'Oh, Mrs Overton, *really*.' He had laughed again, and so had she, and then he had shaken his head and asked, 'Could we perhaps go upstairs, Mrs Overton? I do believe it has become quite pressing for us to find a bed.'

'Only if you stop calling me Mrs Overton and call me Lily instead, Edward,' she had answered with a light laugh.

'And you must call *me* Ned.'

Together they had climbed the stairs and she had not been at all self-conscious; she had led him into her bedroom, then had suddenly turned her head and given him a most cryptic look.

His response had been to immediately take her in his arms, press her close to his body, his hand sliding down onto her buttocks. She had felt so small, feminine and defenceless because he was so tall, broad and masculine, the most masculine man she had ever met.

When he had pressed her even closer, moulding her to him, she had felt his erection against her body, and she had begun to tremble.

As if he understood her instant trepidation he had not made another move, had simply stood perfectly still,

83

looking down at her, his expression suddenly loving. Very slowly, he had begun to remove her clothes, untying the ribbon belt around her waist, letting it drop to the floor, unfastening the rest of the buttons on the front of her dress. Slipping it over her shoulders, it had fallen to the floor, a pool of pale green lace at her feet. A moment after he had started to loosen her undergarments, he stopped and led her over to the bed. Without a word, he had taken off everything else until she was completely naked.

It was only then that he had spoken, saying in an awed voice, 'Oh, Lily, Lily, you are very, very beautiful.'

She had remained silent, simply staring up at him through eyes filled with longing for him, desire written all over her face.

Everything had gone very swiftly after that. He had risen, shed his own clothes quickly, stretched out next to her on the bed. Pushing himself up on one elbow, he had leaned over her, kissed her deeply, passionately, his tongue sliding into her mouth for a moment of true intimacy. All of his movements were slow, gentle, tender, and soon one hand roamed over her, stroking and caressing every part of her until she cried out in pleasure.

Soon after this he had taken her hand and placed it on his groin, and she had been startled by the size of him. But when he entered her he had done so with immense gentleness, and she had found herself opening up to him, thrilled by his virility, knowledge and experience. Their coupling had been rapturous, ecstatic, as they had both known it would be from their first moment of meeting.

Edward had stayed with her for the rest of the day

and into the early evening. She had made supper for him, and he had stayed on and on, in the end not taking his leave of her until the early hours of the morning. He had been insatiable and so had she, and she had realized that night that he was the best lover she had known.

And so had begun the most extraordinary relationship Lily had had with any man, one that over the months had given her unusual happiness.

Ned saw her whenever he came up to London, and occasionally, giving in to his pleading, she visited him in Oxford. With the passing of time she had grown to love him, whilst understanding that the gap in their ages was far too enormous to bridge. Nonetheless, she resolved to remain his mistress for as long as he wanted and needed her.

There was very little she did not know about him, and she understood him completely. He was a highly-sexed, sensual and extremely romantic man; she found him mature for his age and extremely intelligent; he had a brilliant, analytical mind that would sometimes stun her. These attributes aside, his looks were heart-stopping, and yet there was no personal vanity in him about his appearance, and he was kind, compassionate. Perhaps the most unique thing about Ned was his charisma. He possessed a special kind of natural charm that was so captivating it ensnared everyone. This characteristic, plus his amiability and friendliness, immediately put people at ease. All gravitated to him, wanted to be part of his circle.

Yet Lily was very much aware that behind that charming, polished façade there was a wholly different kind of man, one of dogged determination, who harboured great ambition, was full of resourcefulness and had a will of iron that was formidable. Very quickly in their relationship she had come to accept that he could also be absolutely ruthless when he deemed it necessary.

Few people recognized any of these characteristics, because they took him at face value, and also because he did not permit them to know him intimately. Inevitably they underestimated him, much to her amusement and frequent irritation. They tended to characterize him as lazy, indolent and a pretty boy, and therefore dismissed him as a man of no consequence. How wrong they were.

Lily rose from the chair when she heard the front door bang, and her ponderings about Ned and their first meeting were pushed to one side. He was on the staircase, coming back to her, and her look was questioning as he entered the small sitting room. 'Was the cabbie willing to wait?'

'For as long as I wish,' he answered, giving her a faint smile. Striding over to the fireplace he seated himself on the sofa and stretched out his long legs.

'Do you want me to give you a shoulder massage?' she began, and instantly stopped as she saw him shaking his head.

'I just wish to sit here with you, Lily, for a while, and relax, if I can. I'm so filled with grief I feel that anything I did which gave me an ounce of pleasure tonight would be completely wrong.'

Looking across at him, Lily merely inclined her head. A silence fell between them, but it was a compatible silence, and for a while the only sounds were the ticking of the grandfather clock in the corner and the crack-ling of the logs on the fire.

Eventually, Lily ventured, 'I felt the same way as you do now when my first husband died . . . that I shouldn't enjoy anything, that it was somehow disrespectful. But that's not the case, you know. And having a woman love you, and loving a woman in return, is actually a wonderful affirmation of life.' When he made no response, Lily pushed herself to her feet and went to sit next to him on the sofa.

Resting one hand on his leg, she said with great care, 'Do you think that making love to me when you are in mourning would be unseemly? Or something like that, Ned?'

'I suppose so . . .' He left his sentence unfinished, leaned back against the sofa and stared at her, his expression both worried and perplexed.

'I fully understand, and as I said, I have been where you are at this moment in time, so full of sorrow,' Lily murmured. 'It's sorrow mixed with anger, and a sense of helplessness. It's only natural to feel like that, and perhaps worse for you, because you have lost your closest and dearest family.'

He took her hand in his, held it tightly. 'Yes,' he murmured, 'you're correct.'

'I learned long ago that it is important to put death to one side, and get on with *everyday* things. Life *is* for the living, Ned, and understanding that does help to ease the sadness.'

He ran his hand through his red-gold hair and sighed heavily. 'You're wise, Lily, and I agree with you on an *intellectual* level, but it's very difficult to accept that emotionally.' He sighed again and offered her a rueful smile. 'Anyway, I don't think I would be able to make love tonight, I really don't.'

But he was. And he did. With Lily's loving help. Life *was* for the living. And tomorrow was for revenge.

EIGHT

'I don't think there is anything untoward about my coming with you to Deravenels this morning, Ned,' Neville Watkins said, walking across to the fireplace as he spoke, standing with his back to it. 'I consider it quite normal that I accompany you. After all, my father and brother were killed along with yours in Carrara.'

'Oh, I totally agree with you,' Edward was swift to answer, staring at his cousin, perplexed, and then continuing, 'And it was *you* whom Aubrey Masters decided to telephone, once he had received the tragic news. However, why do you bring it up?' Ned frowned. 'Do you envision some sort of problem? By that I mean about *us* arriving together?'

'Not at all. I was just running everything through my mind. Normally, some pernickety member of the staff might wonder out loud about a cousin who has nothing to do with the company arriving on their doorstep with you, that's all. It was always my understanding that several of Henry Grant's employees were a trifle touchy about your father's relatives.'

Edward chuckled. 'Correct, they were, and most especially the French whore, as Father used to call her. She was the most vociferous.'

Neville raised a brow, giving Edward a swift look. 'The French whore,' he repeated, and suddenly began to laugh. 'I remember now, your father did occasionally mutter something or other about the true paternity of her son Edouard. I do believe he wondered aloud about the ability of Henry to perform – well, that was the way he put it.'

'My father was convinced that Henry was impotent, and possibly sterile as well, and he made no bones about it at home. He was truly convinced that their son was fathered by one of Grant's colleagues.'

'Making Edouard a bastard, of course, and therefore not of his blood, and therefore not entitled to take over Deravenels one day.'

Edward nodded. 'Anyway, I have not been in touch with Aubrey Masters. Have you?'

'No. I purposefully chose not to announce our arrival. I thought it would be more interesting to walk in unexpectedly, out of the blue, so to speak.'

'Jolly good idea. And by the way, last night Will volunteered to come with us to Italy. He asked me to ask you if he could. He feels he can be helpful.' Giving Neville a long, questioning glance, he now asked, 'So, what do you say, Neville?'

'It's rather a good idea, actually, Ned. Who knows what we're going to find, and another clever brain and pair of sharp eyes can be most useful. I have decided to have the Thomas Cook agency make all of the travel arrangements, they're very good at that, and I shall merely add Will's name.'

At this moment there was a tap on the Morning Room door, and Swinton walked in, carrying a coffee pot and various accoutrements on a tray, followed by Gertrude, the parlour maid, also with a tray in her hands.

'Coffee and toast as you requested, Mr Edward,' Swinton said as he hurried over to the circular walnut table positioned near the windows. 'And can I bring something for you, Mr Watkins?' he asked, turning to look at Neville, who still stood in front of the fireplace.

'I think not, Swinton, thank you. I've already had breakfast. But I would enjoy a cup of coffee, if that's possible.'

'Not a problem, sir.' Swinton inclined his head and at once turned his attention to the table. After emptying their trays, the butler and the parlour maid then hurried out.

Edward said, 'Do you plan for us to go to Italy via Paris, as you suggested on the train yesterday?'

'Yes, I do. We can take the boat train to Paris, via Le Havre, spend the night in Paris, and then go on to Carrara from there. Do you have any preferences regarding a hotel in Paris, Ned? I thought we should stay at the Ritz in the Place Vendôme if that's all right with you.'

Edward nodded his agreement, and walked over to the table; Neville came to join him, and a moment later Swinton was back with another cup and saucer.

Once they were alone again, Edward took a piece of toast, and spread butter and marmalade on it. As he did, he said, 'At what time should we arrive at Deravenels, do you think?'

'Around eleven o'clock. Any later they'll all be trotting off to their private clubs or fancy restaurants for lunch.'

'Do you have any kind of strategy in mind?' Edward asked, looking across the table at Neville, cocking his head to one side questioningly.

'I'm not all that sure that strategy is really necessary at this stage of the game,' Neville responded, taking a sip of coffee. 'I do believe it would be right and proper for you to take the lead, since your father was on company business when he died. I can then step in with my own comments or questions about my father and Thomas. Basically we need to know how the fire started, how much damage was done, so that we understand what state our fathers' and brothers' bodies were in when they were discovered. Also, we need to know how Deravenels plans to send their bodies back to England for burial.'

'Yes,' Edward said laconically, and sat back in the chair. Sudden sorrow swept across his face, and he was finding it difficult to continue speaking.

Neville remained quiet, sat sipping his coffee, his own face shadowed by pain, his eyes reflective, troubled.

Little else was said between the two men. They took their coffee in total silence, burdened by the knowledge that their trip to Italy was bound to be difficult, fraught with anguish.

Neville Watkins's elegant carriage took the two men around Berkeley Square, into Piccadilly, and through Trafalgar Square, continuing in the direction of the

Strand where the head offices of the Deravenel Company were located.

The splendid horse-drawn carriage finally came to a standstill outside the imposing office building of the great global trading company in the Strand.

Eyes turned as the two men alighted. Both were elegantly dressed in dark suits and black overcoats, the fabric, cut, style and impeccable tailoring proclaiming the garments to be of the finest quality and therefore undoubtedly from Savile Row.

Passers-by, hurrying about their business on this cold January morning, paused to gape at the tall distinguished men as they strode confidently towards the front doors of the Deravenel Company. Gentlemen with a bit of a dash and dazzle, toffs from the upper class, that is how they were perceived, and mostly without any resentment whatsoever. England in 1904 was a world of class distinction, and everyone knew it and accepted it.

The two men went through the ancient portals and stood for a moment in the marble-clad lobby, the ceiling of which soared upward like a great cathedral. The veined marble was in tones of black and a deep terracotta colour, and it covered the walls, the many high-flung circular pillars and the vast floor. Imposing and grand, it reeked of money and success.

A uniformed doorman, who was positioned inside at a small desk in the winter weather, hurried over to them. Immediately he recognized Edward Deravenel. Who could ever forget this tall, good-looking young man with burnished red-gold hair and brilliant blue eyes. The son of the late Richard Deravenel, and wasn't *he* one of the finest gentlemen in the world, the doorman thought, and then said politely, 'Good morning, Mr Edward, Mr Watkins. Please go right up to the first floor.'

'Thank you, Johnson,' Edward answered, giving the commissionnaire a warm smile. 'And how is your son doing? The last time we spoke he was joining the Indian Army.'

Flattered that Edward had recalled their last conversation, he nodded, smiling with real pleasure. 'Very well, sir, thank you. Good of you to remember my Jack, sir.'

Edward inclined his head slightly and he and Neville headed towards the wide, double staircase of carved mahogany that floated upward to a wide landing at the top.

The two men climbed the stairs to the first floor where the executive offices were located, aligned along a wide corridor which ended at the giant double doors leading into the company's board room. Edward thought of that room now . . . As a small boy he had often wished he would one day dominate that room when he grew up. He felt a sudden, peculiar sinking feeling inside as he saw his father's office in his mind's eye. He was not quite certain that he could face going in there today, although perhaps he should. Putting it off was ridiculous, wasn't it? Nonetheless, he baulked at the idea. It smacked of memories and more pain.

Halfway up the red-carpeted stairs, Neville paused, his hand resting on the mahogany banister. 'Once the greetings are over I think it would be wise to move right in with your questions, Ned. Let us avoid procrastination. You know how Aubrey Masters can be.'

'Long-winded, to put it mildly,' Edward answered. 'And you don't have cause for concern. I'm as impatient as you are to get to the bottom of this situation. Let us hope he can supply some of the more important details, give us satisfactory answers. After all, he is the one dealing with Italy.'

Neville nodded and the two continued on up the stairs. They were both anxious, filled with apprehension; they dreaded what they would soon learn about the deaths of their loved ones, and the terrible way they had died in the fire. Although they had not discussed it with each other, both men realized it must have been a brutal and terrifying way to die.

The two staircases came to a stop at the wide landing, more like a room in size and shape. Placed in the centre of this space was a large desk and behind it sat an attractive young woman in a black, long-skirted suit and white blouse.

She glanced up as Edward and Neville approached the desk; her eyes automatically shifted, swung to Edward, whom she recognized at once.

'Oh, Mr Edward, good morning,' she murmured, offering him a small, half smile. She wanted to say something about his father's death but knew it would be improper to make any kind of personal remark to him. It was not her place.

'Good morning, Matilda. This is Mr Watkins. We're here to see Mr Masters.'

She inclined her head in Neville's direction, acknowledging him, and then stood up. 'I'll let Mr Masters know you're here, sir.' She hurried off down the corridor.

Edward and Neville took off their overcoats and hung

them in the coat cupboard, and a moment later Matilda was back.

'Mr Masters will see you immediately,' she said, and led them down the corridor, ushered them into an office and closed the door behind them.

Aubrey Masters came around the desk to greet Edward and Neville. He was a fussy, small, somewhat rotund man in his late forties, dark haired with a florid complexion and brown eyes set close together.

Hurrying forward, grasping Edward's hand, he exclaimed, 'Mr Edward, come in, come in, and sit down!' Turning to Neville, he shook his hand also, and indicated the other chair in front of the desk. 'Welcome to Deravenels, Mr Watkins. It's some time since you've been here. Over a year, if I recall correctly.'

'That's true,' Neville responded and lowered himself into the chair. His gaze remained on Aubrey Masters, who had gone to sit down behind the desk.

'Please accept my condolences, Mr Edward, for this awful loss you have suffered, and you too, Mr Watkins. My deepest condolences to you both,' Masters began. 'This tragedy has been a blight on the company for the last few days, since we received the dreadful news. Everyone has been plunged into sorrow and gloom –'

'Thank you,' Edward said peremptorily, cutting Masters off sharply. 'My cousin and I are most appreciative of your kind thoughts and sympathy, and we certainly thank you for sparing our mothers undue and additional heartache. To have received the news by telephone would have been perfectly ghastly for them both, unbearable actually.'

'Yes, it would. It seemed to me at the time that contacting Mr Watkins was the right and proper way to handle the matter,' Aubrey Masters answered, leaning forward over the desk, his hands clasped together.

'Most sensitive indeed,' Neville interjected, his eyes appraising as he studied Masters, weighing him up.

'Mr Watkins and I are very anxious to know exactly what happened to our fathers and brothers in Carrara, Masters. We have been given only the slightest information about their deaths, and we hope you will now supply more of the details.'

Clearing his throat several times, Aubrey nodded. 'I'm sorry to say I do not have a great deal of information, Mr Edward. All I know is that a fire started in the hotel last Sunday night. I was informed on Monday, by telegram from Carrara.'

'And who sent the telegram?' Edward asked, keeping a tight rein on his emotions. He was re-discovering his inherent antipathy towards Masters, who had never been a particular favourite of his father's either. There was something shifty about him, and Edward was convinced that his loyalty was for sale, and always had been. Edward now wondered about the man's integrity. Certainly it was not a characteristic he associated with the head of the Mining Division.

Aubrey Masters, staring at Edward in return, said in the most matter-of-fact voice he could summon, 'I was informed of the tragedy by Alfredo Oliveri.'

'Isn't he the manager of our business affairs in Carrara?'

'Yes, he is. He works with the superintendent of the mines.'

'I see. And there's another manager in Florence, isn't there?' Edward remarked. 'Fabrizio Dellarosa.'

Masters nodded. 'Dellarosa runs our overall business in Italy, and he was the one who worked most closely with Mr Richard – er, your father.'

'Has he been in touch with you?'

'Yes, he has.' Aubrey sat up a little straighter, more intent on his visitors, looking from Deravenel to Watkins, suddenly detecting hostility. He wondered why. A rush of panic hit him. Had he forgotten something? Did they know more than he did? If there *was* more to know. Clearing his throat, he announced in a clear, firm voice, 'Look, I *have* told you everything I *know*, Mr Edward.'

'Were they badly burned in the fire?' Neville asked, swallowing, not permitting his heartache to surface.

'I'm sorry, I'm afraid I don't know. Oliveri told me by telegram that they were found in the hotel and that their bodies had been taken to the hospital in Florence. That they were being held there until the arrival of the family members. That is yourselves, of course.'

'And that's all you know?' Edward said, incredulity echoing in his voice.

Masters appeared to be mystified by this question. 'There's not much else to know,' he murmured, looking confused and worried.

'Were they all together? Were they in a lounge or the foyer? Or in their bedrooms? How long did the fire burn? Why were they not rescued before it was too late? What did the police report say?' Edward stared hard at Aubrey Masters, his eyes narrowed. 'There's a great deal more *I* want to know about this matter, and so does my cousin.'

'Oh, dear, maybe I've made an error.'

'What do you mean?' Edward asked quickly, fixing his bright blue gaze on Masters.

'Perhaps I should have gone to Italy at once, to look into the situation instead of leaving it to the Italian managers.'

'Perhaps you should,' Edward shot back coldly, glaring at him.

The silence in the room was deafening.

Edward sat perfectly still in the chair, filled with frustration. Was Aubrey Masters really a nincompoop or was he a clever dissembler? He wasn't sure, and suddenly he made up his mind to leave this office at once. There was nothing he and Neville could learn here, that was patently obvious. Once they arrived in Italy in the next few days they would gather the facts themselves.

After leaving the Deravenel offices Edward and Neville went out into the street, where Neville spoke to the driver of his carriage. The two men then walked across the Strand and entered the Savoy Court, the forecourt to both the Savoy Hotel and the adjoining Savoy Theatre.

Neville broke his stride as they approached the theatre, and turning to Edward, he said, 'It's thanks to those Gilbert and Sullivan operettas that Richard D'Oyly Carte was able to build this theatre and the hotel a few years ago, you know. All those profits from them, he made a veritable fortune.'

Edward nodded. 'So my father told me. He loved the operettas, especially *The Mikado* and *H.M.S. Pinafore*.'

'Not to my taste. I much prefer Mozart.'

Once they were seated at their table, Neville ordered a bottle of dry white wine and sat back in the chair, regarding his cousin intently. 'You don't like Aubrey Masters, do you, Ned?' he said at last.

'It's not a question of liking or disliking him . . . I'm not sure that I trust him. He never was a favourite of Father's, and when we were at the offices I began to wonder if he was stupid or a clever dissembler.'

'If he's given to dissimulation then he's a mighty fine actor. Personally, I think he's a trifle dimwitted. Which brings me to a leading question. Why *is* he in that position? Who made him head of the Mining Division?'

'Henry Grant, of course. Aubrey Masters is a relative, a cousin twice removed, I do believe.'

'Nepotism again, eh?' Neville shook his head. 'Weren't you surprised, not hearing from Henry Grant, not receiving condolences?'

'Not really. You see, before Father left for Italy he told me that Henry was out of sorts, not feeling his best, and that he had gone into a religious retreat in Cumbria for two months. So presumably he's still there, and perhaps no one's bothered to inform him of our tragedy.'

'If that is so then I find it quite preposterous he's been kept in the dark.'

'So do I. Never mind that. We have better fish to fry, you and I, Neville. It is imperative that we set off for Italy as soon as possible. Will and I are both prepared to leave immediately. You just have to say the word.'

'We depart on Saturday, Ned. All the arrangements are being made by the Thomas Cook agency, as I

100

mentioned earlier. I merely have to confirm the hotel to them later today.'

'The Ritz is fine, as I told you.'

Neville nodded and picked up a menu. 'I've hardly eaten for days, and I know it's been the same for you. However, I do think we should order a decent meal, if only to keep our strength up.'

'You're right. The problem is I haven't been at all hungry. Lost my appetite.'

Following suit and opening the menu, Edward studied it for a moment, then put it down, and remarked, 'You know, the pious Henry Grant might be purging his soul and revelling in his religion, but his wife is here in London. Condolence letters could easily have been sent to us and our families, don't you think?'

'Look to the source, Edward. That she-wolf doesn't know any better. Now, let's order something to eat and relax. This afternoon we must go over our plans. We have to find a way to get to the bottom of this situation. We really do have to know whether there was foul play or not, and then act accordingly.'

'I'm hoping the two managers in Italy will have more information for us, especially Alfredo Oliveri, since he lives in Carrara. My father always liked him, and often spoke about him. And with some affection, I might add.'

'Then he's our man, and no doubt he'll have the police report. Or at least access to it. That will be a start.'

'I thought Aubrey Masters was most cavalier in his attitude, and it infuriated me,' Edward confided.

'I know it did. I can read your eyes, even when you

keep a poker face, Ned. Anyway, I do feel there is a way to get the better of the Lancashire Deravenels,' Neville said, and went on, 'I predict I will have you sitting in Henry Grant's chair in less than six months.'

Edward was silent for a moment, and then he protested. 'I'm so young, Neville. Let's not forget I am not yet nineteen.'

'Let's not forget that William Pitt the Younger was only twenty-four when he became Prime Minister of England.'

'But –'

'No buts, Ned. You *will* run Deravenels.'

'But only if you are by my side,' Edward exclaimed.

'And I will be, have no fear of that, Cousin,' Neville Watkins promised.

NINE

Florence

They had come here to take the bodies back home to England. But they were also in Florence to find out what had happened to their kin in death. And suddenly, now that they were finally here in Italy, the one thing that Edward dreaded the most was actually viewing the bodies.

He was only too well aware that to gaze upon the waxen, lifeless faces of his father, brother, uncle and cousin would have a devastating effect on him. Conversely, he did *need* to see them, in order to be truly convinced they were *really* dead. In his mind he could not quite accept that this catastrophe had happened.

Edward Deravenel was standing in the window of his hotel room, staring out at the River Arno and the hills of Florence beyond. There was no sun on this cold January morning, and the sky was bloated, bulbous with grey clouds. A mist floated over the surface of the river, obscuring the dark waters, a mist that reminded him of London's winter fogs.

He had arrived here last night from Paris, accompanied by Neville and Will, and they had checked into the Hotel Bristol. This was a well-known hotel, built in the second half of the nineteenth century, much frequented by the English aristocracy, and it had come highly recommended.

Like most of the grand hotels here, it was located on the banks of the Arno, and their rooms faced the river and the scattered hills which stood on the outskirts of the city. He and Will occupied rooms next to each other, while Neville was in a large suite just a few doors down the corridor.

Turning away from the window, Edward strode over to the mirror and began to tie his cravat made of a fine black silk. Once this was arranged to his satisfaction, he added a beautiful pearl pin in the centre of the carefully draped and folded knot. The pearl tiepin was a gift from his father, given to him last year for his eighteenth birthday, and he treasured it more than ever now.

Walking over to the wardrobe, he took out his waistcoat and slipped it on, returned to the cheval mirror, stared at himself, thinking how pale he looked, even haggard. With a small sigh he headed back to the wardrobe to retrieve his jacket.

And it seemed to Edward, as he walked back and forth, that the awful sense of dread he had just experienced trailed along with him, surrounding him like a thin veil, as if it were the mist off the river. He shivered involuntarily, paused next to a chair, rested his hand on it. He closed his eyes and his gaze turned inward.

I must be absolutely in control of myself today, and I must reveal nothing. My face must be unreadable at all times. I share Neville's opinion that there has been foul play, that the fire was no accident. How we will find out the truth I do not know, but we must try. Will is of the same mind. I'm glad he came along. He gets on well with Neville, and we have both enjoyed his company.

Somehow I must get through the ordeal of viewing the bodies later this morning. And then we will go to Carrara, no matter what. I am set on that course. I must see the hotel where they met their untimely end. That is imperative. Then, hopefully, this Italian nightmare will come to an end. Later this week we will take their bodies home, to Yorkshire, where we will bury them in that benign earth, and they will rest in peace . . .

Insistent knocking on the door interrupted Edward's thoughts, and he strode to open it. Will Hasling was standing there, appropriately dressed in a black suit and carrying a black overcoat on his arm.

'I'm not too early, am I?' Will asked, a brow lifting.

Edward shook his head. 'Come in, Will.' He opened the door wider and moved into the room, his friend following closely behind.

'Have you had breakfast?' Edward asked as he took his overcoat out of the wardrobe.

'Yes, thanks, and so have you, I see,' Will responded, glancing over at the tray which stood on a small side table. He frowned. 'Coffee and a roll. Is that all you've eaten?'

'I'm not very hungry.' Edward glanced at the clock on the wall, and continued, 'It's only ten past nine, we're early, I think. Fabrizio Dellarosa is not due here until ten-thirty.'

'I know, but I was certain you would be up, and I thought we could go for a walk, take a breath of fresh air before his arrival. By the way, is Alfredo Oliveri also joining us?'

'Dellarosa didn't mention him in the letter I received last night. But I'm presuming he is. After all, he's the one who lives in Carrara, and will therefore have the most information. At least, in my opinion he will.'

Will nodded in agreement, sat down on a chair and folded his overcoat across his knees. 'Have you ever met him? Or is *he* a stranger, too?'

'He's a stranger, just as Dellarosa is, but my father always spoke so highly of Oliveri. He obviously liked the man and I think the feeling was mutual.' Edward buttoned his three-quarter length jacket, put on his overcoat and said, 'Shall we go, Will?'

'Perhaps we ought to let Neville know we're going out,' Will ventured as they left the room.

'It's not necessary. The arrangement was for us to meet in the main lounge at the given hour. Let's leave it at that, shall we?' Edward's voice was clipped, almost curt.

'That presents no problem to me,' Will answered, stealing a glance at Edward. He knew he was suffering inside, filled with apprehension about what lay ahead in the next few hours. As big and strapping as he was, Will knew, nevertheless, that Ned was a sensitive and compassionate man inside. Just contemplating the manner of their deaths must be an agony for him; this aside, Ned was devoted to his family. They came first with him, and he had been particularly close to his brother Edmund, and his father and he had been closely bonded.

The two men were silent as they went down the wide

staircase which led to the grand entrance foyer, and several opulent lounges. Marble abounded, and there were ceramic tubs holding potted palms placed here and there; on the walls hung a number of lovely paintings of Florence displayed in heavy gilded frames, and pieces of sculpture on plinths were placed along each side of the foyer.

Within a few seconds they found themselves standing outside the Bristol on the Via de' Pescioni, near the Santa Maria Novella and directly opposite the Palazzo Strozzi. This was one of the most elegant districts in the city, where other important hotels were located as well as fine shops, art galleries and museums.

'Here we are, in the greatest Renaissance city in the world, Ned,' Will said, taking hold of his arm. 'Let's stroll along, go this way, and enjoy the sights for a short while.'

Edward nodded. 'I'm sorry, Will, I know I'm being gloomy . . .' He did not finish, merely shook his head, his expression suddenly sorrowful. His enthusiasm for life seemed to have fled.

'Think about this,' Will remarked, ignoring Ned's comment about gloom of a moment ago. 'Here we are in the city of Dante, Petrarch and Boccaccio. Just *think*, Boccaccio wrote the *Decameron* here, and that book became the model for prose the world over, a model that's been popular for hundreds and hundreds of years. And still is.'

Ned glanced at his friend. 'Niccolo Machiavelli lived here and wrote *The Prince* in Florence, let us not forget about *him*. We can all learn quite a lot from Machiavelli, you know.'

Will laughed, catching the mischievous gleam in Ned's eyes. 'I know what you mean, still it is a *wonder* to be here in this city, you know.' He looked at Ned and then all around him, and up at the sky, and said in a voice full of awe, 'We are walking along streets where Leonardo Da Vinci walked *and* Michelangelo *and* Botticelli, some of the world's greatest artists . . . it's unbelievable really, Ned . . . how incredible that this city bred such talent, such genius.'

'Poets, princes and politicians,' Ned murmured. 'And the Medicis. Their dynasty lasted for several centuries, something of a record, wouldn't you say?'

'Indeed I would.'

A silence fell between them, and as they walked Will wondered how to bring a little cheer to Ned, to make him feel better. Instantly he realized nothing could make him feel better at this moment. First he had to deal with the dead, bury his dead, and only then would he be able to move forward, see his way to the future. He needs to close this ghastly affair, Will thought, pick up the pieces and create a life of his own making. A new life.

TEN

Neville Watkins was a striking looking man. Tall, though not quite as tall as Ned, he was of slender build, without an ounce of extra fat on him, very strong and athletic. His face was sharply chiselled; he had an aquiline nose and a smooth, rather high brow. His wide-set eyes under curved black brows were a curious pale blue, almost turquoise in colour. Clear and transparent, they were alive with immense intelligence. His colouring was dark, he had black hair, like most of the Watkins clan, and on occasion he had a strong look of his aunt, Cecily Watkins Deravenel, his father's sister.

This morning he sat at an antique writing table in the sitting room of his suite in the Hotel Bristol, making notes for himself, trying to put some of his thoughts on paper for the meeting with Fabrizio Dellarosa in a short while.

After a few moments he put his pencil down, satisfied he had covered the relevant points. He sat back in the chair, staring out into the room.

Neville's motto, borrowed from his father, was this: Think with the head, not the heart. This he always did in business, and often in his private life, as well. Long ago his father had cautioned him to be ice cold at all times when he dealt in business. Without emotion, inscrutable, revealing nothing. 'Never display weakness, never lose face. That is what your grandfather taught me,' his father had explained when he had first entered the world of commerce. They were words he had never forgotten, and he had always lived by them to this very day.

I must train Ned to be like me, Neville now thought. Certainly his father taught him many things, but I'm not quite certain Richard knew how to teach Ned to be truly cold-hearted. After all, his uncle had been a warm and loving man who should have moved against his treacherous cousin Henry Grant years ago. Grumbling about inequities, and his rights, and what should have been his, and was, in fact, *his*, had accomplished nothing and made many enemies within Deravenels. Deadly enemies, if the truth be known.

Neville's mind remained focused on Ned. His cousin had a superior intelligence, and he was not afraid of anything or anyone. He had enormous self-confidence and an unbelievable charisma, the likes of which Neville had rarely seen. And he could be utterly ruthless if he needed to be. Furthermore, Ned had always had a good head for business, most especially finance.

Convinced that Ned could very easily run the Deravenel Company with the right guidance, direction and help, Neville was ready, willing and able to do all of those things to ensure his success. Together they would rule that empire one day, there was no question in Neville's mind about this. With his own training, knowledge and experience, and Ned's natural abilities and charismatic presence, they could accomplish almost anything. With a little luck of course. Luck always had to be factored into the equation.

Folding the piece of paper on which he had made his notes, he slipped it in the pocket of his jacket and rose. Walking across the room in long strides, Neville stood in front of the window, gazing out at the leaden sky. The sun was beginning to filter through the oppressive greyness, and he decided it might turn out to be a better day after all. He loathed dismal weather, used to it though he was, and craved the sunlight, warmer climes. Just as Cousin Ned did, hence their sojourns in the south of France over the years.

Thoughts of Ned lingered . . . Neville held him dear, admired him. There was only one problem with Ned as far as he could see and that was his overwhelming addiction to women. Older women. And widows, at that. Blonde widows. As long as he remained single there was no problem about his penchant for romantic and sexual dalliances, but when Ned married, which he would one day, he would have to curb his lustful behaviour, or at least be much more discreet than he usually was. Although Ned was not aware of it, Neville knew all about his current alliance with Lily Overton, not that this mattered since they were both single. Still, there were some who thought it inappropriate.

Ah well, he's just a man after all, like all of us, poor creatures that we are, Neville thought with a small wry smile.

The three Englishmen were dressed almost exactly alike. They each wore black suits with the three-quarter length jacket that was currently so fashionable. Their white shirts were impeccable, as were their black silk cravats. Basically they were dressed in mourning clothes, and they cut quite a swathe as they strode across the lobby of the Hotel Bristol, heading towards one of the lounges. Some of the other guests, walking through the lobby, eyed them with curiosity, and several of the women with open admiration. All three men were tall, good looking, obviously English and aristocrats, an appealing combination anywhere, at any time.

As they entered the lounge a waiter came forward, smiling and showing them to a large round table which Neville had reserved a short while before.

Once seated they ordered coffee and when the waiter departed, Neville turned to Edward and said, 'As I did when we went to Deravenels, I am going to let you take the lead in this matter, Ned. After all, Dellarosa is an employee of the company, and at this moment answerable to you.'

'Your father was killed in the fire as well,' Edward murmured, frowning slightly. 'You can say anything you want to him, ask him anything, as far as I'm concerned. We're in this together.'

'Yes, indeed we are,' Neville shot back. 'But do take the lead, Ned, please. It will give me a chance to weigh him up, get a handle on him, and you, Will, can give your attention to Alfredo Oliveri, if you would. I think we should attempt to assess these two men, decide whether they will be allies or adversaries in the future. After all, Deravenels have a lot of business interests in Italy, quite aside from the marble quarries.'

'I understand,' Will answered at once, nodding. 'I

have a feeling Oliveri will be a friend not a foe, from what Ned has said about him so far. Correct, Ned?'

'Oh, yes, Father had enormous respect for him, there is no question about that, as I've already explained. But the strange thing is he wasn't mentioned in Dellarosa's letter to me, so I have an odd feeling he won't be here this morning.'

'Why do you make *that* assumption?' Neville asked, his voice rising, eyeing his cousin in alarm.

'I have a . . . *gut instinct* about it, to use a phrase of yours.'

At this moment the waiter returned with the tray of coffee cups and tall glasses of water, and served them. Again smiling and nodding, he backed away. Neville took a sip of the water. He approved of this Continental custom of always serving a glass of water with other beverages. It was most civilized, he thought.

'Could this be Dellarosa?' Ned muttered quietly a moment or two later, staring at the arched doorway of the lounge, where a well-dressed man stood glancing around. He was of medium height, slim, and blond like many Northern Italians. Ned hurried on, 'He's heading this way, so it is him, I'm certain.'

Edward rose, moved forward in the direction of the Italian, extending his hand. 'Signor Dellarosa, I presume,' he said with a faint smile. 'I'm Edward Deravenel.'

'Good morning, Signor Deravenel,' Dellarosa responded. 'Welcome to Firenze. I wish this occasion was not a sorrowing one. I am sorry for the loss of your family.'

'It is sorrowful, yes,' Edward replied. 'But please,

113

come and meet my cousin Neville Watkins, and our good friend Will Hasling.'

Neville and Will were already on their feet, and after shaking hands and exchanging greetings, the four men sat down together at the circular table.

Dellarosa turned to Neville and murmured, 'I am so sorry, signor, for your loss also.'

'Thank you.' Neville inclined his head, his expression neutral, quite unreadable.

'Would you care for some kind of refreshment? Coffee, tea?' Edward asked.

'*Si, grazie*, Signor Edward. I will partake of the coffee.'

Edward motioned to the hovering waiter, ordered the coffee and then focused all of his attention on Fabrizio Dellarosa. 'What time are we going to view the bodies of our family members?' he asked in a quiet, sombre tone.

Clearing his throat, Dellarosa said, 'In about half an hour. They are at a hospital. Santa Maria Novella. It is nearby. We can walk.'

'I understand. My cousin and I have been wondering why the bodies were brought to Florence?'

Again, Dellarosa cleared his throat. 'Because it was necessary to have them embalmed.'

'I see, and what you are saying is that there are no facilities to do this procedure in Carrara?'

'Yes, Signor Edward, that is so.'

'What did they die of?' Ned asked, startling the Italian.

'Excuse me?' Dellarosa's brow furrowed and he gave Edward a long stare, as if he were uncomprehending.

'Our fathers and brothers were in a fire in the hotel.' Edward's look was intent, focused on Dellarosa. 'So were they badly burned? Did they die of their burns? Or was it smoke inhalation that killed them? We have been told nothing about their deaths.'

'Smoke inhalation, I believe, was the cause of death.'

'And they were not burned at all?' Edward asked, sounding puzzled, shaking his head.

'No. There are no burns on their faces.'

'But perhaps on their bodies? Is that what you're implying?'

'I'm not implying,' Dellarosa shot back swiftly, raising a blond brow. 'I was told they died of smoke inhalation.'

'What information do you have about the fire, how did it start?'

'I do not know, Signor Edward. I was not there.'

'Does anyone else know? Perhaps Alfredo Oliveri?' Ned probed.

'He does not have the information . . . he knows no more than I do.'

'I see. Tell me, Signor Dellarosa . . .' Edward paused, leaned forward. 'Why is Oliveri not here in Florence today? I thought he had been informed we were coming. By the London office. By Aubrey Masters.'

The Italian nodded, looking suddenly worried, and his voice faltered slightly when he replied, 'I told Alfredo Oliveri it wasn't necessary for him to come. I am here, and I run the Deravenel business interests in Italy. He knows nothing. Nothing more than I do.'

'So what you are saying is that the cause of the fire is a genuine mystery. And also that our family members were not even burned in this fire. Very interesting. Very interesting indeed, Dellarosa.'

Fabrizio was silent, staring back at Edward, and asking himself why he suddenly felt both nervous and threatened by this young man, a veritable giant blessed with an extraordinary physique and overwhelming good looks, who had the coldest blue eyes he had ever seen. Steel, Dellarosa thought. *This* Deravenel is made of cold steel. And he was unexpectedly afraid. Edward Deravenel was not like his father, and he would be trouble, of that Fabrizio Dellarosa was convinced. He could not wait to escape, to return to his office and communicate with London.

Edward announced, 'Well, it seems you have nothing more to say, Signor Dellarosa. So let us go. Please take us to the hospital, so that we can finally view the bodies. Oh, and incidentally, what arrangements have you made for the bodies to be taken back to England?'

Dellarosa coughed behind his hand, and then said quickly, in a hurried manner, 'They will go by ship. I have booked passages for you, and Signor Watkins.' He paused, glanced at Will and added, 'I will book passage for you, Mr Hasling. If you wish to accompany your friends.'

'I do,' Will answered at once.

Neville exclaimed, 'I don't think so, Signor Dellarosa! What I mean is, I don't think we shall be travelling by ship. Nor will the bodies of our fathers and brothers.'

Dellarosa gaped at him. 'I am not understanding –'

'Then let me explain,' Neville cut in. 'It is January. The weather is bad. A journey by sea could prove quite dangerous at this time of year. There are far too many storms, rough seas.' He shook his head and gave Dellarosa an odd look. 'I shall make the travel

116

arrangements myself. We will take the bodies back to England by train. So much safer in the long run, wouldn't you say?'

It was the registrar of the hospital, Roberto Del Renzio, who greeted them at the reception desk and led them down a long corridor to the morgue.

A tall, heavy-set man, he was dressed in a starched white shirt with a stiff wing collar, black tie, black jacket and pin-striped trousers. He had a sombre voice but his expression was bland, and it seemed to Edward that the man was lighthearted in spirit, the kind of person who was ready to laugh if the joke was a good one. But he did not laugh or joke or even say very much as he accompanied them to the far end of the hospital, which he explained, was the north wing.

The registrar paused when he came to a waiting room, and turning to Dellarosa, he said, in stilted English, 'Perhaps you would please to be waiting in here.' He swung his eyes to Edward, and asked, 'Just the two of you will enter the morgue?'

'I'm not sure,' Edward answered and looked over at Will. 'Would you like to come in with us?'

'If that's all right with you, yes, I would, Ned. I wish to pay my last respects to them all. Do *you* mind, Neville?'

'So be it,' Neville murmured, and followed the silent Ned and the registrar, with Will Hasling following immediately behind him.

Much to Edward's surprise, the four dead men had

already been brought into the morgue in their closed coffins. He had fully expected them to be in the long metal drawers which were banked around the room.

A moment later, a white-coated doctor joined them, and after being introduced, he proceeded to open the coffins.

Together Edward and Neville viewed the bodies of their fathers and brothers, staring down at their waxen faces. It was true, they had not been burnt. There wasn't a mark on them. At least, not on their faces.

Although they did not know it, both men were thinking the same thing . . . that these were no longer their loved ones, not now that their souls had left them. All that remained were these frozen carcasses.

Edward touched his father's shoulder and closed his eyes. *Goodbye*, he thought, *goodbye*. Then he moved on to look at his dearest brother, his lovely Edmund. But the Edmund he had known and loved was not here either. He touched his shoulder, said goodbye to the boy inside his head, and moved on sadly.

Neville followed suit, silently saying his farewells whilst knowing that what had made these four men so special, so unique, were their spirits . . . They were merely empty shells how, dead flesh. And Will, slowly moving behind them, felt cold inside and utterly bereft. For he, too, understood death now, and its total finality.

Within minutes it was all over.

They collected the relevant papers from the registrar, and took their leave of Dellarosa. They immediately left the hospital, huddled together, hurrying away with speed, heading across the piazza Santa Maria Novella to the hotel.

And Edward wondered why he had so dreaded this viewing of the bodies all day. He had felt nothing.

The letter arrived in the late afternoon. It was pushed under the door of Edward's room. But when he went and opened the door there was no one there. He looked up and down the corridor only to discover it was empty.

Opening the envelope, he took the letter out. It was short, a note.

As he scanned the brief words he felt his stomach lurch, his mind racing. There was no salutation. Only a few lines, brief and to the point:

'*Nothing is the way it seems.*
Come to the place your father visited last.
Tomorrow. Go to the building with a familiar
name. I will be waiting.'

Edward knew immediately that the note was from Alfredo Oliveri. The place his father visited last was Carrara. And the building with the familiar name was Deravenels. Of course.

Folding the letter in half he put it in his pocket and left the room, walked down the corridor to Neville's suite. And he knew deep within himself that tomorrow they would find out the truth at last.

ELEVEN

Carrara

From the moment Edward had arrived in Carrara with Neville and Will earlier that morning, he had wanted to turn around and leave. There was something about this town in Tuscany which truly depressed him.

He knew that, in part, this feeling sprang from the fact that his father and brother, uncle and cousin had died here only last week, and in tragic circumstances. And yet he genuinely disliked certain aspects of the place, found it cold, unwelcoming, and reeking of danger, and there was yet another element that troubled him. He felt oppressed by the range of mountains that encircled Carrara on three sides, and seemed to close it in like a prison.

Marble dominated here. Great slabs of it gleamed whitely high on the mountain sides of the Apuan Alps; its grey-white dust floated on the very air, settled on the buildings and the ground; on the people as well; it penetrated their clothing and hair. There was the constant sound of marble being chipped at, in studios, workshops and apartments along the streets, where artists and artisans were working on sculptures, frescoes, urns and other different kinds of artifacts. Carrara was busy in the town as well as up on the mountain ranges.

Edward fully understood that he must get himself through the meeting with Alfredo Oliveri and then hurry away as fast as he could. In his mind, Carrara would be forever associated with death and grief, and he never wanted to return here as long as he lived.

At this moment he was sitting in a chair in the offices of the Deravenel Company, studying Alfredo Oliveri, who was speaking to Neville, suggesting they should stay the night in Carrara, and adding that he would be happy to have them as guests in his home. 'Far better than a hotel,' he was murmuring.

They had arrived at the offices about twenty minutes ago, having travelled for some hours by hired carriage from Florence, an arrangement made by the head concierge of the Hotel Bristol. It had proved to be a comfortable ride.

Edward already knew that he trusted this man whom he was meeting for the very first time. He now realized why his father had liked him so much, had had such confidence in Oliveri. There was something about him, the expression on his face, his manner, his way of expressing himself that spoke to Edward of integrity, honesty and loyalty.

Alfredo Oliveri was not at all what he had expected. To begin with, he had the brightest of auburn hair, that intense red colour which was usually referred to as 'carrot top' in England. And secondly, he was very English. After they had introduced themselves, and entered Alfredo Oliveri's private office, Neville had commented on Alfredo's perfect command of English.

121

It was then that the other man had explained that he was born of an English mother and an Italian father, that he had spent every summer in London with his maternal grandparents during his childhood. His mother had taken him there with her; later he had attended an English boarding school for four years, returning to Italy for the summers.

'No wonder you sound like an Englishman,' Neville remarked when Oliveri had finished explaining his heritage. 'In fact, you are one, of course,' he added, hoping he hadn't sounded patronizing when he had meant to compliment.

'Half and half,' Alfredo had murmured and smiled faintly, obviously gratified, understanding it was a compliment. 'My Englishness usually takes visitors from the London office by surprise. Although it never surprised Mr Richard.' He looked pointedly at Edward when he added, 'Such a good man, your father was. *Too* good, if the truth be known.'

'You're the one who knows everything about things here, Mr Oliveri,' Edward ventured. 'And the fact that we came at once after I received your note yesterday must tell you something –'

'That you are suspicious,' Alfredo cut in swiftly, his eyes on Edward.

'Yes, we are. What did you mean when you wrote *nothing is the way it seems*?'

'Exactly that.' He gave Edward a keen look. 'So many things appear to be quite straightforward. But when you look beneath the surface, well, that's a different matter altogether. There's very often something else at play. At least, that's the way I've frequently found it.'

'So we are right to be suspicious about their deaths?' Neville asked quietly.

'Indeed,' Alfredo answered. 'I would like to tell you about the night of the fire, tell you everything I personally know and what I subsequently found out later.' He raised a brow quizzically.

'Yes, please do,' Edward encouraged, leaning forward, every part of him alert, expectant, and also somewhat afraid, wondering what awful things Alfredo was about to reveal to them.

'It was Sunday night, just over a week ago. I had dined with your father and uncle, and the two young men, Mr Edmund and Mr Thomas. I left them at the small hotel, the *pensione*, at about eleven o'clock, and went home. As I learned later, the fire apparently broke out in the early hours of Monday morning, around one o'clock. It seemingly started in the right wing, spread to the foyer, and then to the left wing, where your family were staying. It was a sudden fire, and because of the wind that night it kept spreading and, in fact, it became a real conflagration at one point. And –'

'But they weren't burned,' Neville interrupted peremptorily. 'We've seen the bodies, and their faces were not scarred. If it was an inferno, as you suggest, how can that be?'

'The wind suddenly dropped, and it also began to rain. Very heavily. And, anyway, almost immediately the alarm was raised and many of the townsfolk came out with buckets of water, helping to douse the fire.'

'So what you're saying is that the fire was put out quickly, but that our family members died of smoke

123

inhalation at the beginning, when the fire was at its height?' Edward asked.

'That's exactly what the death certificates say,' Neville pointed out to Alfredo. 'Death from smoke inhalation.'

'There was no smoke inhalation,' Alfredo began, and nervously cleared his throat several times. 'They did not die as a result of the fire. They died from their injuries of earlier.'

'*Injuries*?' Edward sat up straighter, once again fixing his vivid blue eyes on Alfredo.

Neville and Will were also on the edge of their chairs, staring intently at the manager of Deravenels in Carrara, aghast at what they were hearing from him.

Alfredo steadied himself, and said in a low tone, 'Your father, uncle and cousin sustained head injuries, Mr Edward,' and then he looked across at Neville, and continued, 'All three men died instantly. Dr Buttafiglio told me –'

'Someone attacked them? Killed them? Are we understanding you correctly?' Edward cut in, his voice rising.

'You are . . . I'm so sorry to give you this dreadful news, and you, too, Mr Watkins. Very, very sorry.'

'And so the fire was started to conceal the crime? Is that what you're suggesting?' Neville asked, his expression grim, his voice hard.

'Yes, I am. That is the doctor's theory, and I concur with him. The men of your family were killed, and the fire was set in order to burn their bodies to a crisp, so that nobody would know that murder had been committed. But whoever did this had not bargained for the rain. It was a *deluge*. It stopped the fire.'

'You mentioned my father, uncle and cousin, but not my brother,' Edward exclaimed, staring at Alfredo. 'What of Edmund?'

Alfredo Oliveri had been dreading this question and for a split second he could not speak. He lost his courage; but he knew that he would have to tell Mr Edward later, if not now, and so he took a deep, steadying breath and said, 'It appears that after I left Mr Richard and the others at the hotel, Mr Edmund went out again. No one knows where he went, and by that I mean the police, who made inquiries later, to no avail. They found out nothing. Anyway, as he was returning to the hotel, probably just before the fire was started, Mr Edmund was waylaid in one of the side streets and attacked. He –'

'*By whom*? Who would attack my young brother?' Edward demanded in a loud voice, his face growing flushed and angry.

'I don't know. No one knows, no one here understands it at all. Everyone is baffled, believe me they are.'

'And no one saw it happening?' Neville asked sceptically, in that same sharp voice, a voice like a whiplash.

'Not the actual attack, no. But Benito Magnanni, the owner of the Colisseum Restaurant, was on his way home after closing up, and he saw two men bending over a body. It just so happens there was a street light on in the alley where they were standing, and he began to run down the alley, shouting at them. They immediately fled. They were English, though.'

'How do you know that?' Will asked quickly, staring hard at Alfredo. He was aware Edward and Neville were too distressed to speak at this moment, and so took charge.

'Because Benito told the police they looked English, and that he heard one of the men say something about London, and the man made a remark like *let's ski diddle*. This phrase didn't make sense to either Benito or the police. But it did to me. I believe that what the man was saying actually was *let's skedaddle back to London*, something like that.'

'How did they kill him?' Edward asked in a voice so inaudible they could barely hear him.

Alfredo hesitated, wondering if he should lie in order to save Edward Deravenel's feelings. But he knew he could not; he must speak the truth. He owed it to Edward and to his father. 'He died very quickly,' Alfredo replied at last. 'Doctor Buttafiglio told me it must have been an instant death.'

'But *how*?' Edward pressed.

'They cut his throat,' Alfredo answered in a shaky voice, one as quiet as Edward's had been.

There was a moment of utter stillness in the room.

Stunned shock filled the air, was a palpable thing almost.

Rigid in the chair, his face draining of all colour, Edward cried out, 'No! Not my lovely Edmund. To die like *that*. Such a brutal way. Oh, no. No, it can't *be*. Who would commit such a foul crime? He was only seventeen, for God's sake, an innocent *boy* –'

Edward broke off, his face crumpling, tears glistening in those bright blue eyes. He brought his hands to his face, and he grieved a second time for his beloved brother.

At once Neville was on his feet, going to Edward. He bent over him, encircled him with his arms. After

126

a moment, Edward struggled to his feet, turned to Neville and clung to him as though his life depended on it. For a while the cousins stood together in tight embrace. They were united more than ever in their mutual grief, shocked and horrified that Edmund had been killed in this heartless, brutish manner. And they shared their sorrow for their other kin who had been so cruelly slain.

Eventually the two men broke their embrace, and went back to their chairs. It was Neville who spoke first. Looking across at Alfredo, he said, 'Let me ask you something . . . do you personally believe that Mr Edmund was killed because he was a Deravenel? That it was not just an odd coincidence that he was attacked that night?'

'I don't think the attack on Mr Edmund was a coincidence. Not at all. He was killed because he was a Deravenel and Mr Richard's son. They did not find him at the hotel when they killed the others, so they went looking for him, in my opinion.' Alfredo shook his head vehemently. 'Nothing will convince me otherwise. They went out searching for him.'

'Do you think Mr Edward is in danger?'

'Yes, I do. Perhaps not here in Carrara, not now. The murderers have fled back to London. But I do think he's in danger. Because he's Mr Richard's son. In my opinion, Mr Watkins, your Uncle Richard was killed because he was the true heir to Deravenels. Everyone knows it in the company . . . Deravenels was stolen sixty years ago by the Lancashire Deravenels. Some of the directors are happy with the status quo, but not everyone. There are those who have always believed Mr Richard should have been sitting in the chairman's seat. Quite a few of us, actually.

Henry Grant is ineffectual, always has been in my opinion. He's been riding on the coat-tails of the two other Grants who went before him. His grandfather, who stole the company, and his father, who made it greater. But it's slipping. Things are not good, take my word for it. He's an absentee landlord, just as Mr Richard always said he was. He has no head for business or finance, and he's dominated by his French wife and her followers. Margot Grant has quite a few supporters, you know, who do her bidding.'

'I did know. My uncle confided in my father.' A deep sigh rippled through Neville, and he shook his head, sorrow shadowing his light blue eyes. 'My father and brother died because they were in the wrong place at the wrong time . . .' His saddened voice filtered away, and he pursed his lips. 'God rest their souls in Heaven.'

'And so Deravenels, the company started by my ancestor, Guy de Ravenel, is actually being run by a young woman who is not even a Deravenel by birth. That has to make you shudder, Neville,' Edward remarked in a voice dripping ice.

'Actually it makes me laugh, if a little hollowly,' Neville retorted. 'That woman is a joke, she doesn't know what she's doing. But of course she's being used by James Cliff and John Summers. It is they who have the power there. Still, I do think she *is* dangerous, she has no conscience whatsoever, and it's more than likely she's behind the murders. Don't you fret, Ned. We *will* have our revenge, as I said we would at Ravenscar. I will not permit a young and incompetent woman to get the better of you, be assured of that.'

TWELVE

Kent

'Why aren't you pursuing the matter with the police?' Lily Overton cried, her face growing flushed, her eyes filling with sudden indignation. 'I don't understand, I really don't, Ned.'

'You should. I've already explained it several times!' Edward shot back, striving to keep his temper in check. 'But I'll try to do so once again. This is *not* a matter for Scotland Yard. The crime was *not* committed here, under their jurisdiction. It occurred in Italy, in Carrara, to be precise, and the –'

'I know that, Ned,' she interrupted. 'I was referring to the police in Carrara. Why aren't they continuing their investigation? *That* is what I meant.'

Clenching his fists, taking a deep breath, Edward answered in as controlled a voice as he could manage, 'Neville and I, and Will, spent hours and hours with the local police chief, attempting to get to the bottom of things. He was very cooperative. Certainly he had done a very detailed investigation before we got there, and came up with nothing. All the police had, in fact, was the information given to them by a local restaurant owner, who told them he had seen two men attacking someone in an alley late at night. He immediately ran to the rescue, shouting at the attackers, who instantly fled. He was too late, of course. The young man, my brother, was dead when he got to him. Benito Magnanni, the restaurant owner, also reported hearing the two men, the attackers, shouting at each other in English. And that is it . . . there is nothing *more*.'

Lily did not respond. She merely sat back on the sofa, staring across at him, shaking her head as if baffled, a nonplussed expression crossing her face.

Staring back at her, Edward realized she looked as if she were about to burst into tears. He unclenched his hands, relaxed his body, adopted a more casual stance in front of the fire roaring up the chimney. He knew she was not a stupid woman, quite the contrary, but she could be maddeningly dense about certain things at times, and this drove him to distraction.

Taking a deep breath, he adopted a lighter, softer tone when he murmured, 'Alberto Oliveri truly went out of his way to probe every aspect of the murders with the police, and, of course, the cause of the fire, its point of origin, everything to do with it, in fact. But there's not very much anyone can do when there are no murderers loitering on street corners, no arsonists hanging around, for that matter. The whole affair is clouded in mystery . . .' He paused, sighed, added, 'Without credible evidence the Carrara police are totally stalled.' He shifted on his feet and another small sigh escaped him as he finished, 'This is not the first case which will go unsolved, Lily, I can assure you of that.'

'And so do I,' Will Hasling said from the doorway,

walking into the study of his sister's house in Kent, where the three of them were spending the weekend with Vicky. He went on, 'It's also extremely frustrating, since we more or less know who is at the root of this ghastly crime, yet there's nothing we can do –'

'Why not?' Lily cut in swiftly, sitting up straighter on the sofa, looking from Will to Ned, who remained standing in front of the fire.

'Because we cannot retaliate in kind,' Edward snapped after a moment, his annoyance with her rising to the surface. 'We can't go around killing people off, just because we think they are behind the deaths of my father and brother, Neville's father and brother. Certainly Scotland Yard would be involved *then* . . . they'd be on *our* backs.'

Lily reached into her pocket for a handkerchief, blew her nose, patted her eyes. 'It's such an . . . agony,' she muttered, crumpling her handkerchief between her long, supple fingers, playing with it nervously. 'I don't know how you can stand it, Ned.'

The room became absolutely still.

Suddenly, the fire spurted, crackled; fabric rustled like a faint whisper as Lily moved on the sofa; light rain began to patter against the window panes. Otherwise there was total silence. Neither man spoke. Lily herself swallowed the sentence on the tip of her tongue, afraid to utter a word, accepting she had just said the wrong thing.

Slowly, almost cautiously, Will walked across the room to the fireplace where his best friend stood rigid and unmoving. Will put a hand on his arm as if to steady Ned, then took a position next to him.

For his part, Edward Deravenel looked perturbed; a veil dropped over his face, obscuring his true feelings. He took a tight rein on himself, breathing deeply.

At last, after a long moment or two, Edward focused his entire attention on Lily Overton. He said, finally, in a cold clipped voice, 'How can I stand it, you ask? If the truth be known, I can't. But I have to. I have no choice. Now, let us bring this discussion to a close, shall we? There is no real point to it. We are helpless, as far as prosecuting those whom we believe are responsible. Neville and I have buried our loved ones . . . they are at peace now. There is nothing to say –' He broke off, leaned forward, staring at her intently, his face resembling a mask of stone. 'The matter is now at an end.'

No, it's not, it's just starting, Will Hasling thought. It won't end until Ned and Neville Watkins have destroyed the Grants. Each and every one of them. That is irrevocable.

And as these thoughts swirled in his head, Will felt the hackles rise on the back of his neck and a cold chill swept over him.

Vicky Forth's second husband Stephen, a well-known banker of some standing, had gone to New York on a business trip, and she had talked her brother into spending a weekend in the country with her.

Will, in turn, had coaxed Ned into joining him. Because Vicky and Lily were close friends, she had been invited to come along as well.

Edward had been delighted to accompany Will, whom

he always enjoyed being with, and the fact that Lily was so obviously welcome was an added bonus.

Stonehurst Farm, located not far from Aldington in Kent, was close to Romney Marsh, and long ago it had ceased to be a working farm. Centuries old, dating back to the 1600s, it had undergone a bold transformation in recent years. Now it resembled a manor house, was, in fact, a gentleman's farm, a country residence. Nothing was grown anymore, except for the vegetables in Vicky's kitchen garden, and there were no livestock, although Vicky did keep a stable of fine horses for riding and hunting.

Although Stonehurst was large and rambling, with several new additions, it boasted a great deal of cosy welcoming warmth. This was due in no small measure to Vicky's perfect taste, and her talent and skill as a decorator.

Comfort abounded everywhere, was evident in the blazing fires, large overstuffed sofas and chairs, thick rugs on the wooden and stone floors, and the velvet draperies at the many windows which kept out the winter chill in the evenings.

Edward had stayed here before, and he had always been given the same room, one which he particularly liked because it looked out towards Romney Marsh and the sea beyond.

Conveniently, and obviously intentionally, Lily's room was located immediately opposite his, just two or three steps across the corridor. They had, so far, enjoyed two nights of passionate lovemaking and had both revelled in the fact that they could share the same bed all night, waking to savour each other in the early morning.

Lily had always managed to soothe him, to lift him out of himself, to chase away the demons that frequently dogged him. But this weekend had been somewhat different, much to his surprise and dismay. Somehow she had done exactly the opposite, upset him on several occasions with her unfortunate desire to bring up the terrible crime which had so afflicted him and his family. He found this hard to comprehend, and she was beginning to get on his nerves, to irritate him. It had never happened before in the relationship.

Now as he sat in front of the fire in his bedroom he asked himself why this rather clever and usually understanding woman was being so insensible to his feelings. What prompted her to constantly mention certain aspects of this tragedy? It was like gouging at a wound on his body, a very deep wound. Why wouldn't she let it heal? He had been shocked a short while before, and had come up here in order to calm down, to settle himself. He closed his eyes, leaning his head against the back of the chair, let himself slide down into his innermost thoughts.

I must remain cool and controlled, in charge of myself. I cannot let Lily agitate me, or distract me away from my purpose. Neville has warned me several times now about allowing women to interfere too much in my life. He told me I must use them, enjoy them, but keep them at arm's length emotionally. Easier said than done, I told him last week, and he agreed with me. But he also reminded me that he and I are about to set out on a very important mission. A campaign to bring down the House of Grant, bring it to its knees. We must win,

Neville informed me, and of course we will. I have more to gain than Neville, because once the Grants are gone Deravenels will be mine, and I will have avenged my father. Not only avenged his murder but the usurpation of Deravenels sixty years ago, which left him to inherit an inferior position within the company. Yes, we will do it, and we will do it fast. I promised my mother that, after the funerals at Ravenscar and at Ripon. In fact, I made a vow to her, and I know this pleased her. I am the head of the Deravenel family now, and I have to protect and look after my mother and my siblings, see to their welfare and their comfort, and to the future. It will be done. I can do it, Neville assured me of that. Of course my mother is safe, because she has her inheritance which Neville will now manage, but I must take from the company all that which is my due. I must find out why my father was always so impoverished, and rectify that situation as soon as I can. And I must find myself a house, a proper place to live. My mother owns the house in Charles Street, and although she offered it to me I cannot take it from her. That would be most unfair since it is actually hers by inheritance from her father.

My mother is self-contained, but then that is her nature, and knowing her as well as I do, I understand that her grief for my father and Edmund is very raw. It will take a long time to heal, if it ever does. But she is stoic and she will go on doggedly, and unbowed, taking care of Richard and George, and my sister Meg, raising them as my father would want them to be raised.

Before I left Ravenscar I informed my mother about the black notebook, which Alfredo Oliveri had

*mentioned to me in Carrara. A notebook constantly
used by my father, who made daily jottings in it. She
and I searched for it, but had no success whatsoever.
She will continue to look for it, as I did in his rooms
at Charles Street before coming down here to Kent. No
luck so far.*

*Oliveri will be most useful to us, and he has prom-
ised to help in any way he can. He is an undoubted
ally. I am lucky to have him on my side. He says we
can win. I believe him.*

Will had been coming to Stonehurst ever since his sister
had bought the place twelve years ago. She had
purchased the property not long after the death of her
first husband Miles Tomlinson, wishing to leave the
hustle and bustle of London for the tranquillity of the
Kentish countryside. She had also turned the restora-
tion of the old farmhouse and its decoration into a
project to help keep grief at bay.

To some extent she had succeeded in this effort, and
Will had been her willing helper over the years. He had
grown to care for Stonehurst as much as she did, in
winter as well as summer. The old farmhouse was
surrounded by a hundred and fifty acres of wonderful
land – there were fields and pastures, as well as a pond
and a bluebell wood, and beyond the vast flower gardens
was the Romney Marsh.

To Will, the Marsh was mysterious, a magical kind
of place with its wild, blowing grasses and winding
paths, its perpetual mists which rose at dusk and floated

over the landscape, obscuring everything. And at this particular twilight hour the salty smell of the sea was carried in on the light breeze, reminding everyone how close the English Channel was.

In olden days the locals had latched their windows at this time of day, believing that the mists caused the ague; others had fastened their shutters tight because they were certain ghosts were at large on the Marsh.

Vicky generally laughed at these old wives' tales which were still told to whomever would listen, and when it came to the mention of ghosts she usually muttered under her breath to Will, 'More like the local smugglers winding their way inland from the sea, hauling their tobacco, their wines and brandy from France.' He agreed with her, fully believed the smugglers still plied their dubious trade here.

This afternoon, as he strode along the flagged path which led from the back terrace to the gardens, he could not help thinking how beautiful the landscape was even on this cold February Saturday. It was growing late, was almost dusk already, and the grey sky of early afternoon had changed, darkened, and was filled with rafts of fiery red and purple along the horizon. Or was that the sea? Some of the low-lying Marsh beyond the gardens was well below sea level, and frequently it seemed to him that the sea in the distance was high in the sky. A most curious illusion.

'Will, Will! Wait for me!'

He swung around at the sound of Ned's voice, and stood waiting as his friend hurried down the path at a fast pace.

'Why didn't you ask me to come for a walk with

137

you?' Ned demanded, peering at Will. 'Or did you feel like being alone? Am I intruding?'

Linking his arm through Ned's, Will shook his head, drew closer to his friend as they walked on together. 'I thought I'd better leave you to your own devices after lunch. You seemed so upset this morning, and were rather silent at lunchtime.'

'I was, and with good reason, don't you think?'

'Yes, I do. Anyway, I knew you were up in your room alone, since Lily and Vicky took the horse and trap into the village after you disappeared. I just saw them coming back and so I ducked out here.'

'For a man who doesn't like rural life, who protests so much about country living, and who prefers the gaiety, bright lights and razzle dazzle of London, you certainly seem rather attached to Stonehurst,' Ned remarked, sneaking a surreptitious glance at Will as they headed down the path together.

'I *have* grown attached to it, actually, perhaps because I helped Vicky bludgeon it into shape, and because we shared something rather special, a unique relationship during that time, just after Miles died. I was fourteen or fifteen, thereabouts, and we worked well together and we bonded. She has always reminded me that I helped her to combat her grief. But to be honest, Ned, I wouldn't want to live in the country permanently. I like to visit Vicky because we're so close. I'm also fascinated by the Marsh. There's something curious about that land out there that spells mystery to me.'

Ned laughed. 'Ah yes, I do understand. It appeals to the young adventurous lad that still exists inside you . . . stories of smugglers, and baccy and brandy-running, and

God knows what else. But I understand what you mean, and I also appreciate that the Romney Marsh has a genuine history to it.' Peering ahead as they came to the edge of the lawns, Ned added, 'And there's romance there, too . . . a fair wind for France tonight, and all that, eh?'

Will had the good grace to smile, knowing full well that Ned was teasing him. 'Well, perhaps you're right, perhaps that's so, the romance of it,' he agreed. Then he changed the subject. In a concerned voice he said, 'You are all right now, Ned, aren't you?'

'I suppose I am. However, I must admit I thought Lily was being as thick as a plank earlier today. And like you, Will, I have always considered her to be, well, rather smart, a clever woman.'

'I agree, I mean about her being somewhat dense this morning. On the other hand, I believe she's intelligent, bright. She's also thirty-two and an experienced woman of the world, wouldn't you say? But you know, I remember now that Vicky once told me Lily thinks she's an expert on the law, knows a lot about legalities, legal proceedings and such, because she was married to a solicitor for a number of years. Obviously she believes she's got one up on all of us, that *she* is *the* expert.'

Ned said, in a soft but emphatic voice, 'I've really tried to place my grief in its own place, deep within myself. It is *there*, and it always will be, but it's buried now, deep in my heart. I have had to do this in order to go on, Will. I must concentrate on the present and the future. My past and those tragic deaths will always be with me. However, I cannot allow feelings of grief to dominate me. I must move forward, and I know *you* understand this, Will.'

139

'I do, and yes, I think that Lily did probe too much. But she wasn't trying to hurt you *intentionally*, she was just being . . . assertive and she probably thought she was showing concern.' He lifted his shoulders in a shrug. 'After all, she's a woman, and who on earth can understand those adorable but tantalizing creatures, understand what they do and say? Not I, for one.'

Edward was silent. The two men walked on, content to be in each other's company. They were, in a sense, like brothers, and their bond of friendship was true and strong. It would last a lifetime, though neither of them knew that.

When they had left the lawns behind and were standing close to the seafront, Will suddenly murmured, 'Fair wind for France indeed, Ned. Just look over there, the lights of the French coastline are shining very brightly, are so *visible*. What a marvellously clear bright night it is.'

'With no mist off the Marsh,' Ned responded. 'And soon there'll be a full moon, mark my words. Not a good night for our smugglers.'

'You're right. But listen, did you know that the Romney Marsh is as famous for its smugglers as the Cornish coast?'

'I did.' Now turning slightly to the right, Ned continued, 'Let's go and sit on that wall for a moment or two. I need to talk to you about something.'

Will nodded his assent. Bundling their scarves and coats around themselves, the two men sat down, staring out towards the encroaching sea. All of a sudden it had grown truly dark; the stars glittered, and far off, in the distance, the Dungeness lighthouse flashed, its wide beams bouncing off the water onto the land and back onto the water.

Knowing that Edward Deravenel would speak in his own time, and only when he was ready, Will waited, wondering what this was about.

At last Ned said, 'What of Oxford, Will? You haven't gone back there to continue your studies. You're long overdue.'

'Oh, but I'm not going back.'

'Not ever?' Ned's surprise was evident in his tone of voice.

'That's correct. I went up to Oxford, saw everyone, bade my farewells, after I had explained my reasons for not finishing my education.'

'And your father? Isn't he angry?' Ned probed curiously.

'He was, but only momentarily. You know, the old man gave up on *me* a long time ago, and I suppose he knew it was futile to argue with me because my mind was made up.'

'Did you go to Leicestershire to see him?'

Will shook his head. 'It just so happened my father was in town on business last week, and we dined at his club. He was annoyed at first, and it was a bit of a sticky wicket for me, but in the end he came around to my way of thinking. He agreed I could lead my life as I wanted, and he actually wished me well. He was a brick really, Ned, since he hasn't withdrawn my monthly allowance.'

'That *was* generous of him,' Ned murmured. Frowning, he then asked, 'But, Will, what are your plans? Do you still wish to join a firm in the City?'

'No, I don't . . .' Will's voice trailed off, and he sat quietly for a moment or two, then continued, 'I would like to work alongside you, Ned, if that would be at all possible.'

Startled, Edward turned to stare at his friend. 'At *Deravenels*? Is that what you mean?'

Will nodded.

'I don't have a job myself, not yet at any rate. So I can't very well give you one, old chap.'

'The day will come when you can. I'm prepared to wait,' Will responded. 'If I know you and Neville Watkins as well as I think I do, I won't have to wait very long.'

'You sound positive about our success,' Ned muttered.

'I don't doubt it for one moment.'

Ned now said, 'I have to present myself there next week, and, frankly, I quite dread it. I know the top brass will simply greet me, give me an office and let me rot, doing nothing, twiddling my thumbs. That's their modus operandi. But I have other ideas, and, for one thing, I'm certainly going to demand my father's office. I'm not going to let them stick me in a poky little room in the back.'

'That's the spirit!' Will exclaimed. 'You *must* have your father's old office. Start the way you mean to go on, that's my advice.'

'I most certainly will do that.'

'Is it agreed then?' Will asked. 'About me working with you?'

'If you wish to work at Deravenels it would certainly please me, but I can't tell you exactly when that would be.'

'As I said, I'll wait.'

'Why?' Ned asked a short while later, as they started walking up the path, going back to the farmhouse. 'Why are you so keen on Deravenels?'

'Because I believe I can be of use to you, and because I want to be with you, Ned, working with you. Now, to change the subject, what are you going to *do* about Lily?'

'Why nothing,' Ned answered swiftly, pausing, turning to Will, staring at him in the moonlight. 'I'm going to walk back into the farmhouse and be as cordial and nice as I possibly can be. After all, there's no point in flogging a dead horse, is there? Anyway, knowing Vicky, she probably put Lily straight, wouldn't you say?'

'I would indeed,' Will answered, pleased that Ned had decided to be his old charming self. His charm had somehow disappeared of late. Perhaps things would become normal again. He felt a ripple of worry then, wondering why he would think things were going to be *normal*. They weren't. Not at all. Their world was about to go mad.

THIRTEEN

London

Neville Watkins was about to meet three men, each one of them very different. As he walked back and forth along the back portico of his Chelsea house he thought about them. He was well aware that each would bring something unique to the meeting; what they said, and what was ultimately agreed upon, would change many lives, some for the worse, others for the better.

As Neville turned and headed back along the paving stones a door suddenly flew open and a child stepped out. It was his small daughter Anne, and as soon as she saw him she ran towards him, her little feet flying down the walkway. She was waving and crying out, 'Papa! Papa! Here I am!'

Laughing, he hurried forward, caught her in his arms and swung her up, held her close to his chest. 'Hello, my little sweetheart,' he said against her glossy light brown hair. 'You should be wearing a coat, you know, my pet. You'll catch a chill in this cold weather.'

'But the sun is shining, Papa,' she answered, staring into his eyes.

'It's still February, Anne.'

'The flowers are coming out,' she countered, pointing to the snowdrops and purple and yellow crocuses peeping up out of the dark earth of the borders set around the lawn. 'Spring flowers Mama says.'

'They are indeed. However, we must go inside, where it's warmer. And you and I, well, we shall see each other later.'

'Mama says Ned is coming. Will he bring Richard with him?'

'I don't think so, sweetheart, not this morning. We are having a business meeting.'

'Today is Saturday, Papa,' she said, sounding reproachful.

He grinned at her. 'I know,' he answered, and suddenly recognized the disappointment in her eyes. Her face had changed, become sad, he thought.

'You like your cousin, don't you?'

She nodded.

By this time Neville had reached the door, and putting her down he ushered her into the house, stepped inside after her. Before they had even moved across the central gallery he heard his wife's footsteps on the polished wood floor. He always recognized them: only she in the household walked with such determination. Slap, slap, slap, her feet went, coming down hard on the wood, and a moment later she was entering the gallery. 'Ah, there you are my little one,' Anne Watkins exclaimed when she spotted her namesake. 'I've been looking all over for you.'

'She came out in search of me,' Neville remarked, walking across the gallery to his wife, putting his hand on her shoulder affectionately. 'She was really looking for young Dick, though, I do believe.' He smiled at her, his eyes full of love. 'You know how attached she is to him, Nan, she's his shadow whenever he's staying at Thorpe Manor with us.'

Anne Watkins, known as Nan all of her life, nodded and reached out, took hold of her daughter's hand. 'She's been attached to him since she took her first steps, and stumbled into his arms . . . arms that were certainly on the ready to catch her.'

Neville was silent for a moment, looking intently at his wife, his face suddenly growing thoughtful, his eyes narrowing. 'A good thing it is Richard she has adopted, taken into her heart and not the other one. I never quite know about *him* . . . the middle one, that is.'

'What do you mean?' Nan asked. She looked slightly puzzled, as if she were unsure of his question, its meaning.

'The breeding is there, but not the stamina.'

'You sound as if you're talking about horseflesh.'

Neville threw back his head and laughed uproariously, highly amused by his wife's comment. But then she frequently amused him with her remarks, brought laughter to his eyes. Shaking his head, he said at last, 'Touché, my dear.'

Nan glanced at him sideways, smiling, flirting with him, and then, looking down at her youngest daughter, she murmured, 'Come along, Anne, it's back to the nursery for you. Miss Deidre is waiting to give you and Isabel a painting lesson.'

'I am here,' a small voice said, and another pretty child came dancing into the gallery, her fair hair gleaming in the sunlight filtering in through the many leaded windows. She moved towards her father, pirouetting, showing off her skills as a budding dancer. 'Good morning, Papa,' she said as she finally came to a standstill.

Bending down, Neville kissed her cheek, hugged her to him, then, holding her away, he gave her a warm smile and told her, 'Aren't you the graceful one, Isabel. I am very impressed with your talent.'

She smiled and bobbed her head prettily, and asked, 'Is Georgie coming with Ned, Papa? Mama told me Ned would be here for lunch today.'

'That's true, darling, Ned *is* coming to have lunch with me. However, it is actually about business. And no, Georgie isn't going to be here, and neither is Dick. You'll have to see your little gentlemen friends another day.'

'Oh.' She pouted a little and shook her curls. 'I thought we could play together . . .' She let her voice trail off as she caught the warning look in her mother's eye, saw the stern expression settling on Nan's face.

Nan said, 'I will talk to Aunt Cecily later, and perhaps we can arrange something. Perhaps –'

'Cecily's still in Yorkshire,' Neville interrupted, shaking his head, pursing his lips. 'She decided to stay at Ravenscar for a little longer before coming up to London.' He gave a light shrug. 'I do believe she's trying to settle herself down, come to grips with . . . things.'

'As is your mother also. I do understand, Neville, it's only to be expected.'

'Go along, my sweethearts,' Neville told his girls. 'Go up to the nursery for your painting lesson. I need to spend a few moments with your mother.'

'Yes, Papa,' they said dutifully and in unison, and ran out together, heading for the grand staircase at the end of the gallery.

Taking hold of her arm, Neville led his wife into the nearby library and closed the door behind them. Turning her to face him, he said in a low voice, his eyes full of concern, 'I'm afraid Cecily and my mother aren't doing too well at the moment. They are still in shock, I think. After all, the deaths were so unexpected and so sudden. There has to be a period of adjustment, and of grieving.'

Nan nodded her head vigorously, 'Of course, of course, Neville. I don't know why the girls are so focused on the two youngest Deravenels at the moment. I really have no clue at all.'

'Well, Anne for one has always been like a little puppy trailing after Richard; as for Isabel, she's seemed to gravitate to George. Although *that* doesn't particularly please me. Still, there's nothing strange, darling, they've known those boys all their lives, grown up together, and after the week we just spent in Yorkshire, and being with them so much at Ravenscar, I think they're missing their little playmates. That's quite understandable, isn't it?'

'Yes, I suppose so.' Standing on tiptoe she kissed his cheek, and led him out of the library. 'I must go and spend a few minutes with them, my dear, show my interest in their painting lesson.'

'I know, I know.' He watched her walking off down the long gallery, thinking how beautiful she was in her rather refined and delicate way. She was the only woman he had ever loved; there had been others, but they had been merely sexual liaisons. His sweet Nan was the love of his life. They were extremely happy together, he and she, and the only thing that caused him the odd moment of regret at times was the lack of an heir. He longed for a son; Nan had had several miscarriages, and she had not yet conceived again. At least not so far. The sudden terrible yearning for a boy child surfaced for a split second, and then he pushed it away. He was a lucky man . . . he counted his blessings. And Nan and he were still young enough to have many more children . . .

Once Nan had disappeared up the staircase, Neville turned around and went outside again. He began to walk up and down along the portico, his thoughts now on business and the impending arrival of his three guests.

The first he expected was his cousin Edward Deravenel. He was very anxious to see him, to listen to what he had to say, and to report. Ned had been working at the Deravenel offices in the Strand for the past week. They had spoken briefly, and he had received several enigmatic notes from Edward, but nothing of real importance had been conveyed. This had been puzzling, and he was somewhat baffled. But he trusted Ned in all things, and especially trusted his judgement, and it was obvious to Neville that Edward was being discreet. Far better to talk in the privacy of his house than on the telephone, and he was well aware how easily notes could get lost, fall into the wrong hands, or be stolen.

Alfredo Oliveri would be the second to come to see him. Oliveri was in London, ostensibly on Deravenel business, but he had really come to see *them* . . . Ned and himself. Oliveri had made his loyalty and devotion to the Yorkshire Deravenels known when they were in Carrara, and to have him on their side was an immense bonus. He was well trusted in the company, and part of the old guard, having worked for them for over twenty years. Although he might not exactly be a member of the inner circle he certainly knew a lot, which could only be useful to them.

Neville had made a plan, and the secret to its success was information; he knew only too well that information was power. The more Oliveri was able to tell him about everyone and everything in the company the more *he* was likely to succeed.

His last guest for lunch was Amos Finnister. *Amos*. He turned the name over in his mind; he had known Amos for twelve years and employed him for ten. He was a private investigator and the best in that line of business, as far as Neville was concerned.

Amos Finnister ran his own firm, which had only one client – Neville Watkins. And it was Neville who actually owned the detective agency through several straw men. This arrangement worked well for both of them.

Now Neville smiled to himself as he continued to think about Amos. Taking the man under his wing all those years ago had been a brilliant piece of strategy on his part. Amos was diligent, logical and persistent, like a dog with a bone when it was necessary. Calm and cool, whatever the circumstances, or the pressure he was under, he was loyal, discreet, and on call night or day. He had a clever knack of picking men to work for him who had similar characteristics to himself.

One of the things Neville considered of unquestionable value were the contacts Amos had . . . in all walks of life. This was one of the main keys to being a successful private investigator.

Before he had left for Italy with Edward and Will Hasling, Neville had given Amos a list of names, for the most part people who worked at Deravenels and were known adherents of Henry Grant, and, therefore, more than likely to be enemies of Edward.

Now, since returning to London, he was more convinced than ever that his cousin needed genuine protection; he had been made truly aware of that by Alfredo Oliveri. But from whom *exactly*?

Who were the real wielders of power at Deravenels? Margot Grant, obviously, and John Summers. But Grant himself?

Maybe. Maybe not. He was a weak man, a trifle lazy, ready to pass on the burdens of business to his wife, who was keen to grab those so-called burdens as fast as she could. And naturally there were others who were against Edward, simply because he was the son of Richard Deravenel, the true heir to the company.

Amos would find out, if he hadn't already; Neville could not wait to see him.

I have to triumph, Neville told himself, as he struck out towards the end of the garden. When he came to the ancient stone wall that fronted onto the River Thames he leaned against it, staring out into the distance. It was a slow moving river today, black as ink, and the sky above had suddenly changed. The pale blue had curdled, become a mix of grey and a strange bluish green.

It's going to rain after all, he decided, lifting his eyes to the sky. And this thought had hardly surfaced when he felt the first drops of cold rain on his upturned face.

Swinging about, Neville hurried up through the garden and went into the house, crossed the central gallery, deposited his overcoat in the hall closet, all this accomplished in the space of a few minutes.

He made his way back to the library, a large and elegantly appointed room, his favourite in the lovely old house that dated back to the Regency period. He had always thought of the library as his haven, one which closed him off from the ugliness of the world outside.

A fire blazed in the hearth and the softly-shaded lamps had all been turned on during his absence in the garden, giving the room a welcoming, roseate glow. He realized he had grown slightly chilled outside, and he went and stood with his back to the fire, warming himself, thawing out.

His mind was alive with ideas and plans. He *was* going to put Ned in the seat of power, however long it took him. And he himself would be the one to wield the power.

FOURTEEN

Ravenscar

The North Sea glittered like highly-polished chain mail, rippling under the light breeze. Above, the sky was a cloudless arc of brilliant azure blue filled with golden sunlight. Sunlight without warmth on this cold wintry morning. Nonetheless, Cecily Deravenel had been lured outside by it, and wrapping herself warmly in heavy woollens and a fur-lined cape she had braved the cold.

At this moment she stood inside the old ruined strong-hold on the promontory, somewhat protected by its high walls, staring out across the sea. Her thoughts were with Edward in London: a week ago he had presented himself at Deravenels, and his professional life had begun. She shivered, but not from the cold. How would they treat him? And how would he fare in the long run? She was well aware that Ned had dreaded going there. In the past week he had told her little, his two phone calls kept to the briefest of conversations. Yet Neville had reassured her, as best he could, that it would be all right. At least for the moment. No one would make any kind of move against Ned. Too soon, he had explained. Also, Alfredo Oliveri was there; ostensibly, he was on a business trip to the London headquarters from his base in Italy. But, more specifically, he was really there to keep an eye on Ned. *Keep an eye on him*. What a silly euphemism that was. Protection was what he would ultimately need. Her son was sitting in the middle of a nest of vipers.

Cecily shivered again and hunched into her warm clothes; her gloved hands fumbled with the ends of the scarf tied around her head. As she tightened it her mind raced.

Neville had been honest with her the other day; he had admitted that all of her sons were in danger. Still, he *had* also managed to convince her that her two youngest were quite safe here at Ravenscar. She trusted her nephew implicitly, knew how clever he was, highly intelligent and brilliant of mind. He was also loyal to family, just as Ned was, and as her father and brother had been . . . family was *all* to them. Rick, her only sibling, was gone forever, and Thomas, his youngest, was dead and buried with him. Now she must rely on Neville, and his brother John, both older than Ned. Dear Johnny. Her face softened at the thought of him. Less flamboyant, less ambitious than his brother, a loving young man, and wholly devoted to Ned.

We are a strong family unit, the Watkins and the Deravenel clans. We will stand together in this battle to come. We will prevail. These thoughts made her suddenly lift her head higher, and with great pride as she remembered who she was, her lineage, and whom she had married: *Richard Deravenel*, rightful heir to the Deravenel business empire. His widow now. She must

154

do his memory justice. Unexpectedly her eyes blazed with a new determination.

She came to a sudden decision. She would not permit herself to be frightened by the likes of Henry Grant and his avaricious French wife, or by their subordinates. Never. She would stand up to them, stand tall, just as her father had taught her to do.

As for her overwhelming grief, caused by her devastating losses, she would bury it deep. Her grief was something private, not for public consumption. Nor for sharing with anyone, not even her children.

Her children. She must focus all of her attention on them now, protect them at all costs, ensure their safety. 'Of course nobody's going to come and murder them in their beds,' Neville had reassured her with a laugh when he was in Yorkshire recently. 'All I'm saying is . . . well, just keep an eye on them.' And that she would certainly do . . . she would protect them with her very life.

Turning around, chilled from the wind coming off the sea, Cecily went back to the house, climbing the steps intersecting the tiered gardens, entering the house through the French doors on the terrace.

She was shedding her cape and heavy jacket in the Long Hall when she heard a yell, almost a war cry, and to her surprise there was George on the stairs, almost hurtling down them, blond hair rumpled, his clothes askew, his face flushed with anger. Margaret was fast on his heels, looking equally distressed. Only Richard, following them slowly, seemed sedate, and perfectly in control.

'Good Heavens! *Children!* What on earth is going on here?' Cecily demanded in her crisp, businesslike tone as she pulled off her gloves and scarf, threw them on top of her outer garments on the chair.

'It's not my fault! Not mine, Mama. I didn't smash the wall in,' George yelled as he scurried towards her down the hall, and as usual flung himself onto her body, clutching at her. 'It's not my fault, Mama,' he repeated. 'I'm not to blame, she pushed me.'

Automatically, Cecily's arms went around the eleven-year-old boy in that particular protective way she had with him, but she looked over his head to his sister Meg, who was straightening her jacket, then smoothing her blonde hair back into the black silk bow at the nape of her neck. She looked as if she had been in a tussle, and obviously with George.

Hesitantly, Meg took a few steps towards her mother, and said in a trembling voice, 'It *was* George's fault. He started it all.'

'No, I didn't!' he shouted back.

'Be quiet!' Cecily exclaimed, staring down at George. Instinctively, she believed Meg, who was usually so loyal to George. Why would she turn on him unless he deserved it? Looking across at her daughter, Cecily continued, 'Please explain the situation to me, Meg, since you at least seem to be in control of yourself.'

'I'm the one in control,' Richard volunteered.

'I see that,' his mother answered. 'Come now, Meg, what *is* this fuss about?'

'We were in the old nursery playroom. Richard was reading, I was working on my stamp collection. George was idling his time away, and growing bored. Suddenly, he swooped down on me and took my album. Actually, Mother, he grabbed it. Then he pranced around the room, waving it in the air. I thought he would damage some of my best stamps which Papa had given me over the years, so I jumped up, tried to get it. But George kept dodging away from me, taunting me, and he made me angry. I lurched towards him, and naturally he tried to avoid me, and as he did so he tripped over a foot stool and fell against the wall next to the fireplace. It caved in, just like that. George fell inside the wall, but it was very strange because there's actually a room there.'

Cecily froze. *The priest hole.* Closed permanently by Richard when Anne, their first child, was born, her husband had decided that the concealed door must be nailed down, and so it was. He was fearful that a small child might lock herself inside and suffocate before she could be rescued. And so he had made it safe. And no one had ever known about the priest hole except them, and the Deravenel ancestors, of course.

Cecily opened her mouth to speak and then closed it as the youngest in the family came forward, slowly approached her. His face was solemn, his eyes grave, thoughtful, as they frequently were. He was totally in control of himself, just as he had said he was, much more so than his siblings.

What had silenced Cecily was the black leather notebook Richard clutched in his hands. Surely it was her husband's missing black notebook, wasn't it? The one she had searched for, and Ned, too, in his father's rooms in London.

'I climbed into the wall,' the boy was saying to her. 'To help Georgie, Mama. He was flat on his back on the floor. Between the walls. That's what I thought at first, but when I went to him I found I was in a *little room*. There's a chest in there, and after I helped Georgie to get up I opened the drawers, well, not all of them because one was locked. Anyway, Mother, I found this.' Moving closer to Cecily, he thrust the black leather book at her.

Cecily disentangled herself from George's clinging embrace, and accepted the book from her youngest child. 'Thank you very much, Dickie,' she murmured.

Holding it in her hands she experienced a wonderful flare of hope. Her husband had jotted notes in it almost every day . . . she opened it eagerly and saw lines and lines of numbers, but few words. There were odd sentences, here and there, but none of them made any sense to her. Disappointment swept through her, and her heart sank. For a brief moment she had thought the book would reveal something important – *important to Ned*. However, the notes in it were an enigma. Unless there was someone who could decipher them. Was this a code of some kind? Perhaps.

Oliveri. Instantly, Cecily thought of the Italian, who had apparently been a close colleague of her husband's, and was obviously so willing to help them in any way he could. Would he know what the numbers meant?

Meg interrupted her thoughts when she said, 'Mother, George *did* take my album, whatever he says. He grabbed it and ran around the room with it.'

'I did not,' George cried, his anger surfacing.

'George, tell me the truth. Did you do what Meg says?' Cecily asked, her tone icy.

'No, I didn't,' he began, and then his voice faltered under his mother's fixed and sharp scrutiny.

'I'm asking you for the final time,' Cecily informed him.

'I only . . . wanted to . . . have a look at the stamps,' he muttered, sounding guilty, looking shamefaced, and he blushed as his mother held him away from her by his shoulders, stared into his eyes.

'I will not tolerate lying, George. Now, apologize to your sister.'

'I'm sorry,' he mumbled without looking around at Meg.

'Please, Meg, come forward. That's right, stand next to George. Now George, turn to your sister and say you are sorry and shake her hand. And Meg, you must apologize, too.'

The two of them did as she asked without any further argument.

Cecily said, 'Well, George, you're not hurt, apparently, none the worse for wear, so do stop whining. *Please.*'

The old nursery playroom at Ravenscar was entirely panelled in dark wood. Except for the gaping hole made when George had fallen, it looked perfectly in order. But Cecily understood that part of the panelling might easily be fragile. After all, it *was* centuries old and some woods did rot with the passing of time.

Ravenscar had been built in the Elizabethan period, almost four hundred years ago, which was when a priest hole had been created behind a wall which adjoined the fireplace. During the early part of Elizabeth Tudor's reign there had been religious persecution after the Catholic risings in the north, and many renowned Catholic families like the Deravenels had built priest holes in which to hide priests in the event of sudden surprise, such as the unexpected arrival of soldiers.

Bending down, Cecily felt the wood around the hole which George had made, and a few pieces instantly crumbled in her hand. It *was* a little fragile, and George, a sturdy boy, had obviously fallen hard against the panelling.

Stepping away from the damaged wall, she tried to recall where, all those years ago, her husband had hammered in the nails, and she was gratified when she had no trouble remembering. Six feet up from the baseboard, at the top of the second panel a couple of feet away from the fireplace . . . that was exactly where he had nailed the small door shut.

Taking a chair from around the circular table in the middle of the room, Cecily pulled it over to the fireplace wall. Tall and athletic, she was agile. Lifting her long black skirt, she climbed onto the chair, and reaching up she felt around for the nails. They weren't there anymore, just as she had suspected. She could actually feel the little holes where the nails had been; they had been darkened over with varnish, or dark boot polish, and quite recently. There was no question in her mind that Richard had pulled them out, just as he had hammered them in place not very long after the first baby, Anne, came into the world.

Stepping cautiously off the chair, Cecily hurried to the fireplace and picked up the poker. Leaning forward, squinting in the bright firelight blazing up the chimney, focusing her eyes intently, she finally spotted the tiny metal lever set in the lower part of the brick fireback. It was hardly visible, covered in soot, and difficult to find even when someone knew exactly where to look for it, as she did.

Lifting the poker she brought it downward, struck the tiny lever, and instantly the panel, no longer nailed shut, slowly swung open, became a door.

After replacing the poker, Cecily went to the priest hole and manoeuvred herself inside through the small door. She was quite startled to find the space relatively clean. Obviously her husband had swept out the dust whenever it was that he had finally opened the priest hole for the first time in years.

Cecily's main target was the chest; it took only a moment to locate the locked drawer, which she managed to pry open with a pair of scissors.

The drawer slid out easily, and she experienced a sense of satisfaction and a rush of hope. She had known full well that there would be something inside the locked drawer, something put there for safety by her husband, and indeed there was. It was a second black leather notebook. This one was slightly larger than the first which Richard had discovered; it had her husband's initials embossed in gold in the bottom corner, and her hand trembled as she reached for it, opened it and began to read. Her excitement grew and grew as she stood there in front of the nursery fire, scanning the pages.

She did not read for long. She had read enough for the moment to know how important it was for Edward to have this. Hurrying downstairs, she went immediately to the small sitting room which adjoined her bedroom and seated herself at the desk.

Placing her hands across the top of the private diary, for that was what it was, she stared off into the distance, thinking. This book had to go to Edward as quickly as possible; how to get it there? She did not want to post it to him, fearing that it might get lost. She could send Jessup up to town with it. A sealed package was safe from prying eyes. Or perhaps she should take it herself? On the other hand, she didn't want to leave her children here alone. She could take them with her, of course. What to do . . . what to do?

PART TWO

Golden Boy
Edward & Lily

'Very tall of personage, exceeding the stature almost of all others, comely of visage, pleasant and broad breasted.'

Polydore Vergil

'He had courage, determination and resourcefulness, which he used to his own advantage, and was pragmatic, generous, witty and ruthless when the occasion demanded it.'

Alison Weir

'She walks in beauty, like the night
Of cloudless climes and starry skies;
And all that's best of dark and bright
Meet in her aspect and her eyes;
Thus mellow'd to that tender light
Which heaven to gaudy day denies.'

Lord Byron

FIFTEEN

Kent

'What to do? What to do?' Lily murmured, staring at Vicky. 'Please tell me what to do, because I really don't know.'

Vicky Forth put down her coffee cup and sat back in the chair, contemplating her friend for a second or two, and then, shaking her head, she answered softly, 'I don't think there *is* anything you *can* do at the moment, my dear. You must let the matter rest, and just wait.'

'That's the hardest part, you know, waiting. Waiting for him to send a note by messenger, or put a letter in the post, or just arrive on my doorstep, as he so often does. This total silence all week is rather unusual, I must admit. I have to think he is still angry with me, perhaps he even wants to break it off?'

'I doubt that. He's much too much enamoured of you, Lily. I know he was a trifle put out with you last weekend; on the other hand, he seemed to calm down later. Also, there's another thing. Edward doesn't bear a grudge, he never has. Very simply, he's just not made that way . . . it's not part of his nature.'

'If you say so then I must believe you, Vicky, and it

cheers me up a little. This whole week without a word from him has been nerve-wracking, seemed like an eternity.'

'And it would, since that's all you've focused on, waiting for a word from Ned. I know for a fact he's been busy. It was his first week at Deravenels, remember.'

'Will told you he's been busy with work? Is that what you're saying?'

'Absolutely. Will hasn't seen him either. Seemingly, Ned has kept to himself. He dropped Will a note saying he was trying to work out the way the company runs, and that Will shouldn't expect to see him until next week, that is the coming week.'

A smile flitted across Lily's face and her eyes sparkled. 'Thank you for telling me this, it makes it easier, knowing that I'm not the only one he's ignoring. Obviously his best friend is going through the same thing.'

Vicky began to laugh, stood up, walked across the small morning room at Stonehurst Farm where the two women were having morning coffee on this windy Saturday. 'If I'm picking up the correct vibrations from my darling brother, I think he has better fish to fry,' she remarked as she brought the coffee pot over to the table. 'Would you care for another cup?'

Lily shook her head. 'No, thanks anyway.'

After filling her own cup, Vicky placed the silver pot on the table and sat down, looking thoughtful. Stirring her coffee and taking a sip, she went on, 'I do believe Will has a new lady in his life.'

Lily stared at her, obviously taken by surprise. 'Really! How odd that Ned hasn't mentioned it to me – after all, they are so close, those two. So he must know.'

'I doubt that Ned would say anything to anyone . . . he'd consider it Will's business. He's not the kind of person to gossip.'

'Edward's an odd duck though, in some ways, don't you think?'

Vicky frowned, not quite understanding what Lily meant by this comment. She gave her friend a questioning look.

As if reading her mind, Lily exclaimed, 'What I mean is he seems much older than his actual age. Also, he certainly has a penchant for seeking out older women. I know for a fact that he had a flirtation with his mother's secretary, a widow.'

'He does have a weakness for older women, and most especially *widows*, but don't complain, Lily. After all, *you're* his favourite, so do be happy.'

'I am happy, although a little worried at the moment.'

'Oh, darling, don't be concerned. You haven't heard from him this week because he's only just stepped into his father's shoes and gone into the family business.'

'It's not his absence or his silence that's really worrying me,' Lily murmured, leaning closer across the table, 'but something else altogether.' Dropping her voice, she now confided, 'I am afraid I might be pregnant, having his baby.'

This was the last thing Vicky had expected to hear and for a moment she was speechless, and then sitting up straighter in her chair, she asked in a quiet tone, 'Are you *sure*?'

Shaking her elegant blonde head, Lily answered swiftly, 'No, not yet. But I have . . . missed . . . a month. Last month. I have to wait and see what

167

happens . . . I'm due in ten days.' Taking a deep breath, Lily added, 'Before you say it, I know he won't marry me if I *am* expecting. And I wouldn't want him to, I'm much too old for him. Anyway, I think it goes without saying that Ned is not really marriage material. He's too much of a Lothario. At the moment. And Edward Deravenel of Deravenels is undoubtedly expected to make a brilliant marriage one day, when the time is right.'

Vicky nodded. 'What you say is true, but what on earth are you going to do if you are carrying his child? There are doctors who . . . well, you know, terminate unwanted pregnancies. But I think that might be a dangerous course to take.'

'Oh, I agree with you! And I would *never* go that route! Believe me, I wouldn't.'

'So what *will* you do?' Vicky pressed, filled with sudden concern.

'I would have the baby, there's nothing else to *do*, if you think about it.'

Vicky was silent for a moment, biting her lip. 'You would have the baby and bring it up yourself, is that what you're saying?'

'Yes.' Lily nodded. 'I would have it, *and* keep it.'

'But Lily, darling, think of the scandal. What will you say? Tell people? And who will you name as the father?'

'Well, I hadn't actually thought of all that, not in great detail. No, I definitely haven't puzzled all that out yet. But I don't suppose I would name Edward. Why would I want to cause trouble for him? After all, I do love him, Vicky, very much. And I do understand that he can never marry me, for a variety of reasons not only because of our age differences. But I think . . . well, you know, I do think I would like to have his baby, and I know I'd enjoy bringing up his child.'

'What lovely sentiments, Lily,' Vicky murmured, smiling at her friend. 'And I'm perfectly certain Ned would help you financially.'

'Oh, but I don't want *money* from him, Victoria! How could you think such a thing, for Heaven's sake? My goodness, I have plenty of money from my late husbands . . . money to burn, in fact. So why would I burden Ned with something like that? Especially since he never has any money of his own. Well, hardly any. He did tell me once that his father had been as poor as a church mouse. The money in the family comes from his late grandfather, Philip Watkins.'

'Yes, I'm aware of that.' Vicky sat quite still, ruminating for a few seconds, and then she nodded to herself and gave Lily a loving smile, her expression one of affection and warmth. 'I must say, you're a most unusual woman, Lily Overton, quite remarkable, in fact.'

'Thank you.' Lily rose, walked over to the window, stood looking out towards Romney Marsh, yet seeing only Ned in her mind's eye. She did love him to distraction, but there was no future for them, not in the long run. She would remain his mistress for as long as he wanted her, she had always known that about herself. She was utterly devoted to him. He was, in a way, a great gift to her, one she had never expected in this life. She had never known such passion or ecstasy before Ned. He had brought her to the height of fulfilment, pleasured her and loved her, introduced passion and sexual excitement to her life. And she knew that in his own way he truly cared about her. And that in itself was enough. Her two marriages had been affectionate, and, of course, she had fulfilled her marital duties. However, lovemaking with her late husbands had been tepid, lacklustre. She was grateful to them in many ways, grateful for the comfort and protection they had provided. Ultimately, they had made her a very wealthy woman, and in so doing had given her total independence.

Swinging around, she said slowly, 'I can well afford to raise a child, Vicky, and that's what I *am* going to do. Bring up Ned's child. In the country. That would be the easiest and the most comfortable place to be. Perhaps here in Kent. Somewhere near here, near you. What do you think?'

'I agree with you, of course I do. Far better to be down here than up in town, where everyone tittle-tattles and pries. And you know I am here, my dear, I'll do anything I can to help.'

Lily walked over to Vicky, gave her a quick embrace and sat down at the table. 'Thank you, Vicky, I'm lucky to have you as a friend. But I might not be pregnant at all, you know.'

Vicky merely smiled, and thought: I'm certain you are. There's a bloom on you and you look wonderful. And Edward Deravenel, almost nineteen, is undoubtedly as virile as any man could ever be.

Vicky awakened with a start. She had slept so deeply she was totally disoriented, at a loss, befuddled, wondering where she was, what time of day it was. As she glanced around, shaking off that deep, almost drugged sleep she realized she was in front of the fire in her bedroom, stretched out on the small sofa. The carriage clock on the mantelshelf told her that it was almost noon.

Pushing herself up, she swung her legs to the floor and waited for a moment until her head cleared. She had come up here just before eleven and fallen asleep as she had been reading *The Times*. There it was on the floor at her feet. She must have been extremely tired to have slept like that, and for almost an hour. But the truth was she had had a restless night.

Leaning back against the cut-velvet cushions, she thought of Lily. She, too, had retreated to her bedroom. Vicky wondered if she was feeling all right, and knew at once she need not worry about her friend, or feel guilty and responsible as she had earlier. Yes, she *had* been the one to introduce Lily to Edward Deravenel, but she hadn't forced them into bed with each other. That had been their choice and theirs alone.

It was an old story . . . a story as old as time itself.

A woman meets a man. They are irresistibly drawn to each other, unable to turn away because the attraction is so strong, overpowering. The woman becomes the man's mistress and inevitably it is she who ends up mired in problems. Never the man. He retains his wife, or if he is not married, has other mistresses, and in a sense he is free as a bird, and does as he wishes.

Well, perhaps that wasn't really fair. And men were not always to blame. In fact, as her brother Will had once said, it takes two. Dear Will. He was so kind and loving. Was there a new woman in *his* life? She wasn't sure but hoped that there was.

She sometimes wondered if his genuine devotion to Ned was too all-consuming, took up too much of his time. But then he was a grown man and he had to lead his own life. A couple of her friends had once hinted, rather meanly, at a more complex relationship between her brother and Ned, but there was nothing strange or queer about it. They were not homosexuals, though they did spend all their free time together. And they did indeed love each other – like brothers and best friends.

Now she asked herself how Ned would react when he found out that Lily was carrying his child. If, in fact, this *was* the case. He would care, of course he would, and he would be devoted to Lily. Until the child was born. And then he would walk away, if he hadn't already done so before the birth. She had known Edward Deravenel for a very long time and she understood him. He did not wish to be encumbered; freedom was his choice.

Did men always have to have a mistress? She was absolutely certain her first husband Miles had been true to her. Certainly it had been a marriage of enormous passion, sexual attraction and commitment. When he had died of a heart attack so unexpectedly she had been devastated, believed her life had been shattered forever. Some years later Stephen had come along. They had fallen madly in love, something she had never anticipated. This, too, was a strong marriage, much like her first, especially when it came to the bedroom and the sexual side of their life together. She would be glad when he returned from New York. She missed him, missed his sense of humour, his loving attention, his brilliant mind.

Leaning down, Vicky picked up *The Times*, turning to the inside pages . . . to the Court Circular. There were mentions of royal engagements during the week. Queen Alexandra had gone *there* . . . the king had been *here* . . . all of their weekly public appearances carefully chronicled.

King Edward VII. Son of Queen Victoria, a middle-aged man before he reached the throne. A man who was now seemingly giving his name to the new era, a man who loved the high life, food and drink, and dancing the night away, a man who perhaps preferred his mistress Mrs Keppel to his wife, Queen Alexandra.

Well, kings *were* notorious when it came to their mistresses, weren't they? Diane de Poitiers sprang into her mind . . . now there was a clever woman, a mistress who had reigned supreme. Her influence over Henry II of France had lasted to the end of his life. Diane had somehow managed to maintain friendly relations with the Queen, Catherine de'Medici, whilst totally eclipsing her. A clever manipulator when it came to politics and politicians, Diane had been a true survivor.

Her thoughts about royal mistresses fled, when she saw the photograph of Madame Marie Curie at her small laboratory in Paris. There she was with her husband, Pierre. They had isolated radium in 1902, and last year this brilliant couple had shared the Nobel Prize in Physics with Henri Becquerel. The caption said she was being considered for a university post. Marie Curie was a woman Vicky admired . . . she admired all those women who went out into the world and did impressive things. The women warriors she called them.

Glancing at the carriage clock again, Vicky jumped up. She must go downstairs to the kitchen and see how Cook was progressing with lunch. No time for daydreaming.

When Vicky went into the kitchen a few minutes later she saw that Cook had everything under control and rolling along in her usual efficient way. Florry, the young woman who came up from the village to help, was beating eggs in a bowl, and she glanced up, smiled cheerily at the sight of Vicky.

Vicky smiled back, nodding, and then said, 'I see all is very much in order in here, as usual, Mrs Bloom, so I'll just leave you to it.'

'That's right, Mum, I'm on schedule, right on time, that I am. The cheese soufflé will be ready at one-thirty, as you requested, and there's no problem with the roast chicken. Fortunately, the bird won't spoil.'

'I'll make sure we sit down at one twenty-five, Mrs Bloom, never fear. Your soufflé is quite safe, it won't drop if I've anything to do with it.'

Mrs Bloom glanced over her shoulder at Vicky, and chuckled.

Vicky hurried out and walked across the hall and into the dining room. It was cosy and welcoming with the fire burning brightly in the grate, and there was the smell of beeswax and pine cones, intermingled with the hint of smoke and the faint scent of ripening apples in the air. It was a mixture of those unique and lovely country smells which never failed to remind Vicky of Compton Hall, the Hasling family seat where she and Will had grown up. That lovely old manor house had always been redolent with the perfume of burning wood, mellow fruit, baking bread, and the sweet scent of homemade honey. She thought of their late mother with a rush of affection, a woman who had turned that ancient pile of stones into a welcoming home where children were loved and cosseted.

Slowly Vicky began to set the table for lunch, selecting a linen cloth with embroidered edges, crystal water tumblers, knives and forks and linen napkins, and as she moved around she thought of her dear friend Lily Overton.

Lily had been very brave earlier that morning when she had discussed her plans, explained what she would do if she *was* pregnant after all. She did have only three choices, Vicky was acutely aware of this. Lily could try to get a termination, a risky business, in more ways than one; she could have the child and give it up for adoption immediately, a miserable, heartbreaking prospect; or she could keep it and bring it up herself.

Lily had elected to do the latter, and Vicky couldn't blame her. She would manage very well, in Vicky's opinion, because she was practical by nature, a good organizer, and fortunately she had her own money, was not dependent on anyone.

That was the key, the money. It protected her and the child.

Having a child out of wedlock was like committing suicide for most women who found themselves in that terrible situation in this day and age. An enormous stigma was attached to illegitimacy, and unless a woman was protected by the man involved she was doomed.

Even in this new Edwardian era, which was more relaxed than in Queen Victoria's time, the stigma remained. Despite the fun-loving antics of the aristocracy and the licentiousness which was so prevalent today, beneath that carefree, glittering façade there remained prudery, snobbery, discrimination, class distinction and –

'I shocked you earlier, didn't I?'

Vicky almost jumped out of her skin. Swinging around, she exclaimed, 'Goodness, Lily! You did give me a start. I didn't hear you coming down the hall.'

'I'm sorry,' Lily apologized. 'But I *did* shock you, didn't I?'

'No, you didn't, actually. *Surprised* me, yes.'

'I've made up my mind not to think about it, for the moment at least . . . it *could* be a false alarm, you know.'

Vicky nodded. 'That's a wise decision.' She fell silent as Lily came to stand next to the fireplace. Vicky couldn't help thinking what a beautiful woman she was, with her perfect pink-and-white complexion, green eyes and blonde hair. Her features were sculpted, very even and smooth, and she looked much younger than her years. No wonder Edward Deravenel was so smitten with her . . . what man wouldn't be?

Margot Grant came in from the garden, and took off her coat, hung it in the armoire, and went into the dining room. She stopped dead in her tracks, staring at the room in horror. What had happened here? *Mon Dieu!* The mahogany dining table had been pushed up against one of the end walls, the twelve antique dining chairs arranged in four rows of three, like the pews in a church, and the table itself had been transformed into some strange homemade altar. And above the table, hanging on the wall, was the crucifixion of Christ. How had Henry managed to nail it up there? she asked herself.

A terrible dismay swept over her, and she did not move for a moment, her mind churning. Henry was off on one of his mad jaunts again, filled with religious fervour, revelling in the belief that he was a monk, and that he had his own church where he preached to a congregation. That there wasn't one present never seemed to bother him at all.

But he wasn't here preaching to the empty chairs now. So where was he? Terrified that he might have wandered out of the garden of their Ascot home, gone onto the main road, she swung around and rushed out into the garden. Shading her eyes from the sunlight, she looked around frantically, calling his name, 'Henry! Henry! Where are you?'

He did not respond to her calls, and she began to search for him. Within the space of a few minutes she saw him flitting through the trees in a small copse at the end of the lawn. Her heart sank. He was wearing the dark brown monk's robe again, and carrying a wooden cross. As she drew closer, she heard him singing, off key as usual.

Margot felt nauseous. He was stark raving mad, there was no question about that. What if someone found out how truly crazy he was? And that he had been in asylums? She might have to put him there again. *Mon Dieu! Mon Dieu!*

'Henry, Henry, *chéri!*' she exclaimed as she moved

into the copse of trees. 'Come along, let us go inside. It is cool today.'

He turned around, gaping at her, his eyes vacant. 'Daughter in Christ,' he mumbled. 'Daughter in Christ, good morrow to you.'

Swallowing her distaste, pushing her spiralling anger to one side, Margot took hold of his arm, and murmuring cajoling words she led him out of the copse, across the lawn and into the house.

Once she had manoeuvred him into his bedroom, she swung on her heels, left his room and locked the door behind her. What a pious, mentally disturbed old fool he was. One thing was absolutely essential. She now had to keep him hidden from the world until he became himself again.

Margot Grant shook her head as she went downstairs. It was better when he went into catatonic shock. At least then he sat in a chair all day not moving, not speaking.

SIXTEEN

London

Edward Deravenel came striding into the library of Neville's Chelsea house, bringing with him a rush of energy, vitality and the most obvious exuberance. Ned's feeling better, Neville thought, putting the grief behind him. He's ready and able to move forward. He was pleased for his young cousin, and relieved at the change in his demeanour.

There was a smile on Edward's face, an apology on his lips. 'Sorry to be late. I'm afraid I had trouble finding a hansom cab this morning.'

'There's no problem, Edward,' Neville murmured, coming forward to greet his cousin. After they had quickly embraced, Neville stepped away, seated himself in a chair near the fireplace.

Edward chose to stand, propped himself against the mantelpiece, and asked, 'What time are the others due to arrive?'

'Alfredo Oliveri will be here in about ten minutes, Amos Finnister fifteen minutes after that.'

'You haven't really explained who Amos Finnister is,' Edward remarked, looking across at Neville, an eager expression settling on his face. 'All you said is that he has worked for you for some years, that you trust him implicitly, and that he will be invaluable to me.'

'He will indeed, I've no doubt. But you'll soon understand about Finnister. Before they arrive please tell me about the past week. Your notes were rather enigmatic, and you were not at all forthcoming when you telephoned.'

Edward nodded, explained, 'There wasn't a lot to tell you, and quite frankly it was a God-awful week. And I loathe Aubrey Masters. I'm putting Oliveri in his place, making him head of the mining division, if we win.'

'*When* we win, but do continue.'

'Masters is bumptious, argumentative and full of his own importance. And basically he's as thick as a plank. I'm more certain than ever that he's there purely because of Grant family connections. Anyway, he was going to give me the worst office in the entire building until I put up a huge fight. I insisted on my father's office, which is the tradition, and he wouldn't hear of it. I went at him hammer and tongs but he was absolutely bloody-minded about it. Obdurate. Finally he brought John Summers in to mediate, and much to Aubrey's shocked surprise Summers agreed with me. Aubrey was furious, but John Summers is his superior at Deravenels. I won. I got my father's old office.'

'So John Summers was on your side, was he?'

'I wouldn't exactly say *that*!' Edward shot back, throwing his cousin a pointed look. 'However, he did insist that I was to be given Father's old office, just brushed aside Masters's objections. After that he disappeared. I never saw him again last week. He went to Wales, so I was told.'

'Did Aubrey Masters give you anything to do?'

'Not a damn thing. I was left to twiddle my thumbs. I went to the office every morning, and was greeted fairly cordially by almost everyone, except for Masters, of course, who was extremely grumpy, almost to the point of rudeness, in fact. However, I will say this, the other men treated me with the utmost civility, and that was that. Then they just ignored my presence.'

'I see. Mmmm. Well, I'm not surprised. They're accepting you because they have no alternative. You have every right to be there. That's the company rule . . . the son steps into the father's shoes, gets his office, becomes a junior director although not on the board, and then works his way up through the ranks. However, they've sort of rendered you ineffectual, simply by not passing on work for you to do. Clever in a sense; on the other hand, it's rather ridiculous of them in the long run. It's so transparent, as transparent as glass.'

'I agree. However, dull and boring though it was I did learn a few things.'

Neville leaned forward, looked at Edward intently. 'About what?'

Edward answered, 'For one thing, about the current state of morale at Deravenels at this moment. It happens to be very low, and quite a few employees believe the company is not only in the doldrums but more than likely in the red. I also managed to ascertain that there are a couple of people who are in our camp, so to speak. And I have begun to understand a little bit about the workings of the company. Also, I now recognize its vastness, how truly enormous it actually is. I have always known, obviously, that it is one of the biggest trading companies in existence today. But Neville, until you're actually faced with it on a day-to-day basis one doesn't really understand completely what *global* means. In the case of Deravenels it is just that . . . the whole bloody world.'

'First things first,' Neville responded. 'Who told you about the morale of the employees?'

'I picked up on the low morale almost immediately, just through chatting to people. Oliveri had steered me in the right direction, pushed me towards those employees he thought might be friendly, who think Henry Grant should be removed. And they were the same ones who muttered about the company being in the red, and not what it once was,' Edward told him. 'As far as the vastness is concerned, Father had always drilled *that* into me, told me there was no other company like ours. But it was only when I stood in front of that huge map in his office and counted the little red flags he had placed there that I *really* understood. Deravenels covers the *world* . . . we seem to be in every country.'

'Almost, yes.' Neville leaned back in his chair, brought his long fingers together in an arc, thinking for a moment, and then he said quietly, 'What you've told me is very good news. A company with low morale, because of bad management I presume, and one which is also in the red is very, *very* vulnerable, Ned. It can be picked off and taken over. *By us.* Of that I am absolutely sure. This is the most heartening information, and it certainly corroborates everything Alfredo has muttered about lately.'

Harrison, the butler, knocked, and opened the door. 'Excuse me, sir, Mr Oliveri has arrived.'

Neville nodded, rose, and walked across the room to greet Alfredo Oliveri, who was being ushered in by the butler.

After shaking hands, the two men walked over to Edward, who hurried to greet Oliveri. They had become friends in Carrara, and in the past week in London that friendship had been carefully cemented.

Neville said, 'Would either of you care for a drink?'

Both men shook their heads, and Edward murmured, 'Perhaps a glass of wine at lunch, but nothing now, thank you.'

Alfredo indicated his agreement, then went on. 'In my considered opinion, and after a lot of chit-chat at the office, I realize you may have more supporters and friends than enemies at Deravenels, Mr Edward. That may surprise you, but I feel sure that I am right.'

Both Edward and Neville appeared taken aback, and then Edward said, 'I did note that several of the men you introduced me to were exceptionally cordial, Alfredo, but I just assumed I had mostly *enemies* there –'

'Oh you do have *some*,' Alfredo cut in, 'those who are cronies of Henry Grant, whose fathers have been allied on his side, usually because of *their* fathers and old loyalties. Let's not forget, that particular faction of the Deravenel family has been in control for sixty years now. A long time.'

'Far too long,' Neville murmured, giving Edward a knowing look.

Edward asked, 'Who *are* my friends within the company? I'd like to know their names.'

Oliveri pulled a piece of paper out of the inside pocket of his jacket, opened it, and began to read: 'Rob

183

Aspen, David Halton, Christopher Green, Frank Lane. Those men are well disposed to you for sure. They've made that perfectly clear to me this week, and of their own volition, I might add. I also believe that Sebastian Johnson and Joshua Kennett are favourable, would be in your corner. Certainly those two have long been dissatisfied with current management, have begun to grumble, and a lot more loudly, about the company being mismanaged.'

'I know that John Summers is my enemy, and also Aubrey Masters,' Edward began and fixed his eyes on Alfredo. 'So who else has me in their sights?'

'James Cliff, who's exceptionally close to Summers and also very chummy with Margot Grant, as is Summers. Then I would add Andrew Trotter, Percy North, Philip Dever and Jack Beaufield. Several of those men are on the board, because of their fathers' connection to the Grants over many years. But, of course, your friends Rob Aspen, David Halton and Frank Lane are board members as well.'

'It looks as if it's fairly evenly balanced,' Neville interjected, sounding pleased. 'The thing is, we must try and win more of the men over, don't you think, Oliveri?'

'Absolutely, and don't forget, *I* am on your side as well, even though I'm in Italy part of the time. But you can always count on me. And I'll come at once if you need me to be in London.'

'That reminds me of something,' Edward said, smiling at Alfredo. 'When we win this war I shall get rid of Aubrey Masters immediately. And I am offering you his job now, Oliveri. It would please me if you'd take it.'

Alfredo chuckled. 'Talk of self-confidence! You

certainly have it. I agree with you, we *will* win, and of course I'll take the job. Thank you. I've wanted to move to London for several years now. I even discussed it with your father, at one point, and he agreed with me that I should really be here. But naturally nothing ever happened.

'What about your wife? Would she mind moving?' Neville asked.

'No, not at all. She's English, as you know, and whilst she loves Italy as much as I do, I know she would welcome a change.' Alfredo smiled at them. 'It's a deal as far as I'm concerned.'

'The news you've brought us today is a real boost, to say the least,' Neville remarked to Alfredo, nodding his head in affirmation of his words. 'We must *all* gather as much information as we can, in order to mount a case against Henry Grant. That is imperative. Information will prove to be our greatest weapon, you'll see, and when Amos Finnister arrives we'll hear what he has discovered. Ah, here he is now,' Neville exclaimed, jumping up, going to greet Amos, who hovered in the doorway with the butler.

After the two men shook hands, Neville said, 'Edward, come and meet my good friend, Amos Finnister . . . This is my cousin, Edward Deravenel, and my other guest is Alfredo Oliveri, whom I've mentioned to you.'

Amos greeted them pleasantly, and the four men sat down in a grouping of chairs near the fireplace. Neville took charge of the meeting and explained. 'Before we went to Italy, I talked to Mr Finnister, and asked him to start digging in Henry Grant's backyard, and also in

185

anyone else's backyard, if he thought it was appropriate to do so. I want to know everything there is to know about our enemies within Deravenels, and Finnister is undoubtedly the best private investigator there is in London – if not in the whole of England.'

Amos smiled faintly, looking at Neville, his gaze steady. 'I don't know if I would go as far as that, Mr Watkins.'

'But I would. Now, what have you dug up? Lots of dirt, I hope.'

'Not so much dirt as facts, sir, which are more important in the long run, wouldn't you say? First off, I'd like to say this . . . In my opinion Henry Grant is not simply pious, scholarly and religious, as everyone claims he is. I believe him to be so seriously unstable, it's more than likely he's actually quite *insane*. I discovered that he has been in two different mental institutions in the last few years. And no, they were not *retreats*, as was claimed at the time. They *were* insane asylums.'

There was a moment of silence, and then Edward said in a low tone, 'Oddly enough, my father once said to me that he thought Henry was extremely unbalanced, but he never took it any further than that, never said anything else. Not to me.'

'Good God!' Neville looked at Edward and then at Amos, obviously aghast. 'Surely that's enough of a reason to have him removed from the chairmanship of Deravenels, isn't it?' He stared hard at Ned, his eyes full of questions.

'Listen,' Alfredo cut in, 'I've heard it said he was off his rocker, a doddering fool, loopy, nutty . . . words like that were used about him. But yes, if he *was* in an asylum it suggests much worse, doesn't it?'

'It does,' Ned finally said. 'And I think you're right, Neville, insanity would justify removal from the board and from the company. And not just at Deravenels either, at any company. Nobody would disagree with you, it's common sense, pure and simple.'

'If I might suggest something,' Amos murmured. 'Perhaps no one ever really believed he was seriously mentally disturbed, perhaps everyone thought he was just an . . . ineffectual sort of chap, and left it at that, let him be.'

'Maybe,' Neville agreed. 'Otherwise he would have been removed promptly, by Summers and his gang, we can be certain of that.'

Alfredo stood up, paced in front of the fire for a few seconds, and then turning to Neville he said, 'I must tell you, this news is lethal, it really is. And it's a huge weapon for us.' Turning to Amos, he asked, 'Do you have *proof*? Hearsay and innuendo won't be enough to convince the Deravenel board. We must have absolute proof that he was in two asylums, at different times, presumably. Otherwise, they'll laugh in our faces.'

'Proof *does* exist, Mr Oliveri, but I don't actually have that proof in my hands at this moment I'm afraid,' Amos replied.

'But could you get it?' Neville asked, giving Amos a sharp look.

'Oh, yes, course I could, Mr Watkins. But you do understand I'd have to have it . . . *stolen*. I would have to get . . . one of my *contacts*, so to speak, a *specialist*

187

in that area, if you get my drift, to break into the two different asylums and pinch their records.'

'Then have it done. At once,' ordered Neville and without any hesitation.

'Would anyone guess *we* had stolen those records? I can't help wondering that.' Edward looked pointedly at Amos.

Amos answered swiftly, 'No, no, they *wouldn't*, because his incarcerations have been secret, or, more accurately, it's been passed around that he was in religious retreats. Correct?'

Edward nodded. 'True.'

'So nobody's going to point a finger at you,' Amos continued. 'Anyway, someone might have *brought* those documents to you . . . as a good deed let's say. Someone who wanted the record set straight for the good of the company.'

'How soon can you get them? Because I do agree with my cousin that you should go after them,' Ned said, staring at Amos.

'How soon? Not sure. It'll take a bit of working out, getting the proper crew together. Can't afford mistakes.'

Alfredo went back to his empty chair. Turning to Edward, he said, 'We can't have any scruples at this moment in time. Very simply, we can't *afford* scruples. There's a great deal at stake here, and not only justice for you, Mr Edward, and you, too, Mr Watkins, because of the deaths of your kin. There's also a huge company at stake. Its very survival, actually. A company that employs thousands of people all over the world. We must think about them, too, they should have a fair shake.'

It was Neville who spoke first. He answered quietly, 'Yes, you're correct, Oliveri, it would be criminal to let Deravenels go down the drain after eight hundred years of trading. Besides, it belongs to Mr Edward, at least the top job belongs to him. It's his inheritance, and I aim to make sure he gets his inheritance and that Deravenels not only survives the thieving Grants, but goes on to become bigger and better than ever under our management.'

Edward pondered for a moment, then addressed Neville. 'Stealing the records to prove Henry Grant is insane is only one step. Surely we need much more to wrest the company from their hands? They could easily put Margot Grant in, to take Henry's place, to run the company until their son Edouard came of age.'

'They wouldn't dare,' Alfredo exclaimed, shaking his head most vehemently. 'Trust me on that. Yes, she manages to insinuate herself these days, but she does not have a role, a position or a title.'

'I have it on good authority that she is extremely unpopular,' Amos told them. 'Disliked by most of the people working there. Only Summers, Cliff and Beaufield are her true adherents, her closest friends. Oh, and by the way, there's a rumour surfacing – people are saying that her son is the half-brother of John Summers, that it was his father who impregnated Margot, not pious old Henry at all.'

'Old? He's only thirty-nine,' Edward muttered.

Neville glanced at him, and said, 'Too old to beat you.' Then turning to Amos, Neville continued, 'So, that old story has sprung up again, has it?' He began to laugh uproariously, and then clearing his throat he said, with another glance at Amos, 'It might be a good idea to get some of those chaps of yours onto it. Blacken the name of the Grants, that's all par for the course.'

Harrison hovered in the doorway. 'Luncheon is served, sir,' he announced.

Nan Watkins sat alone in the conservatory, sipping a tall glass of mint tea and nibbling on a small smoked salmon tea sandwich. She was happy to take her lunch alone here in this sunny glass room filled with potted palms, exotic rubber plants and her prized white orchids. It was a tranquil, peaceful spot in their busy household.

The girls were having lunch upstairs on the nursery floor with Nanny, and Neville was entertaining his guests in the dining room. She herself had planned the menu with Cook, and she hoped they were enjoying her choices.

She had selected Neville's favourites, as usual wanting to please him. The first course was a light vegetable soup, something similar to minestrone, which she knew Alfredo Oliveri would enjoy; the second was grilled plaice, served with parsley sauce, croquette potatoes and peas. For dessert she had asked Cook to make her famous bread pudding, with extra creamy custard and raisins, which was everyone's favourite. She had left the wine selection to her husband.

Her husband. Neville Watkins. A man she had fallen in love with at first sight, when he had come to her family home in Gloucestershire. He had had business with her father, and had ended up marrying her. She had never quite recovered from the shock. That this most handsome and extraordinary man had even deigned to look at her never ceased to amaze her.

In this Nan did herself an injustice, and she knew it. But she still always thought of herself as thin and pale, and not at all enticing. In reality she was fragile and very pretty, with shining, golden-brown hair, huge soulful grey eyes that were flirtatious and beguiling to most men. Apart from an incomparable complexion, she had a perfect, white skin, shapely breasts and lovely long legs. But it was her femininity and fragility that appealed to the opposite sex. Instantly they wanted to protect her, as indeed did Neville Watkins. He not only considered her to be beautiful but had soon discovered she was a very sexual woman as well, a partner who desired him, craved him and showed it in ways no other woman ever had.

Nan knew this because he had confided in her; he had also told her how sexually exciting she was to him. She smiled to herself now, as she thought about their lovemaking earlier that morning. Having complained the night before that he had taken Saturday away from her, a day which belonged to them, he had awakened her very early with intimate kisses and a clamouring sexual desire for her. Their passion had been enormous, their longing slaked, and he had eventually whispered against her neck that perhaps they had made a child together this very day. And this she prayed for, prayed for a son, so that he would have an heir. A baby conceived now would do wonders for him, help to assuage the pain and grief he felt at the loss of his father, and his brother, Thomas.

191

Nan stared into the room absently, thinking of young Tom. How Neville had grieved in the last few weeks. But she had helped him as best she could, and so had his brother John . . . Johnny they all called him, such a kind and gentle young man.

She would never dare say a wrong word about Johnny to Neville, but she knew deep in her heart that it was Ned who held his loyalty and love. She also knew that Edward Deravenel knew this, and sometimes it disturbed her.

Instinct, she thought. I have instinctive feelings about such things, instincts I cannot and must not fault. I'm right more often than I am wrong, aren't I?

It was the same with young Richard. There were times when Neville treated him like the son he had not yet had but hoped one day to have; Richard was the stand-in perhaps, yes, in a sense it *was* that. But Richard's absolute and total loyalty was to his brother Edward first.

Then there was George, the middle Deravenel brother. He had no loyalty to anyone but himself, of that she was utterly certain. One day it will all explode, go up in smoke, Nan said to herself, and then wondered why she had had such an irrational and silly thought.

The two clans of Watkins and Deravenel were intertwined forever. An unbreakable bond. That was what they all said. She just hoped it was true . . .

SEVENTEEN

The four men who were seated at the table in Neville's handsomely-furnished dining room were quite different in style and personality, for the most part as disparate as any men could be.

Seated at the head of the table was the host. A patrician of undoubted aristocratic stock, slender, dark-haired, with those mesmerizing turquoise eyes in his lean, good-looking face, he was elegance personified.

Neville's superbly-cut, dark-grey worsted suit was from the best tailor in London. It looked it. His white shirt, made of the finest blend of Egyptian cotton, was enhanced by a deep-purple silk cravat, elaborately tied in a fancy knot and finished with a discreet diamond pin. He wore a crested signet ring; heavy gold cufflinks fastened his French cuffs; his handmade shoes shone like glass. Neville had dressed with flair and style, and today he more than lived up to his reputation as a dandy, the Beau Brummell of his time.

At the other end of the table sat his cousin Edward Deravenel. Ned dominated the scene because of his height and physique, his handsome face, startling blue eyes and red-gold hair. Edward also wore a well-tailored Savile Row suit, although one not quite as expensive as that of his cousin. Dark blue in colour, it had the popular flared frock coat and narrowed trousers; his shirt was white, his jewellery simple – his father's gold pocket watch and cufflinks. The pearl stick pin which he now treasured so much was fastened in his dark blue cravat.

Edward's overwhelming presence, his aura of raw masculinity and sex appeal was balanced by his charm and amiability, his friendly smile and his genuine interest in other people. Although a man of exceptional personal appeal to women, he was, nonetheless, well liked by other men.

Facing each other across the long mahogany table were Alfredo Oliveri and Amos Finnister. They appeared to be comfortable and at ease with each other, as well as with the patrician cousins and their luxurious surroundings.

Despite having had an Italian father, Alfredo appeared very English in his plain, dark grey suit, with his carrot top red hair, pale skin and freckles. Of medium height, he was slight of build and looked much younger than his forty-one years. A product of the lower middle class, he was a clever man with a good brain who had been well educated, and he was a hard worker. His refined manner and pleasant demeanour attracted people to him, and gave them confidence in him.

Amos Finnister was in his mid-forties, tall and thin with a slight stoop. His jet black hair was touched with strands of grey, but his pencil-thin moustache was as black as his coal-dark eyes. He, too, was from the lower middle class. Intelligent, worldly wise, he was a man with strong instincts about people; it was this psychological insight into people which made him such an excellent private investigator.

Amos had started his professional life as a policeman on the beat, before turning to private investigating. His years with the police force had served him well, and he had continued to nurture most of his contacts long after he had left the force. Contacts who were as diverse as Scotland Yard detectives and coroners, thugs, thieves and underworld characters, with information to deal or information to sell.

Conservatively dressed in a black suit this afternoon, he was always unremarkable in his appearance; Amos could move through the diversely different worlds he travelled without causing a single ripple, or drawing attention to himself. He liked to boast that he was invisible, and this was true.

Despite their differences, the four men were, conversely, very similar. They all had integrity, a deeply ingrained sense of duty and of what was right and wrong. They also now shared the same motive, which was to put Edward Deravenel in the seat of power at Deravenels. They believed, indeed were convinced, that as Richard Deravenel's son he was the true and rightful heir to the company, knew without a trace of doubt that they were righting a terrible wrong committed over sixty years ago.

Each of them had vowed to stop at nothing in order to achieve their goal, fulfil their purpose. And because they were so certain they were fighting a deadly enemy there were no holds barred.

For the last hour over lunch they had touched on

many subjects which interested them, but had not mentioned the business at hand. Neville had made it clear, as they had walked across the hall to the dining room, that it would be wiser to wait until they were alone again before discussing their imminent plans.

Now, as they sipped their coffee and nursed their balloons of Calvados, Neville spoke about their current business.

He said quietly, 'So, let us now review things.' Turning to Amos, he went on, 'You have given us the best ammunition so far, the knowledge that Grant is most probably insane. And you *will* get us the medical records as soon as you can?'

Amos nodded. 'Consider it done. And my people will take any other records pertaining to Grant. We'll make a good job of it, have no fear, sir.'

'Excellent, and I think now would be a good time to fill us in about John Summers and his crew. You did say you had information.'

Amos shifted slightly in the chair, and cleared his throat. 'That's right, Mr Watkins, I do. However, about Summers himself, there's nothing, nothing at all. He's as clean as a whistle. And so is Margot Grant, by the way, except for the resurfacing of that old rumour about her son's legitimacy. But some of the others, well, they're tarnished, sir, and in my opinion that plays in our favour.'

His three companions leaned forward, looked at him eagerly, alertly.

Amos smiled thinly, as he explained, 'They are so tarnished, in fact, they have left themselves wide open to blackmail.'

'Have they now?' Neville exclaimed, his eyes narrowing. But he was not at all surprised, having a low opinion of the Grant faction. 'Please do fill us in, Amos.'

'James Cliff is finding himself in an extremely difficult situation. He has rather foolishly antagonized both his wife and his mistress. He's caught in a vice between the two of them, who are both tough, hard-bitten and cold-hearted females. Each is demanding more of his time, his constant presence. There's a strong rumour that his mistress is pregnant, which would really throw a spanner in the works if it were true, since his wife is the one with the money.' He began to chuckle.

Everyone laughed with Amos, and Neville said disparagingly, 'Yet another fool about to take a fall.'

Amos continued, 'Then there's Philip Dever, a secret homosexual with a hot young buck for his lover. No one knows this, of course, including his wife. And then there is Jack Beaufield, whom, I have discovered, has extremely sticky fingers. Financial problems and complications in his last position at another company. Not too careful, our Jack, when it comes to other people's money. And that's all I have at the moment, but there'll be more, I'm quite sure of that, sir. My operatives are still digging.'

'Well done, very well done indeed,' Neville said, and took a long swallow of the brandy.

'I'm wondering about Aubrey Masters,' Edward began, and his eyes met Oliveri's. Ned went on, 'Finnister, did you manage to get anything at all on the head of the mining division?'

'Not a lot, Mr Edward,' Amos replied. 'Masters is

considered to be a little weird, in fact, by the other employees. He's a vegetarian, and obviously there's nothing amiss in that, except that he does follow a strange diet, consuming roots, seeds, pods, flowers, grains and all manner of rather unusual things, and he's attempted to get others to join him. With no success, I might add. He has a wife but no children, as you no doubt know. The wife stays in the background, a bit of a recluse, seemingly. He's considered to be an indifferent manager by some of his staff, dismissed by many as ineffectual and boring, and he's definitely not popular. Seemingly, he doesn't like to travel, which his staff have taken umbrage to because he *is* the head of the mining division.'

'That's absolutely true about the travelling,' Alfredo said. 'And that was one of the complaints Mr Richard had about him. Masters has long ignored our mining interests abroad, has never gone to India, South Africa or South America, and he's only once been to Carrara. Somehow, Masters has always managed to shove those field trips onto his underlings. I've long doubted his ability, and most people are at odds with him. As for the peculiar diet, I don't know anything about that, and I don't think it really matters.' Shaking his head, Alfredo finished, 'Everyone believes as I do, that he's in that job because he's the cousin of Henry Grant.'

'My father said the same,' Edward murmured, and glanced at Neville, laughed hollowly. 'It's a pity Aubrey Masters is in such good health.'

'Isn't it just,' Neville responded, with a cold smile. 'But please, don't bring up that famous old phrase . . . *who will rid me of this turbulent priest*? Or whatever it was. We don't need murder in the cathedral at this moment.'

'Too true, Cousin. Let us not turn Masters into a martyr like Thomas à Becket.'

Alfredo changed the subject. 'Earlier you asked me how long I would be in London, Mr Edward. I have another week of working at the head office, but I can stretch it to two weeks if you wish. I have a great deal to do on the situation in Carrara, and there are decisions to be made, so it could take longer.'

'Do you think Masters will agree to your suggestion of purchasing new quarries?'

'It's a decision for the board. However, I believe they will listen to me. The old quarries are almost depleted. We must buy new ones to stay in business. What I think –'

Neville interrupted when he exclaimed, 'I think you must try and stay here as long as you can, Oliveri. We need you to gather as much information as possible, since you're our only inside man with access to everyone. You're invaluable, you know, having been so long at Deravenels, and because you are so well trusted. And there is another reason . . . it allows me to breathe easier, knowing you are with Edward on a constant basis.'

Nodding, Alfredo answered, 'I know, and I will do my best to extend my visit. I'm as anxious as you to know what they're planning, and I agree, it's good for me to be able to keep an eye on Mr Edward.'

Focusing on Neville, Amos said in a firm voice, 'Mr Watkins, I know you worry about your cousin, but in my opinion I think Mr Deravenel is perfectly safe, sir. I doubt that John Summers will do anything to hurt him, or have him hurt by others. There's been excessive gossip about the fire in Italy and the family losses. After all, your father and Mr Richard Deravenel were well-known figures in the business world. Summers is far too canny, too astute to do anything rash, he wouldn't want to attract attention to himself or to the Grants. Not after the fire in Carrara. Nor would he want to stir up old animosities . . . The Grants are not particularly popular in the City. Some old hands haven't forgotten about Henry Grant's marauding grandfather.'

Something struck Edward, and he murmured, 'That's another thing, why not get some propaganda going about *that* old story? It won't do us any harm to paint the Grants black, you know. Actually, it would gain us even more sympathy if we remind people about those events, don't you think, Finnister?'

'I do indeed, sir. I'll get my chaps on to it at once.'

For the next hour the four men remained seated at the dining table, discussing their plans. And as the afternoon drew on they became confident of their success and of their ultimate triumph over their enemies.

EIGHTEEN

'I'm so sorry I wasn't able to attend the lunch yesterday,' Will Hasling said, his gaze fixed on Edward, who was sitting opposite him in the hansom cab. 'As I explained to you, I had to be in Leicestershire to meet with the family solicitors. About the legacy my aunt left me.'

'So you said,' Edward replied, then added, 'I hope it was a decent inheritance.'

Will laughed. 'Very decent indeed, Ned. Really generous. I was her only nephew, and as I told you, she never married, so there were no children. I was her sole heir. Anyway, I couldn't get back to London until last night. How was the lunch with Neville and Oliveri?'

'It went very well,' Edward responded. 'I was very impressed with this man Amos Finnister. He's the private investigator Neville is using. I think he's going to prove invaluable to us. He's already dug up a lot of dirt, and, most importantly, he discovered that Henry Grant was incarcerated in two insane asylums. Finnister's convinced Grant is actually insane.'

'Good God!' Will exclaimed, sitting up straighter, his amazement written across his startled face. 'That *is* interesting news, and certainly it works in our favour.'

'Yes, it does. Finnister has to make an attempt to get the medical records, because, as Oliveri pointed out, the board of Deravenels will only be convinced of his insanity by such records. They'll want proof in order to believe.'

'If then,' Will muttered, 'you know the place is riddled with his friends. They'll defend him any way they can, do whatever it takes to keep him in power.'

'Maybe they won't be able to do that,' Edward answered, and in a low, rapid voice began to tell Will about the lunch, and everything that had been said. And ultimately agreed upon.

Once Ned had finished speaking, Will sat back against the seat, looking thoughtful for a few moments, and then he shook his head. 'Certainly this Amos Finnister chap has handed you a number of lethal weapons . . . such as the possibility to blackmail, circulate bad propaganda, those kind of things, but stealing the records might not be quite so easy.'

'Neville assured me that if anyone can do it, it's Finnister. Or rather, some of the men he employs. I get the impression they're professional thieves.'

'Well I certainly trust Neville's judgement. By the way, have you told him I would like to work at Deravenels, once you've taken over?'

Edward began to laugh. 'Another confident soul, I see, not even questioning the outcome. And yes, I have told him, and he was delighted. He even wondered aloud if you would consider working for him at the moment, until you could join me, and I said I would ask you.'

'Neville wants me to work for him? Good God! But look here, Ned, what would I do?' Will Hasling's expression was one of total puzzlement.

'Chiefly, you would be . . . my boon companion,' Edward explained. 'Except you wouldn't be able to accompany me to work, to Deravenels. However, he does want you to be with me at all other times. He's got a bee in his bonnet about my safety, even though Amos Finnister assured him they wouldn't dare make a move against me, *physically* that is, at the moment. Finnister says that the fire in Carrara and those terrible deaths have brought attention to the Grants. There's a lot of gossip going around about the tragedy, and about the Grants, too. Look, Will, Neville feels I shouldn't be wandering around town alone, and he thinks you're the best person to be at my side.'

'But he doesn't have to employ me to do that, Ned! Surely he understands about our friendship.'

'Of course he does. I suppose he wanted to put you on his payroll because he thinks you have to earn a living –'

'That's no longer necessary, because of the money my aunt has left me. It's not a great fortune, Ned, but it's enough to keep me quite comfortably, and my father still gives me a small allowance.'

Edward nodded, and said swiftly, 'I hope you're not offended by his offer of money.'

'Don't be silly, and the answer by the way is *yes*. I will certainly be your boon companion – that's not work, it's total pleasure.'

Both young men laughed, and then Will's face changed, became solemn when he said in a serious voice, 'Rest assured that I *will* protect you. With my life. And

203

always. Because like Neville, I believe the Grants will eventually try to get you in some way. And I don't want my best friend dead . . . I want him alive.'

Edward nodded, gave Will a somewhat wry smile. 'And your friend wants to stay alive, I can assure *you* of *that*.' There was a moment's pause before Ned continued, 'I'm certainly glad my mother decided to come to London, I've worried about them, especially the children. I'll be much happier having them at Charles Street with me. Even though it is perfectly safe at Ravenscar. It's well protected by its location, and the locals are devoted to us. Still, I have been concerned about them being there without me.'

'That I understand, Ned, and you never know in life.' Will sighed. 'You just never know what might happen.' He looked out of the window for a second, and then bringing his steady gaze back to Edward, he asked, 'Do you think your mother was afraid there? Is that why she's coming back to town today? Do you think she considered herself vulnerable at Ravenscar?'

'No, I don't, in all honesty. I know she's always felt safe there, but from what she said on the telephone, last night, she became lonely in Yorkshire without my father. Also, she had previously engaged John Pennington to tutor the boys, and Perdita Willis to act as Meg's governess for the next few months. For those reasons she wanted to return to London. Mind you, Will, she did say they have all missed me.'

'She's done the right thing, coming back, and I feel better myself, having you all in *one* place,' Will confided, and then exclaimed, 'Well, here we are, Ned, King's Cross station!'

A moment later the two men were alighting from the hansom cab. Swinton, the butler, was getting out of a second hansom just behind them, and he came to join Edward and Will.

'I shall go and round up some porters, sir,' Swinton announced. 'Mrs Deravenel told me there would be a quantity of luggage.'

Edward nodded. 'Mr Hasling and I will go to the usual barrier and wait there, Swinton.'

'Right-o, sir.'

Striding out, Edward and Will hurried through the railway station to the platform where the morning train from York would be pulling in within the space of the next few minutes or so.

It was a cold Sunday afternoon, and the two men were heavily bundled up in thick winter overcoats and woollen scarves. The two of them, tall, handsome and well dressed, stood out in the crowd, and it occurred to Will that Edward Deravenel would always stand out anywhere, because of his height and looks and that head of burnished red-gold hair. How to make him invisible? he asked himself. He had no answer. Yet he did know one thing, and it had troubled him for some time.

He was well aware that as soon as the battle between the cousins began in earnest, Ned would be a moving target. How strange to think of murder . . . they lived in a civilized country, in a civilized age . . . and yet he knew that dark powers were at work. Even Cecily Deravenel had said *that* to Edward.

Of all the Deravenels, Edward was the most vulnerable because he could grab the seat of power and take over the company, whereas his two brothers were far

205

too young, just little boys. He is the true threat to the Grants, Will thought, and on the back of his neck his hackles rose.

God help us all when it starts, Will thought, and his mind began to race as he wondered again how he would be able to keep Ned safe. There was no obvious way at this moment, except to surround him with a phalanx of bodyguards. Which Ned wouldn't tolerate. But Neville would, and Neville would pay.

Will's thoughts were interrupted by Edward, who leaned closer to him. 'I went to Belsize Park last night, hoping to see Lily,' he confided. 'The housekeeper told me she had gone to the country for the weekend. Is she with Vicky in Kent, Will?'

'Yes, she is. They were planning to return tomorrow.'

'I hope she's not angry with me, I didn't get a chance to see her last week, I was so preoccupied with Deravenels.'

'Did you leave her a note yesterday?'

'I did.'

'Then she'll be fine, Ned.' Will looked at his friend, and told him in a lowered voice, 'She really loves you.'

'And I love her.'

'It can't go anywhere, though. Now can it?'

'Nowhere at all, Will. But I do want to continue seeing her, for the moment. She's a great comfort to me.'

'We all need a little comfort at times,' Will agreed.

At this moment train whistles began to blow and the York train came chugging along, rumbling towards the barrier at Platform Five where the two men were standing.

Edward noticed Swinton, followed by the two porters with luggage wagons, heading down the platform, and within minutes, through the billowing clouds of steam and smoke, he spotted his mother. She was elegantly dressed in black, surrounded by his siblings. He saw her greet Swinton, and watched her as she indicated the suitcases and trunks being unloaded and placed on the platform.

A moment later, his two brothers became aware he was waiting and they raced along the platform like greyhounds. The two boys were flinging themselves at him, and at Will, and they were unexpectedly entangled in a mass of young arms and legs. And then there was Meg arriving, looking so beautiful and sedate, followed by his mother, who was smiling at him.

Edward knocked on the door of the parlour and waited, entered the room only when his mother called, 'Come in, Edward.'

She was seated at her small, kidney-shaped desk in the bay window, and glanced up as he closed the door behind him.

'Peace reigns at last!' she exclaimed, shaking her head, sighing. 'I thought George would never stop chattering. And that Will would never leave.'

Walking towards her, Edward sat down in the chair facing the desk, and exclaimed, 'Yes, George was unusually garrulous, and as for Will outstaying his welcome, that was all my fault, Mother. I did invite him to have tea with us, and it somehow got out of hand, just seemed endless and rather rowdy, I'm afraid. I'm so sorry.' He studied her for a moment, then asked quietly, 'Are you not feeling well?'

Cecily Deravenel gave him a long puzzled look, frowning. 'I'm perfectly fine, Ned, thank you. And please don't misunderstand – I like Will. No, let me correct myself, I love him, and you know very well he's been like a member of this family for years. The only reason I became so impatient was because I needed to be alone with you, and you seemed so embroiled with the children and Will.'

He laughed. 'Yes, my brothers were all over me like chickenpox.'

She smiled, her love for her eldest son written all over her face. Cecily leaned forward, fixed her soft blue-grey eyes, so like Richard's, on him intently. 'The reason I came to London *today*, instead of in a few weeks' time, was to see you, Ned, and bring you this.' She patted a small package wrapped in silk, which was on the desk.

'What is it?' he asked curiously, eyeing the odd-looking red bundle.

'The famous missing notebook,' she replied a little triumphantly.

'I can't believe it! I thought *that* was lost forever! However did you find it? Where was it?' His excitement was apparent, his blue eyes sparkling.

'In the priest hole.'

'*The priest hole*. There's a priest hole at Ravenscar?'

'Yes, there is,' she answered, and proceeded to tell him what had happened the day before, and explained the history of the old hiding place. When she had finished, she removed the red silk scarf, handed him the notebooks, and added, 'There is a second book, Ned, full of jottings by your father. Most illuminating, *I* think, and it will be more useful to you than the actual notebook.'

As he took the two black leather books from her he seemed puzzled by this comment, and asked, 'But why would that be? I mean, Oliveri said my father always had his nose in the *notebook*.'

'Perhaps he did, but only your father understood what he was writing in it. I don't. It's full of numbers which seem quite meaningless. However, perhaps Oliveri will understand, or perhaps you yourself will. Your father spent a lot of time talking to you about Deravenels over the years.'

'Yes he did, but he never spoke to me about *numbers*, Mother.' Ned opened the smaller notebook, and began to read, scanned several pages, and then shook his head. 'I see what you mean, I'm baffled, too. There *are* sentences here and there, as you no doubt saw, but I don't have a clue as to their meaning. Oh, here's a line that makes some sense. He wrote this . . . "Necessary to talk to my compadre about two and eleven".' Edward glanced up, gazed at Cecily and shrugged his shoulders. 'What on earth can that mean?'

'I have absolutely no idea, Ned. I wondered when I read the sentence yesterday if it might be Oliveri he was referring to as his compadre.'

'Perhaps. But it could be anybody, you know. However, do I have your permission to show the notebook to Oliveri?'

'Of course. And as I said, I think you will find the

second book much more fascinating, and it *is* going to help you achieve your goals.'

Edward jumped up restlessly, began to move away from the desk, obviously excited about the find, and anxious to delve into the pages. At the door, he swung around. 'Thank you for bringing the books to London, Mother, and so promptly.'

'It seemed the safest way to get them to you.'

Edward took the stairs two at a time, rushing to his room. Once inside he locked the door, not wishing to have any intrusions from his younger brothers. They had been so excited to see him, so happy, he half anticipated a visit from one of them, or both. He was glad they were here in London, being so attached to them, but at this moment he wanted total privacy, peace and quiet to read the notebook and the slightly larger book, which looked like a diary to him. From the way his mother had spoken, he believed the diary contained information about Deravenels, Henry Grant and his cronies. And Margot Grant. The look on his mother's face, the intonations in her voice, had indicated this to him. He knew how much she hated the Lancashire faction, *the usurpers*, as she referred to them with great bitterness.

Settling himself in front of the fire, Edward put the diary on the floor, and looked at the notebook first, quickly flipping the pages.

Lines and lines of numbers, page after page; an occasional written comment that was meaningless, although he did realize that the comment usually referred to a number. The numbers two, eleven, thirty-one, and twenty-nine recurred a lot. Unable to decipher the notebook, not understanding what the numbers referred to, Edward impatiently put it on a side table and bent down to retrieve the diary.

After scanning the many pages swiftly, he sat back and turned to page one, the beginning of his father's jottings.

There was no date at the top of the page, so he had no idea when his father had started to write this, except that the condition of the diary told its own story, in a sense. The ink was black, unfaded, the white page crisp, new looking, certainly.

Edward began to read, filled with eagerness and not a little trepidation.

I am at my wit's end. I do not know what to do about Margot Grant. She is worse than ever, and I worry about Harry. My cousin is not a bad man, nor is he evil, like his wife. Actually, Henry is just a poor soul, out of his depth. We were such good friends when we were younger, spent much time together, and I was not only loyal to him, but a devoted cousin, his close friend, just as he was mine.

The trouble with Henry is that he has always been the most pious of men, entangled with priests, full of devotion, wanting only to mingle with the clergy, and he made them his companions, listened to them, took their advice. And he loved to go to church, to study the Bible. His thoughts were always on God, not business, and it is still that way. Deravenels never really meant anything special to him. Nor does it now. Oh yes, he was, and is, proud to be the chairman, sitting in the seat once occupied by his magnificent father, and his grandfather before that. But he did not want to run the company, cannot run it, and he knows that now. He is not capable of it. This is the reason I call him the absentee landlord.

He is a vague, distracted, lazy man; contemplating God is his favourite pastime, and so he lets the Frenchwoman do his job, at least he permits her to give orders to John Summers and James Cliff. They are devoted to her, but they do not follow her guidelines. They dismiss her orders. They are far too clever and smart for that, oh yes. Especially Summers. He takes after his late father – like him he is a handsome man, personable, intelligent. And ambitious. He means to take more and more power, I know that.

I worry about Henry because he's no match for her, or for them. He's daft in the head, I believe. It has come back, the dementia, the illness which so incapacitated him seven years ago. For one year he was like a zombie; he was wandering around, as if in catatonic shock, or in a trance. Until they put him in an asylum for the insane. For treatment. But they lied to all of us in the company, said he was in a religious retreat.

Long before his marriage to the Frenchwoman he made me his heir, because he knew full well I was the true heir, and the board asked me to take charge when he was put away. Put in a padded cell. And I did. I executed my duties well. Then, suddenly, he was back. He had made a remarkable recovery. And I stepped aside, which was only right.

Within days she gave birth to her son, Edouard. Her

heir. But was he Harry's heir? Was he really his son? I doubt it; many doubt it. Henry Grant has always been a monk, lived like a monk. In every way. And the dates were doubtful. Everyone said so.

I was never her enemy, not in the beginning. But she has always treated me as one, and over the years she has been foul, vicious to me and mine. And she has succeeded in turning me into her enemy. What a fool she is.

And I fear for Henry, fear for his welfare. She has such dynastic ambitions. For her son. For herself. For John Summers.

I have no proof, but I do believe he warms her bed at night, as his late father did before him. And surely her son is his half-brother. So Edouard does not have a drop of Deravenel blood in him. Does he?'

Edward sat back, holding the book on his knee, staring into the flames, his thoughts racing.

First of all, his father had confirmed Amos Finnister's story that Henry Grant had been in and out of insane asylums. Well, at least *once*, according to this diary. But wasn't his father also saying that his cousin had always been as mad as a hatter ... *daft in the head*, those were his father's words.

Turning the page, Edward began to read once more, and then he realized that his father was now only writing about Ravenscar, and his great love for his ancestral home.

He scanned the pages swiftly, genuinely wanting to know what his father had to say, yet anxious and impatient to move on to more important entries.

There it was, a new entry on a new page, and the

date was written very clearly: *September the first 1902.* Almost a year and a half ago.

Holding the book tightly, Edward read his father's words rapidly; from the very first line he felt an unexpected tingle of anticipation and excitement.

'I have made my mind up. I am going to do something at last. I shall no longer procrastinate. I shall gather all of my notes together, notes made over the years, and I shall prepare my case. And I do have a case to present to the board of directors. Long, long ago, my ancestors made a new rule – that any director of Deravenels, whether a board member or a junior director, could present a case to them if he had a serious grievance against the company. I do. I have a complaint against Henry Grant. He is allowing Deravenels, one of the greatest trading companies in the world, to be run into the ground. By himself, a man who is daft in the head. I have the proof. I shall use it. I will assert myself. I will take what is mine to take. They cannot refuse to hear me. It is my right as a director, and as a Deravenel, which is even more important. I am going to fight them. I hope I shall win. I think I shall win. The board must remain neutral, and they know this; I believe there is enough neutrality among them to permit justice and fair play to prevail. I must find my copy of the company rules; all of those old documents are important. For back-up. The board won't deny my petition to speak, but it is always a good idea to be prepared.'

There was not a single doubt in Edward's mind that his father had given him powerful weapons to fight the Grants; first, he had confirmed that Henry Grant was a damaged man, mentally deficient and unable to properly run the company. Edward knew enough about the company rules to know that Deravenels could not under any circumstances be run by 'stand-ins', as his mother usually called Grant's cronies. There was *that* fact, to begin with; now there was the old company rule that gave a director the right to present a case to the board.

Obviously, his father had never done what he'd vowed to do. But *he* would. By God, he would.

Edward continued to read the diary for another hour, finding a lot more information that would be useful to them. But as far as he was concerned he had already found the most important.

Later that evening, Edward and his mother discussed his father's diary. They were both in agreement that he had some potent weapons in his hands now.

She promised to find the old documents amongst which were the company rules; he told her all about Amos Finnister and his discoveries.

They made their plans.

NINETEEN

Edward Deravenel knew he would always remember how he felt this morning as he mounted one side of the great double staircase that rose up from the central lobby of Deravenels.

He felt different, felt like a new man.

He was filled with pride; he was happy; his self-assurance was at its height. As he glanced around he felt reassured by this gargantuan building which in a sense was his, and where he now knew he would spend the rest of his life. He was secure in the knowledge that he would win . . . not only a battle or two, either. He would win the war. And he would rule Deravenels. It was his destiny.

His parents had raised him to fully understand who he was, what he was all about, and where he came from. Naturally he had grown up to be self-confident. He was proud of his heritage but there was not one ounce of snobbery in him; he was at ease with himself and with everyone else, whatever walk of life they came from.

When he had started working here last week he

had felt slightly inhibited, and certainly he had been totally on guard. Everyone was suspect, as far as he was concerned; and he was still wary of the men who were employed here, especially Henry Grant's cronies, but he had a better understanding of the various echelons now, thanks to Alfredo Oliveri who had told him much.

He truly understood about his heritage, his right to be head of this ancient company. *He was the rightful heir.* Because of that he would never permit the progeny of usurpers to mismanage it, as Henry Grant was doing; and certainly he would oust the 'stand-ins', the affinity surrounding Grant, along with Grant himself.

Only a Deravenel by birth could be managing director or chairman, and, other than Grant, he was the only one available.

As he strode along the corridor to his father's office which was now his, he thought of the diary. It had hardly been out of his mind since last night when his mother passed it on to him. It was invaluable; there was so much in it; so many guidelines from his father. It was going to be his Bible, and he would live by it. Every word was meaningful, and what possession of it had done was make him feel *entitled*.

He had only just taken off his overcoat and hung it up, when Alfredo came barrelling into the office, his arms full of books and papers. 'Good morning, Mr Edward.' Alfredo gave him a cheery grin from behind the books.

'Good morning, Oliveri. Here, let me help you with all this stuff. And what is it, anyway?'

'Homework, sort of. Yours, to be exact.'

'*Mine?*' Edward gave him a questioning look as he lifted some of the books and papers off the top of the pile. 'Are you serious?'

'Indeed I am.' Oliveri deposited everything he was carrying on the desk, as did Edward, glancing at the titles as he did so. 'Aha! Books on mining I see! And *wine*. And the making of Egyptian *cotton*. You want me to study these so I know something about the various divisions, what we trade in? Am I right?'

'Yes. You said you have a good memory. Is that true?'

'Absolutely. I wouldn't lie to you. But why do you ask?'

'Because you can't just merely read, you've got to memorize some of this material, and there's lots of it. Once you're chairman of the company you will be in charge, and therefore you must know certain things, be able to hold your own with the heads of the various divisions, who are obviously knowledgeable. You're going to be boss, you'll be *IT*. I must make sure you're fully prepared.'

Edward knew that Oliveri was deadly serious, meant every word he was saying, and he was touched that Oliveri had gone to all this trouble for him. 'Thank you for doing this, for bringing all of these books and the material to me. Really, Oliveri, this is decent of you, very decent, and I appreciate it.'

Edward sat down behind the desk, and Alfredo pulled a chair closer, drew up to the desk. 'Now shall we begin? I'd like to start with the Mining Division, because I am involved with that particular division, and you told me the other day you're interested in diamonds, in the mining of them and –'

'Listen to me for a moment,' Edward cut in. 'I have something quite extraordinary to tell you. My mother found the notebook.'

Alfredo's eyes were startled as he gaped at Edward, and for a moment he was speechless.

'Here it is,' Edward said, taking the notebook out of his pocket and handing it to him. 'See if you can make head or tail of it.'

Alone in his own office, Alfredo started at the beginning of the notebook, concentrating on every page, trying to understand the numbers, to decipher them. But they meant nothing to him. He could not fathom what Richard Deravenel had been getting at, nor could he hazard a guess about the person Richard referred to as compadre. Certainly Mr Richard had never called *him* that, nor had he ever discussed numbers.

He thought back to the last time they had seen each other . . . in Carrara, just before Mr Richard had been killed. The older man had complained bitterly about Grant in a most confiding way, and he had said he was alarmed about the spiralling problems in the company, Grant's colleagues, and the problems with the Carrara marble quarries. But that was it. Alfredo had told Mr Edward everything he knew, although Edward Deravenel had somehow seemed to expect *more*. There was nothing more.

After an hour of studying the notebook, growing frustrated, Alfredo got up, put it in his pocket and went back to Edward's office down the corridor.

Knocking, walking in, Alfredo exclaimed, 'I'm sorry, I'm as baffled as you. Bloody annoying it is. The notebook is gibberish.'

Edward was standing in front of the enormous map of the world, which hung on the wall behind the huge Georgian partner's desk. He swung around at the sound of Alfredo's voice. There was a peculiar look on his face as he said slowly, in a low voice, 'Come here, look at this.'

Staring at Edward, he asked, 'But what is it? What's wrong? You have a strange look on your face.'

'Just come over here. Please.'

Alfredo did as he was asked, stood next to Edward in front of the map, remained uncomprehending.

Edward put his middle finger on his tongue, dampened it and touched a small number on the map. The ink ran, bled out. 'Now look closely, see how the ink runs. That's because the number's been written on this map, not printed. And written by my father, of that I am sure. See, it's the number *two*, and it sits up there at the top of India, just between Delhi and the Punjab. See it?'

'Oh yes, indeed I do.'

'Now look over here, at South Africa, that portion of the map. And you'll see the number eleven. Let your eyes sweep over to South America, the number thirty-nine is written there?' Stepping back slightly, looking closely at Oliveri, Edward asked, 'So you tell me . . . what do those three numbers have in common?'

It was obvious that Alfredo was excited. 'The numbers are written on the countries where Deravenels have mines . . . diamond mines in India, gold mines in South Africa, and emerald mines in South America.'

'Correct!' Edward grinned at him.

'My God, how did you discover the numbers?' Glancing at the map, again, Alfredo added, 'They're barely visible, you almost need a magnifying glass to find them.'

Pointing to the books open on his desk, Edward explained swiftly, 'I was reading about diamond mines in India, especially the famous Golconda mines. I knew ours were somewhere nearby, in that vicinity, so I got up to look at the map. I noticed the number there all of a sudden, almost by accident, just below the Punjab, and I realized it hadn't been printed on the map, but *written* by hand. My eyes roved over the entire map, I was so intrigued, and I kept finding numbers . . .' He broke off, shook his head. 'It hit me then! The countries which were numbered were those which were repeated so often in my father's notebook.'

Oliveri was nodding his head slowly, enlightenment spreading across his pale face. 'Listen, your father gave each country a number, and then used the number in the notebook instead of a name. It was a coding system. I think he didn't want anyone to know which countries he was targeting for some reason. Anyone picking the notebook up would be baffled, but not at all baffled if he had written out the names of the countries.'

'But why didn't he want anyone to know which countries he was referring to?'

'I think he stumbled onto something. In Carrara he told me he was not only worried about the quarries there, which were dwindling, but lots of the other mines as well. I asked him if they, too, were dwindling down

221

and he said no, there were other difficulties. But he didn't go any further than that.'

Alfredo took the notebook out of his pocket and passed it to Ned, then went and sat down in the chair. 'You'd better have that. I'd hate to lose it.'

Sitting down himself, Edward confided, 'I think I know who he meant by compadre. My uncle, Rick Watkins.'

Alfredo frowned. 'Why Rick?'

'Because they *were* the best of friends, true compadres, and had been close for donkey's years. Rick was my mother's brother, and therefore family, and obviously someone he trusted absolutely. Then there's yet another thing, Rick Watkins was probably one of the greatest magnates in this country, in fact, there was no other tycoon like him. Therefore, my father could rely on his judgement, any advice he gave. It just made sense to me as I was staring at the map. Rick came into my mind, and I knew I was right.

'I agree. Who better than Rick Watkins to advise your father? Unless it is his son.'

'True. However, I'm sure my father was much closer to Neville's father.'

Sitting back in his chair, staring out into space for a moment or two, Edward seemed lost, drifting into another world, a world only he could envision. Then he sat up abruptly, and looked at Alfredo intently. Lowering his voice, he said, 'That's why Rick and Thomas were killed. They were murdered on purpose. Not because they just happened to be there in Carrara. The Grant faction was afraid of Rick Watkins, his power, his wealth, his brilliance as a businessman. They knew if push came to shove Rick Watkins would throw everything he had at them, to support my father and his claim for the top job at Deravenels. My brother was murdered *because* he was a Deravenel, a contender for the top job if anything happened to me.'

Pale as he was, Alfredo appeared to grow paler. He did not speak for a moment, sat mulling over the things Edward Deravenel had just said. Finally, after a few minutes, he murmured, 'I can't argue with you, Mr Edward, I really can't. I think you are right. And –'

The door of the office burst open, swinging back violently on its hinges. 'So here you are,' a woman's shrill voice exclaimed, and as she strode into the room Edward knew at once that this was Margot Grant.

He had met her several times, but long ago when he was much younger, and he had forgotten how very beautiful she was. Her skin was devoid of colour, absolutely white and flawless, her hair raven black and luxuriant, glossy, upswept into the latest style. Large, luminous black eyes stared out from under perfectly arched black brows. Her incomparable and rather dramatic beauty was matched by her slender, willowy figure and her clothes, which were the height of current fashion and expensively chic.

Coming fully into the room, she closed the door behind her and gave Edward a cursory look, then turned her attention on Alfredo Oliveri furiously.

'I've been looking all over for *you*!' she cried in perfect English only slightly accented. 'How dare you hold these meetings about the Carrara quarries without my presence!'

Alfredo took a deep breath, obviously striving to

control his temper. 'The matter is urgent, and you were not here last week, Mrs Grant. Because of the urgency I held my meetings with Aubrey Masters and other executives involved in the mining division. But you know all this. And there is nothing wrong with my doing that, you know.'

'I represent my husband at this moment in time. I run this company, and I will not tolerate insubordination.'

'There wasn't any,' Alfredo shot back. 'And I won't have you suggesting that there was.'

'You must not speak to me in that tone –'

'Hey, hold on a minute,' Edward cut in peremptorily. 'Let me just point out one thing to you, *madame*. You do not run this company!'

'Oh but I do,' she exclaimed. 'And why are *you* here in the first place? *You* have no right to be here, no right to occupy this office. Pack your possessions and get out.'

'Oh but I do have every right. You had better go and look at the company rules, Mrs Grant. You will quickly discover that I have every right to be here at Deravenels, to occupy my father's office, to be a director of this company, and to work here. For one very simple and undeniable reason. *I am a Deravenel*. You are not a Deravenel by birth, and therefore you cannot run this company. Actually you shouldn't even be here at all. Because in those company rules you will find a clause which says only a woman who is a *born Deravenel* can work in the company and hold a directorship. Other women may work here as secretaries and receptionists, but not hold a position as an executive.'

'*Ah, c'est pas possible!*' she cried, reverting to her native French.

'Oh but it *is* possible!' Edward responded. He moved forward, was suddenly standing in front of her, looking down at her.

Staring up at him, Margot Grant saw the handsomeness of this man, became aware of his raw sex appeal, and she took a step back, glaring. But she was silent for once, unnerved by him, taken aback by his charismatic presence. He overwhelmed her.

Edward continued. 'I will not get out, and don't you ever dare suggest that to me again. You are the one who is a trespasser here, not I, *madame*.'

At a loss for words, feeling unexpectedly humiliated, Margot Grant swung around and left Edward's office without another word.

Once the door had closed behind her, Alfredo grinned at Edward and said, 'That was telling *her* where to get *off*.'

'She's one of the most beautiful women I've ever seen,' Edward said almost wonderingly.

'But she's also a bitch, and evil,' Alfredo pointed out in a low, almost inaudible voice. 'Don't ever forget that. Not ever.'

Neville Watkins met Edward and Oliveri for lunch at Rules later that morning. The wonderful restaurant just off the Strand was a favourite of his, and after Edward's urgent telephone call he had made a reservation for one o'clock and been accommodated immediately.

The three men sat at the best table in the house, studying their menus as they waited for Amos Finnister to arrive.

They had just selected their food and were relaxing with apéritifs when Amos Finnister hurried in.

'So sorry to be late,' he explained, 'but I got caught up with – some of my operatives.' As he took a seat opposite Neville, he added, with a small, satisfied smile, 'I have set things in motion, sir. Regarding those . . . er . . . er records.'

Neville smiled warmly, holding Amos Finnister in great esteem. 'I have no qualms about you. I know how dedicated and efficient you are. Now, have a look at the menu and let's order lunch. In the meantime, would you like to join us in a glass of sherry?'

'Thank you kindly, Mr Watkins, but I won't, if you don't mind. I've got my hands full today. And I'd better be sober.'

Laughing, Neville nodded. 'As you wish, Amos, although I don't think one drink would do any harm.'

Again Amos declined, picked up the menu and studied it. Within a few minutes the four men had ordered, and leaning closer to each other, their heads together, Neville said, 'Now that we're all here, let's have it, Ned, my boy. What is your important news, other than the discovery of the notebooks and your father's diary, which you informed me about already.'

Keeping his voice low, Edward told Neville and Amos about the discovery of the numbers on the map, and what he believed they meant. He also confided that he thought it was Neville's father Rick who had been the person Richard referred to as compadre.

'To tell you the truth, my boy, that had occurred to me, too. Who else would your father trust so implicitly but my father? Now, to the discovery of the numbers on the map, and the meaning of them, let me ask you something. Why did your father keep listing those particular mines in the notebook? Not just because they were *mines*, surely? There's another reason.'

'I think there is probably something wrong with the mines,' Alfredo volunteered. 'What this is I can't hazard a guess. But there's something amiss, I feel positive. Mr Richard was troubled when he was in Carrara, and as I've told you before, the reason *he* came to Italy instead of Aubrey Masters was because he wanted to get to the bottom of the problem there. Which is the dwindling of the marble in the quarries we own. As for the mines in those other countries, maybe they have the same problem.'

'I doubt it,' Neville answered. 'I think my uncle would have told my father, and certainly my father would have mentioned it to me. It's something else.'

'But what?' Edward asked worriedly. 'What *could* it be?'

'I don't know.' Neville shook his head. 'You and Oliveri here have to keep your eyes and ears open. You mustn't miss . . . a trick.'

'I understand,' Edward replied, and then laughed. 'I had quite a run-in with Margot Grant this morning.'

'He was superb, really told her off,' Alfredo said proudly.

'Did you?' Neville raised a brow, his pale blue eyes twinkling.

'I told her she had better go and read the company

rules. That she would soon discover she wasn't even allowed at Deravenels. Well, that's an exaggeration. But she was somewhat perturbed. She left without another word.'

'But I'm afraid we haven't heard the last from her,' Neville muttered. 'Not by a long shot.'

At the end of the afternoon Edward went to see Lily Overton. He had missed her, and he knew he must quickly make amends for neglecting her the previous week.

It was Mrs Dane, the housekeeper, who opened the door to Edward, and her face lit up. 'Why Mr Deravenel, good afternoon, sir. How nice to see you.'

'Good afternoon, Mrs Dane,' he answered politely, and smiled at her warmly.

Her immediate response to his undeniable charm was to open the door wider for him. 'Please come in, Mr Deravenel. I'll tell Mrs Overton you're here.' Closing the door, Mrs Dane continued, 'She hasn't been too well today. Please, do come into the drawing room.'

'Is she ill?' Edward asked, sounding concerned as he followed the housekeeper, entered the drawing room which faced the frosty-looking garden. 'I hope it's nothing serious.'

'Oh no, sir, I think she's just a bit under the weather.' Mrs Dane offered him a small smile, as she hurried away, adding, 'Please excuse me for a moment, sir.'

Edward wandered around the room, feeling slightly on edge, nervous, wondering what could possibly be wrong with his darling Lily. As he thought of her, of her femininity, her blonde beauty, her loveliness and warmth, her kindness to him over the year, he realized something vital about her. Lily's beauty was soft, genuine, angelic; Margot Grant's beauty was dramatic but cold, hard. She was a hard-boiled woman, a woman filled with ambition, a woman on the make . . .

'Mrs Overton would like you to join her in the upstairs parlour,' Mrs Dane was saying from the doorway, interrupting his train of thoughts.

'Thank you,' he answered and hurried out. At the bottom of the staircase he turned to the housekeeper. 'I'll find my own way up, thank you so much, Mrs Dane.'

She nodded and disappeared in the direction of the kitchen. Realizing that he still wore his overcoat, that the flustered housekeeper had forgotten to take it from him, he slipped it off and laid it on a nearby chair.

He was halfway up the staircase when a vision in floating white chiffon and lace appeared at the top of the stairs. '*Edward. Darling!*' Lily exclaimed. 'It's lovely to see you here.'

At the top of the stairs he took her in his arms, and brought her close, kissed her cheek, her neck, her hair. 'I've missed you so much, my darling,' he said softly, then held her away and looked deeply into her face. 'What's wrong? Mrs Dane said you're not feeling well.'

Lily touched his cheek lovingly. 'It's nothing. I felt tired today, Ned, a little weary.' She laughed lightly. 'I suppose I'm getting old.'

'*Old. You? Never.*' Putting his arm around her, he walked her into the parlour. It was as cosy as ever, with

229

a fire burning in the grate; the gas lamps had been lighted, created a roseate glow in the comfortable room, and vases of fresh flowers gave it a feeling of spring.

'I must apologize, Lily,' Edward said, sitting down on the sofa as he usually did. 'I ought to have been in touch last week, but I was swimming in deep waters, so to speak.'

'It's all right,' Lily murmured. 'I wondered what had happened to you, and then this weekend Vicky told me how busy you had been with your work.' She gave him a pretty, dimpled smile, and finished, 'So you're forgiven.'

'I hope to God I am. Because I couldn't do without you, Lil, I really couldn't. You certainly make me feel happier, at ease and more relaxed when I'm with you.' He paused and looked her up and down. 'Amongst the many other *things* you make me feel, you temptress,' he added suggestively, his brilliant sapphire eyes growing most seductive.

Lily was silent for a moment. She pulled her lacey white peignoir around her body, and smoothed a hand over her hair. 'I'm sorry I'm not properly dressed. You see, I was in bed when you arrived.'

'Why don't we go back there, my love? What better place for us to be.' As he spoke he rose, strode across the room, bent over her. Tilting her face to his, he kissed her lightly on the lips. 'Come back to bed, Lily. This time with me. Let me love you, sweetheart, let me pleasure you. We won't do anything too . . . hectic since you're not feeling well. Actually, you don't have to do anything at all. *I* will make love to *you*.'

'Oh Ned, oh Ned, there's no one like you,' she

breathed softly, smiling up at him, all of her anxiety about him instantly blown away.

'I hope not . . . at least, not in *your* heart. Come on, my pet.' He pulled her gently to her feet and led her out of the room, across the landing and into her bedroom. Within moments he had her resting on the bed, and he was kissing her gently. He stopped abruptly, went back to the door and locked it, then he took off his coat and waistcoat, threw them on a chair, unknotted his tie, walked back to the bed. He began to unbutton his shirt as he stood looking down at her, smiling. Once it was unbuttoned, he reached for Lily, brought her to her feet, held her close. 'You'll never know how much I missed you last week,' he murmured, and untied the white silk ribbon at her throat. Slipping the peignoir off to reveal her smooth, creamy shoulders, he went on, 'And I know that you missed me, didn't you?'

Their eyes met. Deep green impaled brilliant blue and locked. Neither looked away. At last he bent into her, kissed her, let his tongue slide into her mouth . . . so warm, so soft. The taste of her thrilled him. He moved the nightgown, gave it a slight pull, and it fell to her feet; he took off his shirt and brought her to him, closed his arms around her. 'Remember what I said, nothing hectic,' he whispered against her tumbling gold hair.

'But I want it to be wonderfully hectic,' she whispered back, and began to unbutton his trousers, fumbling as she did so.

'I'll do it,' he muttered, and she went back to the bed and lay down on her side, watching him finish undressing. As he walked towards her she was momentarily startled. How had he become so aroused, so

231

quickly? She shivered slightly. He seemed so potent, so virile, more than ever at this moment.

One of the things Lily loved about Ned was that he did not rush at her, handle her roughly, or press his cause. He was always gentle, tender, loving, giving her pleasure before he took his own. And this afternoon was no different; he stroked her, touched her, kissed her breasts, brought her nipples to tender points. His hands trailed over her with tenderness, touched her neck, her hair, her stomach, slid between her thighs, encountered her most feminine part, brought her sighing to pleasure until she was calling his name. Entering her, he pressed his hands under her back and lifted her towards him, and their movements together were rhythmic: as always they were in tune with each other, as one. And they soared together, carried upward by their joy in each other, and their ecstasy. And later when he was spent, when he rested against her, sighing and stroking her face, he said quietly, in a low, very serious voice, 'Only you, Lily, only you.'

It was late when Amos Finnister arrived in Whitechapel, almost nine o'clock. As he stepped out of the hansom cab he said to the driver, 'Wait for me here. I'll be about an hour, no longer.'

The driver touched his cap. 'I'll be right 'ere, guv.'

Amos walked away from the hansom, thinking what a lovely night it was. Sky like black velvet, splattered with an array of silver stars. Dazzling. Not too cold. No wind. Yes, a nice night. He stood for a moment looking out towards the Thames. He had always loved this long, flowing river; when he had been a small boy his father had brought him down here to the East End, brought him to the docks, told him wonderful, magical stories . . . stories of the tall ships which sailed in from all over the world, carrying chests of tea from Ceylon, gold from Africa, diamonds from India, sapphires from Burma, spices from the West Indies, silk from China . . . exotic goods transported and traded . . . how adventurous it had sounded to him then. It still did, if the truth be known.

Whitechapel. A mixture of humanity – folk from all over the world. He knew this place so very well, not only from those childhood visits to see the big ships and eat whelks and winkles out of a bag with his father. But from his days on the beat when he had patrolled this place every night. Friend and foe alike down here near the docks. Still, it was colourful, and cheerful, despite the poverty that prevailed, the degradation and the vice, the crime. He had many friends down here . . . some of them were the costermongers, and their pearly kings and queens who ruled the roost, talked rhyming slang and boasted of being born within the sound of Bow bells. Good people.

Not a bad place, Whitechapel. Worse places in this heathen world.

He sniffed. What a fragrant smell that was, floating to him on the night air. He sniffed again, transported to his past for a split second. Thoughts of his father intruding again. His Da, such a good man. Killed too soon, and too young, in the line of duty. A copper like he had been, and perhaps that was why he had become a bobby. For his father, to honour his father's memory.

Amos stopped. Sniffed again. And decided to buy a meat pie. His mouth was watering so much he simply couldn't resist.

Within seconds he spotted the man with the cart and increased his pace. As he drew to a standstill the vendor touched his cap respectfully. 'Evenin', guv. Want a cornish or a meaty?'

'A meat pie. With plenty of gravy, please.'

'Best in Whitechapel me wife is, best cook is wot I means a'course.' The vendor took a pair of tongs, clamped them on a pie and showed it to Amos. 'See its crusty top? Bootiful brown, guv.' As he spoke the man placed the pie in a small white paper bag, picked up a ladle of gravy and dribbled it over the pie.

'How much is it?' Amos asked, anxious to take a bite.

'Tuppence, guv.'

Amos paid, took the bag with the pie, bid the man goodnight and walked off; he was smelling the pie with pleasure, waiting for it to cool. A moment or two later Amos went and sat on a wall under a street gas lamp, and slowly munched on the meat pie, savouring every bite, enjoying himself more than he had in a long time.

The pie was his supper, and such a treat. Much tastier than the slice of bread and cheese Lydia perpetually offered him, or her other mainstay, cold lamb on a bread bun. He sighed to himself, hating his sudden critical thoughts of his wife. She wasn't well, really. Poor Lydia. It was her migraines which bothered her the most. And sometimes rheumatism. Poor Lydia. Full of aches and pains. Always miserable. Never a happy thought these days. Poor Lydia. Indeed.

Amos had demolished the pie in short order, and now as he wended his way down towards Limehouse, he decided he needed a drink. Perhaps a pint to wash down the pie, he decided. Why not?

The Black Swan was hereabouts . . . the Mucky Duck the locals called it. As it hove into sight Amos hurried his steps, was swinging in through the double doors within seconds.

At the bar he asked for a pint of bitter, and swigged some of it down immediately it was in front of him, frothy, delicious. Good beer. He might even have another one.

The bartender came back, peered at him in the murky gaslight. 'Used ter be a copper round 'ere, din't yer?'

'That's right.' Amos smiled at him. 'Retired now. Finnister's the name.'

The bartender chuckled. 'I remembers now. Sinister Finnister we used ter call yer.'

Amos laughed with the man, drank up his beer, put his money on the counter, said goodnight and promptly left. He set out again for Chinatown in Limehouse, an area filled with small shops where all manner of goods were sold, from silks, clothes and jewellery to medicines and herbs; Chinese laundries, Chinese shops, restaurants and even opium dens also dotted the streets. Amos loved the food the Chinese made, and had forgotten about it until this moment. He had fallen hard for the fragrant wafts of the pies of his youth, and had succumbed. Too late now to partake of the Chinese food. Another night.

It was not long before Amos reached his destination. Mr Fu Yung Yen had a small shop set back from the street; the light was burning in the window as Amos hurried towards the door. After rapping several times, and proclaiming, 'It's Amos Finnister,' the door was finally opened.

Fu Yung Yen was dressed in a long black cotton gown with a small standup collar; he had long pigtails and a round porkpie hat was perched on top of his greying hair.

He smiled when he saw Amos, and said in his whispery voice, 'Come inside. Cold night.'

The shop was dimly lit and there was a strong smell of spices, herbs and roots in the air. Mixed in was the whiff of camphor and perfumed oils. It was not an unpleasant smell, and Amos never minded coming to the shop.

'How is wife?' the Chinaman asked, smiling.

'Bad migraines again, Mr Yung Yen. I need her usual headache powders, please.'

The Chinese herbalist nodded and went behind the counter, began taking portions of white powders out of various pots. Finally, after pounding them together, he poured the mixture into a small paper packet, sealed it and handed it to Amos.

'I need the ointment for her aches and pains . . . pains in the limbs.'

'Ah yes. Understand. My balm.' This too was quickly produced, already in its own small glass pot.

Leaning over the counter, looking at Mr Yung Yen intently, Amos handed him a small piece of paper. 'Do you happen to have this in stock?'

The herbalist read it, and nodded. 'How much you need?'

'Whatever you think.'

'For one good long sleep, yes?'

Amos nodded.

'Wait minute.' The Chinaman disappeared through a door and it was a while before he finally returned. He put a small package wrapped in purple paper on the counter.

'Thank you,' Amos said. 'How much do I owe you?'

Smiling, Fu Yung Yen made out a bill.

Amos read it, read it again, took out his money and paid without protest.

After putting the various packets away in his overcoat pockets Amos nodded. 'Good night, Mr Yung Yen. And thank you.'

'Come back.'

'I will,' Amos answered, but as he left the shop he wondered if he ever would.

TWENTY

It was late when Edward Deravenel left Lily's house, much later than he had intended. And now as he crossed Belsize Park Gardens and headed towards the main road he realized hansom cabs were scarce in this area. There was not one in sight.

Glancing around again, noting that the road was almost devoid of traffic, he set out to walk, telling himself he would come across a hansom in no time at all.

Striding out at a rapid pace, heading for Primrose Hill leading towards the centre of London, his mind automatically went to the numbers in the notebook and the conclusion he and Alfredo had finally come to earlier, that there was some kind of trouble with the mines producing gold and precious gems. The number for Burma had not been written in the notebook and so they both presumed the production of sapphires was continuing without problems as it had for some years.

The man who approached him had sprung from up from nowhere, or so it seemed to Edward.

'Egscuse me, guv,' the man said in a guttural Cockney voice. 'Can yer tells me 'ow to get ter 'ampstead? I be lost.'

Edward shook his head. 'I'm so sorry, I'm afraid I can't,' he replied, as polite as always. 'However, if you keep heading north I think you'll be going in the right direction.'

The blow came from behind, the heavy truncheon striking him on the shoulder and then on the back. The brute force of the blows brought him to his knees, and he cried out, clutching at the air as he fell, almost as if he were reaching out for the stranger who had just spoken to him. The man was not there, Edward realized, he had disappeared.

Another blow came down, this time on the crown of his head. Edward fell forward instantly, his face hitting the ground. He was knocked out, unconscious.

There were three men altogether, the pedestrian who had distracted the target and the two giant bruisers who were armed with truncheons. The three men conferred for several seconds, then one of the assailants bent over Edward, peered at him, then straightened.

'Don't t'ink e's breeving, mebbe e's dead,' the assailant whispered, and straightened. 'Best we get goin' afore the bleedin' coppers get 'ere.'

The men ran off down the road. It was so deserted the sound of their boots was like thunder, echoing loudly. Drizzling rain and the wind were keeping everyone at home tonight.

Edward lay on the pavement where he had fallen. The road remained empty, without pedestrians or carriages. No one came for a long time.

Neville sat with Amos Finnister in the waiting room of Guy's Hospital, filled with apprehension, silently praying that Ned would be all right, that he would regain consciousness soon. He had been badly beaten, but it was the blows to the head which were causing the problems.

The two men remained silent. Neville, ashen-faced, his expression bleak, was so troubled and worried he did not want to talk; Amos did not dare. He was afraid to intrude on his distracted employer, who was lost in thought.

The door to the waiting room opened and Neville's wife Nan stood there with Cecily Deravenel. The two women hurried in, and Neville instantly rose, went to greet them. Placing his arm around his aunt, he led her over to a chair, and introduced her to Amos.

Nan had already met him, since he was a frequent visitor to the house. It was she who now turned to Amos and said, 'Thank you, Mr Finnister, for everything you've done for Mr Deravenel. If it hadn't been for you, then I don't know what would have happened to him.'

'It was lucky I happened to have my man on duty, keeping an eye on Mr Edward,' Amos murmured. 'I know the young gentleman will be better in a few days, I feel it in my bones.'

Looking intently at Amos, Cecily said in a warm voice, 'I want to thank you, Mr Finnister, for all you've done for my son. But I'm still not quite sure what exactly happened last night.' She glanced from Amos to Neville. 'Who was it that attacked Ned?'

'We're not sure, Aunt Cecily. The police think it was a random attack, more than likely a robbery. Edward had only loose change on him, no bank notes when he was found. They must have been in a hurry because his gold pocket watch was not taken.' Neville shook his head. 'The problem is the police have no leads.'

'Why do you say *they*, as in . . . they must have been in a hurry?' Cecily asked, staring at her nephew.

'For obvious reasons, Aunt. Edward is unusually tall, taller than most men, and very strong. It would take several men, therefore, to overpower him, in my opinion.'

'Yes, of course, I see what you mean.' Taking a deep breath, she went on softly in a saddened voice, 'You would have told me if there was any news, so I'm making the assumption there isn't any.'

'I'm afraid not.' Neville touched her arm consolingly.

Cecily bit her lip, tears brimming, and she instantly stood up, walked across to the window, remained there looking out until she had recovered her equilibrium.

Returning to the chair, she said to Amos, 'Would you be kind enough to tell me the whole story, Mr Finnister? I'm afraid I'm a little confused, perhaps because I'm so upset.'

'It's not surprising, Mrs Deravenel, under the circumstances. I'd be happy to fill you in, so to speak. It's like this . . . From time to time, Mr Watkins and I have discussed the possibility that Mr Edward might be . . . well, in danger, because of the situation with the Grants. For most of his spare time he's with Mr Will Hasling, but we decided, Mr Watkins and myself, that when he was alone he ought to have, well . . . a bodyguard. My man is on duty every day, but he's not always needed. Late yesterday afternoon when Mr

Edward left the office he was alone. There was no sign of Mr Hasling. My man immediately followed Mr Edward, who went to Belsize Park, and –'

'To see Mrs Overton?' Cecily interrupted.

Surprised though he was to hear this, Amos nodded and went on. 'My man hung around, loitered in the vicinity. Mr Edward was at the house for about three hours, and he left soon after nine. It was very dark last night, and apparently the area was lonely, no one around, and no hansom cabs. My man realized that immediately. He was some short distance behind when Mr Edward was attacked by two very big men and –'

'The bodyguard was outnumbered,' Cecily said quietly.

'That's right, Mrs Deravenel. Once the men, three men altogether, had fled the scene, Harry Forbes, my employee, ran to Mr Edward and was relieved to find him alive. He then went in search of a policeman. Luckily he found one at the top of Primrose Hill. More help was fetched, and Mr Edward was brought here.'

Cecily nodded. 'Thank you, Mr Finnister, now I understand.' Glancing at Neville, resting her hand on his arm, Cecily murmured, 'Could we go outside for a moment, I'd like to talk to you, Neville.'

'Of course.' He helped his aunt up out of the chair, and the two of them walked out of the waiting room and into the corridor.

Once they were alone, Cecily leaned closer to Neville, staring into his face. 'It's the Grants, isn't it?'

'I'm afraid so,' Neville confirmed, grimacing. 'The whole thing was handled very clumsily, badly, and so it's most transparent. His watch was left in his suit pocket, and so was the notebook. Only bank notes were taken. To make it look like a robbery.'

'But he never has very much money on him,' Cecily pointed out. 'As often as not Swinton has to pay the hansom cab out of the household petty cash when Ned comes home.'

'It's the Grants, there's no question in my mind about that. Who else could it be?'

'What are we going to do about them, Neville? They're a menace.'

'Reprisals. There will have to be reprisals, I think. To put them on notice that they have met their match in Ned and myself. However, I want to think things out carefully, not act in haste, or rashly. We must be subtle, and we can't do anything that would involve us with the police. Don't you agree?'

'I do indeed, and I will leave it to you, Neville. You are a clever man, I know . . . you take after my brother, your father.'

'Michael Robertson,' the doctor announced as he came into the waiting room several hours later, just before noon.

He was smiling as he approached Neville, who had risen and was walking towards him.

'Neville Watkins, Dr Robertson. I'm Mr Deravenel's cousin. From your expression I'm encouraged to believe he has regained consciousness.'

'Yes, indeed he has. However, he is sleeping at the

moment, and we feel he must be allowed to sleep, not be disturbed for a while.'

'I understand.' Neville brought Cecily over to the doctor, and introduced her. 'This is Mr Deravenel's mother, Dr Robertson, Mrs Cecily Deravenel.'

After shaking the doctor's hand, Cecily asked, 'Was my son in a coma?'

'Not a coma, no. But he was unconscious, and he still has concussion, but I can assure you he will recover from this ordeal, Mrs Deravenel. He really will.'

TWENTY-ONE

As he blinked in the dim light and slowly awakened, Edward was momentarily disoriented. Blinking again, and endeavouring to push himself up in the bed, he realized that every bone in his body ached.

Looking around the room, so white, pristine, sparsely furnished, he understood at once that he was in a hospital. Sinking back against the pillows, he tried to focus his mind and as he did so he began to remember the events of the night before. Leaving Lily's later than he had intended, walking up from Belsize Park Gardens, looking for a hansom cab. The stranger stopping him, asking for directions, and then the unexpected attack from behind.

Lifting his arm, he gingerly touched his head, felt the bandages, then slowly let his fingers roam over his face. He knew it must be bruised, even a little bit battered, because it was sore, and hurt when he touched it. His shoulders and back ached; now he remembered those heavy blows, the way he had gone down onto his knees so quickly, had lurched forward as additional blows had landed on his head.

Who had attacked him last night? Thieves, wanting

245

to rob him? Or had the attack been arranged by the opposition at Deravenels? He had no idea. Neither did he know who had found him, or how he had been brought to this hospital.

After a few moments, Edward managed to sit up; throwing back the bedclothes he swung his long legs to the floor. For a moment he thought he could not stand but eventually he did, instantly realizing he felt weak and slightly dizzy. He sat down heavily on the bed, wondering how to summon a nurse. He needed to ask questions, needed to know more.

Dizziness overwhelmed him, and he flopped back against the pillows, but he did not have enough strength to lift his legs back onto the bed. He was not quite certain how long he lay sprawled like this, half in and half out of the bed. Perhaps twenty minutes or more. All of a sudden he felt a waft of cool air as the door opened, and he was filled with relief. The nurse at last.

'Good heavens, Mr Deravenel! What on earth are you doing?' a very masculine voice exclaimed, and a split second later the owner of the voice was bending over him, looking concerned.

'Are you all right?' the man asked in a kindly tone.

'Yes. Just felt a trifle dizzy . . . when I tried to get out of bed.'

'I'm not surprised. Come along, let me lift your legs into the bed for you.' As he spoke the man proceeded to get him settled properly. Once this was accomplished, he explained, 'I'm Michael Robertson, by the way. Your doctor, Mr Deravenel.'

'So I've gathered,' Edward answered, attempting to smile. He guessed the doctor was about forty or thereabouts, dark haired, pleasant-looking and wearing a white coat over his dark suit. A stethoscope dangled around his neck. He had an air of competence about him.

'Am I badly hurt?' Edward asked at last, a brow lifting.

Noting the anxiousness echoing in his patient's voice, Dr Robertson was quick to reassure him. 'I believe you are out of danger. You were brought in here unconscious last night. You had concussion. But you appear to be much better. How does your head feel? Any pain? Headache?'

'No, not a headache, but my head does feel . . . well, sort of *top heavy*. And my face is sore.'

'Were you hit in the face, Mr Deravenel?'

'No. But the blows to my back and shoulders were very hard, and I fell forward. My face grazed the pavement. I remember being hit on the head. I obviously passed out. However, I don't think I have any other injuries. Or do I?'

'No, you don't. Not as far as we can tell.'

'So I can go home today?'

'I don't think so, Mr Deravenel. I need to keep you here for a few days. Under observation. Just to be on the safe side. I want to be absolutely certain we haven't missed anything.'

Edward was silent for a moment, and then he asked, 'Has my mother been informed that I am here?'

'She has indeed. She was here at the hospital, in fact, but I understand from Mr Watkins that your mother and Mrs Watkins have gone to your home to have food prepared for you. They will return with a hamper very shortly. In the meantime, your cousin is very anxious to talk to you. Are you able to see him now? Or would you prefer to wait a little longer?'

'No, no, I'm really perfectly all right. Dr Robertson. I would like to see him. And let me thank you for looking after me so well.'

The doctor nodded, and stepped closer to Edward. Bending over him, Michael Robertson put the stethoscope in his ears and listened to Edward's heartbeat. Then he shone a small flashlight in his eyes, and finally placed a cool hand on Edward's forehead. He appeared pleased, well satisfied. He nodded to himself, gave Edward a brief smile and hurried out.

'What I don't understand is how I got here,' Edward murmured, giving Neville a close look, frowning slightly. 'And how did *you* find out? Was my wallet still on me? My name and address are in it, you know. But thieves would have taken the wallet, surely?'

'Indeed they did,' Neville replied swiftly, pulling the chair closer to the bed, and he lowered his voice when he added, 'but thieves they weren't, I'm convinced of it. However, more about all that in a moment, Ned. Since you patronize an excellent Savile Row tailor a small piece of tape with your name on it is always stitched on the reverse side of the pocket which is on the inside of your jacket. That was how you were identified by the police, who brought you to the hospital. But actually there's another story . . . I mean about the way *I* was informed that you had been injured and were here.'

Staring up at Neville, his eyes startlingly blue in his

bruised face, Edward appeared puzzled. 'Do tell me, I'm filled with curiosity.'

A faint rueful smile flitted across Neville's mouth. 'With my permission, Finnister has had one of his operatives following you . . . keeping an eye on you. You were attacked by *two* heavily-built men last night. Finnister's man was outnumbered, and there was nothing he could do to help you . . . except run off looking for the police. Once he had ascertained you were still alive, of course.'

'He saw the attack, did he?'

'From a distance. He also noticed a stranger stop you, and later he saw the same man conferring with the two bruisers . . . before they all made a dash for it.' Neville shook his head. 'Odd, don't you think, that *your* father and *mine*, and my brother, died from fatal blows to the head.'

Edward closed his eyes for a moment, and when he opened them they were stark. He pushed himself up on the pillows, staring into Neville's face. 'Same modus operandi, is that what you're saying?' he muttered bleakly.

'Yes. There is no doubt in my mind that you were attacked by men working for the Grant faction. They're obviously having you followed, just as Finnister was. It was a good thing he took that precaution because his man reported in to him quickly, and Finnister telephoned me as soon as he knew. I, in turn, informed your mother.'

Edward remained silent, turning everything over in his mind, and at last he said softly, 'I know you're going to suggest that I have a proper bodyguard, *several* men, presumably, to look after me, and you will not receive any argument from me, Cousin. Will can now go on your staff, until he works with me at Deravenels, and you and Amos can seek out the other men.'

'Thank you, Ned, for being so sensible. I know what a nuisance it's going to be, but unfortunately it is necessary. I cannot permit anything to happen to you.' Neville reached out, grasped his cousin's hand in his and held on to it tightly. 'We are partners, we are in this together. I promise you I will be your rock.'

'And I will be yours, Neville, there for *you* should *you* ever need me.' He laughed and then instantly grimaced. 'When I move my face it hurts like hell. But I was going to say . . . *not that you will ever need me.*'

'Ah, don't say that, do not tempt Providence . . . we never know when life is going to come and hit us in the face. *Catastrophe* is ever present, a spectre that usually lurks behind every corner. For someone.'

Edward felt an involuntary shiver run down his spine on hearing these words, but he remained silent. The hackles rose on the back of his neck.

Neville released his cousin's hand and sat straighter in the chair. 'I have a good thought, Ned. It occurred to me earlier that my brother could come to London. Johnny and Will and you have often made a good three-some . . . you are old sparring partners.'

'Indeed we are, and Johnny has always been so very special to me. All my life. But can you spare him?'

'Yes, I think so. The managers of the northern offices have all been well trained. By us both. Anyway, my brother needs a change. It will do him good to be here in London . . . and I am sure we can find a place for him later. At Deravenels.'

'Again, if you can spare him,' Edward responded, laughter sparkling in his bright blue eyes. Johnny Watkins was close to his heart.

'We will have to retaliate, you know,' Neville announced.

Edward stared at the other man. '*How?*'

'I don't know. Yet. Don't you worry about it. Something will come to me. In due time. There's no hurry.'

There was a sudden sharp knock on the door, and it opened swiftly, with a burst. And before Edward could catch his breath his mother and Nan, his brothers and sister were rushing into the room, followed by Will Hasling.

Neville jumped up, and went to his aunt, led her forward to the bed, while his wife, Nan, shushed the children, just as Margaret was doing. 'George, do calm down,' Meg told her younger brother, hanging onto his hand. Richard, of course, was silent and worried. His genuine concern shadowed those blue-grey eyes. He could not bear that his adored Ned was hurt.

Cecily clutched her son's hand. 'Ned, oh Ned, your *head*. Your poor bruised face. You took such a beating.' She shook her head, and she, who was usually so controlled, discovered her eyes were filling with tears.

'Not too much damage done, Mother. The doctor says I'm perfectly fine. Please try not to worry. I'll be up and out of here very quickly,' Ned told her, and then looked over at Richard, beckoned for him to come forward. 'I'm alive and well, Little Fish. I do promise you.'

For the first time that day Richard smiled, and ran to the bedside, took hold of Ned's other hand.

'Mama told us you were set upon by thieves, Ned.'

'Were you frightened?' George asked. He had wriggled free of Meg's grasp and was now standing next to Richard by the bed.

'No, he wasn't! Of course he wasn't!' Richard exclaimed, glancing over his shoulder at his brother. 'Ned is *never* afraid, are you, Ned?'

'I didn't have time to be, as it so happens,' Ned responded, his voice full of affection for his younger siblings.

Meg joined her brothers, and gazing down at Ned, she asked, 'Is there anything you need, other than the food Mama and Aunt Nan have brought?'

'To come home to your loving care, Meg darling. But Dr Robertson has suggested I stay here. Overnight. Just to be sure that . . . my old noggin is in working condition.'

'Is there some problem with your head injuries?' his mother asked, her voice rising, alarm flaring on her face.

'No, Mother. It's just a precaution. You know very well how hospitals are.' Turning his head, his eyes met Will's, and he said, 'Thanks for coming, old chap. And what's that you're carrying?'

'A picnic, Ned. Swinton's put together quite a lavish spread, at least so I'm told. I asked the ward nurse if she could find a small table, so I can unpack it, and she was happy to oblige. Oh, here she is now.'

Later that afternoon, after they had had their merry picnic, everyone left except for Neville and Will Hasling.

They wanted to stay with Edward because there were important matters to discuss, and also because the police were coming to ask Edward a few questions. Neville felt they should be with him during the police interview.

Neville had just finished explaining everything in detail to Will, and asked him to join his staff, when Dr Robertson entered the room. He was accompanied by a uniformed policeman and a detective.

Once they had all been introduced, the plainclothes policeman stepped forward, and asked, 'Would you mind telling us exactly what happened to you, Mr Deravenel, please? We do have a police report from the local constable on the beat in Belsize Park, but that's about it. Nothing much at all, sir.'

'Of course, Inspector Laidlaw, I'm glad to do so,' Ned answered. 'I'd been visiting a friend in Belsize Park Gardens, in the late afternoon. I did stay for supper, and I was therefore longer than I'd planned. I left about nine o'clock, and walked up to the main road, seeking transportation. The problem was there were no hansom cabs around. I was surprised. However, there was nothing much I could do about it, and I decided to walk. I was heading for Primrose Hill, where I thought I would probably find a hansom. I was stopped at one point by a pedestrian, who asked me directions to Hampstead. It was when I was speaking with him that I was struck from behind. First across the shoulders and then on my head. I fell forward. And passed out. That's all I know, Inspector. Until I woke up here today.'

Inspector Laidlaw compressed his lips together. 'Not

much to go on, sir, I'm afraid, but it's the truth, nevertheless. The pedestrian who asked directions, can you describe him?'

'Medium height, light eyes, ordinary face. Wearing a cloth cap, a muffler, oh, and a worn looking overcoat. Nondescript sort of chap, actually. I thought at the time that he looked . . . a bit down on his luck.'

'What about his accent? Can you pinpoint it?'

'Oh yes, certainly. A Londoner. Born and bred.'

Nodding his head, the inspector put away his notebook. 'I understand your wallet was taken, Mr Deravenel, but nothing else. Not even your gold pocket watch or your gold cufflinks. So, my question to you, sir, is this . . . was it really a robbery? Or was the attack on you . . . well, let's say, a *personal attack*?'

'Good Lord, Inspector, how on earth would I know!' Ned exclaimed, looking properly askance.

'Any enemies, Mr Deravenel?'

'None, as far as I know.'

'I understand, sir. Well, it looks as if we've hit a brick wall, so to speak. If you do recall anything, anything at all, please get in touch with me, sir.'

'I certainly will, Inspector.'

TWENTY-TWO

John Summers, usually a patient and self-contained man, was agitated. He paced up and down the floor of his office at Deravenels, filled with a mixture of frustration and anger. Unable to sleep the night before, he had risen at dawn and come here earlier than usual. None of his colleagues had yet arrived, therefore he could not question them or confront them. Hence his frustration.

Last evening, just before dinner, he had been informed that Edward Deravenel had been physically attacked and was in hospital, badly injured. His seething anger sprang from this unwelcome news.

He did not need problems at this moment, and an injured Deravenel was indeed a problem. If any of his people were involved they would pay heavily for it.

Finally, he stopped pacing, and walked across to the windows, looked down into the Strand. Even though it was not yet nine o'clock the traffic was heavy . . . horse-drawn carriages, horse-drawn omnibuses, hansom cabs, a few handcarts being pushed, and lots of pedestrians hurrying along, all jostling together, a mass of humanity on the move on this sunny March morning.

Turning away, John Summers went over to his desk and sat down. Steepling his fingers, he gazed out into the large and handsomely furnished room, thinking about the consequences of the attack on Deravenel. The prospect of retaliation alarmed him.

At twenty-eight, John Summers was an attractive man with a pleasant, clean-cut face. Very English in looks, he had a fair complexion, brown hair and light-grey eyes. Slender, almost wiry, and athletic, he was just above average height. John dressed well, but in a most conservative manner which reflected, in a sense, his conservative outlook on life.

He was Henry Grant's man, always had been, as was his father before him. In fact, the Summers family had been allied to the Deravenel Grants of Lancashire for over two hundred years. And now John Summers ran Deravenels. There was no one else to take on the burdens of this vast global company. Henry Grant was a bewildered, absent-minded man these days, pious and harmless, yet far too involved with monks and priests for his own good. Certainly he understood nothing about business now, even though he had in the past.

Henry's French wife, Margot, liked to think she was in charge, but this was a figment of her imagination. She was not shy in coming forward with advice and ideas, many of them ridiculous; John allowed her to rant on, but he paid very little attention to her ravings and edicts, yet was clever enough not to let her know this.

Margot Grant. Beautiful, even beguiling to most men, and dangerous. He sat up straighter in the chair. Could *she* be behind the attack on Edward Deravenel? Was she? He sincerely hoped not.

John did not like Deravenel. He was too fleshily handsome, far too glamorous, oozing charisma and friendly bonhomie. But he was not stupid or soft. Summers knew instinctively that Deravenel had steel in his bones, unlike most other people at Deravenels who thought of him as lazy and a playboy. Not Ned, oh no. He liked women, the good life. But he was driven, ambitious, and strong, a man who was determined to win, no matter what.

That was why Summers was afraid of him. And even more afraid of Deravenel's cousin. *Neville Watkins.* A great magnate, a man of wealth. Cold, hard and ruthless when it came to business. They made a matchless team, in John's opinion, and he loathed the idea that they were ranged against him. Warriors, the two of them, and hellbent on winning. He had to stop them in their tracks, and very soon.

Restlessly, John rose and went out of his office, wandered along the corridor, heading for the reception room at the far end. When he went in a few seconds later, he switched on the crystal chandeliers and glanced around. Hanging on the walls were a collection of portraits of the men who had steered this company over the centuries. Mostly they were Deravenels from Yorkshire; only two Grants hung there – Henry's father and grandfather. Until sixty years ago the Deravenels of Ravenscar had dominated this company. And that was what Edward Deravenel wanted again. As did Neville Watkins.

Leaving the reception room, John flung open the door of the elegant dining room, his eyes scanning the handsome antiques and priceless paintings which hung on the red brocade-covered walls. So many magnificent lunch-eons and dinners had been given here for important clients, politicians and foreign guests over the years. But not lately . . . it was not possible to put Henry Grant on parade because of his mental instability. And, ostensibly at least, it *was* Henry who was head of the company . . . to the outside world.

Retracing his steps down the long corridor, John now considered going to the first floor where many of the heads of the various divisions had their offices. Perhaps Aubrey Masters was already here; he could question Masters, find out what *he* knew, if anything. A reliable ally.

Instantly John changed his mind. Taking out his pocket watch he glanced at it, nodded to himself. In a short while his secretary would arrive, along with the women telephonists and typists, the clerks and other members of the general staff. And certainly by ten o'clock the key executives would be behind their desks.

Although he had managed to calm himself, John felt a sudden flare of apprehension. He did not need prob-lems like the Edward Deravenel matter . . . there were already too many problems in the company to deal with as it was. Trouble loomed. And yet he had to investi-gate the attack on Deravenel, get to the bottom of it. He must put a stop to this sudden . . . *violence*.

'What in God's name is wrong with you?' John Summers demanded, looking from James Cliff to Jack Beaufield, and then more pointedly at Andrew Trotter. 'You're all laughing about the attack on Edward Deravenel, enjoying this . . . *catastrophe*! For that is indeed what it is! When what you *should* be doing is steeling yourself for a powerful retaliation. Are you such fools that you don't understand what's going to happen?'

'Nothing, nothing at all,' Andrew Trotter answered, a grin still lingering on his long, saturnine face. 'That arrogant young pup got a whipping and so what! Hopefully it will teach the little bugger a lesson. Teach him a few manners.'

At this moment there was a knock on the door, and Aubrey Masters hurried in, looking both harried and apologetic at the same time. 'So sorry I'm late, the Strand is jammed with traffic this morning, worse than ever.'

'That's perfectly all right, Masters, do come in and sit down.'

Aubrey Masters took a seat, and then glanced around at his colleagues. Instantly he detected the tension in the room. 'What's wrong, gentlemen?' he asked, frowning.

Summers told him about the Deravenel incident, and then finished, 'I want to know *who* amongst you is behind the attack. And I will find out, whatever it takes.' Now John's eyes settled on James Cliff. 'You're not saying anything at all this morning. So unlike you. Please tell me what you know?'

'Oddly enough, I don't know a damned thing,' Cliff answered in a mild voice. 'I truly don't.'

'*Really*,' John answered swiftly, giving him a cold look. 'Usually you're not squeamish . . . about *anything*, just so long as it serves your purpose.'

'For this company, not my *own* purpose,' Cliff shot back,

and smiled a trifle smugly. 'You know very well I am absolutely devoted to Deravenels, and work for its success. And there's no reason to drip acid on me today, I'm not involved in this bit of . . . *violence*.' Swinging his head, Cliff looked at Jack Beaufield. 'Come on, do confess. You and the lady have been rather cosy lately, wouldn't you say?'

Jack Beaufield's face tightened at this act of treachery, and a small vein started throbbing on the side of his temple. He said, in an icy voice, 'I had nothing to do with the attack on Ned Deravenel. In fact, no one in this room did. However, Cliff is right in that I have been . . . sequestered, shall we say, with the lady of the house, this house, and more than usual. She *is* behind it, Summers. She asked me to hire someone to teach Deravenel a lesson. But I refused. It is my belief she managed it all on her own. It is not so difficult to hire thugs.'

John Summers sat back in his chair and let his eyes roam over the men sitting across the desk from him. Finally his glance settled on Aubrey. He said slowly, 'Now, Masters, you know everything that goes on here, because everyone confides in you. Can you throw any light on the matter?'

'Actually, no, I can't. But I do believe Margot Grant has it in for Deravenel. They had some sort of . . . *run-in*, I suppose one could call it. I think she was determined to clip his ears. Well, that was the expression I heard around the office.'

'Since several fingers have been pointed in that particular direction I shall have to have a word with the lady when she comes in today, if she does come in, that is.'

'She's already here,' Aubrey announced. 'I just saw her, going into her office. Well, into Henry's office.'

John Summers jumped up. 'Let us adjourn, gentlemen. Please excuse me.' Without waiting to hear another thing, Summers hurried out of his office and strode down the corridor.

When he came to the chairman's office he went in without knocking, and immediately stopped short. Margot Grant was sitting behind the giant-sized Georgian partner's desk, whilst her husband Henry lay stretched out on a sofa near the window.

Taken by surprise at the sight of Henry Grant looking somewhat dishevelled, and certainly unwell, John nonetheless recovered himself at once. Always the gentleman, he said pleasantly, 'Good morning, Margot.' And then hurrying over to the sofa, he went on, 'And good morning to you, sir. How're you feeling?'

'Not too badly off, John,' Henry answered in a somewhat feeble voice. 'How're you? And how is your father?'

'I am well, sir, thank you,' John answered, and ignored the question about his late father.

Margot stood up and walked around the desk, came towards John Summers, a wide smile playing on her face. 'Have you heard the news about Deravenel?' she asked, and began to chortle, her merriment reflected in her eyes.

John chose not to respond. Instead he turned to Henry Grant and murmured, 'Would you excuse me, sir? I need to take Margot back to my office. I wish to go over several business matters with her, rather urgently.'

A faint smile glanced across Henry Grant's vacant face, and he waved his hand in a dismissive gesture. 'Go along, my boy, go along.'

Opening the door and standing back, John looked at Margot and said in a low voice, 'After you, please.'

He was silent as he walked with her down the corridor to his office, and it was only when they were inside and he had closed the door that he turned on her, his anger rising. 'I know you are probably responsible for the attack on Deravenel, so please don't deny it. I think you hired thugs to beat him up.'

She looked at him intently, her dark eyes holding his, and then leaning closer, she said softly, 'Why are you so angry, my dear? Apparently he got a whipping. Someone taught him a lesson, and that makes me happy. And that's the end of it. The end of Ned Deravenel. He will not be a problem anymore. Someone did us a favour.' She was jubilant.

Grasping her arm tightly, leaning into her, his face filled with fury, John Summers said in a harsh but controlled voice, 'You foolish, foolish woman. This is not the end of anything. It is the beginning of a war. You have just unleashed a terrible force.'

'Oh John, do not be so silly . . . so *melodramatic* –'

'There's going to be a catastrophe,' he hissed, glaring at her with sudden animosity. 'They will retaliate. I have no doubt about that.'

Margot Grant looked genuinely puzzled. 'I do not understand –'

'No, you don't,' he snapped. 'And there is another matter we must clarify. It is this. Please do not bring Henry to the office until he is in better health. And if that *should* happen, and you do choose to bring him, please make sure he is properly dressed, and not so dishevelled.'

'John, please, let us not quarrel, not you and I. You know I do not wish to upset you. I am your friend, your ally –' Remembering his manners he nodded, and said in a less angry tone, 'I know you mean well, Margot. Now, if you will excuse me, I have work to do.'

She stared at him, still nonplussed by his anger of a moment ago. And without another word she turned sharply on her heels and left.

Once he was alone John Summers gazed at the door, and snapped his eyes shut for a moment. When he opened them he shook his head as he went to his desk.

Why in God's name had he ever succumbed to that woman's charms? But he had, and he had no one else to blame but himself. Thank God, he had never been intimate with her. Their relationship was still only a flirtation, which must now end.

Aubrey Masters left Deravenels early that day.

Once a week he went to see his supplier, and today seemed like a good day to stop by the small shop to purchase his roots and grains. It was a sunny afternoon, quite mild for March, and as he walked up the Strand at a brisk pace he endeavoured to shed his anxieties about business.

John Summers was in a fury about Margot Grant, that was obvious, and he couldn't say he blamed him. She was always interfering in things, and this did not sit right with John or some of the other executives at Deravenels. He himself found her irritating; besides which, there was no room for women in the company.

263

It was not their place to be involved in business. And so Mrs Grant should not be there. Being the wife of Henry Grant was no reason at all to permit her presence in a man's world of commerce.

Aubrey's thoughts veered away from Margot Grant and settled on Alfredo Oliveri. Now there was an enigma. He had never liked the man, had always found him ambitious, competitive and absorbed by his sense of entitlement. Oliveri had worked for the company all of his adult life and believed this made him special, gave him untold privileges.

Years ago Aubrey had wondered if Oliveri wanted his job, and this idea had lately surfaced yet again. Oliveri was hanging around London far too long at the moment, continuing to stretch out his time at the London office. Now Aubrey couldn't help wondering why this was; Oliveri ought to be back in Italy, doing what he was supposed to be doing. Could it be that Oliveri was a traitor? This unexpected thought jolted Aubrey. Was Oliveri in cahoots with Edward Deravenel? Was he now in his camp? Had he changed sides? The more Aubrey thought about it the more he believed it to be true. Why else would Oliveri be hanging around headquarters? Also, he had just learned that Oliveri was helping Deravenel understand the many divisions in the company, from mining to wine-making apparently.

Once again, it struck Aubrey that Oliveri really did want his job, and that was undoubtedly why he had allied himself with Ned Deravenel. Perhaps they had become close in Carrara. I must find a way to discredit Alfredo Oliveri, he thought, get him out of the company, and the sooner the better. This is my priority.

So busy was Aubrey Masters with his planning and plotting, lost in his thoughts, he had not noticed that a well-dressed couple had fallen in behind him and were following him up the Strand, at a distance.

Continuing on his regular route he crossed Trafalgar Square, wending his way through the jostling crowds. Intent on his destination, once more he had no idea at all that another person was now following him as well as the couple. This was a young woman, nicely dressed, but not quite as fashionably as the man and woman. After a quick, brief word with them, the young woman fell in behind them, but again keeping her distance. However, she made certain they were always in her sights, as they had instructed her to do.

Although it was a fairly long walk from the Strand to Piccadilly, Aubrey was enjoying it this afternoon. Striding along the wide thoroughfare he glanced to his left at one moment and immediately noticed how verdant Green Park was looking, living up to its name. Spring was not too far away.

Turning down Half Moon Street, Aubrey was on Curzon Street within seconds. He thought of going into his favourite barbershop to purchase a bottle of his aftershave lotion, and then changed his mind. He was far too anxious to reach Shepherd's Market.

It was at this moment that the young woman who had been following him turned the corner of Half Moon Street herself. And she hurried to catch up with Aubrey Masters. She was a little out of breath when she tapped him on his arm and said, 'Sir, please excuse me.'

Startled, and also irritated, Aubrey swung around forcefully, sharp words springing to his tongue. But when he found himself staring at one of the prettiest girls he had ever seen, the words remained unsaid. Her genuine loveliness startled him, and he found himself asking in a warm voice, 'How can I be of assistance to you, young lady?'

'I'm sorry to trouble you,' she apologized, smiling at him, showing lovely white teeth, 'but I'm not from these parts, and I find myself lost. I'm looking for Shepherd's Market, but I can't find it.'

Struck by the sweetness of her smile and her soft voice, Aubrey beamed at her and exclaimed, 'I will be happy to help you. It just so happens I am going to Shepherd's Market myself. So come along, let us walk there together. It's not far, just up the street.'

The girl smiled again. 'What a relief. And how kind of you, sir, to take me there.' Falling into step with Aubrey, she went on, 'Is it a big place, Shepherd's Market? Do they sell many different things?'

'Oh yes indeed, but it's quite a small area, compact, actually.' Looking down at her, he was struck by her beauty again. She was delightful in his eyes. 'And I suppose you are looking for some pretty things for yourself?' he murmured in a voice that was wholly unfamiliar to him.

The young woman shook her head. 'Oh no, sir, I am hoping to find the shop that sells grains and pods, and other vegetarian things. For my mother. She has been very ill. Her stomach's been acting up, and a friend advised her to forgo such foods as meat and fowl, to eat much more lightly. She now wants to partake of vegetables and the like.'

'How curious!' Aubrey answered, his eyes sparkling. 'I

myself am a vegetarian, and it just so happens I am going to that very shop you're looking for.'

'How lucky I am,' she said, and stopped walking. Thrusting out her hand she added, 'May I introduce myself, sir. I am Phyllida Blue.'

Shaking her hand, full of smiles, Aubrey said, 'And my name is Aubrey Masters. So pleased to meet you, Miss Blue.'

'Please call me Phyllida. Everyone does.'

Walking up Curzon Street together, Aubrey told the young woman about the items he purchased from the shop, and extolled the virtues of vegetables and grains, spoke with knowledge about the importance of vegetarianism. Within a few minutes they were entering the cobbled yards which made up Shepherd's Market, where in the centre of the shops, small restaurants and coffee houses stood the favourite shop of Aubrey Masters.

'Here it is, Phyllida,' he announced, opening the door for her and ushering her inside.

''Ello, Mr Masters,' the man behind the counter said, 'I was expectin' you today.' He eyed the young woman, and, just like Aubrey, he couldn't help smiling at her. What a pretty one *she* was, with her golden curls, large blue eyes and pert mouth. A tasty bit if ever he'd seen one.

Noticing the man's reaction, Aubrey muttered somewhat possessively, 'This is Miss Blue, Phineas. She is looking for certain items for her mother. But I shall show her around first.'

'Please be my guest,' Phineas answered, and as Aubrey turned his back he smiled at the young woman, and winked.

She smiled in return and followed Aubrey, saying, as she did, 'I was told to get dried mushrooms, lentils, sago, and various nuts and pods. And certain dried flowers, and roots as well.'

'Yes, yes, I will help you, my dear,' Aubrey responded, finding himself so attracted to the young woman he was amazed at himself. She looked as if she was in her early twenties, half his age, and she was so lovely she stirred something inside him which had long been dormant. He wondered how he could arrange to see her again. For see her again he must.

'He's hooked,' Phyllida Blue said three hours later when she joined the fashionably dressed couple in the tap room of a pub in Maiden Lane up behind the Strand.

'So tell us all about it,' the man said, grinning at her.

'Easy as eatin' pie,' Phyllida replied, and smiled at the man and his companion. 'He fell for me hook, line and sinker. Took me for coffee afterwards, and he wants me to meet him next week. Same time, same place, Charlie.'

'Good girl.'

The woman eyed her fob watch. 'We'd best be going. We've all got to be at the theatre soon.'

'We're all right for a minute or two, Sadie,' Charlie answered. 'We don't have far to go.'

Looking across at Phyllida, he said with a throaty chuckle, 'You're a good little actress, Maisie. I trained you well.'

'You did, and thanks for watching out for me today,' she replied.

John Summers was so unsettled that evening he found it difficult to eat the excellent dinner his cook had so carefully prepared for him. Finally throwing the white linen napkin down on the table, he left the dining room, swiftly retreated to the library.

A moment later Fellowes, his butler, knocked on the door and came in. 'Is everything all right, sir?'

'Everything's fine, thank you,' John responded in a quiet tone.

'Cook is worried, sir. Did everything suit?'

'Yes, it did. My compliments to Cook, Fellowes, and please pour me a cognac, would you?'

When he was finally alone John Summers settled back in the leather wing chair in front of the blazing fire, nursing the balloon of brandy.

Uppermost in his thoughts were the events of the day. In many ways his eyes had been opened. He knew exactly where he stood with his executives, understood much more about them, knew their weaknesses. Finally. Certainly he had been startled by the knowledge that Margot Grant had a truly ruthless streak in her. He also now realized that she was something of a liability. On the other hand, Henry Grant relied on her, and he loved her . . . if love was an emotion felt by such a lost and demented man.

John sighed to himself and looked across at the small painting of Georgina which stood on the table next to the fireplace. If only his fiancée had not been killed in that accident several years ago his life would be very different now. He would have a wife and a family, and they would have eased his loneliness. As it was, his life was unbearable at times, because he missed Georgina so much, and because he had no confidante, no close friend whom he could trust. He was utterly alone. Except for his brothers, living in Somerset, and they were not all that close these days.

He took a long gulp of the brandy and then put the glass down on a nearby table, closed his eyes, filled with myriad thoughts. One thing was paramount in his mind . . . Thank God he had had the wisdom not to fall into the sexual trap that was Margot Grant. A narrow escape, he thought. And he pitied Jack Beaufield who was apparently her new victim.

John knew he had his work cut out for him in the next few months. The problems at the company would not go away. They had to be solved. He was damned if he was going to let the House of Deravenels fall. Somehow he would find clever solutions. With the help of a few good men, he would bring the company back up on top. He must.

TWENTY-THREE

At times Cecily Deravenel wished she had been born a man. There were many things she could do better and faster than some of the men she knew; but as a child of Victoria's reign and now a woman of the Edwardian era, so much had been, and still was, forbidden to her. Over the years she had suffered her frustration, annoyance and impatience in silence, as had so many other women she knew. Many men, in public and private, complained about Mrs Pankhurst and her fight for the rights of women, but Cecily could not help but admire her, and her efforts on behalf of the female sex.

At this precise moment, Cecily wished she had been standing in her late husband's shoes over the last few years. *She* would have definitely challenged Henry Grant about his mismanagement of Deravenels, and his right to run it. Curiously, Richard had never really done so, perhaps out of sentiment, and a lingering affection for Harry whom he had known throughout his life, since Henry's childhood, in fact.

It was all here, all the documents which would have brought the situation to a head, if Richard had so wished. Earlier that morning she had gone down to the vault in the basement of the Charles Street house and opened it with Swinton's help. Once she was alone, Cecily had removed a large pile of documents, which Richard had secured in a white linen pillow case, and had taken them up to the dining room.

Now these were spread out in front of her, and she studied them carefully. All of the papers were actually copies of ancient documents which dated back hundreds of years, documents so fragile they were stored in the vaults at the Deravenel offices in the Strand.

Long ago, Richard had told her that every five years or so, before the copies themselves yellowed and aged, they were copied afresh. He had gone on to explain that those originals in the office vaults dated as far back as the founding father of the dynasty, Guy de Ravenel, and were very precious and also extremely valuable historically.

As she slowly read, turned the pages, and read on, Cecily quickly understood that everything Richard had written in his diary was correct. She was struck, most forcibly, by the fact that he himself could so easily have presented a case to the board, yet for some reason he had not put that plan into operation. He had only written about doing it.

Once more, she wondered why? Sentiment aside, he was not a fearful man; certainly he was capable of standing up to anyone. He had never been cowardly, just the opposite, in fact. Yet, in this instance, he had backed away from the fight, and had merely continued to grumble about the sixty-year-old usurpation and his inalienable rights and so on, and had angered people in the process. She could not comprehend why he had not acted, given the evidence, and now she would never know. He had taken that reason to the grave with him.

Two hours later, fully informed about the rules and regulations of Deravenels, understanding everything, she collected the papers and carried them up to her bedroom in the pillow case. Placing them on her bed for a moment, she opened a drawer in the chest which stood in the corner, and placed the documents inside.

Later she would show them to Edward, when he returned from lunch with Neville and Will. Even though her husband had never seen fit to take advantage of her many talents and insights when it came to business, she knew her son would. And this pleased her. Ned had always listened to her opinions, paid attention to what she had to say, knowing he would benefit from her wisdom and sage advice.

'I can't believe it's you, Johnny!' Edward exclaimed, rushing across the library of Neville's Chelsea house. 'No one told me you would be here today!'

Hurrying forward to greet his favourite cousin, Johnny Watkins explained, with a wide grin, 'That's because no one knew I would be arriving last night.'

Meeting in the middle of the floor, the two men wore appraising expressions as they eyed one another with great affection. They both laughed, remembering so much. They were not only first cousins but the best of friends, having bonded long ago when they were growing up in Yorkshire – Johnny at Witton Castle, Rick's splendid home in the Dales, Edward at Ravenscar on the high cliffs at the edge of the North Sea. They were regular visitors to each other's homes, and also often stayed with Neville and Nan at Thorpe Manor near Ripon.

Although Johnny was a few years older than Ned, they had always seen eye to eye, shared the same values . . . honour, integrity, loyalty to family, and devotion to friends. These were their sincere and genuine beliefs, and they had remained steadfast in their love for each other and in their friendship.

Standing away from Edward, Johnny's dark-grey eyes swept over his cousin's face, and he said, with a faint smile, 'You don't look like the wounded warrior to me.'

'I'm *not*. Not anymore, Johnny. It's two weeks since the incident, so the bruises are almost gone. I'm no longer black and blue, and the shoulder pains have also fled.'

Johnny touched Ned's arm lightly, his expression serious. 'Thank God you're all right. You could've been killed, you know, Ned. And then where would I have been? Where would all of us have been? After losing my brother Thomas and your Edmund, and our fathers, well, I don't think I could have survived the loss of you.'

There was a moment's silence.

Ned's brilliantly blue eyes turned dark with pain before he said slowly, 'I know, it's still a raw wound, for all of us. But we do have our families, and each other, Johnny.'

'For life,' Johnny answered.

Ned nodded, smiled at his friend and cousin. And at

this moment he had no way of knowing that it would not always be so. Not in the end.

'How is Isabella? And your boy?' Ned asked.

'Wonderful, and if my sojourn here becomes a more permanent situation, she will come with our son to London, live here with me. Neville is well satisfied that things are under control in Yorkshire. The woollen mills in Bradford are turning out the best cloth, a lot of it for export. Our heavy-machinery manufacturing plants in Leeds are booming. The coal mines are operating well, better than ever – in fact all of our industrial interests are at full throttle. My father had everything running smoothly when he was killed –' Johnny broke off, looked away for a second before adding, 'and Neville has always had his business interests on an even keel. That's why he decided I should come here and keep you company, so to speak. Until we take over Deravenels.'

'And that we will certainly be doing in the not-too-distant future!' Neville Watkins announced self-confidently from the doorway, and came striding into the library accompanied by Alfredo Oliveri and Amos Finnister.

Once he had greeted Ned affectionately, he introduced the other two men to his brother John.

Although Neville and Johnny bore a marked family resemblance, they were quite different. Neville, the eldest, was always elegance personified, dressed in the best. Johnny was not at all flamboyant in his choice of attire, and he dressed rather simply in good clothes that were understated.

Johnny was as good looking as all of the Watkins' clan, and like his older brother he bore a strong resemblance to his Aunt Cecily Watkins Deravenel.

As for his character, he was hardworking and disciplined but not quite the slave to business that his brother was. He very frequently teased Neville, told him he lived out of a suitcase as he travelled the length and breadth of England.

Johnny liked the quiet country life, was something of a homebody, unlike Neville and Ned, who thrived amidst luxury, glamour and splendour, and loved the gilded life of society.

Neville indicated the men should sit down near the fireplace. 'Even though it's the beginning of April, it's still rather cold,' he pointed out, and seated himself near the hearth.

A moment later Will Hasling came striding into the library, greeting everyone in his usual breezy and cheerful manner, and then he hurried over to Johnny; they shook hands. They were old friends, good friends, and trusted each other implicitly.

Neville said, 'Oliveri has a few things to tell us, so I suggest he speaks first.'

Alfredo nodded, and sitting slightly forward in the chair, he said, 'The first thing I want to report is the general attitude at Deravenels after Mr Edward was so brutally attacked two weeks ago. I noticed the tense atmosphere myself, but most of my information came from Robert Aspen and Christopher Green. They are on our side. Anyway, they told me, *separately*, by the way, that John Summers was really furious, that he hauled his ex-ecutives over the coals regarding the attack on Mr Edward, and demanded to know who was responsible.'

'I'll wager they all denied having anything to do with it,' Ned exclaimed, glancing across at Neville.

Alfredo nodded vehemently. 'Naturally they did. And then James Cliff did something quite treacherous. He said, rather pointedly, that Jack Beaufield ought to know who was behind it since he was "sequestered" with Margot Grant quite a lot these days.'

'*Really*,' Neville remarked, then laughed at the thought of this. 'Well, we sort of knew that already, didn't we, Finnister?'

The private investigator smiled but remained silent.

'Jack Beaufield admitted that he was friendly with her,' Alfredo explained, 'but insisted he had refused to help her do harm to Ned. He suggested she hire thugs to do her dirty work.'

'It's more than likely she did,' Amos now interjected, 'but we'll never be able to prove it.'

'John Summers has cooled on Margot Grant, angrily turned away from his Queen Bee, but not for long. Christopher Green says they are once more in cahoots, and just as friendly as ever, whilst Jack Beaufield has been relegated to a back bench.' Alfredo sat back, his eyes on Neville.

'None of this is really surprising,' Neville began and then stopped abruptly, considered things for a moment. 'However, come to think of it, it's not such a bad idea, having them all at each other's throats.'

'They won't be for long,' Ned interrupted. 'They are all smitten by that woman, solidly behind her.'

Alfredo said, 'I would like to speak to you all about Aubrey Masters now. Apart from the fact that he's been acting somewhat strangely, he's apparently got it in for me. I hear he is trying to have me thrown out of the company. And out of the country. He's blackening my name, I'm afraid, and I don't like the look of things.'

'He must be stopped. Immediately,' Neville said in a cold, hard voice, staring at Amos. 'He should be induced to retire.'

'He has become a bit of a . . . nuisance,' Amos murmured, struggling to find the right word to describe Aubrey Masters. He looked as if he was about to say something else, but he stopped himself.

'Who will rid me of this turbulent priest,' Will said, a quirky smile playing around his mouth.

Neville glanced at him then said softly, 'I knew we would hear that before long.' Turning to Amos, Neville added, 'Perhaps we can find a way to persuade Aubrey Masters to cease. He must be made to understand he can't speak ill of people and most especially Oliveri here.'

'I will certainly try, sir.' Amos looked doubtful as he said this.

'To my last and perhaps most important discovery,' Alfredo announced, looking from Neville to Ned, and began in a low, confiding voice, 'I think I've found out what's wrong with the mines . . . what your father discovered, too, Mr Edward.'

The room went quiet. No one spoke. No one moved. Everyone was waiting for Alfredo's words.

'Somebody is stealing the product from the mines, skimming diamonds, emeralds and gold. Or money off the top.'

'But who?' Ned asked, incredulity echoing in his voice.

'In my opinion it could be the local managers,' Alfredo answered him.

'They wouldn't dare!' Neville exclaimed. 'Or would they?' His eyes narrowed slightly, and he threw Alfredo a pointed look. 'Unless they had approval from the head office . . . located on the Strand. A partner in Deravenels?'

'That was my guess.' Alfredo nodded. 'And Rob Aspen agrees with me. I'd been working late last week, and so had he; that was when he actually drew my attention to discrepancies he was finding. I knew at once what this meant. I gathered he did, too, had had the same idea. Anyway, I asked him not to reveal this to Masters, or to anyone else. At least for the moment.'

'Why?' Ned asked, and then swiftly added, 'I understand, don't bother to answer my stupid question. If the other side finds out we know about the discrepancies, they'll try to cover them up. Somebody in London *is* running this scheme.'

'Precisely.' Alfredo gave Ned a knowing smile.

'So we're not going to deal with it until we're running Deravenels ourselves, later in the summer,' Neville announced. 'Let's leave this matter in abeyance for the moment. And move on. Finnister informed me several days ago that he now has in his hands all of the records from the insane asylums, where Henry Grant was sequestered a number of times. Let's hear about it, Finnister.'

'Mr Watkins told you the most important part of my story,' Amos began. 'We are indeed in possession of the records. They are very detailed and extremely useful. I have hired a well-known doctor to look at these records, study them, and give a written report on what they mean. In other words, how will Henry Grant behave

279

over the next few years? Is he on the brink of going totally mad? Is he already suffering from dementia? What are his chances of survival? And finally, is he capable of running a company such as Deravenels?'

'I think the doctor will have no problem giving you the best written opinion there is, and no doubt it will be the kind of opinion which will serve us best.' Neville threw Amos a questioning look.

'You are right, sir. The doctor I engaged, Mr Rupert Haversley-Long, is a specialist, a psychiatrist who has been a colleague of the famous Dr Sigmund Freud.'

'I have no fears he will do the job perfectly,' Neville murmured. Rising, Neville continued, 'Let us all go into the dining room. We will be able to discuss everything further over an apéritif before we partake of lunch.'

The others rose and followed Neville out of the library.

Ned said to Alfredo, 'Don't worry, old chap, we'll neutralize Aubrey Masters in some way or other. We can't lose *you*, we especially need you here in London these days. *Permanently.*'

'I agree. When are you returning to the office?'

'On Monday morning. The hospital gave me several examinations this past week, and everything is apparently quite normal. In my opinion, they've been overly cautious, but my mother insisted on these extra tests and I don't think even Dr Robertson had the nerve to contradict Cecily Deravenel.'

Alfredo smiled. 'I know what you mean. There's no one quite like your formidable mother. Anyway, she was right. Head wounds can be dicey, very dicey indeed.'

TWENTY-FOUR

Lily stood in the centre of the drawing room in Vicky Forth's Kensington house, turning her head, taking everything in, a delighted smile on her face. 'It's absolutely beautiful, Vicky,' she said at last. 'But then you've always been so clever in the way you decorate your homes.'

Vicky's eyes lit up, and she exclaimed, 'Oh, I'm so glad you like it. To tell you the truth I've been a little bit worried, wondering if it was all too – *pale*.'

Walking over to Vicky, who was still standing in the doorway, Lily said emphatically, 'Not too pale at all . . . the room is perfect, in fact I love the way you have mixed all of these different creams and whites together, and the touches of green and lilac are charming.'

'It's not too feminine?'

'Of course it isn't. Anyway, the antiques are dark, and help to give the room exactly the right balance.'

'I just pray that Stephen's going to like it.'

'I know he will,' Lily reassured her best friend, and then asked curiously, 'And when is he getting back from New York?'

'In a week. He had to go to San Francisco un-expectedly, and that delayed him, but his business has gone well, and he'll be sailing from New York in a few days. I can't wait to see him, it's been ages.'

'I know what you mean,' Lily murmured, and walked slowly across the room, went and sat down on a plump curving love seat upholstered in pale apple-green damask. As she settled back against the lilac and apple-green silk cushions, she said, with another glance around, 'The flowers are lovely, Vic, you've managed to create a feeling of spring here today.'

'Thank you, darling.' Vicky took a seat in a chair next to Lily, and looking at her intently, she asked, 'Have you told Ned?'

Lily shook her head. 'No, not yet. I only saw him once last week, after he came out of the hospital, and I felt it wasn't quite the right time. But I am going to tell him, please don't worry.'

'Good. I'm glad. Now, you'll be interested to hear that I've found a charming house quite near us in Kent. I think it's lovely and not too big, and I was hoping you could come down to see it with me on Monday or Tuesday, before Stephen arrives in London.'

'Oh, Vicky, darling, how wonderful! I'd love to,' Lily cried, turning to her friend, beaming at her. 'To tell you the truth, I've been thinking about moving from Belsize Park Gardens. Moving to a house I saw in South Audley Street, in Mayfair.'

'I see. I hope you're not taking on too much, in your condition, I mean.'

Lily laughed. 'I really feel wonderful. Very fit and

healthy, and it's only the awful morning sickness getting me down at the moment. Also, the house in Mayfair is not large – compact really, yet very adequate for me, the child and a small staff. I just hate the idea of Ned being stranded the way he was in Belsize Park when he was attacked. I need to be in the West End.'

'I understand.' Vicky fell silent for a few seconds, and then, leaning towards Lily, she asked in a quiet voice, 'You do plan to keep the baby, don't you?'

'Oh yes, I could never give it up! Why, it's part of me and Ned. I might tell him today, Vicky, then I might not. But please be assured that when I do I will explain that I want to be quite independent. I don't want anything from him, as you know.'

'That's rather brave of you, Lily. *I* have something to tell *you*, by the way. It's rather important. At least, I think so.'

Lily looked at her alertly. 'What is it? You seem suddenly very excited.'

'I am. I've made a decision about something I've thought about for a while. I'm definitely going to do voluntary social work with my friend Fenella Fayne –'

'The widow of Lord Jeremy Fayne?'

'Exactly. She's been a friend for years, and as I think I once told you she runs a women's . . . *shelter* in the East End. I've always admired her work, and I want to do something useful with my life. There's so much poverty and misery in London, greatest capital in the world though it might be. I simply can't bear the discrepancy between the lives of the rich, and the desperate, miserable existence of the poor.'

'I'm very happy you finally decided to make a move, you've been hankering after doing work like this for as long as I can remember.' Lily gave her a warm loving smile, and reached out, took hold of her hand. 'You've always wanted to make a contribution, and I think you'll be wonderful at it. Fenella Fayne must be thrilled to have you.'

Vicky began to laugh, looking embarrassed. 'I haven't actually told her yet, but she knows how interested I've been in her work, and for a long time. I plan to visit her next week, and volunteer my services.'

'Stephen won't mind, will he?'

'I don't think so, he understands that I'm . . . well, that I feel women should be able to make contributions if they wish to do so. He thinks I'm rather emancipated really, and he's one of the few men I know who believes Mrs Pankhurst has the right idea . . . about women's rights. Frankly, Lily, he's proud that *I* am emancipated.'

Lily nodded. 'And you're so right about the poverty in London. There are some terrible slums, such as Providence Place, and those ghastly tenements . . . they're called rookeries, aren't they?'

'Yes. And the women who live there are beaten-down and desperate, poor, and frequently in ill health and often abused by their beer-swilling husbands. It makes my blood boil when I think about the wealth in England, and the selfishness of so many people who could help to make a few lives easier –'

Vicky stopped and jumped up, went to the window, saw the carriage coming to a stop.

'Oh, Lily darling, I think it's my brother, with Ned,

284

and, oh my heavens, *Johnny Watkins*. They're earlier than I expected.'

Amos Finnister settled himself at a corner table for four in the Mandarin Garden, the little Chinese restaurant which was his favourite in Limehouse. Six o'clock was early for him to eat his Sunday dinner, but Charlie had requested this time and so he had acquiesced.

His thoughts settled on yesterday's lunch with Neville Watkins and the other men. When he considered the information that had passed between them, the decisions made, he filled with a rush of genuine pleasure and satisfaction. Everything was coming together much faster and much better than he had anticipated it would.

The medical records were in hand, the renowned doctor was studying them; Alfredo had produced valuable information about the Mining Division as well as the names of their allies within the company; and now, thanks to Charlie, he had two men whom he could use to tackle James Cliff, Jack Beaufield and Philip Dever. What the two actors were going to do was pose as gentlemen, as aristocrats, and they would reveal they had lethal information about the private lives of these three men. Information that would prove deadly to their lives and careers. Blackmail, in other words.

Right on time as always, Charlie came hurrying into the restaurant. Amos glanced up, raised his hand in a wave.

A moment later Charlie was sitting opposite him, a grin spreading across his handsome face.

'Evening, Mr Finnister.'

'Good evening, Charlie. Would you like a pot of this jasmine tea I'm having? It's most refreshing.'

'Indeed I would, sir. And thank you very much.' Charlie sat back in the chair and glanced around the restaurant which was still relatively empty. 'It appears we are the sole diners,' he added.

'Playing the toff this evening are we, Charlie?' Amos asked with a wide smile. He was extremely fond of the young actor, and they had worked together on many *projects*, as Charlie was wont to call them. For ten years, at least.

'I *am* the toff tonight, sir. Don't forget I'm stuck with a posh part at the moment, so I try to keep my voice in character with the character, if you get what I mean. Makes my life easier.'

'It's quite extraordinary the way you assume such different voices, can flip from one accent to another,' Amos remarked, giving him a thoughtful look. 'You're the best mimic I know, except for Maisie.'

'Thanks, guv.'

The waiter came hurrying to the table and at once Amos ordered jasmine tea and asked to see the menus, then he continued, 'I think it's a genuine gift, Charlie, your miraculous voice.'

'Mebbe it is, mebbe it ain't.' Charlie grinned at Amos cheekily as he dropped with the greatest of ease into his native Cockney. 'Fings ain't wot they used ter be around 'ere, Mr F., so I'm off to America wiv me sister.'

Startled by this sudden and unexpected announcement Amos sat up straighter in the chair, gazing at Charlie, an expression of disbelief on his face. 'Well,

I'll be blowed! So you made your mind up to do it at last. She must be thrilled.'

'She don't know nuffin' yet. Yer see, I ain't told 'er nuffin'. It's a surprise, guv.'

'Very good, very good indeed, Charlie. I'm delighted you came to this decision, that you're going to remove yourself from these shores. I shall miss you of course, but I think perhaps it's . . . well, a *wise move*, shall we say?'

'Wiv me sister by me side I think we can mek it big in America, Mr F., an' we do 'ave a double act, yer knows.'

'So you've told me, and I –' Amos broke off when the waiter came scurrying back with the pot of jasmine tea and a cup on a tray, along with the menus. He gave these to Amos, poured the tea for Charlie and bowed low, then disappeared again.

Once they were alone Amos leaned across the table and said in a much lower voice, 'Is everything set for tomorrow?'

Answering in his cultivated voice, Charlie murmured softly, 'It is, Mr Finnister. Maisie has arranged to meet Aubrey Masters at the coffee shop in Shepherd's Market. She will explain she's going to be away for a week visiting her grandmother, and she'll give him the going away present.'

Amos simply nodded and reached into his pocket. A second later he placed a small packet on the table between them.

Charlie eyed it, then picked it up and looked at it.

'*Purple paper*. Very fancy.' He slipped it into his pocket without further comment.

'Maisie knows what to do with it?' Amos gave him a penetrating stare.

Charlie nodded. 'She's to mix it in with the grains and pods she's giving him in the brown paper bag.'

'Correct.'

'What is it, by the way? What is it going to do to him.'

'It'll give him a loose bowel for a few days, keep him at home. Away from the office, which is the purpose of this exercise. And for your information it's a mixture of dried herbs and seeds, that's all.'

'That's awright then, innit,' Charlie muttered. Now he pulled a piece of paper out of his jacket pocket. 'Wiv these 'ere two lads yer won't go wrong, guv.'

Amos glanced at the paper. 'Real names?'

'Naw, ain't a good idea ter give real names, yer knows that. Aliases, like my Maisie called 'erself Phyllida Blue. Cor blimey, don't arsk me where she got that from.'

'Has she used that name before, with anyone else?' Amos asked, sounding worried.

'Naw, 'course not, Mr F. I mean, I'm not bleedin' daft, yer knows. Invented it she did an all, on spur of the moment, so she told me.'

'And your two fellow thespians will meet us here in an hour?'

'That's right.'

'So we should order dinner? Or should we wait for them?'

'Naw, naw, they won't be eatin' wiv us. They 'ad Sunday lunch wiv their mums down Whitechapel way.'

'Very good. I shall have duck with orange sauce, and would you like to have your usual, Charlie?'

'I will, thanks. Sweet and sour, and steamed rice, please.'

After Amos had ordered, he looked across at Charlie, his brows furrowing. 'Maisie *is* leaving tomorrow as planned?'

'She is, an' as I told yer, I'm going wiv 'er. Ter Liverpool. On the evening train. Board the ship the next day, that we do. And off we goes, sailin' away ter America where the streets are paved wiv gold.'

Amos nodded, and actually felt a surge of relief that Charlie was leaving London. It would be better in the long run. Too many people knew they were associated, and it was much smarter to terminate their business relationship in view of future events.

'I shall miss you, my friend,' Amos murmured, a sudden sadness creeping into his eyes. Charlie had always brought laughter, a few jokes and loyalty into his life, and he had always been reliable, devoted.

'Same fing for me, Mr F. Yer've been a good 'un, 'elped me out when I've needed it. But now I'm gonna be a good bruvver to Maisie. She deserves it.'

'She does. And by the way just make sure she *never* uses the name Phyllida Blue again. And tell her to dispose of the blonde wig.'

'I got yer, Mr F. I understands.'

Reaching into his inside breast pocket, Amos removed a thick packet and handed it to Charlie. 'Put that money safely away, my lad. Tomorrow there'll be another one like that when I meet you at the railway station. And by the way, don't forget to stay in touch with me when you arrive in New York.'

Charlie's cheeky grin spread across his face once

more, and he reached out and grasped Amos's hand resting on top of the table. 'Friends for life, Mr F.'

And, as it turned out, they were.

Margot Grant stared at herself in the Venetian mirror, viewing her image appraisingly. Satisfied that she was looking her very best tonight she walked away, went and sat down on the big, plump sofa in front of the fire. Leaning back against the many soft cushions, she willed herself to relax at last.

After a moment or two her eyes roamed around her small and intimate private sitting room in the grand house on Upper Grosvenor Street where she lived with Henry Grant – when he was not away on retreat.

The room this evening was just as perfect as she herself was. She had set out to create an enticing roseate glow in this most intimate place in the house, and she realized how well she had succeeded.

The walls were covered in a pale-pink watered silk, while a deeper rose-coloured ribbed silk upholstered this big sofa, several chairs, and a small loveseat set against the back wall. The tied-back draperies at two tall windows were the same rose colour as the sofa and chairs but were made of light, floating taffeta. Beautiful landscapes by French masters hung on the walls, and a number of priceless French *objets d'art* were scattered around.

The lighting was soft. The pink silk shades on the pink alabaster lamps added to the rosy feeling, as did the blazing fire. Margot sighed. It was a room designed by her for seduction and she hoped it would work wonders tonight.

She smiled inwardly. Jack Beaufield, her latest flirtation, had called it the honey trap, and what a fitting name that was. He had added that it was feminine, sexual and with her at the centre even more exciting. But she had made it clear to him that she was unavailable.

There was a faint smell of roses in the air, and she wore the same Attar of Roses perfume. John Summers' favourite. *He* was her favourite. She must win him back, she needed him by her side. How foolish she had been to antagonize him. He had always been her champion; she thought of him as her knight in shining armour, and of herself as his queen.

Despite his genuine adoration of her she had never claimed him in her bed, made him hers as she had his father years ago when she had been only a young girl. But she must do it. Tonight. She could not wait for him any longer. Her whole body raged for him. She lusted after him. Had to have him. It was imperative that she owned him sexually, not only to satisfy her rampant desires but to bind *him* to *her* forever.

Margot closed her eyes, thinking of him. He was a man she had wanted for a long time now, the perfect man for her, and she knew he would be a passionate lover, knew it in her bones. She needed a man she knew she could trust, who would meet her voracious sexual appetite with a raging yearning of his own. *How she had yearned for him.* For so long.

In all of her life, she had never believed she would end up married to a man like Henry Grant. They were total opposites.

She prided herself on her vivid intelligence, her education, her many talents – she played the piano like a true artist, could paint and embroider, and had a knowledge of gourmet food and the great wines of France. Her grandmother had trained her in etiquette and manners; she had taught her how to run great houses and manage country estates. Her father and grandmother had made sure she was a great lady, as was befitting the daughter of a French industrialist such as her father was.

The marriage to Henry Grant had been arranged, was a marriage of convenience. Henry had bestowed on her a famous name, she had brought him a grand dowry. And her father's business holdings and land in Anjou would be his one day, through her.

Proud, spirited and undeniably the most beautiful of women, she had come to England full of anticipation and expectations. She had come to marry Henry, the head of Deravenels, the most famous trading company in the world, and she was excited about the union arranged by her father.

At fifteen she had expected a dashing Englishman. He was twenty-four and she had imagined a vigorous and experienced lover, a man of charm and elegance. She discovered instead that she was marrying . . . a *monk*. More or less. *Mon Dieu!* And a monk who was daft in the head.

She had been married to him for fifteen years, and now, at thirty, she was in full bloom. Frustrated in every way. What she longed for at this moment was a man in her life and in her bed. But not just any man. A particular man, one who was already deep in her heart. And that man was John Summers. Her own female longings aside, he was the man who was actually running Deravenels, and she wanted to be by his side, learning from him for her son's sake.

Looking at the antique ormolu clock on the mantel-piece, Margot suddenly rose and went to the window, stood looking out, hoping he would come soon. She did not have long to wait. Within a few minutes the carriage arrived; he alighted, and she turned, sped across the room and out into the black marble entrance foyer. Before he could lift the knocker she had opened the door.

He appeared startled to see her on the front steps.

'*Chéri*,' she murmured in her low breathy way. 'Come in, come in.'

'Good evening,' he said in his cultured voice, and smiled at her.

Smiling in return, she took his overcoat and placed it on the wooden hall bench, then ushered him into the small private sitting room.

He glanced around, then turned to her and kissed her lightly on the cheek. 'It's nice to see you, Margot,' he murmured, his eyes sweeping over her, taking in the low décolletage of the pink silk gown. This was beautiful and fitted her tightly, showed off to advantage her perfect breasts, tiny waist and curvaceous hips. 'Thank you for your unexpected invitation,' he added, dragging his eyes away from her.

'Sit down, please, here on the sofa in front of the fire. I shall bring you champagne. Yes?'

'That's a good idea,' he said as he sat down, and leaned forward, reached his hands towards the fire. 'It's turned into a cool evening.' He sat back and watched her intently as she floated over to a console table and poured champagne into two crystal flutes. A moment later she was handing one to him.

'Ah, my favourite. Pink champagne.'

She laughed as she seated herself next to him. 'It matches the room.' She clinked her glass next to his. '*Santé.*'

'Your health, my dear. And how is Henry?'

'The same . . . always the same. Resting at this moment.'

'Will he not join us then?'

'*Ah, non, non, c'est pas possible ce soir.*'

'I am sorry he can't come down. So – it's just the two of us then?'

She gave him a careful, guarded look. '*Oui, les deux.*'

He sat back, remained silent, keeping his thoughts to himself.

John Summers was nobody's fool, and he had suspected earlier that she had invited him here to seduce him, that she was about to use all of her wiles on him. But suddenly, unexpectedly, it didn't seem to matter one iota. He was tired and lonely, and frustrated in a variety of different ways; he carried the endless and heavy burdens of Deravenels on his shoulders and never had a moment's joy. Not these days. So let her try, he thought. Let her try to inveigle me into her bed. And let us see what happens.

Mistaking his sudden total silence for lingering anger, after their recent quarrel at the offices, she said softly, 'I am sorry I annoyed you, made you so angry. Please say you forgive me. I want so much to have your forgiveness, and your respect.'

'You have both,' he responded swiftly in a neutral voice.

'Oh, thank you! You have made me so happy. *Merci, Jean*,' she cried, pronouncing his name the French way.

Impulsively, she took hold of his hand. 'I have been so worried you would no longer be my friend. And I am alone, and lonely.'

His mouth twitched with sudden, hidden laughter. He bit it back, and finally remarked, 'But I've been so friendly towards you this past week, we even had lunch together. Didn't you realize I was . . . back in the fold.'

'Are you?'

'Yes.'

She leaned closer, revealing a portion of her beautiful breasts as she did so, and kissed him on the cheek. Then she looked at him pointedly, raising a brow.

He stared at her. Mesmerized. God, she was beautiful. A genuine true beauty. The most beautiful woman he had ever seen. He took in the perfect white skin, the flawless complexion, the arched black brows, the dark eyes full of hidden depths, the cloud of black hair, unbound tonight and worn hanging loose around her heart-shaped face. Her mouth was red, a brilliant red from the lip rouge, and it was luscious. She was luscious. Ripe for the picking. And such a temptress, tempting him. He felt a stirring between his legs as they held each other's eyes.

He said, after a few seconds, 'You have a questioning look on your face.' His voice sounded hoarse to him. 'What is it? Ask me, whatever it is.'

Margot put down the champagne glass, drew closer to him. He could smell the perfume of roses on her neck and breasts, intoxicating him, and he felt himself growing hot. At last, she whispered, 'Will you be mine?'

Before he could stop himself he asked bluntly, 'In the way my father was? Is that what you mean? All of me? Not just my loyalty to your cause? Is that what you want?'

He had startled her. 'Yes,' she answered finally.

'I have a question,' John announced after a moment's consideration.

'Ask me.'

'What of Jack Beaufield? . . . what is there between the two of you?'

'There is nothing between us. There was only a mild flirtation, of no consequence. There has never been anything between me and anyone else. That is, other than your father.' She focused on him intently. 'Truly. I promise. I am not a liar, whatever else I am.'

'I believe you, don't protest so.'

She smiled and then she began to giggle like a young girl.

'What is it?' He frowned, staring at her in bafflement.

'Jack Beaufield said this room was like a honeypot.'

'Did he now?'

There was a long moment of total silence between them, and then quite unexpectedly, all of a sudden, John took hold of her and pulled her almost roughly into his arms. He kissed her on the mouth; it was a deep and passionate kiss, and she returned it fully, sliding her tongue into his mouth, wanting to devour him.

John still held her tightly and kept on kissing her, then abruptly he moved his face and said against her ear, 'But he was wrong. *You* are the honeypot.'

'Your honeypot?' she whispered.

'Ah yes. *Mine*.' After a moment, he said, 'What of Henry? Is he sleeping?'

'I gave him a sedative,' she admitted.

'The staff?'

'It's Sunday. They have the night off.'

'So, we are alone. Nevertheless, I must lock the door, and draw the curtains.'

'Yes, do,' she murmured, leaning back against the cushions, fiddling with the buttons of the peignoir, opening it.

He was gone only a moment. When he came back to the fireplace he switched off two of the lamps, saying as he did, 'It's just a little too bright.'

When he turned around to face her he saw that she had opened the top buttons of the pink gown, then realized it was a robe not a gown at all. Even more of her beautiful breasts were revealed, most provocatively, and she was gazing up at him, a yearning expression on her face, her eyes locked on him.

He took her in his arms and held her close, whispering her name over and over, then began to kiss the voluptuous mouth. Within seconds they were both aflame.

Reaching for his hand, she placed it on her leg. He glanced down, saw that her legs were bare . . . soft, smooth and firm beneath his hand. Instantly he knew it was an invitation to explore. And he did so, running his hand along her inner thigh and across her stomach.

He heard her catch her breath and he looked down at her intently.

'I am yours. Do what you want with me.' As she spoke she tugged at the front of the peignoir and it came open fully.

Now she truly was revealed to him, and as he gazed at her slender white body he caught his breath. 'Oh God, you're beautiful, Margot!' And he leaned over her, buried his face against her breasts.

'Take me, take me,' she moaned against his hair.

It took him a moment to get undressed, but when he was finally free of his jacket and trousers, he flung off his shirt and cravat, lay down with her on the huge sofa which enveloped them like a bed.

Their kissing and touching became more frantic than ever; her arms and legs went around him and he was poised over her, looking down into eyes the colour of jet.

'Please, please,' she begged, 'take me to you.'

And very slowly and very carefully he did so, making himself part of her. They began a long ritual of rhythmic moving, and kissing, and he found himself drowning in her. And then in a moment of sudden and absolute clarity he wondered why he had ever fought her off, fled from her sexual desire for him. She was sheer bliss.

TWENTY-FIVE

Every morning when he arrived at Deravenels, Edward spent several hours studying the books, brochures and pamphlets which Alfredo Oliveri had given him. As Oliveri had intended, Edward was gaining a greater understanding of all the divisions of Deravenels.

Almost immediately he had found himself gravitating to the mining division, discovered he was particularly interested in diamonds and precious stones. In only a few weeks he had become extremely knowledgeable, most especially about one stone – the diamond.

He had always had a prodigious memory, much better than most people's, and when they were at Oxford together Will had announced that Edward had a photographic memory. It was true that after reading something twice he knew it by heart. 'You would have made a good actor,' Will had once told him, and Edward had laughed, and agreed, knowing that there was a lot of the actor in him.

This morning he was immersed in a book about Jean-Baptiste Tavernier, the merchant and traveller who had journeyed from Paris to India in the seventeenth century, usually heading for the famous Golconda mines, now extinct. Tavernier was the first person to bring diamonds back to Europe from the subcontinent of India. Louis XVI had bought diamonds from Tavernier, as had other members of his court who were able to afford them.

As he went on reading eagerly, Edward made notes on a pad. He had recently become intrigued by those very special diamonds which were both big and perfect, and because of this they were given a name. Thus each one became a famous diamond, much valued and coveted. Now he had just discovered that one of the first of these was called the Grand Mazarin, actually named after Cardinal Mazarin, who had owned it. On his death the Cardinal had bequeathed it to Louis XIV.

Unexpectedly, the door of Edward's office burst open, and as he glanced up Alfredo came rushing in looking troubled.

Always pale skinned, Alfredo was as white as chalk, so much so his freckles seemed to stand out most prominently across the bridge of his nose and his cheekbones.

Edward knew at once that something was seriously wrong, and his stomach lurched. He couldn't help wondering if Alfredo had finally been pushed out of the company, or at least instructed to return to Carrara.

Drawing to a standstill in front of the desk, Alfredo stood there staring at Edward, obviously perturbed. He seemed to have lost his voice.

'Whatever's the matter?' Edward asked.

'Aubrey Masters is dead.'

300

Dumbstruck, Edward simply gaped at the other man. He was shocked at this stark announcement, and felt a cold chill run through him.

Alfredo sat down heavily in the chair.

Edward leaned across the desk. 'When did he die?'

'Tuesday . . . last night, that is.'

'Who gave you this news?'

'Rob Aspen. He came into my office a few minutes ago and said, "Masters is no longer with us, he passed away." I was just as shocked as you are now. I had a meeting with him on Monday afternoon, but he told me he'd have to cut it short, because he had an unexpected appointment and he had to hurry off. But he was more cordial than usual, which seemed a bit odd to me. Anyway, he left in a hurry. Yesterday I ran into him in the corridor, and although he was somewhat preoccupied he looked in good health, was quite normal.'

'Did Aspen tell you what Aubrey Masters died of?'

'He didn't know.' Alfredo lifted his hands in a helpless gesture, and added, 'It must have been a heart attack or a stroke, something like that.'

'Whatever it was, it was certainly *sudden*,' Ned remarked, frowning. 'And how did Aspen get the news? From whom?'

'The horse's mouth, of course. *John Summers.* Summers is somehow related to Masters, they're cousins three times removed or some such thing. And as you know they are both related to Henry Grant. Hence their dedication to the Grant cause, and that's the reason they both work here. Or rather did as far as Masters is concerned.'

'I'm not going to play the hypocrite and say I'm sorry he's dead,' Edward said, 'because it doesn't matter to me that he's left this world. He was, after all, my father's enemy, and my enemy as well. And frankly, I've wondered for the last few days whether or not he was involved with the problems in the mining division –' Ned broke off, drew even closer to Alfredo Oliveri. 'You know what I mean, the skimming, or whatever is going on in India, South America and South Africa.'

Alfredo nodded. 'I agree with you. I had the same thoughts.'

There was a knock on the door, and John Summers came in before Edward could say a word.

Summers hovered in the doorway for a moment, then said, 'Good morning, gentlemen.'

They both responded in unison, and Edward said, 'Do come in, Summers.'

As John walked across the office, his eyes on Edward, he said, 'I suppose you must have heard the terrible news . . . about Aubrey Masters.'

It was Alfredo who answered when he said quietly, 'Yes. Rob Aspen came to my office a short while ago and told me, and I have just informed Mr Edward.'

Edward asked, 'What did Aubrey Masters die of, actually?'

'We don't know, as of this moment. His wife telephoned me this morning to inform me of his death. Apparently he came home on Tuesday night and seemed perfectly fit and well. He prepared his own dinner, as usual, his vegetarian dinner, and he ate it alone as always, in his study. About an hour later he staggered out of the study complaining of chest pains. Later he became

302

violently ill. Apparently he was having what Mrs Grant described as convulsions. She had their housekeeper telephone for the doctor, whilst she endeavoured to help her husband. But sadly, to no avail, I'm afraid. The doctor arrived fairly swiftly, only to find that Masters had just passed away.'

'Perhaps it was a stroke,' Edward suggested.

'It's impossible to know anything now,' John responded. 'The doctor arranged for the body to be taken to the hospital, where they are probably doing an autopsy at this very moment.'

'So we should have some news later today,' Alfredo said, making a guess.

'I hope so. In the meantime, I am going to go to their house in Hyde Park Gate, to be with Cousin Mildred. I think I'm about the only family she has, other than her sister. I shall come back to the office as soon as her sister arrives from Gloucestershire.'

All of these last few comments had been directed at Alfredo, who said, 'Yes, of course, and would you like me to have Rob Aspen cover for Aubrey –' He cut himself off, then said, 'Deal with anything Masters was working on.'

'Yes, that will be all right, a good idea actually, Oliveri,' John replied. 'Under your supervision, of course. And by the way, I think perhaps you should postpone your return to Italy. For the moment.'

Later that day, Edward had a short meeting with Neville at Neville's office in the Haymarket. Will Hasling and Johnny Watkins accompanied Edward, and the four men sat together in the vast board room, discussing the death of Aubrey Masters.

'A very sudden death such as his can be any one of a number of things,' Johnny pointed out. 'The obvious things are natural causes such as a heart attack, a massive stroke, a brain haemorrhage, or the ingestion of something poisonous.'

'Talking of poison, he does eat a number of very weird things,' Edward said. 'He could have eaten some sort of poisonous mushrooms, for example. Don't you remember when we were children, one of the stable boys at Ravenscar ate toadstools and was violently ill. Luckily for him he only ate one, that's why he recovered.'

'His name was Sammy Belter, I remember him well,' Johnny replied, and grimaced. 'The poor lad was horribly sick.'

'Didn't Amos say Masters ate pods and seeds, all sorts of strange roots and such?' Edward now asked Neville.

His cousin nodded. 'He did indeed, and perhaps Aubrey Masters ate something that killed him. On the other hand, he could have had a stroke or a heart attack. Look, we're just speculating right now. A waste of time. We'll know soon enough what he died from. What else did Summers have to say?' he asked, changing the subject swiftly.

'That he was going to be with Mildred Masters until her sister arrived from Gloucestershire, that the body had been taken for an autopsy. He also told Oliveri to have Aspen work on Masters's various tasks, under Oliveri's supervision.' Edward leaned back in the leather chair, and said with a wide smile, 'And he made a point of telling Oliveri that he should remain in London for the time being.'

'That's good to know!' Will exclaimed.

'Isn't it just,' Johnny cut in with a laugh.

'How long does it take to get the results of an autopsy, Neville?' Edward now asked quietly.

'Do you know, I've absolutely no idea,' Neville answered. 'A couple of days, perhaps? Unless one knows the pathologist involved. And in this instance we don't.'

'So what you're saying is we'll just have to wait,' Will interjected.

'That's right,' Neville replied, 'and how he died doesn't really matter to us, does it? In the meantime, I just want to say that I for one will not be sending any condolences to the grieving widow, if indeed she is grieving. Finnister led me to believe there was an estrangement in that marriage.'

'And I won't be offering any sympathetic words either,' Edward announced in a sharp voice. 'In view of the fact that we never received any condolences when our fathers and brothers were murdered in Carrara, Neville.'

'Now, gentlemen, shall we repair to my club for a few drinks before dinner?' Neville suggested. 'I think it might be rather nice to raise a glass to each other, under the circumstances.' Neville shook his head, then remarked, 'It's a pity Oliveri's not here.'

'It is rather, I agree,' Edward murmured. 'But his mother is in hospital and he wanted to go and visit her. However, we can toast him, can't we? After all, it looks as if he might well inherit Masters's job.'

'Indeed he might,' Will agreed. 'Let's face it, this sudden death might very well play in our favour.'

At seven o'clock that same evening, Edward arrived at Lily's house in Belsize Park Gardens. As he alighted from Neville's carriage he said to Will and Johnny, 'Enjoy your dinner, and come back around ten o'clock, please. Is that all right, chaps?'

Johnny grinned at his cousin, and saluted. 'Yours to command, sire.'

Edward laughed as he went up the steps to the front door. It was Lily who answered his knock, not the housekeeper, and she opened the door wider, her smile radiant. 'I'm so glad you were able to come tonight, Ned. I must admit, I've missed you.'

As the door closed behind them he took off his overcoat, chuckled and shot back, 'I saw you on Saturday afternoon for tea, at Vicky's for goodness sake!'

'But we weren't alone,' she reminded him in a low voice; slipping her arm through his she led him into the drawing room. 'Would you like to have a whisky?'

Ned shook his head. 'No, thanks anyway. I had several at Neville's club earlier.'

As usual he went and stood in front of the fire with his back to it, looking across at her. She had seated herself on the sofa, and he couldn't help thinking how lovely she looked in the pale blue silk gown with pearls on her neck and ears. He wished he had money so that he could buy her a gift.

'You're looking rather pensive, darling. Is something wrong?'

'No, Lily, nothing's wrong now that I'm here with you. I was just looking at you and thinking how beautiful you are, and wishing I had some money so that I could buy you diamonds and emeralds, cover you in jewels.'

Shaking her head, giving him an indulgent look, Lily laughed. 'Don't be so silly, you don't have to buy me anything! I have everything I could possibly want.' She patted the sofa and said, 'Come and sit down, tell me about your day.'

He did as she asked and seated himself on the loveseat, gazing at her intently. 'You look like a rose in full bloom, Lily, your skin is perfect, your eyes are sparkling . . . simply ravishing, that you are. But a little different somehow.' Leaning forward, he kissed her on the cheek, and sat back. 'Well, you asked about my day, and I can only say that it's been a bit hectic. Aubrey Masters died last night, very suddenly.'

'Oh my goodness!' Lily's eyes narrowed, and she went on swiftly, 'Wasn't he the head of the Mining Division? The one you had the huge argument with about your father's office?'

'He was indeed.'

'Was he ill?'

'Oh no – well, as far as we know he wasn't. John Summers told us that Masters had chest pains last night, and that by the time the doctor arrived he was gone.'

'Masters wasn't very nice to you . . .' Lily slowly shook her head. 'My mother always said God doesn't pay his debts in money,' she added pithily.

Before Edward could respond, there was a light knock on the door and Mrs Dane poked her head around it. 'Dinner's ready, madame,' the housekeeper said, and added, 'Good evening, sir.'

'Evening, Mrs Dane,' Edward responded, smiling, and stood up, offered his hand to Lily, brought her to her feet.

As they went across the hall to the dining room, Lily murmured, 'I asked Mrs Dane to make some of your favourite things – roast leg of lamb and roast potatoes, and I had Fortnum and Mason deliver their best Scotch salmon and Russian caviare, Beluga actually, I –'

'Lily, I'm afraid you're spoiling me!' he cut in, put his arm around her shoulders as they walked into the room together, smiling down at her.

After supper they retreated to the drawing room, and for a few minutes Lily fussed with pouring Edward a cup of coffee and then a balloon of Napoleon brandy. As she was doing so she said in a casual almost offhand way, 'I'm thinking of buying a house in Kent, it's not far from Stonehurst Farm and is rather charming. Fortunately, it's in good condition, not a wreck like Vicky's farm was when she bought it.'

Edward looked at her, his eyebrows drawing together in a jagged line. 'That's always a blessing, not having to engage in remodelling and such. But Lily, why on earth do you want to have a house in Kent? I never realized you had a partiality to the country. Or that you would ever contemplate living there.'

Lily realized at once that he was genuinely puzzled, and she replied quickly, 'Oh, I do enjoy being out of town for part of the time, Ned, as long as there are friends nearby. However, I have another reason for buying the house.' She cleared her throat, sat down on the small sofa, and continued, 'There's something I want to tell you, but please, I don't want you to be upset. I'll take care of everything, you won't have to do a thing, I promise you.'

Frowning again, Edward asked in a puzzled voice, 'Lily, what *are* you talking about?'

'I'm pregnant, Ned,' she announced calmly in a strong, steady voice. 'I'm expecting your baby – our baby.'

He gaped at her in astonishment, and instantly experienced an extraordinary rush of emotion, a sudden sense of happiness. A huge smile spread itself across his face. 'Lily, darling! We're having a baby! And that's what is different about you.' He grinned from ear to ear. 'You've put on weight, not a lot, but you are definitely a little plumper. Not that I mind, it's rather charming.'

Rising, he went to sit next to her on the loveseat, encircled her in his arms and kissed her on the cheek in the most loving manner. '*A baby*. Well, fancy that, we're having a baby.'

'You're not angry with me, are you?' A look of worry crossed her eyes.

'How could I possibly be angry with you of all people?' Drawing away, gazing deeply into her face, he murmured, 'I'm just as responsible as you are for making this child, and I will always feel and *be* responsible for him, or her.'

'You don't have to be, I mean in a financial way,' Lily assured him. 'And I do understand you can't possibly marry me, I'm much too old for you. You will have to make an important marriage one day, you know. But, of course, it would make me happy if you could see our child, spend time with us, visit us.' A gentle smile flitted across her face. 'You must understand I'll never make any demands on you, Ned. Never ever.'

There was an odd expression on his face, and he took her hand, brought it to his lips, kissed it, and held it between his own. 'You're the most extraordinary woman I've ever met. You are very special to me, my darling Lily.'

TWENTY-SIX

'I'm certainly glad you've recovered from that nasty little attack upon your person, Mr Deravenel,' Inspector Laidlaw said in his hearty voice, shaking Edward's hand with a firm grip. 'I'm afraid we came to a dead end on that, sir, no suspects, as you know. Mind you, we've not closed the case. It remains open.'

'I'm perfectly certain you'll never be able to pin it on anyone, Inspector Laidlaw,' Edward replied and chuckled. 'Those boyos were long gone that very night, wouldn't you say?'

'I would indeed.'

'Now, Inspector Laidlaw, I would like you to meet my colleagues, Alfredo Oliveri and Robert Aspen. They both worked rather closely with Aubrey Masters, for a number of years. They'll be happy to answer any questions you have, as will I.'

'Pleased to meet you, gentlemen,' Inspector Laidlaw said, shaking Alfredo's hand and then Rob's. 'I do have a few things I would like to discuss with you both, and Mr Deravenel.'

The four men were standing in the middle of Edward's

office at Deravenels, and he now said, 'I think we might be more comfortable over there near the window where we can all sit down.' As he spoke he walked across the room and seated himself on the sofa; the other three men followed and each took an armchair arranged in a grouping close to the big leather sofa.

'By the way, Inspector, do you have the results of the autopsy yet?'

'Yes, I do, Mr Deravenel. Mr Masters died from the ingestion of digitalis.'

'Isn't that a heart medicine?' Rob Aspen asked in surprise, looking at the Inspector. 'I didn't think one could die from it. My mother has a heart problem and the doctor prescribed digitalis last year.'

In his late thirties, Rob Aspen was a pleasant-looking man who appeared much younger than his years and wore his clothes with a bit of a dash. Women found him attractive, wanted to mother him, but so far he had eluded all of them and was still single.

'It is indeed a heart medicine, Mr Aspen,' the Inspector answered. 'And that was one of the things I wanted to talk to you all about. Did Mr Masters suffer from a heart condition, do you know?'

'I don't think so,' Alfredo answered, 'but then Aspen would know better than I, because he works here in London all the time. I go back and forth to Italy, to Carrara, to be exact.'

Rob exclaimed, 'I'm pretty certain he was in the best of health. He appeared to be, at any rate. On the other hand, how can I be sure? We were business colleagues not close friends, and he did not confide in me. Surely Mrs Masters would know about his health?'

The Inspector nodded, leaned back in the armchair, a reflective look on his face. After a moment's considered thought, he continued slowly, 'Mrs Masters insists that her husband did *not* have a heart condition, and therefore was not taking digitalis. She was most definite about this. I've also spoken to his physician, Dr Fortescue, and went to see him at his surgery. In fact, we had a long chat. The doctor cannot explain the reason Mr Masters took digitalis. He, too, is most baffled. Certainly he did not prescribe it, because Mr Masters did not have a heart condition. The doctor was most firm about that.'

'Could there be another doctor involved, Inspector Laidlaw?' Edward asked, giving the policeman a hard stare. 'Perhaps Aubrey Masters wanted a *second* opinion, if he thought he had a health problem, and certainly he wouldn't have wanted to offend Dr Fortescue. Or perhaps he didn't want his wife to know he had developed a heart condition, and *secretly* went to see another physician or specialist.'

'Or any kind of condition,' Rob volunteered.

'What are you suggesting, Mr Aspen?' the Inspector asked, his eyes on the other man.

'It's something I've just remembered –' Rob left his sentence unfinished, shaking his head. 'No, no, it's a long shot, I'm sure there's nothing to it.'

'To what?' the inspector asked.

'A remark Masters made to me about six months ago. I thought it was an odd comment, and quite out of character, not at all like him. Out of the blue one day, he muttered that life was so much easier for women, that all they had to do was lie down, whereas men had to stand to attention.' Rob shook his head. 'I was being something of a dunce that afternoon, I suppose, because I didn't get the innuendo at first, not until he chuckled and winked at me. Frankly, I was astonished. I realized he was making a reference to his . . . sexuality, or perhaps I should say lack of it. About a week later I took some papers to his office, but he was out. I placed the files on his desk and it was then I noticed a writing pad on which he had drawn a number of hearts in red pencil, doodles really, and just below the hearts was the name Dr Alvin Springer. I thought nothing about it at the time, it just came back to me now.'

'I will have that name checked out, Mr Aspen. Thank you very much indeed,' Inspector Laidlaw said. 'There's a possibility that Dr Springer *is* a heart specialist, in view of those scribbles.'

'It might be a clue, yes,' Rob responded. 'On the other hand, the doctor could be one who specializes in sex therapy. There are a few now practising in London, I hear from a friend of mine, who suffers from . . . well, er, shall we say a certain inadequacy. He has also been going to a psychiatrist, and, in fact, Dr Springer might well be a doctor who treats problems.'

Edward, who had been swallowing sudden and unexpected laughter, now glanced at Inspector Laidlaw. Immediately he saw the laughter in the policeman's eyes, although his expression was one of total solemnity.

Rising, Edward walked over to his desk, trying to turn his spluttering laughter into coughing. A moment later, fully in control he said, 'Do excuse me, I'm so sorry.'

314

The Inspector looked across at him, obviously suppressing *his* laughter, and said, 'Do you need a glass of water, sir?'

Edward walked back to the sofa, shaking his head. 'No, no, thank you, I'm fine.'

Laidlaw now said, 'Mr Aspen, you've been very helpful, and I will personally speak to Dr Springer.' Clearing his throat several times, he then went on, 'I don't suppose any of you would know if there was – well, another woman in his life?'

Edward thought he would burst into laughter at the preposterousness of this idea, but he managed to control himself, as did Oliveri and Aspen. Both of them looked as amused as he was; they simply shook their heads, as did Edward, and kept their faces straight.

After a moment, Edward turned to the Inspector. 'If Aubrey Masters *did* have a heart condition, and had been prescribed digitalis, which is a heart medicine, then why on earth did he die because he took it?'

'It was an overdose, Mr Deravenel. I'm sorry if I didn't make that clear at the outset of this conversation. Accidental or on purpose, we don't know yet. And this leads me to another point, and that is Mr Masters's demeanour. How was he in the last few weeks? Sad? Despondent about anything? Did he appear worried? Or did he perhaps behave differently in some way?' He looked at Alfredo in particular.

'He was totally normal, Inspector,' Alfredo announced in a firm and positive voice. 'Actually, he was in an especially good mood on Monday, although in a bit of a hurry to get away from the meeting we were having. He explained he didn't want to be late for an appointment out of the office. The following day, Tuesday, we bumped into each other in the corridor here, and he was very cordial. But I must admit, he did appear to be preoccupied. That's all I can tell you.'

'He was *very* preoccupied, Inspector,' Rob volunteered. 'And I agree with Oliveri in that I myself thought he was in a good humour on Monday, and certainly normal in everything he did.'

Inspector Laidlaw nodded. 'It's probably all very simple really. No doubt he did have a heart condition he was hiding from his wife and everyone here at his place of work. He must have gone to Dr Springer for that reason, who put him on digitalis. The other night he more than likely misjudged the dose, took too much.'

'Is there going to be an inquest?' Edward asked.

'Oh yes, of course, sir. It will be held next week according to the coroner.' Standing up, Inspector Laidlaw thanked them for their cooperation. 'I'll be in touch with you, gentlemen, as soon as I have more information.'

Edward left his office with the Inspector and escorted him down the corridor in the direction of the grand staircase. As they walked along side by side, Edward said, at one moment, in a low voice, 'There is the possibility he committed suicide, isn't there?'

'Yes, indeed, Mr Deravenel.'

'I didn't know Aubrey Masters well, but he didn't strike me as the kind of man who would misjudge the amount of medication he should take. He was rather precise,' Edward confided in the same quiet voice. 'And yet he did take an overdose, didn't he?'

The policeman nodded, and murmured in an equally

low tone, 'If you have any more thoughts or information to pass on, you can reach me at Scotland Yard, Mr Deravenel.'

When Edward walked back into his office a few minutes later, Alfredo and Rob were laughing hilariously.

'What's the joke?' he asked, and then began to laugh himself. When he finally sobered, Edward said, 'Honestly, Aspen, I thought I was going to explode. There you were, mincing your words, trying to be careful around the Inspector, being ever so discreet. You could have just come out with it and said Masters couldn't get an erection. The Inspector was striving to suppress his own laughter. I saw that immediately.'

Alfredo pulled out his handkerchief and wiped his eyes. 'You sounded like your own maiden aunt, Aspen.'

'I know,' Rob admitted, looking chagrined. 'It was foolish of me, but I was simply trying to say what I had to say without being – bloody vulgar.'

'Inspector Laidlaw's one of the boys, a good sport, I can tell you that,' Edward remarked, grinning again. 'I think he would have appreciated a good laugh, in fact.'

Alfredo walked over to the window and looked down into the Strand for a moment, then swung his head and said to Edward, 'I think Masters might have committed suicide, because of the *skimming*. You and I both think he might be involved in that, and so does Aspen, by the way.'

Rob, who was leaning against the desk nonchalantly,

nodded his head. 'It's bound to come to light in the next few months – unless there's a real cover-up, unless they make it go away. It'll be miraculous if they do.'

'You're correct in that,' Ned answered, and went and sat down behind his desk. 'I told Inspector Laidlaw that I'll be in touch if anything comes to mind, so put your thinking caps on, my lads, and think hard. I'd like to help Laidlaw, if I can. He's a nice chap.'

Alfredo said, 'I couldn't believe it when the Inspector asked if Masters had another woman. Can you imagine that – Aubrey Masters and a lady of the night.'

'Please don't,' Ned muttered, grimacing. 'It's certainly not something I want to think about, I can tell you that. Masters was rather a strange duck in my opinion, and also quite ghastly, actually.'

Rob chuckled. 'You're right, and it's certainly hard to envision him as a ladies' man, even when the lady isn't a lady. Think of that.'

'God forbid!' Ned exclaimed.

TWENTY-SEVEN

He paused, his hand on the knob of the library door, listening acutely, wondering if he had been mistaken. No, he had not. He *could* hear someone sobbing, but he hesitated for a moment before entering. He was not sure who was in there but whoever it was sounded extremely upset.

Quietly, Edward opened the door and looked into the long, elegant room. In the dim light the dark green walls looked even darker at this early hour. Nevertheless, he saw his sister at once. Meg was bent over the mahogany reading table, her head down on her arms, weeping as if her heart would break.

He experienced a swift rush of love and concern for the fifteen-year-old girl, and went into the room, closing the door softly behind him.

Although he was tall and well built, Edward moved lightly and with grace; he was halfway across the floor on silent feet before Meg lifted her head and saw him.

Instantly, she jumped up and flew across the room, threw herself against his body. His arms went around her; he held her tightly, close to him, protectively.

Quietly, in a low, loving voice he attempted to soothe her, stroked her hair. Like many large men, Edward Deravenel was gentle, tender, and especially so with women and his younger siblings.

Within a few minutes her heaving abated, slowed to a few gasps, and bending over her, he lifted her chin and looked into her eyes. 'Too many tears for such a beautiful girl as you, Meg. Now, what's this all about, my love? Why were you crying so hard?'

'I don't know,' she began, her voice faltering, and shook her head. 'I'm worried, I suppose –' She broke off, compressed her lips and the tears welled again, fell down her cheeks unchecked.

'And perhaps a little frightened, I suspect.' Leaning into her, Edward wiped the tears from her face with his fingertips, kissed her forehead. Then he pulled a handkerchief out of his jacket pocket, and offering it to her, he told her, 'Come along, blow your nose, and let's go and sit over there and have a little chat.'

She nodded, took his handkerchief, did as he asked, and walked back to the circular reading table. Edward followed her, glancing around the room, thinking how peaceful and quiet it was on this sunny Saturday morning.

The walls were covered in a dark-green damask fabric, this colour offset by the white painted woodwork, ceiling mouldings, the door, the white marble fireplace, and the line of white-painted bookcases. These were filled with hundreds of volumes collected by his forebears. With its dark-green silk draperies, red leather chairs, Oriental rugs and a Chesterfield sofa covered with paisley-patterned fabric, it was a masculine room, yet not oppressively so.

Edward pulled out a chair next to Meg, and sat down. 'Tell me what's troubling you, sweetheart. Perhaps I can help.'

'I suppose you were right when you said I was frightened, Ned. Such terrible things have happened lately . . . too many for one family to bear. Papa and Edmund murdered, Uncle Rick and Thomas as well, then the attack on you. You could have been killed, all those blows to your head.' A deep sigh rippled through her before she added, 'It's as if the Grants are trying to kill off all the men in our line, render us helpless by turning us into a family of women.'

Edward's blood ran cold as she said this, but nonetheless, he smiled at her and teased, 'You and Mother are my *Amazons*, my warrior queens. Neither of you is helpless, Meg. Just the opposite.' He said this in a mild tone, then when he noticed her frown he continued, 'I'm not trying to make light of what you're saying. A lot *has* happened, but remember bad things do happen to everyone at different times. Life is very hard, you know, and often comes back to hit one in the face. The most important thing is learning how to survive, to fight back, to hold one's own. That's what we must all do.'

'I know, I must be brave,' she murmured. 'I'll try.' She stared at her brother intently. 'I worry about George and Richard, and you, too, Ned, about your safety.'

'Listen to me, Meg darling. None of the Grants are going to destroy *me*. I'm going to get *them* first, don't you know?' He grinned at her, his bright blue eyes full of sparkle. 'As for George and Richard, the Grants wouldn't go after children.' As these words left his mouth he knew, with a sinking feeling, that they would if they had to in order to pursue their cause.

Wanting to calm her, he insisted, 'You're quite safe, Meg, you and the boys, here in this house with Mother and the staff. And *me*. Don't forget, *I* live here, too.'

'You go to work with them, and they could hurt you again.'

'Yes, I do work at Deravenels during the day, and I go out at night, but now I have two bodyguards . . . Will and Johnny. Anyway, I seriously doubt that the Grants will attempt anything in the very near future. They would be very foolish if they did.'

'I hope they won't. I love you, Ned, and so do George and Richard.' She smiled. 'He adores you, your Little Fish.'

'Yes, I know, and I feel the same about him, about all of you, and really, you mustn't worry about the Grants.'

'When will they stop hurting us?'

'Soon.'

'How do you know?'

'We'll make them stop. Neville and I will put an end to them.'

'Why have they been doing bad things to us?'

'It's a long story. Basically though for money and power. They stole those things from us, from our line of the family, sixty years ago, and they are desperately trying to hang onto that power. But they *are* going to lose it, and lose it to us. We are going to reclaim what is ours by rights.'

The fifteen-year-old looked at him, her eyes shining. 'Do you promise me, Ned?'

'I do indeed promise you, Margaret, and I want you to put these worries about the Grants out of your head. *You* must promise *me* that.'

'I do promise.' Leaning back in the chair, she murmured in a quavering voice, 'I miss Papa and Edmund.'

'So do I, and I truly understand your pain, your grief, Meg. I want to tell you something.' Ned leaned closer, said sotto voce, 'I carry them in my heart. Always. And you must do that, too. It helps to hold onto them and the memories of being with them, of having them in our lives.'

Slowly she nodded her head. 'I will do that. And I know I'll never forget them.' She reached out, took his hand in hers, clung to it.

'*I* promise I will always protect *you*,' Ned reassured her.

'And I will stand by you,' she responded, meaning this. And she was to prove her loyalty some years later, and it was a loyalty that never wavered.

'We're going to be fine, the entire family is going to be all right. Trust me, the Grants will fall into oblivion.'

'*When*?'

'I told you, *soon*. However, I see you want me to be more specific. Neville thinks we'll oust them in a few months. By the summer, he says, I'll be running Deravenels. Now, Meg, tell me about your days here. Are you enjoying being in London?'

'I prefer Ravenscar. I wish we were there now.'

'Well, we're going there for Easter, how about that, my girl?'

'Did Mama tell you this?'

'No, she didn't. I just decided it now, on the spur of the moment. So it's *our* secret, for the time being. Now, tell me about Perdita Willis . . . do you like her as much as you did last year?'

'Yes, I do. More, really. She loves botany as much as I do and she's teaching me such a lot of new, interesting things. I was studying a special book before I became sad and started to cry. I want you to look at it, you'll see how lovely the illustrations are.' She pulled the large book towards her, and confided, 'I found this in the library at Ravenscar, and I was fascinated by it. So is Richard. He keeps saying that it's his, that it belongs to him.'

'Why is that?' Edward asked, looking somewhat amused at the idea of his Little Fish asserting himself.

'Because it does have his name on it.' Opening the book, she showed Ned the name inscribed on the faded bookplate on one of the front end papers. In beautiful copperplate it announced: *Richard Deravenel: His Book*.

Looking down at the page Meg was showing him, Edward realized at once how old the book was. Very early Victorian, he thought. It was undoubtedly a gem. At that moment Edward remembered the story of the boy who died, and he exclaimed, 'There *was* another Richard Deravenel, other than Father, many years ago. And that is his name on the bookplate, I feel sure. He died when he was about your age, Meg, of typhoid fever, I think. His full name was Richard Marmaduke

Deravenel. This *did* belong to him, there's no doubt in my mind. It must have been his.'

Edward turned the page and looked at the front. 'What an odd title,' he exclaimed. '*Fatal Flowers* . . . how very weird.' He glanced at his sister a little quizzically.

'It's about flowers that are deadly, so poisonous they can kill. There are lots of them, Ned, growing in everybody's gardens. But please do look at the pictures, they're so lovely.'

'More than lovely, Meg,' Ned remarked as he turned the leaves of the book. 'These watercolours are simply superb, of the highest quality indeed.'

Edward stared at the two pages now open in front of him. He stiffened. There was a painting of the tall and elegant foxglove on the left, and on the right the name of the flower in bold letters:

THE FOXGLOVE (DIGITALIS)

He read the heading again, hardly able to believe his eyes. *Digitalis*, he read once more, and then dropped his eyes to the details of the flower written below. Startled and excited, Edward's eyes widened as he read:

The common foxglove grows in almost every Victorian garden. It is a flower beloved by all. Tall and graceful, it has many other names such as fairy thimbles, fairy gloves, fairy bells, and dead man's thimbles, because its flowers do resemble the fingers of 'fairy gloves'. The curious names originated here in the British Isles where our ancient people believed that the small spots on the bell of the flower were the fingerprints of fairies, hence the name 'folks gloves', meaning the gloves of the little folks. The elegant and colourful foxglove is often referred to as 'dead man's thimbles' because of its shape and the poison it contains. The Latin genus, *Digitalis*, refers to finger or thimble. This beautiful natural ornament for the Victorian garden, so graceful, so tall, is fatal if eaten.

Oh, my God. Edward sat there motionless, frozen in the chair, continuing to stare down at the book, unwilling to lift his head at this moment. He knew that Meg was anxious for his opinion of the book, wanted to talk about it with him. Whereas he wanted to think. Was that how Aubrey Masters had died? Had he eaten foxgloves? Had they been ingested with his vegetarian dinner? An accident? Suicide? Murder? Which was it?

His brain raced. If Masters had been murdered, then who had done it? And how had the perpetrator managed to put foxgloves in his food?

'Ned, Ned,' Meg exclaimed, 'what is it? Why are you so interested in the foxglove in particular?'

Finally he lifted his head and forced a smile. 'Because it's so strange, isn't it, that a thing of such beauty is so deadly. Now I understand the title of the book.'

Will Hasling was waiting for Edward in the library of White's, the gentleman's private club in Whitehall where he and his father were members. Arguably the most famous club in London, many believed it was the first to open its doors, that it had begun as a chocolate house in 1693, and that Pope and Swift were among its regulars. Certainly it was a male bastion where members could go to eat, drink, smoke, gamble, play billiards and read. Women were barred. None of them really wanted to go anyway, preferring the men in their lives to have places where they could be left to their own devices.

Whilst waiting for his friend, Will had been perusing *The Times*, but he had now read enough, and took it back to the table where the newspapers were always placed after use.

As he swung around to return to his chair Edward came rushing into the room, but slowed his steps when he noticed a couple of older members present. Usually the club was deserted on weekends with everyone in the country.

'So sorry I'm late,' Edward said, clasping Will's arm.

'No problem, but shall we go in for lunch? I'm positively ravenous.'

'Let's do that.'

The two young men left the library, crossed the grand entrance foyer with its marble floor and dark mahogany furniture and went into the dining room.

After they were seated and had each ordered a glass of champagne, Will looked at Edward, said, 'This is a nice surprise. I didn't expect to see you today, especially since we're invited to have lunch with Neville and Nan tomorrow.'

'I know, but apart from us and Johnny, there'll be Nan and their girls, my mother and my siblings. It's going to be a family Sunday lunch with all the trimmings, and frankly I don't think we'll have a chance to speak privately.'

'So what's on your mind, Ned? Is something troubling you?'

'I wouldn't say troubling, more like tantalizing.'

'I'm not sure what you mean by that?'

'Did your mother have foxgloves growing in her garden when you were a child?'

'Yes she did, and there are still foxgloves growing at Compton Hall.' Will appeared puzzled when he asked, 'But what are you getting at?'

'She was growing *Digitalis*, and it is still growing in the flower gardens.'

Totally nonplussed, Will shook his head. 'Come on, Ned, you're not talking sense.'

Swiftly, with precision, Ned told him all about the book from Ravenscar, and what he had discovered that morning about the common foxglove.

'Foxglove leaves and seeds are very poisonous indeed, and I think that somehow they got into Aubrey Masters' food. Because nobody really believes he has a heart condition, now do they?'

'No, they don't,' Will answered and paused as the waiter arrived with their flutes of champagne. Once alone, touching his glass to Edward's, Will murmured, 'Cheers.'

Edward went on quickly, 'I telephoned Neville this morning to discuss the matter with him but he had gone to the country for the day with Nan. So I'll mention it tomorrow before lunch, if that's at all possible.'

There was a moment of silence, and the two men exchanged looks.

At last Will asked, 'Do you think that perhaps our side has something to do with that digitalis in Masters' food? If indeed there was some there?'

'I don't know. Anyway, how could they have?'

'God knows,' Will muttered, shaking his head.

Late that afternoon when he arrived home at the Charles Street house, Edward went in search of his mother. He found her in his father's den, working at the desk, and she glanced up as he opened the door and went inside.

'Oh hello, darling,' she said, smiling at her eldest son. 'Nice lunch with Will?'

'Yes, very pleasant, thanks. Is this an inconvenient time to drop in on you, Mother, or do you have a few minutes to spare? You do seem to be rather busy with your accounts.'

'No, they can wait, and I was hoping to have a chat with you anyway, Ned.'

'About something special?' he asked as he walked over and sat down in a chair near the desk.

'No, just things in general, nothing specific. And what about you?'

For a moment his eyes rested on the pile of bills on the desk. After a moment, he said, 'Why did Father never have any money? After all, he was in a good position at Deravenels – assistant managing director. He must have had a decent salary.'

'Not really. Naturally he had a salary, Ned, but it was not very much, of that I can assure you.'

'And what about his father and grandfather? Didn't they leave him any money?'

'They, too, were on low salaries, and the Grants cheated them of their bonuses most of the time, just as they cheated your father later on. There *was* a small annuity from his father, and now that comes to me. Somehow your father always managed to pay for the upkeep and repairs at Ravenscar, but not the staff, I'm afraid.'

'You pay their wages, I know that, Mother, and you maintain this house. I understand all that.' Edward shook his head. 'So unfair, isn't it? The Grants have stolen from us for donkey's years. Stolen our money, but fortunately not our spirit and our pride.'

'True. And it's over sixty years now, to be precise,' she replied in a pithy tone.

'I aim to rectify that,' he exclaimed. 'I vow to you.'

'I hope you will, not out of any avarice on my part, but because Deravenels *does* belong to the Yorkshire branch of the family, and it always has. I think it's about time there was a little justice and fair play.'

'Neville and I will bring it about, Mother, never fear.'

Cecily leaned back in the large desk chair and looked at her son speculatively for a moment, and then she said, 'I've been thinking about money myself. I want to buy a house for you in London, in Mayfair, close to here, and I was wondering how to do it. Actually, I was going to discuss it with Neville.'

'But Mother –'

'No buts, Edward. You're a grown man, you have your own private life now, and I think it's about time you had your own household, your own establishment. Don't you agree?'

'Well, yes, I do in a way. Will has mentioned it several times, and today at lunch he told me that a "set" has come up at the Albany. He wondered if I would be interested.'

Cecily shook her head. 'Those sets of rooms at the Albany wouldn't be correct for you, not big enough, really. No, I think a house in Mayfair is much more appropriate under the circumstances.'

'But that would be costly, I wouldn't want you to dip into your inheritance –'

'Sssh!' She held up her hand. 'I had an idea about how to finance the house the other day.' Rising, she walked around the desk and continued, 'Come with me, Ned. I want to show you something.'

It was gloomy in the cellar, especially when his mother hurried to the far end near the wine racks. All of a sudden, Ned realized she was heading in the direction of the vault, and he called out, 'This electric light isn't very bright. Shall I go and ask Swinton for a few candles?'

'It's not necessary, there are some here, near the vault, and a box of Swan Vestas.'

When he caught up with his mother, she was already lighting the candles, explaining, 'I want you to open the vault, Ned, the handle is a little stiff for me. Now, let me tell you the numbers.'

Within seconds the heavy door of the large vault swung open, and Cecily stepped closer to Edward and pointed to the two dark green leather boxes, and another large one made of dark blue leather. Along with these there was a smaller fourth box, and this was a faded red.

'Let's carry these upstairs, where the light is much better. I'll take the red and blue boxes, they're lighter, Ned.'

'Heavens, the green *are* heavier than I thought!' Ned went along the cellar, following his mother, saying, 'If these are what I think they are, they must be purgatory.'

Cecily laughed, but made no comment and climbed up the stairs to the entrance hall. 'I think we should go into the drawing room, the light is better there,' she pointed out, and led the way. Placing the two leather boxes on a chair, she indicated the sofa to Ned. 'Put those boxes over there. Now, darling, open them please.'

He did as she asked, and gasped when he took out the first tiara. 'Good Lord, Mother, this is extraordinary!' he cried, holding the tiara between his hands, turning it slowly, watching the light strike the diamonds, hundreds of them, catching the rainbow colours. 'Wow, Mother, this is – *something special.*'

'Unique,' she murmured. 'It belonged to my mother.'

Ned put it back in the box, and took out the second tiara. Again, he exclaimed about its beauty. 'And whose was this?'

'Mine,' she answered. 'My father bought it for me after my marriage, and this third tiara was left to me by Mother's best friend, Clarissa Mayes. She had no children and bequeathed it to me, along with this diamond necklace.' As she had been speaking, Cecily had shown him the tiara and necklace, and he seemed a little stunned.

'Mother,' he said at last, 'there's a small fortune here!'

'I know. I've been hoarding all of these diamonds for a rainy day, and now I shall sell them, and buy you a house. What money's left over will pay for your staff.'

'Oh, Mother, it's such a shame to sell these things, why they're family heirlooms. And what of Meg? She will need a tiara one day, after her marriage.'

'*You* shall buy her a tiara, Ned, when the time comes. These are going to be sold so you can have your own establishment.' Her voice brooked no argument.

TWENTY-EIGHT

Edward stood on the threshold of the conservatory in Neville's Chelsea house, watching his brothers play with their cousins, Isabel and Anne.

The two little girls looked charming in their deep-blue woollen dresses, each with a large white satin bow on top of their heads. His brothers were as smartly turned out, in their knee breeches and jackets, black stockings and highly-polished black shoes.

Surrounded by all the plants, and with sunshine pouring in through the many windows, it was an idyllic scene and brought a smile to Edward's face. George seemed to be holding forth about something animatedly, and certainly he had captured Isabel's complete attention. Anne was talking earnestly to Richard, who was nodding his head and looking amused. He felt a little twist in his heart . . . they were so young, so vulnerable.

At the sound of footsteps in the hall, Edward swung around, and smiled at Neville as he approached.

He joined Ned in the doorway, put his hand on his cousin's shoulder, and together they stood watching the children. After a moment, Neville said softly, 'The future,

Ned . . . they are the future of our two families, which are as one, and they must be protected at all cost.'

'I agree, you're quite correct,' Ned answered quietly. 'We must guard them at all times. The Grants will stop at nothing.'

'Unfortunately, you're right . . . I'm sorry I had to leave you to take the telephone call, and just as you were arriving.' Neville glanced around. 'I suppose Cecily and Meg have gone off somewhere with Nan.'

Ned nodded. 'They're in the drawing room.'

'Right. Well, shall we meander along to the library and have a glass of champagne before lunch? Will and Johnny are already there, waiting for us.'

'Why not?'

The two men walked down the entrance hall, but just before they reached the library Edward paused, took hold of Neville's arm, so that he, too, stood still.

'Yes, Ned, what is it?' he asked.

'I need a word with you. Privately.'

'Then tell me now, whilst we are alone here. Are you worried about something?'

'No, no, just curious. About the digitalis. We know Aubrey Masters died of an overdose, but I believe it was in the food. . . his vegetarian dinner, to be precise.'

'Oh. *Really.*'

'Yes. Let me tell you about a book called *Fatal Flowers.*' Swiftly, Edward told Neville of his discovery the day before, and the conclusion he had come to almost at once about the use of foxglove in the vegetarian mix.

'I see what you mean,' Neville replied, nodding. 'But you said you were curious . . . about what exactly?'

'Did *we* have anything to do with Masters's ingestion of digitalis?'

Neville did not respond. He simply stood there, tall, elegant and serene, staring at Ned, his light blue eyes calm, his face without any expression and steady.

Ned, leaning against a pillar, was equally steady. He waited.

After the longest moment, Neville answered. 'I did promise you we would avenge the murders of our fathers and brothers. I never break a promise, Cousin.'

Ned nodded his understanding, his own face wiped clean of all emotion, his eyes locked to his cousin's with intensity. And then he reached out, took hold of Neville's hand and said in a low voice, '*Fidelity unto eternity,*' repeating his family's motto.

Cecily Deravenel was enjoying the luncheon party at her nephew's home in Chelsea. A lovely, flowing house overlooking the Thames, it was beautifully furnished in perfect taste, made a charming setting for this Sunday lunch. And because they were family it was all the more pleasing to her. As for Will Hasling, she always thought of him as family, as another son, having known him for years, and certainly his devotion and loyalty to Edward had forever touched her heart. Yes, he *was* family, no question about that.

Her eyes roamed around the table, rested for a moment on her nephew, Johnny. Dearest Johnny, so fine of character, a man of integrity and honour, Ned's champion. Her glance settled on Neville. How alike the two brothers were in appearance, and certainly they had the Watkins physical characteristics just as she did: dark hair, light eyes, the finest bone structure.

Neville was now the only senior male in the family, and it was on him that she must rely in many ways. Her brother Rick had managed her affairs but now that he was dead it would be his son who would advise her on these matters. Only last week she had told him Ned needed an allowance. He had agreed. She trusted Neville, she had no reason not to do so. He was, after all, her nephew, the richest magnate in England, a powerful man. That was the secret to him, of course, his power. Or rather the secret was his *love* of power. Only the other day she had pointed this out to Ned, and he had smiled and retorted, 'Do you think I don't know that?'

They had laughed together then, and the matter was closed. She knew what her son was all about, was well aware that he had great judgement and a wisdom beyond his years. With Neville by his side, Ned would succeed in taking over Deravenels, it was just a question of time. From what Ned had said recently perhaps it would be sooner than she had anticipated. There was nothing she could do except wait. She wanted their circumstances to change, wanted to know that her children were safe, out of the reaches of the treacherous Grants.

Cecily smiled as her eyes settled on Anne, Neville's youngest daughter. She was an exquisite child, delicate in her beauty, intelligent, like quicksilver. How adoring Anne was of Richard; she trailed after him like a devoted puppy dog. Richard did not seem to mind her attention, was responsive to her and very protective.

Anne was seated opposite Cecily, and as if she had read her aunt's thoughts, she announced in her light, clear voice, 'Richard and I are going to be married, Aunt Cecily.'

Everyone at the table looked at Anne in surprise, and with some amusement. There was a trickle of warm laughter from the adults.

Richard said, 'But not for a long time, Mama. Not until we're grown up.'

'But of course, Dick, we do understand that,' Cecily murmured, smiling at her youngest child.

Ned said, 'Well done, my boy. It's a good idea to stake your claim on a lady early. Just promise me one thing.'

'What is that?' Richard asked solemnly, his grey-blue eyes so serious.

'Promise that I can be your best man.'

Richard beamed at his hero and nodded enthusiastically.

Not to be left out, George now asserted, in a very grand voice for a little boy, 'And I am going to marry Isabel.'

Isabel gazed at him, turned bright pink, said nothing. But she looked pleased if also somewhat startled.

'My goodness, all these sudden announcements,' Cecily responded, staring at George, then smiling at Isabel.

Isabel smiled back, continued to gaze at George through loving eyes, euphoria flooding her face. She looked at her mother shyly.

Neville remarked in a light amused tone, 'All these announcements indeed, Cecily! And yet no one has asked my permission.'

Ned threw back his head and roared with laughter. 'Nor my mother's, nor mine,' he spluttered, his spontaneous laughter infecting the rest of the table.

Richard looked slightly embarrassed, and threw an appealing glance at Edward.

His brother responded at once. 'When you're grown up, Dickie, you can ask Uncle Neville for Anne's hand in marriage. As for me, I give you my permission now.'

'What about *me*?' George demanded, never one to be outdone. 'Do you give me your permission, Ned? After all, I'm older than Richard, and Isabel is older than Anne.'

Yes, and she's the heiress to a vast fortune, Ned thought, if Nan doesn't give him a son. 'Of course you have my permission,' Ned responded at last, smiling at George. But he could not help thinking that his brother was showing some very dubious characteristics, avariciousness being one of them. He bears watching, Ned thought. He might spell trouble when he grows up.

The music washed over him in waves, lulling his senses; slowly he felt the tension easing out of his shoulders and finally he relaxed in the seat. What a blessed relief this was . . . letting go, escaping into this world of thrilling sounds . . . the music was like an enchantment, taking him to another world.

Edward was with Lily at the Bechstein Concert Hall in Wigmore Street, attending the Sunday night concert. He loved music as much as she did, and tonight was special. The featured piece was Rachmaninoff's Piano

Concerto No. 2 in C Minor, a concerto which was a favourite of theirs.

The second movement was coming to a close now, the crescendo engulfing him; he allowed himself to be engulfed, submerged himself in it gratefully. So many of the troubling thoughts running through his head fell away as he gave himself up to the music entirely.

Suddenly it was over. Everyone was on their feet, clapping and cheering. Lily leaned into him and whispered, 'Wasn't it thrilling, darling?'

'Stupendous,' he answered. 'Thank you for bringing me.'

Smiling at him with total adoration, she whispered, 'Who else but you? Now tell me that.' He just laughed. Protectively, he escorted her out of the concert hall and into the street where the carriage she had hired for the evening was waiting for them.

In order to shake off Johnny and Will, his bodyguards, wanting to be alone with Lily tonight, earlier in the day he had explained to his mother exactly where he was going, adding, 'And my friend has hired a carriage. I'll be perfectly safe, Mother.' After a moment's thought she had agreed with him, had excused herself and left the room. She returned a moment later, and had handed him ten guineas. 'But Mother –' he had begun, and she had waved his words away, explaining that he must now have an allowance every week, that it had been arranged with Neville. 'Take Mrs Overton to dinner after the concert, and be the gentleman you are, Ned.'

And so they were going to the Savoy Hotel for supper, and he was excited that for once he could take Lily somewhere elegant and pay for it himself.

Once they were settled in the carriage, he told her about lunch at Neville's that day, and she laughed delightedly when he recounted the story of Anne's announcement that she and Richard were going to marry. In fact, they laughed all the way to the Savoy Hotel in the Strand, chuckling over the antics of the children.

Heads turned as the two of them walked through the hotel lobby. They made a stunning couple, he so tall and handsome, she the most beautiful of women and elegantly dressed in a chic outfit of dark royal blue. After they had been seated in the dining room over-looking the Thames, Ned ordered a whisky for himself and lemonade for Lily.

When they had settled down, Ned asked, 'How are you feeling, darling Lily?'

'Healthy, Ned, thank you. Please don't worry so much about the baby. It's the morning sickness which is truly the worst, but otherwise I'm well. Really and truly.'

He smiled at her, touching her cheek with a fingertip. 'And that's how you look – absolutely well.'

As he savoured his whisky and soda, Edward told her about the tiaras his mother owned, and that she was going to send them to the jewellers to have them appraised and then sold. 'She insists on doing this, Lily, in order to finance the purchase of a house for me. In Mayfair. I understand she's already seen one in Berkeley Square, and thinks it's ideal for me. She wants me to have my own household.'

Lily nodded, smiling and was about to tell him she had seen one for herself nearby in South Audley Street, which she was contemplating buying. But she knew it would be inappropriate. The last thing she wanted was for him to think she was trying to cling, because of the baby she was expecting.

Ned said, 'You looked as if you were about to tell me something, Lily, but changed your mind. What was it?'

'Nothing,' she lied, and went on, 'Shall we look at the menu, I am a little hungry.'

He nodded and signalled to the waiter who was by their side in a split second. He gave them the menus, recommended various items and departed.

Lily said, 'I think I will have Dover sole: it's light.'

'So will I. And what would you like first?'

'Nothing really – well, perhaps a cup of bouillon soup. I find if I eat anything heavy at night I suffer from indigestion these days.'

He smiled, leaned into her, and whispered, 'You poor thing . . . I can't wait to see our child, hold her.'

'Oh you've decided on the sex, have you? A *girl*, eh?'

'Well, you know how much I love women,' he answered before he could stop himself; he could have bitten off his tongue and looked suddenly chagrined, shook his head, seemed somehow helpless.

Lily simply laughed, being a wise woman.

Edward said, 'What shall we call the baby? *Lily*?'

'I'd like to call her after *you*, so I prefer *Edwina*.'

'Edwina Lily, how about that?'

'And Edward, if it's a boy, is that all right with you, Ned?'

'Anything you want, my darling. I do adore you, you know.'

342

The waiter returned and took their order, and they sat back, happy at being together in this elegant restaurant, enjoying each other and sharing the evening, at ease in their relationship.

It was after their first course that Lily suddenly announced in a quiet, rather subdued voice, 'Ned, I want to ask you something. It's really important for me to discuss it with you, and I must have an answer from you tonight.'

Alarmed, he looked at her swiftly, and exclaimed, 'What is it, Lily? Is there something wrong? What on earth's the matter?'

'I'm not sure how to begin, because it's a morbid subject but I have been troubled . . .' She took a deep breath. 'Let me start again. As you know, I was an only child, and my parents are dead. I have no other family, only a few good friends, most particularly Vicky. And because I'm alone in this world I've worried about something quite a lot lately. Women do die in childbirth, you know. It's not unheard of, and I worry that I could die. And then what would happen to the baby? *Our baby.* So I want to know your thoughts on this, Ned. I couldn't bear it if the child were put up for adoption.'

Startled by her words, he was also appalled at the thought of Lily dying and their child being put up for adoption, lost to him forever. He didn't have to think twice before answering her immediately. 'You're not going to die, I promise you that. You're a healthy young woman, and you take good care of yourself. You'll both be fine. But if something ghastly did happen and you . . . died in childbirth, and the baby lived, you know I wouldn't permit our child to be adopted. Never,

Lily. Never. Please trust me on that. I promise you I would take the child, bring it up.'

'You'd do that alone? How would you handle it? What about other women? You'll get married one day. A wife might not be overjoyed at the thought of your illegitimate little girl or boy. Am I not right?'

'Yes, perhaps you are. But I believe my mother would happily raise the child, with the help of a nanny. And of course I would see the child all the time. Does that satisfy you?'

'Yes, it does! And it was the answer I was hoping you would give, Ned. You see, I know women, know how easily the child of another woman could get in the way in a relationship.' Lily gave him a huge smile, and squeezed his arm. 'If anything goes wrong, then your mother can take over . . . I'm so happy you suggested it.'

He took her hand in his, squeezed it. 'Lily, let's not talk about your dying . . . I can't stand that thought, I really can't. Let's be happy tonight, happy that we're together.'

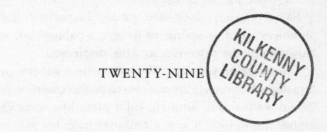

TWENTY-NINE

Edward Deravenel was not easily rattled. In fact, he was almost always composed, in control. This afternoon, as he walked at a measured pace down the corridor to John Summers's office, he was perfectly at ease with himself and with the world. And he had a good idea why he had been sent for by Summers. There was news.

When he arrived at the door of Summers's office he knocked and walked straight in; he was not at all startled to see Inspector Laidlaw sitting there with Rob Aspen. He had expected him to be there.

'Hello, Inspector,' he said, and looked across at the two other men. 'Afternoon, Summers, Aspen.'

They both responded, and John said, 'Come and join us. 'We're waiting for Oliveri so we can begin.'

At this very moment Alfredo knocked and walked in, looking somewhat harassed. 'Afternoon, everyone,' he said in an offhand, rather casual way, and took a chair next to Edward.

Inspector Laidlaw pushed his chair back a little, so that the other four men in the room were in his line of vision. 'Well, gentlemen, I'm here to tell you that I don't

345

have very much news to give you. We have done a very intensive investigation into Aubrey Masters's death, and we've come up empty-handed.'

'What exactly does that mean, Inspector?' John Summers asked, steepling his fingers, a habit of his, and frowning at the detective, looking displeased.

'There are no suspects. We don't believe anyone gave him digitalis, because there seems to be no reason anyone would want to kill him. He led a plain life, somewhat humdrum, in fact. It was a dull marriage, his wife is a bit reclusive, but there were no other women.'

'But did he have a heart condition?' Rob Aspen asked, 'and did you manage to trace Dr Springer?'

'He did *not* have a heart condition, nor was he prescribed digitalis because he didn't need it,' the inspector explained. 'We *did* find Dr Springer, and he turned out to be a psychiatrist, one who is a follower of Dr Freud. He could throw a little light on Mr Masters's life in general, although he did show us the medical files pertaining to Mr Masters. He explained that Masters was concerned with his lack of sexuality, worried that this problem was affecting his relationship with his wife. Apparently he firmly believed that she felt neglected.'

The inspector paused, then added, 'Dr Springer was analysing him.'

'So *did* he die of an overdose of digitalis or not?' Alfredo now asked, a trifle impatiently. He was in a hurry, wanted this meeting to come to a conclusion so he could talk to Edward Deravenel privately.

'Yes, he did,' the inspector confirmed quietly.

'There was an inquest this morning, wasn't there?' Edward said, as he stared at the Scotland Yard man.

'Indeed there was, Mr Deravenel, and the coroner brought in a verdict of accidental death.' Laidlaw paused for a moment, then finished, 'In my opinion there could be no other verdict than this. My sergeant and I believe that Masters accidentally poisoned himself with his vegetarian mix of seeds and pods, the stuff he ate, and apparently had eaten for years. It could have built up, the toxicity. The medical examiner thinks that anyway.'

'Didn't you examine his vegetarian mix at his home?' Edward gave the detective another hard stare.

'We did indeed, but there was nothing much there, and certainly there was no digitalis in the mixture we did find. You see, the idea was to buy everything fresh several times a week, at least so Mrs Masters told us.'

'And where did he buy the mix?' John Summers thought to ask.

'That's the problem: we don't know,' Laidlaw answered, and added, 'His wife told us he brought the mixture home with him in a plain, unmarked brown paper bag, so we have no idea what store he bought it at. I told you, we've come up empty-handed, I'm afraid. Case closed, gentlemen. There was no crime, in our opinion.'

'Thank you very much, Inspector Laidlaw,' Edward said courteously, immediately rising, walking over to the detective, shaking his hand. 'I, *we*, appreciate everything you've done to solve this, and I suppose it will always remain a mystery, won't it.'

'That's right, sir, it will,' Laidlaw answered, and took his leave of them.

Edward followed the detective, walked him down the corridor, as he had in the past, heading in the direction of the grand staircase. When they reached it, Edward turned to Laidlaw and said, 'Inspector, if you ever need anything, need help, whatever it is, please come to me. You've been most diligent, and very courteous. Deravenels and I appreciate everything you've done.'

'Very little it seems to me, sir, and thank you for your kind offer. I'm sorry, too, Mr Deravenel, that we haven't been able to solve the attack on you. It wasn't for the want of trying.'

'Another mystery,' Edward murmured, offering him a warm and genial smile.

A moment later, alone in his office, Edward reached for the phone on his desk and picked up the receiver. Then he instantly replaced it. Why make a telephone call to Neville now? It wasn't necessary. The newspaper boys would soon be out on the streets, touting the latest afternoon editions and screaming the headlines. Best to let sleeping dogs lie, he decided, and waited for Oliveri to come into his office.

He arrived within two minutes.

Seating himself in the chair, Alfredo gave Edward a long questioning stare and said, 'So, what do you think?'

'I think the inspector is a damned fine policeman who has found absolutely no evidence of murder.'

'Do you think Aubrey Masters committed suicide?'

'I'm not sure, to be truthful. He might have killed himself, but let's take the coroner's verdict as the gospel truth, shall we?'

'But naturally, old chap,' Alfredo said, poker-faced. 'However, between you and me, I've found enough evidence to have had him hung, drawn and quartered if he'd been alive. He was definitely skimming, and Jack

Beaufield and James Cliff were in on it with him. And others on the job locally.'

Edward grinned. 'So we've got the two who are still alive by the *cojones*, have we?'

'Oh yes, indeed, we surely do. It's taken a bit of digging, if you'll excuse the unintended pun, by Aspen and Christopher Green but we now have even more evidence required to get those two out. I can't wait to tell Neville Watkins.'

Vicky Forth had the hansom cab take her to Whitechapel; once they arrived at the High Street she alighted, reminding the driver that he was to wait for her.

Hurrying away from the horse-drawn cab, she made her way through several mean, bleak little streets until she arrived at the reclaimed old building now named Haddon House. She knocked on the door and waited, looking up at the darkening sky. A storm threatened and it was beginning to drizzle.

The door was opened within seconds, and the young woman standing on the threshold smiled when she saw Vicky. 'Mrs Forth, how nice to see you again, and so soon! Fenella is in her office, do please come in.' She opened the door wider and ushered Vicky inside.

After hanging Vicky's top coat in the hall cupboard, the young woman said, 'Come along, I'll take you to her office.'

'Thanks, Dora, but I do think I know the way by now,' Vicky replied, laughing.

Fenella Fayne jumped up when she saw Vicky in the doorway of her office and immediately came around the desk, greeted her old friend affectionately.

'Let's sit over there by the fire,' Fenella suggested. 'It's turned chilly today, and it's damp as well.'

'It's not very nice out,' Vicky murmured, sitting down in one of the wooden chairs which Fenella had pulled up to the grate. Clearing her throat, she said, 'I'd like to get straight to the point, Fenella. I've made up my mind. I do want to come and work with you here.'

Fenella's face lit up, and she exclaimed, 'Oh, Vicky! I'm thrilled. And I can truly make use of you.'

'That suits me fine,' Vicky answered, and continued, 'I know you're overworked. I can give you two full days every week. Would you like me Tuesday and Wednesday? Or Wednesday and Thursday?'

Without even having to think twice, Fenella replied, 'Tuesday and Wednesday is so much better, Tuesday being closer to the previous weekend. We get quite a few injured women coming in for help on Mondays and Tuesdays.' Fenella shook her head sadly. 'You see, Vicky, their men have been in the public houses for most of the weekend, and the women get knocked about when the men get home from the pubs.' Fenella grimaced and continued, 'Not a pretty sight, I'm afraid, some of these women. Black eyes, broken bones.'

'I do have a few nursing skills,' Vicky reminded her friend, 'and you said the other day you needed someone who would make stews, soups, that kind of fare. I'm quite a good cook actually.' She smiled. 'But I'll do anything you want, even scrub floors. I just feel I must help in some way. There's such poverty here in the East End.'

'Vicky, there's so much you can do, even taking on some of my paperwork would be a godsend. Now, I would just like to mention there are a few little rules. If I may explain them to you?'

'Yes, of course, please do.'

'You won't be called Mrs Forth once you start working with us, but *Mrs Vicky*. It makes the women feel more at ease, not using a surname, and actually they don't even want to call you by your first name either. They also feel awkward about that, think it's too familiar. So I devised a compromise. The same thing goes for titles . . . I'm not Lady Fayne or Lady Fenella to them but Mrs Fenella, and Dora is not Lady Dora but Miss Dora. Two other rules. Their husbands can visit them if the women are here for a few days. But they must be absolutely sober and they must remain on the ground floor. Finally, we never press the ladies too hard, if they don't want to discuss how they were injured. They are extremely protective of their men, you see. Oh, one other point. Sometimes they bring a small child with them, and we let the child stay here until the mother is well again. And I think that's about *it*.'

'I understand everything, and I'll certainly do the best I can. My heart will be in it, Fenella, I can assure you of that.'

'I know that, my dear, and I can only say thank you from the bottom of my heart for volunteering in this way. You are a sight for sore eyes. How's Lily? I haven't seen her lately.'

'She's very well, Fenella, and she did ask me to give you her love.'

'Thank you, and mine to her. She's such a wonderful

person. Only last week I received several bundles of clothes from her, all of them useful. They can be remade, simplified. I just sent her a note thanking her.' Fenella suddenly stood up, and continued, 'When will you be able to start helping us, Vicky darling?'

'I'll be here next Tuesday morning, if that's all right?'

'It is, and by the way, always remember to book yourself a hansom cab to pick you up in the late afternoon. They are very scarce, hard to find around here.'

A few minutes later as she walked back to the hansom cab waiting for her near the High Street, Vicky thought about her friend.

Fenella was the widow of Lord Jeremy Fayne who had been killed in a hunting accident several years before. She was now twenty-seven, and had once told Vicky that helping the needy and downtrodden women in the East End had helped to assuage her grief to a certain extent, given her a purpose in life. Although she had worked at Haddon House, a charity founded by her aunt, Fenella had been somewhat reclusive in her widowhood until very recently. For the past nine months she had been socializing once more, living in two entirely different worlds. Vicky admired her, admired Fenella's fortitude, strength and generosity of spirit. She was going to do her best for Haddon House.

Edward sat in a comfortable chair in the Smoking Room at White's, waiting for Neville to come. Johnny, Will and he had arrived twenty minutes earlier, but the other two had decided to 'knock a few balls around the table', as Johnny put it, and they had gone into the Billiards Room.

Nursing a whisky and soda Edward drifted with his thoughts, mostly thinking of Deravenels and the detailed plans for the takeover. Everything was coming together.

Occasionally he caught a wisp of conversation from other men in the room, and he smiled inwardly. Men could gossip just as easily as women.

The three men who sat at the table next to him, smoking cigars and relaxing after a day at business, were talking quite loudly. He cocked his ear for a moment.

'The King's going to Biarritz, dragging dray loads of servants with him, of course,' one of the men said.

'And Mrs Keppel, no doubt,' said another.

There were a few titters, and then the third fellow exclaimed, 'Heard what Churchill said recently? That Mrs Keppel should be appointed First Lady of the Bed Chamber.'

All three men laughed and even Edward was amused, had to stifle a chuckle. The King and his long-standing mistress were often the butt of jokes.

Another voice piped up, 'Northcliffe's *Daily Mail* is really backing Balfour and his government.'

'Balfour won't last.'

'The Tories *have* to stay in power.'

'Couldn't agree more, old chap. By the way, I'm thinking of buying an electric car.'

'Good Lord, that's brave of you.'

'Oh, they're perfectly safe.'

'Purchasing one of Mr Ford's models, are you?'

'I'm not yet sure, old chap. Two English engineers, Mr Rolls and Mr Royce, are bringing out their own model. I might just wait for that.'

'Stick with British-made, that's my opinion. That's what it's all about, you know. Got to keep the Empire flourishing. We're the greatest country in the world, don't you know?'

'I'll drink to that, Montague.'

'Kipling has another book out. Amazing the way these chaps keep turning out masterpieces – Galsworthy, too, has a new hit. And George Bernard Shaw is putting on yet another play.'

'Prolific, that's the only word for those writer chaps.'

Edward cut off the chatter at the next table, and fell down into his own thoughts, reminding himself that he had promised his Little Fish another book by Rudyard Kipling. He must order it tomorrow. And Lily's birthday was coming up. He wanted to buy her a beautiful piece of jewellery; he wasn't sure how to do this, unless he borrowed from his mother. *Money.* He needed it badly –

All conversation suddenly stopped, the room went totally quiet. Edward glanced at the door and smiled to himself. Neville was standing there, looking for all the world like the reigning monarch of all he surveyed. Elegantly dressed as always, and supremely self-confident, he strode into the room with panache, nodding to the different men who greeted him. He had arrived with a flourish, had caused quite a stir.

Edward rose and clasped his cousin's hand as Neville drew to a standstill at the table.

'Where are the others?' he asked, sitting down.

Edward, also sitting, explained, 'They went to have a game of billiards.'

Neville nodded, motioned to the waiter, ordered the same as Edward, then settled back in the chair. 'Would you care for a cigar?'

'No thanks,' Edward replied, and went on, 'Inspector Laidlaw came to see us at Deravenels today.' He gave Neville a sharp look.

'I assumed he would. The coroner's verdict is in all of the afternoon papers,' Neville answered. 'Accidental death, so I read.'

Their eyes locked and there was a moment's silence.

Finally, it was Edward who murmured in a low voice, 'Yes, that's what Inspector Laidlaw told us. He said no crime had been committed, also pointed out that there was no reason for Aubrey Masters to commit suicide, at least as far as he had been able to ascertain. The inspector characterized the man's life as humdrum, a plain life.'

Neville nodded, pursed his lips, looked thoughtful. 'The money he stole from Deravenels has to be somewhere, Ned. In his bank account, I presume, which is now his *wife's* bank account. Unless he had another woman in his life, or made other arrangements. It could well be *hidden*.'

'Laidlaw made a point of saying there were no other women around – well, to the best of his knowledge. But that doesn't mean Mildred Masters has it. He might have opened an account with another bank, which she has no inkling of,' Edward suggested.

'Perhaps. In that case, the money is most probably lost, Ned, unless he left instructions with the bank. Or in his will. Regarding the disposal of his wealth. I doubt Deravenels will ever see a penny. If only we had some documentation about his personal finances –' Neville broke off, shaking his head. 'Impossible.'

'I agree, I don't suppose we'll ever get our hands on *that*,' Ned muttered, irritated at the thought.

'You may well be right,' Neville agreed. '*C'est dommage*.'

Neville picked up his whisky and soda, which had arrived a moment or two before. 'Good health, Ned.'

Edward lifted his glass, brought it to touch his cousin's. 'Good health,' he repeated.

'Where would you like to dine tonight?' Neville now asked, wanting to change the subject, not wishing to discuss Masters any further at the moment.

'Wherever you wish,' Edward answered. 'The Savoy? Rules?'

'Ah, here come Johnny and Will! Let's ask them about their preference.'

Margot Grant stared at John Summers and cried, 'Accidental death! This verdict is a travesty! Aubrey was murdered. I *know* he was . . . in my heart I know it. Oh, *mon dieu*, it is a travesty.'

'Margot darling, please calm down. Inspector Laidlaw came to see me today and explained everything. Scotland Yard did a very thorough investigation, and they are absolutely certain no crime was committed.'

'Nonsense! I know he was murdered. *They* did it! *They* killed him.'

John leaned back on the sofa, his eyes on hers. She sat behind the desk in the panelled library of her house in Upper Grosvenor Street, and as usual looked impossibly beautiful, sexually inviting. And imperious. Also somewhat outraged at this moment. When she was angry her voice grew shrill and her French accent became more pronounced, and he always wanted to flee for safety.

Taking a deep breath, John said, 'There is no evidence that the Deravenels did anything. Laidlaw agrees with the coroner's verdict that this was an unfortunate accident. You know as well as I do that Aubrey Masters had the weirdest eating habits. I am certain he ingested digitalis by accident.'

'I do not believe this.'

'If it was not an accident then it must have been intentional, suicide,' John suggested, his voice even and steady, reflecting his unruffled demeanour.

'*Suicide*. Bah, he wouldn't do that! *Non, non, jamais*.'

John remained silent, thinking of the discrepancies he had recently discovered in the accounts which pertained to the mining division. As yet he couldn't quite fathom out what Masters had been up to, and who else might be involved. If there *was* a problem, that is. He decided not to mention this new and troubling development to Margot. She was far too volatile tonight, and he had no intention of inflaming her further.

Suddenly the door opened and Henry Grant stood on the threshold, wearing an old blue velvet dressing gown and slippers and looking rumpled. There was a vacant expression on his face and in his eyes a lost look.

'Ah, Margot, there you are,' Henry began and shuffled into the room, a man old beyond his years.

At once, Margot stood up, went across the floor and took hold of his arm. 'Come, Henry, sit down, John is here, he came to visit you.'

Henry turned. A gentle smile spread across his face when he saw his cousin. He shuffled forward, offering his hand.

Immediately, John was on his feet, shaking Henry's hand, smiling, affecting a look of pleasure. But inside he was troubled and dismayed. More than ever, the head of Deravenels seemed more like a doddering old fool than a captain of industry. He must be kept out of sight. That was imperative.

'Good evening, Henry,' John said, and led the other man over to the sofa. They sat down together, and John went on, 'How're you feeling this evening? A little better, I hope.'

'Oh yes. I was waiting for Father O'Donovan, but perhaps he is late. Mmmmm. Ah well, never mind. And how is your father? Haven't seen him lately.'

Before John could respond, Margot said, 'Now John, Henry, shall we have a *coupe*? A little champagne will be good, no? A healthy drink, my grandmother told me.' Without waiting for an answer she rang the bell on her desk.

'That will be nice,' John responded at last.

Henry said nothing, had lapsed into silence on the other end of the sofa, his eyes already closed. He was drifting with his pious dreams.

The butler appeared in the doorway. 'Can I be of service, madame?'

'*Oui*, Turnbull. Champagne please.'

He inclined his head and left.

Margot moved towards her husband. 'Henry, Henry, are you tired? Are you sleeping?' She bent over him, solicitous.

Henry Grant roused himself and sat up straighter. 'Tired, yes, I think I shall go back to my room.'

'I will help you,' she murmured in a kindly tone.

'No, no, John will accompany me.' He turned to his cousin in a helpless way, and then smiled faintly. 'Please.'

'Of course, Henry,' John replied at once and took hold of the older man's arm, led him out of the library.

Margot stood in the middle of the floor, fulminating inside. *Men.* They were impossible. Henry was a pious, ineffectual idiot; John Summers was a fool. He believed the words of this stupid policeman Laidlaw, believed the coroner's verdict. She was right. She knew it. The Deravenels had murdered Aubrey Masters, and they were getting away with it.

At this moment John came back into the room, followed by Turnbull with the silver bucket of champagne on a silver salver, and crystal flutes.

Within seconds they were both toasting each other with the sparkling wine, and went to sit together on the sofa. Margot made a tremendous effort to curb her anger, and said more softly, with a light smile, 'And did Henry have secrets to confide in you, John darling?'

He shook his head and answered swiftly, frowning. 'He wanted to talk about Edouard. He says he wants me to take him down to Eton to visit his son.' John eyed her carefully, through appraising eyes, always curious when he mentioned the boy who might be *his* father's bastard, his half-brother. 'What do you think of that?'

'It's a splendid idea,' she answered, not in the least put out. 'He has not displayed much interest in Edouard lately. Will you do it?'

'Naturally. But you will accompany us, won't you?' Not waiting for an answer he leaned into her, kissed her full on the mouth. 'It will be unbearable if you don't,' he added.

'I shall come with you. And my *life* is unbearable without you. I need to see you alone, *chéri*, be with you.' She dropped her voice. 'I need to be with you in your bed, in your arms. Ah, John, my life is empty, miserable without you . . .'

Placing his glass of champagne on a side table, he then did the same with hers. Drawing closer, he pulled her into his arms, began to kiss her passionately. She responded with an ardour that more than matched his, and then suddenly pulled away. Against his cheek, she whispered, 'It is not safe here. Let's go out. *Now*. Take me to your house . . . please. *Please*.'

He did as she begged, longing for her just as much as he longed for him. Within minutes they were in his carriage driving across town.

THIRTY

The streets of Whitechapel were dark by the time Amos Finnister arrived there, and after paying off the hansom cab he went in search of his favourite pieman. All afternoon he had dreamed about one of those wonderful meat-filled pies, oozing gravy, and he was now determined to have one, if not indeed two.

Sometimes the vendor had his cart set up on Commercial Street but tonight there was no sign of him. Amos knew he would be around somewhere in the area and set off to find him. He did so ten minutes later; he spotted the cart and the most fragrant smells wafting towards him announced that it was the same chap he had patronized before.

Sure enough it was, and the vendor greeted him with a cheery grin, said in his breezy Cockney way, 'Evenin', guv, I knew yer'd be back 'ere again. Best pies, that I 'ave.'

'You certainly do, and my compliments to your wife. I've never found any more delicious than hers. I'm even tempted to buy two tonight.'

'Go on then, sir, 'ave a splurge.'

Amos nodded 'I think I will.'

The vendor lifted a pie out of the tray with the metal tongs, showed it to Amos and put it in a small white bag, dipped a ladle into a pot, added thick beef gravy on the crust. He followed the same procedure with the second pie, then placed the two white bags into a larger one made of brown paper.

Reaching into his pocket, Amos brought out fourpence, handed the money over, and took the bag. 'I'll be back next week, all being well.'

'See yer, guv,' the vendor said, and saluted, grinning as he did so.

Amos walked through the streets until he found the small cul-de-sac where he had eaten his pies in the past. It was a quiet spot, a bit off the beaten track; a gas lamp nearby added illumination to the area. As he put the bag of pies on the wall and sat down, Amos glanced around. Immediately he noticed the old wooden cart, which hadn't been there before. Somebody had obviously dumped it; without wheels, it was dilapidated and certainly of no use to anyone in its present state.

Taking a pie out of the bag, his mouth watering, he bit into it at once, savouring that first bite. Like this area, the pie reminded him of his father and the carefree time of his childhood long ago. That was the reason he liked to come to Whitechapel so often these days. For the memories.

He had only taken a second bite when he heard a strange mewling sound, like a small animal in pain. He looked around his feet, scanning the ground, but there was no stray dog or cat in sight. There it was again, the mewling. Amos glanced toward the cart and was completely taken aback at the sight of a small face peering over the edge. Light-coloured eyes were just visible under a flat cap, were enormous in the dirty face; the mouth was distorted as if the small boy was in some sort of pain.

Putting the pie down, Amos jumped up, walked across to the cart; instantly, the boy scurried away from the edge, cowering, afraid.

'Now, now, what do we have here?' Amos asked in a soft voice, smiling, not wishing to frighten the child any further.

There was total silence.

He said again, 'So, what do we have here then?'

'Nuffin',' the child answered, 'nuffin'.'

'Oh, but I think you're something.'

'Ain't. I'm nuffin'.'

'My name's Amos. What's yours?'

'Liddle Bugger.'

'No, no, come along, lad, it can't be that. Tell me your name.'

'That's wot 'e calls me.'

'Who?'

'The man, 'im as kicked me out, kilt me muvver, 'e did.'

Amos felt the hackles rising on the back of his neck, and an involuntary shiver ran through him. He asked in the same gentle voice, 'Where do you live, lad?'

''ere.'

'In this neighborhood?'

'Naw, 'ere.'

'Do you mean you live in this cart?'

The boy nodded, and sniffed, then sniffed again.

Amos suddenly understood that the child could smell the pie, and he cursed himself under his breath. Why hadn't he understood that before? The boy had looked out of the cart because of the pie. 'Hungry, lad? Do you want something to eat?'

The boy nodded, suddenly came closer to the edge of the cart and looked at the wall where the pies were.

Amos said nothing more. He reached into the cart and lifted the boy out before he could protest. He was light as a feather, frail, and as Amos put him down on the cobblestones he wobbled slightly, then steadied himself. The child wore an old torn jacket, a pair of ragged pants and broken boots. And he was filthy.

'Come along then, let's have some of that pie,' Amos said cheerily.

Unexpectedly, the boy hung back, all of a sudden wary and cautious, his eyes darting around nervously.

Amos took hold of his hand in an easy way, said, 'Let's tuck in together, shall we, laddie? Get to know each other.'

The boy was silent but put up no struggle. Once they were at the wall Amos lifted him up onto it, opened the brown bag and took out the other pie, handed it to him. 'This is for you.'

The boy hesitated for only a split second, then took it, bit into it, gobbling it ravenously, obviously starving.

Watching him, Amos was suddenly angry and sickened. What sort of country did he live in when little boys could roam the streets, in dire need of food, clothing and shelter? It made his blood boil. All the wealth in this lush Edwardian era and bairns starving on the streets of London. Appalling, it was.

The child suddenly stopped eating, and looking across at Amos he offered him the pie. ''Ere, 'ave a taste.'

Shaking his head, Amos picked up his own pie and began to eat, and after a mouthful or two, he explained, 'One each, you see. I must have known I was going to meet you.'

''Ow yer know'd that then?'

'I've no idea, lad. I suppose I just did. Would you like a drink? Water, milk, something like that?'

The boy nodded, his eyes eager.

'We have to go and get it,' Amos explained, and took a bite out of his pie. 'I'm full,' he murmured, looking at the child. 'Why don't you finish it for me?'

Shaking his head the boy jumped off the wall, stepped backward, looking worried.

'Shame to waste it, really,' Amos muttered almost to himself, and put the remainder of the pie on the wall.

After a moment the child started to reach for it, then paused, his big eyes resting on Amos. He wanted the pie but appeared afraid to touch it.

'It's all right, you can have it. I told you I'm full to bursting,' Amos remarked.

Once the piece had been demolished by the child, Amos stood up, stretched out his hand and said, 'Come on, let's go and find that glass of milk, shall we?'

'Naw, can't go.'

'Why not? It isn't very far.'

'Can't leave me cart.'

'It'll be quite safe, I'm sure of that,' Amos assured him.

''Ow long?'

'You mean how long to get there? How far it is?'

The boy nodded.

'Ten, fifteen minutes, that's all.'

Instantly the boy shrank back, shaking his head vehemently. 'Naw, naw, stayin' 'ere. It's safe 'ere.'

Crouching down, looking into the child's scared face, Amos said in the warmest voice he could muster, 'Tell you what, I know you're tired, how about I carry you there? We'll have a glass of milk and then I'll bring you back to the cart. Or take you wherever you want to go. I promise.'

The child stared back at him, his eyes appearing even larger, and he suddenly smiled. 'Cross yer 'eart an' 'ope ter die?' he said, staring hard at Amos.

'Cross my heart and hope to die.'

Darting to the cart, the boy scrambled inside, and reappeared a moment later clutching a dirty cloth bag tied at the top with string. He clambered out of the cart and stood looking up at Amos.

'What's in the bag?' Amos asked, reaching for it.

The boy clutched it to his body, shaking his head harder than ever, fearful again. 'Naw, naw, it's me fings! Yer can't 'ave it.'

'It's all right, laddie, I don't want it. I thought you might like me to carry it, that's all. Anyway, I'll carry you, and you can carry your bag, and that'll be fine.'

There was only a moment's hesitation, and then the boy confided, 'Me mam says that . . . cross me 'eart an' 'ope ter die.'

'So she's not dead?'

'Yeah, she is . . . she's in Potters Field.'

Cursing himself once more for his thoughtlessness,

Amos bent down and picked the boy up in his arms, carried him out of the cul-de-sac and up towards Commercial Street, singing, 'Onward Christian soldiers, going off to war, with the Cross of Jesus going on before.'

As Amos walked along, singing his favourite hymn half to himself, he felt the little boy go limp in his arms almost immediately; his head rested on Amos's broad shoulder, one hand clutched his precious cloth bag, the other held tightly to the lapel of Amos's overcoat.

Poor little bairn, Amos thought, he's exhausted. Whatever will become of him? And where should I take him after we've had the milk at Haddon House?

It was whilst they were eating the pies in the cul-de-sac that Amos had had the idea to take the boy over to Haddon House, just off Whitechapel High Street. He was quite certain that Lady Fenella would be able to help. He had known her since she and her aunt had opened the safe haven for battered women three years ago, and he admired her, respected her for the extra-ordinary work she was doing in the East End.

After all, she was titled in her own right, being the daughter of the Earl of Tanfield, and, as the widow of Lord Jeremy Fayne, a wealthy woman. She was young, not yet twenty-eight, and considered something of a beauty in society – tall, elegant with blonde hair and grey eyes. As an aristocrat and socialite, she did not have to devote half her life to helping those in distress, yet she did, and did so with great efficiency, kindness, devotion and love. And all those who met her, from all walks of life, succumbed to her charms, fell under her spell.

It was more than likely that she wouldn't be there at this hour of the evening. However, Amos knew that some of her helpers would be at Haddon House because Lady Fenella's policy was to keep the doors open twenty-four hours a day, seven days a week; no one was ever turned away. Perhaps the boy could sleep there tonight, once he had been cleaned up a bit.

Amos loathed the mere thought of taking him back to the cul-de-sac and that decrepit old cart, and, in fact, he had no intention of doing so. It was so unsanitary and unhealthy, and, furthermore, extremely dangerous. For the boy to be sleeping outside on the street the way he was doing begged for trouble. It was inhuman to allow a child to exist in such a terrible way.

He decided he would make inquiries at the local Dr Barnardo's Home tomorrow; perhaps the orphanage would be able to find a place for him.

All of a sudden, as he continued on his way, Amos thought of Charlie and Maisie, wished they were here, that they still lived in Whitechapel. They would have taken the boy in to live with them without a second thought, made him feel most welcome. That's the way they were.

As it was, the brother and sister were in New York, walking those streets they claimed were paved with gold, seeking work as actors. He missed them, most especially Charlie, and looked forward to more cheerful letters from him. One had arrived already, and it seemed that their prospects were good.

Hoisting the boy, holding him close, Amos hurried now, wanting to get to Haddon House. One thing he was certain of was a warm welcome. All of the women who worked there were pleasant, helpful and accommodating. They were the salt of the earth.

THIRTY-ONE

All the lights were blazing when Amos Finnister finally arrived at Haddon House, and they were a most welcome sight, gladdened his heart. Lifting the brass knocker, he banged it several times, and within a couple of seconds the door was opened.

To his utter surprise he stood staring at the familiar and lovely face of Will Hasling's sister, Mrs Vicky Forth. She was looking as surprised as he was himself.

'Goodness gracious, it's you, Mr Finnister!' she gasped, then immediately added, 'Do please come in, won't you?'

'Evening, Mrs Forth,' he replied at once, stepping into the vestibule. 'I didn't expect to see you here, ma'am, and especially in the evening.'

'I'm helping Lady Fenella two days a week,' Vicky explained, 'and my presence here this evening *is* rather unusual, Mr Finnister. There was an emergency, you see, and Lady Fenella asked me to come in to help her deal with it. But please, let us not stand here in the chilly foyer. Come into the great room where there's a fire.' Peering at the sleeping boy with immense curiosity, she then asked, 'And who is this little fellow?'

'I found him out on the streets, Mrs Forth,' Amos answered as together they walked into the large main room where there were several big sofas, plenty of comfortable chairs, as well as a long trestle table covered with a white cloth. 'He was hiding in a cart,' Amos explained and quickly filled her in as they made their way over to the fireplace.

The lamplight, the sudden warmth and the voices caused the boy to stir in Amos's arms, and he suddenly awakened, began to struggle at once. 'Steady on, laddie,' Amos murmured and placed the boy on the floor. Again he seemed a little unsteady on his feet for a second, and then he looked up at Amos, appearing afraid. He was shivering excessively.

'Are you cold, lad?'

The boy nodded.

'Come on then, let's get you settled here by the fire for a little bit. And then I'll get you that nice glass of milk I promised you.'

The boy clung to Amos's hand as they moved towards the roaring fire. 'Sit here, laddie.' The boy hesitated in front of the chair; Amos lifted him up and plopped him down in it.

'You'll soon feel much warmer,' he murmured, and hurried over to Vicky who was hovering near the trestle table, waiting for him. 'Could we get him something to drink, Mrs Forth? Perhaps water, if you can't spare the milk, although I did promise the little mite a glass of milk.'

'Of course he can have some milk, but do you think

he might like a cup of cocoa? Children do love it, and certainly it would warm him up.'

'Oh, what a grand idea, it is indeed! Thank you.'

'I'll go and tell Mrs Barnes to make a jug of cocoa for all of us. You look as if you could use a hot drink yourself. Back in a moment, Mr Finnister.'

Vicky Forth was as good as her word; she returned at once and informed Amos that the cocoa would be made within minutes. 'Now, please tell me more about the boy.'

'I've told you most of what I know, Mrs Forth. He said he'd been kicked out by the man who had killed his mother, but, of course, we don't know if that's true, the bit about the man killing her. However, I do have a strong feeling that his mother really is dead. He said something about her being in Potters Field.'

'Then I agree with you. She probably passed away and the boy could easily have been unwanted after she was gone. Perhaps he was sent into the streets, if the man they were living with was not his father. You told me he said he had no name.'

'That's right. Well, he did give me a name of sorts, but I couldn't possibly repeat it to a lady like you, Mrs Forth.'

Vicky smiled at him. 'Oh you can, Mr Finnister, believe me you certainly can repeat it. You'd be surprised what I've heard around here. Then again, you might not be. After all, you were once a policeman in these parts, so my brother told me.'

'Indeed I was, ma'am, and I do know the area well. My father brought me here quite a lot when I was a boy.' He sighed, and lowering his voice, he muttered, 'He said his name was Liddle Bugger.'

372

'How awful for the child,' Vicky shook her head. 'It staggers the imagination what some people do, the way they wilfully hurt innocent children, harm them in the worst possible way.' She paused, looked toward the kitchen door. 'Ah, here comes Mrs Barnes with the cocoa.'

Mrs Barnes nodded and smiled when she saw Amos. Crossing to the long table she placed the tray with the jug and cups on it, and hurried off in the direction of the kitchen, intent on her business. A volunteer, this was her night to look after the food.

'Thank you, Vanessa,' Vicky called after her. At the table she poured cocoa into the three cups. 'Come along, here's a cup for you, Mr Finnister,' she said and carried a second cup over to the boy, who was curled up in the large armchair.

He raised his head when he saw her, and instantly cowered in a corner of the chair. But then, as he suddenly focused on her properly, his eyes widened and he sat up a little straighter, staring at her intently.

'Hello, little boy,' Vicky said to him, offering the cup. 'Don't be afraid. Look, I've brought you a cup of warm cocoa: it's lovely, it tastes of chocolate. I know you'll enjoy it.' As she spoke he listened most attentively, and his eyes did not leave her face.

Standing in front of the armchair, Vicky leaned toward him, again offering the cup of cocoa. Unexpectedly, with a jerky movement, the boy reached out and touched her hair, then drew back swiftly.

Vicky simply smiled at him, and handed him the cup. For once he let go of the cloth bag he was clutching to him and took the cup from her. His eyes were still wide, the look of surprise lingering on his small face.

She, too, was surprised; in fact, the child had startled her when he had reached out in the way he had. She had almost pulled back, but managed, somehow, to remain perfectly still when he had touched her hair.

She noticed he was not drinking the cocoa; his eyes were fixed on her face; he appeared to be mesmerized by her.

Vicky said softly, 'Have a sip of the cocoa. It's very good. I'm going to have a cup myself.'

The boy finally nodded, did as she said.

Amos had been watching Vicky with the boy, and now he came over to join her by the fireside, bringing the two cups with him. 'Here you are, Mrs Forth,' he murmured, handing her a cup. 'Ah, I see you're enjoying it, laddie. That's good.'

The boy looked at Amos and nodded, then he said in a low mumble, 'Mam . . . like Mam.'

Frowning, Amos glanced at Vicky.

She said, 'I think he's referring to his mother when he says *Mam*. It's Yorkshire. I suppose he might be suggesting I look like her.'

Amos raised a brow, then glanced at the boy, who was now drinking down the cocoa and no longer paying attention to them.

There was the sound of footsteps and as Amos peered across the room he saw Lady Fenella, and, much to his surprise, Chief Inspector Mark Ledbetter of Scotland Yard.

The two of them walked into the great room, and when Mark Ledbetter spotted Amos his face lit up. As he came to a stop he stuck out his hand, and exclaimed, 'How nice to see you, Finnister.' He looked pleased, was smiling broadly.

'Evening, Chief,' Amos replied shaking his hand, and then he turned swiftly to Fenella Fayne. 'Good evening, Lady Fenella.'

'Amos, what a pleasant surprise! It's been a few weeks since you popped in, I've missed seeing you. Those clothes were most welcome, as I told you at the time. It was exceedingly generous of you and your wife, and I do hope you received my letter of thanks.'

'We did indeed, your ladyship. We admire your work, try to help when we can.'

Fenella nodded, and then quickly glanced at the child with the cup in his hand. 'And who is our young guest?' she asked, curious.

Vicky said softly, 'Mr Finnister found him in the streets, Fenella. He seems to have been thrown out of wherever he was living. He had taken refuge in a cart.'

'A cart!' Fenella cried, her eyes startled. She was aghast. 'How horrendous!'

Vicky nodded, and explained, 'Perhaps it would be better if Mr Finnister filled you in. Don't you agree with me, Mr Finnister?'

'Happy to oblige, ma'am.' Amos drew Lady Fenella and the Chief Inspector to one side of the room, and rapidly told them everything that had happened that evening, from the moment he had gone into the cul-de-sac with the meat pies until this exact moment.

They both listened attentively, and Amos finally finished, 'I didn't know what to do with him, Lady Fenella, and then I thought of you and Haddon House. He *can* stay here tonight, can't he? Poor little lad, he seems worn out, exhausted I think, and he was starving. Very hungry and thirsty, and cold.'

'Of course he can stay here tonight, Amos. Where else but here? However, I do think we have to take him into the scullery and give him a bath at once. Don't you agree?'

'Oh yes, indeed, I do, Lady Fenella. He does need a bit of soap and water to make him . . . palatable, no two ways about that.'

At first the boy was reluctant to leave the armchair, but eventually Vicky was able to coax him out of it. Even so, he did not want to leave Amos, who finally had to accompany the two women to the scullery. The boy held onto his hand tightly, looking frightened again.

Vanessa Barnes was standing at the big deal table in the kitchen, cutting up meat and vegetables which she kept putting in the bubbling pot of beef soup on the stove. The boy's nose visibly twitched as they passed by the large black iron oven that also warmed the room. His steps faltered, as if he wanted to stop and eat. The adults noticed this and glances were exchanged but nothing was said. Once they reached the scullery door, Amos got down on his haunches and said to the boy, 'Now listen to me, laddie, I shall be right here in the kitchen with the lady who is making the soup. I won't go away. I'll wait for you, I promise. Cross my heart and hope to die.'

The boy looked up at Amos, and nodded. 'Awright,' he muttered, and allowed himself to be led into the scullery by Vicky.

This was quite a large room, and was used for washing

clothes, for the ironing, and for baths for the abused or destitute women taking refuge at Haddon House. It had a stone floor and one window; there were tall cupboards ranged around the room for linen and supplies, and in one corner a large set-pot where the washing was done. The fire underneath the set-pot was always burning in the grate; tonight it crackled and spurted, and as usual kept the room warm as well as the water heated.

Fenella glanced across at the set-pot and said, 'I know that Vanessa filled it up with water earlier, so there will be plenty for his bath.'

Vicky nodded and went to the end wall where a small zinc bathtub hung on a metal hook on the wall. 'I think this is the best size to use, don't you?'

'I do. I'll get soap and some disinfectant, Vicky. His hair especially will need a lot of attention – for the usual *problem*.'

Within a few minutes the two women were taking jugsful of hot water from the set-pot and filling the bathtub on the floor in the middle of the room. 'Come along,' Vicky said to the boy. 'You have to have a bath now.'

The boy remained standing near the door, a fierce look on his face.

She went on, with a warm smile, 'We must wash all the dirt away.' She smiled again and beckoned to the child.

He remained stock still, clutching his cloth bag next to his little body. He was totally mute.

Finally, Vicky said to Fenella, 'I'd better start undressing him.' Walking over to the boy, she knelt down in front of him. 'We're not going to hurt you, child,' she reassured him in a gentle voice. 'We only wish to make you clean.'

Once again he seemed mesmerized by her, stared into her eyes, and taking advantage of his momentary distraction she whipped the big flat cap off his head before he had a chance to stop her or fight her.

The boy gasped, and so did Vicky and Fenella.

Masses of red curls were tied up in bunches all over his head.

The child began to tremble and hugged the bag tighter. Tears came, slid down the dirt-covered cheeks, making little channels.

Vicky and Fenella exchanged glances, and Vicky asked quietly, 'Are you a little girl?'

At first the child did not answer and then after a long moment there was a nod. 'Yes,' she whispered, her voice barely audible.

The two women were stunned momentarily, and Fenella came over and knelt down next to Vicky. 'Do you have a name, little girl?' she asked, observing her acutely.

The girl shook her head.

'Will you help us? Will you let us undress you so we can wash your beautiful auburn hair, and also bathe you? We want to make you clean and pretty.'

The child nodded, put the cloth bag on the floor and stood on one end of it with both feet. Then she began to untie the filthy muffler around her neck. Vicky helped her to take off the torn jacket, the grubby shirt underneath, and, finally, the old boots were removed. The trousers came off next, but with some difficulty since one foot had to remain on the bag at all times.

Once the little girl was stripped naked, Vicky led her over to the tin bath in the middle of the floor.

Fenella said to her softly, not wanting to frighten the girl, 'I'm afraid I will have to take that bag from you, but only whilst you are having your bath. Otherwise it will get wet.'

The child shook her head frantically, clung to the bag.

Pointing to the large hook where the bath had been hanging, Fenella said, 'I shall put it over there on that hook, where you can see it. And you can have it back when you've been washed.'

'Naw!' the girl cried. 'It's me fings.'

She was looking at Fenella, and once again Vicky acted swiftly. She snatched the bag away from the girl in one deft movement. The child instantly cried out.

Vicky placated her, 'Don't cry. I'm not taking your things.'

She hurried across the floor and put the bag on the hook. 'There! You can see it all the time. Now, get into the bath, please.'

Vicky's sudden rather firm and commanding voice seemed to have the desired effect. The little girl stepped into the bath and sat down with a splash. Vicky rolled up the sleeves of her blouse, leaned over the girl and began to untie the bits of dirty string. Within minutes, a cascade of auburn hair hung around the girl's face.

Taking a face cloth, Vicky dipped it in the water and began to wash the girl's face, removing the dirt. Then she tackled her body, asking the girl to stand up in the tub to ease the process. She did so, and Vicky washed her thoroughly. As she did this she noticed a few old bruises on the girl's body, but they might easily have been caused by sleeping rough in the streets. They did not look serious. The child was thin, but not emaciated, and much smaller than she had appeared when dressed. Vicky realized that the clothes had all been too big for her, and they were a boy's clothes, not a girl's.

Once all the dirt had been washed away, Vicky told the child to sit down in the bath again, and she obediently did as she was told. Vicky, peering at the girl's head, muttered, 'I'm going to need the disinfectant, please, Fenella.'

A moment later Fenella brought a bottle of disinfectant and a large jar of soft liquefied soap, then went to get a comb and towels.

'Cover your face with your hands, please,' Vicky said to the girl, who did so. Vicky explained, 'I'm about to wash your hair and I don't want you to get soap in your eyes.'

At the end of an hour the most beautiful child stood before them dressed in a white flannel nightgown. Her hair had been towelled hard and was almost dry as Vicky brushed it, marvelling at it as she did so. It was a wonderful golden-red, and fell in curls and waves around her lovely face. The other remarkable thing about her was the colour of her eyes. They were an unusual deep blue, almost the shade of cornflowers.

Although Amos had been taken aback to see Mark Ledbetter at Haddon House, his surprise was mostly due to the hour more than anything else. Usually Lady Fenella had gone home by this time, but as Vicky Forth had said, they were there tonight because of an emergency. And perhaps this was the reason Ledbetter was present as well. But not necessarily.

Amos was well aware that the Chief Inspector knew Lady Fenella and her spinster aunt, Lady Philomena Howell. Ledbetter's mother was a close friend of Lady Philomena's; the two women had come out together as debutantes years ago.

He had always liked Mark Ledbetter, had known him for over seventeen years, actually since Ledbetter had started at Scotland Yard. At twenty-two he had been a dashing young aspiring detective, Amos a copper on the beat. They had met in the East End on a strange murder case, and had always got on well since that time.

Mark, who had gone into Fenella's office, returned to the great room carrying two cups. He was a tall, slender, pleasant looking man, with dark wavy hair and warm brown eyes and at thirty-nine, fit and athletic. With a brilliant mind, superior intelligence and dedication to work, he had quickly moved up the ladder at the Yard.

Amos studied him as he strode over to the fireplace, asking himself yet again why a man with Mark's looks, Cambridge education, aristocratic forebears and a wealthy mother would want to be a policeman. He had once asked Mark that question and the younger man had answered that he wanted to help people in despair. Perhaps that philosophy explained his interest in Haddon House, and the support he gave it.

As he came to a standstill Mark said to Amos, with a grin, 'I've just stolen some of Lady Fenella's brandy, but I'm perfectly certain she won't mind.' As he handed the cup to Amos and sat down in the other leather armchair, he added, 'She keeps a bottle in her office . . . for medicinal purposes or emergencies. I need this tonight, and I'm sure you do, too.'

With a nod, Amos took the cup. 'I do. Thank you, and good health, Chief.' Amos took a swallow of the brandy, felt its warmth immediately.

'Cheers,' Ledbetter murmured and tasted the cognac himself, then sat for a moment, looked down into the cup, his expression thoughtful.

After a moment, Amos cleared his throat and asked in a quiet tone, 'What was the emergency here tonight? If you don't mind me asking, Chief? Obviously something serious to bring you here.'

Mark glanced at Amos and pressed his lips together for a moment. 'I'm here by chance, actually. I was at a meeting with Lady Fenella and Hugh Codrill, the barrister. We were discussing ways to improve Haddon House, raise additional funds. Codrill had come along at my request, just to help . . . well, kick a few ideas around, to be honest.'

Mark paused, took a drink, went on, 'We were still at her house on Curzon Street when she received a telephone call from Mrs Barnes, who was here doing the cooking. Anyway, to continue. A local woman had been brought in by two other women . . . neighbours. The woman was badly battered around the face, and appeared to be almost unconscious. The nurse on duty at the time was Clara Foggarty, and she was baffled

382

and worried. She thought the woman might have concussion, and asked Mrs Barnes to contact Lady Fenella. I came along because I was worried.'

'And where is the poor woman now? Here? Or at the hospital?'

'Oh, at the hospital, of course. I immediately sent for an ambulance, and they took her away at once. I was pretty certain that there was concussion. We were just about to leave here and go home when you arrived with the little chap.' Mark shook his head, a sorrowful look sliding onto his face. 'I wish there was more we could do for these destitute boys living on the streets. Despite all the wonderful work done by Dr Barnardo's and others, there are plenty of them out there still. Too numerous to count.'

'I know that, sir. I used to think mudlarks and urchins and all the little street thieves had disappeared finally, been rehabilitated. But I'm not so sure. I can't help thinking it's as bad now as it was when Charles Dickens was writing about them.'

'That wasn't so long ago, you know –' Mark stopped abruptly, and his expression changed. He looked across the room towards the kitchen door, bafflement flooding his face.

Amos followed the direction of his gaze, his eyes widening in amazement as he stared at Lady Fenella and Mrs Worth. Both were ushering a little girl into the room. A beautiful girl at that, with amazing golden-red hair. *Oh, my God.* The girl was clutching the cloth bag. It couldn't be . . . she wasn't the boy, was she? It wasn't possible.

Almost as if she had read his mind, Vicky said, 'Look what emerged from underneath all the dirt and grime, Mr

Finnister. This lovely girl who had been wearing a boy's clothes – a disguise. From what she told me, her mother dressed her like that most of the time. More than likely to protect her, I should think.'

Jumping up, smiling hugely, Amos came across the floor, stood in front of the two women and the child. He reached out, touched the child's glorious red hair, and murmured, 'Will you tell me your name now, little one?'

'Mam . . . she call me her liddle rosebud,' the girl answered, gazing up at him through her brilliant blue eyes. Her face was serious, her eyes suddenly sad.

'That's a pretty name indeed,' Amos answered, smiling at her, then lifting his head, looking at Vicky, he raised a brow questioningly.

Vicky bent down to the child's level. 'But that isn't your *real* name, is it?'

'Dunno . . .' The child's voice trailed off and she looked bewildered.

Vicky noticed that the girl's hands had tightened on the bag and she wondered what was inside. Possibly information they needed, something which might explain who she was. How to get the bag away from her? It was an impossible task.

Fenella now knelt down in front of the girl, and said slowly, 'I am Fenella. And this,' she glanced up at Vicky, 'is Vicky. And the gentleman who found you is Amos. Over there is Mark. And you are . . . *who*? Tell me your name so we can call you by it.'

The little girl shook her head and then addressed Vicky, 'Rosebud . . . Mam say.'

Vicky smiled at her and knelt down on the floor next

to Fenella, gazed at the child through eyes that were warm and tender. 'All right then, that will be *your* name. We shall call you Rose. Do you like that?'

The child nodded. A faint smile flicked and was gone.

Vicky reached for the bag, saying, as she did, 'Let me lock this up for you, to keep it safe.'

'Naw! Naw!' the girl cried and clutched it even tighter.

'That's all right, don't cry,' Vicky murmured, 'come, let us go and have another cup of cocoa.'

An hour later, after the little girl had been put to bed, still clutching the cloth bag, Fenella and Vicky sat with Mark and Amos discussing the situation.

'We cannot put that lovely little girl into an orphanage,' Vicky announced at one moment, shaking her head. 'I won't allow it. She's far too beautiful and vulnerable. Something bad will happen to her. I feel it in my bones.'

There was a moment's silence, and then Fenella exclaimed, 'She must stay *here*. There's no real reason why she can't, you know. Perhaps you can make some discreet inquiries in the area, Amos? Find out whether a little girl has gone missing.'

'I will, Lady Fenella, but I doubt very much that anyone will claim her. I think she told the truth when she said her mother was dead and that she had been tossed out onto the street. If only we had a name –' Amos's voice trailed off and he shrugged helplessly.

'If only,' Mark muttered, shaking his head. 'I tend to agree with you, Amos, about her mother. And certainly with Mrs Forth and Lady Fenella. Of course she must stay at Haddon House until we decide what's best for her. Are we all agreed on this course?'

The three of them said they were.

Vicky found herself filling with relief. The little girl they now called Rose was safe. For the moment.

THIRTY-TWO

Ravenscar

Richard had pestered and then begged to go fishing all morning. Finally, after lunch, Edward had succumbed to his entreaties and taken him down to the beach.

Even though it was the middle of April and sunny, there was a high wind blowing across the North Sea and it was raw and icy, lashing at their cheeks and making their noses red.

'It's a good thing Meg wrapped you up well, Dickie boy,' Edward said, staring at his brother, who was fumbling with his fishing rod. It was obvious that his woollen gloves were in the way, but somehow Richard was managing.

Edward smiled at the way Meg had protected the boy against the weather. She was always worrying about her beloved younger brother, and today she had cocooned Richard in layers of clothing, had added, as a final touch, a red scarf wrapped around his head and neck. She had placed a red knitted cap on top of the scarf, completely covering his head.

She would have cocooned *him* in the same way if Ned had allowed it, but, of course, he had not let her get anywhere near him. However, he had seen the wisdom in wrapping a woollen scarf around his head, copying the way she had used one on Richard to protect his ears. But instead of a red woollen cap with a pompom on top, Ned wore a tweed cap over his grey scarf, which was more sedate.

They crunched along together in their Wellington boots, making for a spot Ned preferred for fishing. The beach was a shingle bed of rock where old fossils were often found, along with pretty shells and all manner of odd sea specimens dredged in by the tides, and seaweed.

They did not talk much as they tramped ahead, both of them lost in their own thoughts. Edward was thinking of Lily, wondering how she was, what she was doing, and Richard was congratulating himself, overjoyed that he had managed to get Edward all to himself. George was always hanging around these days, trying to curry favour with their elder brother. But he didn't really succeed; Ned held back, and Richard was beginning to ask himself why.

Suddenly Richard cried, 'Look, Ned! The Cormorant Rock!' Before Edward could restrain him the boy had started to run along the beach hell for leather. A worried frown struck Edward's face, and he held his breath, praying the boy wouldn't go sprawling.

Within minutes Richard had reached the Cormorant Rock and was already clambering over the smaller rocks to get to it. Then in a flash, there he was, standing on top of it. Triumphant, grinning, waving to Ned, beckoning to him.

His elder brother waved back and trudged on, remembering how their father had brought him here with his brother Edmund all those years ago. It was from his father that he had learned some of the local fishermen's lore . . . Cormorant Rock was so called because the cormorants would emerge from the waves to stand on that one particular rock, with their wings outstretched, drying them.

His father had always said that he couldn't understand why a species of bird that spent a great amount of time in the sea had not evolved efficient waterproofing like so many other marine birds had. He constantly muttered that it was a mystery of nature, quite unfathomable.

Arriving at the cluster of rocks, Edward climbed up to join his brother, and when he was standing next to him on this perch high above the frothing, foaming sea he said, 'Just be careful, my Little Fish. I don't want to be . . . fishing you out, have you on the end of my line instead of a plump little cod.'

Richard laughed, his eyes dancing. 'Yes, this is the place for cod! Papa told me that, and he also said that if you want to catch haddock you must take a boat out a mile from the shore. That is where all the haddock are.'

'That's right,' Ned replied, and pushed away the sudden image of Edmund, at the age of ten, saying almost the same words. He snapped his eyes shut to obliterate the image of Edmund's innocent young face, and then opened them almost at once.

'Let's put out our lines, Tiddler,' Ned said to his youngest sibling, and cast his line into the sea as he spoke.

Richard followed suit. They stayed there for over an

hour, caught only a few fish. Freezing cold, their eyes watering, their faces bright red from the wind, they finally abandoned Cormorant Rock to the cormorants and headed back along the beach. Their destination was the steps cut into the cliff face. These would lead them up to the lowest part of the moorland that flowed down to the North Sea.

As they climbed slowly towards the low stretch of moorland, Richard chattered away to Edward, interrupting his thoughts, which were mostly about Deravenels and those who currently ran it. The boy was forcing Ned to pull himself out of his sudden and rather reflective mood.

'Ask me questions about sea lore,' Richard requested at one moment, staring up at Edward, tugging at his arm.

Understanding that he would have to comply, Edward nodded, and remembered that this was a game they had played with their father only last summer.

Taking a deep breath, stifling the rush of unexpected and sudden emotions, Edward finally said, 'All right then, let's do just that, Little Fish. Let's see how sharp your wits are today.'

'Very sharp,' Richard shot back.

'What is the one thing you must not do with a ship or a boat?'

'Change its name!'

'Correct. But why is that so, Little Fish?'

'Because it's *unlucky* to change the name of a sailing vessel.'

'Very good indeed, Dick. Now here's another . . . what were Admiral Nelson's last words?'

'Kiss me, Hardy.'

'Clever lad, that you are. Now, which was Nelson's greatest battle?'

'Trafalgar.'

'That's it and Waterloo is another one. What else do sailors consider unlucky, especially when they're out at sea?' This was something of a tricky question, and Edward wondered if Richard had remembered what it was, that it was partially a joke amongst sailors.

'*Mermaids*! And I know I'm right. Edmund told me this . . . never take mermaids on board. Yes, he told me that lastsummer –' The boy's voice faded away and he fell silent, his eyes grown dark, the colour of slate. He fell down into his sadness, didn't say much for a while, and then he murmured, 'I thought of Edmund, Ned, and that made me want to cry. I miss him . . . do you?'

'Very much,' Ned answered, and hoisted the fishing basket higher on his shoulder. It contained the cod, which were not heavy, but the leather strap kept slipping. 'Let's keep going with the game, my lad,' he went on, asked, 'When you go up the gangplank of a British battleship, what's the first thing you see when you step onto the deck?'

'A plaque that says, *Fear God. Honour the King.*'

'You have an excellent memory, Dickie. I know Father taught you a great deal of this stuff, didn't he?'

'Yes, and he said he would have liked to have been a sailor in the Royal Navy. I think I would, too.'

'Talking of the Navy, what do you do when you unexpectedly see a sailor?'

'Touch his collar for luck.'

Edward began to laugh, and through his chuckles he murmured, 'I think I'm actually running out of things to ask you about sea lore, do you know that?'

'It's all right, Ned, we're almost at the top of the steps. Are we going to give the fish to Cook? Perhaps she'll make it for supper.'

'Perhaps, although I think the cod are going to end up as fish cakes, because they *are* quite small, you know.'

It was Will Hasling who greeted them when they went back into the stable yard. He was standing at the back door waiting for them and he waved, and exclaimed, 'Do you two have a big catch then?' He was grinning from ear to ear, and seemed anxious to talk to Edward.

'What's the matter?' Edward asked, as they went inside the house together. 'You look *excited*.'

'Not really excited, but well, sort of relieved, perhaps that's the best way to describe my feelings.'

'Do tell me,' Edward answered, putting the fishing basket down along with his rod, struggling out of the cap and scarf and layers of clothes, then helping Richard to do the same.

'Neville telephoned whilst you were out. Apparently Oliveri has had a telegram from his contact in Delhi. It looks as if his little team out there have come up with just the evidence we need. David Westmouth is going to send it all in a series of telegrams – seemingly that's the quickest way.'

'Thank God we've heard from the fellow at last, I'd almost given up on him,' Edward replied, and this good news brought a smile to his face. 'Now, Tiddler,' he remarked, turning to Richard. 'Here's the catch of the day. Take it along to the kitchen and tell Cook it's *our present* to her. If she wants to keep the cod for herself, she can. Will you tell her that?' Lifting the fishing basket, Edward placed the strap on Richard's shoulder. 'Oh, and do me a favour, please, Little Fish. Ask her to please send hot tea and crumpets to the library, will you, my boy?'

Richard nodded. ''Course I will, Ned.'

The boy hurried off with the small haul of fish, walking rapidly down the corridor.

Will and Edward followed at a slower pace, a compatible silence between them. After they went into the library Will said, 'Once we have that information, everything can go ahead according to Neville. There's nothing else we're waiting for, not really.'

Walking across the floor, going to stand in front of the roaring fire, still chilled from his sojourn on the beach, Edward nodded. 'I'm anxious to get things moving, to be honest. The sooner the better. There's no real reason to wait, once those telegrams are received. I don't want John Summers and that bloody woman to do any more damage.'

He sighed and went to sit in a chair nearby, looked across at Will. 'There's a lot of rebuilding to do, of that I am absolutely certain. Rob Aspen and Alfredo Oliveri, and Christopher Green as well actually, will quickly pull the mining division into shape, but the vineyards in France are in need of an overhaul, and somebody will have to look after the northern offices. Things have grown slack, in my estimation.'

'Perhaps Johnny will agree to do that,' Will suggested. 'After all, he has a fund of knowledge about the north, after working for Neville all these years, and he has a family home in Yorkshire.'

'I expect he will have to take on that burden, if only for a short while. But I'll miss him, Will, he's invaluable.' Edward smiled at his friend with affection, swiftly added, 'I certainly can't let you work up here in the north. I need you in London with me.'

'And that's where I want to be. By the way, Ned, I spoke to Vicky while you were off fishing. And –'

'Did she mention Lily?' Ned asked eagerly, cutting across him.

'She certainly did. Lily is fine, and she's expecting you next week. If you go up to town I'll go with you, and Johnny will have to come, too. You know Neville's a stickler about protecting you.'

'Of course, there's no question about that. Is that all she had to say about Lily?'

'She confided that your darling Lily was looking beautiful, that she was in good health, and that the baby was showing a little, and that was about it.'

Edward grinned. 'Can you imagine that I'm going to become a father? It's hard to believe, isn't it?'

Will merely grinned, and exclaimed, 'And Vicky might well become a mother, Ned. She and Stephen are thinking about adopting that little girl Amos found in a cart. Don't you remember, he told us all about it at the last meeting we had. He seemed oddly touched by the child, and so is Vicky. More than that, actually, old chap. She's gone a bit potty about her, according to Stephen. However, he's all for the adoption because Vicky hasn't been able to become pregnant.'

'I think that's wonderful, and such a kindness to the child,' Edward replied. 'From what Finnister told us, the girl is rather pretty, isn't she?'

'Yes. Still, they don't know anything about her. Vicky told me that when they took her in at Haddon House she was sort of . . . well, permanently attached to a cloth bag and wouldn't be separated from it. Eventually they did get her to show them some of the things inside. There was nothing to explain who she was. So they call her Rose.'

'*Can* they adopt her?' Edward wondered out loud. 'I mean, *who* are they adopting her *from*? She was homeless, on her own, can't they just . . . take her in and bring her up as theirs? It's ludicrous to talk of adoption.'

'Good Lord, I hadn't thought about that!' Will exclaimed. 'Perhaps you're correct, maybe they don't have to do anything legal. Anyway, Fenella knows Hugh Codrill, the barrister, and he's apparently going to advise them.'

'Then they're in good hands.'

Before dinner that night, Edward went to his mother's upstairs sitting room. She was alone, reading a book in front of the fire; she looked up, and put it down when he came into the small boudoir.

'Yes, Ned, what is it?' she asked, smiling at him, beckoning him to enter.

'Can we talk for a few moments?'

'But of course we can. Is something troubling you?'

'Well, yes, as a matter of fact it is. I'm troubled about the tiaras, Mother. I don't want you to sell them so that you can buy me a house, in order for me to create my own household.'

'Ned, there's no other way to do it!'

'I think there will be and really rather soon.'

Cecily frowned. 'You do? Please explain, darling.'

'We have an enormous amount of evidence against the Grants and their adherents,' Ned confided. 'It's going to sink them once and for all. Actually, we could go ahead now, but Neville wants to wait until we have some telegrams which are coming soon from India. Oliveri has a good friend out there, a man called David Westmouth, and he's finally got the goods on Aubrey Masters and his dealings with the locals, those who are involved in the skimming I told you about. So, we're mounting a case and then we'll request permission to present it to the board.'

'I understand . . . when do you think you will do this?' she asked, her excitement reflected in her eyes, her expression eager.

'I hope it will be only a few weeks from now. In May.'

Now Cecily could not keep the smile off her face. She beamed at her eldest son and asked, 'Why are you still standing there? Come and sit with me for a moment, and tell me more.'

He did as she asked, lowered himself into a chair next to the fire, and explained, 'There's not a lot to tell, Mother. You already know most of it.'

'When are you going to London?'

'Next week. For a few days only, and then I'll be back for about a week. After that I'm going to be needed in town. You do understand, don't you?'

'Oh yes, I do, darling, I really do. I plan to remain here at Ravenscar for the summer. I know the London Season's not over, but that doesn't matter since we are a family in mourning and cannot participate. Therefore, in my opinion, we're better off here, and I think the children agree.'

'I know Richard does . . . he loves Ravenscar.'

'So does George, you know.'

'Yes, that's true,' Edward agreed, and thought: he would love it for himself.

'You will be running Deravenels, won't you, Ned?' Cecily suddenly asked, startling him.

'I will.'

'And Neville?'

'Ah yes, Cousin Neville. Mmmmm. Let me think . . . he will be advising me, helping me wherever he can, as will Johnny and Will.'

There was a pause.

Cecily was totally silent.

'What is it, Mother?' he asked finally when she remained mute.

'What does Neville hope to gain from all of this, Ned? He is the greatest magnate in England, and probably the richest. He already has everything. He doesn't need to help you run Deravenels . . .'

'I know that as well as you do, and I suppose he does, too. On the other hand, his father backed my father, the true heir to Deravenels. I believe he feels totally committed to do the same for me. There's his pride involved you know, and honour. And another thing. I would say he wants . . . *power*.'

'Oh, Ned, surely he has enough power.'

'When is enough *enough* for an ambitious man?'

'So what you are saying is that Neville wants power through you. Is that it?'

'To a certain extent.'

'Oh, Ned, be careful.'

'I am not a toy on a string, he is not my puppet-master. He doesn't control me. I am my own man.'

'Ah, but does *he* know that?'

'I should think so . . . Why Neville has known me all my life, and has only my interests at heart.'

'I say again, be careful, Ned. Be very careful.'

THIRTY-THREE

'It's becoming very painful for me to leave the child at Haddon House,' Vicky explained, looking from Fenella to her husband Stephen. 'And I worry about her so much when I'm not here, it's upsetting my life, my concentration, and almost everything I do.'

'I know it is, my dear,' Stephen said, reaching out, touching her arm lovingly. 'And I can't say I blame you. I realize you think there's a chance someone might come and claim her, or that she might run out into the streets and disappear. However, I don't believe there is the remotest chance of either of those things happening.'

'Neither do I!' Fenella exclaimed. 'She has become very attached to you, Vicky, we understand that. She took to you the day Amos brought her, and she can't wait for the days when you come here.'

Stephen Forth sat back in his chair, a reflective expression shadowing his eyes. At forty-two he was a successful banker with a rising career. A man of independent means, through his mother's family inheritance, he was a Harrow boy and a Cambridge graduate, and something of an intellectual. He was also a practical man, very down to earth, who believed in all things English, in the King, and in God, in that order. He had an enormous sense of justice, of fairness, and he was known for his kindness and charity. His looks were typically English. He had light brown hair and a fair complexion, and his warm brown eyes could fill with compassion or twinkle with fun and mischief. He was usually characterized by everyone as a nice man . . . nice looking, nice by nature.

Fenella was thinking exactly that at this moment when she said, 'So you are in agreement with Vicky, Stephen? About adopting Rose?'

'Oh yes, very much so. I think she is the most adorable child, and we can offer her so much.' He glanced at Vicky, and added with a smile, 'Vicky wants her, needs her in a sense, and so do I. Therefore, I will do anything I can to accomplish the adoption. Also, Fenella, Rose loves Vicky, we see that with our own eyes.'

'Of course she does –' There was a knock and Fenella broke off, looked at the door of her office, said, 'Come in!'

Amos Finnister appeared on the threshold and smiled at them all as he entered. 'Good afternoon, Lady Fenella, Mrs Forth, Mr Forth. I'm sorry I'm a bit late, but I was delayed on some other business.'

They greeted him warmly, and Fenella said briskly, 'Thank you for coming this afternoon, Amos, we really do appreciate it. Please, come and sit down.'

Amos did so, and observing the expectant expression on Fenella's face, he shook his head, and said, 'I'm sorry, I haven't been able to find out a thing about little Rose. There are no children missing in the area, in the local streets. I've inquired everywhere and I've even gone farther afield. Let me put it this way: if a girl *is* missing nobody's admitting it, or claiming her.'

Stephen said, 'And there was nothing in that old cloth bag was there, Vicky? Nothing to give us a clue to her origins?'

Vicky bit her lip. 'Absolutely not. Unfortunately. Yes, there were some interesting things, but they don't mean anything to *us*, in that they don't reveal anything about her. Obviously they do mean a lot to the child, she becomes frantic when we put the bag away for safe-keeping.'

'Perhaps I could have a look at the things again, later,' Amos murmured, 'after we've had our meeting. Talk to her about them.'

Vicky agreed. 'I think that's a good idea.'

Fenella now said, 'Well, I do have some good news. I have spoken to Hugh Codrill, and he says he can find no legal reason why you and Stephen cannot adopt Rose, Vicky. Legalities aside, he made inquiries at one of the local Dr Barnardo's Homes, and they have a good system when they take in children, whether they are off the streets or given up by parents who cannot keep them. For health or financial reasons. Every child is registered at Barnardo's. Name, date of birth, other family details. When a couple come looking to adopt a child, they are given a copy of the registration certificate, and if they are approved they receive adoption papers drawn up by Barnardo's.'

Leaning forward over her desk, Fenella finished, 'And he recommends that we do exactly the same, follow their example.'

Vicky beamed at her. 'That's such a relief.' She glanced

at Amos. 'As I told Lady Fenella, the other day Will asked me how we could adopt a child, when we didn't know *who* we were adopting her from. And Mr Codrill has given us the perfect solution.'

'He has indeed,' Fenella concurred. 'He is currently drawing up the appropriate documents, a registration agreement for Haddon House to use now, in order to register Rose and the details of her arrival here. It will be a document that we can have printed later, to use if any other children are found on the streets and brought here. However, I cannot encourage that, since we are not an orphanage but a safe house for destitute and battered women, as you know.'

'I presume Mr Codrill is also preparing documents for us to sign, Fenella?' Stephen asked. 'In other words, proper *legal* adoption papers?'

'Exactly, and they will be as watertight as he can make them.'

'And when will you have the documents, Fenella?' Vicky asked, her eagerness and excitement apparent.

'Within the week, but now that Hugh has done his legal research he just advised me that you may take Rose today if you wish.'

On hearing this news tears came into Vicky's eyes, and she gave Fenella a faltering smile and said, 'Thank you! Oh, thank you, Fenella,' her voice thick with emotion.

Her beaming husband put his arm around her shoulders. 'You see, my darling, everything has worked out perfectly, after all.'

'I must say, it's a wonderful relief for me, too,' Amos murmured, his face also ringed with smiles. 'I've worried about the little bairn for weeks now.' He smiled at Fenella and said, 'Thank you, your ladyship. Little Rose owes you a lot – well, we all do, really.'

It was Vanessa Barnes who took charge of the tea in the great room, with Vicky and Fenella helping her. As the women busied themselves, setting up cups and saucers and other accoutrements on the trestle table, Amos and Stephen Forth sat and talked for a few minutes about the mysterious circumstances surrounding Rose.

'I just can't understand it,' Stephen said, sounding astonished. 'How anyone could push a child like Rose out onto the streets, abandon her in such a way, staggers the imagination. It's frightening to even contemplate such a thing, never mind knowing it's actually being done.'

'There are a lot of monsters passing for human beings out there, Mr Forth,' Amos said in a sombre voice. 'Take my word for it. Long before I became a private investigator, working for myself, I was a copper on the beat, right here in Whitechapel.' He shook his head sadly. 'I can't begin to tell you what I've seen in my day – the most hair-raising things you could possibly conceive.' He gave Stephen a long look, and continued, after a moment, 'How any person could throw Rose away like rubbish I'll never understand. She's such a beautiful child.'

'Very, I agree,' Stephen was quick to say, and then asked, 'How old do you think she is, Mr Finnister?'

'Please call me Amos, everyone does. I must admit,

her age is hard to figure out. I don't think she can be any more than five, do you?'

'Isn't she a bit tall for five?' Stephen asked. 'My wife thinks she's four, though. And I suppose we'll never know.'

'I believe she's more than four, she's very bright and intelligent, but not *more* than five, I'm certain of that. I tried to find out how long she had been on the streets, but she wasn't able to tell me. She doesn't have any sense of real time, very few children do as a matter of fact. But she was very dirty, and her clothes were unusually filthy, so I can only think she was out there living in cubby holes and corners, scavenging for herself, for at least three or four weeks, possibly longer.'

An involuntary shudder passed through Stephen and he closed his eyes for a moment; when he opened them there was a strange look in them, a mixture of sorrow and pain most acute. He made no response to Amos's comment, just sat there looking sickened.

Finally, after a few seconds, Stephen said, 'When we saw her earlier this afternoon she was bubbling over with happiness that we were here. There's something quite lovely about her personality, when she's not so tense.'

'I know exactly what you mean, Mr Forth,' Amos replied. 'She's full of life.'

'That's a good way of describing her. Yes, Rose *is* full of *joie de vivre*.'

'Amos! Amos!' a child's voice rang out, and a moment later Rose was rushing across the floor to greet her friend.

As he watched her draw closer Amos thought she

404

had never looked bonnier. There was a big white ribbon tied on top of her auburn hair, and she wore black stockings, a navy wool dress and a starched white pinafore. He knew they were clothes Vicky had bought for her.

As she drew to a stop Amos grinned and picked her up, and swirled her around. And then he placed her on the floor, noticing at once how steady she was now, not wobbling the way she had when he had first found her.

'Hello, Rose,' he said, giving her a broad smile. 'You look beautiful in your new clothes.'

'Fank yer,' she said, and bobbed. 'Mrs Vicky give 'em ter me. She's like me Mam.'

Amos took hold of Rose's hand and led her across to the sofa, where he sat down, and brought her close to his knees, looked into her bright blue eyes. 'Rose, will you do something for me, please?'

'Summfink 'ard, is it?' she asked, looking at him keenly, her head on one side.

'No, no, it's not hard. It's easy. I want you to go to Mrs Vicky and ask her to unlock the special cupboard, so I can take a look at your things in your cloth bag.'

'Wot yer wanna look at me fings for?' she demanded, frowning, suspicious all of a sudden.

'We want to try and find out how old you are. It's possible something in the bag will tell us.'

Reaching inside the neck of her dress, Rose pulled out a piece of black ribbon on which hung the key. 'Mrs Vicky put the key 'ere 'cos I cried for me fings wen she took 'em.'

'Isn't she a nice lady? Well, come along, little one, let's go to the cupboard.'

Smiling up at him, taking his hand in hers, Rose led him across the floor to a series of cupboards built along the wall facing the trestle table. She pulled the ribbon over her head, and opened the cupboard. Then she reached inside for the cloth bag.

Rose was careful to lock the cupboard, and put the ribbon around her neck, before they went back to the sofa. When Vicky saw what they were doing she hurried to join them. She and Amos sat down on a sofa, and a moment later Stephen walked over, carrying a cup of tea for Vicky. After handing it to her, he said to Amos, 'Would you like a cup?'

'Not at the moment, thanks, Mr Forth. I want to concentrate on these items here.' He indicated the cloth bag with his head.

Rose looked at Amos and asked, 'Wot yer wanna see?'

'What about the photograph you showed me last time?'

Without a word Rose took the photograph out of the cloth bag and handed it to Amos. He stared at it for a moment then stared at Rose, and asked, 'Is this Mam?'

She nodded several times and said vehemently. 'Yeah.'

'She always says that,' Vicky volunteered.

Amos studied the photograph. It had been taken in a studio, no doubt in his mind about that, and it was by a good photographer. So it had cost money. Poor people did not have cash to spare to have their photographs taken.

Did this young woman in the picture come from money? She looked as if she did. Her hair was swept up on top of her head, with all the curls coming forward to the front. This was the current fashionable style, one favoured by the society women, who copied Queen Alexandra.

She wore a dark dress, and the lace collar was beautiful, came across her shoulders and chest, and it had the latest stylish high neck. Matching lace cuffs trimmed the long sleeves. As he peered at the photograph he noticed the young woman was wearing a star-shaped brooch which looked as if it was set with diamonds. He had not noticed it before because he had been concentrating on the woman's features. He also noticed the earrings sparkling, and they looked real.

The face was lovely; her eyes were large and she had a wide brow. The first word that came into his head was *class*. She had it, in Amos's opinion. She obviously came from good stock. Suddenly, he knew deep inside himself that this was true. He glanced surreptitiously at Rose, who was talking to Stephen and Vicky, and caught a glimpse, fleeting though it was, of the young woman in the photograph. She *was* Rose's mother, he truly believed that.

Turning the picture over, Amos looked again to see if there was a photographer's name on it. No luck, there wasn't. If there had been a name they would have noticed it when Rose had first allowed them to open the bag.

'What can you show me next, Rose?' Amos asked, and she turned from Vicky and Stephen, looked in the bag and brought out a key. She handed it to him.

It was a plain key, no name or markings on it. Amos shook his head. 'I don't know what this is for. Do you, Rose?'

'Mam's key,' she answered and looked at Vicky as if she could supply the answer.

Amos handed the key to the child. After putting it away she brought out a piece of flannel, a scrap really. He knew what it was – the gold wedding ring. He took it out of the cloth, his eyes resting on it for a moment, and then he wrapped it carefully and once more she took it, placed it in the bag.

There were other small things, which she showed him, mostly a child's treasures, things she had saved for herself. Several coloured glass marbles, a pressed flower between two sheets of paper, a handkerchief, and a small prayer book. Inside he saw again the neat inscription: 'To Grace from Mother.' No date. Nothing else. Not a word.

A brick wall, he thought. We're facing a brick wall. Looking at Vicky and Stephen, his eyes full of disappointment, Amos murmured, 'It's the same as last time, I'm afraid. I haven't found a clue amongst her things. I somehow thought I might, that there would be something there that would be a lead, a clue, something I'd missed before. I'm afraid it's wishful thinking on my part.'

'We understand,' Vicky said. 'And anyway, it will be like starting afresh, won't it, Amos? The three of us together . . . a new family.'

Pushing herself to her feet Vicky went over to Fenella standing near the table. She slipped her arm through hers, and said in a low voice, 'Thank you for everything you've done, my dear, dear friend. I shall be forever grateful.'

'Vicky, darling, I'm thrilled for you and Stephen, and for that simply gorgeous child. She's lucky, we're all lucky.'

'If it hadn't been for Amos and Haddon House –' Vicky broke off and shook her head. 'Imagine what might have happened to our little rosebud if Amos hadn't found her and you hadn't opened Haddon House three years ago?'

Fenella nodded and smiled. All of a sudden she seemed on the brink of tears. She swallowed them back, took control of herself, and together the two women walked across to the big sofa near the fire. As usual, the child was clutching the cloth bag, and appeared to be suddenly alarmed as the two women approached.

Vicky said, 'Don't look so frightened, Rose. I'm going home now –'

'Naw! Naw!' the child whimpered, and her face crumpled. Tears ran down her cheeks. 'Please doan go.'

'Ssssh,' Vicky said softly, and knelt down in front of her. 'You're going to come, too, Rose, with me and Stephen, to our house. And you shall live there with us, and we shall look after you always, and we shall keep you safe.'

THIRTY-FOUR

The sunlight filtering in through the many glass windows in the conservatory cast a soft golden glow on everything on this sunny May Saturday.

Amos Finnister glanced around, admiring the room, which was airy and lighthearted, yet extremely comfortable with wicker chairs and sofas filled with plump cushions, and matching occasional tables. It overflowed with white orchids and others of more brilliant hues. Nan Watkins's pride and joy, they were glorious, and Neville's wife had created an indoor garden that was serene and peaceful, a quiet haven.

Will Hasling, who was sitting with Amos, broke the silence when he said, 'I have finally met Rose, and she is the loveliest little girl. My sister and Mr Forth are thrilled to have her, and Rose is lucky to have fallen into their laps, so to speak, thanks to you.'

Amos looked across at Will, inclined his head. He had grown to like this young man, found him admirable in many ways, not the least in his devotion to Edward Deravenel, his genuine loyalty to him. Will was also intelligent, well informed about business and politics, and a warm-hearted, kind person.

'I wonder if you understand how *truly* lucky the child has been?' Amos asked in a low voice.

'To a certain extent, yes, I do. She could have died out there alone on the streets, from hunger or exposure, or she could have been seriously injured in some way. Or taken by the wrong kind of person, someone who might have easily abused her, hurt her.'

A shadow crossed Amos's face, his mouth tightened; there was a long reflective pause before he finally said, 'The latter would have been the worst, in my opinion. If you're dead you're free . . . certainly from further harm. Injured, you're in hospital hopefully, or being looked after somewhere safe. On the other hand, if you're grabbed by the wrong people, forget it.' He shook his head and there was a sudden sorrow on his face. 'Those kind are *unscrupulous*. They're the ones who sell children to brothels and to white slave-traders, who ship them abroad to be re-sold like so much cattle in markets dealing in humans. Boys as well as girls. Sold to brothels, where they are in bondage for the rest of their lives. They never escape.' Amos paused, and for a moment he looked pained, his eyes weary, his face pale. He sighed, then he noticed that Will was watching him closely, obviously interested in what he was saying.

Amos continued more slowly, 'Then there are those criminals who run gangs of children, they teach *them* how to be criminals, to steal in the streets and on the river ferries crossing the Thames . . . they are trained to be pickpockets, and they become dangerous little thieves, and they, too, are doomed to a life of crime and degradation.'

Will Hasling sat back, staring at Amos, a man whom he had come to like, respect and trust. After a moment, Will remarked, 'There's a whole world out there that few people are aware of. Especially people like me, who don't know much about crime and criminals and the East End.' He grimaced and added, 'We're not all that well informed, I'm afraid, are we?'

'That's true, sir. And you know, it takes all sorts to make a world,' Amos answered. 'Some of the worst types reside in Whitechapel, Limehouse, Southwark, and the environs. On the other hand, by the same token, there are innumerable good, upstanding, law-abiding citizens living there as well. Rose could have ended up being taken in by good people. However, more than likely they would have been very poor, and she would have been an extra mouth to feed. It would have made it tough on them, and she would have been a terrible burden.'

'Rose had a narrow escape, I understand what you've been saying,' Will murmured quietly. 'And I do have a bit of knowledge from my sister. She has told me a little about those awful places – the rookeries, in particular. They sound vile.'

'They're foul. Unspeakable broken-down tenements surrounded by dark alleys and cul-de-sacs, underground tunnels, dead-end ginnels and yards. The rookeries are enormous slums, and dangerous, Will, hard for you to comprehend. It's a violent world in there, not even the police go in unless they have to, and they never go in alone or even in twos and threes. They enter as a large posse so that they can protect each other.'

Leaning forward, Will now said, 'You've painted

quite a picture, a terrible picture, and what I don't understand is why they're not torn down?'

'And where would they *go*, the poor who live there? Answer me that.'

'I don't know, but what you've described is something inhuman.' Will shook his head vehemently, his eyes bleak, anger flickering there. 'Here we are, you and I, sitting in this beautiful house in Chelsea, living in the greatest, most influential, and biggest capital city in the entire world. *London*. Centre of a great Empire, the greatest there has ever been. We are a prosperous, innovative, industrious nation. We are influential around the world. Money is plentiful. London – in fact the whole country – is flourishing. And we are a kindly, humane race by nature. So, *you* tell *me* why the rookeries exist.'

'I wish I could. I've often asked myself that, and I've come up with no real answers. There are people who try to help such as Dr Barnardo, who started the homes for waifs and strays. He has been most successful. Other open-handed wealthy people, women in particular, have done much to alleviate terrible situations, and then there's the home Lady Fenella and her aunt started for destitute women. Mind you, I understand what you're saying . . . why doesn't the government do something? Am I right?'

'Exactly. It's so appalling, it makes me feel sickened, and ashamed, and now I truly understand why my sister has wanted to work with Lady Fenella and has given her money for Haddon House.' He smiled. 'By helping those much less fortunate she has found the child she has dreamed about. As for Rose, she must have a guardian angel watching over her.'

'And she has a few angels here,' Amos pointed out,

some of the tension leaving him. He went on, with a sudden warmth, 'Not only Lady Fenella, Mrs Forth and Mr Forth, but also Hugh Codrill. He has arranged everything in the most proper and legal way. Your sister and her husband have nothing to worry about, from what I understand. No one can take Rose from them now. She's their child, and she will have a good life.'

'I want you to do something,' Margot Grant said, glancing at John Summers. 'We must retaliate. I know they are responsible for Aubrey's death. *Jean, chéri, s'il vous plaît . . .*'

Reining in his black stallion, John Summers stared back at Margot, who also reined in her horse. She gazed into his face, a face that she had come to love, and whispered, 'I have a terrible foreboding . . . *les choses mauvais –*' She left her sentence unfinished.

There was a moment's silence. The two of them had been riding along Rotten Row in Hyde Park for the past half hour, and now under the spreading branches of the trees they rested their horses. It was warm on this May Saturday, a beautiful spring day.

John let out a small sigh, and murmured, 'How can I possibly retaliate? I've nothing to go on. I can hardly accuse Edward Deravenel of murdering Aubrey Masters. The police say he died an accidental death, it's not even suicide. They've dismissed the idea of murder. I must admit I'm torn, Margot darling . . . part of me thinks that Aubrey died because of his own carelessness, his strange eating habits. Yet another part tells me it has been a most *convenient* death for Edward Deravenel and his clique within the company. So yes, I'm suspicious, like you, but I must be careful what I do, for your sake as well as mine.'

Margot nodded and suddenly smiled at him. Her face became radiant in the sunlight filtering through the leafy branches, and his breath caught in his throat for a moment. How beautiful she was this morning; her black hair was pulled back in a chignon, and she wore a jaunty royal-blue bowler hat with a tiny spotted veil. The crisp white linen jabot brought a touch of femininity to her tailored royal-blue riding jacket which she wore with a long matching skirt and boots. Her black eyes were luminous in her pale oval-shaped face, and she beguiled and tempted him as always. Margot held a fatal attraction for him, and there were times when he asked himself why he had allowed himself to become so involved with her. For besotted he was. Like father, like son, he thought, and pushed those implications away from him.

Reaching out, resting her gloved hand on his arm, Margot said, 'I know you think Edward Deravenel is an amiable, pleasant young man with little in his empty head except chasing women. But I think you misjudge him, John.'

Shaking her head, her eyes piercing his, she added, 'I see him differently, ah yes, I do. Very much so. He is clever. And he uses his lighthearted personality to conceal his ruthlessness.'

'You've said that before, my dear, and I must say I do see it. I'm not dismissing Deravenel as empty-headed, no, not at all.'

'What *I* have *seen* is the way he has charmed his colleagues at Deravenels, at least those who have always had a leaning towards the Deravenels of Yorkshire. Such as Alfredo Oliveri and Rob Aspen. They appear to hang on his words. And *what* of Oliveri? You promoted him to be head of the mining division, and this, too, worries me. He has too much power now.'

John laughed. 'Oliveri is doing an excellent job,' he answered crisply, although he was himself more than ever suspicious of Oliveri's true loyalties. Changing the subject adroitly, he asked, 'How is Henry? You have kept him in the country for quite a while now.'

'You were the one who told me not to bring him to the office. That he was looking frail and ill. So yes, he is resting in the country.' Her black eyes suddenly danced and she smiled invitingly. 'Perhaps we can have lunch together . . . I can prepare a *pique-nique*.'

'What about your staff?' he asked, raising a brow eloquently.

'I have given them the day off . . . the weekend off, in all truth, John.'

'I see,' he murmured, and could not keep the smile off his face. 'So, we have a whole weekend at our disposal?'

'*Mais oui*.' Glancing around, seeing no one in sight, she leaned into him and kissed his cheek, whispered in his ear what she planned for that afternoon.

He did not respond, merely stared at her.

They set off at a walk, continuing down Rotten Row. Margot's brain was whirling, filled with so many thoughts. But the most important was how to persuade John Summers to take revenge against Edward

Deravenel. She was convinced he and his colleagues were behind the death of Aubrey Masters, one of Henry's true followers.

The Saturday lunch at Neville's house had become something of a ritual. Whenever they were all in London the six men met there to review their progress and enjoy a pleasant meal together.

The six of them stood in the handsome library, savouring an apéritif before going into the dining room. Edward Deravenel, as always, loomed over them, looking taller than ever, and even more handsome, if that were possible. He was talking earnestly to his cousin Johnny, who was listening attentively.

Edward had embarked on a discussion about libraries and books, and was confiding that one day, when he had a house, and money, he planned to have a library of his own.

'Like this one, perhaps?' Johnny asked. 'Except for the one at Ravenscar, I don't know of any other that is more beautiful, or better in any way.'

'That's true,' Edward agreed, and then turned at the sound of Neville's voice. His cousin had closed the library door, and was asking them to come and sit down near the fireplace.

They all did so at once, curious to know what Neville was going to say. For it was quite obvious he intended to speak; he took up a stance in front of the fireplace, without a fire today because it was mild weather.

'I am happy to announce that we are almost ready

417

to confront the Grants and their gang, and to bring them down. At long last,' Neville said. 'After sixty years of ruling the roost at Deravenels they will be hounded out of office.'

'I do sincerely hope God is listening to you, Neville,' Edward remarked, staring hard at his cousin. 'Because whilst I believe we should strike them soon, I do want *us* to win.'

'Oh, we will win,' Neville assured him, with a bright, confident smile. 'Finnister has everything ready.' Neville glanced questioningly at the private investigator, who nodded and stood up.

'I have now finished all of my work. The records from the asylums have been studied by numerous doctors, and all of them believe the records do indicate that Henry Grant is an ill man, suffering from dementia. There is absolutely no problem regarding my two colleagues, the thespians, who have already ingratiated themselves with Beaufield, Cliff and Dever, the three directors of Deravenels with unsavoury private lives. They *can* be blackmailed, I'm positive of that. Many of my other operatives have been spreading rumours about the Grants, rumours that have taken hold and paint them in a bad light. Yes, we are ready.' Amos sat down and smiled as the others applauded him. 'Thank you,' he acknowledged.

Neville said, 'I think you have something to say now, Oliveri, do you not?'

'I certainly do,' Alfredo answered and rose. 'Over the last few weeks I have kept you all informed about my old friend David Westmouth, and the situation in India. He has been working for us. I have received much documentation from him, which reveals the massive theft, and skimming, at our mines there. Westmouth is already on the high seas, en route to England, and he is bringing more evidence with him.'

'When will he arrive?' Edward asked eagerly, leaning forward.

'Within the next ten days,' Alfredo answered. 'And as you know, Beaufield, Cliff and Dever are implicated in some of the stealing that has gone on in India, apart from their scurrilous behaviour which Amos discovered.'

'So they are doubly condemned,' Edward murmured. 'I have good news to report, in that I have discovered I have many friends within the company these days, all of whom can't wait to see the last of the Grants. We can rely on their unanimous support.'

'Let us proceed into lunch, gentlemen,' Neville announced with a wide smile. 'I think we can celebrate, toast each other in anticipation of our success. Because I know we cannot fail.'

THIRTY-FIVE

Vicky glanced at herself in the dressing-table mirror, adjusted her hat slightly, and then left her bedroom. As she climbed the staircase to the third floor, now known as the nursery floor, she reminded herself not to forget the envelope Stephen had given her before leaving this morning. It was a bank draft for Haddon House, a gift from them to Fenella, in appreciation of all she had done in the matter of Rose's adoption.

As Vicky went into the playroom, Rose looked up and broke into smiles when she saw her. She jumped off the chair and ran across the floor, her little face shining with happiness.

Bending down, Vicky hugged her, then taking her hand she led her back to the table where she had been drawing pictures with a crayon in a drawing book.

'Where yer goin'' the child asked glumly, eyeing Vicky, a troubled look in her clear blue eyes at the sight of Vicky all dressed up.

'To see Lady Fenella,' Vicky replied. 'I am going to have lunch with her.'

'Me come?' she asked eagerly, instantly smiling. 'Fenella nice leidy.'

'Yes, she is, and she loves you, Rose, but it's not possible today. I will take you to see her very soon. Please don't worry, darling, I won't be gone for very long.'

Rose nodded her understanding, but her body had tensed, and that apprehensive expression Vicky had come to know so well now flickered on her face. She always became upset and worried when Vicky went out.

'I promise I will be back in time to have tea with you,' Vicky said, smiling reassuringly, squeezing the child's hand. 'Frances will look after you.' A frown brought Vicky's eyebrows together in a jagged line as she scrutinized the child. She was suddenly concerned. 'You *do* like Frances, don't you?'

'Yeah.' Rose leaned back in the chair, and bit her lip, then asked in a low tone, 'I live 'ere wiv yer fer ever?'

'Of course you will! I keep telling you that this is now your home, and it always will be, Rose. *Forever.* Until you're grown up at any rate, and then you can do whatever you wish.' Leaning across the table, she added, 'Don't you remember, darling, I told you that Stephen and I have adopted you?'

'Wot's it mean?' Rose asked, her puzzlement apparent, her eyes growing huge in her face.

'It means that *you* are *our* little girl. You belong to us, and we belong to you, and nobody can take you away from us. We are your parents.' When she saw that Rose did not quite understand what this meant, she explained, 'We are . . . your mother and father.'

A wide smile spread across the child's face. 'Yer me muvver?'

'Now I am, yes, yes, *I am*. But I wouldn't want you to ever forget your first mother . . . *Mam*.'

Sliding off the chair, Rose ran across the floor to her bedroom and went inside. When she came to the bedside chest she opened the top drawer, took out the photograph and the prayer book which had been amongst her treasures in the cloth bag.

Vicky had followed her, now stood watching her from the doorway, wondering what this was all about.

A split-second later Rose came back to her, pointed to the woman in the photograph, and said, '*Mam* . . . 'ere's Mam.' And then she offered Vicky the prayer book. 'Mam . . . she gimme it. Mam put summfink in it fer me wiv 'er pen.'

Vicky experienced a sudden rush of excitement on hearing these words, and she held herself very still as she opened the prayer book and looked at the inscription. Out loud she read, 'To Grace from Mother.'

Rose was smiling and nodding. 'Yeah. Mam put it in.'

'So this is *your* book? Not Mam's book?'

'Yeah.'

'Then your name must be . . . *Grace*.'

'Yeah, yeah.'

'*You* are Grace?'

'Yeah, I jest tells yer that. *Me*.' She patted her chest. 'Me is Grace.'

Several hours later Vicky was recounting the story of the prayer book to Fenella and Lily. The three women were lunching together in Fenella's summer dining room which opened onto the garden of her house in Mayfair. White wallpaper patterned with green ivy leaves, a plethora of flowering plants and white-painted furniture made the room an extension of the garden. The overall effect was charming, light and airy.

'I wonder why she never told us her name was Grace before now?' Fenella murmured in a puzzled voice, frowning.

'I can't know for certain, obviously,' Vicky answered, 'but I do have several thoughts about that. When we first questioned her about her name, she told us her mother called her *liddle rosebud*, and I think that's the name that stayed in her mind after her mother died. Assuming she *is* dead, of course. I have a feeling that the name Grace is associated with her past. Another time, another place, not London at all.'

'Why do you say that?' Lily asked at once, sounding perplexed.

'Because I am fairly certain she and her mother lived near the sea. When Stephen and I took her to Stonehurst a couple of weeks ago she was so happy when we went to Romney Marsh. The first thing she did when we were drawing close to the sea and the beach was to sit down, take off her shoes and her stockings. She wants to go paddling, she announced. When I questioned her about this she literally *glowed* when she told me she had done that with Mam. She also wanted to look for seashells, became excited when she found a strand of seaweed. All in all it was a very happy weekend for her. Another thought of mine is that she must have been in stunned shock when her mother died and she was thrown out onto the streets. It's perfectly obvious she was *still* in shock when Amos found her.' Vicky paused, took a sip of water, and went on, 'Fenella, I'm positive your friend Dr Juno Newman would agree with me. Shock causes terrible problems for adults, never mind children. I'm sure it's worse for them. *Liddle rosebud* is what she's clung to because it is associated in her mind with her *mother* and *now*, rather than the past.'

'So where do you think she and her mother lived by the sea?' Lily asked, putting down her soup spoon, staring at Vicky.

'I'm sure they lived near the sea in the north, more than likely Yorkshire,' Vicky responded, her voice full of confidence.

'Because she uses the name Mam, rather than Mum or Mother?' Fenella raised a brow quizzically.

'Yes.'

'But you've told me she has such a Cockney accent,' Lily reminded Vicky.

'Not all of the time, I've noticed,' Vicky swiftly replied. 'Sometimes she says *yes* instead of *yeah*, *isn't* instead of *ain't*, and so on. She was full of tension when Amos found her in the cart and brought her to Haddon House, as you well know, Fenella. Stephen thinks that she has begun to relax, to feel safe with us, and that she's changing in many of the things she says, the way she speaks.'

'That makes sense,' Fenella said. 'But I am still curious, nevertheless.'

'Well, she says thank you, rather than *fank*, and the Cockney F is being replaced with TH, with certain words. But the shock aside, she's grieving for her mother,

I'm sure. I've found her crying at different times, and when I ask her what's wrong she just says "*Mam*", in a desperate little voice, and comes into my arms for comfort, sobbing.'

'Oh that poor child,' Lily exclaimed. 'I would like to know who the fiend is who threw her out on the streets of Whitechapel. I'd have him horse-whipped.'

'So would I,' Fenella agreed, then shook her head. 'It's odd, isn't it, Vicky, that we all thought the prayer book belonged to her mother and that it was her mother who was called Grace.'

'Yes, but Rose was so specific this morning, very sure when she said it was *her* prayer book, that her mother had given it to her, and that she was Grace.'

'What shall we call her?' Fenella now wondered out loud, looking across at Vicky, then at Lily. 'Rose or Grace?'

'I prefer to call her by what is obviously her real name . . . Grace,' Vicky said. 'But I could ask *her*, and we can always attach the name Rose anyway.'

'So she would be Grace Rose Forth,' Lily said, smiling. 'That sounds rather nice. Anyway, I can't wait to meet her. I'm so sorry I haven't been well enough to come for tea as you've suggested several times, Vicky darling.'

'You *are* feeling better, aren't you?' Vicky peered at her dearest friend. 'There's nothing wrong with your pregnancy, is there, Lily?'

'No, I'm in good health really, it's just the ghastly morning sickness sometimes, it gets me down.' She smiled. 'Ned fusses so much about me. Frankly, I'm glad he's gone to Ravenscar with Will.'

'They're going to stay up there through Whitsuntide,'

425

Vicky said. 'Will has really been looking forward to it.'
A sudden smile illuminated her face with radiance, and
she continued, 'I rather think there is a new lady in his
life, and that she lives in Yorkshire.'

'Oh who is it, do tell us,' Lily cajoled, her eyes
sparkling, filled with interest.

'I would if I knew, but I don't have a name, not yet
at least. However, he seems very happy, and I've never
seen my brother looking so well, so handsome.'

'As usual, Ned hasn't said a word to me about it,
he's very close-mouthed,' Lily pointed out. 'He never
discusses anyone's business. Very discreet, my Ned.'

Fenella laughed. 'That may be so, but I do think most
men gossip as much as women.'

She rang the bell for the butler as she spoke and
within minutes the soup bowls had been removed and
the fish served.

The three friends chatted enthusiastically about
various matters during lunch, but the most important
topic they addressed was improving Haddon House.
Their aim was to find ways to better help those women
less fortunate than they.

THIRTY-SIX

The two women who walked down the steps of the tall house in Curzon Street were good looking, fashionable, and elegantly dressed. Because of their stunning appearance many heads turned, especially those of the opposite sex, as they glided forward across the pavement to the open carriage waiting in the street.

Vicky was dressed in a silver-grey silk taffeta dress with a tight waist and long flowing skirt, topped by a matching jacket trimmed with pale-green ric-rac. On her head she wore a cartwheel hat of grey leghorn which had pale green and grey osprey feathers fastened to the wide brim.

Lily was in her favourite pale blue. Her loose-fitting silk dress had a matching capelet that fell to her hips, and helped to conceal her condition. Her hat was an unusual tricorn shape made of pale blue silk, with white ostrich plumes attached at one side, and she wore it with great panache, as stylish as she always was.

The driver of the carriage, Lily's favourite landau, helped her in first, and then Vicky followed. The two women sat together in the low-slung carriage with its low half doors, spreading out their gowns, making themselves comfortable.

The landau was open to the world, its double, soft, folding tops at the front and back folded down on this beautiful May afternoon. One of the reasons Lily loved this luxury carriage, which was only ever used in the city, was because its low shell provided great visibility, showed off the occupants. It was often referred to as a women's carriage since their clothes were displayed to great advantage.

Once Robin, the driver, had climbed up onto his bench just above the two horses, Lily said, 'We are taking Mrs Forth home to Kensington, but let us drive through Hyde Park, it's such lovely weather.'

'Right-o, ma'am,' Robin responded, made a clicking sound with his tongue, and set off up Curzon Street making for Park Lane.

Lily turned to Vicky and said, 'Perhaps I'll come in for tea. If that's all right?'

'Oh Lily, darling, that's wonderful!' Vicky exclaimed. 'You know how much I've wanted you to meet Rose . . . goodness me, I'll have to get used to calling her Grace, won't I?'

Laughing, Lily nodded. 'Yes, I think you will. On the other hand, she might wish to remain Rose, it's such a pretty name.' Lily eyed her best friend carefully, dropped her voice, and added, 'I'm so glad you and Stephen adopted her . . . you might even become pregnant now . . . that often happens, you know.'

Vicky smiled but made no comment.

'It was very generous of you both to give Fenella a

thousand pounds for Haddon House. She was thrilled,' Lily murmured.

'We wanted to help, and she can make good use of the money, as you're well aware. You've been generous yourself these last three years, Lily, have given her rather a lot of money.'

'It's for an important, worthy cause, and I have so much, so many good things in my life. I *have* to give back, I just can't be any other way. When I think of those poor women and the straits they're in I go cold inside.'

'I do, too. Their plight makes me wonder what Grace's mother went through. She was obviously living with some man who probably mistreated her.'

'I agree, and I'm coming round to your idea that Grace and her mother did come from the north.'

'Look, Fenella spotted the child's use of the word Mam for Mother immediately, because she comes from Yorkshire. As you well know, their family seat is just outside Ripon, and I was also instantly aware of it because I've spent so much time at Ravenscar with Will and the Deravenels.'

'Yes, I know, and I suppose she must have picked up the Cockney accent in the last couple of years, don't you think?'

'It's more than likely –' Vicky broke off, turned to Lily and said, 'Doesn't Hyde Park look pretty today? I can't wait to drive through it.'

'I knew you'd enjoy it.' Leaning forward slightly, Lily said to the driver, 'Where are you going to enter the park, Robin?'

'At the top of Park Lane, Mrs Overton. I thought you'd get to see a bit more of it that way.'

'Thank you, that's a splendid idea.'

The two women went on chatting about Grace Rose, as Lily had suddenly started to call her, and also touched on the child she herself was carrying. 'I'm glad I have purchased the house near you in Kent, Vicky. It will be a lovely, comfortable home for us, for me and the baby, and if Ned wants to come and stay sometimes he can. But as I've told him many times, there's no pressure.'

'I know he wants to be involved.'

'Did he tell you that, Vicky?' Lily asked, her eyes sparkling, her face eager.

'No, he didn't, but I can see how much he cares for you, cossets you, is solicitous of your well-being, Lily. I've been surprised actually, because I always thought he would just . . . abandon you, let you get on with it all by yourself.'

Lily laughed out loud. 'As a matter of fact, so did I! And I didn't care, I wasn't worried about myself, or the baby. As you know, I'm perfectly safe, because of my late husbands, and the money they both left me. But I can't say I'm not glad Ned's happy about the baby, because I am. Obviously he means to be part of our lives. And, before you remind me yet again, I know he won't marry me. He can't, and I don't want him to.' Eyeing Vicky, Lily now murmured, 'You think of him as the great womanizer, don't you?'

'Yes, don't you?' Vicky gave her an intent look, frowning slightly.

'Of course I do. He's always been a womanizer, and he always will be,' Lily answered. 'Women are his drug, he's addicted to them.' Suddenly her laughter broke out

430

again, and leaning closer to her dearest friend, she whispered, 'He once told me that he had been seduced by a young married woman when he was *thirteen*, and that he'd never looked back.'

Vicky couldn't help but join in Lily's laughter, and eventually, as she calmed herself, she said, 'Well, one cannot say that he's not *honest*.'

'Always, and too honest sometimes,' Lily shot back.

The two women fell silent, and shortly after this the carriage entered Hyde Park, the dappled grey horses trotting forward at an easy, gentle pace.

The trees were in bloom, leafy green bowers filled with sunlight above their heads, and the shrubs and bushes were alive with colour, their flowers bursting into bloom. It was the beginning of the last week of May, and spring was truly full blown in this year of 1904.

Lily felt exceptionally happy this afternoon. The morning sickness seemed to have subsided in the last couple of days, and she was really feeling very well at the moment. Ned had been particularly attentive, and very loving before going to Yorkshire for Whitsuntide.

It seemed to her that all was well with the world. Although she had not told Vicky or anyone else, Lily had purchased a lovely and rather compact house in South Audley Street, and fully intended to live in it part of the time.

Glancing around, she noticed a number of children playing on the grass. Some were rolling hoops, others were throwing balls to each other, and they all seemed to be so happy and carefree. There was nothing like the frolicking of children to cheer the spirits.

A few women were taking an afternoon stroll, walking along in pairs; there were several nannies out, pushing large perambulators in front of them; and she spotted several courting couples arm-in-arm, moving slowly under the trees.

Otherwise there was not much other traffic in the park today, only a couple of carriages in the distance. How tranquil it was, this little green haven in the middle of the largest and most important city in the world.

'Good Lord!' Vicky exclaimed shrilly. 'What's going on ahead of us? Look at the rider on that big charcoal stallion! Oh my God, he can't control the horse! It seems to be having some sort of a fit, stamping its hooves and rearing. Look now, Lily. Look how he is rearing up on his hind legs.'

'I can't see!' Lily craned her neck even more, shuddered involuntarily and cried to her driver, 'Robin! Please pay attention to that horse up ahead. There's something wrong with it. Oh my God, it's bolted. It's heading this way, with the rider clinging on for dear life!'

Vicky was staring ahead, keeping her eyes pinned on the rider and the horse, her heart in her mouth. The man was endeavouring to restrain the stallion, but it appeared to be beyond him. The horse was coming towards them, hell bent for leather, throwing its head backwards, snorting, its nostrils flaring. There was foam on its wide mouth; it bared its big white teeth. The rider seemed panicked, and as he drew closer to their carriage Vicky noticed that he was handsome in a fleshy way, with dark eyes and hair, and a long scar on one cheek. He looked foreign to her. He stared at her for a brief moment through

432

hard eyes. He glanced longer at Lily, Vicky thought. She felt herself recoil, shivering.

'Robin, try to calm the greys!' Vicky shouted.

'Stop moving! Stop!' Lily screamed. 'For God's sake stop the carriage moving, Robin. There's going to be an accident.'

'I can't curb them, Mrs Overton,' Robin shouted back over his shoulder, every muscle straining as he pulled on the reins.

Everyone had seen the horse and rider, and children were brought onto the grass, were running under the trees, away from the main avenue which cut through the park.

Suddenly the horse and rider were upon them, only a few feet away from the landau. The great horse reared up on its back legs, snorting and tossing its head again, now immediately in front of the greys. They instantly reacted, stamping their feet. And then they bolted.

They were moving too fast now, Lily understood that at once. Robin was struggling, pulling on the reins but the horses and the landau had taken off at high speed. The animals had been totally frightened by the stallion and were out of control.

It seemed to Vicky that everything happened very fast. Lily was shouting orders, as was she; Robin was doing his best to bring the greys to a halt, but with no success. Suddenly the horses increased their pace. Vicky clung to the side of the carriage, as did Lily. And then it happened. The carriage tipped over.

Vicky felt herself flying up out of her seat and being thrown sideways. She screamed. A moment later she was lying on the grass at the side of the avenue, stunned.

Lily had tried to grab hold of Vicky with no success,

and had been thrown out of the carriage as well; she herself was now sprawled on the ground, and a portion of the landau was covering her lower body, pinning her down.

Pandemonium broke out.

People were hurrying to them.

Robin, bathed in perspiration, his face stricken, was trying to reach Lily, who was partially on the grass, partially on the road.

Groaning, swallowing, Vicky opened her eyes and immediately saw horses' hooves and she recoiled at once, crying out, thinking it was the wild stallion.

'It's Mrs Forth, isn't it? Stephen Forth's wife?' a cultured voice was asking her.

Vicky raised her eyes, saw a man dressed in proper English riding clothes; he was mounted on a roan, looking down at her through worried eyes.

She nodded, and whispered, 'Yes.'

'My name is Horace Bainbridge, Stephen and I belong to the same club. I'm sure you're hurt. Do you think you are, Mrs Forth? You must be.'

'I don't know,' Vicky responded, her voice raspy. 'My leg hurts. It could be broken.' Glancing towards Lily, she went on urgently, '*Please*. Go and help my friend, help her driver. He's trying to lift the carriage off her body.'

'Certainly I will, at once. And I shall telephone your husband at the bank. Ah, I see policemen coming. I shall tell them ambulances are required.'

'Thank you,' Vicky whispered.

The man on the horse had trotted off; she could see him talking to the police. Now he was coming back, heading for the landau to help Robin.

Vicky pushed herself up on her elbows, began to drag herself across the grass to Lily. As she drew closer her throat tightened; dread flooded through her. Finally she reached her friend, took hold of her hand, held it tightly in hers.

She could see Lily better now. The images hurt her eyes . . . the blue tricorn hat lying on the ground . . . the white ostrich feathers fluttering in the breeze . . . Lily's white face . . . oh so very white. And the blood . . . so much blood . . . staining the pale blue silk . . .

THIRTY-SEVEN

Ravenscar

Edward sat reading in a corner of the library, immersed in *Our Mutual Friend*, one of the novels by Charles Dickens which he had not read before. It had been published in 1865, and was one of the author's last books. Edward was enjoying it, found it fascinating, even though the rowdiness from the other side of the library was beginning to annoy him.

Suddenly he sat up straighter and banged the book down on the small occasional table. 'Stop it, George! You're being intolerable,' he exclaimed, glaring at his brother.

'It's not me making the racket, it's Richard!' George cried, glaring back.

'Why are you always so ridiculous, George? And such a little liar. Of course it's not Richard, it's *your* voice I hear. Do you think I'm deaf? Or that I cannot distinguish the difference in your voices?'

George's bravado fled; he sat back in the chair, looking sulky, his mouth drooping at the corners. For a moment he hated his older brother.

Richard said, 'It's all right, Ned, I don't mind that

he shouts a lot, although I do care that George says I don't know how to play chess.'

'I don't blame you, Little Fish. And you certainly *can* play, and very well. After all, I taught you, and you've beaten me many times.'

Will began to laugh. 'You all sound just like my brothers . . . Goodness me, I might well be at home at this very moment.'

'But you *are* at home,' Ned shot back, laughing. 'My home is your home, and it always will be wherever I am in this world.'

At this moment Jessup came in carrying a tray with a coffee pot on it and cups and saucers. After placing it at the end of the long magazine table, he looked across at Edward and asked, 'I was wondering if you and Mr Hasling would like a *digestif* with your coffee, Mr Edward? Perhaps a cognac?'

'I think I would, thank you, Jessup. How about you, Will?' He glanced at his friend, smiling, his geniality restored.

'Why not? Thank you very much.'

George said, 'I'd like a brandy, Jessup.'

'Not on your life!' Edward said swiftly. 'Just bring the two cognacs please, Jessup.'

The butler nodded and hurried out.

'When *can* I have a cognac after dinner then?' George asked, suddenly belligerent, a tone which Edward well recognized.

'Not for a very, very long time,' Edward shot back. 'When you're grown up, not until then, rest assured of that.'

George did not respond; he lolled in the chair, his

sulky expression settling on his face. Moody and put out, he retreated into himself as he did when he felt thwarted.

Richard, aware of the sudden tension in the room, said in a placating voice, 'It was kind of Uncle Neville to invite us to Thorpe Manor for lunch on Whit Sunday, wasn't it, Ned?'

'Indeed it was. I'm looking forward to it, and I'm sure you are, too. You'll see Anne, and you, George, will see Isabel –' Edward broke off as Jessup appeared in the doorway.

'Yes, Jessup, what is it?' he asked.

'A telephone call, sir, for Mr Hasling.'

Will put down the *London Illustrated* he was reading and rose, hurried across the floor, glancing at Ned, shrugging to indicate his bafflement. He said, 'Please excuse me, Ned. I wonder who it can be calling at this hour?'

A moment later Will was picking up the receiver in the Long Hall. 'Will Hasling here.'

'Hello, Will, it's Stephen.'

'Stephen!' he exclaimed, surprised to hear from his brother-in-law, frowning. 'Is everything all right?'

There was a moment's hesitation at the other end of the line, and then Stephen Forth answered in a tightly controlled voice, 'I'm afraid not. There's been a dreadful accident, a terrible accident, Will. Vicky and Lily were involved. They were injured today –'

'Oh my God, no!' Will cut in, and clutched the receiver tighter. 'What happened? Tell me what happened. Are they seriously hurt?'

Stephen began to speak, his voice shaking at times

as he explained what had occurred in Hyde Park that afternoon, and Will sat down heavily on the wooden hall chair, his heart sinking as he heard the disastrous news.

After he had hung up the telephone, Will sat for a moment or two trying to compose himself. Finally he rose, a little shakily, and as he turned around he saw Ned coming out of the library into the Long Hall.

'You were so long on the telephone, Will, I began to think something was amiss –' Ned broke off when he saw Will's face, and he exclaimed, 'You're as white as a sheet! There's something the matter.' Edward hurried forward, took hold of his friend's arm, saw the distress reflected in his eyes, felt Will's entire body trembling.

'What is it? Please tell me.'

Will nodded, then swallowed. 'Let's go somewhere private, I need to speak to you alone.'

'The Morning Room,' Edward answered, and guided Will across the hall, wondering what on earth had happened to make him so upset. He just hoped it wasn't something to do with his father's health.

Once inside the Morning Room, Will sat down in a chair and indicated that Edward should sit opposite.

He did so, and said again, 'Tell me what's upsetting you, Will, *please*.'

'It's Vicky,' Will began, and took a deep breath, tried to steady himself, 'And Lily. They were in an accident this afternoon, and –'

'Oh my God! Are they badly hurt?' Edward asked,

leaning forward, his eyes on Will, suddenly filled with apprehension.

'Vicky has a broken leg and a broken rib, and her face is very, very badly bruised,' Will began, and realized that his voice was shaking. He swallowed, and went on, 'Lily has a broken shoulder and two fractured ribs –'

'Thank God they're both alive!' Edward interjected, relief rushing through him. 'Broken bones do eventually mend.'

'Ned, Lily has . . . concussion . . .' Will paused, shook his head, and added in a voice that was almost inaudible, 'I'm so sorry . . .' He shook his head once more, whispered hoarsely, 'She lost . . . the baby, Ned.'

'*Oh, no, no,*' Ned muttered in a tone that was nothing much more than a whisper, and closed his eyes. After a few moments he opened them and stared at Will, sounding stunned as he said, 'She so much wanted the child, and so did I, you know. I really did.' He brought his hands to his face and wept.

Will rose, went to Ned, and bending down, he put his arm around him. 'I'm so sorry, so very, very sorry.'

Ned clasped his friend's hand, held it for a moment, and then he sat up straighter, looked into Will's eyes. 'Lily . . . and Vicky . . . they *are* going to be all right, aren't they? You're not holding anything back, are you, Will?'

'No, not really,' Will answered, his voice cracking. 'Lily . . . well . . . actually she's in a coma.'

Edward said nothing, just gaped at Will and tears brimmed once again but remained unshed. His mouth was trembling as he asked, 'People do come out of comas, Will, don't they? She will, won't she?'

'Stephen was very hopeful, very positive. And they are now in the best of hands. Stephen has had them moved to the Masterson Private Clinic in Harley Street, and they are getting proper attention, the very best of medical care.'

'I must go to London tomorrow, first thing,' Ned announced softly, taking out his handkerchief, wiping his tear-streaked face.

'I know you must. So must I. We will go together. We should catch the first train leaving York. At the crack of dawn.'

'I'm so sorry about Vicky, Will. She's not injured more than you're saying?'

'No. Vicky sustained the injuries I mentioned, and that's all.'

'What kind of an accident was it? You haven't said anything to me about that.'

'I know, but I wanted to inform you of their injuries first, and explain Lily's condition, and –' He stopped abruptly; he couldn't say it again, he couldn't mention the loss of the baby.

Edward seemed to understand this without being told, and he murmured, 'I always thought the baby would be a girl, I don't know why but I did . . .' His sentence trailed off and he leaned back in the chair, staring at Will, frowning. His bright blue eyes were red-rimmed. 'Tell me how it happened, won't you?'

'Vicky and Lily lunched with Fenella today. At her house in Curzon Street. After lunching, Lily and Vicky went for a drive through Hyde Park . . . because it was such a lovely day, and anyway Lily was taking Vicky home to Kensington. Apparently a big horse, a huge charcoal stallion, suddenly went berserk on the main thoroughfare, and the rider was unable to control it. It galloped forward, caused Lily's calm little greys to become upset, and they were so frightened they bolted. They just shot forward, trying to get away from the rampaging horse. They were going at quite a pace, very fast, and the landau overturned.' Will shook his head, his distress apparent. 'Stephen says that this style of carriage has a high centre of gravity, and that when it's moving at great speed it's not so manoeuvreable, that it's prone to tilt to one side, and to roll over.'

'And that's what happened, isn't it?' Edward said in a low worried voice. 'Christ Almighty! Lily and Vicky are very lucky they weren't killed outright.'

'I know,' Will agreed. 'Fortunately the police were on the scene within minutes, and an ambulance was sent for. Lily and Vicky were taken to the hospital at Hyde Park Corner, but later Stephen had them moved to the private clinic.'

Edward took a deep breath, then blew out air, shook his head vehemently. 'I've seen some really wild riders in the park lately, especially when I've been on Rotten Row. A lot of them don't seem to be very good equestrians. And another thing, Will, what sort of man is it that cannot control his horse? I ask you that?'

Will was silent, thinking of the things he was holding back, wondering whether or not he should reveal everything Stephen had told him.

Almost as if reading his friend's mind, Edward asked, 'You have told me *all* of it, haven't you? Is there anything else I should know?'

When Will did not respond, Edward probed, '*Is* there something else? Please don't keep me in the dark. This is all too serious. And don't do my thinking for me either, especially if it's about Lily and her condition.'

'There is something, yes, Ned, but it's not about Lily's condition,' Will finally responded. 'It's about Vicky actually, however, not her injuries. What it's about is . . . well, she has a theory, Ned, about the accident.'

'A theory?' he repeated and frowned, perplexed.

'She's not sure it was an accident, she thinks it might have been deliberate.'

'*Deliberate*? How could it have been deliberate? You said the horse went out of control –' Edward paused and fixed his eyes on Will, giving him a shrewd look. 'We're both pretty damned good equestrians, you and I, and I suppose we could do a lot of things to a horse to make it run wild, make it bolt. And if we gave it certain medications, potions, we could engender excitement, agitation in it, now couldn't we?'

'This is exactly what Stephen said. Any good rider who knows horses can manipulate them, especially if the animal has been doctored with something beforehand.'

'Is Vicky suggesting that Lily . . . was a target?'

'Yes, I'm afraid so.'

'She thinks it's the Grant faction?'

'That's what she's suggesting, Ned. When Stephen told me this, I asked him why she would think such a thing. He answered that Vicky hadn't liked the look of the manon the horse. She described him as dark-haired, with dark eyes, hard, knowing eyes was the way she put it. And that he had a long scar on one cheek. She also thought he looked foreign.'

'A hired hand?'

'That's the general idea . . . she said that the rider had looked at her for a long moment, but stared even harder at Lily. Vicky explained there was a malevolence about him that she couldn't quite define, and that it had made her recoil.'

A terrible coldness settled over Edward. Deep down he suddenly knew that Vicky was right. He leaned forward, pinned his eyes on Will. 'But *how* would they know Lily would be driving through the park? Answer me that.'

'I think it's a relatively easy thing to figure out, Ned,' Will answered. 'Let's say Lily was being followed on a permanent basis, as we know *you* are. When she left Belsize Park Gardens this morning she would have been spotted immediately in her landau, and tailed. She goes to Curzon Street, to Lady Fenella Fayne's house. Vicky, who lives in Kensington, arrives in a hansom cab which is dismissed. When Lily leaves after lunch she takes Vicky in the carriage with her . . . a clever private investigator could have easily worked that out in advance. Earlier he would have anticipated that Lily would take Vicky home, drive with her through the park to Kensington. On the main avenue. The rider could have been stationed somewhere along the route during the ladies' luncheon, ready to make a move against them if they suddenly appeared. If they didn't, well, nothing lost.'

'A staged event, is that what you mean?'

'Yes,' Will said, 'and women are so *predictable*, you know. Most would want to drive through Hyde Park on a beautiful day, and a true lady, with manners bred in the bone, would always take her best friend home.

444

If someone did cause the accident, they were relying on predictable behaviour.'

In the still of the night, when the din of the evening had passed, Edward lay in his bed unable to sleep. He was fully aware that as long as Lily was in danger sleep *would* elude him.

The shocking accident had driven everything else out of his mind; all he could think of was his darling Lily, her condition, and the loss of the child she was carrying.

He felt the pain of this most acutely, and he knew only too well how stricken she would be. Not long ago she had explained how much she wanted to have the baby. 'I know that I can't have *you*, Ned, at least not forever. One day you will leave me, to go and start a whole new life . . . and that's one of the reasons I want our child . . . so that I can have a part of you with me for as long as I live.' He had realized that night how much she truly loved him; tonight he had understood, finally, how much he loved her.

His mind ran on, filled with disturbing thoughts and worries. Would she come out of the coma? If she did, would her mind be impaired in any way? Would her physical injuries leave her damaged? On and on . . . he tossed and turned, restless, full of anxieties.

New demons began to creep into his head as he suddenly focused on Vicky's injuries, and *her* wellbeing. And he began to struggle with her suspicions about the accident, weighed the possibility that she could be right.

Edward trusted Vicky's judgement, had always

445

respected her, admired her, considered her to be rock solid, just like her brother, Will. If she suspected foul play and evil hands at work, then so did he. How to find out, how to ascertain whether the Grant faction at Deravenels had been behind this ghastly occurrence?

By the time the clock in the corridor outside his room began to strike four, Edward finally flung back the bedclothes and got up. He went into his adjoining bathroom, shaved and bathed; in the bedroom, he dressed in his travelling clothes, then he went downstairs. He had packed a few things last night, and his small suitcase was in the vestibule, just off the Long Hall; next to it stood Will's luggage.

He walked along the corridor to the kitchen and went into Mrs Latham's private domain. But of course she was not there, not at four-thirty in the morning. He ran the tap at the sink, filled a glass with cold water and carried it back to his father's office.

Once seated at the desk, he took a piece of writing paper and began a letter to his mother. Mostly he thanked her for her concern of the night before, and her kindness to him, her heartfelt sympathy. She was a great lady, Cecily Deravenel; she had shown him nothing but compassion, love and understanding in his grief, and when he had confided that Lily had miscarried his child in the accident his mother had wept.

When he came to the end of the letter he told her he would remain in London until Lily was out of danger and well on the way to recovery. Only then would he contemplate returning to Ravenscar, most probably in July or August, to spend time with the family.

He had just sealed the letter when the telephone on

the desk began to ring, and he picked it up at once. 'Ravenscar,' he said, 'Edward Deravenel here.'

'Oh, Ned, it's you . . . er . . . er . . . actually I expected Jessup to answer, it's Stephen.'

'Good morning, Stephen. Do you wish to speak to Will? Or is it me you're looking for?'

There was a hesitation, a painful silence, and somehow, deep in his soul, Edward Deravenel knew what Stephen Forth was about to say to him. Instinctively, he braced himself.

'I'm so sorry to call at this hour . . . However, Will said you would be leaving at dawn for London, I didn't want to miss you. Ned . . . I have the worst news . . .' His voice took on a quavery tone and he could not continue.

Edward said, 'Is it about . . . Lily?'

'Yes,' Stephen whispered.

'She's dead, isn't she?'

'I'm so sorry, so very sorry, Ned.'

'Thank you for calling,' he answered, his voice husky. He hung up, unable to speak another word.

He sat staring out into the room, a room he had always loved but which now seemed so alien to him. Blinded by tears, he pushed himself to his feet and rushed out, knocking over a small occasional table in his haste, not even bothering to stand it up. Unlocking the French windows he went down the steps cut through the hanging gardens, moving at breakneck speed and he did not stop until he came to the ancient stronghold on the promontory overlooking the North Sea.

As he went into the circular ruin which had once been a watchtower the light changed, and dawn suddenly broke. A pure crystalline light silvered the edge of the horizon, spread upward to illuminate the skies with radiance.

'Lily! Lily!' he cried out loud, lifting his eyes to the sky. Then leaning against the stone wall, he wept for her and for their baby until there were no tears left in him.

As he straightened and wiped his face with his hands an icy coldness settled over him, and his heart turned to steel. He stood there looking out to sea, and cursed the Grants. Those bloody bastards . . . they had killed his father and his brother, his uncle and his cousin, and now his woman and his child.

'I swear to God I shall not rest until I have destroyed the Grants of Lancaster,' he screamed into the wind. Then he turned and strode towards the chapel . . . To say a prayer for Lily and the child he had never known.

THIRTY-EIGHT

London

'I'm all right, really I am,' Vicky said, looking up at Fenella. 'I'm perfectly comfortable.'

'I just want to put another pillow behind your back,' Fenella Fayne answered, and did so swiftly. 'I had a broken rib myself once, and I felt much better sitting up rather than lying down.'

'It's true,' Vicky replied. 'I didn't realize you were something of a Florence Nightingale! And thank you for the flowers, they're lovely. You're spoiling me, Fenella.'

Her friend merely smiled, seated herself in the chair next to the large sofa in Vicky's downstairs parlour, where Vicky was spending most of her time. Her leg, because of a break in the shin bone, was in a plaster-of-paris cast, and she found it difficult to climb the steep stairs to the upper floors in the house.

Before she could stop herself, Fenella now leaned forward and straightened the colourful, crocheted wool afghan which covered Vicky's legs. Leaning back in the chair, she asked, 'How is Edward Deravenel? Have you seen him again?'

'Yes, he came for tea yesterday, with Will. He's taking it hard. Not that you would know it, actually. He's very self-controlled, holds himself in check, but I know how much he feels it inside. He loved Lily. The accident, the loss of their child and her death . . . well, all I can say is that he is utterly *devastated*.'

'I'm not surprised, Vicky, I've known him for years and I've always liked him. So many people dismiss him as an empty-headed, amiable young man who spends his time chasing the ladies but I'm acquainted with a different Edward. Also, my father has a lot of time for him, thinks he's quite brilliant. Much brighter and more focused and ambitious than his father Richard ever was, according to Papa.'

'Will would only agree with you,' Vicky murmured, and fell silent. After a few seconds, she continued in a worried voice, 'I'm afraid Will is rather angry with me. He said I shouldn't have told you about my suspicions regarding the accident, and that you shouldn't have told Mark Ledbetter.'

Fenella frowned. 'But why on earth shouldn't you tell me? We're old friends, close friends! I mentioned it in passing to Mark because he's with Scotland Yard. It occurred to me that he might be able to find that incompetent rider, who wasn't all *that* incompetent after all, was he? If he did set out to cause an accident. Surely you want some sort of justice, don't you, Vicky?'

'That's just it, *the Scotland Yard part*. Will says Edward doesn't want Scotland Yard poking around in Deravenel business.'

'I see,' Fenella replied. 'I'm sorry if I've caused problems, Vicky, but I'm afraid it's too late. Mark said he would come this morning, around eleven o'clock to have coffee with us. He wanted to ask you a few questions.'

Vicky sighed and bit her lip. 'Then I shall answer them, Fenella, there's nothing else I can do. But I do hope Mark's investigation dies a natural death . . . that's what Will and Edward hope, too.'

No sooner had these words left her mouth than the doorbell rang, and she glanced through the open door of the parlour, saw the housekeeper, Mrs Dixon, hurrying to answer it. Glancing at the clock on the white marble mantlepiece, she said, 'If this is Mark, he's a little early.'

As Chief Inspector Mark Ledbetter came into the parlour, Fenella quickly stood up, and went to greet him. 'You are so very prompt. Always,' Fenella said, as he bent to kiss her on the cheek.

Mark smiled. 'Only by a few minutes,' he murmured and went across the room, leaned over and took Vicky's hand, kissed it with a small show of old-fashioned gallantry. 'Good morning, Vicky, I do hope you're feeling a trifle more comfortable.'

'Yes, I am, thank you, Mark. And good morning.' Vicky looked up at him, and added, 'Why don't you sit in the chair near the fireplace, it's very comfortable.'

'Of course,' he agreed, and did as she asked.

Fenella said, 'Mrs Dixon will be bringing coffee in a few minutes, Mark, unless you would prefer tea.'

'Coffee's fine, thank you very much,' he answered, leaning back in the armchair. Glancing over at Vicky, he sounded sympathetic as he said, 'It was quite an ordeal you had on Monday. I was saddened to hear of

451

Mrs Overton's death. Such a terrible tragedy. I'm so sorry.'

Vicky nodded, and her eyes filled with tears. This happened a lot at the moment; she blinked them away.

Fenella, deciding to jump right in, and possibly diffuse the situation, said, 'Mark, I'm afraid Vicky is now beginning to think she might have been overly-imaginative in her theories about the incident in Hyde Park. Not that Vicky is given to flights of fancy, mind you, she's really very down to earth. Nevertheless, she's rather sorry I troubled you.'

'I've always been a firm believer in women's intuition, Fenella, you should know that by now. And you, Vicky, were an eye-witness to an unusual occurrence, one that does leave me wondering a little. It sounds quite bizarre.'

'It does, and it was,' Vicky responded. 'Everything happened so suddenly, so quickly . . . I'm sure there's never ever been an accident quite like that before, especially in Hyde Park.'

Mark nodded his agreement, went on in a conversational tone, 'Why don't you tell me what happened on Monday morning, from the moment you left this house and went to Fenella's in Curzon Street, to later, when the landau entered the park.'

'All right,' Vicky agreed, and did so, carefully taking him through her activities that day.

Mark listened attentively, and when she had finished he said, 'Could you please describe the man again, the rider?'

'He was dark-haired, had dark eyes. I thought they were hard, knowing, perhaps even cruel. There was a

. . . malevolence about him, the way he looked at me and at Lily. And he had the appearance of a foreigner.'

'What makes you say that?' Mark asked curiously, his eyes not leaving her face.

'I'm not sure, but it did strike me that he wasn't English.' Vicky stared off into the distance, narrowing her eyes, trying to remember, and then turning back to Mark, she said, 'His skin was a little . . . *swarthy*, I think that's the best word to use. Then the long scar down one cheek gave him a devilish look, piratical. He just wasn't . . . *normal* in his appearance, not the kind of rider one would expect to see in Hyde Park on a spring afternoon.'

'What about his clothes?' Mark probed. 'Were they the sort of togs an Englishman would wear for riding?'

'No . . .' Vicky paused, sounding hesitant. 'I remember thinking how English and properly dressed Horace Bainbridge was – he's the man who knows Stephen and came to speak to me after the carriage overturned. I remember thinking that he was wearing proper riding clothes . . . I may have been making a comparison. The dark-haired man wore a burgundy jacket . . . the cut and the tailoring were off.' She nodded her head. 'Yes, now that I really am thinking, I realize the jacket was more European in style, and he had on strange trousers, not riding breeches. Actually, Mark, I do believe they were the trousers of a suit . . . yes, they matched the jacket. He must have pushed them into his riding boots.'

Mark reached into the inside pocket of his jacket, brought out a folded piece of paper, walked across to Vicky and handed it to her. 'Is this the man, do you think?'

453

Opening the piece of paper, Vicky stared down at the sketch on it, and immediately caught her breath. 'Why yes, Mark, it is! That's him. How did you get this?'

At this moment Mrs Dixon and Elsie, the parlour maid, came into the room, each carrying a silver tray. 'Excuse me, madame,' the housekeeper said to Vicky with a small smile, and hurried to a console table under the window. She placed the tray holding the coffee pot and cups and saucers on one end of the table, and made room for the tray Elsie was carrying. Coffee was poured, cream and sugar offered, and Elsie then took the plate of biscuits around to everyone. Within seconds the two women had departed.

Mark took a sip of his coffee, then began to explain. 'Last night a dead body was found in the East End, down near the docks in Limehouse. The man had a gunshot wound to his head, and it certainly looks as if he was murdered. From the angle of the wound it could not have been self-inflicted. When this murder was brought to my attention early this morning, it struck me that the description fitted the one Fenella had passed on to me. I had one of my men make the sketch, and I later went to the morgue myself to view the victim and look at his clothes. Although all the labels had been cut out, the clothing did appear to be European-made.' Mark nodded and pursing his lips, he added, 'And as you've probably guessed, the jacket and trousers were both cut from burgundy coloured cloth. But even without taking the clothes into consideration, the long scar on one cheek was enough to identify him as the rider who caused the accident. At least to me.'

'There's no question in my mind either,' Vicky said in a firm tone. 'This is the man. Most definitely.'

Mark finished his coffee, stood up, walked across to the console table, put the cup and saucer on the tray. Returning to the fireplace, he stood with his back to it, his expression reflective. Finally, he said, 'Maybe this foreign-looking fellow was merely a poor rider, an incompetent, unable to handle his steed well, and he therefore got into trouble with an overly skittish, disturbed horse, and panicked. Perhaps it was, pure and simple, a terrible accident that led to an enormous tragedy.' He looked from Fenella to Vicky, focused on the latter. 'That *could* be true, couldn't it?'

'Yes,' she agreed.

'On the other hand, what if it wasn't? Let's just suppose it was all staged. Why would anyone target you and Lily Overton, Vicky? *Who* would want to do either of you harm? And real harm at that?'

Vicky swallowed, steadying herself, and remembered the written words which had been given to her last night by Edward. Words she had memorized, following Will's most explicit instructions. Slowly, she began, 'I don't think anyone wished to harm me, no, not at all. If there was a target it was Lily.' Now she paused, as Will had instructed her to do, and waited for Mark to ask his next question.

'Why would someone wish to harm Lily?' Mark asked.

Edward had predicted he would focus on Lily now, and she was ready with her answer. 'My brother, Will Hasling, has felt for a long time that Edward Deravenel has an enemy, or indeed *enemies*, who wish to cause

455

him harm. Some months ago, Edward was himself attacked one night, and badly beaten up. So much so he was in hospital. I know from Will that it was an Inspector Laidlaw who looked into the attack. No culprit was ever found, nor do my brother, or Edward, know why anyone would wish to hurt him, or who those enemies might be. It's all a bit of a mystery.'

'So Lily Overton was a target because of her friendship with Edward Deravenel, that *is* what you're saying, isn't it?' Mark sounded momentarily puzzled.

'I am,' Vicky answered. 'Unless, of course, I'm being a little imaginative about the rider of the horse that went berserk. It could have been accidental, as we agreed a moment ago.'

'I understand what you mean. On the other hand, perhaps you're not imagining anything. After all, the rider is now a murder victim. If he *was* hired they certainly got rid of him awfully quickly. The accident was Monday, he died last night, which was Wednesday. The disposal of the only genuine witness to a staged killing, the killer himself, has been rendered ineffectual, and most rapidly, wouldn't you say? All very convenient.'

Vicky simply nodded, since she had been instructed to say nothing more than she had already said.

Fenella glanced at Mark, and asked, 'So what's the next step? What are you going to do?'

'We will endeavour to put a name to the body, and obviously we must attempt to find the person who shot the man. Hopefully we'll be lucky, and come up with something.' Mark shrugged, 'However, some of these cases are hard to crack.'

'It all sounds like a wild-goose chase to me,' Vicky

pronounced in a strong tone, silently praying Mark Ledbetter would drop the case, sooner rather than later. She hated the idea that she might have caused more heartache for Edward. Better the whole thing remained a mystery rather than have Mark digging into things which did not concern Scotland Yard.

THIRTY-NINE

Lily Overton had died on Monday. On Friday afternoon of the same week she was buried.

There were six pallbearers: Edward Deravenel, his cousins Neville and Johnny Watkins, his best friend Will Hasling, Stephen Forth, Vicky's husband, and Amos Finnister.

Only a small number of Lily's friends had been formally invited to attend the funeral service and burial in Hampstead, and Vicky and Fenella had been quite unprepared for the number of people who did attend in the end. The church was full: all of her friends and the people she had known had shown up to pay their respects.

There were a few gasps and whispers when the coffin was carried into the church and down the central nave by the six pallbearers, all of them men who were either unusually good looking or distinguished in appearance.

Because Vicky was on crutches she gave the eulogy in front of the three small steps which led up to the altar below the huge stained glass window, positioned immediately behind the coffin. Fenella also spoke, as did Will Hasling, from the pulpit.

All of them touched on Lily's generosity of spirit, her loving nature, the charities she had so generously supported, most especially Haddon House.

At Edward's request it was Johnny who read the twenty-third psalm, his voice only wavering slightly when he first began with the words, 'The Lord is my shepherd, I shall not want.' It grew stronger with each line, and because he had a mellifluous voice, everyone listened attentively.

Edward sat staring at Lily's coffin at the bottom of the altar steps, covered in the white lilies he had sent. He was lost in despair, the deepest despair he had ever known, and he wondered how he was going to pull himself out of it. How he would go on.

As the service proceeded, and the vicar gave a brief sermon, and hymns were sung, prayers said, he asked himself why she had died so tragically. Lily had been cut down at the prime of her life . . . And then he thought of their unborn baby, and his heart tightened, shrivelled within him. He was a man alone now that his darling Lily was gone.

Later it was Will who took his arm and led him back to the coffin. As he hoisted it up on his shoulder with the other five men and carried it out of the church, he thought of John Summers and the Grants. Edward was convinced he could place her death on their doorstep. He knew it deep in his bones, and his bones never lied to him. How would he revenge her death?

Neville Watkins took Amos Finnister to one side, and asked 'Did you get information out of Mark Ledbetter? Has he discovered anything?'

Amos drew closer to Neville and whispered, 'It's more than likely the rider was French. I got that from Paul Coleman, Mark's police sergeant who works with him.'

The two men were standing in a corner of Vicky Forth's drawing room in her Kensington house. All of those who had been invited to attend the funeral had come for refreshments after the burial, guests of Vicky and her husband.

Amos glanced around, and said in the same low voice, 'I think we need to be in private, Mr Watkins. Let me ask Mrs Forth if we can use another room.'

Neville nodded, and watched Amos pick his way through the small group of people who were sipping tea, nibbling on sandwiches, and reminiscing about Lily Overton.

A few seconds later Amos returned. 'Mrs Forth says we can go into the library.' As he spoke he ushered Neville out of the drawing room and across the hall.

Once they were inside the library overlooking the large garden, Amos closed the door and strode over to join Neville, who was standing near the French doors.

'To continue,' Amos murmured. 'Sergeant Coleman didn't have much more information to offer, at least that's what he said. However, I went down to Whitechapel last night, made inquiries of my own. I picked up a few things. One of my contacts told me that a Corsican, who had once been in a circus troop on the Continent, had been seeking a job, mostly asking around about working with horses. My contact said the man had a deeply indented scar on one cheek, was dark-haired and had black eyes.'

'From the sound of it, that has to be the rider of the stallion,' Neville ventured.

'The description certainly fits,' Amos answered, and continued, 'Apparently the man's nickname was Nappo, short for Napoleon because he came from Corsica, too. No one knew his real name, it seems. My chappie sent him up West, to Mayfair and environs, and he said that later he'd heard that Nappo had secured a job driving a carriage for some fancy French family, or rather, a fancy French lady. My contact added, "a real beauty she is, so I'm told."'

Neville smiled a small smile, staring at Amos; he finally nodded his head. 'A French lady, eh? Well, well, I can certainly think of one French lady who is a real beauty, and so can you.'

'Yes, sir, I can. Margot Grant be the name.'

'That does give us food for thought, doesn't it? Perhaps you can attempt to confirm that this Nappo worked for the Grants?'

'I'm already on it, Mr Watkins.'

'Very good. Was the incident in Hyde Park retaliation for Aubrey Masters's death, I wonder? What do *you* think?'

'More than likely.'

'You told me a few weeks go that I was being followed, so why wouldn't Mrs Overton have been followed as well? We're both closely connected to Edward, at least she *was*. I still am. And the Grant faction have a lot of money . . . they can afford to employ an army of private investigators, if the truth be known.'

At this moment the door of the library opened a crack and a small burnished head of red-gold curls peeped around it. 'Amos! Amos!' the child cried when she saw her beloved friend and rushed into the room.

As she flew across the floor to him, Amos bent down and she came straight into his arms, hugged him tightly. He hugged her back, and glanced up at Neville, and was surprised to see the most startled expression crossing the other man's face.

Releasing the child, straightening, Amos explained, 'This is the little girl I found in Whitechapel, Mr Watkins. Her name is Grace Rose and she now lives here with the Forths.'

Neville said in a kindly way, 'Hello, Grace Rose.'

The child dipped, gave a slightly wobbly curtsy. ''Ello,' she answered solemnly, her face serious.

Suddenly, the door flew open and Edward marched in, saying as he did, 'Vicky told me I would find you in here –' He broke off when he noticed the child standing near the French doors. She turned her head, and when she saw Edward, broke into smiles.

Cornflower blue eyes gazed into cornflower blue eyes, and locked. It was Edward who finally blinked and looked away. A faint memory touched his mind, but fleetingly so. He tried to grasp it but it was elusive, was gone in a fraction of a second.

At last Edward took a step further into the room, and said gently, 'Hello.' The little girl simply smiled at him again but said nothing.

Amos said, 'This is the child I found, Mr Edward, her name's Grace Rose.'

'My goodness, here you are, Grace!' Vicky exclaimed as she came rushing into the library on the heels of Edward. 'I've been looking all over for you.'

'It's all right, Mrs Forth,' Amos murmured. 'She's not really disturbing us.'

'You're so kind, Amos,' Vicky replied graciously, taking hold of Grace's hand, leading her across the floor. 'And I'm so sorry she intruded,' she added, glancing from Neville to Edward, smiling faintly, apologetically.

As the door closed behind them, Edward said, 'I think we must make our moves against the Grants, Neville. I don't want to wait any longer. Surely we are now fully prepared to go to battle with them?'

'Indeed we are, Cousin.' Neville smiled broadly. 'And it shall be done. *Now*.'

Margot Grant stood staring down at the boy sleeping in the narrow bed. Dark lashes lay against his creamy skin, a small hand was resting under his cheek. *Her beloved Edouard.* Her son. Seven years old now, and the most important person in the world to her. He was her joy and her pride, an intelligent boy, with a vivid imagination and such determination. He was so quick and smart and eager to win.

There was no one like him, as far as she was concerned, especially in his personality and character. Henry twiddled his thumbs and said constant pious prayers, did nothing; Edouard reached out eagerly to the world, wanting everything, knowing he could take it all, and he would, one day.

He was the heir to Deravenels. She was going to make sure he inherited the mantle now worn by his father.

'*Margot.*'

The whisper of her name made her turn around.

John Summers stood in the doorway; he was staring at her longingly, and when she beckoned he came into the bedroom immediately.

He put his arm around her waist and drew her closer, stared into her eyes. Against her hair he whispered, 'I have to go back to London soon.'

Margot nodded, then swung her gaze to the child sleeping so soundly. 'Isn't he the most beautiful thing?'

'After you, yes,' he answered softly. It was on the tip of his tongue again, the tantalizing question which always remained unasked. Was this boy his half-brother? His father's son? He dare not ask her. And even if he did, she would never answer him. Certainly she would never tell him the truth. The boy must always be seen as Henry Grant's only child, and the heir apparent to Deravenels. He understood that necessity. He was the future of the Grant dynasty, young Edouard.

Leaning down, Margot touched the boy's cheek lightly, and then turned away, and together she and John left the bedroom on tiptoe.

Once outside in the corridor, he asked, 'Where is Henry? I should say goodbye before I leave for London.'

'He's dozing in his bedroom, as usual,' Margot answered, and took hold of John's arm, grasped it tightly. 'Come with me for a moment, *chéri*. Let us take our leave of each other in the best way possible.' A moment later she opened the door to a small sitting room and led him inside. Locking the door behind her, she stepped into his waiting arms, kissed him deeply, and let her hand slide down his leg. She felt her senses swimming, her legs were suddenly weak, her heart pounded.

John Summers pressed her hand against his crotch.

'See what you do to me?' he whispered, and then he lifted her up in his arms and carried her over to the sofa.

She lay back against the pillows, smiled up at him; he joined her on the huge couch, lifted the skirts of her loose summer dress, and slid his hand up a bare leg. There were no underclothes to hamper him, and after touching her intimately for a few minutes, making her gasp, he stood up, threw off his jacket and trousers. Lowering himself on top of her, he took her to him passionately. And she responded with her usual ardour, her desire for this man flaming through her; when they came to a climax together, she had to cover her mouth with her hand in order not to scream out with pleasure.

A short while later she went downstairs with him, and they shared a glass of wine on the terrace over-looking the lawns.

'I adore you, Margot,' he said in a low voice, touching his crystal goblet to hers. 'And I'm sorry I must leave you here in the country. As always, business calls, matters at Deravenels must be attended to.'

'I know. I know, *chéri*, and I thank you from the bottom of my heart for holding the company for my son.'

He put his glass down on the wooden garden table, and turned to face her. 'Margot, there has been a new development. I haven't mentioned it for the last few days, because I wanted us both to enjoy our brief time together. However, I must inform you now that the mistress of Edward Deravenel died in a terrible accident earlier this week.'

'Oh,' was her only response.

465

John explained, 'There's gossip floating . . . gossip that this wasn't an accident at all . . . that it was a staged accident.'

'How strange,' she murmured, and leaned back on the garden seat, seemed almost uninterested as she gazed into the distance.

John waited for a moment or two, expecting her to make some sort of comment, but she did not. He took a deep breath, and jumped in with both feet. 'Please tell me we didn't have anything to do with this, Margot, that you did not take matters into your hands.'

'Oh no, *chéri*, I did not. Why would I?'

'You *were* behind the attack on Edward Deravenel.'

'This woman Lily Overton . . . what did she mean to me? *Rien* . . . nothing. I think the suggestion that it was something created is ridiculous. Who can make a horse become crazed? Now I ask you to explain that to me. *C'est pas possible.*'

John gaped at her, rendered speechless for a moment. He had not said a word about a horse going berserk, in fact he had not given any details at all. Leaning forward, he picked up his glass, gulped down the last of the wine.

It took him a moment or two, but eventually he calmed himself, stilled the violent machinations revolving in his mind. He must not even *think* that they were somehow involved.

Rising, he forced a smile onto his face, offered her his hand.

She took it.

He gently pulled her to her feet.

Margot said, 'I will walk with you to the stables, to

your carriage. I'm so glad you came.' She tucked her arm through his, and went on, 'I am so bored here in Ascot . . . and I miss you.'

He made no response, merely nodded. He was too perturbed to say even a single word to her.

FORTY

Ravenscar

'Do you think you can remember *everything*?' Neville
Watkins asked quietly, looking across the small bridge
table at Edward.

'Oh yes, Neville. Please be assured of that. However,
to make sure, I will commit some important bits to
memory.' Edward leaned forward, patted the pile of
papers on the table between them. 'I've already memorized certain salient points from my father's diary, if one
can call it that. It's really a lot of notes, jottings, his odd
thoughts about Deravenels, but useful nonetheless.'

'And the company rules?'

Edward smiled faintly. 'I have them down pat, thanks
to my mother.'

Leaning back in the leather wing chair, Neville now
asked, 'Do you mind if I smoke a cigar, Ned?'

'Please do,' was his laconic response.

Neville went through the process of clipping the end
of the cigar, lighting it, striking several matches to do
so, and puffing hard. Finally, it ignited, and he relaxed,
settled into the chair.

Although he had not shown it in any way, Neville was

beginning to worry about his cousin. Since Lily's death, two weeks ago now, he had seemed depressed, withdrawn even, which was not like him at all. There was an aura of sadness around Ned, and it showed in his sorrowful eyes, his gloomy expression. What struck Neville most forcibly was the quietness, almost a resignation, in the younger man.

As he glanced at him surreptitiously, Neville noticed the dark smudges under his eyes, which were lacklustre, and he appeared thinner in the face. He's not sleeping well, Neville decided, and he's grieving. But then why wouldn't he be? He had, after all, loved Lily; Neville had come to understand that. *Time*. He needs time to heal. But he's young, he'll spring back.

These thoughts brought a certain comfort to Neville, and he turned his mind to the board meeting which would be held in London in a few days. Ned would present his case against Henry Grant, and Neville was praying that he would win. *He had to win*.

For his part, Edward was focused on another meeting, one which had taken place last week. In the offices of Lily's solicitors, to be exact.

He had been meaning to tell Neville about this, yet he had not found the right time to do so. Deciding it was now, at this very moment, Edward announced, 'Lily left me everything, Neville.'

Taken by surprise, Neville sat up straighter and stared at Edward through startled eyes. '*Everything*,' he repeated, sounding incredulous.

'Yes.'

'You mean she made you her heir?'

'That's correct.'

'What of her family? Are they not put out?' Neville's light blue eyes narrowed. 'Surely there will be some sort of reaction, trouble about this? Or is the will watertight?'

'It's watertight all right, but there is no problem, Neville. Lily was an only child, well . . . actually her brother died when he was a little boy, of meningitis. So she ended up being the only child of wealthy parents. There are no other relatives. Lily was alone, except for me. And Vicky, her best friend.'

'I see.' Neville puffed on his cigar for a moment, and then murmured, 'It's always been my understanding that her late husbands left her very well taken care of indeed. Isn't that so?'

'It is, and she had a very shrewd head on her. Lily made some excellent investments.'

'It's a large estate?'

'Oh yes. Lily left me her house in Belsize Park Gardens, the house she recently bought in Kent, and another house she purchased about a month ago in South Audley Street. And –'

'Good Lord!' Neville exclaimed, cutting across Edward. 'She has made you a wealthy man, Ned, hasn't she?'

He sighed, and pursed his lips. 'She has. However, I'd much prefer to have her living and breathing and here in this room with us, rather than dead and buried in the ground.'

'Of course you would, I fully understand your feelings.'

'She left most of her jewellery to Vicky,' Ned went on, 'except for a few things she bequeathed to Fenella, and some of her antiques to Vicky, other pieces to me.

The rest of her furniture will go to Haddon House. Actually, Lily was rather generous to them, Neville. And to several of her other favourite charities as well, as a matter of fact. The residue of her estate comes to me.'

Neville sat back, his eyes focused on Edward. After a moment's reflection, he said slowly, 'I imagine the residue is quite large.'

'Yes,' Ned murmured, 'it is . . .' He decided to say no more.

Ever since he had returned to Ravenscar, Edward had lain awake at night, finding it hard to fall asleep. Nothing was different tonight. The moment he had closed his eyes his mind had begun to work, numerous worrying thoughts jostling for prominence, and sleep was, once more, elusive.

There was a full moon visible through the window, and it was coating everything in the room with a light layer of silver. Earlier he had opened the window and in the past hour the weather had grown colder than ever. It was always chilly at night here on the North Sea, even in summer, and he realized it must be bitter outside for the room to have grown this icy. The wind was blowing the curtains, and they were billowing out like the sails of a ship.

Jumping out of bed, he went to close the casement, then walked over to the fireplace, threw another log onto the glowing embers. The log instantly flared and crackled, sparks flew up the chimney, and he knew that within minutes the room would be much warmer.

Struggling into his woollen dressing gown and fastening the belt, he found his slippers, seated himself in a chair, pulled it closer to the hearth. His busy thoughts swirled in his head as he hunched down, leaned forward to warm his hands.

Unexpectedly, a small smile flickered on his mouth and was almost instantly gone . . . it was the first time he had been even faintly amused since Lily's death . . . The look on Neville's face this afternoon had been quite priceless. He had known instantly that his cousin was flabbergasted about Lily's will, even if he had taken the news in his stride.

Resting his head on the back of the chair, Edward closed his eyes, and thought of Lily; her generosity to him had been astounding. He heard her solicitor's voice echoing in the inner recesses of his mind, as Mr Jolliet had read from the will made three months before. 'If a child or children of mine do not survive me, and if I am not married, I do give and bequeath to my friend Edward Thomas Deravenel all of my worldly goods, as listed herein, and with the exception of . . .' And then Mr Jolliet had read out the other bequests and the recipients.

Oh Lily, Lily, if only you were here, he thought, his heart contracting. How I miss you, and how I wish I had told you just how much I cared for you. I did love you, Lily, I truly did, and with all of my heart. His thoughts drifted; he fell down into himself.

Catastrophe lurks around every corner . . . life comes at you hard, to hit you in the face. Life is full of

surprises, some of them good but most of them . . .
catastrophic. That is what my mother asked me . . .
has no one ever told you that life is catastrophic? Well,
I know now that it is. That is the way it has always
been, my cousin Johnny says, and that what matters
most is the way one handles catastrophes and
heartaches, the pain of it all. He told me the other day
that I cannot let Lily's death get me down. That I have
to keep my eyes on the goal: On Deravenels, he means.
And he is right, just as Neville is, too. I am glad it has
now all come to a head. Glad that the board have
accepted my request to bring a complaint against Henry
Grant. I am well prepared for the board meeting. I
have re-read my father's notes, gone through all of the
Deravenel papers, made my own notes, committed them
to memory wherever necessary.

Neville and I have met with Hugh Codrill, the famous
barrister, and he has reviewed everything for us, all of the
medical papers Amos acquired, the medical reports and
analyses. He has recommended a highly reputable law
firm, solicitors with whom we have met, and who will
advise me. No one can go to the meeting with me. Neville,
Johnny and Will are not part of the company and there-
fore cannot be present. But I have Alfredo Oliveri, Rob
Aspen and Christopher Green. The three of them happen
to be board members, and they are on my side.

Oliveri explained to me that after I have presented
my case, the board will take a recess, discuss every-
thing, and return to meet with me within two hours.
At that time they will tell me if I have a genuine case
or not. If I don't, then nothing more can happen. If
they agree that I have a strong complaint, due cause,

they will confer between themselves for several days, in order to make an ultimate decision. I will be summoned to a second meeting with them, and they will pass judgement. That is the procedure, and it has been in place for hundreds of years. Oliveri and Aspen have helped me to keep my spirits up. They are strong, loyal, level headed.

My cause is just. I must not lose. My father and my brother died at the hands of the Grants, so did Uncle Rick and my cousin Thomas. And Lily and my unborn child. I keep saying to myself that I want revenge. But what I really want is justice for those who died. My cause is right. Henry Grant has given up his power to John Summers and his wife, Margot Grant. And over sixty years ago his grandfather was the usurper.

I am the true heir.

I aim to win.

There was a light tapping on the door, and it brought Edward out of his reverie. Sitting up, he pushed himself to his feet and strode across the room.

Standing outside in the shadowy corridor was his youngest brother, shivering in his dressing gown, pale faced, his slate-grey eyes grown dark, almost black, genuine worry shadowing them.

'Good Lord, Little Fish! What are you doing here at this hour?' As he spoke Edward grabbed Richard and pulled him into his arms, then swept him into the room.

'I'm worried,' Richard murmured, his voice low, subdued.

'Come here, sit on my knee, and let's get ourselves warm. And you can tell me why a boy like you should be worried. After all, you have a mother and a big brother to look after you.'

Climbing onto Edward's knee, Richard settled himself against Edward's broad chest, and explained, 'I'm not worried for me, I am worried for *you*. George told me that your friend died, your lady friend, that is, and that you were broken-hearted. Is that true, Ned, are you broken-hearted and devastated? That's what George says.'

'And I wonder where Mr Know-It-All-George gets *his* information? Not from me, I can assure you of that, Tiddler.' Edward hugged his brother, and then tilted his face upward. 'I'm going to be all right, my lad, and thank you for your concern. You mustn't worry about me any longer. Don't listen to George. I can look after myself, and I say again, I will be fine.'

'Do you promise me that, Ned?'

'I *do* promise you that, Richard.'

'I want you to know that I am here, if you need me,' Richard now announced, looking up at his brother adoringly. 'I will always be here, as long as we both shall live. I want you to know that I will stand by you no matter what, especially when you have the fight with the man from Deravenels.' Richard frowned. 'Who *is* the man you have to fight?'

'I have to fight Henry Grant and the men who are on his side within Deravenels. His associates. But we are not going to . . . well, it's not a physical fight, with our hands up, going at each other, like in a boxing match. It's not that kind of fight at all.'

'What is it then?' Richard asked.

Edward told him slowly, and carefully, explaining everything, and once Richard had nodded his understanding, Edward slid his brother off his knee and stood up. 'Now, let's go down to the kitchen and raid Cook's larder. We'll have a midnight snack and then you can share my bed if you wish, Little Fish.'

His answer was the radiant smile of Richard's face.

FORTY-ONE

Ripon

Nan Watkins turned on her side sleepily, reaching out for Neville. He was not there; instantly she opened her eyes, saw the bedclothes thrown back, and her gaze flitted across to the windows in their bedroom.

Neville was standing at one of them, gazing out. Tall, erect, and very very still, his stance suggested he was deep in thought.

There was a full moon tonight and it filled the room with clear, bright light, made everything perfectly visible. His face, in profile, was vividly illuminated, and as she usually did she thought how handsome he was. Her heart fluttered inside her. He was her whole life; without him she would be nothing, would barely exist. She genuinely loved her daughters; but her husband came first: he always had.

There had been other women before her, but none since their marriage. He had told her this countless times, but she would have known it even if he had not said a word. Neville adored her, was always sexually potent, and he spent most of his free time with her. There was also something else . . . his character.

Neville had never played the field. He had always been attached to one, and only one. Yes, he had moved on frequently, yet he had remained faithful when in a relationship. In fact, he was the total opposite of his cousin Ned in that respect, who seemed able to handle several women at once. Such a talent was missing in *her* husband.

Nan compressed her lips, remembering her conversation with Neville the other day. She now must correct herself on the long-held assumption that Ned was the proverbial swordsman. According to Neville, Ned had been faithful to Lily Overton. Poor woman, Nan thought, dying like that, so tragically. And she had been young, in her thirties.

Long ago she had seen another accident with a landau, but fortunately no one had been killed. Her father had always warned her that they could be dangerous carriages if driven at high speed, and her father had rarely been wrong.

Stretching her long legs, moving up in the bed, she settled against the headboard. It rattled slightly, and Neville swung around at once on hearing the noise.

When he saw her sitting up, leaning against the mound of white pillows, he said softly, 'Oh darling, I awakened you.'

'No you didn't,' she responded, and stared at him, realizing she desired him, needed him. She stretched out her arms, and he came to her, sat down on the bed, leaned to her. Putting her arms around his neck, she whispered against his hair, 'I have such a hunger for you . . . I long for you, and need you. Make love to me, Neville . . . Perhaps tonight is the night to make that son and heir you crave.'

'It is *you* I crave, my dearest heart.'

Within seconds they lay naked in each other's arms.

He kissed her face, her eyelids, her neck, and swiftly moved his head down to her breasts, kissing them, smoothing his hand over them. Sliding down the bed, he now ran his hand over her flat stomach, down her thigh, until it came to rest between her legs. When he touched her most intimate part she moaned softly, and whispered, 'Please, darling, please.' And so he brought his tongue to her, kissing her womanhood until she shivered in ecstasy.

He took her to him swiftly, entering her with urgency and his own overwhelming need, plunging deep inside her until she cried out. 'Now, Neville, now, oh please, now,' and when she began to cleave to him and shudder excessively he threw off all his constraints and came with her when she came.

Together they lay joined for a long time. He did not want to leave her, and she wanted him to stay where he was. He rested his head against her face, and they drifted in a gentle haze, saying nothing, simply enjoying the aftermath of their lovemaking.

Eventually Nan spoke. 'You once said I am the only one now. Is that true?'

He smiled against her cheek. 'Don't you trust me?'

'I do!' she cried, and tried to sit up.

Neville held her down on the pillow, kept her body under his. 'I know you do, and you can be certain there is no other woman for me, my Nan. Why should I want anyone else when I have you? These perfect breasts, your long shapely legs, your slender, elegant body. And you do have such a lovely face. Not to mention *this* miraculous part of you.' He slipped out of her and slid his fingers inside her, and within minutes brought her to ecstasy again.

'I think you might have made me pregnant tonight, darling,' Nan said a short while later, staring at him.

Neville had rolled off her, and was propped up next to her sharing her pillow. 'I hope so,' he answered, 'but it doesn't really matter in the long run, Nan. I can well manage without an heir.'

'You're thinking of Richard, aren't you? He's becoming your surrogate son, isn't he? He's spending so much time here with you.'

'Not really . . . No, Nan, he isn't becoming my son. I just like the boy.'

'And George? What of him?'

'George is rather strange, I must admit. An enigma to me. I sometimes think he might not be very trustworthy, do you know that?'

'But he's always so charming . . .' Her voice trailed off.

'Let us not mistake personality for character, my darling.'

'You're worried about something, Neville, something important. I know you are. I saw it in your eyes over dinner. And then when I saw you standing at the bedroom window, staring out, I was fairly sure you had burdens . . . things on your mind.'

Pushing himself up on his elbow, looking down at her, Neville shook his dark head. 'I cannot hide a thing from you, can I?'

'No, I don't suppose you can. I know you so well.' She looked into his light turquoise eyes, saw his love for her shining there, but almost instantly those eyes darkened, were suddenly shadowed over. 'There *is* something wrong.'

Neville sighed, continued to look into her face. He rarely burdened her down with business, but somehow she always instinctively knew when to question him, like tonight. Sighing once again, he said in a low, concerned voice, 'I'm worried about Edward and the board meeting at Deravenels in a few days. It might not go quite as well as we expected after all.'

'Why is that?' Nan cried, astonished, her eyes full of alarm.

'The telephone call I took tonight was from Amos Finnister.'

She nodded.

'He had hoped that two of his men would be able to persuade three board members from the Grant faction to resign, and –'

'Why would they do that?'

'Because Amos Finnister had information about them that would be ruinous to them on all levels if made public. Unfortunately, they haven't quite responded in the way he wanted.'

'And if they don't resign?'

'They will vote against Ned at the meeting, and he could lose his chance to bring his case against Grant to the board.'

'What are you going to do?'

'I shall have to find some sort of weapon which will bring them around to our way of thinking . . . otherwise it will be a disaster.'

FORTY-TWO

London

Vicky finished pinning her hair on top of her head, arranged the curls at the front and added the two tortoise-shell combs on either side at the back to hold everything in place. She stared at herself in her dressing-table mirror for a moment, decided she was looking so much better, for the first time in several weeks. Since the incident in the park, in fact.

A brunette with hazel eyes and a creamy complexion, Vicky Forth had a lovely face which drew much of its quiet loveliness from the calm and tranquillity which dwelt there.

Smoothing her hand over the high guipure lace collar of her cream blouse with its leg o'mutton sleeves, she clipped on pearl earrings, then, holding onto the dressing table, she levered herself up. Her leg was still in plaster, somewhat cumbersome, but she had learned to manoeuvre herself around the house, including mounting the stairs, and descending them. She was rather proud of herself and her new-found agility and skill despite the cast.

Glancing at the clock on the white marble mantel-piece, she realized she had an hour to waste before

Nanny and Amos brought Grace back from Harrods, where they had gone to have lunch and to do some special shopping. It was supposedly a secret from her, and she was amused that Grace and Nanny had managed to talk Amos into the expedition. She guessed the outing was to buy her a small gift for her upcoming birthday.

Vicky left her bedroom and went out into the corridor, heading for the staircase. Holding onto the polished mahogany bannister, she went up the stairs carefully, clutching her long cream-coloured gabardine skirt, lifting it so she wouldn't trip.

When she entered Grace's bedroom she smiled to herself. The child had a penchant for neatness. Everything was in its place, exactly where it should be, and, of course, there was her mother's photograph, propped up on the small bedside table. Vicky remembered how pleased she had been when Grace had placed it against the lamp, understanding the child finally felt safe here, truly knew no one would steal her mother's photograph.

Picking it up, Vicky carried it back into the playroom which adjoined the bedroom and seated herself at the circular table. The photograph needed a frame and yesterday Stephen had gone to the silver shop they patronized and found one which was the right size and not overly ornate. Vicky took it out of the box, removed its wooden back covered in dark blue velvet, and attempted to fit the photograph in, then realized it was rather bulky. The velvet-covered back would not sit correctly and she was unable to fasten it down with the side clips.

Vicky took her spectacles out of her skirt pocket, opened the case, and put them on, examined the photograph. She realized for the first time that it was made of quite thick paper, heavier stock, and had a mount around it which framed the actual picture. The discoloured mount was spotted here and there and Vicky decided the spots had been made by water. No doubt the mount had been damaged when Grace had dragged the cloth bag around. Suddenly she noticed the faint lines on the mount, lines which had been made by a frame, no question about that.

She stared at Mam's face, as she always thought of her, and nodded to herself. She had been a very pretty woman indeed. Turning the photograph over, Vicky noticed that the brown paper backing was coming away from the picture at the edges, peeling on several corners. She decided it needed new backing, and began to pull on one corner of the brown paper. It loosened but was not quite as easy to remove as she thought. Suddenly she was afraid of damaging the photograph; Grace would be hysterical if anything happened to this one genuine memento of her mother, and to Vicky that was quite understandable.

Rising, leaving the playroom, Vicky manoeuvred herself down the stairs to her bedroom, found a nail-file and a pair of nail scissors in her manicure case, went carefully back upstairs to the playroom.

Sitting down at the table, she very gently inserted the nailfile and began to lift off the brown paper backing. It was a slow job, but within ten minutes she had loosened one side, and began to work on the edge across the bottom.

The moment she pulled the backing off completely, Vicky saw the large piece of folded paper laying on the photograph; she knew instantly and without question that the brown paper backing had been put there by Grace's mother, not the photographer, as she had originally believed.

For a moment she did not touch the piece of folded paper, simply stared at it worriedly, wondering what it was. In a sense she was almost afraid to reach for it, afraid of what might be written on it, what she would discover.

Coward, she told herself, and finally picked up the large piece of paper and unfolded it.

Vicky had thought it would most probably be a letter, but it wasn't. It was a birth certificate. However, inside the folds of the birth certificate there was another piece of paper. She placed this on the table, anxious to read the birth certificate.

A woman's name was written on it, a name Vicky did not recognize, and the square where the father's name should have been written was totally blank. She's illegitimate, Vicky thought. Grace is illegitimate. Her eyes went to the top of the birth certificate, and she now read: *County of Yorkshire*, and underneath: *WHITBY*, the name of the town. At least she now knew two more things about Grace: her mother's name and her place of birth. Anxious now to know even more, she reached for the smaller piece of paper and opened it. A lock of red hair fell out; Vicky put this on the birth certificate, almost absently, and looked down at the paper in her hand, reading swiftly.

'Oh my God!' Vicky exclaimed out loud. 'Oh my God!' she cried again, and her eyes, unexpectedly, filled with tears. She blinked them away and read the short note once again, took the lock of hair, put it back inside the note and folded it. To her surprise, Vicky discovered her hands were shaking as she replaced the note inside the birth certificate. Swiftly, she put both in her skirt pocket, and sat back in the chair, too stunned to think straight for a moment, utterly astounded.

It was the carriage clock on the mantlepiece chiming the half hour which brought Vicky Forth out of her reverie. She blinked, sat up straighter in the chair, glancing at the clock. It occurred to her that she had only half an hour to put a new backing on the photograph and get it inside the silver frame before Amos, Nanny and Grace returned.

Standing up, she went to the bell at the side of the mantlepiece and pressed it. Within seconds Elsie, the parlour maid, was hurrying into the room. 'Is there something you need, Mrs Forth?'

'Elsie, please do me a favour. Bring me a roll of the brown wrapping paper, a pot of glue and a pair of scissors. I want to tidy up this photograph before putting it in the new frame.'

Elsie nodded. 'Right away, mum.' She dashed out.

Vicky sat gazing at the picture of Grace's mother, wondering whether to keep the discoloured cream mount surrounding it. She made a decision and lifted it off. Printed in a type of scrolled handwriting was the name of the photographer, and underneath the town: *Whitby*. Without the discoloured mount, the photographer's name was revealed. For the moment Vicky did not want anyone else to know a single thing about Grace's background, and so she put the mount back in place even though it was a bit grubby.

Once Elsie returned with the items she requested, Vicky cut out a piece of the brown paper, glued it on the back of the photograph, and put the picture in the frame.

'Now it fits,' she muttered under her breath as she replaced the wooden back covered in blue velvet. Turning it around, standing it up on the table, she nodded to herself, pleased with her handiwork, thinking how happy Grace would be when she saw her mother's photographic portrait in the handsome silver frame.

FORTY-THREE

'Fer a rozzer yer not a bad chap,' Albert Draper muttered, staring at Amos Finnister. 'Even if yer bold as brass, askin' me agin abart Nappo. I told yer all I knows afore.'

'First of all, Albert, I'm not a copper anymore. I'm a private detective,' Amos explained, shaking his head, looking into Albert's eyes. 'And you know it. Also –'

'Once a copper allus a copper,' Albert cut in, grinning hugely.

'I concede you might have a point there, Bertie, but please help me. I must find out who this Nappo fellow worked for up West. It's worth quite a lot to me.'

''Ow much?'

'Definitely a fiver . . .'

'Five quid! My Gawd! 'E must've done sumfink awful, a real bleedin' 'orrible crime. I wus goin' ter arsk yer for ten bob. Changed me mind, though.'

'Why did you do that? I'd always give it to you, Bertie. Anytime.'

'Changed me mind 'cos I ain't no cadger, can't stand cadgers, Amos. Bad way ter make a livin', innit?'

'I suppose it is, and I know how proud you are. Come on, Bertie, you've got the goods on Nappo, so let's have it.' Reaching into his pocket, Amos put some loose change on the counter and called out, 'Two more pints of bitter, please.'

The bartender of the Mucky Duck called back, 'Comin' right up.'

Turning to Albert, Amos continued in a low voice, 'Nappo was bumped off a few weeks ago. It wasn't suicide, you know that as well as I do. The Yard have come up with nothing, and I just need to know *who* it was he worked for up West.'

Albert bit his lip, shook his head, looking worried.

Amos said, 'Nappo caused a terrible accident in Hyde Park – a good woman was killed, another wonderful woman injured. Both of them have been involved in Haddon House. Hasn't your sister Gladys had a lot of help from them in the past . . . when that no-good husband of hers beat her up?'

'Beat 'er to bleedin' pulp, 'e did, bleedin' bastard. If I ever gets me 'ands on 'im, I'll do 'im!' Bertie hissed, keeping his voice low. 'So them fancy bits wus 'elping Lady Fenella? A saint I calls 'er. That wot yer sayin', Amos?'

'I am.'

Bertie nodded, his mind made up after hearing the name Haddon House, and drew even closer to Amos. 'Wot I've 'eard is this . . . it's the Frenchie wus employin' Nappo as a driver of 'er carriage, so I 'ears from me mate, 'im as knew Nappo. *Margo*, that's 'er name. Can't think of 'er last name.'

'*Grant*, Margot Grant,' Amos said swiftly, his excitement obvious. 'Is that the name?'

'It is! That's it!' Bertie exclaimed, grinning from ear to ear. 'Tells me mate 'e fancied 'er, wanted ter get 'er up the apples and pears, would've paid a king's ransom ter do 'er,' Bertie explained. 'Oh, yeah, Nappo fancied 'er awright. Wishful thinkin', innit?'

'Only too true. Are you certain of the name?'

'I am that. Let me think a minit . . . Grosvenor Street . . . no, not right . . . Upper, that's wot's missing . . . Upper Grosvernor Street, up West, that's where Nappo worked and dreamed of feckin' the Frenchie woman.'

Amos felt a rush of relief flood through him. He wanted to shout out with glee, but restrained himself. 'A name, Bert? Surely your mate knew Nappo's actual name.'

Albert began to chuckle. 'Yer knows wot, Amos, 'is real name wus Napoleon, t'weren't a nickname, the bugger wus called Napoleon by 'is muvver.'

'His last name?' Amos probed.

Grinning again, Bertie said, 'Sure as 'ell t'weren't Bonaparte.' The Cockney began to laugh.

Amos couldn't help laughing with him, even though he had one other horrendous problem to deal with. He had always liked Albert Draper's Cockney humour and wit. 'So, come on, lad, let's have it.'

'Dupon, or Dupont.' Albert emphasized the T. 'That wus the geezer's name. Or Dupond.'

'Thank you, Albert.' Amos put his hand in his pocket and brought out a small packet. 'A fiver in there for you, and I appreciate your help.'

After pocketing the envelope of money, Albert looked hard at Amos, his eyes narrowing. 'They did for 'im, did they, them buggers up West?'

490

'In my opinion, yes.'

'D'ya think Nappo got in 'er knickers? That why they did 'im?'

'No, I doubt very much that he got anywhere with her. They had him killed because he knew too much.'

'Bloody 'ell!'

'Thanks again, Bertie, you've been a genuine help.'

Albert Draper nodded. 'Ta fer me dosh, Amos, yer a good un.'

Amos nodded, picked up his pint and drank half of it, put the glass back on the counter. 'I've got to be going, and thanks again, Bertie.'

'See ya, Amos.'

Once he was outside in the street, Amos pulled out his pocket watch and looked at the time. It was almost seven o'clock. He had told the two actors he would meet them at the Mandarin Garden at half past seven, so he must hurry now.

As he strode along the wharves, he sniffed, grimacing, fully aware of the stink of the Thames on this warm June evening. It was the most beautiful river in the world to him, but it was the dirtiest, and it was rank in warm weather.

Walking at a rapid pace, he thought about the information Albert Draper had given him. He had known Albert for many years, since he had been on the beat here in Whitechapel, and he trusted him implicitly. He now had a name to give to Neville Watkins – more importantly a positive identification of Margot Grant as Nappo's employer. This tied her and possibly Henry Grant to the crime. At least he had done something right. The failure of the two actors to persuade Beaufield, Deever and Clifford to resign was the most unhappy conclusion to that particular part of his work for Neville Watkins.

Charlie had told him the actors were good, often played toffs in the theatre, and that they would do a proper job. Those were Charlie's exact words, 'a proper job', just before he had sailed off to New York. To the New World. To a new life.

Amos made it to the Chinese restaurant in record time, and, as he was shown to his favourite table in an isolated corner, he asked the waiter for jasmine tea. He sat down, a bit out of breath, thirsty, and relieved to see he was the first to arrive.

But he did not have to wait long. Ten minutes later the two thespians appeared, and were suddenly sitting down opposite him. Justin St Marr, as he called himself, in reality Alfie Rains, and his companion, Harry Lansford, who was really Jimmy Smithers. Two good-looking Cockney lads, old friends of Charlie, talented actors by profession. Nice lads, he decided, looking across at them. But somewhere they had gone wrong on the job for him. He aimed to find out how.

'Good evening, chaps,' Amos said cheerily, smiling at them.

'Good evening, Mr Finnister,' they said in unison, speaking in upper-class voices. They were staying in character for the moment.

'Care for refreshments?' Amos asked, raising a brow.

'The same as you, I think, jasmine tea, please,' Justin replied in his plummy tone.

'I'll have tea also,' Harry added, equally posh.

Once the order for the tea had been given, Amos leaned across the table and said in a low voice, 'I've got a real problem, lads, and I certainly need you to help me solve it.'

They both nodded, looked at him eagerly, obviously wanting to please.

The waiter deposited the teapots and teacups, and hurried away.

Amos leaned forward once more, speaking in the same low voice. 'I want you to tell me again what happened when you finally pulled the rabbit out of the hat so to speak, and told those chaps you would expose them to the world. Expose their guilty secrets.'

'They laughed,' Justin answered. 'They just didn't seem to care, did they, Harry?'

'Justin's right, Mr Finnister, they were totally unconcerned, acted as though it didn't matter one iota.'

'Think, lads, go back over it in your minds. Didn't they say anything about the board, their immediate superiors, the consequences?'

'No,' Justin said, shaking his blond head, biting his lip.

Harry looked as though he was remembering something; his eyes narrowed as he stared out into the room above Amos's head. 'Well, there was *one* thing . . . something Jack Beaufield said, and it struck me as being rather odd, sort of . . . well, out of context.'

'What did Beaufield say?' Amos demanded, his heart tightening in anticipation.

'He said there would be no more summers in France if they were thrown off the board, and all three seemed to think it was funny. But I didn't get it, not at all.'

Oh, but I do, Amos thought, his heart leaping. They know something about Summers and Margot, something explosive. An affair? I do believe they think they've got him by the *cojones*. But we'll see about that, won't we?

Harry now asked in a puzzled voice, 'You look extremely pleased, Mr Finnister, do you know what Beaufield was talking about?'

'I'm not quite sure,' Amos answered cagily, and then smiled. 'But I think my boss will, and he'll certainly know what to do. Now, lads, the treat's on me. What would you like for your supper? Have anything, anything at all.' He lifted his hand, summoned the waiter. He suddenly felt light-headed with happiness. Perhaps he hadn't failed after all.

FORTY-FOUR

Today it was Tuesday, June 21st in the year 1904.

It might turn out to be an auspicious day. Certainly today *his* destiny would be sealed, of that he was absolutely sure.

Edward Deravenel stood at the window in his office at Deravenels, looking down into the Strand, thinking about the ordeal which awaited him.

In a short while he would go into the boardroom and face seventeen men, the members of the board who would either champion his cause, or defeat him.

His cousin Neville Watkins, his mentor, had told him it was up to him to convince them his was a just cause, a rightful cause.

'You are a *seducer*, Ned, not just of women, but of . . . well, just about *everyone*,' Neville had told him earlier this morning, over breakfast at the Charles Street house. 'You can convince *anybody*, when you so wish. Do it today, Ned: charm them, beguile them, make them want *you* to win, not Henry Grant. But remember, you must do it with a cold heart. You must be ruthless.'

'I know that,' Edward had answered his cousin. 'And

your own motto is engraved on my heart . . . *never display weakness, never show face.*'

Neville had nodded and smiled, patted him on the back, and added, 'Be inscrutable. Show no visible emotion, reveal nothing of yourself. Bear those points in mind and you will succeed.'

Last night they had had a long session with Amos over dinner, and the private detective had told them about two meetings he had recently had.

One had been with a contact in Whitechapel. This man had given Finnister information about the Corsican, the rider of the horse, perpetrator of the accident in Hyde Park. According to Amos, the Corsican had been employed by Margot Grant as one of her drivers: she was irrevocably tied to the accident, which was not an accident at all, as far as Amos Finnister was concerned. 'Premeditated,' was the way he had put it. 'Murder, in fact, to my way of thinking. The Corsican *did* set out to kill Mrs Overton.'

The private detective had then gone on to tell them about the actors Justin St Marr and Harry Lansford, who had inveigled themselves into the tight-knit social circle where Beaufield, Cliff and Deever were prime movers.

Each actor had tackled the men individually – first Beaufield, then Deever, finally James Cliff. They had explained that they knew dangerous secrets and would reveal them to the world if each man did not resign from Deravenels.

The actors had really believed they had succeeded in convincing them all to step down in order to avoid a huge public scandal.

'And then suddenly everything changed,' Finnister had said. 'Deever and Cliff told Justin and Harry to go to hell. It was a case of publish and be damned, that sort of attitude. My actors were a bit flumoxed, I don't mind telling you. Later they were even more taken aback when they ran into the toffs at White's, and the three men laughed in their faces. It was Beaufield who then said something about "no more summers in France" if they were kicked off the Deravenel board.'

'He was alluding to John Summers and Margot Grant. As you surmised, they must be meeting secretly. There is no doubt there's a sexual liaison there,' Neville remarked.

'No doubt whatsoever, sir. I got it from the horse's mouth – this morning. The butler at the Grant house in Upper Grosvenor Street is about to vacate his position and was happy to blab.'

Edward had jumped into the discussion at this point, and directed a question at Finnister. 'Do you think that Beaufield, Deever and Cliff conferred with each other and decided to brazen it out?'

'That is my conclusion, Mr Edward. I thought at first they might have spotted my two thespians, and realized they were imposters. But I've changed my mind. We know those fellows are in cahoots, and have benefitted from the Indian skimming situation. Therefore, I think they know everything there is to know about each other. Birds of a feather, and all that.'

Neville had laughed, then turning to Ned he had pointed out, 'But the other board members don't know a thing, and you, my dear Ned, are going to give them all the gory details. No holds barred.'

When he had arrived home last night Edward had made innumerable notes, committed everything to memory, like an actor memorizing his lines. That was the way he had thought of it then, and now. When he walked into that boardroom he had to dominate, as a leading actor dominated a stage. He had to persuade, convince, beguile, and conquer his audience. *He had to make them his.*

'They're waiting for you,' Alfredo Oliveri said from the doorway.

Startled, Edward swung around, and nodded, half smiled when he saw his colleague and friend. As he walked across the floor he noticed Oliveri's pallor; his freckles always seemed much more pronounced when he was pale like this. He was obviously worried.

Ned put his hand on Oliveri's shoulder and said in a calm and steady voice, 'Don't fret. I am fine, and it *will* be all right, I promise you. Now, who is in there?'

'Everyone we expected, except for Henry Grant, of course. He hasn't shown up.'

'I knew he wouldn't come. He can't. And they can't let him. He's pitiful these days, at least so I hear. There *are* seventeen board members, then?'

'Correct.'

'I'm glad you went onto the board automatically, when you were promoted to Aubrey Masters's job. Who's there in *his* place?'

'A new board member, by the name of Peter Lister.

He was appointed by vote, of course, but originally recommended by Martin Rollins. He's neutral, by the way, Rollins I mean. Nice chap, very honourable, has good judgement. He's been on the board of Deravenels for donkey's years, and sort of guides it really, in an unofficial way. He liked your father. He'll be fair, *just*, perhaps even sympathetic. But he may play devil's advocate.'

'Good to know. Who are the other outside directors? Remind me again,' Ned said.

'Victor Sheen,' Alfredo answered. 'Also neutral, I think. Matthew Reynolds and Paul Loomis, they're a bit wishy-washy, I've noticed. Don't carry much weight.'

'Let's go then. Let's get it over with.' Edward moved towards the desk, picked up a pile of folders, went to the door.

Alfredo reached out, held him back, and said, 'It will go exactly the way I explained. The procedure is quite simple. Martin Rollins will ask you to present your grievance, your case. And you will do that. The board members will ask you questions, perhaps, may ask if you can produce evidence to back your case. There's just one thing I want you to remember. We're there to help you, if you need us. Me, Rob Aspen, Christopher Green and Frank Lane. If you should need one of us just look at us, or say our names. We'll jump right in with corroborating evidence, if that's what you need. We're your backup.'

Edward nodded. 'I remember everything you've told me, and thank you. Thank you for being supportive today.'

Together they left Edward's office and walked down

the corridor together, heading for the boardroom. Neither of them spoke, both lost in their thoughts.

Alfredo was worrying himself sick, praying that Ned would handle himself well, would not see red and explode, as he occasionally could.

For his part, Edward Deravenel was keeping himself perfectly steady and calm. He was convinced that he must be ruthless in order to win.

When he walked into the boardroom a few moments after Oliveri, all conversation ceased. Edward glanced around, saw only one empty seat at the far end of the table. He walked down to it, stood behind the chair. 'Good morning, gentlemen. For those who do not know me, I am Edward Deravenel.'

There were mumbled good mornings, and Martin Rollins said, 'Please take the seat in front of you. It was kept for you.'

'Thank you, but I prefer to stand,' Edward answered, and then placed the folders he was holding on the mahogany conference table in front of him.

Rollins nodded, and announced, 'Let us begin the proceedings. Mr Deravenel, it is our understanding that you have a grievance with Deravenels, and wish to present a case against an individual. Is that correct?'

'Yes, it is, sir. I wish to present a case against Henry Grant, chairman of Deravenels.' Edward was going to do more than that, but for the moment he kept quiet.

'Mr Grant is unable to attend today, due to an illness,' Rollins said. 'However, you may proceed, since we do have a full board present with the exception of Mr Grant.'

'Henry Grant is chairman of this company, but he is not the person running it,' Edward began in an icy voice. 'And, therefore, I believe he should be removed from the company. Because he is not running Deravenels on a day-to-day basis he must be retired, as of today. The man running Deravenels is John Summers, and he has no right to be managing director. He is not a Deravenel by birth, and, according to ancient company rules, only a Deravenel can be the head of Deravenels.'

For a moment there was a flutter of asides, exclamations, mumblings, and Martin Rollins exclaimed, 'Please, gentlemen, silence please.' Looking down the length of the table, he focused on Edward. 'I am vaguely familiar with this rule, but it has never been brought up before, not by anyone. Mr Summers has been in charge for a number of years.' Rollins was frowning, seemed puzzled.

'Mr Summers was supposedly assisting Henry Grant, but Henry Grant was and is an absentee landlord, as my father Richard Deravenel called him. And why was he an absentee landlord?' Edward paused dramatically, let his eyes roam around the table, focused on the men seated at each side. No one spoke. Some met his gaze, others did not.

Edward continued in that steely voice, 'I shall tell you why he was never here, and relegated his job to John Summers. He was in a variety of different mental asylums over these many years. Mr Grant is suffering from dementia. He is not merely a pious and religious fellow, devoted to God, as some of you characterize him. The man is mentally disturbed and therefore incapable of running this company. Or any other company for that matter.'

No one spoke. Everyone looked at Edward. Some were stunned, others pleased, yet others filled with sudden fear, apprehensive about what would be said next.

'That is quite an accusation, Mr Deravenel!' Martin Rollins announced in a cold, clear voice, obviously stunned. 'A *dastardly* accusation, if it is not true, and I doubt that it is.'

'It is absolutely true!' Edward contradicted him, his voice louder, fierce, emphatic. 'I have the evidence here for perusal later.' He glanced down at the pile of folders on the conference table in front of him, and continued, 'I have all the medical records from the various asylums where he was being treated. I have doctors' opinions from those mad houses, and I also have various medical opinions from a number of highly-respected psychiatrists, including Mr Rupert Haversley-Long, of Harley Street, a most respected doctor who has worked with Dr Sigmund Freud. In his opinion Mr Grant is no longer sane. He has not been sane for years.'

'And has this psychiatrist, Haversley-Long, examined Mr Grant?' Rollins asked, a brow lifting sceptically.

'No. But he has studied innumerable medical records, and has spoken to those doctors who looked after Mr Grant in the various asylums.'

Martin Rollins, a reasonable man, now fully understood that Edward spoke the truth. He looked saddened as he asked, 'And you say you have these medical records and reports here with you today, Mr Deravenel?'

'Yes, I do, sir.' Edward gave the older man a bleak little smile, added, '*Copies*, of course. But they can be examined by the board members later, at their convenience. However, they have been reviewed by some board members already.'

'Is that so!' John Summers spluttered, glaring at Edward, but holding his temper in check. He was fulminating with rage inside.

'Yes, it is,' Edward answered, his tone quiet, even mild. He looked at Christopher Green, and raised a brow. 'I think Mr Green might have a word to say to the board.'

Christopher Green nodded, and rose, feeling better when he stood up. Almost as tall as Edward, he knew his height was effective at times, especially at board meetings. 'What Mr Deravenel says is perfectly true, Mr Rollins and fellow board members. The records I have studied do indeed show that Mr Grant was treated in a number of mental institutions over the years. In my opinion, he is not able to run this company. I concur with Mr Deravenel.'

'John Summers is doing a wonderful job,' James Cliff cut in, in a loud voice. 'If Henry Grant is considered redundant because of ill health, then John Summers can continue as before. He's a good man!'

'Hear, hear,' some board members cried, backing James Cliff's opinion.

'Oh no, not *hear*, *hear* at all!' Edward Deravenel exclaimed, his voice rising. 'I do not believe Mr Summers has been a good caretaker of Deravenels, not at all. But this point aside for the moment, he is not a Deravenel, he is not even *remotely* related to the Deravenels. He is, in fact, a second cousin once removed of Henry Grant. He has no right to the job.'

'And who *do* you think should run Deravenels?' Jack Beaufield asked with a sneer.

You will regret asking that question, you bastard, Edward thought, staring back at Beaufield coldly. He was remembering that Beaufield was more than likely involved in the deaths of his father, young Edmund and Neville's kin. A murderer.

'I am the true heir to Deravenels,' Ned finally said. 'And more so than Henry Grant ever was. Over sixty years ago now, Henry Grant's grandfather stole the company. His grandfather did not run the company very well, it did poorly under him, although his father did a magnificent job. But, and it is a big *but*, the Grants should never have been at the helm of this company in the first place. Through the laws of primogeniture, as we know those laws today, I am the rightful heir, as a true and direct descendant of Guy de Ravenel, through my father Richard Deravenel, who was also the true heir before me.'

There was a silence in the boardroom.

No one spoke. Several men shifted in their seats. Jack Beaufield glanced around, expecting someone to denounce Edward Deravenel's claim but no one did.

Beaufield said, sarcastically, 'You're just a young pup. Only nineteen. Why do you think *you* could run this company? Now tell me that, lad?'

Edward did not rise to the bait. He merely smiled at Beaufield, and answered quietly, 'My age has absolutely nothing to do with anything at all, certainly not my ability. Let us not forget that William Pitt the Younger became Prime Minister of this great country of ours when he was only twenty-four.'

Alfredo Oliveri, Rob Aspen and Frank Lane all clapped, laughing.

'Just so,' Martin Rollins murmured. 'But what about experience, Mr Deravenel? Surely that counts for something, doesn't it?'

'Yes, indeed it does, Mr Rollins. For the last six months I have been working at Deravenels, and learning about every division. I have had some wonderful teachers in Mr Oliveri, Mr Aspen, Mr Green and Mr Lane. I know a lot about our mining division, the vineyards in France, the quarries in Carrara, and our northern companies in Yorkshire. I have learned about our cloth-manufacturing mills in Bradford, our ready-made clothing companies in Leeds, our coalmines in Sheffield.' Edward paused, smiled at Rollins, and then cast his glance over to the men he had just mentioned. 'I think you may wish to talk to my colleagues later, get their opinions about me.'

Rollins nodded, looking impressed and rather beguiled by the handsome and articulate young man who stood so proudly at the far end of the boardroom. Finally, he said, 'So your case is against Henry Grant, chairman of Deravenels? Whom you say is no longer capable of running the company. And you are suggesting yourself as his replacement. In fact, you are asking for the removal from the company of Mr Grant *and* Mr Summers.'

'I am indeed,' Edward answered simply.

'Over my dead body!' John Summers shouted, jumping up, waving his fist at Edward. 'You young pup!

505

How dare you come in here today and propose such a ridiculous thing. You are the one who is out of his mind, not Henry Grant. You should be ashamed.'

'And you, Mr Summers, are an enemy of Deravenels! You are a cheat, a liar and an adulterer. You are the man who should be *ashamed*. You are the lover of Margot Grant, the wife of Henry Grant. It is you who has cuckolded him.'

Not one man in the room moved. Nor did anyone speak. They did not dare. Martin Rollins, aghast, looked as if he had gone into sudden shock.

John Summers still stood, his face purple with embarrassment and rage. He, too, had lost his voice, so stupefied was he. It took him a moment to recoup, to gather his swimming senses.

Finally he said, 'Only a lad of your age would make such an *empty* accusation.' But as he spoke John Summers knew in the depths of his soul that he had met his true adversary. Edward Deravenel was cold, ruthless, and formidable, not to mention ambitious. He suddenly began to tremble inside, knowing that perhaps all was lost. Yet he remained standing, deciding to brazen it out. Fool though he was about Margot Grant, he nonetheless had a certain courage.

'I do not make empty accusations, Mr Summers,' Edward responded in a low and dangerous voice. 'I have evidence that you have been having an affair with Mrs Grant for some time now. And I have that evidence in these folders here.' He motioned to them. His eyes did not leave John Summers's face. 'A Mr Clarence Turnbull, butler to Mrs Grant, has given a statement, revealing your sexual liaison with her. It is a sworn statement.'

John Summers sat down heavily. He made no comment whatsoever. He was a ruined man.

Edward looked directly at Martin Rollins, and continued, 'I bring specific charges against Jack Beaufield, James Cliff and Philip Deever. These three men have been systematically robbing Deravenels. They have stolen vast amounts of money by skimming off the top at our diamond mines in India. And stealing diamonds. Aubrey Masters, now deceased, was also involved.'

'Mr Deravenel! These are very serious charges indeed,' Rollins cried, wondering what was coming next. He was utterly appalled.

'I do have the evidence here. Mr Oliveri and Mr Aspen, who work in the mining division, first came across this crime some months ago. Mr Oliveri hired Mr David Westmouth, an expert in diamond mining, in India, and Mr Westmouth has given us all the evidence we need. Charges can be brought against these three men. Immediately. Mr Westmouth is now in London.'

James Cliff cried, 'Just try it, laddie!'

'Oh, I will indeed, Mr Cliff. And at the same time, perhaps you had better make arrangements for your illegitimate child to be taken care of properly. And your mistress. I'm sure Mrs Cliff won't be doing that.'

'*You bastard*,' Cliff shouted, jumping up, looking not only irate but dangerous. 'I'll bloody well get you for this, you bastard!'

'I doubt it,' Edward answered softly. 'You won't be able to do very much from behind bars. As for you, Mr Beaufield, this is not the first time your hand has been in the till, and you will soon have other charges brought against you by your previous employers. And you, Mr Deever, will no doubt be in the divorce courts as well as the criminal courts, once your wife discovers you have a lover. A male lover at that.'

Deever did not answer. He jumped up, almost ran across the floor, left the boardroom. A frightened Beaufield followed him, and then Cliff hurried to join them. Only John Summers remained, flabbergasted, rooted to the spot. And then he, too, made for the door, following his colleagues, knowing that he had been totally defeated by Edward Deravenel, his nemesis.

Martin Rollins cleared his throat, and began carefully, 'Mr Deravenel, you have made horrendous statements, implied terrible things about these men who have long served Deravenels –'

'Served themselves,' Edward interrupted.

Rollins ignored this comment, and continued. 'I just hope you really do have the evidence to uphold your accusations, otherwise you are going to be in serious trouble, sir.'

'I can assure you that I have the evidence of everything I have just accused these men of . . . *absolute proof*. And various other board members know that I am speaking the truth, Mr Rollins. You see, they have helped me to gather the evidence. It is they who have served Deravenels well, not the Grant faction. Please be assured of that.'

Rollins nodded. 'Thank you, Mr Deravenel. You are excused. I would like you to pass me the documents you have for our perusal. We shall see you again shortly. Thank you.'

'And thank you, Mr Rollins, for allowing me to bring the case, and hopefully to serve this company well.'

All of the board members were silent; most were aghast at the unexpected downfall of men they had long known and respected.

Edward rose, walked the length of the room and gave the pile of folders to Martin Rollins. Then he slipped out of the boardroom, closing the door after him softly. Justice for my family, justice for Lily and the baby, he thought as he walked back to his office.

Exactly one week later, on Tuesday, June 28, 1904, Edward Deravenel was appointed managing director of Deravenels. The position of chairman was left open. It would never be filled during his lifetime. He was the sole ruler of Deravenels, his domain.

At a luncheon later in the company dining room, which had not been used for years, Edward sat down to a lavish repast with his mother and siblings, Meg, George and Richard, his Little Fish. Also present were all of the Deravenel executives who had supported him in his fight to gain control of the company, as well as his comrade-in-arms, Neville, and Nan Watkins, Neville's wife, his boon companions Johnny Watkins and Will Hasling, and Amos Finnister, who had contributed so much. The rest of the board were also present. They had voted him in unanimously, and were his admirers now, totally charmed by this charismatic man.

Earlier that morning he had given Neville, Johnny, Will, Amos Finnister and Alfredo Oliveri a memento of this day. It was a round gold medallion on a slender gold chain. On one side was the Deravenel family emblem of the white rose and a fetterlock, the rose enamelled in white; on the other side was the sun in splendour, commemorating this happy day. Around the edge of the medallion on the side of the rose, was engraved the Deravenel family motto: *Fidelity unto eternity*.

'I'll wear it 'til I die, and even after that,' Johnny said, smiling wryly at Edward as he added, 'And to think you didn't even attempt to seduce the board, from what Oliveri told me.'

'I didn't really get a chance, to be truthful,' Edward confessed, grinning. 'The only thing I could do, actually, was go in for the kill with the Grant faction.'

'But it obviously worked,' Will murmured, his hand on Edward's arm.

'Only too true,' Neville interjected. 'And I am very proud of you, Ned, very proud of you indeed.'

Lifting his glass of champagne, Edward toasted them. 'Here's to friends and friendship. May they last forever.'

Margot Grant was speechless. She just stood there, staring at John Summers, looking dumbfounded. After a few seconds she said slowly, in a puzzled voice, 'Are you telling me they ran out of the board meeting? Is that what you are saying, John?'

'Yes, that is exactly what I'm saying. They did run too, like scared rabbits. I was appalled.'

'And what did you do?'

He sighed, admitted, 'After a moment or two, I left

myself, there wasn't much point staying there. It was palpably obvious Deravenel had taken the board by storm, convinced them of his rights, and he did seem to have the facts about Cliff, Deever and Beaufield. I'm afraid he was holding all of the cards.'

'Oh how stupid they were!' she cried and went and sat down on the sofa in front of the fireplace in her Upper Grosvenor Street house.

John moved across the room, draped himself against the fireplace, and stared at her.

She stared back, raising a curved black brow.

He said, 'We might have lost this battle, but it is only a *battle*. We haven't lost the war.'

'It sounds as if we have to me,' she snapped, sitting up straighter. 'What are we going to do?'

'At this moment, I don't know actually. I think we should go to Paris, you and I, and have a break from all this business, have an intimate weekend together. *Chez toi.*'

Her face lit up.

'I can see the thought of being alone with me in your flat in Paris makes you happy,' John said, a pleased expression in his eyes. 'And the thought of it sends *my* head spinning. However, we must get back to business for a moment, Margot. Deravenel will soon be sitting in my chair, the managing director's chair, and there's nothing that I can do about it. On the other hand, the Grants do own a huge amount of shares in the company, and I think there has to be a Grant on the board, or there as a spokesman. I'm going to have to go back to the company rules, look a few things up.'

'We can't let Edward Deravenel win, and –'

'He has, Margot, if only for the moment, of course.'

She nodded. 'You have to find a way to . . . unseat him.'

'Indeed I will,' John answered, and went and sat down next to her on the sofa. 'And what are we going to do with Henry whilst *we* are in Paris? He can't be left alone, you know.'

'I understand that. He is perfectly happy at Ascot, and the butler there knows how to take care of him. He will do so, following my instructions.'

'That makes me feel easier.' He stood. 'I must go, I want to arm myself with enough facts, so that I know what I'm talking about when the time comes.'

PART THREE

Glittering Temptations

Edward & Elizabeth

'He pursued with no discrimination the married and the unmarried, the noble and the lowly: however, he took none by force.'

Dominic Mancini

'She was of medium height, with a good figure, and she was beautiful, having long gilt-blonde hair and an alluring smile.'

Alison Weir

'Where Beauty & Beauty met,
Earth's still a-tremble there,
And winds are scented yet,
And memory-soft the air,
Bosoming, folding glints of light,
And shreds of shadowy laughter;
Not the tears that fill the years
After – after –'

Rupert Brooke

FORTY-FIVE

London 1907

The spring supper dance was already underway at Lady Tillotson's splendid house in Berkeley Square. The strains of the orchestra playing music for the popular dance The Cakewalk came floating in from the magnificent ballroom, and there was a sense of festivity and gaiety in the air. It was a gaiety which seemed to prevail everywhere in London these days, with King Edward VII leading the way in this extraordinarily prosperous year of his reign, his sixth on the throne of England. London was the greatest capital in existence; the Empire ruled the world, and all was well under English skies.

In the charming and beautiful drawing room which adjoined the ballroom, guests stood around or were sitting on gold-framed chairs, small sofas and banquettes, sipping champagne and chatting to each other.

Tall, airy palms in heavy cream-coloured porcelain tubs were stationed in corners, and there were flowers everywhere . . . banks of lilies, peonies, roses, rhododendrons and hydrangeas introduced rafts of pinks, cream and white, lilac, purple and different reds, bringing vibrant colour to the backdrop of the cream, silk-covered walls and cream-and-gold painted wood-work. The air itself was filled with the delicate fragrance of the mingled flowers and the more heady scents favoured by the glamorous women who were present tonight, arrayed in all their finery.

Two glittering crystal chandeliers hung from the ceiling at each end of the drawing room, and were balanced by matching crystal wall sconces. The brilliant light from the Waterford crystal pieces brought additional sparkle to the room, and enabled all of the women to view each other's gowns with ease. And every woman was elegantly dressed in the latest Paris and London styles, bought from the most famous fashion houses in both cities and worn with magnificent jewels which highlighted their elegance.

Like the women, the men were equally elegant in their impeccably-tailored black tails, starched white shirts, white bow ties and matching white waistcoats.

Glancing around, the woman in black realized she was the only one wearing a dark colour. Every other woman had chosen a pastel shade for her gown, so appropriate for spring. She did not care; she liked her choice, and it *was* appropriate for *her*.

She glanced to her left and saw her cousin Arthur Forrester heading in her direction, carrying a glass of champagne for her. 'Thank you, Arthur,' she said as he handed it to her and offered her a warm smile.

'Do you mind if I leave you alone for a few seconds?' he asked, as always scrupulously polite. 'I'd like to smoke a cigar on the terrace with Woodstock and Hopkins, two old friends of mine from my Eton days. Haven't seen those blighters for months.'

'No, not at all,' she murmured. 'I'm sure Mama will descend on me at any moment.'

He laughed with her and hurried off in the direction of the terrace, obviously looking forward to catching up with his old friends, she could see that. There was an eagerness in his eyes and a spring to his step.

Leaning back against the deep cream plush-velvet banquette, she glanced around, admiring some of the gowns, thinking that others were overdone, as was, indeed, much of the jewellery. Yet again, current fashion prevailed, and every woman wanted to ape Queen Alexandra with her ornate chokers and collars of pearls and precious stones, the matching long strings of pearls and diamonds, all worn together. However, not all women had a long swan-like neck, as the Queen did. She smiled to herself, suddenly feeling pleased that she had kept her toilette simple tonight. It made her stand out, she thought, set her apart from every other woman present.

She saw him the moment he arrived.

He caused quite a flurry of excitement as he hesitated in the entrance to the drawing room, glancing around. People rushed to him, surrounded him, obviously wanted to welcome him, fête him. She wondered who he was.

He was very tall and broad chested, and in the brilliant light of the room his luxuriant hair looked silver. He was so handsome she was genuinely startled, taken aback by his exceptional good looks. She had never set eyes on a man quite like him.

With immense confidence he entered the room boldly, yet he moved lightly on his feet as he rushed, quite suddenly, towards a woman he obviously knew. She was a pretty brunette seated on the banquette opposite her. Catching her breath, now that she had an even better view of him, Elizabeth realized he was indeed a big man. Yet there was no excess fat on him; he appeared athletic, very fit.

She was actually close enough to notice that everything about him was scrupulously clean, shining almost, and the silver hair was not silver at all, she could see that now: it was a burnished red-gold; he was very fair in colouring, his skin pink and white, and so *clean* looking. Like a freshly scrubbed schoolboy, was her unexpected thought.

He had seated himself next to the woman opposite; one arm stretched along the back of the banquette, rested between himself and the woman, and his right hand lay there, curled open slightly. He had beautiful hands with long fingers.

To her absolute amazement she suddenly knew she wanted those hands on her. Wanted him. Wanted every conceivable part of him. So intense and real was this feeling she felt her face becoming hot. How amazing . . . she was blushing. She hadn't blushed in years.

He must have dressed hastily. She noticed, suddenly, that the right cuff of his white dress shirt was open, loosely hanging out of the sleeve of his superbly-cut black evening suit. He leaned to the woman and kissed her on the cheek, almost as an afterthought, it seemed to her. He was talking to the woman earnestly, seemingly unaware of anyone else, even the others standing nearby, obviously wanting his attention.

'Elizabeth, what on earth's got into you?' her brother Anthony asked a trifle sharply, startling her, staring into her face as he bent towards her. 'Gaping at that fellow like a common street girl! *Really*, darling.'

Elizabeth stared back at her brother, who had so suddenly appeared at her side, and asked curiously, 'Who *is* he? I don't know him.'

Anthony was surprised to hear this, and he frowned. 'You must be the only woman in London, if not indeed in the whole of England, who doesn't recognize *him*. That's Edward Deravenel, and please don't tell me you've never heard of him, because I certainly won't believe you. Others might, but not I. Everyone knows who Deravenel is, and especially members of *your* sex.'

'*That's* Edward Deravenel! Good heavens, Anthony, I thought Deravenel was a much older man! Certainly a man in his thirties, even early forties.' She glanced across the room, and went on, 'Why, *he* looks to be in his twenties.'

'Indeed he is, about twenty-three, something like that, not exactly sure. But young.'

'I've read about him in the newspapers. He gives very fancy parties, goes to all the best occasions given by others, and is quite the social animal, isn't he?' Not waiting for a response, she rushed on, 'They say he's a genius in business. Is that true?'

'Don't really know, Lizzie darling.'

'Anthony, please don't address me as Lizzie. You know I don't like it, and Mother *certainly* doesn't.'

He ignored her comments. 'Whether Deravenel is a genius or not doesn't really matter. He has very clever men working for him at Deravenels, and he is supremely lucky in that he has his cousin Neville Watkins by his side, guiding him. Watkins is this country's greatest tycoon today. Some people says it's actually Watkins who runs Deravenels, and holds the power, not our young friend over there.'

'*Is* he a friend of yours?' Elizabeth asked swiftly, staring hard at her brother.

'Unfortunately not – he's an acquaintance, and merely a nodding acquaintance, at that. We did do business some years ago with Deravenels, with the other branch of the family, the Grants, when they managed the company. Not since then, though, more's the pity.' Turning his head, Anthony exclaimed, 'Oh darling, here's Agatha. I do believe I promised her this dance. Please excuse me, Lizzie.' He winked at her mischievously, knowing how much she loathed any abbreviation of her name, this one most particularly.

'Of course, do run along with you, Anthony,' she murmured in a slightly dismissive voice, and sat back on the plush-velvet banquette. Now that she was alone again she stole another look at Edward Deravenel.

At this precise moment he himself moved, drew away from the lovely brunette. He looked around, then glanced across the room.

His eyes met hers.

Her breath caught in her throat.

His blue eyes were the bluest eyes she had ever seen, startlingly so.

To her mortification, she felt herself blushing again, not only because he had caught her watching him surreptitiously, but because his eyes were suddenly and unwaveringly focused on her. And with intensity.

520

Very slowly, a lazy, almost amused smile spread across his face.

For a moment Elizabeth couldn't look away, and then through the corner of her eye she saw her mother approaching, and she stood up, rapidly moved in the opposite direction, found herself heading towards the terrace. Within seconds she was opening the French doors and stepping outside. She looked about, saw that it was empty. Obviously, her cousin and his old schoolfriends had gone for a walk in the garden below.

Although it was a pleasant April evening, it was, nonetheless, growing cooler, and she realized her error. But she wouldn't mind standing here for a moment. She was warm, and her face felt flushed when she touched it; moving closer to the balustrade, she placed her hands on the marble, liking the coolness.

She heard steps on the gravel footpath in the garden; voices drifted up to her, and she recognized Arthur's voice as he said, 'He might have gone to Harrow, but why do we care? I think Churchill's a bloody good chap. He's done an excellent job as Under-Secretary of State at the Colonial Office, and obviously Campbell-Bannerman has a lot of faith in him.'

'I've heard that Campbell-Bannerman's not well,' Hopkins said.

'Good Lord, Hopkins, where did you hear *that*?' Arthur demanded.

'*I* told him,' Woodstock answered. 'My father's close to the Prime Minister – he told him he'll probably step down next year.'

'Good God!' Arthur exclaimed. There was a fractional pause before he went on, 'If he does step down as Prime Minister, it'll be Asquith who succeeds him. There's nobody else.'

'There'll be no election,' Hopkins announced in a firm tone. 'The Liberals swept to power last year and they aim to stay. Churchill was lucky. When he crossed the floor of the House to join them he knew what he was doing –'

'Hey, wait a minute! He crossed the floor because he was not happy with Tory policies,' Arthur interjected, sounding annoyed as he hit back.

'There are some who say he's a traitor to the Tory Party and to his class,' Hopkins muttered.

'I beg to differ,' Arthur replied, lightening his voice. He laughed. 'Come on, chaps, let's go back in and have a bit of the old bubbly, flirt with the ladies.'

'I want to finish my cigar,' Woodstock mumbled. 'There's a bench over there, let's go and sit for a while.'

Their voices drifted away, and Elizabeth leaned forward, looked out into the garden. Men and their politics, she thought impatiently, they drive me to distraction. But then again politics were very much part of daily social life within the upper classes.

She sighed to herself. Hopkins was something of an argumentative chap; she rather agreed with Arthur. He was right, Churchill was a very promising politician. Her father had a lot of time for him, had always said he would go far.

FORTY-SIX

A few moments after the woman in black left the drawing room, Edward turned to Vicky, and asked, 'Do you know who that was? The young woman who was seated on the banquette at the other side of the room.'

Vicky shook her head. 'I've no idea, I really didn't pay too much attention, actually, Ned darling, I was listening to you. However, just before you arrived I did notice a lovely blonde sitting down there.' Vicky began to laugh merrily. 'That's still your weakness, I gather. Blondes. You can't resist them, can you?'

'He certainly can't,' her brother agreed, strolling towards them, accompanied by Johnny Watkins. 'I noticed the lady earlier myself. Rather striking. I've no idea who she is either,' Will remarked.

'Ask our hostess, Ned,' Johnny suggested, studying his cousin. 'She wouldn't be here if she weren't some-body of importance . . . you know dear Maude, she's a terrible snob.'

Ned laughed, stood up. 'Please excuse me, Vicky. I can see Maude over there, talking to Lord Gosford.

I think I should take your advice, Johnny, and inquire of our hostess who the lady in question is, don't you?'

His cousin grinned, rolled his eyes theatrically.

'Come back quickly,' Vicky said. 'You promised me the next dance, Ned.'

'Now *that* I certainly won't miss,' Edward answered, smiling.

Elizabeth had come to Maude Tillotson's dance because the renowned hostess was her mother's best friend. She had received one of the first invitations, and naturally her mother had pressed her to accept, and to accompany them, along with her brother Anthony and their cousin Arthur Forrester.

She hadn't really wanted to attend, in the first place; now she was frantically wondering how to escape, so she could go home. The dance held no meaning for her, and she could not bear to be here. Edward Deravenel had unsettled her, unnerved her. I must leave, she decided, and right now . . .

'I hope I'm not intruding on your privacy, or any important reflections,' a mellifluous masculine voice said.

Elizabeth knew at once that it was *him* before she even looked behind her. The curious thing was, she hadn't heard him approaching. She finally turned around, found herself standing face-to-face with Edward Deravenel. Her throat went dry, and she swallowed. He was larger than life, stood there in front of her, very close, so tall and distinguished. He was overwhelming. His presence, his charisma and masculinity seemed to radiate from him.

She discovered she couldn't speak for a moment, and gratefully leaned against the balustrade, relieved that it was there; her legs were suddenly weak and she was shaking inside.

Finally, growing conscious of the stillness surrounding them, her lack of response to him, she said hurriedly, 'Oh no, you're not intruding at all. I simply came out . . . for a little air.'

'It *was* warm inside.' He paused, stared at her intently.

To Edward she was extraordinarily beautiful. Her face was a perfect oval, with high cheekbones and a broad brow. Her eyes, large and set wide apart, were a light blue, sky blue; she had wonderfully arched blonde brows and a sensual mouth. Like most women of today who were fashionable, her hair was worn swept up on top of her head, piled high with a mass of curls at the front. But it was the colour of her hair that captivated. Pure silver gilt, he thought. She wasn't very tall, of medium height, but a quick, glance told him she had a lovely figure and high, firm breasts. Her dress, simple yet elegant, was made of black chiffon and lace, with a square neckline and slashed sleeves. The skirt floated around her, swirling in the light breeze. The gown was in the new style, long, flowing and full, and without the once-popular semi-bustle.

She cleared her throat softly.

He said swiftly, 'I beg your pardon, how rude I'm

being, staring at you. Please forgive me. Actually, I have a feeling we've met before. We have, haven't we?' He knew they hadn't; he would not have forgotten this beauty. But he needed words to bridge the silence.

She was shaking her head. 'No, we've never met, not ever. I would have remembered,' she said, echoing his own thoughts without knowing that she did, and without any artifice.

'I am Edward Deravenel.' He thrust out his hand.

She took it. For a moment he held it tightly in his – too long, in fact – and then he let go of it very quickly. Her skin felt scorched.

She noticed, unexpectedly, the open cuff again.

'And you are?' he asked, raising a brow questioningly, his eyes searching.

'Elizabeth Wyland.'

'I'm very pleased to meet you, very pleased indeed.' He bowed slightly, and as he did he noticed the gold wedding ring on her finger. Straightening, he asked, 'And you are no doubt here with . . . Mr Wyland?'

'Yes, my brother. That was whom I was talking to earlier.'

Edward frowned, looked slightly perplexed.

She said quietly, 'I'm a widow, Mr Deravenel. I was married to Colonel Simon Gratton. He was in the British army.'

'Oh. I see.' He seemed even more perplexed. 'But you did say Wyland?'

'Yes, I did, my maiden name.' She shrugged lightly, dismissing this point. 'My husband was wounded in the

Boer War, and when he came home to England from Africa in 1900 he was not the same man at all. The war killed his spirit, Mr Deravenel. He was a different person altogether, and he suffered from the after-effects of his wounds. Sadly for me, he died several years ago, in 1904. My mother said death was a relief for him, that his suffering was over . . .'

'I am so very sorry. My condolences.'

She inclined her head. 'Thank you,' was all she said.

'So here you are Elizabeth!' Anthony exclaimed, walking out onto the terrace, joining them. 'I've been looking all over for you. Mother would like to have a word with you, my dear.'

Elizabeth merely nodded, then said, 'This is Mr Edward Deravenel.' Glancing at Edward she added, 'This is my brother, Anthony Wyland.'

The two men shook hands, and Edward said, 'I'm not certain, but I do believe we have met before, Wyland. Am I not correct?'

'We have indeed met before, Deravenel. With my father.'

Edward nodded politely, then turned to Elizabeth, said, 'Thank you for your courtesy.' He flashed her a brilliant smile. 'With your permission, I would like to call on you in the near future, if I may?'

'That would be acceptable,' she answered, then couldn't resist saying, 'Your right cuff is undone, did you know?'

He glanced down at it, smiled wryly. 'Could you fasten it for me?' He reached into his pocket, brought out a lapis lazuli cufflink that matched his shirt studs. 'Here you are,' he added, offering it to her.

She hesitated fractionally, and then took it.

He shot his sleeve down so that she could insert the link in the cuff. Without looking at him, her eyes on his sleeve, she murmured, 'I receive friends at four every afternoon.'

When Edward returned to the drawing room a few minutes later, Vicky was waiting for him. The orchestra was playing a waltz, and as he led her onto the floor Vicky looked up at him, and asked, 'So who *was* the beautiful blonde?'

'I never found out,' he lied, although he did not know why he did this. 'Maude was leading Gosford off into the other drawing room, so I abandoned the quest.' He laughed. 'Got caught up with an old friend for a few minutes,' he improvised, in order to explain his absence.

Vicky wasn't sure if she believed him, but she let the matter drop. There was no point pressing it, and it wasn't any of her business. She knew that Edward had not had a permanent relationship since Lily's death, just lots of women hanging around him.

Her brother Will called them 'Ned's carnal relationships', and would laugh and say blithely, 'Women are crazy about him. So much so, some chaps say he never has his trousers on. But I know differently, I'm with him at work every day, and he works like a galley slave, believe you me.'

She knew this was true. Ned was a lot like his cousin Neville Watkins, another man who spent most of his time at his office. Defying demons and driven by ambition, the two of them, she thought. She liked Neville, he was a man of his word and considerate. As for Edward, she loved him dearly like another brother, but sometimes she had problems understanding certain aspects of him. Ned was a hard taskmaster with himself, and yet he had, somehow, managed to acquire a reputation for being very much the ladies' man. But why not?

At almost twenty-three, Ned was determined to live the big life. And he was entitled; after all, he was young and single, and he had the world in his hands. Edward Deravenel had money, position and background, therefore he was in demand at all the dances, cotillions and balls, dinner parties and every other kind of high-profile social event in London. Because of his wealth, success and power, and that awesome charm of his, Ned was the most eligible young man in London these days. Since he was also stunning looking and known to be a great lover, every woman wanted him; even older married women played up to him. No wonder he was just a little bit spoilt by women . . . women of all ages.

'Penny for your thoughts, sweet Vicky,' Ned said, looking down at her. She had always been a favourite of his, and he went on gently, 'You seem miles away. In New York, I've no doubt, with Stephen?' His bright blue eyes were searching, questioning.

'That's right.' She smiled up at him. 'I miss Stephen so much Ned, and so does little Grace Rose.'

'When does he get back to London?'

'In about ten days, two weeks at the latest. Talking

about that, I'm giving a party for Grace, when he returns. I'd love you to come, Ned. With Fenella.'

'Thank you, I will, and who else are you going to invite?'

'Amos, of course. Grace loves him.'

'Good old Finnister, he's the salt of the earth. Splendid chap. I suppose my boon companion is coming, too.'

'I haven't asked Will yet, but I'll mention it tonight. The only person other than you I actually did invite so far is Fenella. She's always shown such an interest in Grace.'

'And done a great deal of detective work on her behalf,' Ned pointed out, laughing. 'Amazing how persistent Fenella was.'

A little smile played around Vicky's mouth. 'Yes, she was, and I for one am very glad.'

They finished the waltz in silence.

A short while later Edward found Will standing at the bar alone, drinking a glass of champagne. As he reached his closest friend, Edward said, 'You're looking glum. What's wrong?'

'I miss Kathleen rather more than I thought I would,' Will said in a low voice. 'I think I'm finally going to have to take that *fatal* step. Get married.'

'I think you should,' Edward answered swiftly, fully approving of Will's involvement with his cousin, Kathleen Watkins, sister of Neville and Johnny. 'She adores you, you know.'

Will nodded, and suddenly smiled. 'That's good to know.'

'Don't act daft, Hasling! You damn well know how she feels.'

Will grinned, and took a swallow of champagne, asked, 'And did you find out who the mysterious blonde is?'

'I did.'

'And?' Will stared at Edward, frowning, 'Why the long face?'

'She's a Wyland.'

'God, no!' Will leaned closer to Edward and said, sotto voce, 'Her father used to be very close to the Grants, very close indeed, although I must admit I don't know where he stands today, now that the Grants are living in France. But surely you knew the Wylands did business with the Grants. And for years . . . they go back a long time, that I *do* know.'

'My father once told me that the Wylands had been involved with Deravenels for over a hundred years, so they do go back, far back. I met her brother: he seems like a pleasant chap.'

'Nicest of the bunch, so I've heard.'

'She's a stunning woman, Will. I was bowled over. Captivated. I have to see her again . . . By the way, she's a widow.'

'Oh Christ, no! Why is it that you always fall head over heels for blondes who are widows? You certainly have a peculiar knack for it, Ned. It's uncanny. Come to think of it, she's probably older than you.'

'Probably.'

'Make it a short run, Ned, short and sweet, and then

say farewell. She's from the enemy camp. Don't *you* forget that.'

Edward gave him an odd look but made no further comment.

FORTY-SEVEN

'I'm so very sorry, Elinor, but I really must be getting back to the office,' Edward Deravenel said, smiling at the woman who was seated opposite him.

'I understand, darling, but I am so disappointed,' she murmured. 'I thought we could spend the afternoon here . . . we are alone, you know, as I told you my house-keeper is off today. We could be . . . *together*.'

'I had planned to be here with you, but unfortunately something came up at the office this morning, and it needs my immediate attention. I have a meeting at three.'

Elinor Burton nodded. 'I realize you have a huge business empire to run. I don't know how you do it.'

'Not alone, I can tell you that,' he replied, with a smile, standing up. 'Thank you for lunch, it was delicious.'

'All prepared by Fortnum and Mason,' she laughed and also rose, and together they left her dining room, went out into the entrance foyer of her small house in Belgravia. 'When will I see you again?' she asked.

'I'll try to come down to the country next week, I'll let you know.' He pulled her towards him, held her tightly in his arms, and then kissed her passionately on the mouth. She clung to him, responding enthusiastically.

After a moment, they stood apart, and she said, 'You shouldn't have done that, Ned, it was far too tantalizing.'

He merely laughed, gazing down at her, thinking how lovely she looked today, with her shining blonde hair and hazel eyes that were golden in certain light. 'Oh, Elinor, you are a true beauty,' he murmured, genuinely meaning this, and took hold of her again, suddenly aroused.

Elinor held him at bay, laughed lightly. 'Oh darling Ned, you're incorrigible. But not *now*. I will not be blamed for interfering with your business.'

'Sanity usually reigns when I'm with *you*.' Flashing her his brightest smile, he let himself out of the house, and within minutes his mind was focused on business.

And then he stopped, thinking of Elinor. He had not been very nice to her today, and she really was the loveliest of women, sweet and gentle, and almost Madonna-like in her appearance. Turning around he walked back to the front door and lifted the brass knocker.

Surprise filled her eyes as she opened the door and saw him. 'Edward!' she exclaimed, staring at him. 'Did you forget something?'

He smiled at her. 'Yes, I forgot for a moment how much I care about you, my darling. Can I come in for a short while?'

'Of course,' she answered, opening the door wider. 'But I'm confused. You said you had an important meeting to attend.'

'I do,' he said, turning to her in the entrance foyer.

'But it's only one fifteen – we had a very early lunch, you know. Noon . . . a little bit too early for me. Never mind, let's go upstairs, as you wanted to before.' He took her in his arms, and kissed her, and then led her upstairs to the next floor. She did not protest.

She was wearing a loose, navy-blue silk dress, with a dropped waistline, and she turned to him when they were in her bedroom and asked, 'Could you unbutton me, please, Ned.'

He laughed as he started on the buttons, kissing the back of her neck and her lovely blonde hair as he did so. The dress fell to the floor; she stepped over it, turned to him, smiled into his face.

'How lovely you are, my sweet,' he whispered, touching her cheek. There was something truly innocent about her face, and in her eyes there was nothing but peacefulness, and love for him. He had wanted her from the moment he had met her, attracted to her because of the innocence and simplicity in her. Of course she had fended him off, being a very proper widow, and virtuous; he had exercised every ounce of his charm. And eventually she had succumbed to him, and given herself to him most wholeheartedly.

'What are you thinking about?' she asked, staring up into his eyes.

'I was thinking how your reluctance to start an affair with me actually made me want you all the more. In any other woman I might think the reluctance was a ruse, but with you I know you were sincere.'

'Oh yes, I was, Ned, but I'm glad now that we are together. You are so important to me. Let us go to bed, so I can show you how important.'

Elinor was always ready for him, and after kissing her and smoothing his hands over her long slender body, he knew she was growing more and more hot under his hands, agitated even, and so he took her to him swiftly, entering her with ease. She was truly ready, opening herself up to him like a flower, and the heat of her body aroused him further. He was unable to hold back. Against her neck he whispered, 'Now, Nell, now, come to me.' And she did so, clinging to him, her body trembling with joy under his.

As they lay together later, talking softly, she suddenly said, 'You will come to the country this weekend, won't you?'

'I will. Where else would I want to be but with you?' he answered, knowing full well that he would visit her at her country cottage. He was not going to treat her lightly.

Edward had only been back in his office at Deravenels for half an hour when Will Hasling knocked on the door and came in. 'There you are. It's almost three so let's go to the boardroom, and Oliveri and Aspen will join us in a few minutes. How was lunch?'

'Pleasant. Marsden is a nice chap, but I don't think we'll be able to do any business with him.'

'Where did you lunch? At White's?'

'No, *his* club. The Reform. But it was very quick, he was in a hurry,' Ned answered, glad that he had indeed met Marsden at his club for a drink before rushing over to Elinor's pied-à-terre for their private luncheon. It gave him an alibi. The affair with her was a secret; they both wanted it that way, at least for the moment.

'By the way,' Will went on, 'Neville has finalized the plans for the Paris trip, to meet with Louis Charpentier. He telephoned a short while ago and said he'll have all the details later. But he's going in a few days.'

'Very good. Shall we go into the boardroom?'

Ever since Edward had become managing director of Deravenels, Will had worked with him closely, as his personal assistant. But he was also in charge of a pet project of Edward's, one which they were about to discuss.

Within seconds Alfredo Oliveri and Rob Aspen joined them and sat down at the conference table. After greetings had been exchanged, Edward said, 'Well, tell me the big news.'

'It's not *big* news,' Alfredo answered. 'But our contacts in Persia have confirmed that the company called Onpeg is definitely still there, continuing to drill for oil. At Masjid-I-Sulaiman.'

'That's in southwest Persia,' Rob Aspen explained.

'But they haven't struck oil yet, have they?' Edward asked, frowning. He glanced at Will as he spoke. 'Nothing much has changed, has it?'

'Several other companies are out there already, drilling in other parts of Persia, and I think we ought to do what you've always wanted to do – send a team of our own to look around, investigate,' Will said.

'Then let's plan it,' Edward agreed, always sure of himself, of his ability in business. It had served him well for the last three years. He had brought Deravenels back to a large extent, had ensured its future, and

rectified much of the damage done by Grant mismanagement in the past. He was aiming to make it more
important than it had ever been.

'So,' he went on, 'who's to go? What about you,
Oliveri? Do you want to hop out there to the desert
sands of Persia?'

'If you want me to, I will.' Alfredo grinned. 'You
know I love adventure.'

'I'll go too, if you think I can be useful,' Rob Aspen
interjected.

'I'm game. Persia appeals to me,' Will announced.

'Oh no, not you, Will. I'm afraid you'll have to stay
put. Now, chaps, let's discuss this further,' Edward said.
'Definitely make the proper plans. I believe oil is going
to be the big commodity of the future. And we must
be in on its discovery. We need our own oilfields, they're
vital . . .'

'Under no circumstances are you to allow him to climb
into your bed,' Jocelyn Wyland said, giving her daughter
Elizabeth a hard and cautionary stare. 'He has something of a reputation, you know, as a womanizer. And
if you become intimate with him, that's it. You will
soon be discarded by him.'

'Mother, I've no intention of becoming intimate with
Edward Deravenel! How could you think such a thing?'
Elizabeth looked askance.

'Because if I were your age I'd take him into my bed
at the drop of a hat!'

'Mother! *Really.*'

538

Jocelyn Wyland smiled. 'I know I'm contradicting myself, but he is quite extraordinary, and, I will add, irresistible to most women. Why should *you* be any different?'

'I'm not, and you're correct, Mother, but I'm not a fool. I'm hardly going to sleep with him now, when I want to marry him. That's my aim. Nothing less than marriage will do for *me*.'

Jocelyn beamed at her eldest daughter. 'I'm delighted to know that you have the right attitude about this. After all, sex is sex and it can be most enjoyable. With the right man. But we are playing for bigger stakes here, Elizabeth. Let's not forget you're a widow with two young sons, and not much of an income from Simon's estate. Your father and I will continue to support you in the way you should be supported. However, I have big hopes for you, dreams of a good marriage.'

'I know that, Mother, and I won't let you down. I know how to keep a check on . . . my emotions, my feelings.'

'You're a great beauty, and most men would do anything to possess you, my dear. But only the one who puts a wedding band on your left hand will do.'

Elizabeth nodded, stood up, walked across the small sitting room of her house in Cadogan Square, stood looking out into the leafy square, thinking of Edward Deravenel. She wanted him desperately. After a moment she said, 'I haven't seen him a lot, you know. Only twice . . . he came for tea.'

'Hasn't he invited you anywhere, darling?' her mother asked, frowning slightly. 'To the opera? A concert? Perhaps to dinner at the Ritz. That hotel's the most popular place with the denizens of society since it opened last year.'

'No, he hasn't invited me out,' Elizabeth said again.

'How peculiar. So how has he behaved when he's come for tea? What has he said? What happened?'

Elizabeth stared at her mother, frowning slightly, wondering whether to tell her the truth or not. Opting for the truth, she said quietly, 'He's talked to me affectionately, attempted to be amorous with me, kissed me on the cheek, the last time on the mouth, and he's tried to touch me . . . But I fended him off.'

Jocelyn had always been able to talk openly with her eldest daughter, more so than with any of her other children, and now she dropped her voice, and asked, 'Was he . . . *anxious*? Aroused?'

Elizabeth nodded. 'Very much so, and the last time he was here he left in an angry mood, because he was . . . rampant, raging to possess me.'

'His frustration at not having his way with you got the better of him.'

'I think so. He said I was a temptress, in a very annoyed voice.'

Jocelyn burst out laughing. 'Continue to tempt him, my darling, but don't let him get anywhere near you. Instinctively, I know the likes of him . . . a man who can't resist women soon moves on to fresher fields once he's picked the flowers in the field he's standing in.'

Elizabeth laughed at this analogy, then confessed, 'I'm head over heels in love with him, Mother.'

'Keep yourself in check, Elizabeth. Save that love for later, after he's married you. Don't give him what he wants until then. Do you hear me?'

'Yes, I do. You have my promise.'

'Has he made any attempt to see you again?'

'He sent a note this morning.' Elizabeth glanced at the carriage clock on the mantelpiece. 'He's coming in a few hours . . . this evening. Between six and seven.'

'Has he invited you out to dinner tonight?'

'No, he said in the note that he would come for a drink.'

'Perfect. And if he does want you to dine with him, say you cannot. I think I'd prefer you not to be seen in public with him at this moment. He's the most eligible man in London, and I don't want people to think he's had his way with you and then dropped you . . . that is, if nothing comes of this . . .'

'I understand.'

'I trust you do, darling. Your future depends on your chastity.'

FORTY-EIGHT

Yorkshire

Thorpe Manor was one of the loveliest houses in Yorkshire. Beautifully proportioned, with a flowing front façade, many windows and two towers with cream domes and shining spires, it was a perfect example of late Elizabethan architecture. Built of local pale pink stone, the window and door surrounds were outlined in cream limestone, and the whole building was soft and gentle in all of its aspects.

The house was set in a vast parkland of sweeping green lawns and great spreading oak and sycamore trees, flower gardens, walled rose gardens, and several ornamental lakes. Swans floated on the surface of the lakes, and elegant peacocks strutted proudly on the terraces and lawns, colourful sentinels guarding this great manor house. It had been in the Watkins family for centuries, gifted to Neville by his father when he had married Nan. It had been their country home ever since.

Today the house was a hive of activity. The staff bustled everywhere; florists were filling urns and vases with roses and other flowers; chefs were preparing delicious food in the kitchen; caterers were arranging small gold chairs around the circular tables on the long terrace, straightening rose-pink organdie cloths.

In a few hours Kathleen Watkins, sister of Neville, would be married to Will Hasling in the private chapel on the estate. And afterwards the family and guests would mingle outside at the reception, a summer garden party. It was a glorious June Saturday, a perfect day for a wedding.

Will Hasling stood in his bedroom, staring at Edward worriedly. 'Are you sure my cravat is correctly arranged?' he asked. 'Do I look all right, Ned?'

'Never better, old chap. In fact, if I were a woman I'd marry you in a shot,' Ned joked, grinning at his best friend.

'Oh, do be serious!' Will exclaimed, sounding impatient, shaking his head, looking exasperated.

'All right, I'll be serious. *You've never looked better*,' Ned reassured him. 'Tall, handsome, and Savile Row perfect down to the glassy toes of your shoes. Do stop being the proverbial nervous bridegroom, and stand still so that I can attach your boutonnière.'

Once the white rose was in place on Will's jacket, Edward handed another white rose to him and said, 'Now it's your turn to fix mine.' Both men were elegantly attired in morning suits – impeccably-tailored black frock coats, striped trousers and white waistcoats. Their cravats were of soft dove-grey silk, each held in place with a pearl stick pin.

Stepping away from Ned, Will eyed his friend, and joked, 'And *I* would marry *you* at the drop of a hat, if I were a woman.'

The two friends laughed together, and then Ned said,

'Do you feel a bit constrained? Having Neville in Paris when you're on your honeymoon there?'

Will shrugged, looked unconcerned. 'Not really. Actually, Kathleen and I will only be there for a couple of days before going on to the Côte d'Azur. Anyway, I doubt that we'll see Neville. He's going to be in meetings with Louis Charpentier on the few days he's in Paris.'

'Yes, that's true. Actually, he'll be finalizing the deal to take over the Charpentier silk mills in Lyons.'

Hearing the lack of interest in Edward's voice, Will glanced at him swiftly. '*You* don't sound very enthusiastic.'

'I'm not, I couldn't care less, Will. I know Charpentier has a big business empire in France, and Neville craves it for us, but Deravenels is pretty solid these days. I don't think we need the Charpentier French holdings, not really. I'm more interested in *oil*. I'm glad we sent that team of geologists to Persia with Oliveri and Aspen. I hope we can stake a claim out there, I really do. In fact, I'm becoming fanatical about it.'

'You've always said oil is the future, and I agree. After the honeymoon maybe *we* ought to go out to Persia, Ned, take a look round, you and I.'

'Maybe. Although I have my hands full at the moment, as you well know. I have those Americans coming next month. They want to sell us their cotton plantations outright, and I've a mind to buy them out. It makes great sense to me.'

There was a light tap on the door, and Johnny Watkins walked in, looking as elegant as Ned and Will in his morning suit. 'Ah, there you are,' he said to Ned, 'and *you* have the tray of white roses, I see. I need one, old chap, and so do the other ushers. And Neville.'

'There's plenty here, and there's even one for Richard, Johnny. I don't want my Little Fish to feel left out.'

'And George, what about *him*?' Will asked, throwing Ned a cautionary look. We don't want a temper tantrum today of all days.'

'Only too true. There is a rose for George,' Ned answered quietly. George could be troublesome these days; he worried Ned.

Ned attached the white rose to the lapel of Johnny's jacket, and went on, 'I hope you're wearing your other white rose. You are, aren't you?'

Johnny smiled at him, his light grey eyes sparkling. 'I'll never take it off, Ned. I told you, I'll wear it 'til the day I die and even after.' Picking up the small silver tray, Johnny now headed towards the bedroom door, explaining, 'I must go downstairs and rally the troops, get them lined up.'

Will watched Johnny go, and then swinging to Ned he said in a low voice, 'Has Johnny asked you about the blonde you spotted at Maude Tillotson's dance?'

'No. Why?' Ned's eyes narrowed slightly.

'Because he *did* ask *me*, quite recently. He wanted to know if you'd found out who she was, and I actually lied to him, Ned.' Will shook his head. 'God knows why I did that . . . I just felt I'd better not say she was a Wyland. I know Neville has never liked them, always been suspicious of the family, because of their long-held friendship, and connection, to the Grants.'

'Thanks for being protective of me, Will, I appreciate it. But actually I haven't seen her again. I mean, after the last time I had drinks with her at her house. She wasn't very ... *cooperative*, shall we say? Not at all willing to share her favours with me, so I backed off. Too much trouble ... a widow with two young sons.'

'I'll say!'

There was another tap on the door and Vicky looked in, smiling at Will and Ned. 'I've been sent to fetch the bridegroom and his best man.' As she spoke she came into the room, looking beautiful in a pale blue gown. She was a matron-of-honour with Fenella Fayne. 'Let me correct myself, chaps. I volunteered, so I could give you both a kiss.' She walked across to her brother, and added, 'And I want to wish you much happiness, Will darling, and all the luck in the world.'

Like her brothers, Kathleen Watkins had a strong resemblance to her aunt, Cecily Deravenel. She was a lovely-looking young woman, with a cloud of russet-brown hair, large pellucid grey eyes and a slender, aristocratic face, finely boned.

As she walked down the aisle of the small chapel on the arm of her brother Neville, she felt as though her life was just beginning. She had been in love with Will for years, since she was sixteen, and now her dream was about to come true. When she left the chapel she would be his wife. She would belong to him, he to her. He would be her husband. Her happiness soared.

Will, waiting at the altar for Kathleen, thought she had never looked lovelier than she did today. As she walked towards him on her brother's arm, all of his nervousness fled.

He suddenly felt utterly calm, confident. He knew he was doing the right thing, marrying this special young woman. He felt Ned squeeze his arm, looked at him quickly, and nodded. 'I'm all right,' Will whispered, answering the questioning look in Ned's eyes.

As for Edward Deravenel, the best man, he was relaxed and at ease with himself. He was happy for Will, knowing how much his friend had wanted to be married. He was lucky he had found the right person, someone who loved him so much in return.

Here she came now, his cousin Kathleen, a vision in white satin and white lace. There was the glint of pearls and orange blossoms in the small coronet on her head, and the tulle veil itself was like a great cumulus cloud around her face, soft, enfolding. She carried a magnificent bouquet of white roses, freesias, gardenias and orchids, and as she drew closer he caught a fleeting whiff of their mingled perfumes.

Behind her came her two matrons-of-honour, Vicky and Fenella, and behind them the bridesmaids, his sister Margaret, Neville's daughters Isabel and Anne, and lastly, the flower girl, Grace Rose. All of the attendants were wearing pale blue silk, and the little girls, in particular, looked adorable, Ned thought.

In the background the organ was being played, and a lone soprano voice suddenly rang out:

'O perfect Love, all human thought
      transcending,
Lowly we kneel in prayer before thy throne,

That theirs may be the love which knows no
    ending,
Whom thou for evermore dost join in one.'

Neville and Kathleen finally came to a standstill in front
of the altar. The organ music faded away, and the
Watkins family priest was in place standing before the
bride and Neville.

Ned felt around in his pocket for the wedding rings.
They were there. *Safe*. He relaxed once more.

And the marriage ceremony began.

Satin and lace. Flower petals and confetti. Laughter and
tears. Happiness and joy to overflowing. Champagne in
crystal flutes. Sunlight shimmering. Shady seats under leafy
trees. Music in the air. Mozart and Brahms. English country
airs. Popular songs. Glamorous people. Beautiful clothes.
Jewellery glittering.

People talking, laughing, moving . . . all around him.
The garden party was a success, Ned already knew that.
But he wanted to move away from the lawn, move up
onto the terrace, to sit down, to reflect for a moment.
His mind was so full . . .

He walked fast, moving through the crowd,
climbing the broad stone steps to the smaller terrace,
which had been decorated with comfortable white
wicker chairs and loveseats. As he sank down into
one of the chairs, he saw his mother coming towards
the terrace, and he raised his hand, waved. A moment
later, he noticed Vicky, holding Grace Rose's hand,

and they too were wandering across the lawn heading in his direction.

As his mother came up the steps, he stood, waiting for her, a wide smile on his face.

'How beautiful Kathleen looked,' Cecily said. 'Such a lovely ceremony, Ned, wasn't it?'

'It was indeed, Mother.'

Suddenly Grace Rose was running towards them, and as she came to a standstill, Ned crouched down. 'Hello, Grace Rose, you were the perfect bridesmaid,' he murmured.

'Was I really, Uncle Ned?' she asked, smiling prettily.

'Oh yes, indeed!'

Turning to Vicky, Grace cried, 'Mumma, did you hear that? Hear what Uncle Ned said?'

'I did, my darling. Now, come along, we must go inside for a moment.' Vicky smiled at Cecily and said, 'Hello, Mrs Deravenel, it's such a happy day, isn't it?'

'It is indeed, Vicky, my dear.' Cecily glanced at the child. 'And your name is Grace Rose, is it?'

'Yes,' Grace said, bobbing a small curtsy.

'Well, hello, Grace Rose,' Cecily murmured, and smiled.

'Hello,' Grace answered shyly, and then she put her hand in Vicky's and the two of them left.

Cecily Deravenel watched them go into the house, and then she turned to Edward and asked, 'Is that Vicky's child, Ned? She called her Mumma.'

'Thereby hangs a long tale,' he answered. 'Sit down, and I'll tell you.'

After Edward recounted the story of how Amos had found Grace on the streets and brought her to Haddon

House, he then told her about the birth certificate in the photograph frame.

Cecily sat up straighter in the wicker chair, and frowned. 'So Vicky found out who the child's parents were. How amazing!'

'She discovered who the mother was. The father's name was not on the birth certificate.'

'*Illegitimate*. Grace Rose is illegitimate then.' Cecily frowned. 'And what did the note reveal, Ned?'

'The name of the father.'

'And who is the father?'

'Actually, Mother, I am.'

FORTY-NINE

Cecily sat staring at him. She was perfectly still, her face devoid of all expression. And she did not say a word.

Finally, Edward spoke. 'You don't appear to be surprised, Mother.'

'I am, then, yet again, I am not. The moment I set eyes on that child walking behind the bridesmaids down the aisle in the chapel, I was struck at once by her extraordinary resemblance to you. At that moment I didn't actually know who she was. When I saw her with Vicky on the terrace, saw how you were so gentle and sweet with her, I assumed . . .' Cecily sighed, shook her head. 'Forgive me, Ned, but I thought you and Vicky had had an affair, and that Grace Rose was the result.'

'*Mother*. How could you think such a thing? Vicky's a married woman!'

'When has that ever stopped you?'

'My God!' Ned shook his head. 'I must have the most dreadful reputation.'

'Well, I don't know that I would use that word . . .

from what *I* hear, most men envy you, and most women would . . . well, let's leave it at that. The less said about women and their sex lives, the better.'

Edward couldn't help chuckling. After a moment, he said, 'There's no one like *you*, Mama. No one at all.'

'So who is, or was, the mother of Grace Rose? I'm assuming the child was correct when she said her mother was dead.'

'She is dead, yes. At least so I believe. Fenella thinks so, too, but actually I'm jumping ahead. Let me explain something . . . Grace's mother was Tabitha James. She was the wife of the choirmaster at a church in Scarborough. I met her when –' Edward paused, compressed his mouth, then said vaguely, 'when I was very young. We became . . . involved, but she was afraid we'd be caught out, and disappeared from my young life, but then I ran into her again one day. In Whitby. She was widowed by this time, and had gone to live there with her sister-in-law, her husband's spinster sister. Toby James had left her . . . destitute.'

'And you picked up with her again, is that what you're about to tell me?'

Edward gave his mother a direct look, and nodded. 'Yes, I did.'

Cecily frowned, shaking her head, and then said slowly. 'But Ned, you must have been very *young*.'

He bit his lip, and didn't answer for a moment, then took a deep breath, blew out air. 'When Tabitha lived in Scarborough, when I first met her, I was thirteen . . . *she* seduced *me* at the age of thirteen. Later, when I saw her in Whitby, I was fourteen.'

Although she was appalled to hear how young he had been when he had come to know a woman intimately, at the same time Cecily realized that her eldest son was not like most men. First of all he was tall and strapping, and had been extremely well developed as a boy of thirteen. And he had appeared much older than his true years, not only in his appearance but also in his demeanour. Ned had always been rather grown up for his age, more sophisticated than other boys of the same age.

Leaning forward, Cecily now put her hand on Edward's arm and her gaze was full of understanding. 'How old were you when Grace Rose was born?' she asked softly.

'I must have been fifteen, Mother. I did try to stand by Tabitha as best I could.' A faint smile flickered and he said in a subdued voice, 'There wasn't too much I could do . . . about giving her money. I didn't have any. But I would ask Cook for a picnic every time I rode over to see Tabitha, which was often. So I did provide food for her during her pregnancy.'

Cecily closed her eyes again, asking herself why children never came to their parents when they had problems, whatever those problems were. But she knew the answer. They were afraid to confide. And rightly so. If Ned had come to them, told them of the predicament he was in, he would have been sent away to boarding school instead of being tutored at Ravenscar. So he had struggled on his own, done his best.

'Are you all right, Mother?' Ned asked, looking at her worriedly.

'Yes, Ned, I am,' she murmured, and opened her eyes.

He searched her face. 'I tried to be responsible, you know.'

She nodded. 'Then the baby was born . . . and what happened?'

'If you remember, I had bronchitis when I was fifteen, and was really quite ill for some weeks. When I finally got better, I rode over to Whitby. Tabitha was gone. In fact, other people lived in the cottage. I made inquiries, and apparently the sister-in-law had died and Tabitha had gone to London. That was all I knew.'

'I see. You must have been upset, weren't you?'

'I was. Yes. But I told myself that Tabitha was in her twenties and capable. I thought she had probably gone to stay with a friend in London. She once told me she had a schoolfriend who lived in Chelsea.'

'And so you got on with your life, I presume.' Cecily raised a brow quizzically.

'There wasn't anything else I could do,' Ned replied.

'And then one day you met your child. With Vicky. Am I correct?'

'You are. I was struck at once by Grace Rose's looks, and so was Will. But we never actually discussed it. He never asked me if she was mine.'

'Not even Vicky? Didn't she spot the curious resemblance?'

'I think she did, Mother, but the circumstances were so strange. The way Finnister had found the child in a cart in Whitechapel threw everyone off. So *I* believe. How could that child be *mine*? Vicky thought Grace's colouring was just a peculiar coincidence. She told me that later.'

'Once the birth certificate had been found, and the

note, of course everything was out in the open. Is that the way it was?' Cecily stared at her son again.

'Let's just say six people knew . . . Vicky, Stephen, Fenella, Finnister, and Will. And me. You see, Tabitha had named me as the father in the note, asking that I be contacted. There was a lock of my hair inside the note.'

'And your address? Was that not given?' Cecily wondered aloud.

'Just Ravenscar, that's all.'

'But no one ever did find the note to contact you, am I not correct? Because no one ever removed the brown paper from the photograph until Vicky did.'

'You are correct, Mother. Actually, I didn't know much myself. I told Vicky that Tabitha had gone to London and disappeared from my life.'

'You mentioned Fenella a short while ago. How did she come into it?'

'Fenella knows Whitby rather well, as it turns out. Although she grew up in Tanfield, she and her brother were taken to Whitby every summer by their nanny when they were children. For their seaside holidays. She was going up to Yorkshire to stay with her father, just after the note was found, so she decided to do a bit of detective work in Whitby. She went over there, talked to Tabitha's former neighbours, as well as the local trades people, and she found out two things. That Tabitha James wasn't who she said she was – by that I mean her background was quite different than most people realized. She was seemingly the only daughter of a titled family, and had run off with her music teacher, Toby James. Fenella was also given a name. Sophie

555

Fox-Lannigan. This woman was seemingly the old schoolfriend of Tabitha's, who lived in Chelsea.'

'Goodness me! Who would ever have thought that Fenella would be such a clever detective, and go to all that trouble.' Cecily was impressed, and showed it.

'Actually, you don't *really* mean that, Mother, if you think about it. Of course Fenella would want to help. And just think of the way she runs Haddon House. That's who she is, you know, a very caring person.'

'That's true. She's also very inquisitive. Fortunately.' Cecily threw Edward a knowing look, and continued, 'And I suppose Fenella went to see this lady, Sophie Fox-Lannigan, to ascertain what *she* knew.'

'She did indeed look up Mrs Fox-Lannigan. Tabitha's old friend still lived in Chelsea. Unfortunately, Sophie didn't know too much. She told Fenella that Tabitha had stayed with her and her husband for a few months, and had then gone off with a man she had met through friends of the Fox-Lannigans. He was a former guards officer, and a gambler, by the name of Cedric Crawford.'

'And Fenella found him. Is that it?'

'No. Mrs Fox-Lannigan told Fenella that Tabitha had ended up living with Crawford in Whitechapel, in a terrible hovel of a place. Mrs Fox-Lannigan had gone to see her a few times, taking money and food, and begging her to leave this man. But Tabitha seemed fearful of Crawford, and wouldn't budge. Sophie was so troubled she kept going back, and one day when she went to see Tabitha in Whitechapel, she had disappeared. All of them had. *Gone*. Just like that, without a trace.'

'What a dreadful way for poor Tabitha to end up. She was never found, I suppose?'

'No. And obviously Crawford had flown the coop, disappeared into oblivion. Probably after Tabitha died. The child originally said to Amos Finnister that the man had killed her mother. But we have no proof of that.'

'This man Crawford pushed Grace Rose out onto the streets once her mother was gone, of that I'm positive.'

'More than likely he did,' Ned agreed.

'Who was she really? Tabitha?'

'She was the daughter of the Earl of Brockhaven, and therefore had a title in her own right. Before she married Toby James she was Lady Tabitha Brockhaven.'

'Has anyone been in contact with her family?'

'There is no family left, Mother. The Earl and Countess had no sons, only Tabitha. She was the only child. Now the Earl and Countess are dead, the title is extinct. They were rather an impoverished family, according to Mrs Fox-Lannigan.'

'I see. How sad . . . what terrible lives people do have.' Cecily shook her head sorrowfully. 'We all of us suffer such hardships at times and in such different ways.'

Edward Deravenel, at this precise moment, thought of the word *catastrophe*, and instantly pushed it away. He looked off into the distance, and then, finally turning back to his mother, he murmured, 'That's more or less the whole story . . . except for one thing. Sophie Fox-Lannigan had a small trunk belonging to Tabitha. Once Tabitha and Grace had disappeared she simply put it in the attic of her house, loth to throw it out. She mentioned this trunk to Fenella, who remembered a key in Grace's cloth bag.'

Cecily nodded. 'I know what you're going to tell me . . . the key in the bag fit the trunk. It did, didn't it, Ned?'

'It did.'

'And what did the trunk contain?'

'Notes from me to Tabitha. Letters from her father, begging her to come home, letters that said all was forgiven. A few bits of jewellery, not worth very much. Odds and ends that Vicky will give to Grace Rose when she's old enough to have them.'

'And what does the child know, Ned? Does she know *you* are her real father?'

'No, no, not at all! I would never do that to Stephen Forth and Vicky. They adore the child. We discussed it at length, and I was the one who asked them to allow things to remain exactly as they were. No big revelations. I did say I would like to be part of Grace Rose's life . . . but only as Uncle Ned. Also, you should know that now I am head of Deravenels, and have money, I have created a trust for Grace Rose. However, she mustn't know anything about my being her natural father. It's the best way, Mother, really it is. No one gets hurt.'

'I absolutely agree with you, Ned. You have done the right thing . . . Despite what some people might think, you always do. In your own way.' Cecily gave him a loving smile that had a hint of pride in it. 'And so Grace Rose is . . . *seven* years old. Am I right?'

'Yes, you are. She was four when Finnister found her, but because she's tall, like I am, Fenella was always convinced that she was five, perhaps older. Naturally, the birth certificate confirms her age.'

'Thank you for telling me the story of Grace Rose. Now, perhaps we should go and find some of our family members, take part in the wedding tea.' Rising, Cecily walked towards the stone steps, followed by her son. As they went down the steps together she told him, 'I'd like to see Grace Rose again, Ned. A little later. Just to talk to her for a short while.'

'I think that's a good idea, Mother. You should get to know her.'

They made their way to the larger terrace where the two families and guests were starting to gather, and were looking for their seats.

Neville came striding towards Ned and his mother, exclaiming, 'There you both are! We wondered what had happened to you.'

'Just catching up,' Cecily remarked, smiling at Neville, wondering suddenly how much her nephew knew.

'You look perfectly beautiful, Aunt Cecily,' Neville said as he led his aunt toward her place at the family table. 'This lovely delphinium blue suits you enormously.'

'Why thank you, Neville, and I must congratulate you and Nan. You are giving the most beautiful wedding I have been to in a very, very long time. It's superb, and the idea of a garden party was inspired.'

A few minutes later Neville drew Edward aside, and said, in a low, confiding tone, 'Are you sure you don't want to come with me on Monday, to Paris to meet Louis?'

Oh, so it's Louis now, Edward thought, but said, 'Thanks, but no thanks, Neville. It's your deal, and I think you should be the one to follow it through. Close it.'

'Very well. Consider it done,' Neville answered with a bright smile, placing a hand on Edward's shoulder. 'We make the best team, you and I.'

Much later, after all of the wedding speeches had been made, and toasts drunk, the dancing began in the Great Hall. Many of the guests flocked inside, while others walked around the gardens, enjoying the beautiful evening.

It was then that Cecily Deravenel went in search of Vicky. She found her sitting at one end of the Great Hall with her husband Stephen.

'Vicky darling, may I have a word with you?' Cecily asked as Vicky looked up and smiled as she approached.

'But of course, Mrs Deravenel. Excuse me for a moment, Stephen.'

He had risen when Cecily had come to stop in front of them, and now he smiled at her. 'It's a lovely day, isn't it, Mrs Deravenel?'

'It is, Stephen, and a lovely wedding. I'm glad our families are joined.'

Taking hold of Vicky's arm, Cecily quickly led her to the far end of the Great Hall, and out into a courtyard that opened off it. 'Vicky, I know everything,' Cecily began, wanting to get to the point at once. 'Ned told me everything about Grace Rose. Just now, this afternoon.'

'I always thought that you, more than anyone else, would notice the extraordinary resemblance between Ned and the child once you saw Grace Rose.'

'I did. But I thought it might just be a coincidence.'

Vicky smiled, nodded. 'Coincidence plays such an important part in our lives, doesn't it? And sometimes lives are built entirely on *ifs* . . . *If* Fenella hadn't opened Haddon House, Amos Finnister wouldn't have known where to take Grace . . . and *if* he hadn't worked for Neville he wouldn't have known *me* . . . and on and on, so many *ifs* in all of our lives.'

'Yes, indeed, it's amazing at times. Could we go and find Grace Rose? I would love to look at her again, Vicky, just hold her . . .' Cecily's voice trailed off.

'Yes, yes, let us go and find her!' Vicky exclaimed enthusiastically. Cecily Deravenel had had so many terrible things happen to her, so many losses in the last few years, Vicky wanted her to have a moment of joy now.

They hurried back to the centre of the Great Hall, where people were dancing. Music filled the air, and the sound of voices and of laughter swirled around them. The evening was just getting started. Supper would be served at eight.

Grace spotted Vicky first, and came running to her. The child's beautiful face was full of smiles. She came to a stop and said, 'I've been dancing with Richard . . . he swirled me around and around, Mumma. It was fun.'

Vicky laughed. 'You remember this lady, don't you, Grace? You met her earlier with Uncle Ned.'

Grace nodded, and offered Cecily Deravenel a small, shy smile.

Cecily bent down, took hold of Grace's hand. 'I forgot to tell you something, Grace Rose . . . I am Uncle Ned's mother, and I want you to call me Aunt Cecily. Will you do that?'

The child nodded. 'I love Uncle Ned! He's my friend.'

'Can *I* be your friend?' Cecily asked.

'Oh yes,' Grace Rose answered solemnly, staring at Cecily.

And then suddenly, much to Cecily's surprise, and Vicky's too, Grace moved closer to Cecily Deravenel, put her plump little arms around her neck and nuzzled Cecily's cheek, as if they were old friends.

Cecily held the little girl tightly in her arms, and thought: This is my grandchild, my first grandchild, and I can never claim her as mine. But I can surely love Grace Rose. I can surely do that.

FIFTY

Whenever she came to stay at Thorpe Manor, her nephew Neville and his wife Nan gave Cecily the room which had been hers when she was a child and a young woman, growing up here. This had been her father's favourite residence of all the houses he owned, perhaps because he himself had been born and grown up at the manor.

Philip Watkins had spent a great deal of time here in Ripon with his wife and children after he had inherited the manor from his father Edgar, who in turn had inherited it from *his* father; in fact, the house had been in the Watkins family for centuries, and they were the squires in this little village in the Dales.

Cecily loved this old place, with its well-proportioned, airy rooms filled with light from the many leaded windows, the highly-polished wood floors, the carved fireplaces, the funny little nooks and crannies, eccentricities so frequently found in Tudor architecture.

The reception room which Cecily liked the best was the Great Hall. Large and rather long, stretching almost the entire length of the house, it had a soaring brick fireplace and a unique carved overmantle, a beamed ceiling and tall mullioned windows.

Now, as she sat in the window seat in her bedroom, Cecily's thoughts went back to the evening which had only just ended an hour ago . . . the dancing in the Great Hall, the elegant supper in the formal dining room, and the continuation of the dancing later. It had been an effortless evening, one full of music, merriment, and laughter, and Neville and Nan had been superb hosts. It seemed to Cecily that everyone had enjoyed themselves, and guests had stayed late.

Leaning her dark head against the window, she gazed out at the gardens. There was a large full moon tonight, a June moon, and its radiant silvery light gave the garden a magical look.

She sighed to herself. How often she had sat here as a young girl, dreaming of romance and marriage, of starting a family of her own. So long ago, at least so it seemed to her now.

Thoughts of her husband crept into her mind, but she instantly pushed them away. She could not bear that particular pain tonight, the pain of his loss, and the loss of her son Edmund, her brother Rick and her nephew Thomas . . . the bride's young brother . . . all should have been here today . . .

Cecily, always self-contained and protective of herself, allowed these unhappy thoughts to slide away, fully aware of her responsibilities. There were still two young sons to take care of, George and Richard, and Meg, her darling Meg, eighteen now and beautiful.

She smiled as she thought of Meg as she was a few hours ago. How lovely she had looked, how happy she had been, dancing mostly with Edward. He had captured her for many dances, and the eighteen-year-old had been in her element with her brother, whirling around the Great Hall, light as air, her eyes sparkling.

Edward. The story of Grace Rose had captivated her; she had been fascinated, touched and appalled, all at the same time. Of course Edward had always been impulsive, yet also loyal to family and friends, caring of them, and brilliant in so many different ways. But impulsive, yes. And easily tempted by women. Women threw themselves at him shamelessly. They had done so even when he was only twelve and thirteen. She had noticed it, as had his father; they had endeavoured to ignore it. Too much temptation had always been put in Ned's way.

Well, Tabitha had enticed him into her arms when he was thirteen, although, in fairness, Cecily believed Tabitha James had not known his true age. He was a strapping young man, very tall even then, and he had looked so much older. To impregnate a woman at fourteen, to become a father at fifteen, simply stunned her.

Cecily started to chuckle quietly all of a sudden, shaking her head, thinking what a product of the Victorian Age *she* must be . . . Centuries ago, young women had given birth at twelve, and boys of fourteen and fifteen had been fathers. But we don't live in medieval times anymore, she told herself reprovingly.

No matter what, Grace Rose was always going to be loved and looked after, and protected. Vicky and Stephen would not fail to do that, and Ned would always be there for his daughter. He was already there for her. Just as she was herself. Grace Rose had suffered;

however, the child would never suffer again, if she had anything to do with it.

Cecily turned her face to the window, once more looked down into the gardens, continuing to think of Ned. Observing him surreptitiously tonight, at moments when he was occupied with family and friends, she noticed that he appeared troubled. Despite the gaiety, the frivolity, the *bonhomie* that flowed from him, his bright blue eyes had been shadowed, dulled. She suspected that there was something wrong, something amiss in his life.

Trouble with women, she decided. That had to be what it was. She left the windowseat and climbed into the four-poster bed. On the other hand, he usually threw off trouble with women; they were just part of his everyday life. What occupied Ned the most, and engaged him totally, was Deravenels. And the running of the company he had inherited. *Was there a problem with Neville?* Ned had made a few curious remarks earlier this evening which had seemed oddly sarcastic, now that she focused on them.

She lay in the dark, staring up at the ceiling, thinking of her father Philip Watkins. He had been one of the greatest industrialists of the Victorian Age, a man who had made an immense fortune before he was twenty-five. Everything he touched had turned to gold. Tonight Ned had made mention of this, remarking to her that the Watkins family would have been nothing without her father and grandfather, Edgar, who had spun gold from the grim Northern pits, mills and factories of Victorian England.

Had her son meant that her brother Rick and his son Neville would not have been successful on their own? That their background and the family money they had inherited had eased their way. Of course it had, no doubt about that. And yet the implication, somehow, was that Rick and Neville owed everything to their forebears and nothing to their own abilities. No, that's not true. My brother was brilliant, and so is Neville.

Neville . . . Did he pull the strings? Was her son just a puppet? No, that could not be possible. Ned was made of stronger stuff than that. He had a backbone of steel. An iron will. And most importantly of all, perhaps, *total concentration*. That was the key to Edward Deravenel. His concentration, and his determination to win at all costs, no matter who stood in his way.

I mustn't worry about Ned, Cecily told herself, turning on her side, closing her eyes. My son knows what he is doing; he *will* be all right.

FIFTY-ONE

Edward sat in the Red Library, nursing a balloon of Napoleon brandy, staring into the dying embers of the fire. Even in June the nights were cool in Yorkshire, and the fires were always burning at Thorpe Manor just as they were at Ravenscar.

He had spent half an hour in here with Neville, after everyone had left, going over the details of the French deal. He'd had to muster up great enthusiasm, which he didn't truly feel, in order to delude Neville into thinking that he did indeed care. Fortunately, it hadn't been too difficult a task, and Neville had been very receptive.

Edward knew it was going to be rather strange at Deravenels for the next week or so. Alfredo Oliveri and Rob Aspen were still in Persia with the geologists, and they were now much closer to staking a claim for oil. Only the other day he had sent them a telegram giving them the authority to make a deal with the Shah of Persia for rights to a parcel of land that looked highly promising.

Will would also be away, on his honeymoon, touring

the South of France, visiting Cannes, Nice and Monte Carlo. And Neville's plans were taking him off to Paris. Even Johnny was to remain in the north this coming week, checking on their various holdings.

And so he would be all alone at Deravenels, minding the business by himself. He would miss Will Hasling, since they were enormously close, and the absence of his other colleagues would also leave a gap.

However, he would be busy. He did have a series of reports to read, written by a young oil-speculator from Texas. Jarvis Merson was a wildcatter, and had been introduced to Ned several weeks ago. Merson could teach him a great deal about oil. According to Merson. Maybe this was true, and he did need to know more, that was why he was gathering as much information as he could. *Oil.* He aimed to make it a big part of the future, the future of Deravenels.

He moved on in his head, suddenly starting to think of personal problems.

Elinor. She is my problem really. What to do about her? She isn't well, I know that. That's why she hasn't been up to town for several weeks. She did seem listless, somewhat withdrawn, when I went to Devon, and I begged her to tell me what was ailing her. She wouldn't. The problem is I've lost interest in her, at least as a lover. Can she sense that? Women are very intuitive. I'm not a cruel man, and I must let her down lightly, try not to hurt her too much. But I know myself, and I'm not very clever at faking interest when it has fled.

Then there is Elizabeth, the most beautiful woman I have ever come across. Well, not quite. Lily was very beautiful.

He closed his eyes, thinking of his darling Lily, and then he fell down into his innermost thoughts once more.

There will never be a woman like Lily. I know that. I must put her out of my mind. But she lingers there, I'm afraid. Lily was not just beautiful, she was a good woman. And how often do you find that? Not very frequently, I'm certain.

Elizabeth is a cracking beauty, but I think her character is different, and her personality as well. She's not like Lily at all; I have a feeling she can be tough, determined to get her way. I think it's best I leave her to her own devices at the moment. Nothing to be gained by seeing her. Anyway, she's not in London; she has gone to Gloucestershire for a holiday.

I'm glad Will tipped me off about Neville's feelings about the Wylands. They have always been chummy with the Grants, but that doesn't mean they are beyond the pale. Anyway, the matter won't arise.

Neville has something up his sleeve. I just know it. He is hugging a secret, one which brings a smile to his face now and then. Perhaps he believes he is getting the better of Charpentier in the deal. But I doubt that he could. Louis is known to be a wily fox.

Elinor. Elizabeth. Neither can hold a candle to Lily. Poor Elinor. She had had such hopes for our relationship . . . wanting it to continue forever. But I'm no longer fascinated by her. Sadly. When she was married to Angus Talbot I eyed her with lust, coveting her; as a widow she has grown quickly stale . . . I mustn't be unkind. I will send a letter and flowers next week. I must try to cheer her up.

He went to the console, lifted the bottle of Napoleon, poured it into the balloon, returned to the fireside.

Women. They are the bane of my existence. I couldn't do without them, though. I suppose they are my weakness, my drug. What a strong woman my mother is, quite remarkable. I'm pleased she has taken the advent of Grace Rose in our lives so well. I had a feeling all this would happen, that I would have to tell her the truth. I was certain she would spot Grace's resemblance to me.

I think about Tabitha a lot, wonder about her fate. She was a sweet and lovely young woman and there were times when I was convinced she was an aristocrat, and I was right in that. I also wonder about the rotter Cedric Crawford, the guards officer. An officer and a gentleman, so they say. He is certainly not a gentleman. Is he still alive? Did he simply do a moonlight flit? If I ever come across him I shall give him the thrashing of his life.

The other day Will said that Grace Rose being on the streets may have saved her from a terrible fate. Who knows what Crawford might have done with her if she had remained with him. Poor Tabitha . . . what a life of tragedy hers was. At least the child has been saved. My little Grace Rose. My daughter.

I can do a lot for her. Apart from the money I earn at Deravenels, there is the money I inherited from Lily, all of it now well invested. Yes, I can and will use some of that money for Grace Rose . . .

'Ned, could I talk to you for a moment? *Please.*'

His brother so startled him, Edward almost dropped his brandy. Sitting up in the chair, glancing over his shoulder, he muttered, 'Yes, of course you can, Little Fish. But don't creep up on me like that in future. You gave me quite a start.'

'Oh, sorry,' Richard muttered, walking over to the other chair in front of the dying fire. 'It's just that I'm a bit troubled by several things, and I thought I could discuss them with you.'

'Come on, Dick lad, come and sit with me,' Ned said, smiling at the boy. 'Would you like a drop of Napoleon?'

Richard began to laugh. 'Mother would be furious with you if she knew you'd offered me brandy! *Alcohol*.'

Ned grinned at his favourite. 'I didn't mean it, actually,' he admitted. 'It was a slip of the tongue, I'm afraid. You sounded like such a young gentleman. However, I do hope you know I would not have poured even one drop for you.'

'I do.' Richard now leaned forward and said, 'I need to talk to you . . . about Anne Watkins.'

Nodding, Ned took a swallow of the brandy, and looked across at his brother with interest. 'Go on, then, Dick, what about Anne?'

'When I marry her will the marriage take place here or at Ravenscar?'

It took Edward a moment to answer this question. He tried hard to swallow the laughter rising in his throat, to disguise his amusement. Finally, keeping a straight face, he responded, 'It isn't really very pressing at this moment, is it? Surely not? After all, you are only eleven, Richard. Let's talk about this nearer the wedding, in about ten years' time, shall we say?'

'I actually need the matter settled now, Ned. *Please*.

I shall worry about it, and quite a lot otherwise.' Richard sounded taut, and his voice was insistent. 'George says he won't allow me to marry Anne here at Thorpe Manor. When I told him it was the tradition that a bride was married from her home, he laughed in my face. I said it wasn't his house, it didn't belong to him, and he said that it would be his one day. He was adamant that we couldn't have the reception here either.' Richard stared at his adored brother, waiting.

Sudden annoyance rushed through Edward. George was becoming a persistent troublemaker these days, and his behaviour was worrying.

Keeping his irritation in check, Edward smiled, almost languidly, and then he laughed. 'Oh Richard, my boy, don't pay any attention to George. I do believe he is suffering from delusions . . . empty dreams of glory. His own. Naturally you will marry Anne here at Thorpe Manor – her father does own this house, you know. Actually, it's been in their family for hundreds of years. It will never belong to George. However, as I said, you won't be marrying Anne for a very long time, and perhaps you might even change your mind about her when you're older.'

Richard shook his head; those grey-blue eyes turned the colour of slate, and his narrow mouth tightened. 'I will only ever marry Anne. And she will only ever marry me. If we don't marry each other, we won't marry at all.'

Edward smiled indulgently. 'Do you want some lemonade? There is some in a jug over there.'

'No, thank you, Ned, and thank you for telling me

KILKENNY COUNTY LIBRARY

the truth. May I have your permission to relay your words to George?'

'If you want to,' Ned answered, smiling at Richard's attempts to sound very grown up. 'You said you had several matters to discuss.'

'Oh yes, the other one is rather . . . well, it's not nice. I mean, what George said . . . about *you*, Ned.'

Edward rose, walked to the fireplace, stood with his back to it, regarding the youngster. Before Richard said another word he knew what scurrilous things George had probably passed around today. Ned had much insight into people, and particularly his brother George. For years he had acknowledged George's jealousy and envy. George wanted it all.

'I'm waiting,' Edward said, his cornflower blue eyes resting on Richard.

'When George saw Grace Rose at the wedding he said she was your illegitimate daughter, and that this was obvious because she looked so much like you. It was Meg who reminded him that Grace was the child of Vicky and Stephen Forth. He answered her by saying you had had an affair with her, I mean with Mrs Forth, but I know that's not true. And I said so to George. It isn't, is it?'

'You are absolutely correct, Little Fish. I have never had an affair with Will's sister, Vicky Forth. That was a wretched thing for George to say, and it was very wrong of him to impugn the reputation of a respectable woman. I shall certainly have to reprimand him.'

'How?'

'I don't know yet. But I will think of something appropriate.'

'When, Ned?'

'Tomorrow, you can rest assured of that.' Edward wished he could tell Richard the truth; he detested lying to anyone, most especially his youngest brother, his favourite. But he did not dare speak out, for fear of hurting Vicky and Stephen. They saw the child as their own now, and there was also Grace Rose to consider. The less she knew about her past now, the better.

After a second, Edward cleared his throat and asked, 'Who else did he tell, other than you and Meg?'

'I'm not sure. He sort of whispered it to me and Meg. He didn't shout it out, the way he often does when he has something mean to say about . . . someone. You know he can be nasty about people.'

Ned nodded, and then he muttered, 'Chinese whispers.'

'What are they? Chinese whispers?' Richard looked perplexed.

'Little tiny whispers . . . whispers that go from one person to the next, tiny, tiny whispers that become a crescendo, cause mountains of trouble. For everyone. Don't ever fall into that trap, Richard. Promise me you won't whisper behind people's backs, or gossip.'

'I won't! I do promise you, Ned. You'll never hear Chinese whispers from me.'

'I believe you, Little Fish.'

The two brothers continued to sit and talk for a while longer, Richard waiting for Ned to finish his brandy. They spoke of Will and Kathleen and their wedding, all the excitement and happiness of this special day. And then as the clock struck midnight Edward put down his glass, and together he and Richard left the Red Library, crossed the Great Hall and went upstairs to bed.

Later, alone in his room, Ned thought about George for some time, and he knew, without a single doubt, that he would always have to watch his back where George was concerned. Over the years he had discovered his brother was a liar, treacherous, and therefore dangerous. One day George would do him ill, if he could. Edward realized that now.

There were moments when he missed Lily so acutely there was an ache inside him, a longing so overwhelming it brought him to a sudden standstill. He had to be alone when this happened, to draw on his inner resources, to steady himself. And he had to remind himself that his beautiful, soft, feminine Lily was dead. He could not win her back. How could he? Death was the most final thing on this earth.

Immediately he thought of Elizabeth Wyland. A beautiful woman, a woman beyond belief. Everyone who had ever seen her agreed with him. The white, flawless skin, the long silver-gilt hair, the pale blue eyes. It was an imcomparable face, and yet hers was a frosty beauty.

The Ice Queen, he suddenly thought, and then smiled to himself. Outwardly frosty, yes, but he was certain there was an inner fire. He wanted to possess her completely, because of her awesome beauty. Yes, she was a challenge to him. The more she resisted his charms the more he wanted her. He had a need to break through those icy barriers, take her to him, arrive at the core of the woman.

Perhaps he would one day. He would certainly try when he found the right opportunity. He just had to possess this untouchable beauty, whatever the cost.

He closed his eyes, drifted off to sleep thinking of Elizabeth Wyland.

FIFTY-TWO

London

'Neville looks pleased with himself,' Will Hasling said in a low voice, drawing closer to Edward. 'Perhaps he has *finally* finished his negotiations with Louis Charpentier.'

'I hope so. They seem to have dragged on for months. I suppose it's not a bad idea to acquire the silk factories after all, and the vineyards, since the real estate involved is worth a lot. We can't lose.'

'You still don't sound particularly excited about this deal, Ned.' Will gave him a hard stare, frowning. 'Does something bother you about it?'

'I don't know. Not sure, really, Will, why it nags at me so much. I feel uneasy about it, although don't say anything. I've never expressed these feelings to Neville.' Edward let out a long sigh, and finished, 'Look, he's never made a bad deal in his life. He only ever makes good deals, and I trust him. *Absolutely*. It'll be all right, you'll see.'

'If you say so.' Will turned, glanced around the private dining room at Deravenels.

Ever since Ned had taken over as managing director

of the company, three years ago, he gave a lunch every Wednesday, inviting different executives. Will, Neville and Johnny Watkins were always invited since they were the closest to Ned.

From across the room, Neville caught Will's eye and moved his head slightly; Will nodded in return. He touched Edward's arm. 'I think Neville wants to talk to me. Please excuse me.'

Ned grinned. 'Of course. I need to have a word with Oliveri anyway. I want his opinion of my wildcatter, Jarvis Merson.'

Will simply rolled his eyes, and moved across the floor towards the window, where Neville was standing talking with his brother Johnny.

Edward strolled over to Alfredo Oliveri, and said, 'So, tell me what you think about my Texan friend, Mr Merson.'

'I think he has a lot of knowledge, and he's very useful to us. There's a bit of bragging and that puts some people off, but basically I believe he's a good chap. Sincere.'

'We're in agreement then, because in my judgement he's honest. And sincere, as you say. I'd like him to go out to Persia, the next time you and Aspen go. What do you think?'

'I'm all for it,' Oliveri replied. 'Aspen will be, too, we both like Merson. To tell you the truth, I think he's as straight as a dye, even if he does get carried away occasionally.'

'He just likes to tell tall tales, is that it, eh?' Edward laughed as he said this, and Alfredo joined in. Then Edward said, 'I think perhaps we should go to the table,

Oliveri. I have an appointment this afternoon. Out of the office. I can't be late.'

Alfredo nodded and the two of them walked across to the round table in the centre of the room. Today it was set for the six men who were already present: Edward Deravenel, Neville Watkins, Johnny Watkins, Will Hasling, Alfredo Oliveri and Rob Aspen.

Edward had greeted everyone as they had wandered into the dining room, a short while before, and now he said, 'Enjoy lunch, gentlemen.'

As white wine was poured for the fish course the men began to talk amongst themselves, discussing business, the Stock Exchange, politicians and politics. After the first course of sole, lamb chops were served with mixed vegetables and roast potatoes, and after that bread-and-butter pudding for dessert.

Will, who was sitting next to Edward, murmured quietly, 'I think Neville *does* have some good news about Louis Charpentier. He sort of intimated that to me earlier, but look surprised if he mentions it during lunch.'

Edward merely nodded, then said to Rob Aspen, 'I may very well take you up on your suggestion that I come to Persia with you, the next time you go.'

'It would be a great experience for you, and especially if you're there when we hit a gusher, as Merson calls it.'

Edward plied Aspen with many questions during the rest of the lunch, once more expressing his belief in oil, and his determination to drill in other parts of Persia. 'I want oil for Deravenels. We must have it, Aspen. It's imperative.'

Once lunch was over, and just before the coffee was served, Neville stood up, tapped a spoon on his water glass. 'Just a moment of your time, gentlemen, please.'

Everyone stopped talking and looked at him. Neville nodded and smiled. 'I would like to propose a toast.' He picked up his wine glass, and went on, 'As you all know, we have been negotiating with Louis Charpentier for some of his holdings. Everything is completed now except for one thing. However, I think we can safely drink a toast today . . . to Deravenels and its new acquisition in France.'

'To Deravenels!' they said in unison, and all raised their glasses and drank.

Edward exclaimed, 'Well done, Neville! We should now toast you, since it is you who have brought this about.' Lifting his goblet, looking around the table, Edward, smiling at them all, said, 'To Neville Watkins.'

'Thank you, thank you.' Looking pleased and happy, Neville sat down.

A short while after this toast Alfredo Oliveri and Rob Aspen excused themselves and left for their afternoon appointments.

Edward, finishing his coffee, looked across at Neville.

'You mentioned that there was one last thing . . . to conclude. What can be left? You seem to have covered everything in the last two months.'

'Actually, Ned, it concerns you,' Neville answered, smiling with geniality. 'You know, I've asked you many times to come with me to Paris, and you have always found an excuse not to come and meet Louis Charpentier. But now it can no longer be put off. You have to come with me next week, to meet Louis, and also Blanche.'

'Who's Blanche?' Edward asked, looking slightly puzzled.

'Why, his daughter, of course.'

Edward stared at Neville, and something appalling dawned on him. *He* was part of the deal. Neville must have made an arrangement with Charpentier: *Let us buy you out, and in return Edward Deravenel is yours.* But he did not voice these thoughts, he simply sat there gaping at his cousin, speechless.

Neville, appearing just as puzzled as Edward, now said, 'I told you last year, Ned, that Louis Charpentier would only sell his major holdings if his daughter married the buyer –'

'But I'm not the buyer,' Edward cut in peremptorily. 'A *company* is buying the Charpentier holdings, not *a man. Not me!*'

'Come now, Ned, you're splitting hairs.'

'I don't recall you telling me any of this!' Edward exclaimed, speaking the truth. 'You really didn't, Neville, because I would have never agreed. Tell me, did I agree to this?'

'You didn't actually say *yes* –'

'Right! I never uttered that word. Because I never understood what you were saying.'

'Blanche Charpentier is a beautiful young woman, Edward, blonde and blue-eyed. She is well educated, charming, and cultured. An only child, and therefore the heiress to the entire Charpentier fortune. A vast fortune. When you meet her you will be captivated.'

'I doubt it.'

'I know your taste in women, Ned,' Neville said with

a light laugh. 'She's your type. Nineteen, gorgeous, and utterly . . . magical. That's the only word I can use.'

Edward shook his head. '*No.*'

'I made an agreement with Louis,' Neville now explained patiently, his voice firm. 'A binding marriage contract, in fact, and the whole negotiation hangs on that contract. If you don't marry Blanche then the deal is off.'

'I can't marry her.'

'Ned, listen to me. Blanche is a Frenchwoman, sophisticated. She won't make a problem if you have mistresses. My God, her father has had a mistress for years. It hasn't disturbed his marriage.'

'I just told you, I can't marry this woman.'

'You mean you *won't*,' Neville shot back sharply, suddenly irritated with his cousin. He knew full well that Edward Deravenel couldn't be faithful to any woman. So what difference did it make if he married Blanche Charpentier? He was baffled by Edward's total stubbornness, and his indifference to the consequences, and what they involved. The deal would blow up if Edward did not fulfil the marriage contract and he knew that.

Taking a deep breath, Neville said in a most placating tone, 'Come now, Ned, let's compromise –'

'I can't marry her. Or any other woman.'

Neville frowned. 'What are you trying to say . . . why can't you marry?'

'Because I'm already married.'

Johnny Watkins gasped, glancing at Ned and then looking at his brother, expecting an explosion.

Neville was truly stunned, and he did not speak. He

could not speak. He had never been so shocked in his life.

Wanting to break the tension, Will took a deep breath and asked, 'And who is the lucky lady who deigned to become your wife, Ned?'

For a moment Edward did not respond. He simply sat there, gazing blankly at the three other men in the room.

Neville, staring back at him through cold blue eyes, asked in a contained neutral voice, 'Who *did* you marry, Ned? Do we know her?'

'Elizabeth Wyland,' he said at last.

There was a grim silence. It was so quiet in the room a pin dropping would have sounded like thunder. None of the men spoke. The four of them just sat there, continuing to stare at each other as if dumbfounded. Even Edward was shocked; he had not anticipated this kind of reaction to his news. But then he hadn't known about those secret marital plans his cousin had made for him with Charpentier. And they *had* been secret. He hadn't been told.

Although he was further enraged, Neville managed to hold his temper in check. At last he spoke. 'Why didn't any of us know about your marriage, Ned? And why weren't we invited to participate, to celebrate with you?'

Avoiding the first part of this question, Edward said swiftly, 'We eloped, Neville.'

'When was this?'

'At the end of June.'

'Three months ago . . . well, well, well.' Neville pushed a smile onto his face. 'Congratulations, Ned,' he said steadily, utterly in control of himself despite his rage.

Following his brother's lead, Johnny exclaimed, 'The best of luck, Ned! You're a rascal, though, you know, keeping us in the dark.'

'Yes, congratulations, Ned,' Will murmured, and stood up, went to shake Edward's hand.

Rising, Edward took hold of Will's hand, and a moment later he looked at Neville, his gaze intense, and very direct. 'I suppose our deal with Charpentier is now in shreds?' He raised a brow.

'It is.' Neville again forced a smile. 'So be it,' he answered, 'so be it.'

FIFTY-THREE

'I'll grant you that he was cordial,' Will said, giving Edward a quick glance, 'because he is, after all, very clever. And he can hold himself in check. But let me tell you this: despite his constraint, Neville was fuming when he left.'

Edward sat back in his office chair and returned Will Hasling's steadfast gaze, nodding his head. 'I know all this, Will. Don't forget I grew up with him, I've been around Neville all my life. Of course he's angry . . . beyond that, he's in a rage, but the point is I *am* married, and there's nothing he or anyone else can do about it.'

Will sat staring at his closest friend, a man who had his total devotion and loyalty; for a moment he did not speak, and then he murmured very softly, 'I think he is affronted, and that quite possibly he feels humiliated. Remember, he now has to go to Louis Charpentier and tell him you don't want to marry his daughter. Or that you cannot marry his daughter, because you're already married. He's going to look like a complete and utter fool. Louis will not close the deal, and Neville doesn't like not closing deals. In fact, he detests the mere idea of it. He'll think he looks like a loser, well, actually he *is* the loser, in a certain sense. Oh God, how he hates that! It's going to rankle, and rankle a lot.'

'Will, listen to me, Neville did bring this on himself.' Edward leaned over the desk, holding Will's eyes with his own. 'I did not understand what he had in mind, what he was doing, that he was using me as a negotiating tool. I truly didn't. He was not merely obtuse, he was rather forgetful. He forgot to mention the word marriage. He didn't explain anything to me, I promise you.'

Will, struck by the honesty in Ned's steady blue gaze, exclaimed, 'Listen, I believe you. And if that's the case, as you say, then Neville has misjudged you. Surely he knew he couldn't make an arranged marriage for *you* . . . *you* of all people.'

Edward suddenly began to laugh, shaking his head. 'Once I'd recovered from the shock of what he was saying an hour ago, I had exactly that same thought. He must have been deluding himself, having fantasies, don't you think?'

'Delusions, fantasies, what do I know! I only know this, Ned, he's angry with you. Bloody angry right now.'

'The anger won't last, he'll get over it, you'll see.'

Will forced a smile. 'If you say so. I thought Johnny looked awfully queasy when he left, worried, and uneasy. You know he's caught between the two of you, he loves you both.'

'I know that. But Johnny's a congenital worrier. Look, it'll be fine. Trust me, they will both come around, they will accept my marriage to Elizabeth.'

Pursing his lips, Will eyed Edward speculatively, then he replied slowly, 'I was a bit suspicious of you from time to time this summer, you know. You started to become secretive, evasive, never said where you were going. And when I asked you once about Elizabeth, you brushed the idea of her to one side, very abruptly for you. You were very dismissive of her, in fact.'

'I had to be.'

'Why, Ned?'

'Because I knew that Neville and Johnny and my mother would see Elizabeth as the enemy. Because of her family's connection to the Grants over the years. Her father *did* do business with Henry Grant, and the Wyland merchant bank did make money with them, at one point.' Ned shrugged. 'I just knew she wouldn't be acceptable. Even though I also knew from her brother that they haven't done business with the Grants for years. They don't see them anymore, and haven't for some time.'

'You could have told *me*, Ned. I'm your dearest and most trusted friend, am I not?'

'Yes, you are, and you always will be. I didn't say anything because I didn't want you to be cast in the role of accomplice. I didn't want Neville castigating you, attempting to fix the blame to you in any way, or chastising you.'

'I understand, and I suppose I should say thank you for protecting me. But you could have told me.'

'Don't be hurt.'

'I'm not.' There was a moment's pause, and then Will said slowly, 'You wanted her, that's it, isn't it? You lusted after her, and she spurned you, and because you had to have her you married her. Am I right?'

'Absolutely correct, old chap. She kept saying no, no,

no. She wouldn't let me get near her, fended me off all the time. One afternoon, when I was losing my patience, and pressing her hard to succumb . . . to my charms, shall we say, she became *indignant*. She said that she might not be good enough to be my wife, but that she was far too good to be my mistress.'

'Anne Boleyn,' Will said, grinning, laughter in his eyes.

'What?'

'Anne Boleyn said that to Henry VIII, didn't you learn that at school?'

'I must have forgotten. Anyway, I thought about those words afterwards, when I was alone, and I sort of . . .' Ned paused, and let out a burst of unexpected laughter. 'I agreed with her, Will!'

'And you got married in secret and bedded her *immediately*, I've no doubt of that.'

Ned smiled, that warm, languid, indulgent smile that women loved, and nodded his head. 'Yes. We were married at her aunt's house in Gloucestershire in the private chapel, married by the family priest, with her mother and her aunt in attendance.'

'I wish I'd been there, standing up for you, Edward, I really do.'

'I do, too, but I didn't want you involved.'

'If you don't mind me asking, has it been worth it? Has she . . . lived up to your expectations?'

'Beyond my expectations.'

'You've been going to the country a lot lately. To Cirencester, I presume.'

'That's right. She is still staying with her aunt at Avingdon Chase. For the moment. She understands all of the ramifications . . . she's very bright, and she is happy to comply with my wishes.' Ned now rose, walked over to the window, stared out for a moment, then swung around. 'It's not only lust, Will. We are in love with each other. Truly in love.'

Will smiled at him but remained silent, ruminating on everything, feeling somewhat apprehensive despite Ned's obvious good humour, his equanimity. 'I'm glad of that,' he said at last. 'I'm really genuinely happy for you. Being married to the right woman is so important, I've come to understand that. My Kathleen is wonderful.'

'I do believe I can say the same thing about Elizabeth,' Ned murmured, strolling back to the desk.

Watching him, Will couldn't help thinking how extraordinary Edward Deravenel looked today. Nobody like him that *I* know of, Will thought, and tried to crush the persistent idea that trouble was brewing for them. Edward appeared impossibly nonchalant, as if he didn't have a care in the world, appeared to be happy, full of bonhomie, good will and wellbeing. Didn't he understand that he had shown his independence, taken his fate into his own hands, and in doing so had deeply offended his cousin who credited *himself* with Ned's success as the head of Deravenels. We haven't heard the end of this, Will thought. Neville won't let us.

'Well, enough of this,' Will murmured. 'You said you wanted me to go somewhere with you, that you had a surprise for me.'

'That's true.' Edward moved towards the door of his office.

Will strode after him, exclaiming, 'Then lead the way, and tell me where we're going.'

'I can't do that, Will. If I did, it wouldn't be a surprise.'

It was a glorious September afternoon, and the two young men walked up the Strand, through Leicester Square and on to Piccadilly Circus. It was a busy afternoon, with traffic jamming Piccadilly: carriages and hansom cabs, horse-drawn buses and several of the new electric motorcars from America, the invention of a Mr Henry Ford. And floods of pedestrians as well, jostling each other on the pavements.

Spotting one of the electric cars, Edward grabbed Will's arm, and exclaimed, 'Look at the new invention, the horseless carriages.'

'They *are* quite remarkable,' Will agreed. 'I remember my aunt telling me that she first saw one in 1904. It belonged to the Duchess of Marlborough . . . you know, the American heiress Consuelo Vanderbilt. Her mother Alva sent it to her from New York. Marlborough married her for the money, you know. No other reason.'

'He needed the money, Will, to keep Blenheim going, and she's not bad looking, quite aside from all that money. And who looks at the mantelpiece . . . if you know what I mean.'

Will grinned, and the two of them walked on in silence. Unexpectedly, Ned said confidingly, 'You know what, Will Hasling, I am going to order us both electric motorcars, from Mr Rolls and Mr Royce, who are starting to make them in some quantity at last.'

591

'My God, Ned, they cost a fortune! You can't do that.'

'Of course I can . . . and I shall be paying with my own funds, so you don't have to worry about Deravenels.'

'I certainly won't in that case, and thank you.'

Fifteen minutes later, as they walked across Berkeley Square, Will Hasling suddenly understood where Ned was leading him. To the house he had purchased almost a year ago. It was a beautiful house, tall and stately, overlooking the leafy square right in the heart of Mayfair, Edward Deravenel's favourite part of London.

'It's finished, isn't it?' Will said as they mounted the front steps together.

'Indeed it is, and I think you're going to be surprised by what it's become, what I've made out of it.' As he spoke Ned inserted the key in the lock and opened the heavy mahogany door, and stepped into the entrance foyer. 'No staff, as yet, Will, other than a caretaker who occupies the basement. I haven't actually moved in yet.'

'And when will you do that?' Will glanced around, already impressed with what he was seeing.

'Next week. Now that my secret marriage is out in the open, I shall bring Elizabeth back to London in a few days. We shall start our married life here.'

'And what's going to happen to your house in South Audley Street?'

Edward made a small grimace. 'I will have to sell it, I'm afraid. I've always loved that house . . . Lily's house I call it, as you well know. But I've no use for two houses, and Lily's house is a bit too small for me. It always has been really, and now that I'm married it does have to go. I did need this house for the space, so I'm putting the South Audley house on the market next week.'

'No, no, don't do that! I have the perfect buyer for you,' Will told him, sounding excited.

'And who's that, might I ask?' Edward's brow lifted.

'An old acquaintance of mine, Bryan Shaw. He's a wine merchant, in quite a big way, actually. An importer. He and his wife Jane have been looking for a Mayfair residence, and money is no object.'

'I must meet with them as soon as possible.'

'I'll arrange it,' Will answered, 'and now, give me a tour of your new home, which is why you brought me here in the first place.'

FIFTY-FOUR

Nan Watkins stood perfectly still outside the library, filled with unexpected alarm.

Neville, a man who rarely raised his voice, was shouting at someone. He sounded furious, more angry than she had ever heard him in all their years together.

Because she detested eavesdroppers she immediately knocked on the door and walked into the library, closing the door behind her.

Neville swung around, glaring at her.

Johnny was standing near the window. He also had an angry look on his face, although he attempted a half-hearted smile, and nodded.

Nan gazed at her husband, received no reaction from him. Quite suddenly, she was afraid. Neville's face was grim, and as white as death. It struck her that he looked ill.

'What is it?' she asked tremulously. 'What's happened?'

Neither men answered her, and she came further into the room, then hesitated. She was unexpectedly shaking, and her alarm made her voice shrill when she asked again, 'What's *wrong*, darling?'

Neville was silent.

Johnny, walking towards her, responded in as steady a voice as he could, 'It's Edward. He's . . .' Johnny's voice trailed off; he was unable to finish.

'What *about* Ned?' she demanded, her eyes swinging from Johnny to Neville. 'Is he all right?'

'Of course he's all right!' Neville snapped. 'When is he not *all right*, as you put it. *But I'm not all right!* He's done something quite terrible to me, put me in the most untenable situation. I've never been in such a mess in my entire career in business.'

Nan reached out, put a hand on the back of a wing chair to steady herself, knowing that whatever Ned had done it was extremely serious and her husband had taken it very badly. Slowly, she began, 'What has gone wrong?'

'*My French deal*. That is what has gone wrong. It will explode later this week, and all because that young pup can't keep his –' Neville broke off, cleared his throat, remembering he was speaking to his wife. 'As you know, I've been dealing with Louis Charpentier for months, and I brokered one of the greatest deals in history. The merging of two enormous empires . . . Deravenels and Charpentiers in France. Louis had agreed to sell to Deravenels his silk mills and his vineyards, and at an excellent price, with the stipulation that once his daughter Blanche was married to Edward Deravenel, he, Louis, would sign another contract which, in effect, would *give* the rest of his empire to Deravenels upon Louis's retirement, or his death. It was the dream deal of the century. However, it won't happen. And all because of that arrogant, pig-headed, sex-driven cousin of mine. He's a fool!'

'Oh, come now, Neville, you know very well Ned's not arrogant,' Johnny interjected. 'Anything but, and it was obvious this afternoon that he hadn't ever understood the ramifications of your deal. He really hadn't, let's be fair.'

'You'll always defend him, won't you, Johnny? I've long noticed that. But I do believe your loyalty should be given to me, and not to Edward Deravenel, in this instance.'

'I'm loyal to you both, and I care about you both. I do think you're being unfair, Neville. It's so unlike you.'

Neville glared at his brother, and turned away, strode over to the console table, poured himself a brandy.

Nan said, 'Perhaps you can talk to Edward, darling. After all, he's a reasonable man. If he's made to understand, surely he will at least go and meet Louis's daughter, because he hasn't, I do realize that. He's never gone to Paris with you, as you've wanted. Now I understand why you were so insistent. Is she pretty? Desirable?'

Swinging around, Neville answered in a clipped tone, 'Beautiful, young, and Louis's only child. *His heiress*. But taking Ned to see her won't make a damn bit of difference, I'm afraid. It's all too late.'

'But why?'

'Because Edward Deravenel is already married.'

Nan was stunned. She stood gaping at her husband.

Neville took a long swallow of the cognac, glanced at his younger brother. 'Would you like something to drink, Johnny?'

'No, thank you, Neville.' Johnny eyed the clock, and went on, 'I'm afraid I do have to leave. We're going to Covent Garden tonight. Emma Calvé is performing in *Carmen*, and I don't want to be late for the curtain.'

Neville simply nodded. 'Thank you, Johnny, for your support. I do *know* you are loyal, forgive me for implying otherwise. I'm afraid my rage with Ned did get the better of me.' Neville put down the brandy balloon, and said in a more even voice, 'Let me see you out.'

'No, no, old chap, I'm fine,' Johnny replied, and smiled at Neville. He went over to his brother, put a hand on his shoulder, and murmured softly, 'Please, do take it easy. Let's have lunch tomorrow. At Wilton's? At one?'

'I'll be there.' Neville managed a smile.

Once they were alone, Nan hurried to Neville, and took hold of his hand. 'Come and sit down, and tell me everything. And who on earth is Ned married to?'

'Elizabeth Wyland, if you can believe *that*. He married her in secret. Three months ago.'

'Oh, my God, no! *Not her*. She's quite dreadful, Neville.'

'Very beautiful, though.'

'Probably the most beautiful woman in England, if not indeed in Europe. I won't say the world, because perhaps that's going a bit too far, but she is a beauty, everyone says so. However, she's also known to be . . . well, *difficult*, to put it mildly.'

'I've heard she's a bitch,' Neville exclaimed, almost spitting out the word.

'Neville, really.' Nan shook her head reprovingly. 'She's avaricious, arrogant, ambitious for herself, her two sons, *and* her entire family. There are a lot of Wylands, Neville, and she is going to surround Ned with them, you'll see.'

'There's nothing much I can do about that or his marriage, Nan,' Neville muttered.

Nan was relieved he was sounding calmer, and she led him over to the sofa. They sat down together; Nan continued speaking in a low voice. 'I think Elizabeth Wyland is going to lead him a merry dance, she's not the easiest person, I'm told.'

'Who is it that knows her so well? Whom you know?' Neville asked, his curiosity getting the better of him.

'Maude Tillotson. She's very friendly with Elizabeth's mother.'

'Obviously Maude doesn't like the new Mrs Deravenel.' Neville's brow lifted, and then he nodded. 'She may well lead Ned a merry dance, as you call it, but he's not going to be tamed. Whatever she might think, he will continue to live his life the way he has always lived it. He won't be faithful to her, I'll wager you that.'

'I agree with you.' Nan settled back against the sofa, and looked off into the distance. After a moment, she said, 'He just can't help himself, he doesn't know the meaning of the word fidelity.'

Neville sighed. 'I shall have to go to Paris as soon as possible, to see Louis.'

'What on earth are you going to say to him? How will you explain?'

Neville shook his head, sighed. 'I believe in telling the truth in this instance. I shall do just that, explain that Ned eloped. I'll have to put a good face on it, darling. He's embarrassed me no end, I'm afraid. I'm going to look rather foolish in Louis's eyes.'

'Perhaps, but Ned is young, can't you blame it on his youth?' she suggested.

Neville laughed hollowly. 'Oh darling, don't you think Louis knows all about Edward Deravenel and his reputation as a womanizer? Of course he does! Louis hasn't left anything to chance. I'm sure he's had Edward investigated. However, it obviously didn't matter to Louis – Ned's reputation, that is. After all, he's a sophisticated Frenchman, and he probably merely chuckled about it. You know, men will be men, that sort of thing, and I know for a fact that Louis Charpentier has had several mistresses over the years. His own infidelity hasn't affected his marriage to Solange.'

'I see.' Nan bit her lip, looked at Neville worriedly. 'What are you going to do . . . I mean about Ned?'

Neville stared at her intently, his expression startled. 'I don't believe I'm following you, Nan. What do you mean exactly?'

'Well, he's let you down, to put it mildly. He's acted independently of you, without conferring with you, and after all, you are his mentor, you've done so much for him –'

'I certainly have! I put him in the seat of power at Deravenels. He wouldn't be there without me.'

'So, what are you going to do? What are *we* going to do about him and Elizabeth? After all, he *is* family.'

'I don't think I'm going to do anything,' Neville responded slowly, his expression thoughtful. 'I do believe that the best course is to behave as though nothing *untoward* has happened . . . we'll just go on together as usual. I shall be my concerned, cordial, usual self. Certainly I will not allow this matter to come between us. After all, his marriage is private, personal, quite a separate thing. It has nothing whatsoever to do with business. And we are in business together. The fact is, Ned's been good for Deravenels, he's done rather well for the company. Actually, I'm quite proud of him, Nan.'

'But it is you who has guided him!' his wife asserted.

'Yes, that's true, I have. On the other hand, he's done a number of extraordinary things in three years. He and Oliveri have pulled off several *coups* . . . finding and buying those new marble quarries in Carrara, reorganizing the diamond mines in India, with the help of David Westmouth, of course. And Ned has set Deravenels on a new course with his development of oil. That will be a big one, if it happens. These things aside, he's brought the vineyards in France back to life. They'd been badly neglected.'

'That's one of the things I love about you, Neville, you always do give credit where credit is due.'

He gave her a warm smile, relaxing. His tension was leaving him.

'Nan, darling, I have an idea. I think we should behave as we have always behaved with the Deravenels – with love and family devotion. We must put on a very good face with Ned and Elizabeth, and give a wedding reception for them. Here at the house. And very soon. Heal wounds, if there are any.'

'That's a wonderful idea! We'll invite the entire family, and all the Wylands, and friends. That will put things right between you, won't it?'

'It will.'

'Things will be back to normal, won't they?' she asked again, still concerned.

'Yes,' Neville answered, and thought: But I'll never trust him again.

FIFTY-FIVE

Paris – 1908

'But of course you can trust me,' Edward said, smiling his languid, amused smile. 'I would never betray you, I do promise you that.'

Elizabeth, who was seated at the dressing table in the bedroom of their suite at the Ritz Hotel, finally swung around and looked across at him.

How impossibly handsome he was, that was her first thought. Edward lay sprawled on the large bed, lounging against a mound of white linen pillows, wearing a sapphire-blue silk robe. It was a colour that made his dazzlingly blue eyes look all that much bluer.

A few minutes ago he had attempted to lure her into that bed, and she had pushed him away. He had been very annoyed with her; instantly she had regretted her actions, wished she had been sweeter, and had succumbed to his pleas to make love, accepted his endearments graciously.

She knew how aroused he had been, and that he had wanted her desperately, and yes she had spurned him. That had been a most foolish move. If there was anything he truly hated, it was being turned down. Women never turned Edward Deravenel down. But she, his wife, envied by all, had indeed turned him down and in no uncertain terms. Then she had been even more stupid, reckless even, and had pouted and told him that she knew he had been unfaithful to her.

Staring across at him, she wondered how to make amends. Seduce him, give him what he wants, and more. Indulge him, use the sexual tricks he's taught you, and taught you so well. He loves that. Yes, I must make amends; I mustn't drive him away; I must have a child. I must become pregnant. I must bind him to me through a child.

This last thought caused Elizabeth to stand up, and slowly she walked towards the bed, smiling at him, hoping to entrance him. Her eyes did not leave his face as she said softly, 'Forgive me, Ned darling . . . it's just that I love you so much, I can't bear the thought of you touching another woman . . . I'm so very jealous, you do know that.'

He smiled back at her. 'Why would I look for another woman when I have *the* most beautiful woman as my wife. The most luscious, sexual, enticing woman to call my own. Why would I touch any other? Tell me that.'

She did not respond.

When she reached the bed he stared up at her for a long moment, and then he plucked at the robe she was wearing. Made of pale blue chiffon shot through with silver threads, it was a light and floating robe cut like a kimono. It slipped off her shoulders as he tugged at it again. She stood before him naked, still smiling, looking down at him. 'Well,' she said. 'Here I am. I'm yours. Do what you will with me.'

'Oh yes, oh yes. I intend to do everything to you,' he breathed. 'You're so beautiful. *How* could you think I'd want anyone else but you? You silly, silly girl.' He laughed then, very lightly, and pushed himself up, got out of the bed. Taking hold of her hand he led her to the dressing table. 'Sit here and don't move,' he ordered, and disappeared.

A moment later he came back carrying a small suitcase. This he opened on the bed, took out another leather case and opened it.

Walking over to the dressing table, he said, 'Close your eyes.'

She did as he asked. But when she felt something cold on her neck she opened her eyes. And gasped. Ned was fastening a diamond necklace around her throat, a necklace the likes of which she had never seen.

'Oh Ned,' she gasped. 'Oh Ned . . . it's magnificent.'

'Like you.' As he spoke, he picked up a handful of silver-gilt hair which fell down her back to her thighs. 'All that glitters,' he murmured, almost to himself. 'Glittering temptations,' and then looking at her in the mirror he said, 'This necklace was made for an Empress. The Empress Eugénie of France. When the crown jewels of France were sold off at the auction of the Diamonds of the Crown of France in 1887, many of them were bought by the famous jeweller Boucheron. This necklace was amongst the pieces. It's changed hands since then. I bought it for *you*. Now it is yours. An anniversary present. Next month we will have been married for one year, Elizabeth.'

'I know.' She smiled at him in the mirror. 'Thank you, Ned. Thank you for this . . . it's fabulous.'

'Get up,' he commanded, and when she did so he led her towards the bed. 'Isn't it time you gave me a son and heir, madame?' he asked. 'I certainly think we should try . . . all night, if necessary.'

'For as long as you want,' she answered quietly.

'Forever,' he answered in a low voice, pressing her down onto the pillows, stretching out alongside her. 'I knew you'd love the diamond necklace . . .' He kissed her deeply on the mouth. He loved the taste of her, just as he loved the scent of her. The overpowering scent of a woman who lusted for him as he lusted for her. That scent was on her now.

'Just as I know how much you love me to do this to you,' he added a few moments later, as he reached down between her thighs and let his fingers move into her lovingly and with great expertise.

She sighed under his insistent touching, and whispered, 'Oh yes, Ned. Don't stop.'

She looked up into the blue haze of his eyes, and began to tremble, her excitement growing as he increased his pressure, his fingers tantalizing her. 'Make me yours,' she whispered against his neck, and he whispered back that he was going to take her to him. And he told her of his longings and desires, and what he wanted from her, and wished to do to her.

'You will be mine in a moment,' he murmured, touching her hair. 'I'm going to take you as never before. Just so you understand there is no other woman but you, my love, my wife. And then you will make me yours, as only you can, the way I taught you.' His voice was urgent, hoarse with his desire for her.

She slid down the bed at his sudden, urgent request;

he was hard, ready for her. She touched him, kissed him, the way he liked, and she thought of the first moment she had seen him, seen his beautiful hands, had wanted them all over her. And how she had wanted *him*. These thoughts excited her. She gave him pleasure the way he always sought from her, a special pleasure he vowed no other woman had ever given him, and she believed him, was certain he told the truth.

Suddenly he moved her head, and moved her, rolling them both over so that he was on top of her. He took her to him almost roughly, urgently; they moved together with passion and joy, soaring upward, and when they shuddered in ecstasy they clung to each other, gasping and breathless, saying each other's names.

'I don't want to go out to dinner,' Edward said, stretching his long limbs, turning on his side, throwing an arm over Elizabeth in a possessive manner.

'Then I won't go to dinner either.'

'Let us stay right here and do this.' When she did not answer him, he said, 'Shall we?'

'Yes, why not. It's a lovely idea.'

'*Exciting*. And you're a very exciting woman . . . you do know how much you excite me, don't you?'

'More than anyone else ever has?'

'Yes,' he murmured, and smiled. She never failed to ask this.

'I heard rumours . . . that you'd been with another woman recently, Ned. It's not true, is it?'

Although he was annoyed that she was harping on this again, he held his temper in check. 'Of course it's not true. How many times do I have to tell you?'

'Then why do people say these things?'

'What people?' he demanded, giving her an odd look.

'Women I know.'

'Because they're jealous, envious of you. And our marriage. You shouldn't listen to them. They're telling lies.'

'I believe you.'

'I think you should.'

'I hope you've made me pregnant.'

'I hope so, too. But just in case I haven't, let us try again, shall we?'

'*Now*?' She sounded surprised. 'Do you think you can, I mean so quickly.'

'Oh yes, ma'am, I surely can. Have you forgotten, I'm younger than you!'

Pushing herself up on one elbow, she looked down into his face, touched it lightly with one finger. 'Prove it to me, Edward Deravenel, prove to me that you can take me on another pleasure ride. Because I don't think you can.'

He did not respond verbally. He simply took her to him, and made love to her for the rest of the night. 'Just to prove a point,' he told her later.

FIFTY-SIX

Paris was Edward Deravenel's favourite city after London. The City of Light, as it was known, had always fascinated and captivated him, and beckoned him to return time and again.

He loved its wide and spacious boulevards, its tree-lined streets, and its glorious ancient monuments. He had become, over the years, something of a Francophile, and a devotee of most things French.

On this current trip to Paris with Elizabeth, her first visit, he had taken her to his preferred haute couture designers; to the House of Lanvin, the House of Paquin, and also to view clothes by Jacques Doucet and Poiret. He had bought her a collection of the most fashionable gowns and suits from these designers, and purchased other jewels as well as the famous diamond necklace which had once graced the neck of Empress Eugénie. Elizabeth was the most beautiful of women, and he wanted her to be decked out in great finery, the best that money could buy. When she was on his arm she had to outshine every other woman, and, of course, she did so with her perfect face, her unique silver-gilt hair and slender, shapely figure.

He thought of his wife this morning as he left the Ritz Hotel and crossed the Place Vendôme, as usual taking a morning walk through his favourite parts of the city. Although it was after ten o'clock, Elizabeth was still sleeping. She always slept late, never took breakfast with him, and, as was his habit in Paris, he usually went out to a sidewalk café to have his *café au lait* and croissants.

He preferred to do this rather than linger in the hotel suite. He liked to be alone, to think about his business, his plans for Deravenels, and other weighty matters, problems to be solved. These were things which did not interest Elizabeth at all. But then he wasn't sure what did interest her, other than clothes, jewels, gossip, and the betterment of her family.

She had more relatives than he had realized when he had first met her: seven sisters and five brothers, and a very avaricious mother. He liked her father and her brother Anthony, but had little time for the rest of this good-looking bunch. For good-looking they were, no question about that.

The Wylands got their looks from their father. He and his siblings got their quickness, alertness, beauty of face and spirit from their lovely, truly graceful mother, Cecily Watkins Deravenel. She still outshone everyone in their family, even Nan Watkins, who was unusually lovely. However, for beauty of face and figure his mother had met her match in Elizabeth Wyland.

After these considerations, his mother won hands down. She was charming, gracious, thoughtful, a woman who ran her homes with great skill, was charitable and caring of the staff and the villagers at Ravenscar. In other words, she was a great lady with impeccable manners, not to mention an understanding heart.

Elizabeth did not have these inbred qualities actually. She couldn't run their house in Berkeley Square because she had never been trained to run an important home. God knows what she would do when it came to running Ravenscar one day. She would be lost. This aside, she never asked a question about his work and business, unless it was to beg a position for another relative.

Then there was the matter of conception. They had had an active sex life ever since their wedding night, and she was not with child yet.

He corrected himself. At the beginning of the week, the night he had presented her with the necklace, they had spent many passionate hours together. Perhaps she *was* with child now, after their unusually hectic, busy evening. He hoped so.

Edward wanted a family, wanted children, and a proper household. Only then would this marriage work. It *had* been a little ill-conceived, he knew that now; however, he accepted it, and comforted himself with the thought that she was a gorgeous-looking woman, and she wasn't frigid in bed as some women were.

Edward smiled to himself, thinking of her innocence – and that was the only word for it – when he had bedded her the night of their secret marriage. God knows what she had done with her husband when they had been in bed. He had discovered to his amazement that she was a novice, knew nothing, and he had had to teach her what to do, how to satisfy a man. She was a widow, had borne two sons, and was five years older than him. And yet so unskilled sexually. He had promptly dealt with that, teaching her most assiduously.

Striding out rapidly, turning a corner, lost in thought, Edward collided with a woman. He was in such a hurry he would have knocked her down to the pavement had he not grabbed hold of her at once, clasping her arms.

'*Excusez-moi*!' he exclaimed, holding her up, then stepping away, staring at her, hoping she was all right.

'Mr Deravenel, good morning,' the woman said, smiling up at him.

He stared back, frowning slightly, and then he suddenly recognized her.

Before he could say anything, she began to laugh. 'It's Jane Shaw, Mr Deravenel. Don't you remember me? My husband and I bought your lovely house in South Audley Street last year.'

'Mrs Shaw, good morning! I do hope you're not hurt, I was such a clumsy oaf, rushing around the corner like that.'

'I'm perfectly all right, thank you very much. How is Mrs Deravenel?'

'Very well, thanks. At the hotel at this moment. And Mr Shaw? How is he?'

'Also very well. He is actually in Provence for a few days, visiting the vineyards he buys from. As you probably know, he is a wine-importer.'

'Yes, I did know that. And how are you enjoying my house? Oh, do forgive me, *your* house I mean.'

'I've never been happier in a house . . . there is something really rather special about it. A friendliness, a warmth, it welcomes one, don't you think?'

'Why, yes, you're correct. It *is* a welcoming house. I, too, was happy living there . . .' He paused and a sudden feeling of loneliness came over him, and before he could stop himself, he found himself saying, 'It was a gift. Someone I loved very much left it to me. She was a most lovely and special person.' He couldn't help wondering why he had said this to a woman who was, essentially, a total stranger. A woman he had met once.

'Yes . . .' Jane Shaw replied, hesitated, then said, 'I knew her, you know. You *are* speaking about Mrs Overton, aren't you?'

He nodded, his blue eyes lighting up. 'You knew Lily?'

'Why yes, I did. She and I worked for several charitable causes, and we became quite friendly.' Jane Shaw paused, looked up at him through soft, caring eyes, and said quietly, in her melodious voice, 'I am so sorry for your loss, Mr Deravenel. She was indeed very special, perhaps the most unique woman *I've* ever known.'

'I thought so, too,' he exclaimed, and then impulsively, he said, 'I wonder if you would care to join me for breakfast, Mrs Shaw? I was just on my way to a café near here. But of course, you're probably rather busy: women usually are in Paris, so many lovely things to buy, and all that sort of thing.'

'I'm not busy at all, Mr Deravenel, and I can think of nothing more enjoyable than taking breakfast with you. Actually, I'm quite hungry.'

He beamed at her. 'Well, come along then, Mrs Shaw. Let us go, the café isn't far away.'

'Oh, that doesn't matter,' she replied, falling into step beside him. 'I love walking, and especially in Paris.' She glanced up. 'What a beautiful day it is, isn't it? Look at the sky, it's as blue as speedwells. I just adore Paris, it's my favourite city.'

'Where have you been?' Elizabeth demanded when Edward walked into their hotel suite hours later. 'You just disappear without so much as a by-your-leave, and stay out for hours! I've been waiting to go to lunch with you since noon. It's now one thirty!'

Edward stood in the middle of the floor in the sitting room, looking startled, staring at her, noting her cold blue eyes, the rigid set of her face. That she was angry was apparent.

'I've been walking,' he said mildly. 'You know how much I like to walk in Paris. And then I had breakfast, as I usually do, at a café.'

She rushed across the floor, came and stood in front of him, looking up at him. Then she sniffed, wrinkled her nose, and cried, 'You've been with another woman! I can smell her on you! What's wrong with you? Can't you keep your hands off other women? Even during the day?'

Edward glanced at her and stepped away, disgusted with her behaviour. She had accused him of being unfaithful since the first day they were married, and it was beginning to get on his nerves. For a whole year he had lived with her accusations. He *had* strayed occasionally, although not of late. But even so, the women he slept with meant nothing, were casual and short-lived encounters, of no consequence.

He knew he did not smell of Jane Shaw's perfume, because he had not been close to her other than when he had prevented her from falling. This idea of perfume was in Elizabeth's imagination.

'Your jealousy is totally unfounded,' he said finally, in an even tone. 'And I'm not going to stand here listening to your ridiculous rantings, Elizabeth. In any case, I usually come back around this time, and I have every day since we've been in Paris, so there's nothing different.'

'There's perfume on you,' she shrieked.

He gazed at her, frowning, incredulity crossing his face. And as his eyes rested on her he realized, all of a sudden, that she looked rather ugly in her fury. That such a beautiful woman should change like that in an instant took him by surprise. Her face was distorted.

'You see, you're not even denying it now,' she went on, her voice rising on a shriller note.

'Oh, don't be so damned ridiculous, you silly woman.' His voice was suddenly cold, hard. Without another word he swung around, left the suite.

He went down in the lift and was crossing the lobby when one of the concierges hurried towards him. '*Bonjour, Monsieur Deravenel.*'

The concierge offered him a silver tray. '*Pour vous, Monsieur.*'

Smiling, nodding, Edward took the telegram on the tray, and went to one side of the foyer, opened it, read: 'Just heard we struck oil May 26 at 1180 feet at Masjid-I-Sulaiman. Whoopee. Will Hasling.'

His bad temper, his irritation with Elizabeth, instantly fled, and a wide smile broke across his face. As he stuffed the telegram in his jacket pocket he began to stroll towards the lift, then paused, changed his mind.

Why go up to the suite to face more of her wrongful accusations, her wrath? Instead Edward walked over to the concierge desk, and spoke quickly to Jacques. Within minutes he was sitting in a small telephone booth, speaking to Will in his office at Deravenels. 'What great news!' Will was shouting down the line. 'Come home soon, so we can celebrate.'

'Tomorrow. I'll be back in London tomorrow night. I'll be in the office the day after. Can't wait, Will. This is the best news I've had in a long time.'

Edward left the Ritz and walked across the Place Vendôme, heading . . . nowhere in particular, he decided. He wanted desperately to celebrate, to tell someone of his extraordinary news. *Deravenels had struck oil*. His dream for the future was coming true.

And there was no one to celebrate with. Certainly not his wife, ranting and raving and making ridiculous accusations, upstairs in the suite, in the hotel towering behind him.

He bent his head, sniffed his jacket lapels, wondering if he *did* smell of Jane Shaw's perfume. After all, he had grabbed her to stop her falling; perhaps she had brushed against his clothing when this happened. But he couldn't smell anything. It *was* all in Elizabeth's head.

Jane Shaw. His mind focused on her for a moment. She had been charming, rather nice to talk to, particularly about art, artists in Paris and the school called

Post-Impressionism; and such Impressionist painters as Van Gogh and Gauguin. A very lovely woman, a friend of his darling Lily. And actually, now that he thought about it, rather like Lily in so many ways. He had enjoyed having breakfast with her.

Again on an impulse, he walked over to the rue de la Paix and the small hotel where she was staying and which he had escorted her to after breakfast.

As he crossed the small entrance foyer, he spotted her walking down the staircase. She was wearing a white-and-lavender lace dress, and a white organdy picture hat trimmed with violets. She looked so lovely he caught his breath in surprise. Why, she was a truly beautiful woman.

He stood there looking across at her as she came towards him, surprise reflected on her face, and he thought of Lily. Unexpectedly, his heart twisted inside him . . . His darling Lily seemed to be somehow reborn in Jane Shaw at this moment.

'Mr Deravenel,' she said a little breathlessly. 'Is something wrong? You have the oddest look on your face.'

He shook his head, slightly bemused. 'You'll think I'm rather silly, I realize that, but do you know, when you were coming down the stairs, walking towards me, you reminded me so much of Lily.'

She put her gloved hand on his arm, and said, 'It's not silly, and it has been said before, actually. People did quite frequently mistake her for me, and me for her. We had a strong look of each other.'

He nodded, continuing to stand there, feeling strangely happy that he had run into her earlier in the day.

'Are you looking for me, Mr Deravenel?' Jane Shaw asked at last.

'I am actually. I just had the most wonderful news, and I wanted to share it with you.'

'How nice of you. I do enjoy good news. What is it?'

'Deravenels, my company, just struck oil in Persia.'

'That is stupendous news, Mr Deravenel. Stupendous. Congratulations.'

'Are you going out to lunch? If not, could you, would you, can you have lunch with *me*?'

'I would love to have lunch with you.'

'That's excellent,' he answered, delighted, and smiled at her. 'It's very hot outside, I'm wondering, should we perhaps eat here at your hotel? What do you think? How is the food?'

'It's delicious, and we don't need to rush around Paris, especially in this heat, seeking a restaurant, now, do we? Not when there's one right over there.' She tucked her arm through his and guided him across the foyer, saying, 'I'm so flattered you thought of me, Mr Deravenel.'

Within minutes he was ordering champagne, and they were toasting each other and celebrating his great news.

At one moment, she said to him rather shyly, 'I hope you don't mind me telling you this, Mr Deravenel, but I sometimes think of you . . . when I am at the South Audley Street house. Yes, you often come into my mind.'

'I do?' He threw her a questioning glance, his brows furrowing.

I shouldn't have told him that, she thought, and swiftly added, 'Yes, and that's probably because I knew

Lily. I think of *her* often, too. We were such good friends.'

'Did she ever mention me?'

'No, Mr Deravenel, she didn't. Lily was extremely discreet.'

'Are you discreet, Mrs Shaw?'

'Certainly . . . it's always important to have discretion, don't you think?' She lowered her head, looked up at him from under her lashes.

She's flirting with me, he thought, and discovered this made him feel rather happy. 'I'm glad you like where you now live . . . I miss that house myself sometimes.'

'In that case, you must come to tea with me when we're back in London.'

'I will enjoy that, Mrs Shaw.'

'And so will I.' She lifted the champagne flute, took a sip, and smiled at him over the rim of the glass. Placing the glass on the table, she licked her bottom lip with her tongue, then patted her mouth with the napkin.

He knew at that precise moment that he wanted her for himself. And he aimed to get her, however long it took him. This was his kind of woman, this pretty blonde with the face of an angel, so like Lily and obviously older than him, as Lily had been. Women like Jane Shaw appealed to him, had always given him a certain solace.

So naturally he went to tea with her. He hadn't been able to resist. A week after he had returned from Paris, Edward sent Jane Shaw a short and very simple note, merely asking her to telephone him regarding the house in South Audley Street. An innocuous note should it fall into anybody else's hands.

618

Jane had telephoned him immediately, and had invited him to tea the following afternoon.

When he walked in, the first thing he thought was that she was living in Lily's house. Of course Lily had never lived there, and yet it pleased him that Jane now occupied it. After all, she was living where he himself had resided; it somehow made him feel close to her.

As she led him into the drawing room he smiled and nodded; she spoke to him of trivialities. He was not really paying attention. He was stunned by the way she looked today. Her soft blonde beauty was more appealing to him than ever. Jane Shaw was ravishing, wearing a soft lavender-coloured silk dress.

The tea tray had already been placed on a low table in front of the sofa, and she sat down there so that she had easy access, could pour the tea herself. 'Come and sit next to me, Mr Deravenel.'

'I will if you'll stop calling me that. My name is Edward, but my close friends call me Ned.'

'Then I shall too, and you must call me Jane.'

She poured his tea, dropped in a slice of lemon, remembering how he had taken it in Paris. Pouring a cup for herself, she thought of Paris, and felt a sudden rush of excitement inside, remembering the way he had looked at her, with such open desire written across his face; the way her skin tingled when he had held her hand. He made her feel desirable, very womanly, and wanted: a feeling long missing in her life. And of course she wanted him. How could any woman resist this most exceptional looking man, who was warm, charming and eager to please.

Becoming aware of the silence between them, Edward

said, 'I was very happy living in this charming little house. Are you?'

A startled look crossed her face and she replied, 'I love the house, it's really very different, and comfortable.'

He frowned, and put down the tea cup. 'But you're not happy living here?' he probed.

There was a pause. 'Not happy,' she responded at last.

Edward understood immediately what she was endeavouring to convey. He nodded. 'I'm so sorry.' When she remained silent, he continued, 'You're not happy with your husband, are you?'

Jane sighed. 'He's a nice man, pleasant, very kind to me. It's just that . . . well, we're not compatible, I believe that is the best word to use. And also, he's . . . away a great deal.'

Clearing his throat Edward said softly, 'Dare I hope that we might lunch or dine together when you are . . . alone. No doubt the most convenient time for you.'

'I would like that, yes, I truly would, Ned.' She smiled at him as she said his name. 'I could lunch with you tomorrow. My husband has gone to Provence again. He left this morning. But . . .' She left her sentence unfinished.

'But what?' he asked, looking at her intently.

'Where could we go for lunch? We are both married . . . it would be a little unseemly to be spotted together in a public place.'

'Perhaps, yes, you have a point,' he answered, thinking suddenly of Elizabeth's jealousy, her volcanic rages when she imagined he had been with a woman.

'I do want to, you know,' Jane said somewhat tentatively, staring at him, momentarily dazed by the blueness of those eyes.

He took hold of her hand impulsively, kissed her palm, folded it over, then he smiled at her. 'We can meet at the Cavendish Hotel in Jermyn Street, and –'

'Oh no, surely not. The hotel has a . . . curious reputation.'

'No, it doesn't, not really. Yes, a lot of toffs use the place for a rendezvous, but it's all very discreet. Rosa Lewis, the owner, is a good friend of mine. I shall book a suite there for lunch tomorrow.'

'I'll be seen going in,' she murmured worriedly.

'Just wear a hat with a heavy veil, dark clothes. No one will recognize you.'

There was only a moment's hesitation before Jane nodded. 'All right then,' she murmured, looking at him.

Before he could stop himself, Edward leaned forward and kissed her on the mouth, letting his tongue linger.

Jane responded with passion, clutching his arm, but suddenly pulled away. 'I'm afraid the parlour maid might come in at any moment.'

Edward smiled at her. 'I can wait until tomorrow, when I will kiss you properly,' he said.

The following morning he arrived at the Cavendish an hour early, to make sure everything was perfect. And it was. Rosa Lewis, smiling and chatting with him, showed him the suite.

'The best in the house, Mr Deravenel,' she said,

glancing around. 'And I put extra flowers in the bedroom as well as the sitting room, as you requested. The champagne will come up in a moment, on ice. However, you didn't say what time you wished lunch to be served.'

'I think at two o'clock, Mrs Lewis, that will be about right.' Edward glanced at the grandfather clock in the corner of the sitting room. 'My guest will arrive at noon, and we can have a leisurely drink before eating.'

'Oh yes, very good, Mr Deravenel.' With a smile and a nod, the proprietor of the hotel bustled out, her skirts swishing as she left.

Edward meandered around the suite, pleased with it. Furnished in perfect taste, it was decorated in pale colours, greys and pale blues, and the furniture was light in scale. What a relief to see rooms which were not burdened down with Victorian pieces, too much clutter and dark colours.

A moment later there was a knock on the door and as Edward called 'Come in,' the waiter entered, carrying a silver ice bucket and a bottle of champagne.

Nodding to the waiter, tipping him generously, Edward left the suite and went down to the lobby. As the grandfather clock struck noon Jane came through the front door of the hotel and glanced around.

'Good morning,' Ned greeted her, and taking hold of her arm he led her up the stairs to the first floor where the suite was located. Once they were inside the sitting room, Jane lifted her veil and smiled at Edward.

Smiling in return, he went and poured champagne and gave her a glass. 'Lunch a little later. I thought we could sit and have a leisurely drink first.'

They went and sat down on the sofa together, and he

continued, 'We both know why we are here . . . because we have a need for each other, a need to be alone in private. To be with each other . . .'

'I think we were both aware of each other, were attracted when we met in Paris. And I do know this is not about having lunch,' Jane said, and then shook her head 'I never thought that I would have an illicit relationship with a man, never in my life.'

'I'm glad I am that man, darling.' He put his glass down on a nearby table, and so did she. Drawing closer to her, he took her in his arms, kissed her.

Her arms went around him, and they clung to each other, kissing passionately. Unexpectedly, Edward let go of her and rose. He extended his hand to her and she took it. He pulled her up from the sofa and led her into the adjoining bedroom.

'I have such an intolerable need for you, Jane,' he murmured. 'I can hardly bear it.'

'And I for you, Ned. A need I've never known before.'

He drew the curtains and then went over to her where she was standing in the middle of the floor. He removed her hat, threw it onto a chair, brought her into his arms and kissed her on the mouth, letting his tongue rest against hers. After a moment, he drew away, looked into her face. 'Let's find that bed.'

They lay together for a long time, touching, kissing, and stroking each other. 'I want to learn you, learn your body,' he whispered, and she responded, 'And I you.'

And so they did: loving each other with enormous passion and then with tenderness. Lunch was forgotten. Jane had never known such joy. Edward knew with the utmost certainty that he had found a woman who was like Lily. This knowledge gave him an unexpected inner peace . . . there was a sudden absence of pain.

And so their love affair began.

It lasted for months and months, and they saw each other as much as they could. And in that time she never gave him a moment's heartache.

Not until the day she ended it. Fear of discovery intruded, brought their romantic liaison to an end. Edward was bereft, unable to forget her.

FIFTY-SEVEN

London – 1912

'I'm going to ask you a question, Neville, and I absolutely insist you tell me the truth,' Edward said, and gave his cousin a very direct look. 'Promise me you'll tell me the truth.'

Neville stared back and smiled, shaking his head. 'I have a rather strong feeling this is what I think of as a *dicey* question. And I've discovered that when you tell people the truth they don't always want to hear it. You know that to be correct, old chap.'

Edward began to laugh, and protested, 'I'm not like that, and you know it. I'm very straightforward, and I want you to be, too. I'll accept what you say.'

'All right, what is this *dicey* question?'

Beckoning to the waiter, Edward ordered champagne for them both, and asked, 'That does suit, doesn't it? A drop of chilled bubbly?'

Neville nodded, and remarked, 'Come along, Edward, ask me this very important question so that we can then relax.'

Leaning forward over the small occasional table,

Edward lowered his voice and said, 'Why does everyone hate my wife?'

Neville recoiled slightly, and gave Edward a long, questioning stare. 'Ned, this is a very, very difficult question for me to answer.'

'Because you think I won't like it if you tell the truth? Is that what you mean?'

'No, no, not at all, it's just that, well . . . actually, Ned, I suppose people dislike Elizabeth for different reasons.'

'I see . . . would you name some of those reasons for me . . . *please*.'

'I don't like to speak for others, you know.'

'Then speak for yourself.'

'All right, I will. Firstly, let me just say this . . . I think some members of the family, and our family friends, don't like her because she doesn't like us, and them, and she makes them aware of her dislike, and us, too.'

'That's not very clever, is it, Neville? Rather stupid, if you ask me.'

'Well, you said it, not I,' Neville shot back. 'There's something else, I'm afraid, as far as I'm concerned, that is.'

Again Edward leaned forward eagerly, wanting to hear what his cousin had to say. The upset in their relationship, the discord of several years ago had been just that: *momentary*. They had swiftly repaired any damage done between them, and Neville's wedding reception for Edward and Elizabeth had been so beautiful, lavish and expensive, that all wounds, if there were any, had quickly healed. The two men had gone back to behaving normally with each other quickly, the Louis Charpentier debacle forgotten, and were as deeply involved in business today as they had always been since 1904. Tonight they were seated in the Long Gallery of the Ritz Hotel in Piccadilly, which had opened in 1906, and was the English replica of the Ritz in the Place Vendôme in Paris.

Edward said, 'What sort of problem do you personally have with Elizabeth? Is it new? Or has it always been there?'

'To tell you the truth, I feel certain she has always had a problem with me, because I really believe she sees me as having far too much influence over you. People sometimes do call you my protégé and I think she resents that as well. Then there's the personal level . . . she does not like me as a *man*, actually. I believe she's afraid of me, for some reason. What that can be I don't know.'

'Obviously, she doesn't have a lot of judgement, but then I've always known that,' Ned murmured. 'She's not stupid, not really, but there's a lack of interest in things, a genuine lack of curiosity, and this makes her appear a dullard.'

'That's possible, of course. However, she also knows I don't really approve of all these Wyland relatives working at Deravenels –' Neville broke off, shook his head. 'Did you *have* to give jobs to so many of them, Ned?'

This was said in such a comical way, although unintentionally so, that Ned burst out laughing. 'Anthony Wyland is all right, Neville, and her father is decent. As for two of her brothers, I let them go this past week. It was top heavy with Wylands, and those two are incompetent.'

'I'm glad to hear you got rid of some of them. I do agree with you though that Anthony's quite a good chap.'

'Why doesn't Nan like her?' Ned probed.

Neville let out a long sigh. 'Mostly because Elizabeth's haughty, a trifle arrogant, lords it over everyone, all of us, in fact. Richard, your Little Fish, got it right when he said she thought she was the Queen Bee.'

Edward laughed. 'Richard can be witty, and he has really grown up in the past few years, don't you think?'

'I do, Ned, I'm rather proud of him. And George, too.'

'*George*? I don't know about George, he troubles me at times. But let's face it, he's always been a law unto himself.'

Clinking their glasses together, Edward said, 'Here's to you, Neville. And thank you for being honest with me.'

'To you,' Neville responded in kind, and took a long swallow of the champagne. He then asked, 'What time are you meeting Aunt Cecily?'

'My mother will be here at seven-thirty. Why? Are you in a hurry to get off?'

'No, no, I was just wondering what time you would be dining?'

Ned nodded, and said slowly, 'Going back to my wife, I know what Elizabeth is . . . she's very ambitious for herself and her family, and she wants money and power. There's an enormous unquenchable greed there, but somehow we're managing to make this marriage of ours work.'

'I realize that, Ned, but I'm sure it's *you* who invests the most energy, makes the biggest effort.'

Ned merely smiled and took a sip of champagne.

His commanding height and astonishing good looks apart, Edward Deravenel was now extremely well-known in London, and he was automatically given the best table in the Ritz Restaurant. It was in a secluded rather private corner at the far end of the spacious room and overlooked Green Park.

'So much snow,' his mother said to him, glancing out of the window. 'It's been one of the worst Januarys I've known for years. The traffic's been terrible in London, hasn't it?'

Edward grinned at her, and exclaimed, 'Just be glad we're not up at Ravenscar. There's no traffic there, I'll concede that, but you'd be already frozen into a block of ice, Mama. We all would.'

Cecily Deravenel laughed with her son, and took a sip of the Pouilly Fuissé, remarking, 'This is a lovely wine, Ned. Your father always enjoyed it, and so do I. It's my favourite.'

Edward merely nodded, preoccupied for a moment, thinking how truly elegant his mother looked this evening. She was wearing a deep-purple silk gown, trimmed with the same coloured lace, and the triple string of pearls he had given her for Christmas looked wonderful against the purple. Her hair was smoothed back from her face, worn in a French twist, and her face was remarkably unlined for a woman in her early fifties.

'You're *gawping* at me, Ned,' she murmured, using a very North Country word, emphasizing it. 'Is there something wrong with my appearance?'

'I'm sorry, how rude,' he apologized. Then he smiled, shook his head. 'Nothing is wrong. In fact, I was thinking how elegant you look tonight, really *beautiful*, Mother. No one would ever guess you're a grandmother.'

'Thank you, darling, and tell me, how are the girls?'

His face lit up, and his bright blue eyes sparkled, 'Just marvellous – so quick and alert and bright as new pennies, they're lovely little things.'

'I'm very proud of them. It doesn't seem possible that Bess will be three in February. Time does fly, you know, it seems like only yesterday she was being christened in the chapel at Ravenscar.' She chuckled. 'I've never seen anyone look as awkward as Neville did, when he was holding Bess at the font. I truly thought he was going to drop her.'

'I knew he wouldn't, Mother . . . he didn't dare,' Ned answered and drank from his tall glass of water.

Cecily said, 'How is Elizabeth? Is she feeling all right?'

'She's absolutely fine, Mother, in the best of health, as she always is, actually. But I know she'll be relieved when the baby is born in March. She says she's beginning to feel top heavy.'

'I remember that feeling from my own child-bearing years. Anyway, she only has another two months. And how are you? Is everything all right between you both?' Cecily disliked probing, asking questions about her son's marriage, but there had been some rocky moments over the past few years, and she worried a lot.

'We're like an old well-married couple these days, trudging along together,' he answered good-naturedly. 'I go to work and Elizabeth has babies one after the other. First Bess, then Mary, and now there'll be another one any moment.'

'I hope it's a boy, and I'm sure you do, don't you?'

Edward nodded, then gave a small shrug. 'A boy would be nice, but I know one will come along eventually, if not this time. We are a very fertile family, and so are the Wylands. And we both want a big family.'

The waiter came and cleared away their fish plates, and they fell silent until they were alone again. Edward then leaned across the dinner table, and said, 'Earlier I was talking to Neville about Elizabeth, Mother.'

Cecily appeared startled by this remark, and she frowned. 'Is there something wrong, Ned?'

'No, no, but I knew he of all people would give me a very straight answer, and I wanted to know *why* it is that everyone in the family dislikes my wife.'

Cecily was more astounded than ever, and murmured after a moment's reflection, 'But why didn't you ask me? After all, I'm your mother.'

'I wanted to get a man's opinion,' he answered lamely, and made a face. 'I should have asked you first, though, you're right. Do forgive me. So, why do people hate her?'

'Oh Ned, really, I do think the word *hate* is an exaggeration, and overly strong, darling. The family don't hate her, that's a silly statement.'

'So how do they feel?'

'Some feel overwhelmed by her, others are intimidated, they don't all feel the same way, you know.'

'What about you?' He gave her a long, questioning look. 'You're going to say you are the mother-in-law, and therefore shouldn't answer, but give me your opinion, won't you?'

'I don't hate your wife, Ned, in fact, I've been getting along quite nicely with her lately. However, I suppose I was initially upset when you married her, mainly because I felt you had married . . . beneath you. I never thought she was good enough for you.'

'I suppose you still think that?'

'In certain ways, not others,' she said diplomatically, not wanting to drive a wedge between her son and his wife. It was a turbulent relationship as it was. And with Elizabeth now pregnant with their third child, this was not the time to create problems for her eldest son.

Edward was silent.

Taking a deep breath, Cecily continued, 'She's very beautiful, and she has managed to keep her looks and her figure despite the child-bearing. Therefore, she looks wonderful wherever she goes and does you credit. She's the perfect hostess for you, she entertains well, and she manages to find the right staff. Somehow you've taught her how to run a grand home smoothly. All these things are commendable in my opinion.'

'Those things are true, yes. You mentioned the pros. Tell me the cons.'

'There's still that haughtiness, Ned. It's remained in place, and people do occasionally take exception to it. She's not Queen Mary, after all.'

He grinned. 'No, Elizabeth is much more decorative, wouldn't you say?'

Cecily started to laugh. 'You're correct. But I'm sure King George thinks his wife is beautiful, and certainly she's elegant.'

Several waiters came to the table, one of them pushing the meat trolley, and the two of them waited for the Angus beef to be carved, topped with gravy, and placed in front of them.

'I'm famished,' Edward said, cutting the meat. 'I just remembered, I didn't have time to go out for lunch today. This is delicious, Mother, isn't it?' He looked across at her, a brow lifting.

'It is. By the way, are you inviting Grace Rose to Bess's birthday party?'

'As a matter of fact, we are.'

'So Elizabeth is all right with that, is she, Ned?'

'Very much so, believe it or not. Of course, no one at home other than Elizabeth knows Grace Rose is mine. Still, Elizabeth is not at all stiff or cold, and she makes Grace Rose feel at home, and certainly she's always been cordial with Vicky.'

'I'm glad to hear it.'

'There's something else I need to ask you about, Mother.'

'Then ask me, darling. You said you had a family matter to discuss, when you invited me for dinner.'

'It's about George, actually. At Christmas he mumbled something to me about not wanting to remain at Oxford, that he preferred to come and work with me at Deravenels. I said I'd discuss it with you. What *is* your feeling about it?'

'I'm not surprised he wants to leave Oxford. You know as well as I do that George is not the best student. He'll be nineteen this year, and perhaps we ought to try to persuade him to stay on . . .' She paused, shook her head. 'Whether he will do that I just don't know.'

'I don't either, he's always been a law unto himself, old George has.' Edward sighed. 'He seems to think that because I went to work at nineteen he should do the same, but my circumstances were awfully different.'

Cecily remained silent, not wanting to let her mind go back to that terrible January eight years ago, when her husband and son, brother and nephew had died in Carrara. She couldn't bear the pain.

Ned told her, 'I'm hearing the same song from Richard, too. He wants to leave Eton and come to Deravenels. To be my personal secretary, he says.'

'Now why doesn't that surprise me?' Cecily remarked with a warm smile, thinking of her last child. 'He's always worshipped you.'

'And been extremely loyal to me as well,' Edward murmured. He shook his head. 'I know Richard doesn't really like Elizabeth, but at least he makes an effort to be civil, even cordial. However, George is the bitter end, quite ghastly at times, *rude*, and he loathes my wife. I can't imagine why. He doesn't even know her very well.'

'If only she could be less . . . *cold*, I think that's the best word to use. Not so grand, so . . . proud.'

'I do love her,' Edward said, staring across the table at his mother. 'And she loves me. Of course there are problems . . . at times, but then all married couples have problems on occasion.'

'I hope you're not . . . leaving her alone too much in the evenings,' Cecily began, and then hesitated, wondering whether she should continue, say more. She was on thin ice with this, she was well aware.

Her son saved her the trouble of continuing when he exclaimed quietly, 'I don't have a mistress, Mother, if that's what you're thinking, and I haven't been *straying*. I promise you that.'

Cecily simply stared hard at him eloquently.

Laughter bubbled in his throat, and then he said, 'I know you don't believe me, but I'm quite reformed.'

'For how long?' she asked before she could stop herself.

'I don't know,' he admitted, and gave her a regretful look.

The butler let Edward into his house on Berkeley Square. 'Evening, Mallet,' he said as he shrugged out of his overcoat and handed it to the other man. 'Mrs Deravenel asleep, is she?'

'Yes, sir, I believe so.'

'Right-o. Pour me a cognac please, Mallet, and put it in the library. I've some work to do before I go to bed.'

'Certainly, sir.'

'And you can lock up and retire yourself,' Edward added as he moved toward the staircase.

'Thank you, sir. And goodnight, sir.'

'Goodnight, Mallet.'

Edward climbed the stairs two at a time, and went quietly down the corridor to Elizabeth's bedroom. Opening the door as gently as possible, he went in.

Much to his surprise she was sitting up in bed, the *Illustrated London News* in her hands.

She glanced at him and smiled. 'How was your mother?'

'Very well and she sends you her best.'

'Did she say if she's coming to the birthday party for Bess?'

'She didn't, but she mentioned it, and I'm sure she's coming, sweetheart. What grandmother would miss the third birthday celebration of her little grand-daughter?'

Elizabeth nodded. 'I hope *I'm* there. I feel as big as a whale tonight . . . I might well give birth tomorrow and not March, as the doctor says I will.'

He bent down, kissed her lightly on the cheek. 'Everything's going to be fine, don't worry so much. You're healthy and strong.' He moved across the floor of her bedroom, opened the door to his room which adjoined, struggling out of his jacket.

A moment later he came back into Elizabeth's bedroom wearing a silk robe over his shirt and trousers. 'I have to go downstairs and work for a while, darling. So don't stay awake, I'll be quite a while.'

'But you will sleep here with me tonight, won't you, Ned?' she asked. 'I do miss you when you use your own bedroom.'

'If you're sure I won't disturb you in your condi-tion.'

'No, no, I prefer it when you're by my side.'

'Then I'll be here . . . when I've finished my work.'

He went out into the corridor and climbed the stair-case to the next floor, the nursery floor. Again he crept across the landing, not wanting to awaken the nanny, and quietly opened the door to the girls' room. There was a tiny night light burning on a chest-of-drawers, and he could see that his daughters were fast asleep in their narrow beds. He went over, looked down at Bess; her red-gold hair was just like his and it tumbled all over her pillow. He smiled to himself, and glanced at Mary. The two-year-old was as blonde as Elizabeth, and very pretty. Fast asleep and sucking her thumb.

'Sweet dreams, my sweethearts,' he whispered, and crept out.

Before going downstairs Edward returned to his own bedroom, moving quietly so as not to disturb Elizabeth. He took a piece of paper out of his jacket and put it in his trouser pocket. God forbid Elizabeth found it. Not that she would know what it actually meant. But he had no wish to inflame her in any way.

Although he had remained with her, there had been times when he had felt like walking out, leaving her for good. She was difficult to live with, especially when something came over her and she went berserk. Like the scene she created with Richard a few months ago, when he had come into the library at Ravenscar to find her behaving like a harridan with his brother. At this moment he could see her in his mind's eye: her face twisted with fury, Richard looking puzzled, as if he had been taken by surprise in some way, and didn't understand her anger.

'What's going on?' he had demanded, staring at Elizabeth, going to Richard and putting his arm around his youngest brother.

'He knows what's going on,' Elizabeth had shouted. 'Ask him.'

'You sound like a fish wife,' he had snapped at her, and looked at Richard. 'Is there something you want to tell me, Dickie?'

'I was taking a book out of the library, and Elizabeth became angry, I'm not sure why, except she said I couldn't take books. That the books belonged to her children, not to anyone else.'

'Are you going insane?' he had demanded of his wife, a cold anger taking hold of him. 'My brother can have anything in this house. *Absolutely anything.* Do you understand that? And you're not to scream and shout at him the way you do. My God, you're like a virago. Mind your manners, woman.'

He recalled that look on her face so easily, a look of hauteur, and of pride. 'I merely said I didn't want it to get lost, that's all, Ned. The book is part of the leather bound sets of Shakespeare's tragedies, extremely valuable.'

'I don't give a damn if they're worth a million pounds. You're not going to inflict your ill humour and temper on my family. And that goes for all of them, not only Richard. You are cold and mean with them, and I won't have it, do you hear?'

She had nodded, turned on her heel and walked out of the library, and he had sat with Richard for a while, comforting him. His brother frequently suffered at Elizabeth's hands. She liked to torment the boy, possibly because she was jealous of the relationship, jealous of his love.

Edward sighed, closed the door of the armoire,

walked across his bedroom, looked at himself in the mirror on the chest of drawers. The bruise on his temple had faded, was almost invisible now. Ten days ago it had been purple, and he had told everyone he had walked into a door. In reality, Elizabeth had thrown a heavy glass paperweight at him during another of her temper tantrums. Even though he had dodged when she had hurled it at him it had glanced across his temple, and left the bruise.

He remembered now how he had sat down heavily, holding his head. She had come to him, of course, full of apologies, worried that she had injured him, and she had. He had thrown off her hand on his arm, pushed her away as he had risen, and gone into the bathroom to examine himself. Now he glanced at the small writing desk where the paperweight sat. It could have killed him. She had been standing in this very room, going through the pockets of his jackets and trousers, looking for God knows what, evidence of infidelity he supposed. They had had one of their worst rows and she had thrown the paperweight, and if he hadn't been swift he might well be dead.

Shaking his head, Edward turned away from the mirror, and slipped out of his bedroom, went slowly downstairs. She was a bitch at times, no two ways about it. She had led him quite a dance since their marriage. And yet she could come to him, wheedle herself into his good graces again, suffuse him with passion and sensuality in bed, and make her peace with him. For a while at least. She would never change, he knew that now. And neither would he. He stayed with her because of the two girls, and because he wanted a family life.

She was tranquil now, but he never quite knew when she would explode, start a quarrel with him, or insult his relations.

Ah well, he thought. So be it.

Mallet had not only poured him a large cognac and placed it on his desk, but the butler had also stoked the fire. It was burning brightly up the chimney and looked as if it would burn on for hours.

Striding over to his desk, Ned sat down and shuffled the papers, looking for the notes he had made several days before. After months of digging he and Alfredo Oliveri had finally found the money Aubrey Masters had skimmed from their diamond mines in India, and hidden. Well, to be honest, he and Oliveri had not found it, the remarkable Amos Finnister had. When they had finally come up empty-handed after years of investigating, Finnister had decided to have Mildred Masters followed. It had been the widow woman who had eventually led them to her accounts – in various banks in the suburbs of London. Who would have thought of looking there? To avoid prosecution she had surrendered the accounts which contained the stolen Deravenel funds.

Edward had invested the cash, six years ago now, and from his recent notes he saw that he had quadrupled the money. He clipped the notes to the latest balance sheets, and closed the folder.

He went through another pile of papers, initialled many so that his secretary could file them away, and then he sat back in his chair, glancing around the library.

He nodded to himself, liking this room, remembering how he had planned the library so carefully, wanting it to be perfect. Johnny had helped him, had given him some ideas. But in the end he had not copied either the Red Library at Thorpe Manor, which was far too red for him, nor his mother's library swathed in dark green and white. Instead, he had used wood panelling.

The room was lined with silver birch, and had burgundy-leather bound books from floor to ceiling on either side of the intricately carved fireplace. Above the fireplace was one of his favourite paintings, an oil by Alfred Sisley called *Le Givre*, and painted in 1872. It was a wintry landscape of bare trees and snow-covered moors, which reminded him so much of Ravenscar.

Bookshelves made of silver birch lined the other walls, and there were touches of dark burgundy in the heavy brocade curtains at the windows, and the sofa and armchairs upholstered in a similar burgundy velvet, while the floor was covered with a valuable Oriental carpet patterned in dark reds, blues and greens.

The house had been finished by the time he had married Elizabeth; fortunately, she had never wanted to change anything, sharing his taste for opulence, luxury, extravagant fabrics and mellow antiques. He remembered now how relieved he had been at the time.

He was also relieved that she had been relatively peaceful through *this* pregnancy. But then he had given her no reason to be challenging or contentious. He had not told his mother the truth earlier that evening when he had said he was reformed, and that he didn't have a mistress, that he hadn't strayed.

Rising, Edward walked across the room with his brandy balloon, and sat down in one of the big armchairs near the fire. After a few swallows of the Napoleon he put the glass down, reached into a trouser pocket and took out the note delivered to him at the office that afternoon.

He read it again: *I am now free.* That was all it said.

Leaning forward, he threw it into the fire and watched it curling into black shreds.

He had left his office immediately and gone directly to South Audley Street. Jane Shaw was waiting for him in her drawing room. She had known he would come at once, and had sent her staff out on various errands, given the housekeeper the afternoon off. He had sat with her in that room which he had always liked when he had owned the house, and sipped a cup of tea, and she had told him that she was now divorced at last from Bryan Shaw.

'I am not asking anything from you,' she had told him, 'except to go back to the way we were the first year we met. If you still want to. I don't expect you to change your life in any way. I just wanted you to know that I am free now, Ned.'

'No, you're not,' he had murmured, going and sitting next to her on the sofa. 'You're mine now, Jane, just as I am yours. For as long as you'll put up with me.'

'For as long as *you* want to be with *me*,' she had answered, and smiling softly she had said in a low, sincere voice, 'You know I will be discreet, never cause you a moment's embarrassment, nor make any demands. So, do we have a bargain?'

'We do indeed have a bargain,' he had replied. And

they sealed their bargain by going upstairs to his old bedroom, now hers, where they had made love, filled with relief that they were finally back together. Their separation had been painful.

Edward closed his eyes and thought of Lily, his darling Lily.

She would approve of Jane, I know she would. Just as I've always known Lily would not like Elizabeth. My wife is too cold, calculating and greedy for the kind of woman Lily was. Jane is so like her. I thought that from the moment we collided in Paris in 1908. She is affectionate and filled with warmth, kind and considerate, makes few demands of me, other than wanting my love. And I do love Jane. I gave her up because I loved her. She was so afraid of a scandal, I ended our affair in 1909. Then we resumed it in 1910 for a short while. Finally I went away because she became ill with anxiety, worry and guilt. But her marriage to Bryan Shaw had never been happy. It was sexless, and when she had discovered he had a mistress she came to me, asked me what she should do, and I told her to get a divorce, said that I would look after her financially, although that has not been necessary. Shaw was generous with her since he was the guilty party, and he wanted to end his marriage. And in the time we have been apart I have been faithful, have had no women other than my wife.

Elizabeth is difficult. But I care for her in my own way. She is still the most beautiful of women, and she has great taste in clothes, and immense style, and I love her glamour. She has, under my tutelage, learned to run this rather grand house, and the lovely old manor I bought in Kent a few years ago, on the Romney Marshes.

She is the mother of my daughters, and she is carrying my third child. And she will be the mother of my heir, if not this time, then the next. There can be no divorce. Jane understands that. She knows I must have sons, and she cannot have children. That had been one of the problems in her marriage to Shaw.

As my mother said tonight, Elizabeth is an excellent hostess, gracious and skilled at entertaining, and everything runs smoothly at our homes. Life seems to be on an even keel.

My mother knows deep down that I am not happy with my wife. I'm quite sure she realizes I have compromised, made an accommodation, as indeed I have. Elizabeth and I have nothing in common except our children, and our routine family life. Yes, we are compatible in bed, and she is passionate sexually. But we have nothing much to say to each other. She's basically a dull woman in many ways, although she can be entertaining when she discusses friends, gossips to me about the people we know. She does occasionally like to go with me to the theatre, which she realizes I enjoy, and to concerts, although she knows nothing about music. And I've hardly ever seen her read a book.

I can only be glad that I have my work. I love Deravenels with a passion and in the last few years I have made the company stronger than ever. And I enjoy every minute I'm at the office. But sometimes a man needs a woman to talk to, to share things with. Jane and I share a love of art; she has taught me so much about it. She is the one who found me the Sisley, and two years ago she spotted the Renoir which now hangs in my bedroom. She has a wonderful eye when it comes to paintings, and she loves books as much as I do.

So . . . I have a mistress again.

I made a bargain. I aim to keep it.

Sitting up in the chair, Edward lifted the brandy balloon to his lips and took a swallow, put the glass down, and stared into the blazing fire, thinking about his cousin Neville.

I don't trust him anymore. He's up to something. I know it. Will senses it, too. It's never been the same really since I married Elizabeth. He's always resented that I acted on my own. Tonight I wanted to see him, to test the waters. It was just an excuse, my questions about his attitude towards my wife. He was clever in his answers, he always is somewhat foxy. Still, things are now very different. I challenged his authority when I picked a wife for myself and he's not the kind of man to be thwarted. Will has warned me that he is becoming ever closer to George. Well, they're cousins, but George is ambitious, envious, and I know he is jealous of my relationship with my Little Fish. He always has been. Meg constantly sided with George, he has long been her favourite. She's not here to defend him these days, though. Yes, I must keep an eye on George . . .

As for Neville, he does play the game, keeps on working at my side, but there's a gap between us now. I almost laughed out loud tonight when he said people think of me as his protégé . . . no one has thought such a thing for years. They've all come to understand I'm not his puppet, that I never have been . . .

'Papa! Papa!'

Edward instantly turned around and saw a miniature

645

replica of himself standing there in the doorway of the library, his little daughter Bess in her white nightgown. Her burnished red hair was tumbling down over her shoulders, and her vivid blue eyes were focused intently on him.

He jumped up and went to her, picked her up in his arms and carried her back to the fireplace. Sitting down in the chair, cradling her, he looked into her face, and asked, 'Sweetheart, what are you doing down here in the middle of the night?'

'I woke up and it was dark and I was afraid. I went looking for *you*, Papa.'

'But what happened to your night light?'

'It went out . . . I went to your bedroom, Papa, and Mama's room.' She shook her head. 'I just wanted to find you. I was afraid.'

He kissed her cheek, hugged her to him. 'I'm here, I'll always be here to look after you. I love you, Bess.'

'Will you love me when the boy comes . . . the heir? Mama says she's giving you the boy . . . the heir . . .'

'Now how could I ever stop loving you, my darling! You are my first born, Bess, and so you are very, very special to me.'

She smiled up at him, and a most beautiful smile filled her face with radiance.

At the age of nineteen George Deravenel was a strapping young man with light blond hair and unusual smokey-green eyes. He had inherited the superior good looks of the Deravenel family, and was somewhat vain.

He thought he gave his brother Edward competition. But this was not true at all. He did not have Edward's unique height, nor beauty of face, and he certainly did not possess Edward's charisma and presence.

Because he did not know this he had developed a sort of swagger, and a confident manner that sometimes could border on the belligerent if he was crossed. He walked with a spring in his step, a regal tilt to his head, and of course women were attracted to him. However, George was only interested in one woman. Isabel Watkins. He had always hankered after her since childhood, and he aimed to have her. Neville was all for it; Ned objected. But Ned was going to be overruled. By Neville.

Now as he stood waiting for his cousin, looking out of the window into the Haymarket, he wondered what news Neville had for him this morning. He had been summoned to Neville's office urgently.

'Sorry to keep you,' Neville said as he came striding into the boardroom. 'How are you, George, my boy?'

'In fine fettle, Cousin,' George said, shaking Neville's hand.

'Let's sit down, have a chat for a few minutes. I know you're anxious to know what this is about.'

'Yes, I am.'

'How do you feel about taking over the top job at Deravenels?'

Startled, George sat up straighter in the chair. He frowned. 'How can I do that? Ned has the top job.'

'I put him in that seat. And I can take him out of it.'

George leaned closer, intrigued. A wide smile spread

across his face. 'Unseat Ned? Never. You couldn't do that.'

'Oh but I can. I have so much dirt on him I can twist his arm if necessary.'

'If you mean about women, don't even bother. Elizabeth knows about his extramarital activities, and if she cares she tries not to show it. She wants the money and the position. She'll turn a blind eye.'

'Not if she knows that he's about to buy his current mistress a house, and that he lavishes thousands and thousands on her. Elizabeth won't stand for that.'

'Well, you do have a good point. So, you'll twist his arm and put me in his place. Is that what you are getting at?'

'I am indeed.'

'Why?'

'Because Ned won't take Deravenels higher, as I've recommended. He's making a mistake. I want us to buy all of the holdings of Louis Charpentier. Deravenels will become the biggest in the world.

'I thought we already were.'

'Yes, But what about even *bigger*.'

'Does Charpentier want to sell . . . I thought that all died with Edward's marriage to Elizabeth.'

'It did for a while, but I've revived it. Naturally Deravenels will have to pay more now, because Blanche has married someone. Nevertheless, it will be a good deal.'

'I don't know whether I can run the company, Neville,' George began, but stopped when Neville held up his hand.

'I will be there to guide you, I will be your mentor as I was Ned's mentor.' Neville said.

'I see.' George nodded.

'And you will have help from John Summers.'

'Why John Summers? He's the enemy!'

'No, not necessarily. You see, the Grants do own a massive amount of shares in the company, and they should, by rights, be represented by someone. And there is no one better than John. Also he knows how to handle Deravenels on the inside. He would work with you.'

There was a knock on the door, and Neville rose, went to open it. 'Oh John, do come in, we've been waiting for you,' he said, and led John Summers into the boardroom.

George stood, and the two men shook hands. Then the three of them sat down at the table, and began to talk Deravenel business. At the end of half an hour, John Summers rose, and said, 'Thank you, Neville, for explaining. Everything is now perfectly clear to me. I look forward to our meetings in Paris with Louis Charpentier.'

John looked at George and gave him the benefit of a warm smile. 'And I certainly look forward to working with you at Deravenels.'

'I simply don't understand why this is suddenly happening,' Margot Grant said, giving John Summers a long, questioning look. 'It beggars belief.'

'No, no, it doesn't. It is perfect in its simplicity. Replace Edward Deravenel with George. The younger brother is easy to manipulate and control. I shall be working along-side him, and it will be the perfect situation.'

'*Why*? Why is Neville Watkins suddenly on our side? Tell me that.'

'In my opinion he has lost control of Edward Deravenel and did so a long time ago. He was also extremely humiliated when he had to go back to Louis and tell him that Edward, the intended bridegroom in the arranged marriage with Blanche, was in fact already married. And to marry a Wyland at that. Neville was fit to be tied, I am positive. He couldn't stomach that his beloved protégé had married the enemy. And in general, he's lost favour over the years. Oh they keep up a pretence, but that's what it is really, *a pretence*.'

Margot jumped up, began to pace up and down the dining room in her Upper Grosvenor Street house, ignoring her lunch, so agitated was she.

John, looking slightly alarmed, put down his fork, and exclaimed, 'Good Lord, Margot, why are you so excited?'

'I just feel uneasy about Neville Watkins coming over to our side.'

'It's going to be all right, I promise you,' John soothed. 'In any case, it's certainly worth investigating, going along with everyone. For the moment. I shall meet with them in Paris as arranged. Louis Charpentier is anxious to talk to George, who is going to Paris with Neville. We will be meeting in a few days.'

'All right,' she murmured, and went and sat down, adding, 'I trust you, John. With my life.'

'I'll do my best to make it work, don't worry, Margot,' John answered in an assured and confident voice, but his demeanour was somewhat fraudulent. He was going along with Watkins and Charpentier because he knew he had nothing to lose. However, he was fully aware that Edward Deravenel had a complete grip on the company. Furthermore *he* had never underestimated the man, whom he knew was clever, ambitious and ruthless. John thought that Neville Watkins might well be deluding himself about unseating Edward and putting George in his place. In his opinion George Deravenel was a fool, easily led, filled with conceit and very few brains.

We shall see, John Summers thought. We shall indeed see who comes out the winner. And he wasn't going to put his money on Watkins.

FIFTY-EIGHT

'Read all abart it! Read all abart it!' the newspaper boy shouted at the top of his lungs. '*Titanic* sinks! Hundreds dead!'

Amos Finnister, hurrying down the Strand, stopped in his tracks, and gaped at the paperboy, stared at the large white poster he was holding, which was obviously hot off the presses.

TITANIC DISASTER, it read, and underneath: **GREAT LOSS OF LIFE,** and then the name of the paper in slightly smaller print: *Evening News.*

Rushing over to the paperboy, Amos slipped his hand into his pocket, pulled out a few coins and gave them to the boy, almost snatching the newspaper from him.

'Bad news, guv,' the boy said. 'Summfink 'orrible, it is.'

Nodding, moving up against the wall of a building, Amos read the headline again, and then opened the paper and began to read the first page inside.

And what he was reading chilled him to the bone. This great ocean-going liner, the *unsinkable Titanic* they called it, had sunk.

Unbelievable, he thought, and went on reading, gobbling the words down.

The lookouts had seen the iceberg ahead, at around 11:40 p.m. on the night of Sunday, April 14. Then the iceberg had struck the *Titanic* on the starboard side of her bow. At 11:50, only ten minutes later, water had poured in and risen 14 feet in the front part of the ship.

At 12 midnight the captain had been informed the ship could only stay afloat for a couple of hours. He told the radio operators to send out signals for help, and orders were given to uncover the lifeboats and to get passengers and crew ready on deck. There was only enough room in the lifeboats for half the estimated 2,227 people on board.

Jesus Christ! God help me! Amos muttered, horrified. He read on, and learned that the *Carpathia*, southeast of the *Titanic* by fifty-eight miles, had picked up the distress calls and headed full speed to the rescue. The first lifeboat was lowered safely, and left – with only twenty-eight passengers, when it could have carried sixty-five. Distress signals were sent up. The last lifeboat eventually left at 2:05 a.m. and there were still 1,500 people on the ship as it tilted precariously, the deck of the *Titanic* growing steeper and steeper.

Amos stopped reading. His hands were shaking uncontrollably; he could hardly stand. All he could think of was Charlie and Maisie and what a narrow escape they had had. The brother and sister had been due to sail on the *Titanic*, going back to New York. They had been in London for three months, having a holiday, full of their success, fame and glory as popular stars on the New York stage. And then Maisie had fallen sick, with pneumonia, of all things to get in the spring, and their passage had been cancelled. They were staying in Whitechapel with friends while Maisie recuperated.

Thank God, he muttered again, and tucking the paper under his arm, he continued on down the Strand, heading for Deravenel House.

All of the staff knew him well, and he went right in, across the large foyer and up the stairs, nodding to those he knew as he did. His appointment was with Mr Deravenel, and as he glanced at the wall clock he saw that he was right on time. It was just ten-thirty.

'How are you doing, Finnister?' Edward asked a few moments later, coming around the desk, shaking Amos's hand.

'Not too badly, sir, thank you,' Amos replied, nodding. 'And I can see you too are in good health, if you don't mind me saying so, sir.'

'Yes, I am well, Finnister, but I'm not so sure about your good self. You look a bit peaked to me. Is anything wrong?'

'Well, no, sir, not exactly. It's just that I've been reading about the *Titanic* going down before coming here. It gave me a bit of a shock. A couple of friends of mine were going to New York on it, but they had to cancel.'

'Thank God they did! Ghastly thing, this disaster,' Ned went on, shaking his head. 'There will have to be a bit of an investigation, in my opinion. I've been reading about it myself in *The Times*, and it seems to me a lot of mistakes were made in the last twenty-four hours. God only knows why they didn't slow down after the warnings. Why weren't there more lifeboats?'

'It does seem odd, Mr Deravenel, yes, sir.'

'Please sit down, Finnister. You said on the telephone you needed to speak to me privately, and very urgently. What's this all about?'

Amos gave Edward a very direct look and began, in a low, steady voice, 'Mr Deravenel, I'm going to do something now I never dreamed I would do in my whole life. I'm afraid I have no option. My conscience tells me that I must do it.'

Edward leaned across the desk, staring at Amos, his eyes narrowing slightly. 'What are you going to do? Please tell me, won't you?'

'I am going to betray one man to protect another – a man I have the most tremendous regard for, and that is you, Mr Deravenel. And I have to betray your cousin in order to save you.'

Edward nodded slowly. 'Obviously what you're going to tell me must be in confidence, am I correct?'

'Yes, sir.'

'You have my promise, Finnister. It will be confidential, that I do promise you. I will never repeat what you tell me to anyone.'

'I trust you, sir, and I just want to say this, in case you're wondering why I come to you, come to warn you, betray your cousin's trust. Over the years I have grown to respect you enormously, and I know that you're a good man. Decent, fair, and honest. And you've been good to Grace Rose. You made sure she'll always be safe, and that is a wonderful thing to know, sir. I have a bit of an interest, you see.'

'Thank you,' Edward murmured. 'I know how much you care about her.'

655

'Your cousin, Mr Neville Watkins, assigned me to follow you . . . and I did this, Mr Deravenel, I have to admit it. He wanted to know everything about your personal and private life. I did discover that you go frequently to your old house in South Audley Street.'

'Do you know who lives there at present?' Edward asked quietly.

'Yes, sir. But as far as I'm concerned you've never been near the place since you sold it. You're as clean as a whistle, Mr Edward. I just want you to know that. Not a blemish.'

Although he had been inordinately shocked by Finnister's words, Edward had managed to keep a neutral expression on his face, and held his temper in check as he had listened to the private investigator.

But now, as he sat alone in his office later that Monday morning, he discovered he wasn't all that surprised. Ever since January, when he and Neville had had drinks at the Ritz, four months ago now, Edward's suspicions had grown. His cousin Neville maintained a cordial demeanour, but underneath that pleasant façade he detected genuine anger, albeit contained. He knew within himself that their loving friendship had never recovered from the blow he had dealt Neville. His cousin's pride had been hurt by his secret marriage to Elizabeth, no two ways about it. Will had been right . . . it *had* rankled.

Unfortunately, his wife hadn't helped the situation. It seemed to Edward that she was always hostile to Neville and Johnny. Her father and brothers resented his cousins, perhaps because they believed that Neville, in particular, exercised a certain power over him . . . Even Neville had made mention of that to him in January.

But Edward knew that he had been his own man for years, and acting without Neville's permission had been a step towards independence.

So, the wound had festered, apparently. Neville was moving against him now. Or trying to, at least. Otherwise why had he ordered Finnister to dig for dirt in his private life?

He was grateful for Amos Finnister's loyalty to him. He had long known that the older man liked and respected him and not only because of Grace Rose.

Well, he had been warned. He must now take more care, not be quite so casual and easy going about his relationship with Jane. He had no intention of giving her up. They had become closer than ever. She was his true companion, gave him so much intellectual stimulation as well as sexual satisfaction. Intelligent, cultured, and clever, she had become his sounding board on so many different things in his life. He needed her, he could talk to her.

He had been lucky in a way. Ever since their third daughter was born in March, Elizabeth had been particularly involved with this child. She had not been so enthralled with either Bess or Mary when they were first born, perhaps because of disappointment that they weren't boys. The new baby was named Cecily, after his mother, who had been delighted by this friendly gesture on his wife's part.

Now his problem was how to spend time with Jane discreetly. He chastised himself when he thought of his easy-going ways, the careless visits to South Audley Street – far too close to Berkeley Square for comfort.

It came to him, almost immediately. He must purchase a new house for Jane, either in the Hyde Park area, just north of Park Lane, or in Belgravia. Both were removed from Mayfair, enough to be safe, but not so far away that it would take him too much time to get there. In the meantime, how would he manage to see her without being noticed going into her house? An impossibility.

Rising, walking across his office, he stood looking out of the window, and his eye suddenly caught sight of the corner of the Savoy Hotel courtyard. It was on the other side of the Strand, a little way up. That was it! *The Savoy*. A perfect place to rendezvous. Jane must take a suite there. Immediately. For the next week. He would book a room for the same period. He could then visit her quite easily without anyone being any the wiser. He would explain this to her tonight, and he knew she would agree.

Edward went back to his desk and his work. His main interest at the moment was oil. After his people struck oil in May of 1908 work had continued. They had pumped oil for a year and made money, but in 1909 he had taken the decision to sell the Deravenel fields to Anglo-Persian Oil, a large company. Even though Deravenels no longer had a stake in Persia he hoped they would start drilling there again soon. Oliveri and Aspen were currently back in that country, negotiating with the Shah. Recently he had backed Jarvis Merson and his new team, who were at this moment drilling in Texas. He was keeping his fingers crossed they hit a gusher.

Edward knew there was a huge future in oil, especially for British battleships. Six years ago, in 1906, the first modern battleship the HMS *Dreadnought* had been launched. Churchill, the politician he trusted the most, was First Lord of the Admiralty, and he was constantly endeavouring to get his Naval estimates through Parliament, wanting to build more of these modern battleships. Churchill was nervous of the growing size of the German navy, and suspicious of Germany's intent. As was he. Edward knew that country bore watching, just as Winston did.

'I have something very strange to report,' Will Hasling said, staring at Edward across the latter's desk, his eyes on his closest friend and colleague.

'What is it? You look terrible.'

'I've felt terrible all the way back from Paris on the boat train, Ned. I think we're facing a huge disaster.'

Edward scowled. 'If there's something wrong with the vineyards it won't ruin us, you know . . . it would be a problem but hardly a disaster. We're in the black, and very much so.'

'I know that, and actually this has nothing to do with the vineyards and my business over there. It's to do with . . . *Neville*.'

Sitting up straighter in his chair, an alert look immediately settling on his face, Edward said wearily, 'Tell me then. Let's get it over with, Will.'

'I saw him in Paris – what I mean is, I got a *glimpse* of him. At the Grand Vefour. I had been dining there with Alphonse Arnaud, and I was just leaving the restaurant when I noticed him at a table in a corner. I fled immediately. Obviously I didn't want him to see me.'

Edward nodded. 'He was with somebody he shouldn't have been with, in your opinion. Is that it?'

'Louis Charpentier, John Summers, and, listen to this, *George*.'

'My George! My brother George?' Edward exclaimed, in astonishment, shock reflected in his bright blue eyes.

'That's right. *Your brother George*. Quite a cosy quartet, wouldn't you say?'

'I would indeed . . .' Edward paused, looked down at his engagement book which was open on his desk. 'Today is Thursday, April the eighteenth. You left on Sunday for your Monday and Tuesday meetings in Paris. So when did you see him?'

'Tuesday night. I travelled back yesterday, got in early evening. But I didn't want to tell you this on the phone,' Will explained.

'I understand, and there's no urgency I suppose? But it's better to know that they're . . . *plotting*? Is that what *you* think?'

'There's something afoot,' Will answered. 'Otherwise why would Neville be with John Summers all of a sudden? *The enemy*. Margot Grant's right-hand man, and Henry Grant's, as a matter of fact.'

'Neville and the Grants! I just can't believe it,' Edward muttered. '*And why*?'

'What about *why* George Deravenel was with them?' Will asked, his eyes on Ned.

Edward shook his head. '*He* should be at Oxford, studying. Still, perhaps he had gone to see our sister . . . you know how close he has always been to Meg.'

'Perhaps he was there to see her, but he was also at that very suspicious dinner. Listen to me, Ned, I had time to really think about this, coming back on the boat train yesterday, and I've got a theory. It's this – George to replace you at Deravenels, so that Neville can control him, and therefore control the company, and do exactly what he likes with it, make any deals he wishes, and with whom he wants.'

Edward paled. 'To put George in there he would have to get rid of me.'

'*Exactly*.'

'Blanche Charpentier is now married,' Edward muttered. 'So he can't have been thinking of her becoming George's bride.'

'No, of course not!' Will exclaimed. 'But I've noticed from the *Financial Times* that Louis has been expanding his business interests in the last few years. And all over the world. I'm positive Neville would want to be in on that. You know how much he loves power, loves wielding it.'

'He could make deals with Louis on behalf of his own companies,' Ned pointed out. 'Let's not forget he's still the biggest tycoon in this country,' Edward held Will's gaze; his face was paler than ever and still.

'Maybe Louis is not interested in Neville's companies, or doing business with him for those companies. Perhaps he's only interested in Deravenels.'

'I think you're right,' Edward agreed, sounding worried.

'George would go along with them, you know that without me telling you.'

'Of course I know he would. He's always envied me. He wants to be *me*.'

'What can we do?' Will asked softly.

'At this moment, *nothing*. But if Neville is wheeling and dealing with the Grants, then he's really treacherous. We're going to outsmart him, my dear friend. I know we can.'

'How nice to see you here, Finnister!' Edward exclaimed, shaking Amos's hand. 'And I see you've made Grace Rose happy, coming to her twelfth birthday party.'

'I think she *was* glad to see me, yes, and doesn't she look lovely, Mr Edward?'

The two men were standing at one end of Vicky Forth's drawing room in her Kensington house, their eyes on Grace Rose. She was rather tall for twelve, a beautiful girl with red-gold hair falling to her shoulders, and cornflower blue eyes so like Edward's. They were sparkling today, filled with happiness. She wore a blue silk dress and had a large blue bow in her hair.

Edward took a moment to answer, and then he said, 'Yes, she is indeed quite the beauty. An amazing looking girl.'

'Your spitting image, sir, if you don't mind me saying so.'

Edward began to chuckle. 'I know, Finnister, I know she is. Well, shall we stroll over there and join Hasling and Ledbetter?' Edward then added, 'I wouldn't mind a cup of tea either.'

Will, Mark, Stephen, Fenella and Vicky were grouped

near the buffet table at one side of the room, while Grace Rose was sitting down at a round table with Edward's daughters Bess and Mary, and several of her little friends. All the children were enjoying the party, eating tea sandwiches and laughing amongst themselves.

Edward had already noticed how caring Grace Rose was of his two daughters, and he smiled inwardly. Grace was a good child, devoted to the little girls, whom she tried to mother. Did she not see her likeness to him? he wondered, and then instantly dropped the thought when Finnister murmured something about Neville.

'I'm sorry, Finnister, I didn't quite catch what you said.'

'I made mention of the fact that I'm leaving Mr Neville's employ, Mr Deravenel.'

This announcement truly startled Edward and he looked at Amos swiftly, frowning. 'I hope there's nothing . . . gone amiss between you?'

'Oh, no, no, sir, nothing like that. Not at all. I told Mr Watkins that I wanted to retire. Ever since my poor Lydia died two years ago now, I've wanted to be a bit freer, wanted to work less. I'd like to do a few things I enjoy. I explained all this to Mr Watkins, told him that I didn't want a full-time job anymore.'

'How about a part-time job? With me?' Edward said before he could stop himself.

Amos stood staring at Edward, his face totally bland as he asked sotto voce, 'Doing what, sir?'

'Watching my back,' Edward answered.

Amos Finnister smiled, and stuck out his hand. 'Happy to oblige, Mr Deravenel.'

Edward grinned, delighted at this sudden and most

unexpected turn of events, and he said once again, 'Let's get a cup of tea, Finnister, and have a few of those delicious sandwiches before Mrs Forth cuts Grace Rose's birthday cake.'

Last year his sister Meg had been married, and Edward had not seen her since then. Now on this hot July day he thought she looked lovely in her pale green dress and smart hat. And, most importantly, very happy.

She had arrived in London several days ago, en route to Ravenscar for a month's holiday with her mother. Charles Feraud, her husband of exactly one year, would join her for the last two weeks.

'For the Glorious Twelfth,' Meg said, referring to the first day of grouse-shooting across the moors of England. 'He's a good shot, Ned, marvellous. One of the best, and he loves the sport.'

'I'm glad to hear it. We'll be coming up at the beginning of August, Meg darling, so we'll be one big happy family again for a short while.'

She smiled at him, as loyal and loving as she had always been since their childhood days. 'What a beautiful baby Cecily is, Ned. Another blonde,' she laughed. 'And quite large.'

Edward had invited his sister to lunch at the Ritz Hotel, and as usual he had been given his favourite table in the corner, overlooking Green Park. Bringing his head closer to hers, he asked, 'You are happy, Meg, aren't you? Since I was the one who tried to foster this union I've worried about you at times.'

'You didn't have to, I wouldn't have married Charles if I hadn't wanted to, you know. I'm like you, Ned, very independent, and I detest arranged marriages. Charles and I are extremely compatible, and we do love each other. So, the answer is, yes I'm happy. Very.'

'I'm relieved to hear it. How do you like your new home?'

'Burgundy is quite beautiful, and you know the château, you've seen it, it's entrancing. I've been busy from morning to night since I arrived there as Charles's bride. He's terribly busy running the vineyards, and it's quite an undertaking.'

'I can imagine.' Lifting his glass of champagne, Edward said, 'Welcome home for a few days, and may your happiness continue, Meg.'

'Thank you, and to you, Ned. You look wonderful.' She touched her flute to his. 'But then you're the handsomest man I know.'

'You're my sister, so you're prejudiced!'

Meg nodded, and said slowly, 'Ned, I've something to tell you, which I've actually been asked to tell you . . . Please, don't be too angry.'

His bright burnished head came up from the menu he had been studying, and he glanced at her swiftly, his eyes narrowing. She had sounded very serious. 'Why would I be angry? This must be something . . . *problematical*?'

Meg was silent for a moment, and looked across the room, scowling. Finally she brought her gaze back to his, and said, 'George married Isabel Watkins yesterday.'

'What!' he exploded, although he kept his voice down to a low hiss. 'Why wasn't I informed beforehand?'

His sister shook her fair head, and muttered, 'I don't

know, I don't understand any of this really. Nan came to see me at the Charles Street house this morning. To tell me. And to ask me to tell you.'

'And where's her mighty husband? Hiding behind her skirts?'

'She didn't mention Neville, except to say that *they* didn't know before it happened.'

'That takes some believing.'

'They eloped, Ned. To Gretna Green. Several days ago.'

For a moment Edward digested this, looking reflective, biting his lip, and then rubbing his mouth with his hand. He said, very slowly, and quietly emphatic, 'Neville and Nan *had* to know. Because the law changed in Scotland a long time ago. One of the parties to a marriage has to spend twenty-one days in Scotland before a marriage can take place, even if it's at Gretna Green. Since George was running all over London for the last few weeks, it must have been Isabel who was residing in Scotland for those twenty-one days. Didn't they know where their daughter was, Meg? After all, she's not yet twenty-one, around about seventeen or so, if I remember correctly.'

'Are you sure about the law, Ned?'

'I am, and I'll tell you why. I wrote an essay about marriage and the law when I was at Oxford, and I remember my research. Gretna Green has been famous for runaway marriages since the 1700s, and in the middle of the 1800s the law *was* changed. One of the parties must reside in Scotland for twenty-one days before a licence can be issued. And, by the way, cousins *can* marry each other.'

'Good Lord, you are a mine of information,' Meg said, shaking her head, adding, 'I'm so glad you're not angry.'

'Oh, but I am!' he said sharply. 'I'm just refraining from displaying that anger here. After all, we are in a public place. Neither am I all that *surprised*.'

Meg laughed, relieved he had taken it so well. 'I remember, they were always saying they were going to marry when they were children.'

'True. Did Nan say where *they* are at this moment?'

'On their honeymoon.'

'And who's footing that bill? Oh, I needn't ask,' he exclaimed, the anger surfacing. 'Her father, no doubt. And now I suppose it's your job to tell our mother, because I'm perfectly certain she hasn't been informed yet.'

'I promised Nan I would tell Mama when I get to Ravenscar tomorrow.'

'Where are they spending their honeymoon?'

'Nan didn't say, but if I hazard a guess I do think it's probably Thorpe Manor.'

'I see. Well, make sure George and Isabel go over to see Mother, promise me that, Meg.'

'I will, Ned, I will.'

'Now let's order lunch, I've a busy afternoon,' he said, somewhat snappishly, she thought.

Later, after he had returned to Deravenels, Edward called Will Hasling to come to his office. The moment the door closed, Ned told him the news, and for a

good ten minutes ranted and raved about the elopement, walking up and down furiously.

'Calm down, Ned,' Will said at one moment. 'It's
not worth getting het up about.'

'Maybe not. Neville and George planned this. Those
two have been hand in glove for a long time,' he cried,
his face flushed with his inner rage. 'Birds of a feather,
eh, Will?' He shrugged, and walked over to his desk.
'George is after Isabel's fortune, and Neville wants
Deravenels. Well, not the company, but the power it
would give him. And brother George is his tool.'

FIFTY-NINE

Ravenscar – 1914

Johnny Watkins drove the Daimler into the yard of
the stable block at Ravenscar, pulled on the brake
and turned off the ignition. Swivelling in his seat, he
looked at his brother Neville, and said, 'Let me go
in alone, talk to Ned, and then I'll come and get
you.'

Neville shook his head; Johnny noticed that a nerve
in his brother's cheek twitched. 'I think this is a big
mistake,' Neville muttered. 'A stupid move, Johnny,
probably the worst mistake we could be making.'

'No, no, I don't agree. We've got to try and bring
this ridiculous feud to an end.' Johnny sighed, his gaze,
fastened on his brother's light blue eyes, imploring.
'*We're family*. Let's not forget that. Our father died in
Carrara because of his love and friendship for Uncle
Richard, and our brother Thomas died with them. Ned's
mother is a Watkins, part of our *clan*. We cannot remain
estranged. It's wrong.'

'It's been two years since we had our last big
confrontation, about George's marriage to Isabel, and
Ned was adamant that I was to blame, that I wanted

to unseat him at Deravenels. What makes you think he will have changed his mind now?'

'I don't know that he has. But perhaps if we talk to him, offer him an olive branch, he might just accept that we are genuinely sincere. It's worth trying, Neville. Don't you think *he* also might be tired of this bickering and back-biting that goes on between us all the time?'

'No, I don't. I think that young pup thrives on it.'

'Neville, *don't*! This is altogether the wrong attitude to have.'

Neville simply sighed.

Johnny stared at him, thinking that his elder brother looked tired. He was in his early forties now, and there was a weariness about his drawn face, little lines around his eyes and mouth. He was still a handsome man, and fit, yet Johnny detected an air of exhaustion about him this morning.

'Sit here and wait, Neville. And please, I beg you, try to relax, get rid of some of this tension.'

'Are you certain they're here? What makes you think they came for Easter?'

'Ned comes to Ravenscar for most of the main holidays, and you know that. Anyway, Kathleen told me that she and Will would be here with Ned and his family.'

'Our sister is here? Why isn't she staying at Thorpe Hall with us, as you and your family are?'

'She's married to Will, and Will is Ned's best friend, and business colleague, and sparring partner, and they are always together . . . you don't need me to tell you that.'

Neville was silent.

Johnny opened the door of the car and got out. He

pushed his head inside and said, 'I won't be long. Try and relax. *Please.*'

Neville nodded, said nothing.

Johnny closed the car door and walked around to the other side of the house, deciding it might be more appropriate to enter from the front. There was something very intimate, rather casual about going in at the back, taking everyone by surprise. He didn't want to get off on the wrong foot. It was more than likely they were persona non grata here these days.

A moment later Johnny was ringing the bell, and within seconds the door was opened by Jessup.

'Oh, good morning, Mr Watkins,' Jessup said, opening the door wider, ushering him inside.

'Good morning, Jessup,' Johnny replied, giving the butler a slight nod. 'Is Mr Deravenel at home?'

'Mr Edward is here, yes. Everyone else is out, sir. The entire family have gone to Scarborough for lunch. Including the children. Oh yes, Master Richard and Mr Hasling stayed at home, sir.'

There's nothing unusual about that, Johnny thought, as he followed Jessup into the Long Hall. Will and Richard were Ned's favourites, and they believed he could do no wrong, so of course they were here, keeping him company.

'I'll go and find Mr Edward, sir,' Jessup murmured and disappeared.

Johnny wandered down the Long Hall, stood looking at a large plaque on one of the walls. It was the Deravenel family crest, the white rose of York, the fetterlock and the sun in its brilliance: written in scrolled lettering at the bottom were the words *Fidelity Unto Eternity*, the

Deravenel family motto. He did not move for a moment or two, simply stood in front of the plaque, studying the crest, digesting the motto.

The hall was beautiful this morning, with sunlight pouring in through the leaded windows. He turned and stared out towards the sparkling North Sea, noticed little dust motes flying up into the long rafts of sunlight that filtered into the hall.

How peaceful it is here, Johnny thought, and he remembered the days of his youth when he had played here with his cousin, his dearest companion.

Peace again, he thought. That's what I want to bring about . . . peace in this family. An end to all the quarrelling, the anger and the pain.

He heard a step and swung around and saw Edward approaching. They hadn't seen each other for a while, and he was as handsome as ever. But at twenty-nine he had a new maturity, a greater self-confidence, if that were at all possible. He looked more alluring than ever, in Johnny's eyes.

'Hello, Johnny,' Edward said quietly, and came closer, holding out his hand. He was surprised, taken aback, in fact, but did not show it.

Johnny went forward to greet him, saw at once that his cousin's eyes were warm, welcoming, and that there was a hint of a smile on his mouth.

For his part Edward thought Johnny looked well, like his old self, except there was a sense of restraint in him, as if he were holding back.

The cousins shook hands, and Edward said, 'Let's go to the library. Can I ask Jessup to bring you something to drink?'

'No, thanks,' Johnny answered.

The two men stood in the middle of the library, staring at each other. Edward spoke first, when he said in the same quiet voice, 'How have you been?'

'Good, and I can see you are in the best of health.'

'Have you been in Yorkshire or in town?'

'I've been in the north quite a lot.'

'That's why I haven't run into you in London then.'

Johnny nodded, and cleared his throat. 'I'll get to the point, Ned. I come here with an olive branch today . . . I'm so sick of this bickering and quarrelling in the family, and I want to put things right between us, I really do. *If we can.*'

'We've been so close, you and I, Johnny,' Edward remarked. He forced a smile. 'It would be nice to get everything . . . on an even keel, I agree.'

'That's my feeling, too.' Johnny felt some of his tenseness slipping away. 'Do you think that might be possible?'

'Perhaps. Are we talking just about you and me? Or is Neville going to be part of this . . . reconciliation?'

'I want it to be the three of us,' Johnny answered. 'Neville's outside, waiting in the car –'

'No, I'm not, I'm here,' Neville said from the doorway.

Edward and Johnny swung to face him; both were surprised.

Edward nodded. 'Cousin,' he murmured, eyeing Neville. 'Come in, won't you?'

Neville entered the beautiful old library, glancing around approvingly, and then he offered his hand to Edward, who took it. They shook hands, and Edward moved away, went to stand near the window, glancing out at the sea.

'Well, where do we begin?' Johnny looked from his brother to Ned and back to Neville.

There was a moment of silence.

They all simply stood there, staring at each other.

Finally Neville spoke. 'I think we should begin with an apology. The *last* time we saw each other, you accused me of plotting your downfall, Edward. You made a mistake –'

'No, I didn't!' Edward shot back, standing up straighter. 'You wanted to put George in my place at Deravenels. You were hell bent on it!' He was furious but endeavoured to hold his temper in check.

'This is something in your imagination!' Neville cried, his face flushing. 'A year ago you were full of accusations again, saying I arranged for George to marry Isabel, convinced I planned their elopement to Gretna Green. Another empty accusation.'

'Oh, come on,' Edward exclaimed. 'You *were* behind it.'

'They wanted to marry when they were children, and you know it.'

'And how convenient for you, Neville. With George, your son-in-law, in your back pocket you had another Deravenel under your control.'

'Don't be so ridiculous.'

'It's not ridiculous. I know the rules of the company only too well. *Only a Deravenel can run Deravenels*. I studied those rules before I took over the company.'

'Listen to me! *I* am the one who put you where you are today. If I hadn't thrown all my energy, wealth, and experience behind you, I know you would have never made it to that managing director's chair. Never in a hundred years.'

'I admit you helped me. And I've always thanked you, and repaid you in countless ways. But I also accomplished a lot myself. I steeped myself in the rules of the company, followed my father's notes, memorized everything, hundreds of pages, studied every division, learned how they were run, and then I went and faced the board. I made my case. And I won. You didn't win for me.'

'I'm ready to give credit where it's due!' Neville snapped. 'Why can't you?'

'I just did. And there's another thing. You're the one who let the wolf in the door. *Louis Charpentier*. He's been after the company ever since you started your wheeling and dealing with him. I've been battling him for years. He undermines us everywhere, competes for companies we've wanted to buy, sabotages us. And all with your help, *Cousin*! And you are in cahoots with the Grants as well. You're treacherous. You betrayed me.'

'That's not true!' Neville yelled, his face now crimson with rage.

Johnny had been so shocked by this sudden storm between the two he had been rendered speechless. Flabbergasted, in stunned shock, he had been unable to intervene. Now he moved, hurried to his brother, put a restraining hand on him. 'Neville, for God's sake, please calm down! You're going to have a heart attack if you're not careful.'

'I'm fine. But I'm done here.'

Johnny looked across at Edward, shaking his head; he was aware Edward's resentment had been festering for years, and he understood, but he regretted it had come out at this moment. 'Can't we begin again?' he begged.

'Not as far as I'm concerned,' Neville shouted, turning on his heel. 'I'm finished. I told you this would never work.' Neville rushed out of the library, almost knocking Richard down in his hurry.

Johnny gave Edward a rueful look, and threw up his hands, raced after his brother.

Richard came into the library followed by Will. They were both white-faced, looked shaken. 'What was all that about?' Richard asked, staring at Edward.

'Johnny was trying for a reconciliation. Neville wanted none of it, I'm afraid.'

Richard shook his head, said in a faltering voice, 'Ned, let's go after them, *please*. Let's try to sort this all out.'

For a moment Edward did not budge, and then he nodded. 'What is there to lose? Let's go after them.'

The Daimler had turned out of the stable block and was on the drive, heading for the gates of Ravenscar by the time the three men came rushing out of the house.

Ned began to run, chasing the car, shouting, 'Johnny! Neville! Wait!'

Will and Richard were running alongside him, then with a sudden spurt of energy Will sprinted forward, yelling, 'Wait for us! Slow down!'

The car kept on going, swept through the gates and out onto the cliff road, moving at an even greater speed.

Edward and Will followed the car onto the road. Richard had lagged behind but soon caught up again, the three of them racing forward, almost abreast. Then Edward stopped dead in his tracks, shaking his head. His heart was thundering in his chest and he was gasping for breath, sweat running down his face.

'It's no good,' he managed to say, panting, wiping his face with his handkerchief. 'We can't catch up. They had a head start. Anyway they don't want to stop. At least Neville doesn't.'

Richard, his chest heaving, gasped. 'Let's go back and get the car.'

'Good idea,' Will agreed, pulling his handkerchief out of his pocket and patting his face. 'Let's drive to Thorpe Manor, Ned. Settle this once and for all.'

When Edward did not respond, Will glanced at him, and frowned. He saw a look of fear spreading across Edward's face, and exclaimed in alarm, 'What is it?'

'Johnny's driving too fast. I know this road like the back of my hand. There's a dangerous curve coming up –' Edward did not finish his sentence. He stood there, frozen, watching in horror as the Daimler appeared to fly up into the air as it went over the edge of the cliff, spun in mid-air and fell, disappearing from sight.

'Oh, my God! We've got to get there!' Ned shouted, and started running down the cliff road, followed by his brother and Will.

They were all out of breath and heaving when they came to the curve in the road, and Edward put out his hand, held them back from the edge of the cliff. 'It's a six hundred foot drop, get back,' he instructed. Edging carefully onto the grass bordering the road, he looked down at the beach.

He could see the Daimler far below, overturned and on its side. Neville's body was nearby but there was no sign of Johnny. His heart was beating so rapidly he thought it would burst out of his chest, and fear shot through him. He was shaking, for a moment felt sick. He stepped back, looked at Richard and Will, said in a hoarse voice, 'Neville's lying on the beach . . . I can't see Johnny. Maybe he's still in the car.'

Not waiting for any response, Edward set off at a run, making for the steps which cut through the lower part of the moorland and swept down to the beach. The others ran after him at full speed.

Half running, half falling, Edward stumbled down the steps and onto the shingle in minutes, and he saw Johnny immediately. He lay near the overturned car; Neville was a few feet away.

Ned saw Neville move, and ran to him, knelt down by his side. Then he realized it was the wind that had ruffled his cousin's clothes.

Edward felt his pulse. Neville was dead. There was blood on his face, and his head was askew. Edward was certain he had broken his neck as he was thrown out of the car. As he looked down into Neville's face he noticed how clear his eyes were, as clear as they had been in life, a pure turquoise. Such unique eyes, such a unique man. He closed the lids gently, and walked over to Johnny.

Will and Richard were kneeling next to Johnny's body.

Will shook his head. 'No pulse . . . he's gone,' Will murmured in a choked, voice, his face wet with tears.

Richard, who was sobbing, looked up when he saw his brother approach. 'I thought Johnny was still alive,' he gasped between sobs. 'I opened his collar. Look, he still wore your medallion.'

Edward nodded, then said almost harshly, 'Let's carry Johnny over to Neville. So they can be together.'

Once the bodies were side by side, Edward knelt down on the shingle with his Little Fish and Will, and said a prayer for them. And he wept for Neville, and all that they had meant to each other in the past. And he wept for Johnny, whom he had loved.

They stayed for a while with the bodies, none of them wanting to leave the two men who had been such a major part of their lives. A stillness surrounded them. It was as if the world had stopped. The only sound was the waves swishing up onto the beach and rolling back, and the cries of the kittiwakes as they floated high above in the cloud-filled Yorkshire sky.

Much later that day, after an ambulance had taken the bodies to the morgue in Scarborough, Richard found Edward alone in the ruined stronghold.

Speaking softly, his youngest brother said, 'Ned, can I come in?'

Turning, Edward nodded. His face was ravaged with grief.

Without a word, Richard handed his brother the white rose medallion which Johnny had still worn.

Edward's hand closed on it; he put it in his pocket. And later that night he took off his own medallion and fastened Johnny's around his neck. And he wore it for the rest of his life.

SIXTY

London

Four months later Edward's personal grief was swept to one side, as the guns of August roared.

Europe was engulfed in war after the assassination of Archduke Franz Ferdinand, heir to the Holy Roman Austro-Hungarian Empire, and his wife the Duchess of Hohenberg, in Sarajevo. Within days most countries were involved in the fearful conflict caused by this act of terrorism in a small Balkan state.

Edward sat in his office at Deravenels, reading *The Times*, his attention caught by an interview with David Lloyd George, the Chancellor of the Exchequer: '*I felt like a man standing on a planet that had been suddenly wrenched from its orbit by a demonic hand and that was spinning wildly into the unknown,*' Lloyd George was quoted as saying last night, the night of August fourth, when Britain declared war on Germany.

Dismay flooded through Edward. He knew they were in for a long fight; he also knew it would be a war that would spread to the far corners of the globe. He dreaded it; he was still unable to understand why people were so excited about going to war, why people were rushing through the streets of London filled with a strange kind of jubilation when war heralded nothing but death and destruction.

He picked up the *Daily Mail*, one of Northcliffe's newspapers, and scanned the front-page headline: **BRITAIN DECLARES WAR ON GERMANY.** There were other smaller cross-headlines inside: *Belgium Invaded. Two New Battleships for our Navy. British Minelayer Sunk. War Risk at Sea.*

Thank God Winston Churchill is First Lord of the Admiralty, Edward thought, sitting back in his chair, the *Mail* discarded for the moment. Only Churchill and a few other enlightened men had seen the menace of war approaching, and had tried to make ready for it.

There was a knock on the door, and Will came in, a bleak expression in his eyes. 'We're in for a long siege, I think, Ned, don't you?'

Edward nodded. 'Churchill told me that the other night. I can only say that it's a good thing he recognized the threat of increasing Germany sea power in 1911. By withdrawing our Fleet from abroad and concentrating it in the North Sea, he's certainly increased our strength.'

'Not to mention *safety*,' Will pointed out.

'I've been told I cannot even attempt to join up,' Edward said in a low voice. 'Because I run this sprawling global company I'm required to remain in this seat for the duration. However long that will be.'

'I read somewhere that the German Chancellor, von Bethmann-Hollweg, predicted in Berlin the other day that the war would be very short, maybe three to four months. But I say more like three years.' Finally sitting down, Will continued, 'Anyway, *this* is where you are meant to sit. You have no right to even contemplate marching off to war carrying a gun with a bayonet fixed to it. Whereas, I –'

'Stop right there!' Edward exclaimed, holding up a hand. 'You're not joining up either.'

'I'd thought about it, Ned.'

'No, no, you can't. Anyway, the government is only calling up single men. You're married.'

'So is George, but he is going to enlist, so he told me only half an hour ago.'

'I don't think he'll pass the medical. George has always had bad eyes, he doesn't see very well. So, he won't make it. Please rest assured of that, Will.'

'This memo you sent me, about the factories in Leeds. Am I to understand that the government's going to requisition them? That we're to make army and navy uniforms?'

'Yes, exactly that. But the government's not requisitioning the clothing factories. They just want us to switch our production to uniforms.'

'No problem. I wasn't quite understanding. Anyway, I really came in to see if you're free for lunch today.'

'I am. I didn't make any lunch dates, since I thought I would be in Yorkshire for the grouse. War has put paid to that, I'm afraid, and a lot of other things.'

'I know. I've just cancelled our trip to Paris. I was taking Kathleen there in September. Well, we can say farewell to the *belle époque*, Ned. France is gearing up for war, just as we are. I'm a bit worried about the vineyards, you know, but there's nothing we can do.'

'I realize that we have just to sit tight . . .' Edward shook his head. 'It's all so disheartening. But we must hope for the best, as far as our French vineyards are concerned.'

'Shall we go to White's?' Will asked.

'No place better,' Edward answered. 'I can't make it before one, though.'

'I'll pick you up at twelve forty-five.'

Will slipped out of the office and Edward went over the letters his secretary had left on his desk, and then he sat back, a worried expression crossing his face. If the whole world was engulfed by this war, what would happen to them all?

He stood up, went to look at the map his father had hung there years before. It seemed to him now that there wasn't a country in the world where they didn't have offices.

He suddenly laughed to himself. Deravenels had existed for well over eight hundred years, so why should it falter now? But then there had never been a war like this one was going to be.

'Let's have a drink before lunch,' Will said, as they walked into White's around ten past one. 'I think I need one to cheer me up.'

Edward smiled. 'You've taken the words right out of my mouth, old chap.'

The two of them sat down at a table, and Will ordered for them, then said to Ned in a quiet tone, 'I heard last night, at a dinner party we attended, that the navy is the only service that's strong. The army is apparently not at all well organized, and we have only minimal air power, even though Churchill has attempted to boost it lately.' Will took a cigarette out of a gold Cartier case and lit it, drew on it. 'We're in a bloody mess, actually, Ned, if the truth be known.'

'We need a new Secretary of State for War,' Edward told him.

'Do you think Asquith will appoint one?' Will looked at him alertly. Edward knew more than he did; he had politicians as friends.

'He'll have to, he can't be Prime Minister and run the War Office as well,' Ned replied. 'I hope he appoints Lord Kitchener. He's a great General, and also a national hero.'

Will nodded. 'He would have a very uplifting effect on the public, yes.'

The two of them fell silent, sipped their sherry, and smoked, listening to the different conversations flowing around them. The Smoking Room was packed today, and the only talk was talk of war.

'We don't have a compulsory draft system,' a voice said at a table behind them.

'I didn't know *that*, Hartley,' his companion replied.

'Well, it's true, and we'll have to raise an army to fight this bloody war. We'll have to start a campaign to recruit single men, that's a fact.'

'Asquith knows what he's doing, he's been an excellent Prime Minister,' another voice intoned from the right.

'And Churchill has the right attitude. Beat 'em before they beat us,' a fourth man pronounced.

Will shook his head, and murmured, 'What about Meg? Will she stay in France, do you think?'

Edward sighed. 'I don't know. When I spoke to her yesterday at Ravenscar she said Charles was already talking of going back to Paris immediately, and on to Burgundy. I'm sure he has to, he can't just leave his vineyards at a time like this. And listen, Will, don't worry about ours. They're in good hands, we have wonderful managers.' Ned nodded. 'You'll see, everything will be all right. As far as Meg is concerned, knowing her, I do believe my sister will go back to France with her husband and she'll stay there until the war is over.'

As the war dragged on through August, September, and October, right up until the end of 1914, Edward realized he was dedicating most of his time to Deravenels. His work load was enormous at the best of times, and this was the worst. It seemed to him that he had to have a single-minded sense of purpose in order to get through every day. But there was a big war effort on, and everybody was in the same situation as he was, working day and night, trying to do their bit.

The guns of August 1914 roared on through 1915 and 1916, without cease. Hundreds of thousands of young men died on the bloody fields of Europe, felled in the trenches as they bravely fought the enemy. The overall losses were so monumentally high the world was horrified.

Many of the men who worked at Deravenels had

joined the forces, and in May of 1916 Edward was alarmed one morning in May when he began to realize how many single men now had to enlist because of the bill that had been passed earlier that year: compulsory military service was now enforced. He knew that it would soon be married men who would be called up to fight for their country at the Front. He was not worried for himself, but for Will, Oliveri and Christopher Green. All were married, young and fit. They would most certainly pass the physical.

He was somewhat surprised that evening when he arrived home, to discover that Elizabeth, who rarely read anything, had spotted an item in the *Evening News*.

As he went into the small parlour of the house in Berkeley Square, she glanced up and waved the newspaper at him. 'Ned, have you seen this in today's paper?' Not waiting for his reply, she added, 'Married men will be called up soon. The Prime Minister is introducing another Military Service Bill, and if it passes the House then married men will have to go and fight the Boche.'

'But I won't, sweetheart,' he soothed as he went in and sat down in a chair next to her. 'I told you, I'm exempt because I run a huge company.'

A smile of relief crossed her face. 'I'm so glad. I couldn't bear it if you had to go to war.' She frowned, added worriedly, 'My brothers will though.'

'Yes, I know, darling. But let's not dwell on war tonight. I'm going to go upstairs to see the children, and then I'll have a glass of wine before I go to the theatre.'

'I'll come up with you. I think I have to rest.'

Elizabeth was pregnant again, and they mounted the stairs together so that he could support her. She went into her bedroom; Edward climbed to the next floor, the nursery floor, the domain of all the young Deravenels.

The moment he went in, three girls and one little boy, all with reddish-blond hair and eyes of varying shades of blue, flung themselves at him.

Laughing, crouching down, he opened his arms, and they scrambled close to him, and cries of 'Papa! Papa!' filled the nursery.

His son, Young Edward had been born in 1913, and he was now two and a half, a sweet, docile child with a happy temperament and the looks of a Botticelli angel. He was terribly spoilt, because he was the youngest in the household, and also very beautiful.

Edward unscrambled his little scramblers, as he called them, and reaching down he lifted Young Edward into his arms, and held him close. 'You know what we shall do on Saturday, Edward?' Ned asked his small son, kissing him on his warm pink cheek.

'No, Papa.'

'Have you forgotten already, sweetheart?'

The boy shook his head, looked puzzled, and then his face lit up, and he cried, 'Buy the puppy! You promised, Papa!'

'It's true, I did indeed, and I will, but that's not what I meant. I told you that when we went down to Kent this weekend I would take you to paddle in the sea, and that we might even go sailing on a special boat, a new boat.'

'Oh Papa! The boat! Oh, oh, I can't wait.' The child began to squeal with delight.

Edward, smiling into his son's eyes, felt a tug on his jacket and he glanced down.

Bess said, 'Can I come on the boat, too, Papa?' She sounded so woeful, Edward put the boy down on the floor, and took hold of her hand, led her over to a chair. Seating himself, he brought the seven-year-old forward into his arms, and said gently, 'Of course, you can. It's a new boat for *all of us*. And do you know what it's called?'

She shook her head.

'It's called *The Brave Bess*, after you, because you are brave and beautiful, my dearest little one.'

'You do still love me the *best*, don't you Papa?' she whispered against his cheek. 'The heir comes first, I know, but I'm your favourite aren't I, Papa?'

'Yes,' he whispered back, 'but don't tell anyone. It's our secret.'

As usual, when we came home tonight, Elizabeth went straight up to bed, and here am I, sitting with my brandy in the library, in front of a roaring fire, thanks to my devoted Mallet who looks after me so well. Which is more than I can say about my wife. She's cantankerous and difficult these days, perhaps because she is tired of giving birth. We have had a new addition to our already large family, another girl, christened Anne. Now I have six children: Bess, Mary, Cecily, Edward, Richard, born in 1916, and the latest.

I must make allowance for Elizabeth, I keep telling myself that. Although she has nothing much to say to me, and isn't really interested in anything I do, she is my ready, willing and able partner in our bed. Always passionate, still extremely jealous, continuing to be suspicious, and very proprietary about me. She doesn't like to have me out of her sight for too long. But I manage, and I go to my Jane all the time, and she keeps me sane, gives me great happiness. Things aren't so bad for me, not bad at all, and I really don't have anything to complain about. The children are bright and beautiful, my darling Bess is extraordinary and gives me much comfort, and Jane is my solace.

It is Friday the thirteenth of November in the year of our Lord 1918. Friday the thirteenth is supposed to be unlucky, but I don't believe the world thinks that tonight. No, not at all. Two days ago, on November the eleventh, in a railway car in the Forest of Compiègne in France, German delegates signed an armistice ending the war. Ever since then the world has gone mad rejoicing. I saw jubilant workers in the Strand jumping on passing omnibuses, waving flags and banners. Men, women and children danced and sang in the streets of Paris, I heard, and a huge victory parade marched down Fifth Avenue in New York, according to the newspapers. Even in Berlin the relieved citizens seemingly welcomed the end of this grotesque world war.

They're calling it the war to end all wars, and I sincerely hope that it is. A conflagration like this cannot happen again, it just cannot. It seemed to me that the world went mad for a while, all the fighting and the killing. And then there was the Russian Revolution. The Czar and Czarina assassinated in 1917, murdered in cold blood, a whole family. I tremble when I think of that horrendous act of brutality, an act of terrorism against a family . . . I think of my own children and I tremble more.

I've kept Deravenels safe. In fact, it's flourishing as it never has before. War always boosts business, it's sad to say, but that's just the way it is, and it has certainly boosted my company. And thankfully most of my men are safe. George didn't pass the physical, just as I knew he wouldn't with those bad eyes of his. And Richard, my beloved and loyal Little Fish, also has remained at my side. His wonky shoulder made him exempt.

As for Will Hasling, he did go to war. My dearest friend. They sent him to the Somme, and he fought through that entire battle. And he lived. So did my devoted Oliveri, who did his duty in Flanders. But not Rob Aspen and Christopher Green. I lost those two grand men, who gave me their all, their loyalty and devotion. They died fighting at Verdun, and now they are buried in some far corner of a foreign field. I shall always remember them with pride because of their endeavours.

My sweet sister Meg survived the war in France, stood side by side with her husband and fought off the Boche.

And Mama is flourishing. She's as fit as she's always been, and just as beautiful, and her dearest friend and companion is our lovely Grace Rose, grown up now, and a friend to us all. She knows I am her father. I decided to tell her in 1916, but before I got around to it Bess explained to me one day that she and Grace Rose knew that Grace was my daughter, and that Grace Rose wanted to know about her mother. And so, persuaded by the very persuasive Bess – so like me – I did tell them both about Tabitha. Grace Rose confided

691

that she knew I was her father the day I first saw her at Vicky Forth's house, the day of Lily's funeral.

She explained that her mother had once told her when she was very small that her father was tall and strong like a tree in the forest, with hair the colour of autumn leaves, eyes the shade of bluebells that grew in the woods. And when she saw me she just knew, she said, and that was why she had smiled at me. Ever since then I've understood that one never knows what children know and keep secret in their hearts.

I can't believe this war is finally over. Four years that seem like forty. So many dead. Eight million men who fought to save the world have died. The flower of English youth were felled on the blood-soaked fields of Flanders in Northern France, and England will never be the same without them. The world will never be the same. It was turned upside down, and that is the way it will remain.

I drink a toast tonight, here in my library in my house in Berkeley Square. It is heartfelt. I drink to those I loved and lost, to those I love who remain, and to those who are yet to be born.

I am Edward Deravenel. I am thirty-three years old, and I still have a life to live.

Author's Note

This is a modern novel, told in the modern vernacular, and set in the early part of the twentieth century. However, I have to a certain extent based my protagonist Edward Deravenel on the English medieval king, Edward IV. Born Edward Plantagenet, the Earl of March, he was the eldest son of the mighty Duke of York and his Duchess. Edward's father was a prince of the blood and a royal duke, head of the royal House of York, rightful heir to the throne of England.

When Edward's father was killed in the Battle of Sandal Castle in Yorkshire in 1460, during the Wars of the Roses, Edward assumed his father's hereditary title and became Duke of York. He continued his father's fight to win back the throne from his cousin, Henry VI, Duke of Lancaster. He was aided in this struggle by his cousin, Richard Neville, the Earl of Warwick, later known in history as the Kingmaker.

The throne of England had been usurped by the House of Lancaster from the House of York some sixty years earlier, and it was in 1461 that Edward

Plantagenet took that throne back when he defeated Henry VI and became king that same year.

Apart from 'borrowing' the exceptional good looks of Edward Plantagenet, and his height of six feet four, unusual for those times, I have used some aspects of his character and personality in the depiction of Edward Deravenel. Significant events in the life of the medieval king are used in a modern form as the basis, in part, of Edward Deravenel's story.

New York, 2006

For more information on the Ravenscar series, and the inspiration behind it, go to www.barbarataylor bradford.com.

Bibliography

Edwardian London by Felix Barker (Laurence King Publishing)

Eminent Edwardians by Piers Brendon (André Deutsch)

Victorian & Edwardian Décor by Jeremy Cooper (Abbeville Press)

The Lives of the Kings & Queens of England edited by Antonia Fraser (Weidenfeld & Nicolson)

Born To Rule by Julia P. Gelardi (St Martin's Press Inc.)

The Edwardians by Roy Hattersley (Little Brown)

Churchill by Roy Jenkins (Farrar, Straus & Giroux Inc.)

Richard the Third by Paul Murray Kendall (W. W. Norton & Co. Inc.)

Warwick The Kingmaker by Paul Murray Kendall (Allen and Unwin Ltd.)

The Wars of the Roses by J. R. Lander (Sutton Publishing Ltd)

The Wars of the Roses by Robin Neilland (Brockhampton Press)

Victorian & Edwardian Fashions from '*La Mode Illustrée*' edited by JoAnne Olian (Dover Publications Inc.)

The Edwardian Garden by David Ottewill (Yale University Press)

The Edwardians by J. B. Priestley (Sphere Books Ltd.)

Edward IV by Charles Ross (Eyre Methuen)

Consuelo & Alva by Amanda Mackenzie Stuart (HarperCollins Publishers)

Lancaster & York: The Wars of the Roses by Alison Weir (Pimlico)

The Princes in the Tower by Alison Weir (Pimlico)